Maiden Voyage

Maiden Voyage
Graham Masterton

St. Martin's Press
New York

Acknowledgments

The author wishes to thank the chairman and directors of Keys Shipping Line Ltd. for their invaluable and patient assistance in the preparation of this book. He also wishes to thank the Beeney Memorial Library in Boston, Massachusetts, for access to the letters and business papers of Mr. Mark Beeney. Thanks also to Constance Spratt, who so diligently typed the manuscript. Thanks to Messrs. Sussman & Bergman for permission to use the words of "Moonlight Promenade" (copyright © Harris and Harris, 1924); and for the lyrics from "Let's Talk Turkey" (copyright © Godber and Mesdag, 1922).

Passengers will remember how romantically the glowing phosphorescent waves curled back in the ship's wake, falling forever in flakes of diamond and pearl. They will remember how readily the damsel of their choice could be persuaded to a secluded spot in order to observe this poetic phenomenon. They will remember quite a lot of things, we have no doubt.
—*Cunard advertisement*

One

She was making cinnamon toast in the kitchen, quite naked except for her pink velvet slippers and a pink velvet hair riband, when they arrived at the house to give her the news that her father had died in the night. Nigel came into the kitchen in his purple and turquoise jazz-age dressing gown, and said seriously, "You'd better pop something on. Mr. Fearson's outside and says it's rather drastic."

That was probably her last ever carefree moment, her last completely carefree moment, and Nigel would remember it for years to come, even when he was married and living in Oxfordshire with a wife called Penelope, three Shetland ponies, a duck, and a pair of overweight twin daughters with Fair Isle sweaters and freckles. He would see it as an illuminated picture postcard: Catriona standing by the New World gas stove, her white face already turning towards him, and those slightly slanted eyes already beginning to cloud, her dark curly hair tied back with the riband, and the long bare curve of her back limned by the eleven o'clock sunlight. Eleven o'clock in the morning on Thursday, June 12, 1924: what a time and a day to be twenty-three years old and in love, especially with Catriona. She had her mother's height and her mother's figure, tall and unfashionably large-breasted for 1924, but with narrow hips. And she was easily the most devastating girl that Nigel had ever known, even more of a goddess than Rosebud Wilkinson; and he eyed her nakedness possessively as she walked across the kitchen, lifted her pink satin robe from the back of the kitchen chair, and slipped it on.

"Cat, old girl," said Nigel, grasping her shoulders. He was conscious of the slight sway of a heavy breast beneath slippery satin. "I do hope it's nothing frightful."

She nodded but didn't say anything. Nigel hesitated for a moment, his lips pursed indecisively, then he opened the door wider to let her through into the passage. He held back for a second or two, but then he followed her, clawing quickly at his blond marcelled hair to smarten himself up. He knew the news was serious, and he felt inexplicably ratty. Chaps had no right to come knocking on a chap's door with serious news, not when a chap was just about to have breakfast.

As he passed the foot of the stairs, Nigel could hear the phonograph in the bedroom still squawking out the last few lines of "My Rambler Rose." He had bought the record for Rosebud, but in the past few weeks it had become the song that would always remind him of Catriona's body and Catriona's spirit. He suddenly felt that he might never play "My Rambler Rose" on his phonograph again, might not be able to bear to.

Mr. Fearson was waiting in the cocktail room and so was Mr. Thurrock. Against the snazzy black and gold wallpaper with its pattern of tipsy highball glasses, they looked unrelievedly staid and discomfited, visitors from another age and another morality, before short skirts and bobbed hair and fox trotting had ever been imagined, even in the most indecent of fantasies. Neither Mr. Fearson nor Mr. Thurrock had sat himself in either of the armchairs that Nigel had offered them. In one of the armchairs was a discarded peach-coloured camisole, and in the other was a dirty bread-and-butter plate on which someone had crushed out a purple cigarette.

"Well?" asked Catriona, her hand still on the doorknob. "I'm surprised to see you."

Mr. Fearson's black morning coat was buttoned tightly over a chest that was as solid as the boiler of a small riverboat, and his cheeks were still ruddy from his kipper breakfast. He said in a blurting voice, "It's not what you think, miss. It's not the Pop." The Pop was what she and Mr. Fearson had irreverently christened those occasional visits that Mr. Fearson was called upon to make whenever company business brought him down south from Formby. "Your father said I should just pop in to see how you were." Because in spite of all their arguing; in spite of their constant clashes over clothes and smoking and going out with fast friends, Catriona's father had always prized her and protected her, and wanted to know that she was safe. The newspapers these days were full of stories about cocaine and white slavery and unprincipled mashers.

Catriona looked at Mr. Thurrock, but Mr. Thurrock could do nothing more than remove his spectacles, fold them, and stare shortsightedly back at her out of eyes like pale blue marbles.

"We came down on the first train," said Mr. Fearson. "We thought of the telephone or a telegram, but your mother thought it wiser to tell you in person. It's bad news, I'm sorry to say. Your father died, just gone midnight last night, of a heart attack. Had he lived, Dr. Whitby said, he would have lived the life of a vegetable."

"A cabbage," put in Mr. Thurrock, as if it were necessary to specify which variety of vegetable.

"He's *dead?*" said Catriona. She was still holding the doorknob. "I

2

don't understand you."

"Cat, my *dear girl,*" said Nigel and attempted to take her arm, but she tugged it away. She could feel the tears in her eyes, but somehow they didn't seem to do anything but blur her vision and turn Mr. Fearson and Mr. Thurrock into dark dancing outlines. The tears didn't relieve the rising lump of grief in her ribcage, nor explain why these two solemn men had suddenly appeared to give her this hateful news on a sunny June morning when it seemed nothing so tragic could possibly have happened. There were blue skies outside those curtains, and birds, and motorcar horns parping in the street. How could her father have died?

"Your mother would like it very much if you could come back with us," said Mr. Fearson. He sniffed in one nostril and looked very unhappy.

"The rest of the family are coming tomorrow like," added Mr. Thurrock. "Your cousins and all."

"Was it quick?" asked Catriona.

Mr. Fearson blinked. He didn't quite know what she meant.

"Was it quick?" she repeated. "The heart attack?"

"Oh, quick," said Mr. Fearson. "Oh, yes, quick." He snapped his fingers and then obviously wished that he hadn't. "Quick as a candle snuffed out, that's what Dr. Whitby said. With us one second and in the bosom of the Lord the next. Not even time for last words."

Catriona touched the tears in her eyes with her fingertips. "I don't suppose he would have wanted any last words," she said. "He always said that deeds made talking redundant."

There was a long silence. Then Mr. Fearson said, "I'm very sorry, miss. You do have my sympathy. It's a very sad loss."

"Well, yes, it is," said Catriona. She looked at him and gave him a tight, puckered smile. "I suppose the worst of it is that the last time I saw him, we argued."

"They say that fathers and daughters only clash because they're like each other," said Mr. Thurrock. "Same as magnets, you know. Opposite poles attract. Like poles repel."

"Yes," said Catriona. Her voice was as soft as a sheet of tissue paper falling from between the leaves of a photograph album. And the photograph she would always recall, whenever she thought of her father, was the one of them walking side by side through the sandhills at Formby, when she was only eight; and both of them, she and her father, had their hands clasped obstinately behind their backs, as if to make absolutely certain that they would not hold hands with each other, not for anything.

Stubborn, stubborn, stubborn, she thought. A whole life of being stubborn, and what for? To die, as quick as a snuffed-out candle, at the age of fifty-three. For some reason, she thought of her father carving the Sunday joint; she could almost smell the roast lamb and picture his square-fingered hands holding the bone-handled carving knife, and the vision coaxed up more tears.

"Would you like a drink, old girl?" asked Nigel anxiously. "Cup of coffee? Brandy maybe? I must say you look like something out of Tutankhamen's tomb."

"Make me a . . . gin and bitters," she said. She held her pink dressing gown around herself as if she were feeling cold. "Bring it upstairs. I'll have to pack. There's a darling."

Nigel looked over her shoulder at Mr. Fearson and Mr. Thurrock, his face questioning. Mr. Fearson shrugged. It was one of those things. Nothing that anybody could do about it. Sorry, like, but there you are. Catriona left the cocktail room and the three men heard the clack-clack of her high-heeled slippers going up the stairs.

"Well," said Nigel, feeling deflated. "Can I get you gentlemen anything?"

"Bit early for me, thanks," said Mr. Thurrock stolidly.

Nigel went to the black and silver cocktail bar, found a bottle of gin with a piddling measure left in the bottom, and turned it upside down into a martini glass.

"Party last night?" asked Mr. Fearson, nodding at the untidy room.

"What?" said Nigel. "Oh, no, not really. Just a few friends. You know the kind of thing. Few drinks."

Mr. Thurrock said, "Bit of a high time you have down here in London, then, by and large?"

Nigel shook angostura into Catriona's drink and stirred it with a glass swizzle stick. "You could say so. Cat enjoys it. I mean Miss Keys."

He disappeared behind the bar, clinking bottles in his search for the whisky. "I suppose you'll have to postpone the *Arcadia*'s maiden voyage, won't you? Next week, wasn't it?"

"Tuesday she sails." Mr. Fearson nodded.

Nigel reappeared holding up a bottle of Crawford's. "And she still will?"

Mr. Fearson made a face. "I think Mr. Keys would have wanted her to. That's the way I look at it. Mind you, I reckon it's all up to Mrs. Keys now whether she sails or not. You have to respect a widow's wishes."

"Bit ominous, though, isn't it?" Nigel said in a bright voice. "The largest passenger liner since the *Titanic*, and the owner pops off the week before the first voyage? Bit ominous, I'd say."

"Well, this is your own house, sir," said Mr. Fearson, "and in your own house, I suppose you're entitled to say whatever comes into your head."

Nigel stared at him, his face as sharp as an ice pick. He looked as if he didn't know whether to stamp his foot or demand that Mr. Fearson leave the house at once or blow up in a shower of smoke and confetti. As it was, he picked up the drinks from the bar, and snapped, "*I* see!"

Mr. Fearson said, "You'll ask Miss Keys to make haste, won't you, sir?"

"I'll see to it that she doesn't keep you waiting too much longer than necessary," Nigel retorted.

"Obliged, sir," replied Mr. Fearson with a smile.

Upstairs, in the brilliantly sunny bedroom, NIgel banged the drinks down on the glass-topped dressing table and said, "Bit damned Thomas Hardy, your Mr. Fearson."

Catriona had opened her buffalo-hide suitcase on the bed and was folding up her white tennis skirt. She was reflected in the semicircular mirror which stood at the head of the bed, and reflected again in the mirror on top of the dressing table, so that the whole bedroom appeared to be peopled with Catrionas in different stages of packing. Nigel stood with his ankles crossed, feeling peevish.

"I don't suppose you know when you might be back?" he asked her. She shook her head.

"Well, funerals don't take that long, do they?" he said. "I mean, after a chap's dead, you can't keep a chap above ground for too long, can you?"

"Nigel," she warned him. He recognised the tone of her voice and raised his hand, fingers spread, like an exasperated Italian tenor. *Mamamia.* Before Catriona had come into his life, he had never even known that anything he said was in dubious taste. His lack of sensitivity had been part of his charm. There was no doubt about it, she had given him some wonderful times. She had even enabled him to glimpse ecstasy. But she had definitely provincialised him. His friend Tommy Tompkins had said to him only two or three days ago, after he had been talking about hare coursing, or showing respect for one's parents, or some such subject, "That's a frightfully *Formby* thing to say."

Yet how frustrating it all was. She was so beautiful.

"You'll give me a tinkle when you arrive," he said.

She looked up. "I don't know. I may. Do you really want me to?"

He pouted at himself in the dressing-table mirror. "Do what you like," he said, more to his reflected face than to her.

She paused in her packing. Then she came across to him and took his hands in hers and kissed him on the cheek and then on the mouth, very precisely but also very tenderly.

"You think I'm going for good, don't you?" she said softly.

He swivelled his eyes around, partly because he was clowning and partly because he was trying to stop himself from crying. "The thought had actually crossed a chap's mind."

"Don't be sad," she insisted. "That was why I fell for you when I first met you, because you looked like the kind of man who would never be sad."

"I see," he said. "Life and soul, that kind of thing."

"That's right. And you're famous. What more could a girl want?"

"Famous, hah!" he said scornfully. "Two small parts in two medium-to-average West End musicals, and I'm famous! My dear girl, the name of Nigel Myers might twinkle and shine in the saloon bar of the Queen's Elm, but scarcely anywhere else. I shouldn't think a single soul in *Ongar* has ever heard of me."

Catriona stroked his unshaven cheek, prickled with blond. "I've never heard you so modest," she said. "You're not trying to tell me something, are you? Nigel?"

"Why should I be?"

She lowered her hand. Her two reflections lowered their hands.

Nigel said, "I could be trying to ask you to come back as quickly as you possibly can. As soon as this beastly Formby business is all over."

"I'll have to make sure my mother is taken care of."

Nigel sighed. "Yes, of course you will."

"And then there'll be the question of probate."

"Of course. Mother and probate and all the rest of the tackle that goes with having a family. When should I expect you? Nineteen twenty-nine?"

"Nigel," she chided him, "we've had such fun together."

"Now I *know* you're not coming back."

She turned away, back towards the bed, where her half-packed case lay open. She had always known in a strangely lucid way that if ever she left Nigel she would never be able to return to him. Not because she didn't actually love him; she did. He was fast and funny and he knew everybody in London who was worth knowing. He had a red Gwynne eight-horse-power runabout with a back end like a small boat, and she would remember their harum-scarum drives through the summer villages of Surrey for as long as she lived. But she was twenty-one now, and the family into which she had been born, for all of her rebellion against it, was calling her back. You can't have the wind in your hair forever. You can't grow old amongst actors.

"I promise you, NIgel, I *will* let you know how I'm getting on," she said. "I do promise you that."

Nigel looked at her steadily and then pulled a wry sort of expression —a little too theatrical, but easier than having to show her how he really felt. "Well, old girl, you don't have to make me any promises, you know. Just one: that you'll make sure you're always happy, and that you don't go chaining yourself for life to some dunce who doesn't appreciate what a rare treasure you are."

Catriona picked up a pale blue angora cardigan and folded the sleeves over. She couldn't say anything at all, not without crying; and just now she didn't want to cry, not in front of Nigel. She wanted him to think

6

that she had left him bravely and cheerfully, and that they could still be friends. But when she thought of the way they had run headlong down Box Hill on an August afternoon, and of beer and sandwiches in smoky country pubs, it was difficult not to feel so sad and nostalgic that the tears ran down her cheeks anyway.

"You'd better go, my love," said Nigel. "I don't want to make things worse for you than they are already."

She nodded and tied up the last of her lipsticks and her jars of rouge in her washbag.

"I'll bring the case down," Nigel told her.

By now, Mr. Fearson and Mr. Thurrock had moved into the hallway, and Mr. Fearson had his hand on the door handle. Outside in the sunshine a taxicab was waiting, its driver reading a copy of the *Daily Mirror*. Mr. Fearson took Catriona's arm as she came down the stairs and led her out into Royal Hospital Road. Mr. Thurrock mutely offered to take the suitcase from Nigel, but Nigel insisted on stowing it onto the taxi's luggage platform himself.

"You'll take care then, old thing," said Nigel as the cabbie opened the door and Catriona lowered her head to climb in.

"You too," she whispered, and then got inside and sat in the shadow of the far corner. Nigel had an unusual view of the broad shiny seat of Mr. Fearson's black trousers as he hefted himself in after her; and Mr. Thurrock, who was last, raised his hat to Nigel with all the morbid impudence of an undertaker.

"We're indebted, you know," he said.

Nigel stood on the pavement in his flashy dressing gown as the taxi pulled away from the curb and chugged off in the direction of Sloane Street. The tiny oval window in the back of the taxi's hood was tinted dark brown, and so he saw nothing of Catriona as she drove out of his life, not even the brim of her hat. A Chelsea pensioner in his bright scarlet military tunic came across the road to where Nigel was standing and watched the disappearing taxi with equal interest.

"They're not worth it, you know," he remarked in a phlegmy voice as the cab turned the corner.

Nigel looked at him. "What aren't?"

"Women," said the pensioner. "They say they're going to wait for you, but they never do. Women and their promises! Mine didn't wait."

Nigel said, "Oh. I'm sorry," and then went back into the house.

TWO

Her mother was resting in the day room when Catriona arrived home. She was propped up in a white-painted basketwork chair with far too many cushions, and she was wearing a tiny and menacing pair of sunglasses, presumably to hide her swollen eyes. She had just finished a mug of Home & Colonial Beef Tea, but she hadn't been able to touch the ham salad that cook had prepared for her.

The day room had always been her mother's room; it was a small pretty parlour with French windows which gave out on to a flight of stone steps, and on to that part of the garden which her father had always liked to call the nattery—where Mother's friends would gather on summer afternoons to natter. Unlike almost every other room in the house, there were no etchings or oil paintings of ships in the day room, just pink flowery wallpaper and gilded mirrors. In the corner stood an unfinished embroidery of Balmoral Castle.

"You *came,* darling," Catriona's mother cried tearfully, lifting her hands. "Oh, my dear Catriona, they brought you back."

Catriona crossed the room and knelt beside her mother's chair. They embraced each other, tightly and awkwardly. Catriona stroked her mother's auburn-tinted hair and scratched her hand on one of her mother's diamond combs. Her mother wept and trembled in a tussle of frustration and grief, and Catriona knew that there was nothing she could say or do to help her, not now, and maybe not ever. Her father had been the firm ground on which her mother had walked and the vault of heaven above her head. His death had been more than the loss of a husband; it had been the sudden and utter vanishing of every recognisable landmark in her life. It was as if she had been abruptly blinded as she was walking across an unfamiliar pasture.

"I was afraid you weren't going to cuh-uh-ome," sobbed her mother. She had to take off her dark spectacles to dab at her eyes with the corner of her handkerchief. "After what happened last time, well, I just didn't *know.*"

"Mother, of course I came," Catriona soothed her. She took her hand and squeezed it twice. Her mother's hands were knobbly with diamond and sapphire rings—ugly Victorian rings that were probably worth thousands and thousands of pounds. She always wore them, and even today she hadn't forgotten to put them on. But her dress was plain and unfamiliar and black, with a jet brooch at her neck and double pleats of black lace over the bust, and she wore black shoes and black stockings. Her mother had always looked like Catriona expected *she* would look in twenty years' time, and somehow the black dress reinforced that impression. A black and white photograph from tomorrow.

"Is Isabelle here?" asked Catriona. "I saw the Crossley parked outside."

"Mr. Fearson sent her a telegraph very first thing," said her mother. "She's having a light supper now, with Mrs. Brackenthorpe. She's been wonderful, of course. Everybody's been wonderful. But your poor *father,* my darling. It was such a shock. And so young, and so *vigorous.*"

"Hush, Mother," said Catriona, but her mother didn't seem to hear her.

"He went to church as regularly as anyone," she said. "Every Sunday, Holy Communion and Evensong both. So how could the Lord have taken him so young? Only fifty-three! His life only two-thirds lived! And to think of the sinners and the ruffians who live to a ripe old age, and have never once seen the inside of a chapel! That's what I've been asking myself today. How could the Lord have taken so obedient a servant so young?"

Catriona stood up and brushed her skirt straight. "Mother," she said, "you really must try to rest. It's no good thinking about why Father died. You have to start thinking about helping yourself now. That's the way he would have wished it, wouldn't he?"

Her mother let out a wretched sob, her lips as wet as a child's. "How do *I* know what he would have wanted? He never told *me* what he wanted. He was just *there.*"

"Mother, rest. I'll see if Isabelle can get something to help you sleep."

"Sleep? How can I sleep? The last time I slept I woke up to find that I'd lost the only person I've ever cared about. I never want to sleep again."

"Mother," said Catriona, and bent forward to hug her mother very close to her. "I do love you, Mother."

At that very moment the door opened and Isabelle came in with a piece of blackberry and apple pie on a plate. When she saw the uneaten salad and Catriona she said, "Oh," in an affronted tone, as if all of her painstaking nursing was being thrown back in her face. Isabelle was her mother's younger sister, a narrower, thinner, sourer version of her mother, with skimpier hair, a sharper nose, smaller breasts, and bonier ankles; Catriona's father always used to say that when Isabelle had been younger she had been "quite a dazzler." But care and jealousy had prematurely worn her out, while Catriona's mother, by contrast, had grown smooth-faced and placid.

"You're going to have to eat something sometime, you know, dear," said Isabelle. "And cook did make a special effort to give you something light and tasty. Hallo, Catriona. I'm surprised to see you back so prompt."

"My father's dead," said Catriona simply, standing up straight.

Isabelle ignored her. "You really ought to make an effort with the salad, dear," she persisted. "Cook will be frightfully hurt if you don't even make an effort."

Catriona's mother looked sideways at her supper tray. Catriona said, "You don't have to eat it if you don't want to, Mother. I don't think ham salad is the best antidote to grief anyway."

Catriona's mother continued to stare at the supper tray, and two large tears rolled out from under her dark glasses and down her cheeks. She was thinking, probably, as Catriona was thinking, that this was the first supper she was having to eat without her husband. Her first supper alone, and all of those lonely suppers ahead of her, for the rest of her life. She could never conceive of marrying anyone else. What other man was so much a part of the fabric and the firmament of Formby; what other man was big enough to build the world's largest passenger liner and still care for everything that his wife wished for?

"I'll send Gwen for the tray then," said Isabelle.

Catriona said clearly, "No, Aunt Isabelle. Please, I'd really appreciate it if you took the tray away now."

Isabelle hesitated by the door. Then fussily she came across and picked up the tray. "I hope you don't think that *you'll* be running things around here," she said in a voice as sharp as a lemon drop. "Not after *your* scarlet goings-on. Actors and the like. I've heard all about it, don't you worry."

"I'm not worried," Catriona told her levelly.

"Not even ashamed, I shouldn't wonder," said Isabelle.

"Izzy," put in Catriona's mother wanly. "I do wish you wouldn't. Not now."

"Well, I'm sorry, I'm sure, but even at the worst of times some things have to be said, don't they?" Isabelle retorted. "She wasn't what you'd call a model daughter, was she? Never did a solitary thing that Stanley wanted. But now he's been taken, she's around the honeypot soon enough, isn't she, the busy little bee?"

Catriona pressed her hands together as if she were praying and lowered her head. She could never get to grips with Isabelle's bitterness. It was like a wriggling sour-tempered porcupine that hated its life but refused to be helped. The whole family knew why Isabelle was so bitter, of course; and Isabelle knew they knew. But she couldn't help herself. When she was seventeen she had been far prettier than Catriona's mother, and she had always had dozens of boyfriends. She had eloped with Tony, a dashing young commercial traveller who had dazzled her into believing that he was going to make a million out of selling Brooke's Monkey Brand soap throughout the northwest of England. But now Tony was a shop assistant in Liverpool, selling ready-made gents' suits and celluloid collars, and Isabelle was having to make do on six pounds, seven and nine a week; while Catriona's mother, who had gradually developed during her twenties into a young Victorian woman of ravishing looks, had at last married Stanley Keys, the self-made shipping magnate, after meeting him at a teatime concert in Formby, and was now the mistress of five large houses, seven motorcars, and a fleet of passenger liners that were universally acknowledged to be the fastest and most gracious ships afloat. Of course, Catriona's mother had always helped Isabelle out with occasional gifts of money. The Crossley motorcar had been a birthday present. But Isabelle's bitterness had not been softened by her inability to say no. Isabelle had her pride, naturally, but not *that* much pride.

"I'm just pleased that Catriona is here," her mother told Isabelle in a gentle voice. "This is a time when I'm going to need all of my family around me, without any prejudice or favour shown to anyone. And if you do think of poor Stanley's fortune as a honeypot, well, just remember that Stanley never denied any of his relatives or friends any of the honey. He was a Christian, a man who believed that everybody had a right to a fair share of luxury, if there was any luxury ever to be had."

Isabelle gave a petulant shrug. "I'd better instruct Cook about dinner tonight, if Mr. Deacon's coming. And I suppose Mr. Fearson will want to stay, too."

"I would like it if he were to," said Catriona's mother.

"I just hope we have enough cutlets to go around," Isabelle replied, as if someone had already plucked her dinner off the end of her fork.

When she was gone, Catriona took her mother's hand again and stroked it.

"I'm sorry," said Catriona's mother.

"There's no need to be," Catriona told her. "I think I'm used to Aunt Isabelle after all these years."

"It's not her fault, really," said Catriona's mother. "I can understand how she feels. Fate is very unjust sometimes, or at least it appears to be. She doesn't seem to realise that I would gladly give up everything—the house, the shipping line—just for one more day with Stanley. Just for one more minute. We were very happy, you know. Very much in love."

Catriona smiled.

"Are you going to be staying long?" asked her mother. "You don't have to rush back to London straightaway?"

"I'll stay for as long as you need me."

"But there's nobody waiting for you, is there? What about that actor boy, Terence?"

"Nigel."

"Oh, yes. Nigel. Won't he be waiting for you?"

Catriona stood up and walked across to the French windows. It was dark outside now, and she could see her own reflection in the glass, like a ghostly waif standing outside in the garden without even the courage to knock.

"I think I've left Nigel."

"For good?"

"I think so."

Her mother turned around in her chair and looked at her sympathetically. She felt sorry for Catriona, but of course it was also good news. Catriona's waywardness with boys had been the cause of more family dissention than almost anything else, and the Yorkshire relatives in particular had been so scandalised that they had sent Catriona no birthday presents since she was fifteen. The day that her father had discovered that Catriona was playing around in bed with Monsieur Nasillard, her young French tutor, he had furiously sent her off to live with his spinster sister in Morecambe. Every visit of Catriona's to Formby after that had been short, sharp, and attended by hellish arguments. Stanley Keys had loved his daughter too much to disinherit her, or punish her too severely or for too long; but he had come to believe at last that she was a girl with a will and a passion of her own, and when she was eighteen he had given her enough money to go to London and stay with one of his retired liner captains and his wife, knowing quite well that she would soon find her own friends and lovers, and her own place to live.

He may never have really known how much Catriona had adored him, nor how much she had wanted him simply to say that she could continue to stay at home and live with the family in a state of truce, even if they couldn't actually live together in accord. It probably wouldn't have worked anyway. He had probably done the right thing, letting her have her head. But if only he had *asked*. It would have meant that at least one of her parents understood that she wasn't really the confident, casual, promiscuous girl she appeared to be.

At least one of her parents would have known that she needed more love and encouragement than most children, that her prettiness and her brashness were masks behind which she hid a baffling uncertainty about herself and an almost addictive need for reassurance. But she realised now that expecting her father to penetrate her personality as deeply as that had been too much. He had been a rich, busy man, and he had been preoccupied with the financing and the building of the world's largest and most luxurious ocean passenger liner, the *Arcadia*. Apart from loving her, plainly and straightforwardly, what else could he have found the time to do? She thought it was strange that she could not remember what his face had actually looked like. Did people vanish from memory so quickly when they died? Yesterday he had been alive. He had made telephone calls and eaten a mutton pie. Today he might just as well never have existed.

"Nigel was a nice chap, wasn't he?" Catriona's mother asked her carefully. "He didn't—well, he didn't treat you roughly, did he?"

Catriona gave her mother a brief, rueful smile. "No, Mother. He didn't treat me roughly. He was a bit of a harebrain. Father would have called him a 'rumble-seat Roger.' But he was very fond of me. He could be marvellous. And when he was on the stage, you wouldn't have believed it was the same man."

"Well, anyway," said Catriona's mother, smoothing her dress. There were tears in her eyes again and Catriona knew that another wave of grief was coming over her, in spite of the beef tea and the sedatives that Dr. Whitby had given her.

"I'll stay, Mother, don't worry," Catriona told her softly.

"It's the ship," said her mother. "It's so *sad* about the ship. The finest ship that ever was, and he never saw it sail."

"I know, Mother," whispered Catriona. "But try to be brave. He wouldn't have asked for a better way to be remembered, would he? Whenever anyone mentions the *Arcadia*, they'll always think of Stanley Keys."

At that moment Catriona raised her eyes, and there on the small Regency table beside the window was a photograph of her father in a silver frame. The picture must have been taken on a windy day, because his hand was blurred as it went up to catch his cap. But he was smiling, brightly and confidently, a man who was very pleased with himself, and very pleased with life, and quite certain about the future.

Three

Edgar Deacon arrived late, at a quarter past nine, when they were already at dinner. He came straight into the mahogany-panelled dining room in his black clawhammer coat and kissed Catriona's hand. He bowed to Isabelle and said, "Good evening, Percy," to Mr. Fearson. Then he took his seat at the far end of the table and meticulously opened out his napkin. Still red-eyed from crying, Lettice the maid ladled out tomato soup for him, although he raised his hand after two helpings to show that he only wanted a little.

"I can't say that it's really been the kind of day that whets one's appetite," he remarked, sprinkling salt over his soup before he had tasted it, and stirring it with his spoon. "Too many sad duties to perform, don't you know." He turned to Catriona and said, "I can't tell you how sorry I am, my dear. The whole business has been a frightful shock. You and your mother have the condolences of the entire company, both board and managerial. Yes, and clerical, too."

"And manual," put in Mr. Fearson, breaking a bread roll.

"Well, of course," said Edgar. "Manual, too. Plenty of honest tears have been spilled down at the quayside and in the warehouse. Your father was an exceptional man, missed by all."

Catriona managed an evanescent smile. She had never quite known what to make of Edgar Deacon, although her father had always seemed to trust him implicitly. "The very devil when it comes to accounts," her father had always said of him, "and likes to gamble, too, although you wouldn't think it, not to look at him."

Edgar Deacon had been managing director of Keys Shipping for four years now, and for two years before that he had been works manager and chief engineer. Stanley Keys had come across him in India, on one of the first exploratory cruises he had made after the war, when Keys were busily planning for the prosperous and peaceful future. The war to end all wars was over, and Stanley Keys had envisioned a luxury shipping operation that would carry the wealthy and the curious to every country on the map, mundane or exotic, from Antwerp to Surabaja.

They had shared a tonga along English Laundry Road in Calcutta, on their way to the Bengal Club. When Stanley Keys had told Edgar who he was and why he had come to India, Edgar had nodded in approval. "You're quite right, of course. Luxury travel is about to come into its own. I've been trying to tell that to the directors of the Calcutta railway for absolutely *years.*"

He had taken out an Indian ivory cigarette holder and inserted a Players Perfectos No. 1 into it with the firm twist of an engineer. "You should make your shipping line appear to be as élitist as possible. That's the way to reap the greatest rewards. You may carry any number of second- and steerage-class passengers, of course, to pay for your bread and butter; but make the first class as exclusive as you possibly can. Make it almost impossible for anyone to buy a ticket, and then charge monstrous prices for it. Give your passengers the pleasure of being able to tilt their noses up into the air and say, '*I* travel Keys, don't y'know.'"

Stanley Keys had been amused. "And where did you learn *that* philosophy?" he had asked as Edgar lit his cigarette.

"At the Bengal Club," Edgar had said between clenched teeth. "I took over the running of the District Engineer's Ball three years ago. It had always been a dismal affair, or so I was told. So I trebled the price of the tickets to twenty rupees and made it as inconvenient as I could for anyone to get hold of one; and lo and behold it became the most sought-after social event on the calendar."

That evening, on the verandah of the Bengal Club, Stanley had approached Edgar and asked him quite bluntly, "Do you want a job?"

Edgar had been standing with his hands in his pockets watching the sunset, puffing away at his cigarette holder. "You don't know the first thing about me," he had said.

"I know that you run a shipfitting business down at Diamond Harbour, and that you're very well thought of."

"By some," Edgar had said cryptically. And then, without taking his cigarette holder out of his mouth, "Very well. I accept. I think it's time I went home, anyway."

As Stanley Keys had enlarged and built up his shipping line, he and Edgar had become closer and closer, sharing an office and taking all of their working lunches together. They were so close, sometimes, that other directors like Percy Fearson had begun uncomfortably to feel that Keys Shipping was a two-man company. But Edgar was a ferociously hard worker—punctilious, correct, and tireless, even if he could be a trifle distant with the staff, and that was probably nothing more than a hang-over from India. Anyone who still called the winter months the "cold weather" and referred to the works canteen staff as *khitmutgârs* could hardly be expected to be chummy with anyone on the shop floor.

Edgar had never been seen with a woman; but although Mr. Thurrock insisted that he was "one of those," Mr. Fearson said that he was probably more interested in his work than in petty flirtations. Edgar lived by himself in a severe grey house in the better part of Formby and was not to be drawn on the subject.

He was thin, with black polished hair and drawn-in cheeks, rather like one of the sketches of Sherlock Holmes in *The Strand Magazine*. He wore half-glasses to read, and his only concession to British life was a rather shorter cigarette holder than the one he had customarily used in Calcutta.

"I didn't really want to discuss business tonight," he remarked, cracking open his bread roll. "Unfortunately, I think that there is something with which you should be acquainted as soon as possible."

Catriona said, "I really don't know anything about business at all."

"Nonetheless, it is important that you hear what I have to say."

Catriona looked across at Percy Fearson, and Percy Fearson gave her an approving nod. She felt sophisticated enough tonight to talk about business, she supposed, and sad enough, too. Her hair was drawn tightly back from her face and tied with two strings of pearls from her mother's jewellery box. She wore a black silk dress with batwing sleeves, pinned together at the front with a clustered-pearl brooch. Her father would have considered that the gown was cut too low for an occasion as sombre as this, and in a peculiar way Catriona felt upset that she was able to wear it without being admonished.

Edgar said, "Your father was a great man, you know, Miss Keys. He was one of those few fellows who become giants in their own lifetime. When they come to write the history of the greatest ships and how they were built, your father's name will be emblazoned next to those of Ismay and Cunard and Ballin."

"Rather we didn't make comparisons with the Hun," put in Percy Fearson gruffly.

Isabelle, who was struggling with her cutlet, glanced across and gave Edgar a tight little smile to show that she, too, had always believed that Stanley Keys was a hero. She rather cared for Edgar Deacon and pooh-poohed the idea that he might be susceptible to the kind of affections that dare not speak their name. "He's *mysterious*, that's all," she used to say; and one morning she had had a dozing dream that he had taken down her thirteen-shilling cami-knickers and smacked her bare bottom. Tony of course was terrible in bed, even when he wasn't drunk on Newcastle Brown. You could only describe Tony's as a winkle.

"I haven't yet broached this matter with your mother," said Edgar. "I feel that it might be better to leave financial matters until after the funeral."

"She's very shocked, of course," Catriona told him. "But Dr. Whitby gave her some sedative tablets, and she's asleep now; although she swore that she'd never be able to."

"Sleep is the best medicine of all," said Edgar. "But how do *you* feel? You must be tired yourself after travelling all the way up from London."

"I'm numb, actually," said Catriona. "I don't think any of it has quite sunk in yet."

"Well, be careful when it does," Edgar cautioned her. "We're going to be needing you over the next few weeks. After your mother, you are, of course, the sole heiress to Keys Shipping, and your father's death has already entitled you to quite an inheritance of voting stock."

Catriona's eyes widened over the rim of her lifted wineglass. Then carefully she set the glass down on the table again. Although she said nothing, it was quite clear from her expression that she expected Edgar to explain exactly how he would need her, and why.

Edgar meticulously took a last spoonful of soup and then sat up very straight. "We had an *ad hoc* meeting of directors today," he said, steadily. "We talked about a difficulty which has been besetting us for some time, but a difficulty with which we could cope as long as Stanley was still alive. Now, tragically and prematurely, he has passed from amongst us. And the problem is that we have lost not only a dear friend and colleague, and a man whom we respected and loved, but the single most creditworthy asset which Keys Shipping ever owned."

"Surely you're not trying to suggest that the company can't continue without Stanley?"

"The problem is almost as serious as that." Edgar nodded. "The whole point, in plain English, without any Hobson-Jobson, is that Keys Shipping should never have attempted to build the *Arcadia* at all."

"What on earth does that mean?" asked Catriona. "Why not? She's a beautiful ship."

"Beautiful, yes," said Edgar. "But paid for, no."

"You mean the company's in debt?"

"Not just the company, my dear. Your whole family fortune, too. The Keys Shipping Line is so financially overstretched that we could be declared bankrupt at any moment. Your father, you see, gave personal guarantees for all of the company's debts. While he was alive, the banks considered these to be quite acceptable. But, now that he's gone . . ."

Catriona frowned quickly at Percy Fearson, but all Percy could do was nod and say, "It's true, I'm afraid."

"But we own so many ships," Catriona protested. "How could we possibly be bankrupt? And the *Arcadia* is the most luxurious passenger liner in the world. I don't understand."

Edgar remained silent while Lettice came in to take his soup bowl away and serve him with his lamb cutlet. Then, when she had gone, he said in that precise voice of his, "Keys Shipping is paying the same penalty that White Star is paying—namely, the penalty of having been one of the first shipping companies to build a grand ocean-cruising fleet. Before the war, of course, Keys was one of the most vigorous fleets on the Atlantic. But our ships are growing older now and less fashionable, and as you know for yourself, the oceangoing public is notoriously fickle about which ships are *pukkah* and which aren't. That was the principal reason your father wanted to lay down the *Arcadia*—to own a liner that could challenge the *Aquitania* and the *Berengaria* and the *Majestic*. 'A gleaming ferryboat for the rich and titled,' that's what he called her; a ship that would be glamorous and fabled in her own right and would also lend lustre to the rest of the fleet. But, she has cost us nearly four million pounds to build and to fit out, and this expense has come at a time when we have been losing money steadily on the greater part of the rest of our fleet. We have been systematically refitting the older ships, of course. You wait until you see the magnificent job that John Brown's have done on the *Iliad*. But refitting has been vastly expensive, too; and we've run out of credit, as simple as that. The bank won't underwrite us for any more for another six months, and the Government have told us quite bluntly that they won't lend us any money unless we consider a merger with Cunard."

"I wasn't aware of any of this," said Catriona.

"Well, you wouldn't have been, would you, living away from your family?" put in Isabelle sharply. She didn't quite have the vinegar to say "in sin" but the intimation was there.

Edgar cut the meat from his cutlet and began to chew. "We used to have a lamb cutlet every Thursday night at Peliti's Restaurant in Calcutta, don't y'know, myself and all the other chaps from my chummery. Lamb cutlet and mint sauce every Thursday. Always think it's Thursday when I eat lamb; can't shake it off."

Catriona said, "What are we going to do?"

"Do?"

"About the debts? How are we going to pay them off?"

"Well, we have a choice," said Edgar. He helped himself to a small sip of wine. "We can hope that the *Arcadia* puts up such a stunning performance on her maiden voyage that the banks can be persuaded to change their minds, although I have to be truthful and say that the chances of that happening are pretty remote. We'd have to take the Blue Riband for the fastest Atlantic crossing first go; and apart from that we'd have to show firm bookings that were up by at least twenty per cent, if not more. That can happen, of course. After the *Kronprinzessin Cecilie* took the Blue Riband, sales of North German Lloyd tickets went up twenty-six per cent. But it takes so long for ticket sales to be realised as profit that the banks may not wish to cooperate."

"What else can we do?" asked Isabelle. "Are there any alternatives?"

"Oh, yes. Several. We could dismantle the Keys fleet and sell it off piecemeal; but that, of course, would mean that we would sacrifice the jobs of every man who works for us, two thousand seven hundred men in all, not counting casual labour. We would ruin this entire community overnight, no doubt at all, and after everything that Stanley has done for it, I hardly think that we should consider any step as drastic as that."

"I'm against it, for one," said Percy Fearson.

"Then . . . we have had some preliminary approaches from International Mercantile Marine, in America. Their foreign business manager, George Welterman, has been in London for the past three weeks and will be sailing back to New York on the maiden voyage. He was talking to your father on the telephone last week about buying up the Keys fleet. Of course, your father refused; but this afternoon George Welterman called again and suggested that we might care to reconsider his offer."

"Which is?" asked Catriona.

"Better than most, as far as I can see," said Edgar. "Eighteen million in gold for the entire Keys Shipping Line, and a guarantee that it will be kept intact and that all existing employment agreements will be honoured for three years."

"But that means we'll lose the shipping line entirely," said Catriona.

Edgar chewed and nodded. "It will pass under the control of International Mercantile Marine lock, stock, and barrel. Or rather, it will pass under the control of a British board of directors who are directly answerable to IMM, since no British ship can be sold to a foreigner."

Catriona said, "Eighteen million in gold—how far will that stretch?"

"It will pay off our debts and the interest on our debts, and it will probably leave us with slightly less than a million pounds. Enough to invest in something afresh, if you have a mind to."

"But the end of the Keys fleet as a Keys family business?"

"Unless Mr. Welterman decides to appoint you or your mother as chairman," said Edgar. The tone of his voice was quite flat, but Catriona was alert enough to recognise the sarcasm in what he was saying. All that was left of the Keys family after her father's death was her mother, dithery and self-indulgent; Isabelle and Tony, neither of whom had the very first clue about business; and herself, a twenty-one-year-old flapper with no experience and a naughty reputation.

"You mentioned *several* alternatives," said Catriona as coldly as she could. "What were the others?"

Lettice, freshly red-eyed, came in to collect up the plates. She did it very noisily and managed to drop a lot of knives and forks, and then pick them up again, and then drop them again in the doorway. "There's only cheese," she said, miserably.

Catriona said, "Don't worry, Lettice. We'll help ourselves. Aunt Isabelle, would you mind awfully getting the water biscuits from the sideboard?"

Isabelle, bustling a little, fetched the crackers. Percy Fearson poured the port. They spooned ripe blue-veined Stilton onto their plates and ate it with olives and fresh celery.

Edgar Deacon said, "We could go into voluntary liquidation. That's always a possibility."

"Not one that *I'd* consider," said Percy Fearson.

"Well, it may be forced on us," replied Edgar. He brushed crumbs from the side of his mouth with a prissy gesture of his napkin. "It may also be one way of surviving. We could buy back the ships we wanted from the receiver and start up again under a different flag."

"I won't hear of it," said Percy Fearson. "It took Stanley years to build up the reputation of Keys Shipping as honest and upright, and that kind of financial jiggery-pokery just won't do."

"I was asked for alternatives," said Edgar.

"Honourable alternatives, yes," Percy Fearson retorted.

"Well, there's only one other," said Edgar. "And that is to sell the *Arcadia* separately."

"Would anyone be interested?" asked Isabelle.

"Stanley was visited several times by representatives of American TransAtlantic asking if he might consider selling or lending the *Arcadia*. But they were never offering enough money. Three million was about their best for an outright sale; and in any case, Stanley was determined *not* to sell, at any price. The *Arcadia* was Stanley's dream. He thought she would transform the entire shipping line overnight. It's true, of course, she has. She's almost broken us."

"In any case, selling the *Arcadia* separately wouldn't do much to solve our problems," said Percy Fearson. "We'd be left with the rest of the fleet and scarcely enough profit to pay mooring fees. And we'd have lost our most glamorous asset, present company excepted."

Catriona gave Percy a fleeting smile. She liked him when he pretended to be flirtatious. "Who runs American TransAtlantic?" she asked. "Isn't it Mark Beeney?"

"That's right. Thirty-one years old, almost implausibly handsome, and a dollar millionaire twenty times over. Well, on paper, anyway."

"I think I read about him in the *Evening Standard* a couple of days ago," said Catriona. "They said he was the most eligible man in the world. And he's in London, too."

"He'll be sailing on the *Arcadia*'s maiden voyage," said Percy.

"Really? I know that Douglas Fairbanks and Mary Pickford are going to be on her."

Edgar Deacon lifted his hand and ticked off his fingers one by one. "Douglas Fairbanks, Mary Pickford, Princess Xenia of Russia, Jack Dempsey, Dame Clara Butt"—he raised his other hand and carried on counting—"Madge Bellamy, Lenore Ulric, Charles Schwab of Bethlehem Steel, and even Señora Zelmira Paz de Gainza, with her ten maids, four motorcars, and a chambermaid."

Isabelle remarked, "It sounds like the Ark."

"Well, we do have some animals, too," said Edgar. "A two-thousand-pound chow dog called Choonam Brilliantine, whom we have to feed with fresh raw eggs for his lunch every day; and Pyramid, the horse which won last year's Derby. He's going to be shipped in a special padded stable, and he's going to be taking his own blacksmith with him."

Catriona held her glass towards Percy Fearson for a little more port. Percy Fearson hesitated at first, but Edgar Deacon nodded at him to fill her glass up. "After what Mr. Thurrock told me about your young man's cocktails I'm sure a little 1911 port won't go to your head." He smiled. His smile was as thin as celluloid.

Catriona said, "This still doesn't solve the problem of how we're going to save Keys Shipping."

"We have some time left to consider the matter, of course," said Edgar. "But by the time the *Arcadia* docks in New York, we will have had to have made up our minds. The sheer cost of refuelling her and victualling her up for the return journey will be beyond us, unless we can be sure of a sale, or some further credit. And I would very much dislike to have her impounded in a foreign port."

"Why send her to New York at all, if we can't afford it?" asked

Isabelle.

"We can't afford *not* to send her either," Edgar explained. "We have scores of cargo contracts to fulfil, contracts which have already been paid for; we've bought food and drink and fuel. How are we going to settle with all of our creditors if we don't sail, and have to refund our passengers' ticket money? Not to sail would sink us faster than sailing will. And besides, if we fail to take the *Arcadia* out, if we fail to show her as a fast and exciting and fashionable ship, her value on the shipping market will be seriously—disastrously—undermined."

Catriona said, "You really believe that we'll have to sell Keys Shipping?"

Edgar set down his butter knife. "I wish I could say no, but I cannot."

"And you think that George Welterman is the man to sell it to?"

"He will, after all, keep the existing company intact."

"What did Father think of him?"

"Your father disliked him; but then George Welterman is not a particularly easy man to like. Nonetheless, he is probably the most powerful single man in American shipping today, apart from his masters at IMM."

"How can we think of selling Keys to a man whom Father disliked?"

Edgar said, "I regret, Miss Keys, that we often have to deal with people we dislike, as a matter of expediency."

"There *must* be another way of raising money somehow," said Catriona. "To think of selling everything that Father worked for all these years, and right at the moment of his greatest success . . ."

"You have to think of more than your immediate family," Edgar told her. "The families of scores of Liverpool men depend on us, too. The most important thing is to pay off what we owe and keep the company in one piece. That may not be everything that your father wanted; but it will leave him with a very fitting memorial."

"Well, I just hope that I don't have to meet this George Welterman," said Catriona.

"Oh, I'm afraid that you will," said Edgar. "You're coming along on the maiden voyage, after all; and Mr. Welterman will be joining us."

"*I'm* coming?" asked Catriona.

"Of course. Who else is there to represent the Keys family? Your mother can't come, she's just not up to it, and somebody has to be sweet to the bankers and the food suppliers."

"Your father always talked about cajoling you into coming along." Percy Fearson smiled. "He wanted to attract the younger travellers, you see, the bright young things, so that if they got the idea it was smart to travel Keys, he'd have loyal new passengers who would travel with Keys forever after."

"But I don't see where *I* come into it," said Catriona.

"He was going to publicise you as the Queen of the Atlantic," said Percy. "He was going to have you dressed by Paris designers, and buy you jewellery and furs and you name it. There's a whole file on it down at the office."

"He never told me," said Catriona. "The last time we met, we had that awful row, and he never told me."

"I think he was almost afraid you wouldn't agree to do it," said Percy.

"Afraid?" Catriona frowned. She couldn't imagine her father ever having been afraid.

"He wanted you to be the star of the whole voyage," Percy told her gently. "He loved you, you know; and I sometimes think that when he built the *Arcadia* he built it for you."

Isabelle stared at Catriona with an expression of such jealousy that she could have made a herring curl up. Catriona felt giddy, and the table seemed to tilt away from her. She was used to Nigel's poisonous Chicago cocktails, but not to Château Mouton Rothschild form her father's cellars. But perhaps it wasn't the wine at all. Perhaps it was the way in which her life had so suddenly tricked her. She had thought she was free of her father, and relieved of all involvement in the Keys family. A carefree, heel-kicking flapper. But now she had discovered that freedom is something which is granted—by a government to its people, by a parent to his child—and when death supervenes, the grant of freedom is automatically withdrawn and has to be renewed.

"Mr. Deacon," she said, "I really don't know what to say. You'll have to give me time to think about it."

"There isn't much time, my dear," said Mr. Fearson. "The *Arcadia* has to sail on Tuesday, whatever."

"You can't even delay her until Father's buried?"

Edgar shook his head. "The cost of even one day's delay would be more than we could stand. And apart from that, the *Arcadia* must start off her active life with a reputation for reliability."

Catriona sat where she was, and then discovered that tears were sliding down her cheeks.

"Forgive me, Miss Keys," said Edgar. "I didn't intend to upset you today of all days."

"No, no. It's not your fault," said Catriona. "I'm just tired, that's all."

"Dottie has your room ready for you, if you wish to withdraw."

Percy Fearson escorted Catriona out of the dining room; and in the dark timbered hallway he gave her over to Dottie, the upstairs maid, a ruddy-faced young girl who had come into service with the Keys family when she was fourteen. Dottie took Catriona's arm and led her solicitously upstairs to the green-wallpapered guest bedroom at the end of the landing.

22

Catriona's old bedroom was being redecorated, and there was a sharp smell of lead paint and wallpaper paste around.

The night was so warm that the diamond-leaded window which gave out on to the main sweep of the garden had been left wide open, and the full moon could be seen rising from behind the poplars. Moths pattered and battered against the green and white frosted bedside lamp. "I'll squirt them with Flit if you want," Dottie suggested.

Catriona stood with her arms by her sides, her eyes closed, while Dottie unhooked her black dress for her and lifted it over her head. She wore no slip or corset; she thought her figure looked more boyish if she went without. Dottie helped her to roll down her black silk stockings and step out of her crepe-de-chine panties.

Catriona said to her, "What was the last thing my father ever said to you, Dottie? Can you remember?"

Dottie had to think about that. She was holding up Catriona's biscuit-on-cream pleated voile nightgown, and she was obviously astonished by the shortness and the airiness of it. "I don't know, miss," she said. "I think I'm still perplexed by it all."

"You can't remember anything?"

Dottie frowned. "Now, then. I remember I saw him in the hallway just before he went upstairs to bed. He said, 'You won't forget to remind Cook that I want my Food of Life, will you, Dottie?' That's what he said."

Catriona sat down on the edge of the bed and started to unpin her hair. "Food of Life," she whispered sadly, and she thought of the little nursery rhyme her father used to sing her, the one which he had invented himself.

> Where the fish swim free, child,
> And never bite the line;
> Keep your nose in your own soup
> And keep it out of mine.

Four

Mark Beeney said, "I've always been an Anglophile. I love your climate, I love your women, I love your mutton pies. But God Almighty, I've never understood your cricket."

Philip Carter-Helm lifted his boater off his neatly trimmed hair and wiped around the leather sweatband with his handkerchief. "You can't really understand cricket until you understand loafing," he said. "You must never listen to any explanations of the rules of cricket, byes or fours or leg before wicket, or any tommyrot like that. It's the mental attitude that counts. The British love to loaf; but unlike Americans, they have to find an excuse for it. Hence, cricket."

Mark and Philip were strolling in Hyde Park late in the afternoon, within sight of the Albert Memorial. Some small boys were playing cricket under the trees, their single stump casting a long sundial shadow across the marmalade-coloured grass. Their cries as they played were like the cries of small birds. There was a smell of soft-mown grass in the air, and London evenings.

Mark said, "You're a little *cynical,* aren't you?"

"Ah," said Philip, "but all Englishmen are. Our cynicism protects us from our sentimentality."

Mark stooped to pick up a long whippy branch. As he walked, he swished it in the air. "You want to talk about the *Arcadia?*" he asked.

Philip Carter-Helm was tall and well built, with the kind of open-faced good looks that characterised Old Boys from minor public schools, especially those whose photographs appeared in the school magazine after they had been killed at Omdurman or Killa Khasi. He had chestnut hair and very clear grey eyes and a bump on the bridge of his nose from boxing. He spoke in that clipped newsreel accent that made Americans believe that every Briton must be a relative of the King; but English ears could pick up the slightest of Northern intonations. He said "path" with a short "a," instead of the drawled-out aristocratic "parth".

Mark had been disinclined to talk to Philip at first, since he was on a furious tour of all his European interests, and London was his last and busiest stop before sailing back to the States. In two months Mark had visited Zurich, Hamburg, Copenhagen, Frederikshaven, Naples, Capri, and Marseilles. In all, he had visited seventeen cities and nine countries, and now he was anxious to get back to Boston; not just to assess the state of his business interests from a detached distance, but to see Juliet again, the girl he had met only days before he had sailed for Europe. She was the only daughter of the Harrises, the Newport Harrises, and she was not only dark-eyed and curiously beautiful, she was awash with inherited dollars. Mark had an unashamed liking both for looks and money. After all, he had both attributes himself.

The popular magazines called him "boyishly handsome." He had irrepressibly curly hair and the firm square jawline of a Boston Irishman. He wore his grey tweed suit with casual but assertive style, and his collars and cuffs were almost unnaturally white. He walked straight-backed, like the horse rider and yachtsman he was.

Philip Carter-Helm had left him a letter that morning at his hotel. It had said simply, "I know you covet the *Arcadia*. Perhaps I can assist." The message had been cryptic enough and arrogant enough for Mark to cancel an afternoon meeting with his underwriters at Lloyd's and take a walk with Philip in the park.

"There isn't any question that the *Arcadia* is the most advanced and luxurious passenger ship ever built," said Philip. "She's *years* ahead of anything currently afloat; and it's going to take Cunard and White Star another five years even to catch up with her. There's no doubt in my mind, either, that the future lies with giant-sized liners. Look how fast passenger ships have developed in the past fifty years. In 1874, the biggest Cunard steamers were the *Bothnia* and the *Scythia*, 420 feet long, with a gross tonnage that was less than 5,000 tons. Now look what they've built —a 960-footer like the *Arcadia*, 53,000 tons."

"You have it all at your fingertips," Mark said dryly.

"Well, it's my job. But when I look at your fleet, American TransAtlantic, I can see that you sorely need a fast prestige express liner to give you not only glamour and style but carrying capacity, too."

"I can't disagree with you," said Mark. "I've been saying the same thing to my board of directors for the past three years. Unfortunately, there doesn't seem to be much likelihood of my being able to buy the *Arcadia* on her own, as a one-off purchase. I know Stanley Keys is having his money troubles, but he's resisted all of my offers so far; and I don't see much hope of him changing his mind."

"That may be possible," said Philip. Mark glanced across at him quickly, alerted by a noticeable sense of what?—sadness, regret?—in Philip's voice.

"You wouldn't like to tell me *how?*"

"Well . . . let me put it theoretically. Supposing Stanley Keys were to give up his share of Keys Shipping?"

"Give it up? I can't see him doing that. What would he want to give it up for? Stanley Keys *is* Keys Shipping. Besides, he's as stubborn as a pickaxe handle." Mark paused, and then he said, "Do you know something that I don't know?"

They had reached the Serpentine now; drowned cumulus clouds lay beneath the ruffled blue surface, and toy boats spanked across the water at a sharp diagonal. Philip thrust his hands into the pockets of his summer flannels and said, "I'm in the business, that's all. Shipping, maritime insurance, that kind of thing."

"All right, then," said Mark cautiously. "Supposing Stanley Keys *did* give up his share of Keys Shipping?"

"Well, then, you'd find that you had an interesting situation as far as the distribution of voting stock was concerned. You see, Stanley Keys has always kept a controlling interest in Keys Shipping, with fifty-one per cent of the stock. The other stock owners are International Mercantile Marine, with twelve per cent; Thistle Maritime in Glasgow, with five per cent; the Eire Credit Bank, with five per cent; Mr. Deacon and Mr. Fearson, who are both directors of Keys, with two per cent apiece; Mr. Thurrock, with one per cent; Mrs. Keys' sister Isabelle, with two per cent; Mr. Rogers and Mr. Peabody, half a per cent each; and then a collection of trusts and individuals and insurance companies who hold the balance of nineteen per cent."

"Yes?" asked Mark. "What of it? I can find out all of this down at Lloyd's."

"Of course. But what you *can't* find out at Lloyd's is that Stanley Keys has willed his fifty-one per cent share of the company to his wife Doris and his daughter Catriona. Doris gets twenty-six per cent, Catriona gets twenty-five per cent."

"That isn't unusual. My father willed my mother and me just about the same percentage of American TransAtlantic."

"I'm not saying it's unusual. I'm just saying that, once the bequest is made, there will be a fascinating lineup of opposing interests. Considering the financial trouble that Keys is now going through, I suspect that Mr. Deacon, the managing director, will try to put forward a proposal that Keys should be sold to IMM, who have been after Keys for ages. Of course, IMM will back that proposal, with their twelve per cent of the vote, and there's no doubt that Eire Credit Bank will, too. *They've* never been deliriously happy about lending Keys so much money. The rest of the Keys board will go along with Mr. Deacon, and Mrs. Keys will undoubtedly go along with the board."

It had already dawned on Mark that what Philip was telling him was not theoretical at all. He stopped where he was, the evening wind blowing his uncovered curls, and he held the cuff of Philip's coat, as if it were necessary to cling to him in order to make sure that he stayed here by the Serpentine and told him everything.

A snotty-nosed boy came up and said, "Gissa penny, mister," but Mark waved him away.

"Shitface," the boy said gratuitously.

Philip said, "On the other hand, you have Thistle Maritime, who handle a good proportion of Keys' cargoes, and they would certainly vote against a sale to IMM, since IMM always use their own forwarding agencies. And most of the various small trusts and insurance companies who hold nineteen per cent of the stock would oppose a sale to IMM because it would take effective control of the company out of England.

"The unknown quantity in this lineup is Stanley Keys' daughter Catriona," said Philip. "With a twenty-five per cent holding, she would obviously hold the balance of power between those who favoured a sale to IMM and those who wanted Keys either to remain completely independent or at worst to sell off some of the company's assets in order to keep the greater part of the fleet in Keys family hands. Assets like the *Arcadia*, for instance."

Mark released Philip's sleeve but didn't take his eyes off him. "What you're telling me is that Stanley Keys is dead," he said hoarsely.

Philip said, "Yes."

"When did this happen? I haven't heard anything about it."

"Last night, very late. It'll probably be out in this evening's papers."

Mark said, "How did you get to hear about it?"

"It's my business. You won't get anywhere in shipping unless you keep your ear to the ground."

"So Stanley Keys is dead," said Mark, reflectively. "He couldn't have been all that old. Fifty?"

"Fifty-three. I understand he had a heart attack."

"Well, the way he used to work, I'm not surprised. And he never even got to see the *Arcadia* sail. That's a little sad, isn't it? Boy, that's sad."

Philip nodded. "Yes. Very sad."

"And that's what's going to happen?" Mark wanted to know. "His fifty-one per cent share in the company gets split up between his wife and his daughter?"

"That's right."

"So what's *your* interest in it?"

They started to walk back towards Park Lane. Fleets of black upright taxicabs drove backwards and forwards through the park, and the late sun lit up the pale grimy columns of Marble Arch. Philip said, "I represent a number of the small stockholders, as a matter of fact, including Thistle. Their interest is in seeing Keys remain independent. My interest obviously is in my fee if I succeed in ensuring that this happens."

"So how do you intend to do that?"

"Plainly the first step is to persuade Miss Catriona Keys that selling to IMM is not necessarily the wisest course of action."

"She's coming along on the maiden voyage, isn't she?"

"That's right. She's a very attractive young girl; I'm sure you'll get on famously. A little wayward, her father always used to say, but I think he respected her for it, too."

"You sound as if you knew Stanley Keys pretty well."

Philip shrugged. "On and off. He wasn't a particularly easy man to get close to."

They passed Apsley House, the former residence of the Duke of Wellington, and parted company at Hyde Park Corner. As they shook hands, Mark said, "I'll keep in touch. You can expect a call from my company secretary tomorrow morning."

"Oh, well, don't worry about that. I'm coming along on the *Arcadia*, too."

"Sounds as if it's going to be a regular party."

"I'm sure it is," said Philip. "Well, cheer-ho."

"Cheer-ho," replied Mark self-consciously.

As he began to walk back to his hotel, however, he began to feel that in spite of all the British *bonhomie* of their encounter, Philip had only allowed him to be privy to part of the story. He frowned as he walked, trying to work out what it was that hadn't quite fitted together.

A newsboy yelped out, "Pape-ear, pape-ear, famous shipping magnate dead, pape-ear!"

He dug into his pocket for a penny and bought the *Evening Standard.*

Five

He was staying at Brown's, on the Albemarle Street side, in a suite of rooms which cost seven pounds the night. As he entered the lobby, the porter called, "Messages, Mr. Beeney!" and hurried across with a sheaf of envelopes.

Mark sorted through the messages quickly, then tipped the porter half a crown, although a florin would have been enough. The porter said, "Obliged, Mr. Beeney, sir," and retreated to his cubbyhole. Mark walked along the corridor to his suite, tearing open the messages one by one, feeling unusually despondent. Or perhaps it wasn't despondency at all;

perhaps it was just that unsettling sensation that the world of shipping had somehow changed, and changed forever, now that one of its pivotal personalities had so suddenly disappeared.

"Mr. Beeney, sir, glad to have you with us," said the assistant manager, gliding past him on the left-hand side like a ballroom dancer.

Mark opened the door of his suite and stepped inside, kicking the door closed behind him with his foot.

"Damn it," he said aloud. Philip Carter-Helm had really aroused his curiosity; and he hated curiosity, especially his own.

Something tumultuous must be happening at Keys, not only within the Keys boardroom but within the Keys family itself. Carter-Helm had given him one version of it, but there had to be others. Was it true that Stanley Keys had left a quarter of his voting stock to his twenty-one-year-old daughter? Was it true that most of the small shareholders and insurance companies wanted Keys to remain independent? It was crucial to Mark if they did, because he coveted the *Arcadia* more than any other vessel in the world. She was the ship he would have built as his own flagship, if the board of American TransAtlantic hadn't so consistently counselled him to hold back. They agreed in principle with the idea of building or acquiring a new express flagship, but did it really have to be a gilded barge like the *Arcadia?* The future of travel lay not with the first-class passenger, whose tastes and expectations required prodigious numbers of trained staff and extraordinary feats of catering, but with the second- and third-class passenger, who required only a bed, a chair, a little deck space, and plain good cooking. One director had even suggested that transcontinental aeroplanes could soon take over from the giant liners, and that in ten years' time the grand shipping companies would all be out of business.

That, of course, was somewhat farfetched. As another American TransAtlantic director had retorted, "Your first-class passenger wouldn't contemplate crossing the Atlantic without his full quota of luggage and at least some rudimentary entertainment *en route.* By the time you've loaded an aeroplane with a hundred pieces of Swaine, Adeney and Brigg luggage and a Steinway grand piano, where's the room even for *one* passenger, leave alone hundreds?"

Mark had been torn. He recognised that tourist-class fares were going to bring American TransAtlantic the steady profits of the next decade; and he was modern-minded enough to accept that air travel might one day cream off some of the business trade. After all, there were many passengers who would be prepared to sacrifice luxury for speed. But he still believed that American TransAtlantic needed a glittering flagship, a ship which would carry the company name into high social currency all over the world, and which would lure passengers to travel American TransAtlantic in the same way that the *Mauretania*'s glamour attracted passengers to travel Cunard.

He stripped off his tweed coat and tossed it onto a chair. Just then his manservant Wallis appeared, buttoning up his vest. "Mr. Crombey has been waiting for you for some time, sir," he said, collecting up Mark's coat and folding it neatly over his arm. "He's back in his room now, sir, and asks if you could be kind enough to call him when you come in."

Wallis was a grey-haired Louisiana negro whom Mark's father had met on board the Mississippi steamer *Alonzo Child* in the 1880s. He had been a deckhand then, but Joe Beeney had taught him the rudiments of social grace, and Chloe Beeney had eventually turned him into one of the best black butlers in Boston.

Mark's father often used to say that when he met Mark's mother, "the whole damned Western Hemisphere trembled." There was no doubt that Mark was the product of one of the most passionate collisions of wilful and headstrong people that the nineteenth century had ever witnessed; and his father often used to compare his meeting with Mark's mother with the poem that Thomas Hardy had written to commemorate the sinking of the *Titanic* by an iceberg.

> Alien they seemed to be:
> no mortal eye could see
> The intimate welding of their later history.
> Or sign that they were bent
> By paths coincident
> On being anon twin halves of one august event.

Mark's mother, Chloe McKeown Amery, had been the daughter of one of Boston's noblest and wealthiest families. When Chloe's father had earnestly complained at a public luncheon that he was taxed ninety-two per cent, one wag in the audience had shouted out that he would certainly like to try to live on the remaining eight per cent. The Amerys' money was in property, in railroad stocks, in mercantile insurance, and shipping; and it was through the shipping side of their business that Chloe had accidentally come to meet Joshua Marblehead Beeney, the captain of one of the Amerys' largest passenger vessels, *Seraphic*. Chloe had always been an obstinate girl, and when she had been dispatched to Switzerland at the age of eighteen to "finish", her mother had entrusted her into Captain Beeney's personal custody; little realising that this blunt, rugged, oddly becoming man would promptly and insatiably fall in love with Chloe, and that she would just as promptly and with equal ferocity fall in love with *him*. When he had found out about their affair, Chloe's father had thrown a fit of rage close to the epileptic, but Chloe had been as persistent as ever, and in the same way that she had persuaded her father to buy her a rocking horse when she was four, she had persuaded him to let her marry

Joe Beeney. Part of her dowry had been a sizeable interest in Amery Shipping; and after the death of Chloe's father in 1893, Joe Beeney had taken over the entire company. Tragically, he had died himself only four years later, drowned while sailing his yacht off Point Gammon, Massachusetts. And so, at the age of twenty-three, Mark Beeney had inherited a shipping line that was second only to United States Lines, and an incalculable fortune in property, stocks, paintings, racehorses, and land. It was hardly surprising that he was considered to be one of the world's most eligible young men.

Mark shook open the *Evening Standard* that he had bought and said, "Get me a drink before you call Mr. Crombey, will you? Did you know that Stanley Keys is dead?"

"No, sir. Mr. Stanley Keys of Keys Shipping, sir?"

"The very same. Look, here it is in the paper."

The story was on the front page, under advertisements for Dr. J. Collis Brown's Chlorodyne and a Thursday night "Souper Dansant" at the Metropole. Stanley Keys, chairman, founder, and principal stockholder of Keys Shipping Line, had died the previous night of a massive heart seizure. So far the company had not announced a successor, but the directors were adamant that Mr. Keys would have wished the new luxury liner *Arcadia* to leave Liverpool on Tuesday, as scheduled, for her maiden voyage.

> Mr. Keys' only child, his twenty-one-year-old daughter, Miss Catriona Keys, is understood to have returned to the family home from London, where she has become well known in recent months in theatrical circles. She recently denied suggestions that she was engaged to marry musical actor Mr. Nigel Myers, who is currently appearing in *Daydreams of 1924* at the Prince Edward.

Mark turned the City pages, but apart from a note that "Keys Shipping shares drop 1½d" there was nothing about the company's future plans, or how dangerously in debt they were. Wallis brought him a bourbon and seltzer, and he sipped it thoughtfully.

The last time he had met Stanley Keys, in the bar of Scott's restaurant in Piccadilly, he had openly expressed his admiration of the *Arcadia*, and said, "If ever you need liquidity, Mr. Keys, I'll buy her from you for cash."

Stanley Keys had given Mark that quizzical, amused look which either charmed or infuriated the people he met, and replied, "I'll never be *that* hard up, my lad. The *Arcadia*'s more than just a ship; she's my own flesh and blood. Aye, and my spirit, too. You don't go selling your spirit."

Nonetheless, it was common knowledge in the shipping business that

Keys had desperately overstretched their resources by building such a lavish flagship; and it had always been Mark's intuition that Stanley Keys would sacrifice her at the very last if it meant that he could keep the rest of his fleet alive. Stanley Keys had always been a fleet man, rather than a devotee to one particular ship. He had been just as happy crossing the Atlantic in one of his small single-class steamers as he had been in the best of his luxury liners. Given the right historical circumstances, and a better social background, Stanley Keys would have made a fine naval commander.

But now he was abruptly gone, and it was almost impossible for Mark to guess what the board of Keys would do to remain solvent. It was quite possible that they would auction off the entire fleet, and they would probably come under heavy pressure from George Welterman to make a bargain offer to IMM.

One thing was certain: they would have to let the *Arcadia* sail on Tuesday. They would have far too much capital and prestige invested in the maiden voyage to cancel or postpone it now. But what then? If Mark knew anything about Keys' finances, they would scarcely be able to afford to bring her back to Liverpool again. He said to Wallis, "Bring me the telephone, will you? I think I'd better make a few calls."

"You're dining in tonight, sir?"

"Maybe. I'll see how hungry I feel. I was toying with the idea of going to Rule's for a pork chop."

Wallis brought him the white candlestick telephone, and he asked the hotel operator to connect him with Mr. Edgar Deacon, of Formby, in Lancashire. Then he said to Wallis, "Call Mr. Crombey, will you? And tell him to bring in all the Italian figures, and all the reports on De Freitas."

"Yes, sir. But I have to say that Mr. Crombey's not in a happy mood tonight, sir."

"I don't care what kind of a mood he's in. Will you call him?"

"Yes, sir."

"Operator?" said Mark. "Ah, good. Do you have the number? Formby what? Two-oh-fife-fower? Hey, don't you feel a bally ass having to pronounce numbers like that? Oh, well, I didn't mean it. I'm sorry. Yes, I'll make a note of it. All right. Now, could you please connect me?"

There was a knock at the sitting-room door. Mark waved Wallis to go answer it, and the butler tugged at his lapels, opened the door, and inquired, "Who is it, please?"

At the same time, Edgar Deacon came on the line. He was just about to have dinner with Catriona, and he sounded vaguely exasperated. "Who is it?" he asked, his voice tinny and distant.

"It's Mark Beeney," shouted Mark. "Can you hear me?" He felt as if he were trying to shout to someone on the opposite rim of the Grand

32

Canyon. "I was talking to Mr. Keys not long ago about buying the *Arcadia.*"

"Yes, Mr. Beeney. Quite so. What can I do for you?"

"I read the papers tonight. I'm sorry to hear about Stanley. It was a great shock."

"Well, thank you for your condolences," said Edgar, "but is that all you rang for? I'm really very busy. I expect you can imagine that it's been a frightfully gruelling day."

"I'm sure of it, and I'm sorry," Mark told him. "But listen, that isn't all. What I wanted to do was repeat my offer. I'd very much like to buy the *Arcadia* as the flagship of American TransAtlantic. I'm prepared to pay four million pounds cash, subject to survey, and I'm prepared to settle the deal right away, even before she's cut her teeth."

There was a silence, punctuated only by the crackling of long-distance telephone lines. Then Edgar Deacon said, with all the correctness of an experienced office *wallah*, "You realise, Mr. Beeney, that you cannot actually *buy* the *Arcadia*. A ship in British law is a small piece of the Kingdom, whether it is at sea or at anchor. No alien can actually own a British ship or any share of it, and even if he were to acquire one by accident or good fortune, he would immediately forfeit it to the Crown, although he would undoubtedly be compensated for his loss. A foreigner may not even serve as an officer on a British vessel."

"Mr. Deacon, I know all of that, and it entrances me," said Mark. "But I don't intend to buy the *Arcadia* as an individual. I simply want control of the *Arcadia* transferred to Amery, London, so that my British board of directors will control the *Arcadia* for me at two removes. All legal and correct, but the money's just as good."

There was a long silence. Mark said, "Hello? You still there?"

"Yes, I'm still here, Mr. Beeney," said Edgar Deacon. "But I must say that I'm really not used to doing business over the telephone. You're coming along on the voyage, aren't you? Perhaps we can discuss the matter then, in a more civilised manner, over a chota peg."

"A what?"

"Two fingers to you, old chap."

"I beg your pardon?" asked Mark, perplexed, but still trying to sound British.

"Two fingers of gin, or whatever it is you drink. *Burra peg* is three fingers. But listen, we'll have plenty of time to talk about this later. Poor Stanley is still warm in his coffin. It's hardly appropriate to discuss this now. The *Arcadia* was like a daughter to him, closer in some ways than his own daughter was. And I have yet to discuss this matter in any detail with my board of directors."

"You won't get a better offer, nor such a fast one," said Mark.

"It's very generous," Edgar acknowledged. "And please don't think that I'm turning you down out of hand."

"Well, of course you can have some time to think about it," said Mark. "But I don't want to have to wait indefinitely. Four million is a great deal of money to lay my hands on in cash; and there'll be some financial planning to do."

"I understand completely," said Edgar. "But, if you could excuse me —"

"Sure," said Mark. "I'm sorry I called you on a question of business on a day like today."

"Stanley wouldn't have minded," Edgar replied. "Stanley would have recognised that respect for the dead has to wait for the needs of the living."

Mark was a little baffled by that remark. He said, "Sure, okay," and hung up the earpiece.

"I don't think I can ever quite get the hang of dealing with the British," he remarked, turning around to Wallis. But it was then that he saw who it was that Wallis had let into the room, and his frown faded immediately, and he spread his arms in welcome and said, "*Marcia*, I thought you were in Paris."

Marcia Conroy came flowing towards him across the sitting room, the sleeves of her silvery dress rippling in the breeze of her own coming, tall and blond, with shingled hair and pearl earrings that danced and swung (in Wallis' words) "like the drip on the end of a Mississippi river pilot's beezer."

Marcia had been graced with what was easily the most beautiful profile of any of the debutantes of 1922, but she was one of the few who had remained unmarried. She had contrived to meet Mark at last year's Ascot, by deliberately tipping strawberries and cream down the left leg of his trousers, and since then they had carried on a spasmodic, combative, irregular affair whenever their paths happened to cross.

Marcia's seasonal cycle took her to Paris in the springtime, then home to England for the Derby and Ascot and London's high season; then to the regatta at Cowes, off to Germany for a cure at Marienbad, Scotland for the fall shooting; followed by a winter cruise of the Mediterranean. Her friends always knew where Marcia was by the social calendar, but Mark only ever ran into her by accident. That was what made their affair so exciting: the fact that after each brief bout of lovemaking they might never actually meet again, ever. But they never said goodbye.

"I was *astonished* when Bangers told me you were here," said Marcia, kissing Mark on both cheeks as if he had just been awarded the Croix de Guerre. She threw her silvery evening purse down on the sofa and opened the onyx cigarette box on the table.

Mark offered her a light. "Who the hell's Bangers?" he wanted to know.

34

"The Honorable Phoebe Tawthorne-Bangs," said Marcia, blowing smoke out of her nostrils. "She said she'd seen you at the Criterion, in the crush bar, but the crush had been too crushing to reach you. She did shout 'cooee,' but she's never had a very convincing voice."

"Can *anybody* say 'cooee' convincingly?" Mark grinned.

"Bangers can't," said Marcia.

"Wallis," asked Mark, "will you bring me a fresh drink, please? A Ward Eight; and what's yours, Marcia?"

"Anything but champagne," said Marcia. "One gets so *tired* of champagne."

Mark sat down on the sofa and Marcia perched herself on his lap, her cigarette held at the very tips of her fingers. She tugged up the long hem of her dress so that she might be more comfortable, and also more provocative. Underneath the silver satin she wore silver silk stockings, with silver garters. Mark knew from experience that she rarely wore panties. She had an aura of perfume around her that was heavy with Guerlain's fashionable new Chamade.

"Paris was so *tiring* this year," she said. Her eyes were the blandest blue that Mark could ever remember seeing, like a clear sky glimpsed through a frozen windowpane. "There were so many Americans there, begging your national pardon. I was taken to dinner at the Ritz one evening by Duc de Gramont, and all around me there was a positive *ocean* of Americans: Berry Wall, Mrs. Stuyvesant Fish, the Dolly sisters. And all *braying,* my darling, like hounds."

Mark touched her cheek and twisted one of her curls around his finger. "I'm sorry about the braying," he said. "I'll speak to Olivier about it."

"Oh, it wasn't really so bad," Marcia said, kissing the veins on the inside of Mark's wrist. "I was just feeling unusually vexatious. I feel better now that I'm here with you. You have a wonderfully calming effect on me. You're like a *good lunch.*"

"Well"—Mark smiled—"I've been compared to one or two things in my life: an ass and a thick-headed bullock. But never a good lunch."

Wallis came in with a tray of drinks—a Ward Eight for Mark, he being a good Bostonian, and a glass of very cold Polish vodka for Marcia, so frigid that it smoked. The Ward Eight was a kind of bourbon sling, devised at Locke-Ober's Winter Palace Wine Rooms in Boston in the 1890s, and it was said to make the experience of being struck by lightning seem comparatively mild.

Once Wallis had retired to his quarters, with instructions not to disturb them, Mark and Marcia raised their glasses to each other. Marcia said, "Your man murmured that I shouldn't keep you longer than necessary. He said you had an important meeting with your company secretary."

"All my company secretary can do is to nag me about the deficiencies in my long-term planning. Besides that, he's in one of his bates. Isn't that what the English call it, a bate?"

They clinked glasses and sipped their drinks. "Cherry vodka," said Marcia appreciatively, shifting herself on Mark's lap. "Your man may be fussy, but he has taste."

"We Americans aren't as ignorant as we seem," Mark told her with the smile of an impudent boy. "We don't want very much out of life, but then there isn't ever very much of the best, is there?"

They kissed, with a fierceness and a hungriness that would have startled anyone who was secretly watching. The insides of their mouths were cold with ice and aromatic with spirits, and their tongues sought each other's teeth like chilly seals in Arctic waters.

"I always think I'm going to hate you when I see you again," breathed Marcia. "I always think I'm going to walk into the room and think how ugly you are, and how dull you are. But I never do. You always make me feel so abandoned. You make me feel as if I'm being swept away by a hurricane."

Mark said nothing, but sought her mouth again, and kissed her into breathless silence.

"Music," she said. "Why isn't there music?"

"They don't have victrolas in the rooms, that's why. I can hum, if you want me to. How about 'Little Alabama Coon'? My father taught me that. I do the baby cry and the clog noises, too."

"God, you Americans are so romantic," said Marcia in mock disdain. "I want music to dance to, music to make love to."

Mark shrugged and tipped Marcia off his lap. He went across to the telephone and tapped the bar for the hotel operator. "Get me the manager, will you? This is Mark Beeney. That's right."

Marcia, sitting on the floor with her back against the sofa and her dress right up to her slender thighs, sipped her drink and watched him with the smouldering coldness of a lascivious Ice Queen. He smiled at her, and one by one began to undo the buttons of his black vest.

"Is that the manager? This is Mark Beeney. Yes, fine. Everything's really fine. Well, I have a favour to ask. Sure. You had a string quartet playing at dinner this evening, am I right? I heard it on the way in. Do you think if they're all through in the restaurant they could come down to my room and play a little dance music outside of my door? Would that be too much to ask?"

Marcia threw her head back and laughed out loud. "You're mad," she said. "Quite mad, but I adore you."

And so it was that in ten minutes' time Mark and Marcia were dancing cheek-to-cheek around the sitting room to the muffled waltz music of the Albemarle Quartet, who sat outside in the corridor on gilt chairs provided by the hotel management. Mark was naked; Marcia wore nothing but her pearls. As they danced, she pressed her small rose-nippled breasts against his chest, and he pressed the stiffened thrust of his penis against her bare stomach.

They made love on the Turkey rug, violently and greedily, while the quartet outside played "Les Roses" and then "We'll Meet Beyond the River." Marcia clutched her legs around Mark's back and closed her eyes tight as he pushed and pushed inside her. He grasped her breasts so tightly that the flesh and nipples bulged between his fingers.

There was a moment for both of them when there was neither music nor light; no hotel, no rug, no day, and no night. Then, his chest shiny with sweat, Mark knelt upright, and looked down at Marcia with that same stunned expression that Paavo Nurmi had had after running two miles in nine minutes. Marcia turned her face away, and that perfect 1922 profile was outlined by the pattern on the carpet. Her neck was flushed, and there were scarlet finger marks on her breasts.

"God, you're beautiful," she said, as if she were addressing the leg of the table. "But thank God I don't have to marry you. I think we'd drive each other *mad*."

Outside the hotel room, the music abruptly scraped and died. His body still sticky, Mark got up, went to the bedroom to find his blue silk bathrobe, and then went to the door.

"I'm afraid we have to finish now, sir," said the violinist. "We don't wish to disturb the other guests."

"You did a magnificent job." Mark smiled. He took four ten-pound notes out of his wallet and handed them one each. For each of them, ten pounds was the equivalent to three weeks' earnings.

Mark closed the door and came back into the sitting room. Marcia was still naked, sitting in a deliberately dryadic pose on the sofa, the white pearls of Mark's semen clinging to the close-trimmed curls of her pubic hair. She sipped her vodka and followed him with her cold, cold eyes.

"I suppose you're going back to America soon," she said.

He nodded. "I'm sailing on the *Arcadia* on Tuesday."

"Sailing on the competition? You surprise me."

"I'm looking forward to it. They've billed it as the most luxurious passenger liner afloat. I want to see if they can live up to their billing."

Marcia smiled at him provocatively. "How would you bill me, if you had to?"

"You? I'd bill you as the Mistress of the Century."

"You disappoint me. Not the millennium?"

"Give it time."

Marcia thought for a moment. Then she stood up, came across to him, and reached out her hand so that her fingertips were touching his lips. "I don't want you to say anything," she said, "but I think I'm going to come to America with you."

He frowned and was about to say something, but she pressed his lips to keep him silent. "I just have a feeling, that's all," she told him. "I don't think I'm ever going to see you again, not unless I come with you."

"You always said that you didn't mind if we saw each other again or not."

"Well, suddenly I do mind. Is that so terrible?"

"I don't know. You might as well understand that I'm not going to marry you."

"I don't expect you to," said Marcia. "I don't expect you to marry anybody. There isn't a girl alive who could keep you happy, not on her own."

Mark said, "What are you going to do? Sail on the *Arcadia* with me? All my staterooms are taken. Claude Graham-White's got one, and Victor Sorbay has the other."

"I'll book one for myself."

"They're all booked up."

"Then I'll make sure that somebody unbooks one. I'm coming, Mark, whether you want me to or not."

"I don't understand the panic," said Mark. "This isn't you. This isn't the cool, sophisticated Marcia Conroy, daughter of Lord and Lady Conroy of some muddy place in the English countryside I can't immediately remember."

Marcia was suddenly quiet. "I have a premonition, that's all," she said. "I felt a shiver come over me, like cold water."

"Here, borrow my bathrobe. You're feeling chilly, that's all."

"It's not that. I was always supposed to be rather psychic."

Mark stripped off his bathrobe and hung it around Marcia's shoulders. "A warm bath does wonders for a case of the premonitions," he told her and kissed her close-cropped hair.

She looked up at him. "Yes, I suppose you're right. I am being rather absurd. Do you think your man could bring me another of those vodkas? I need to drink myself cheerful again."

They kissed once more, and then Marcia went through to the bedroom suite to take a bath. Mark watched her go and stood in the centre of the room for a while, his hand thoughtfully covering his mouth, until the sound of faucets gushing disturbed his reverie.

He was about to pick up the telephone when the door opened and John Crombey stepped in. As usual, John was dressed with utter correctness, right up to the highly starched linen collar and the rosebud in his buttonhole. Only someone who knew him very well, as Mark did, could have guessed how angry he was. His nostrils were slightly widened, like an anxious thoroughbred horse, and there was a whiteness around his eyes which betrayed his sense of outrage and shock.

"You're *naked*," he pronounced in his marked Philadelphia accent.

"You could have knocked," Mark replied.

John Crombey turned around with exaggerated care and stared at the door as if it should have knocked for him. "We had a meeting arranged for an hour ago," he said, still rigid with indignation. "I have all the figures you asked for: the Italian figures, how many long tons went in and out of Naples; the French figures, how many passengers sailed in and out of Cherbourg. I also have a comprehensive analysis of our entire business dealings with De Freitas: bills of lading, end-of-year accounts, financial prognoses. I understand from Wallis, however, that other considerations proved more attractive."

"Well," said Mark, "you're right. They did."

"I can't say that I'm not disappointed," said John Crombey. He pursed his lips.

"Oh? Well, I'm sorry, because *I'm* not," Mark told him. "And you can do something for me."

"Yes?" asked John, with cautious ire. His eyes were as black as a boiled lobster's.

"I want you to call the offices of Keys Shipping in Liverpool, if they're still open, and see if they have a single spare stateroom in first class. If they don't, ask them to mail you a passenger list right away. Then go through it from A to Z and see if you can't persuade someone to give up their stateroom for twice what they paid for it. I want just one first-class stateroom, that's all; but I want it booked in the name of the Honorable Miss Marcia Conroy. You got that?"

John Crombey said, "I see," suddenly deflated. He laid his sheaf of accounts and company reports down on the table in front of him. Mark looked up and Marcia was standing in the doorway wearing a pink hotel bathcap and wrapped in a huge white towel. Her face was pretty but unreadable. She might have been smiling. She might have been annoyed. Mark couldn't tell.

He said, "Are you through with my robe yet, Marcia? I'm beginning to feel like the Old Adam, standing here."

John Crombey thought for a second that Marcia was going to unwrap herself there and then, and flinched as if someone had thrown a baseball directly at his face.

Six

It was the summer of 1924. In England, bright young men were striding about in those voluminous grey flannel trousers known as Oxford bags. In France, Gloria Swanson was being courted by her husband-to-be, the Marquis de la Falaise de la Coudray. It was the summer of mah-jongg, crossword puzzles, and the last fading popularity of "Yes, We Have No Bananas." On the day that Stanley Keys died, the Republican Convention in Cleveland nominated Calvin Coolidge to be their Presidential candidate for the November elections.

The mood in the world was changing. There was fresh frivolity, fresh hope, silly songs, rolled-down stockings. The Prince of Wales visited Long Island and spent most of his time dancing, playing polo, or motorboating. A new movie was advertised as featuring "beautiful jazz babes, champagne baths, petting parties in the purple dawn." Two rich and spoiled young men called Leopold and Loeb murdered an innocent boy named Bobby Franks for the sheer hell of it, and escaped with life sentences.

It was all so different from the summer of 1920. Harry Pakenow, for one, knew just how much, and could never forget.

On Saturday morning, June 14th, Harry was standing in the kitchen of a narrow Victorian terraced house in Bootle, not far from Liverpool, frying himself some breakfast.

He was bespectacled, narrow-chested, with spiky hedgehog hair; but he had an attractive vulnerability about him, an apparent helplessness that made him immediately magnetic to shopgirls and waitresses and even to the fat ladies who stood behind the jellied-eel stalls in Bootle market. He was the kind of young man that almost every woman over thirty wanted to take home and mother.

Harry was originally from Hoboken, New Jersey, although he had been living near Liverpool for so long now that his accent had almost completely flattened out. Just like a Liverpudlian, he said "sters" instead of "stairs," and came out with phrases like "Chance'll be a fine thing" and "Did he heck as like." In his rolled-up shirtsleeves, yellow suspenders, and baggy pants, he looked like any other clerk for the Mersey Docks and Harbour Company; he even had mauve indelible ink on his fingers.

Harry fried his two eggs and his single rasher of bacon in his charred-black frying pan with the wonky handle, while outside the window the sheets of the woman who lived upstairs snapped and billowed on the line (she had no husband to speak of, and a ten-year-old boy mysteriously called Romulus who wet the bed). He whistled a jazz refrain that had been popular when he was last in New York in September 1920: "The Fall I Fell for You."

From the next room, a girl's voice called, "Harry? Have you seen my pink shoes?"

"You left them in the outhouse," he called back. "There was dogshit on them."

"Oh, bugger it. Didn't you clean them for me?"

Harry didn't answer. He turned off the gas, and then carried the frying pan across to the kitchen table, where an empty plate was waiting, already flanked by two doorstep slices of bread and butter and a mug of bright orange tea. He shovelled his eggs and bacon onto his plate, and then sniffed and sat down to eat. He would take a mouthful of egg, a big bite of bread, and then wash everything down with tea, in that order. He was indistinguishable from any other British workingman at his breakfast.

"I'll be *late*, Harry," said a pretty young girl in a short pink and white dress, hopping into the kitchen in one slipper. She had bright blond hair, spiky eyelashes, and two vivid spots of rouge on her cheeks. She had read how to make herself up like that in *Movie Secrets*.

"If you think I'm going to go scraping dogshit off your shoes right in the middle of breakfast, you can think again," Harry told her.

"But it's five past eight *already*. Mrs. Carson will *kill* me."

"Let her kill you. If she kills you, you can sue."

"Oh, you're not much bleeding help, are you? I shall have to change my dress now, and wear my green ones."

"*Green*," said Harry, mopping up egg yolk, as if that was the most obnoxious word he'd heard for a week.

But when the pretty young girl came dancing in a few moments later, all ready for work in a green shimmy dress and a green headband, Harry reached out and grabbed her arm, sat her down on his lap and kissed her.

"One day," he told her, staring at her intently through his bacon-spattered spectacles, "one day you'll understand just how much you've done for me, Miss Janice Bignor, of Bootle."

Janice tugged at his hair and kissed him back. "It's mutual, innit?" she told him. "Now, I've got to run for that bleeding bus, or else she really *will* kill me."

Harry followed her to the front door in his carpet slippers and watched her run down the sloping windy road to the bus stop on the corner. The woman next door, with a scarf on her head and a cigarette hanging out of her mouth, was scratching at her corsets in her front window. When she saw Harry looking, she scowled. Harry smiled and went back inside.

He always felt that the house was quiet and unsettled without Janice. Whenever she went to work on Saturday mornings, leaving him alone, he would prowl around for almost half an hour, taking three times as long as usual to clear up his breakfast plate and to tidy the narrow brass bed in which they slept together in what had once been the "best parlour." There was still "best parlour" wallpaper on the walls—faded brown flowers, with a green and brown border all the way round.

Today, before he went back to the kitchen, he went into the bedroom and pulled out from under the bed a small tin box with a padlock. He found the key in his trouser pocket and unlocked it, and then laid out on the rumpled bedspread the three most important papers in his whole life as if they were tarot cards.

On the right was a third-class ticket for passage to New York on the SS *Arcadia*'s maiden voyage, on Tuesday, June 17th. In the centre was an American passport, its olive-green cover circled by teacup stains. On the left was a yellowed newspaper clipping from *The New York Times* of September 17th, 1920.

The newspaper clipping described how at 11:59 in the morning of September 16th, a horse-drawn wagon loaded with dynamite and scrap iron had exploded at Broad and Wall Streets, outside the offices of J. P. Morgan & Company, the merchant bankers, killing thirty-eight people and injuring hundreds more. Windows had been smashed for blocks around, and an iron bolt had been driven through the window of the Bankers Club, on the thirty-fourth floor of the Equitable Building. The street had been glossed red with the blood of the dead and the dying.

Harry touched each of these papers with his fingertips, in the way that mediums familiarise themselves with their tarot cards. This, the explosion on Wall Street, is what came before. This, the Irish passport, represents the means to the end. And this, the third-class ticket on the *Arcadia*'s maiden voyage, is the significator.

Outraged, the press and the police had assumed at once that the Wall Street explosion had been the work of Bolshevists. Their wild investigations had led them around and around in circles for days, and then months, and then years. Detectives had discovered that the iron bolts which had penetrated the buildings all around were window sash weights, cut in two. Next they had examined every single fragment of the remaining scrap iron, including the shoes of the blown-up horse. The most promising piece had been the knob of a safe door, which had been traced by a particularly dogged detective from the day of its manufacture, from America to France, and then back again. But the trail had gone cold in Hoboken, New Jersey, at a scrap dealer on Willow Avenue. He sold scrap by the fifty-ton load. "Who knows what they're going to use it for?"

It had taken a long time for the echoes of the Wall Street explosion to fade away. But now the Red Scare of 1919 and the early 1920s was old news, and the Communist purges first incited by A. Mitchell Palmer, President Woodrow Wilson's attorney general, were faltering for lack of genuine evidence against the suspected revolutionaries, and even more from lack of public interest. Jazz, sex, Rudolph Valentino, and the Ku Klux Klan were all much more exciting than Bolshevists with beards. The thirty-eight victims of the blast had long been buried, the injured had recovered, and a supposed Red who had tried to blow up A. Mitchell Palmer's house had only succeeded in blowing himself up instead.

In nearly four years, nobody had discovered that the perpetrator of the explosion was Harry Pakenow, onetime economics student, and by far the most active and aggressive member of a society called Young American Workers. To Harry, the capitalist institutions of Wall Street had been, and still were, a grotesque affront to the workingmen of America. Behind those façades, fat and uncaring, the capitalists gorged themselves on fine foods at the expense of the ordinary man. Harry still felt angry when he thought of all those workers who had been unjustly arrested and imprisoned under suspicion of being "sinister and subversive agitators." He had been to Boston in 1920 after one of Palmer's raids and seen how a hundred men had been kept prisoner in a bullpen measuring thirty feet by twenty-four feet for a whole week; and he had read in the papers how men from Hartford had been beaten by police and humiliated in front of their families. All because they were suspected Reds.

Harry wasn't violent by nature. He had never punched anyone, not very hard anyway, and he was always telling Janice that he would much rather argue than fight. Janice, of course, had no idea of what he had done, or why. But when he was a boy, Harry had seen his father sacked from his job at the Nagel shoe factory for going to listen to Eugene Debs preaching socialism from his "Red Special" train, in the marshalling yard at Paterson; and he had known the meaning of Wobbly before he had understood long division. Harry came from tough stock. His father had worked hard and well, cutting leather patterns for Oxford brogues, but had believed implicitly in the Wobblys' uncompromising slogan, "Good Pay or Bum Work." His mother had kept the family together, God knows how, when there was no money and no credit and nothing left to hock. Harry always ate a rasher of bacon for breakfast these days, because when he was a boy there had never been any bacon, ever. He had seen a newspaper cartoon in 1912 of "Capitalism" in the shape of a grossly distended hog sprawling over the mines and the factories and the legislatures of America; and he had promised himself, tight-fisted, that as soon as he could afford to buy bacon he would personally devour that hog, slice by slice.

He put away his papers and his tin box, straightened the bedcover, and then went into the kitchen to put on the kettle for a fresh cup of tea.

He could make tea like an Englishman now: warming the thick brown china teapot first, then adding one teaspoonful of tea per person, and one for luck. It seemed strange that he would probably never come back to England again, even if he survived.

His *Arcadia* plan had come to him almost a year ago, when she had been launched from John Brown's shipyard on the Clyde. The *Arcadia* had been described in Keys Shipping advertising as "the last word in de luxe travel . . . a city afloat, in which the scintillating manners and style of high society of both continents will be the order of the day, and of the night . . ." A first-class suite, one way, would be competitively priced at $4,118, a couple of hundred dollars cheaper than the *Aquitania*.

When Harry had read about the dancing and the parties and the luxury foods that would be taken aboard for each voyage, he had felt bitter to the point of illness. He had left his supper of herring and boiled potatoes untouched. It wasn't that he was personally jealous of the rich. He didn't crave luxury for himself. It was simply that he couldn't bear the manifest injustice of one man, in one meal, pushing into his face food that would have fed a whole working-class family for a whole day, and spending on a week's accommodation the same amount of money that would have enabled that same family to buy their apartment outright and live rent-free for the rest of their lives.

The kettle started to boil and he made his pot of tea. Outside in the yard, the woman from upstairs was unpegging her sheets. Her grey-streaked hair flapped in the breeze, and her face looked impossibly care-worn, as creased as the tissue paper they used for wrapping shoes in. He thought it was both sad and strange that she would still be here, pegging and unpegging these sheets, long after he had gone.

He didn't particularly want to be a martyr, but he knew what he had to do. He had to strike again at the heart of capitalism, violently and expressively. The junction of Wall Street and Broad Street had been the very nub of capitalism on land; the *Arcadia* symbolised it on the high seas.

Janice had sensed that Harry had changed in recent weeks, become tenser, as the date for the maiden voyage came nearer. But she had never sought explanations from him. He would miss Janice, in the same way that he would miss the narrow Victorian streets of Bootle, and the meat pies, and the warm beer at twopence a pint. He would miss the rain. England had a kind of gritty reality about it that he had never experienced anywhere else, even in Hoboken. You were allowed to be as mad as you liked in England, and nobody cared. That was what made it so real; you could keep your own sense of reality intact, no matter how potty that sense of reality actually might be.

He had not yet made up his mind how real the moment was going to be when he detonated thirty sticks of dynamite in the cargo hold of the *Arcadia*, but it was enough for him to know that he was going to do it.

The woman from upstairs tapped on the window and said, "Harry, love? Are you going out this morning?"

He raised his mug. "After my tea."

"Would you get us a packet of five Woodys, please? I'll pay you Thursday."

He paused, sipped his tea, and then said, "Okay." He rather liked the idea that he wouldn't be here to collect his money.

It was beginning to shower with rain as he banged the front door of the house behind him and started to walk down the road. He wore a brown tweed cap and a thin brown overcoat with a belt. The rain speckled his glasses. On the corner, an old man sitting on a front-garden wall waiting for the Liverpool motorbus said, "Aye up."

Harry thought about Janice as the bus ground its way slowly southwards down the wet lengths of Stanley Road and Scotland Road. He had met Janice his first week in England, in the comb and brush department of Wavertree's, the gloomy Edwardian department store in which she still worked. He had been making his way from counter to counter stocking up with all of those things that he had left behind in New York when he escaped. Toothbrush, shirt, pyjamas, socks. The Young American Workers had got up a collection and given him $108 getaway money.

Janice had been living at home with her mother then, after leaving her new husband of only three weeks. She was only just twenty now; she had been a chubby seventeen when she had been taken to the altar of St. Matilda's Church by a nineteen-year-old butcher's assistant to become Mrs. Philip Snowball.

Philip Snowball's idea of what a wife should expect out of married life had been washing and ironing his shirts, cooking his tea, and staying at home darning his mustard-soled socks while he went out in the evening and got so drunk that he vomited into the fireplace. He had never touched her, Philip Snowball, not once. He probably hadn't even known what to do.

Harry, isolated in Liverpool, worried, confused, had asked Janice to step out with him just for the sake of having someone young and friendly to talk to. He had taken her to a restaurant and bought her a pork chop with apple stuffing, and a cup of tea. She had never met a man as gentle and yet as individual as him before. That night, back at her mother's house, with no light but the glow of the dying coals on the kitchen range, and no perfume but the lingering sprats from her old dad's supper, they had made love sitting on a plain wooden chair, she with her plump thighs wide apart, he with his eyes tight shut and his spectacles on the table next to the cheese.

Janice didn't want anything from Harry but love. He wondered what she would think when she came back from work on Tuesday and found him gone.

Seven

It was raining much harder by the time Harry crossed the wooden boards of the landing stage at Liverpool's pierhead, pausing to let a puttering lorry pass in front of him with a load of clanking casks, and then dodging into the doorway of a small office building with a corrugated-iron roof. He turned left once he was inside the building and walked along the corridor until he reached a small untidy workshop at the end. A fair-haired young man in a long leather apron was standing at a bench filing noisily at a length of copper piping. On the wall was a calendar for 1923 with a photograph of Ann Pennington, the Ziegfeld girl with the "dimpled knees."

Harry took off his cap and slapped the rain from it. "Good morning, Dennis," he said loudly.

Dennis stopped filing, as if he hadn't been very interested in it anyway, and tossed the rasp onto the workbench with a loud clatter. "You're early, wacker," he said. "Janice kick you out of bed?"

"She's at work. I thought I'd come by here before I went over to Lime Street to see Jim."

Dennis nodded towards the workshop window. "Nice drop of rain, don't you think? Bring me leeks on. Do you fancy a cup of char?"

Harry shook his head. "I was wondering how the loading was going."

Dennis propped his bony hands on his hips. "All right, as far as I know." There was a hint of challenge in his voice.

"Any suitable automobiles? Anything that's taken your eye?"

"Not especially."

"But there are automobiles here, ready to go on board?"

Dennis was silent for a moment. Then he said, "Some, yes. That's right."

Harry thoughtfully walked around the workbench and went up to the window. Beyond the clutter of low pierhead buildings, flagstaffs, and lamp standards; beyond the jostle of lorries and automobiles and people hurrying backwards and forwards in the showery wind, the outline of the *Arcadia* rose like a great black and white castle, towering nearly a hundred feet out of the water.

Even from here, it was difficult to grasp the size of her. She was nearly a sixth of a mile long, and when she moved away from Liverpool's landing stage on Tuesday she would be carrying 2,275 passengers and crew. Pennants were already flapping from her masts and from her three huge yellow-painted funnels; and the red ensign furled and unfurled at her stern counter with laconic pride, stirred by the wind, untroubled by the rain.

Harry could see only a part of the *Arcadia*'s hull from where he was standing, but she was the largest luxury liner in the world, from her sharp cruising prow to her shapely overhanging stern. Her oil-fired reciprocating engines, the very latest design, were easily capable of twenty-eight knots. Keys Shipping, of course, hoped that she could go much faster, and take the Blue Riband for the fastest Atlantic crossing from the *Mauretania*, which had held it since 1907.

As Harry looked at the black-painted liner, and the scores of dockers and officials who clustered around her, he was reminded of the journalist who had said that "if you were followed by a cab coming out of Pennsylvania Station at twenty-five miles per hour, you would think nothing of it. But if Pennsylvania Station *itself* were following you down the street at twenty-five miles per hour, then you would have some conception of the *Arcadia* at speed."

He said to Dennis, "You've got something on your mind, haven't you? You're backing out."

Dennis shrugged. "It's not so much backing out, Harry. It's not that. It's a question of conscience. I mean, how many people on board that ship are going to be just plain people, like you and me? Working class. You're talking about drowning the very people you're supposed to be saving."

Harry turned away from the window. "When did you work all this out?"

"You only have to look at the passenger roster," Dennis insisted. "Three hundred and seventeen first class, two hundred and fifty second class, six hundred and fifty steerage. You're going to drown nine hundred of ours just to get at three hundred of theirs? And children, too? It doesn't make sense."

Harry rubbed his eyes, as if he were thinking. "You thought it made sense before."

"I know. But I hadn't worked it out then."

"You've forgotten the ship itself," said Harry. "The ship itself is an embodiment of capitalist exploitation."

"Well, yes. Yes, it is. I've always said that. But the trouble is, our people are going to be on it. I mean, it's *our* people what are going to be thrashing around in the sea."

Harry said, "There always have to be casualties, in any war. This is a war, Dennis, make no mistake about it."

Dennis untied his apron and folded it and laid it over the workbench. "I know you get your accidental casualties," he said. "But this is too cold-blooded for me. Because what's going to happen when she goes down? Same as on the *Titanic*, I shouldn't wonder. They saved over half of the first-class passengers on the *Titanic*, but less than a quarter of the steerage. And then there's the crew, over a thousand of them. A thousand workingmen. Are you going to risk *their* lives, too?"

Harry turned away from the window. "You're getting hysterical about this, Dennis. If everything goes to plan, then nobody need drown. Not one single person, rich or poor."

"I suppose you can guarantee that," said Dennis, crossing his arms in the way that workingmen do when they feel defiant.

Harry smiled. "I can't guarantee anything. Dynamite doesn't come with any kind of assurances about what it's going to do. It doesn't have a recommendation on every box, 'as used by Bolshevists everywhere.' "

"You don't have to make fun of me," Dennis told him.

"I'm not, Dennis. But all that's going to happen here is a concentrated explosion in one of the cargo holds. The *Arcadia* has plenty of watertight compartments, and it will take her a long while to sink. It took the *Titanic* over three and a half hours to go down, and she was torn open for a third of her whole length. Besides, unlike the *Titanic*, there are quite enough lifeboats for everybody."

Dennis was silent. Harry came up to him and put an arm around his shoulders and gave him a gentle, affectionate punch on the arm. "Listen, Dennis, this is your chance to do something historical. This is your chance to strike a blow against capitalism that people are going to remember forever. The night the *Arcadia* sank. Think of it!"

Dennis said reluctantly, "I suppose you're right."

"Right? You know I'm right! I'll tell you how you can be sure that I'm right. You go take a look at those first-class staterooms on the *Arcadia*, with all their decorated panels and their soft beds and their silk drapes, and then you take a walk through Bootle or Arnfield and look at the way the ordinary people have to live there. That ship was built as a monument to the arrogance of the rich; it's like the wealthy people of this world deliberately taunting the poor. 'We've got all of the money, and by God, we're going to waste it right in front of your noses, just to remind you that you have to live on herring and pies and potatoes, while we fill ourselves with caviar and lobster and ripe pheasant!' "

Dennis looked at Harry seriously. He had a slight squint in his pale green eyes, which made him appear slightly retarded. He was a hard-working young Socialist, however, and he never made up his mind about anything without considering it in detail. At last, with obvious reluctance, he nodded and said, "All right. As long as you're sure that nobody's going to be hurt."

"That's the Dennis I know and love," said Harry. "You've got an automobile?"

"There's one special one I had in mind," said Dennis. "It arrived last night, quite late, so we haven't had time to load it yet. It's a Marmon Big Eight, real posh job. They've got it parked in the warehouse."

"You can get the keys?"

"Don't need keys," Dennis told him smugly. "Any automobile lock you ever heard of, I can open it up with a bit of wire."

"You're sure about that?"

"Try me."

"I intend to. Do you think we can load the stuff now?"

Dennis sniffed and looked up at the clock on the workshop wall. "I don't see why not. Give it five minutes. That's when Wally goes off for his lunchtime pint. We'll have the place to ourselves then."

Harry cleared a space on the workbench and hoisted himself up so that he was sitting on the edge of it with his legs swinging. "You know something, Dennis," he said. "I think for the first time in my life I've felt like I'm really fulfilling myself."

"You're not scared?" asked Dennis.

Harry glanced at him through the distorting lenses of his spectacles. Dennis had always wondered how somebody who looked so vulnerable could be such a dedicated fanatic. Harry said, "Of course I'm scared. Aren't you scared? Jesus, Dennis, destiny is always scary."

Dennis said, "Yes," in a way that sounded as if he confronted destiny every morning after breakfast. Then he went to the pegs where his raincoat was hanging, and took a paper packet of sandwiches out of one of the pockets. The sandwiches looked decidedly squashed.

"Cheese butty?" he asked Harry. "Might as well have something to eat while you're waiting. It's Cheshire."

Harry shook his head. He was too agitated to think about chewing and swallowing a cheese sandwich. "How do you know when Wally's gone off for his drink?" he wanted to know.

His mouth crammed with sandwich, Dennis pointed towards the window. "Walks past. Has to."

They waited another five minutes; and then a round-shouldered man in a cloth cap passed the window on his routine way to the Queen Victoria public house outside the dock area, little realising that he was acting out the most historically important moment of his whole life. "All right," said Harry, "let's get the stuff out and go."

"The stuff" was in a wooden chest about three feet by two feet by two feet, bound with cheap lacquered hinges. Stencilled on the top of the chest in black were the words NOT WANTED ON VOYAGE. Dennis dragged it out from under the workbench, and they both stood looking at it for a moment before Harry said, "Come on, then. We haven't got all day."

Outside, the rain clouds had all rolled eastwards towards Runcorn, and the wet planking of the landing stage had been gilded with morning sunlight. Carrying the wooden chest between them, Harry and Dennis walked between the rows of wet iron bollards to the warehouse where passengers' cars were kept before they were swung aboard by cranes and stowed in the liner's holds.

The air was sharp with the smell of brine and fuel oil, and seagulls sloped and feathered around the tall funnels of the *Arcadia* and dived for scraps. The *Arcadia* was so huge that she was almost impossible to look at. Harry noticed that the dockers and victuallers who crowded the landing stage hardly ever glanced at the ship at all. In the same way, people who live and work in the shadow of high ranges of mountains never stand back and focus on the massive terrain which dominates them.

Harry was reminded of the newspaper story of the man who had hurried aboard the *Titanic* so late that he had no time to take a good look at her. He had promised himself that he would take an appreciative stroll alongside her once she was berthed in New York.

Dennis said, "This is it," and pushed open a green-painted door with his shoulder. Inside, the warehouse was silent and gloomy, irradiated by light that was strained the colour of cold tea. There were thirty or forty automobiles parked there, bumper to bumper, all facing towards the large closed gates through which they would eventually be driven out to the ship.

Harry carefully lowered the wooden chest onto the cobbled floor. There were at least ten Rolls-Royces here, in varying shades of cream and mauve and brown. There were Bentleys, Daimler touring cars, and an Angus-Sanderson. The whole warehouse smelled of motoring spirit, wax polish, and leather. It was the heady aroma of the newly mobile rich.

"The car we want is round the other side," said Dennis. They hefted up the chest again and carried it between the rows of automobiles, trying not to let it bump against the mudguards and headlamps all around them. Blowing up the *Arcadia* was one thing; blowing up a few cars and themselves as well wasn't what Harry had in mind.

The Marmon was parked on its own. It was long and black, and its chauffeur had buffed it up to a mirrorlike shine. Harry could see himself and Dennis approaching it in the reflection paintwork of the fenders like two dark dwarfs.

"All right, set the stuff down here," whispered Dennis. He looked around over the tops of the cars to make sure that they were alone. In any event they were quite well hidden, because the custom-built coachwork of most of the cars was higher than usual, to accommodate their owners' top hats.

"Just open the trunk and let's get it loaded," Harry whispered back.

Dennis crouched down at the back of the Marmon, fiddling with the lock on the trunk, while Harry kept a lookout.

"I was talking to the chauffeur about this car when he first brung it in," said Dennis. "Do you know how much this car cost? Nearly twelve thousand dollars, fittings included. It's got a gold vanity by Cartier, built-in, and solid silver ice tongs for the bar, and all the fabric inside is handmade French what-jum-acallit, tapestry."

"Just the goddamned automobile to blow up," said Harry.

"I thought you'd appreciate it." Dennis grimaced, still wrestling with the lock.

"Can you hurry it up?" Harry told him.

There was a moment when Dennis, teeth gritted, had to force the last lever of the lock. "Don't break it, for God's sake," Harry warned him. But then the lock gave way with a loud click, and the trunk door came down on well-lubricated hinges. Inside there were two shooting sticks, a locked binocular case, and a picnic basket which bore the name of Abercrombie & Fitch. Plenty of extra room for a wooden chest packed with thirty sticks of dynamite.

"Right, drag the stuff over here." Dennis beckoned. "I'll pack it right behind the picnic basket, where it's more difficult for anyone to see."

"What about the lock?" asked Harry as he shuffled over with the case of dynamite. "How do I get back into the trunk when I want to set everything off?"

"I'll fix it so that you can hook it open with a piece of wire," Dennis told him. "Then all you have to do is connect up the leads of the clock with the detonators inside the lid, and you're away." He suddenly looked abashed. "Well, when I say *away*—"

"I'm not going to take any more risks than I have to," Harry told him.

Together they picked up the wooden chest and lifted it onto the open door of the Marmon's trunk. But just as they were sliding it past the picnic basket into the inner recesses of the trunk, they heard a door open on the far side of the warehouse and the sudden sound of voices. They both crouched down and froze.

"You can load most of them today, can't you?" said a loud Liverpudlian voice that echoed around the vaulted ceiling.

"Well, some, Mr. Pollard. It depends on the lads."

"What do you mean, it depends on the lads? I was down the Queen Victoria ten minutes since, and most of the so-called *lads* were propping up the sawdust bar, half stewed. The *lads* can put their backs into it and get these motors loaded by tomorrow, or else they can find something else to do, like delivering letters maybe, or digging coal."

"I'll see what I can do. That's all I can say."

"Well, do your best. If Mr. Keys were still with us, you'd be doing it, and no mistake. See if you can do it for me."

"All right, Mr. Pollard. But I can't promise miracles."

Harry and Dennis waited for almost five minutes after the door had slammed shut again before they dared to move. Then, without exchanging a single word, they pushed the wooden chest deep into the Marmon's trunk and quietly relocked it.

"I've fixed it so that it's only held shut by one lever," explained Dennis in a hoarse voice. "All you have to do is push a metal strip into the lock, twist it, and it should spring open straightaway."

"What if it doesn't?"

"Then try again."

"And what if it *still* doesn't?"

"If it still doesn't, you can assume that God is on the side of the rich, and enjoy the rest of your trip as per normal."

"You daft bugger."

They crept across the warehouse as quietly as they could. Dennis peeked through the outside door to make sure that nobody was looking their way, and then they both strolled back to the workshop, trying to appear as nonchalant as possible. They were given a suspicious stare by a man in a droopy mustache and a Derby hat who was obviously keeping his eyes open for pilferage, especially now that the *Arcadia* had been fitted out with her brass firehose rings, but when they turned in to the workshop instead of making for the main gate he lost interest in them.

"If only he knew," said Dennis, inclining his head back towards the security man.

"Nobody's going to search the cars now, are they?" asked Harry.

"Why should they?" said Dennis. "There's nothing in that Marmon's trunk that anybody's going to want until they get across the Atlantic. Relax. All you have to do now is creep down to the hold one night, set your clock, and you're done. Well, when I say you're *done*—"

"You don't think any of the dockers might break into the car before the *Arcadia* sails?"

Dennis led Harry back into the workshop and picked up his leather apron. "Well, there's always a risk of that. Dockers and shipfitters have always believed in their divine right to supplement their wages with just about anything they can lay their hands on. Do you know we had to replace the copper piping in the first-class staterooms three times in some cases? What the fitters do is bang a nail through a likely looking pipe, and if no water comes out, they rip it out. Then they walk out of the gate with it stuffed down their trouser legs. Most of the pubs around here take copper pipe instead of cash."

Harry picked up his cap. "I guess that's nothing more than social justice. The capitalist robs the workingman, and the workingman tries to rob the capitalist in return. I just hope that none of the workingmen decide to take a look inside of that Marmon, that's all."

"They don't usually tamper with the cars, not as a rule."

Harry said, "You don't know whose car it is, do you? It would be real social justice if it was somebody very respectable, and they got blamed for sabotage."

Dennis smiled. "That's part of the fun of this particular car."

"What do you mean? You mean it really does belong to somebody special?"

"Oh, yes. That was part of the reason I chose it. It belongs to Mr. Mark Beeney, the fellow who owns American TransAtlantic. He's the biggest rival that Keys Shipping have got. If there's anybody in the whole world who would like to see the *Arcadia* sink to the bottom of the ocean, it's him."

Harry looked at Dennis for a while, his mouth slanted in amusement. Then he ruffled Dennis' blond hair, and said, "I have to be going, okay? But I think you're a genius. You know that? I think you're a complete genius."

Past the window, as round-shouldered as before, Wally returned from the Queen Victoria to take charge of his automobiles again. "There he goes," said Dennis with a grin. "I hope he gets *his* name in the newspapers, too."

Eight

Dottie tapped on Catriona's bedroom door and said, "Are you ready, miss? Mr. Deacon says you have to leave in a moment. No more than five minutes, he said."

Catriona had been ready for almost half an hour. She had been sitting at her dressing table staring at herself in the mirror and wondering who she was and whether she actually liked herself. She had drunk two large gin and bitters since teatime, and smoked three Craven-A cigarettes, and if it hadn't been for the fact that whenever she tilted her head her mirror image tilted her head, too, she would have been quite sure that it was some other girl in the glass altogether.

She had to admit that Edgar had arranged everything spectacularly. Since her return to Formby last week, he had brought a hairdresser around to the house to bob her hair, as well as a milliner with so many cloche hats that her bedroom had looked like a multicoloured mushroom farm, and a dressmaker who had brought her gowns of velvet and silk and crepe-de-chine, gorgeous evening gowns that floated as she walked, short day dresses in vivid Japanese prints, smart touring suits in French brocades, tennis skirts and sun frocks and bathing costumes with designs by Pablo Picasso. There hadn't been time for Catriona to have her whole new wardrobe made to measure, but after a morning in which she had felt as if she were drowning in voile and rayon and marabout-trimmed velour, she had spent on the Keys Shipping account something approaching £ 3,200, and she owned a lavish modern wardrobe which was going to take eleven trunks to pack.

Then there had been shoes—handmade pumps and high-heeled slippers in pink and purple and eau-de-Nil—and pocketbooks in everything from lizard to sequins. And jewellery—rhinestones and emeralds, paste and platinum, enamelled peacocks with rubies for eyes, zigzags of lightning made out of pavé-set diamonds.

Her pleasure and vanity, however, were both sharply reduced by her grief at losing her father. He would have adored to have seen her now; even if they would have argued over which dresses were too saucy, and which earrings were too ostentatious. It hurt her, too, to think that if her father were still alive, she might not have agreed to come at all; and yet there on the list of first-class passengers, in her father's own stubby handwriting, was the name Miss Catriona Keys next to the number of her stateroom. Had it been optimism? Or pride? Or a fatherly knowledge that she would have said yes, after all?

She hoped very much that it hadn't been a premonition that he himself wouldn't be sailing.

It was Monday evening, just past six o'clock. The marmalade-coloured sunlight glistened through the cypress trees in the garden, and somewhere very far away a young dog was yapping. Catriona lit another cigarette and sat with her elbow on the glass top of the dressing table, her eyes lowered so that her reflection in the mirror wouldn't see what she was thinking.

Her eleven trunks were already aboard, and Edgar had announced to the press that if they gathered at Liverpool's landing stage at eight o'clock tonight, they would have their first opportunity to photograph the fashionable young "Queen of the Atlantic."

It was all so glamorous. Nigel would have called it "ritzy." But she knew that it meant an end to her freedom, and even an end to herself —at least as she knew herself now. She had already changed beyond instant recognition. She could have strutted past Nigel in Royal Hospital Road and he wouldn't have known who she was. At least she thought he probably wouldn't. She didn't *feel* like herself at all.

She went to the open window and stood there smoking, her right elbow couched in the palm of her left hand, her eyes half closed, watching the smoke stream out over the window ledge.

There was another knock. This time it was her mother. She was wearing a black V-necked dress and two strings of pearls, and there were plummy circles under her eyes. Dr. Whitby had prescribed her some new sleeping pills, but she still woke up every night at three or four o'clock in the morning and walked around the house with her hair plaited, like Lady Macbeth in search of Cadbury's cocoa.

"Are you ready, darling?" her mother asked. "I think Edgar's becoming a little restive."

"I suppose I'm ready," said Catriona. "If anyone is *ever* really ready, then, yes, I suppose I am."

"It's such a lovely dress, you know," said her mother. "The grey silk and the white lace edging. Very respectful, but so becoming. And your hair!"

Catriona touched her short-cropped head. "I don't know," she said. "I think I rather miss my hair."

"But you look perfect. So pretty! Haven't they made your eyes up well? Oh, my darling, I so wish that your father could have seen you."

Catriona came over and took her mother's hands. "Mother," she said, "if father had been alive to see me now, I wouldn't have been here. It's one of those dreams that never could have happened, not even in dreams."

Her mother's eyes winced a little, and then she looked away. "You don't despise me, do you, for wanting you to do this?" she asked, in a reedy voice.

"Why should I? He was my father, as well as your husband. We both loved him, in our different ways."

"*Did* you love him, Catriona?" her mother asked urgently.

Catriona smiled, although her smile was a little vague. "I think I did. I must have done."

Her mother took her hands away, like someone who has been forgetting herself. "We're going to bury him tomorrow," she said. "The moment that the *Arcadia* starts out over the open sea, at three tomorrow afternoon, we're going to bury him."

Catriona went to her dressing table and came back with a small gold locket. She pressed it into her mother's hand. "Tomorrow," she said gently "can you throw this on his coffin for me?"

Her mother's eyes blurred with tears. "What is it?" she said. "I don't think I've ever seen it before."

"I bought it in London, with money that father sent me for my birthday."

Fumbling because she couldn't focus through her weeping, Catriona's mother opened the locket. Inside was a small photograph of Catriona on a summer's day in Cambridge, taken a year ago. There was a lock of her hair, too, tied with ribbon. Then there was a carefully cut oval of paper on which Catriona had written, "To My Beloved Father, in Memory of All the Happy Times We Had Together, and All the Times We Didn't, But Should Have, Your Only Daughter."

Catriona's mother closed the locket and then held her very tight. "I know that you'll make him so proud," she sobbed. "I know that, wherever he is, you'll make him proud."

Dottie knocked hesitantly at the door again, and said, "Miss? Are you nearly ready? Mr. Deacon's getting worried that you might miss your press appearance, and he says it's ever so important."

Catriona kissed her mother on the forehead, and then brushed her mother's tears with the tip of her finger. "I'll make him proud," she said, although behind those words her uncertainty was as vertiginous as a lift descending down a bottomless shaft.

Edgar Deacon was waiting tightly in the hallway in a black suit and a stiff white collar, his hat held behind his back. Catriona came down the stairs twice as slowly as she normally would have done, allowing the billowing sleeves of her dress to flow down all around her. She thought to herself, If Edgar is going to make me a queen, then I'm darn well going to behave like one.

"We have to be going," said Edgar with a grimace of impatience. "This whole press reception is timed like clockwork and I want to make sure it *happens* like clockwork. Besides, we have a little detour to make on the way."

Isabelle appeared from the sitting room wearing a hat that covered her head like a black cooking pot, and a lifeless dress of black rayon. "It's about *time*," she said. "You really can be the most inconsiderate of people at times. I suppose you think you can keep God waiting on Judgement Day?"

Catriona smiled at her. "Aunt Isabelle, when they exalt you into even a minor deity, I promise that I'll be more punctual."

"Baggage," snapped Aunt Isabelle, and bustled out of the front door so quickly that Edgar Deacon scarcely had time to open it for her.

"You look beautiful," said Edgar, although he sounded clipped and objective, as if he were complimenting an Anglo-Indian *burra-mem* on her begonias. "I'm sure the press will love you."

"Well, we'll see," said Catriona. She waited while Lettice brought her coat, a black belted wool coat with a spray of diamonds on the lapel.

They left the house and walked across the gravel drive in the warmth of the evening. A laurel-green Rolls-Royce tourer with red coaching stripes was drawn up by the ornamental fountain, its engine warbling. Isabelle was already sitting in the back, her profile lifted in haughty disapproval. Edgar ushered Catriona inside, and then nodded to the chauffeur.

As they drove away from the family house down the long curving driveway, Catriona turned and looked back at the elegant grey 1860s facades, the grey Gothic chimneys, and the rows of bay trees like children's green lollipops.

"It's funny, you know," she told Edgar. "I never thought of this house as my home, but now I do."

Edgar, holding on to the braided silk hand strap, smiled and said, "You were too much of a kind, you and your father, don't y'know. Too competitive. Now he's gone, I think you'll probably find that just about everything in your life will be very much more straightforward."

"Well, *that's* not a very nice thing to say," protested Isabelle.

"I wasn't trying to be *nice*, my dear," Edgar told her. "Just truthful."

Isabelle turned away, but managed to remark, "I still don't see why Tony couldn't at least have been asked to *help.*"

"Believe me," said Edgar, "if the *Arcadia* had been a haberdasher's shop or a hardware store instead of an ocean liner, I would have called on Tony at once. But I had to select only those people who were suitable."

"If you think Catriona's suitable, you must regard the *Arcadia* as a floating house of ill repute," snapped Isabelle. Then immediately, flustered at herself, she said, "I'm sorry. I didn't mean that. I'm just overwrought. What with your mother's weeping fits, and Tony ringing up all the time to ask what's going on, I'm afraid it's all got on top of me."

Catriona took Isabelle's hand and held it between hers. It was thin and scaly with eczema, like the claw of a bird. "You've done wonders, Aunt Isabelle. Don't get ill and spoil it all."

Isabelle took her hand away immediately. "I hope you don't think I'm *ill.* I'm not *ill.*"

Edgar glanced at Catriona and gave her an almost imperceptible shake of his head, as if to say that she should leave Isabelle alone with her jealousy and her tantrums and her inexhaustible grievances against the Keys family. Catriona sat back on the soft velour seat as the Rolls-Royce carried them swiftly through the suburbs of Liverpool to the docks, and didn't try to speak to Isabelle again.

On an angled sunlit corner, as they passed, Catriona glimpsed two barefoot children sitting on the curb, their cheeks fat with gobstoppers. A woman in a straw hat was just coming out of the doorway of a small shop where posters in the window advertised Pear's soap, Player's Navy Cut, and Monkey brand soap—which was a sharp reminder to Isabelle of her husband's shortcomings.

"Now," said Edgar to the chauffeur, leaning forward in his seat.

"Down Breeze Hill, sir?"

"That's it, then right at Stonecroft Terrace, and pull up."

"We don't have much time, sir."

"We have time for this."

The Rolls-Royce drove down a steep cobbled hill, then turned into the top of a sloping street of narrow stone-fronted houses. These were the "backs," the small tied houses where so many of Keys' employees lived: stokers and deckhands and fitters and welders. Edgar said, "Stop here, please," and the Rolls-Royce drew into the curb with a squelch of tyres.

"I'll not want to be waiting here *too* long, sir," said the chauffeur, inclining his head uncomfortably across the terrace towards a gang of small boys with patched and baggy shorts, who were whistling and shouting and kicking an empty tomato tin around on the pavement. "A motor like this is a red rag to scruffs like them. Last time I stopped in Bootle some little blighter rubbed a sheet of wet-and-dry all the way down the bonnet, begging your pardon.'

"We won't be long," Edgar assured him. He waited patiently in his seat while the chauffeur walked around the car to open the door for him. Then he stepped down and held out his hand to Catriona.

"I've never been down here before," said Catriona, and she rather wished that she wasn't here now. She stood in the late-afternoon sunlight smelling the curious aroma of coal fires, boiling vegetables, sweat, cats, and stale hallways. A man walking down the other side of the street with his hands in his pockets stopped and stared at her openly.

"Percy Fearson is really your man when it comes to a guided tour of the backs," said Edgar. "But come with me; let me show you something."

They walked down a few doors until they reached No. 17. There was a peeling maroon-painted door, left ajar to catch the last of the sun; and on the doorstep sat an old woman in a flowery-print housecoat, knitting with knobby arthritic fingers.

"Hellow, grandmama," said Edgar. "Is Mrs. Colehill in?"

"Hellow, Mr. Deacon, sir," replied the old woman toothlessly. "Fine afternoon, sir. Good for me bones."

"Is Mrs. Colehill in?" Edgar repeated, louder.

"In the back, Mr. Deacon, sir. Beating the rug."

"Follow me, Miss Keys," Edgar asked her, and led the way through a narrow hallway with crumbling plaster and brown wallpaper that smelled of kippers and mould. Catriona glanced anxiously into the front parlour. There was a dilapidated sofa sprouting horsehair, and sheets of newspaper on the floor. Two kittens dashed from one side of the newspaper to the other. On the wall was a picture of Jesus smiling beatifically into the middle distance.

They walked through the kitchen. A single green-corroded faucet dripped stains into a sink that was beyond cleaning. On a shelf above the sink was the family's entire larder: a tin of Rowntree's cocoa, a small jar of Marmite yeast extract, a half-empty tin of Hartley's plum jam, a packet of tea, a saucer of cooking fat, a piece of sweaty Cheddar, and a bottle of HP sauce.

Through the misted glass of the back window, Catriona could see a thin ferret-faced woman beating a worn-out rug with a carpet beater. A small boy stood dutifully beside her in a skimpy green sweater with holes at the elbows and boots without laces. A ten-month-old baby banged a wooden spoon in imitation of his mother.

Edgar called, "Mrs. Colehill?"

The woman stopped beating and turned to see who it was.

"Mrs. Colehill, it's Mr. Deacon. I told your Ernest that I'd stop by, just to speak to you. I've brought Miss Keys with me."

"Oh," said Mrs. Colehill, flustered. She came into the kitchen wiping her hands on her apron. The boy followed her, pinched and silent. "You should have let me know, I'd have had some cake."

She shook Catriona's hand and bobbed a little curtsy. "I was ever so upset to hear about Mr. Stanley," she said. "It was ever so young to go, wasn't it? We're all right sorry."

"Thank you," said Catriona, gently.

"Would you like a cup of tea?" Mrs. Colehill asked them. "It won't take a minute to put the kettle on."

"That's quite all right, Mrs. Colehill," said Edgar. "We have to get down to the pier in a very short while. I just wanted Miss Keys to meet some of the important people in Keys Shipping before she meets the ones who only *think* that they're important. Mr. Colehill is one of our riggers, Miss Keys; been at Keys for nine years, longer than I have."

"I suppose he's down at the landing stage seeing the *Arcadia* off," said Catriona. "He must be just as excited as I am."

"Well, he would have given his right arm to have sailed on her, seeing as how he worked so hard on her; but of course you couldn't take along every Tom, Dick, and Harry who wanted a free trip, could you?"

There was no sarcasm in her voice at all. Edgar reached out and held her arm solicitously, and said, "Tell Mr. Colehill not to worry. We'll find a place on the *Arcadia* for him sooner or later. And remember that Mr. Keys promised a one-pound bonus for every man who worked on the ship when she arrives in New York, and two-pounds if she takes the Blue Riband."

"Well," said Mrs. Colehill, smiling respectfully at Catriona, "that'll come in handy. A pound's a pound, after all; and it isn't easy for anyone to make ends meet these days, is it? Don't think that I'm complaining, mind. Two pounds, sixteen shillings the week is good money by any standards. There's plenty who have to make do with less."

Edgar nodded towards the pale young boy in the torn green sweater. "How's young Godfrey?"

"Making progress, thank you, sir. The doctor says he should be well enough to go back to school in a month or so, after the summer holidays perhaps."

"How do you feel, Godfrey?" asked Edgar sharply. Godfrey said nothing, but hid his face behind his mother's skirts.

Edgar smiled and reached into his pocket for sixpence, which he held out to Godfrey as bait to come out into the open.

"Perhaps I should explain that young Godfrey was suffering from a severe case of rickets," Edgar said to Catriona, still smiling, still teasing the boy with the silvery sixpence. "It's quite common here in the backs, what with the lack of fresh air in the winter and the poor diet that many of our lower-paid workers have to put up with. If only the company could afford to pay them more. But young Godfrey's condition came to your father's personal attention, and he paid for Godfrey out of his own money to be treated by a specialist in Manchester, and for a regular supply of fresh milk and cod-liver oil to be delivered here to improve his health."

Mrs. Colehill said earnestly, "If it hadn't have been for your father, miss, he might never have walked. As it is, he's going to be bandy; but his da says that he could always be a jockey, seeing as how his legs would fit around an 'orse."

Catriona leaned forward and held out her hand. Godfrey watched her suspiciously at first, but at last he reached out with his own thin hand and took it.

"It's been lovely to meet you, Godfrey," she said gently. "When I come back from New York, I'll bring you a present. What would you like more than anything else in the world?"

"Come on, chuck," his mother chided him. "What would you like for a present from America? Miss Keys won't buy you nothing at all unless you tell her what you want."

Godfrey cleared his throat, and then he whispered, "Raspberry junket."

Catriona said, "Is that all? No toys?"

"A lead sailor, if they do them, please."

"A lead sailor and a raspberry junket?"

Godfrey nodded.

Catriona squeezed his hand and kissed his forehead and said, "If that's what you want, that's exactly what you shall have."

They talked to Mrs. Colehill for a few minutes about the baby, who was sleeping badly; but then Edgar took out his pocket watch and said that they would have to be leaving if they were going to get to the landing stage on time. Mrs. Colehill bobbed Catriona another curtsy, and then they left and walked back up the street to where the chauffeur was zealously standing guard over the Rolls-Royce.

Edgar said as they approached the car, "I expect you're wondering why I brought you here."

Catriona looked at him. "You said it was to show me who the really important people were."

"Yes, well it was. Well, partly. It was also to show you where your father always believed our responsibilities lay. You see, your father and I spent a great deal of time together. We became very tight chums, don't y'know, and I learned after a number of years what really made him tick. Apart from being a remarkable engineer and a well-respected commander, he was also a philanthropist. He believed that his duty in life was to help the human race, rich and poor, and that no enterprise should be undertaken unless it eventually produced some ultimate benefit for the world as a whole."

Catriona said nothing, but waited by the open car door for Edgar to finish.

"The thing is, you see," said Edgar, "if we *do* have to sell Keys Shipping, we must think of families like the Colehills. If we sell it off piecemeal, then the Colehills and all the other people who live in these backs will be out of work. You have seen for yourself what a hard existence they have. Unless we make sure that Keys remains intact, and that the company keeps running, we will be condemning each and every one of them to indescribable misery."

Catriona said, "You never gave me the impression before that you cared very much about the shipyard workers. Didn't you once call them 'the next worse scourge to rust'?"

Edgar gave Catriona a very thin smile, thin as a celluloid collar. "Just because your common dockside labourers are difficult men to deal with —untrustworthy, most of them, and none of them past wholesale thieving —that doesn't mean that one doesn't have a moral obligation to take care of them. Stanley, your father, saw Keys Shipping as a family, and in every family there are delinquents. That, however, does nothing to make it any less of a family, nor any less deserving of being kept together."

"We'd better leave now, sir," put in the chauffeur. "I'd hate to have to speed the last couple of miles, begging your pardon."

"Quite right," said Edgar. Then, to Catriona, "Shall we? I think it's time for the great adventure to begin."

"Peter Pan said that to die would be a great adventure," said Catriona.

"Well, that's J. M. Barrie for you," Edgar remarked obtusely.

"I always saw myself as Wendy, as matter of fact," put in Isabelle.

"Wendy," said Edgar, "was skewered by an arrow." He gave Isabelle a bland and unreadable smirk. "Hardly a fate deserved by the most personable lady in the entire family."

"Hm," purred Isabelle, and looked across at Catriona to see what she thought of *that.*

Nine

They arrived at last at the landing stage, and the chauffeur nudged the Rolls-Royce through the tangle of taxis and wagons and jostling people until he reached the entrance to the terminus. A police constable opened the car door for them, and they stepped out onto a wide red runner. There was a smattering of applause from the pressing crowds all around, although few of them had any idea who Catriona was, or what she was doing here. Most of them were waiting to see Douglas Fairbanks and Mary Pickford. Five or six press cameras popped and flashed, and Edgar gripped Catriona's arm and muttered, "You have to *smile*. You have to look as if you're enjoying yourself."

Catriona managed a wave and a nervous smile. Then she was pushed unceremoniously through the terminus building to the main concourse, where there were flowers, and even more crowds, and a silver band playing "Goodbye, Dolly Gray." Edgar led her forward to a cluster of stout smiling dignitaries, and there was the Lord Mayor of Liverpool, with his fur-trimmed robes and his chains, and he grasped her hand in his sweaty chipolata fingers and raised it to his lips.

"I have to tell you how proud we are of the good ship *Arcadia*," he said. "Wherever she goes in the world, she'll carry on her stern the name of Liverpool—a fine ship from a fine city."

There was more applause, and the band tore into "Land of Hope and Glory" as if they were trying to finish it in under a minute. Someone released a shower of coloured balloons, which filled the inside of the terminus and clung to the glass-roofed ceiling, although one or two of them escaped through a skylight and fled into the bright summer sky. More cameras dazzled and flashed, and Catriona found that she was suddenly being rushed to the covered gangway that would take her aboard the *Arcadia*.

"Miss Keys!" the photographers kept shouting, holding up their plate cameras. "Miss Keys, this way please! This way!"

She was aboard the *Arcadia* before she knew it. She suddenly found herself being hurried up a wide staircase of sweeping semicircular stairs lit by bronze statues of dryads with Lalique torches in their hands. The noise and the bustle were utterly confusing. Edgar stayed close by her side, but her vision seemed to be nothing more than a kaleidoscope of intense, excited faces, both men and women, and cameras, and running feet.

"*Miss Keys!*" they shouted at her. "*Miss Keys, please!*"

For a moment she was out on the promenade deck, and the warm evening wind was blowing in her face. But then Edgar had propelled her to her stateroom, and the door was closed on all those flashes and pops and all those eager bright-red faces. There were two or three knocks and something of a scuffle, but when Edgar shouted, "Go away! Miss Keys will be out in ten minutes!" the commotion seemed to die down.

Edgar came away from the door, his hands in his trouser pockets, smiling. "Well," he said, "what do you think? This is where the Queen of the Atlantic begins her reign."

"I'm completely bewildered," said Catriona. "What happened down there?"

Edgar walked across the thick aquamarine carpeting to the inlaid walnut cocktail cabinet. "Would you like a drink?" he asked her.

"A gin and bitters."

He took ice out of a silver ice bucket, and clinked it into two handmade Lalique glasses with frosted stems in the shape of stylised nudes.

"What happened down there was your official civic reception."

"But it was like a *whirlwind.* I didn't even get the chance to say thank you."

"I didn't want you to have the chance to say thank you. I'm trying to make you into a queen, not the Lady Mayoress. You don't give speeches and you don't say thank you. You don't mingle. You take it for granted that you're the glittering star that all of these people want to see. Come on, that's how Gloria Swanson and Clara Bow do it. They keep that little bit distant from their public. They make people thirst for even the slightest glimpse of them."

"I see," said Catriona, taking off her hat and laying it down on a polished onyx table next to her. Edgar brought over her drink and she swallowed half of it in one ice-cold gulp.

"This is all about *mystique,*" Edgar said in his most matter-of-fact voice. "You have a lot of it already, so you must know what I'm talking about. But at the moment, your appeal is what one might call a kind of 'jazz-baby' cuteness. Don't misunderstand me, I'm not trying to be rude; it's very attractive in its way, and it sets a lot of chaps back on their heels. But you're going to have to develop yourself from there—give yourself more aloofness and style. Think to yourself that you're a queen, and you'll start behaving like one."

"When do we go to meet the captain?" asked Catriona.

Edgar smiled. "That's exactly what I was talking about. *You* don't go to see the captain; the captain comes to see you. After all, twenty-five per cent of the ship will soon be yours."

"Do you have some music in here?" asked Catriona.

Edgar raised a finger. Then he went across to what looked like a bureau. He slid out the front panel, and inside was a gramophone, balanced on gimbals so that it could be played even in rough weather. "What takes your fancy?" he asked her.

"Something soothing," she said.

While the thin clarinet warbling of Johnny de Droit filled the room, Catriona had a chance to look around. There were 385 first-class staterooms on the *Arcadia,* and every single one of them was decorated according to a different theme. Catriona's suite was "The Wind," and two entire walls of the sitting room had been veneered with a ribboned pattern of bird's-eye maple and Cuban mahogany, to represent streamers flying in a breeze. There was a bronze sculpture by Bruno Zach in the centre of the long modern sideboard, a girl with her hair blowing out behind her. The furniture was all strictly modern, though eclectic: Italian-designed chairs upholstered with patterns of clouds, French tables in three different shades of blue grass, and a writing desk of inlaid ebony, yew, and box, by Gordon Russell. On the wall was a Cubist print of "A Windy Day in Paris" by Gino Severini.

"You should see 'The Jungle' stateroom," said Edgar, who had been watching her. "It has bamboo furniture, bronze palm trees, and a whole collection of porcelain monkeys."

"This is *extraordinary,*" said Catriona. "I was expecting gilt and plush and stuffy old-fashioned furniture."

"That was what most of the Keys directors wanted," said Edgar. "You know what they're like. All tweed waistcoats and old-fashioned ways. But your father insisted that we should bring in the most advanced interior designers we could. This is the ship of the future, he said; we don't want it to be out of date before it starts. He didn't like half of the staterooms, not himself. They weren't to his taste. Most of them aren't to mine, either. But he recognised brilliant design when he saw it. He used to say, 'How can you expect a flapper in a short skirt to sit in a Louis Quatorze chair?'"

Catriona put down her drink and walked through to the bathroom. There was a huge bath of solid Sicilian marble, as well as white velvet draperies, gold-washed faucets, and a multicoloured mirror on the wall showing white mirror clouds blowing over a range of softly curving blue mirror hills.

"I think it's amazing," she said. "You would hardly believe that you're on board a ship at all."

Edgar took out his pocket watch and squinted at it. "The press should be ready for you in about ten minutes, if they're not queuing up outside already. I expect we'll have quite a few people from the shipbuilders and the company, too. Do you want to get changed now? I can send your maid in."

"Not just yet," said Catriona. "I just want to wallow for a while." She peered out of one of her portholes at the sparkling reaches of the Mersey estuary. The reedy jazz music made her feel like dancing around and around. She felt as if she must be dreaming or drunk. There was a brisk knock at the stateroom door, but it was only the florist with a huge bunch of fifty white roses to symbolise the *Arcadia*'s maiden voyage, and then more sprays of red and yellow roses and freesias and orchids than she could count. The sofa and the floor were knee-deep in flowers. Catriona could have waded in them, and their perfume was so heavy that she had to ask Edgar to open the porthole.

The telephone rang. Edgar picked it up and said, "Miss Keys' suite?" Then he covered the mouthpiece with his hand and said, "It's Sir Peregrine. He hopes you're comfortably settled in your stateroom, and he wants to know if he might come up to present you with his compliments?"

"Tell him to come up straightaway," said Catriona. "I feel like another drink before I get changed, anyway."

Edgar cautioned, "You shouldn't keep the press waiting for too long."

Catriona lay back amongst the flowers, Ophelia amongst the orchids, and stretched her arms luxuriously. "Surely that's all part of this mystique you're trying to cultivate in me, being unpunctual. All the top film stars are late on the set. You know that."

Edgar gave a tight, impatient shrug. "It's up to you. As long as you don't overdo it."

It took Sir Peregrine Arrowsmith only four or five minutes to reach Catriona's staterooms from the bridge deck below, but in that time the restless newspaper reporters had managed to force open the door at least half a dozen times, and several of them had even tried to pop off "candid" photographs of Catriona as she sat drinking her cocktail. There had also been a ceaseless in-and-out traffic of beige-jacketed stewards, carrying in boxes of candies tied up with ribbons, bottles of Chanel and Guerlain perfumes, sugared plums, more flowers, jeroboams of Irroy champagne, silver trays heaped up with greetings, telegraphs, and a china doll dressed in the gold-buttoned livery of Keys Shipping Lines.

At last Sir Peregrine elbowed his way in, and while Edgar forcibly closed the door on the newspaper reporters behind him, he stood tall and dignified as an old stork, brushing the gold-braided sleeves of his uniform. "A menagerie," he said with trembling disapproval.

Catriona had met quite a variety of elderly men recently, mostly with Nigel. Theatrical producers, bankers, impresarios, and ageing princes of the footlights. By now, she'd grown accustomed to the nakedness of elderly men's fears. Unlike the young men she knew, who had all of their lives before them and hadn't yet scraped the keel of their ambition on the unexpectedly shallow bottom of their own shortcomings, men like Sir Peregrine had become all too familiar with the precise measure of their limitations, and how little time was left to them. They betrayed their desperate anxiety that they might never be able to achieve anything worthwhile like signal flags.

She could tell that Sir Peregrine was considerably discomfited by having to leave the bridge and come to her stateroom to welcome her, and that it rocked the security he felt in the traditions of the sea. On board a liner, the captain was the Absolute Presence, and even Catriona's father wouldn't have expected a man of Sir Peregrine's stature to have to jostle his way through crowds of reporters to a passenger's stateroom—whether the passenger was heir to the whole shipping line or not.

Sir Peregrine was numbered amongst those legendary liner captains like Sir James Charles, of the *Aquitania*, and Sir Arthur Rostron. Sir James was a man of Brodignagian proportions who ran his dining table like Henry VIII, insisting on evening dress and full decorations at every meal, and directing the ship's orchestra to play Elgar while he led full-blooded assaults on citadels of pastry with moats of turtle stew. Sir Arthur, on the other hand, who had commanded the *Carpathia* when she picked up the survivors of the *Titanic* disaster, presided over a table which was noted for its severe regard of all the maritime proprieties, and its chilly lack of affability.

Handsome in the hollow-cheeked, cadaverous way that very thin men can be when they reach the age of sixty, Sir Peregrine was the last surviving son of the Marquis of Walburton. From babyhood he had irritated his father so much that at the age of fifteen he had been sent off to Portsmouth and apprenticed in sail. Unabashed, he had worked his way to his master's certificate and his extra master's certificate on the violent seas of Cape Horn and the Indian Ocean. He had joined Keys Shipping as fourth officer before the war, after seven years with Cunard, and had commanded the liner *Samaria* when she was a troopship. For the way in which he had sailed his vessel right into the Greek coast under fierce enemy fire in 1916 he had been knighted. Only his first officer had known that he was devastatingly drunk at the time; although when he was given the command of Keys Shipping's best liner, the *Aurora*, his determined way with bottles of Old Haitian rum had gradually become more noticeable—first to the management, and then to the passengers.

There had been two near-collisions, and then a frightening night when he had refused to heave-to against a storm that had wrecked half of the *Aurora*'s superstructure and drowned three passengers. One morning he had failed to give a clear instruction from the bridge, and the *Aurora* had rammed the Keys Shipping Line pier at New York harbour at three knots, reducing its length by forty-one feet.

Several of the company's directors had fiercely opposed Sir Peregrine's appointment as captain of the *Arcadia*. But Sir Peregrine had allies in exalted places. His younger sister, Hattie, was married to Cecil, Duke of Ashurst, chairman of Maritime Finance, which had underwritten thousands of pounds of Keys debts; his closest friend, Roger Wallington, was one of the louder noises at Lloyd's; and after entertaining the Prince of Wales on board the *Aurora*, he had regularly made up shooting parties at Sandringham. The pressure on Stanley Keys to appoint him master had been, in the end, irresistible; particularly since it was essential for the captain of a luxury liner to have high social *ton*. But privately he had made Sir Peregrine swear to give up the bottle.

The man most sharply disappointed by Sir Peregrine's appointment had been Rudyard Philips, the energetic young Welsh captain who had taken over the *Aurora*. Since the *Aurora* was presently in dry dock, Mr. Philips was sailing on the *Arcadia*'s maiden voyage as Sir Peregrine's first officer, but Sir Peregrine had made it transparently clear that he would put up with no interference and no quibbling, especially from a sprat like *him*.

Sir Peregrine's crustiness did little to intimidate Edgar, however. Edgar Deacon knew most things that went on in Keys Shipping, and he knew just how heavily the commodore could drink. That was why Sir Peregrine had reluctantly answered Edgar's summons to Catriona's staterooms; he wanted to keep the *Arcadia* for himself and go down in history with a shining reputation for being a great and glorious master of the Atlantic. It was that fear, and that ambition, that Catriona had immediately sensed in him.

"It's a considerable pleasure to have you aboard, Miss Keys," said Sir Peregrine with exaggerated formality, coming over and taking Catriona's hand. "I was, you know, a lifetime admirer of your father, and you have the sincerest condolences of myself and my crew. A sad, sudden demise. He should have been here today, so that he could have rejoiced with the rest of us."

"Thank you, Commodore," said Catriona. "Won't you have a drink? I'm having one."

Sir Peregrine, his cap wedged under his arm, glanced uncertainly towards Edgar, who was standing by the bar. Edgar shrugged as if to say that one drink wouldn't hurt.

"I'll have a mineral water, if you don't mind," said Sir Peregrine.

"Miss Keys caused quite a stir when she came on board," remarked Edgar. "I think she's going to bring us luck."

"I heard the ballyhoo." Sir Peregrine nodded. He took his glass of sparkling water and said, "Thank you. Let's drink to the *Arcadia*, shall we?"

"*Arcadia*," they said in unison.

"Sit down for a moment, Commodore," Catriona told him, and when he actually did she was so pleased with herself that she couldn't hold back a smile. From being nobody more important than Nigel Myers' flapper girlfriend to Queen of the Atlantic in one week was more amusing than she could have imagined. "Aren't you nervous?" she asked Sir Peregrine. "I would be, having to steer a ship as expensive as this, especially for the first time."

Sir Peregrine gave her an embarrassed grimace. "I *have* sailed her before, you know. She has undergone quite extensive sea trials. So I'm not quite as nervous as you seem to think that I may be. She's expensive, yes. But each liner has to be handled with equal care, no matter how many passengers she has aboard, and no matter how much she cost."

"Like the *Aurora*," put in Edgar.

Catriona raised an eyebrow. She had read about the *Aurora* in the newspapers. She looked at Edgar and suddenly began to understand that there was more behind Sir Peregrine's welcoming visit to her stateroom than the dutiful homage of an old company retainer to the bright new company figurehead.

"Well," said Sir Peregrine, "the *Aurora* always was a quirky old girl."

"What about the *Arcadia?*" asked Catriona. "Is she quirky, too?"

"Every vessel has her particular fancies," said Sir Peregrine. He wasn't looking at Edgar directly but he was obviously conscious of every move that Edgar made as he packed up and down the stateroom behind him. "The *Arcadia* lists very slightly to starboard, and probably always will do. But she's fast and lively and less inclined to roll than the *Mauretania*, or some of the Frenchies. There won't be so much seasickness on the *Arcadia*, I dare say; and since the carpets cost so much, that's probably just as well."

"I'm told that champagne is the best preventive against seasickness," said Catriona. Her mother had told her that, actually, the day before yesterday: Drink as much champagne as you like, dear, but on *no account* eat ice cream.

"Champagne and silk pyjamas, that's what they say," Sir Peregrine asserted, and fixed Catriona with such a penetrating stare that she felt she had to turn away. It was almost as if he were trying to imagine what she would look like dressed in silk pyjamas, or even less. What a funny old bird he was.

"There's no *sure* cure, of course," put in Edgar. "Even aboard the greatest and grandest liners people get sick. The *Berengaria*'s one of the worst: a very tender ship. I once saw sixty or seventy third-class passengers in a row on board the *Berengaria* all being sick at once, like an orchestra."

Sir Peregrine stood up. "I'm sure Miss Keys doesn't really want to be disturbed by that kind of talk, Mr. Deacon," he said. "But can I have a quiet word of business with you before I get back to the bridge?"

"Anything you can say to me I'm sure that you can say in front of Miss Keys," said Edgar, his voice very steady. "She's going to be more than just a figurehead, don't y'know. More than just a company mascot."

Sir Peregrine turned around and looked at Catriona, then back at Edgar. It was clear that he mistrusted Edgar in the way that he mistrusted submerged rocks or icebergs. You could never be absolutely sure when you were going to glance against them and have your hull ripped out.

"It's a personal matter, Mr. Deacon," insisted Sir Peregrine.

"All the more reason to confide in Miss Keys." Edgar smiled coldly. "She has a very personal touch."

Sir Peregrine's stringlike sinews tightened in his neck. "Perhaps this is the wrong moment," he said. "I'm sure Miss Keys must be impatient to meet the press, just as they are obviously agog to meet her."

"It's about Mr. Philips?" asked Edgar.

Sir Peregrine breathed deeply but didn't answer.

"You know my feelings about Mr. Philips already," said Edgar. "I have complete faith in him. Just as I have in you, of course."

"Mr. Philips," said Sir Peregrine, as if the name were two fairy-tale toads which came out of his mouth when he spoke, "is the kind of first officer who might well put his ambition before the safety of his ship."

"What does that mean?" asked Catriona pointedly. She knew nothing of the rancour between Sir Peregrine and Rudyard Philips—in fact, she didn't even know who Rudyard Philips was. But she thought, as the heiress to Keys Shipping, that she ought to sound authoritative and sharp.

"It simply *means,*" said Sir Peregrine, drawing up his pointed shoulder blades so that his gold epaulets bristled, "it simply *means* that Mr. Philips, in a moment of crisis, might conceivably put his career before the principles of good seamanship, and not assist me to the best of his ability. He might prefer to see me take the blame for any mishaps, and thereby enhance his own prospects of commanding this ship."

"You mean he might cheerfully allow the *Arcadia* to be damaged and the lives of its passengers put at risk—just for the sake of showing you up in a bad light?" asked Catriona.

"It is not entirely beyond the bounds of possibility," said Sir Peregrine uncomfortably. He was aware that when they were phrased as bluntly as Catriona had phrased them his insinuations against Rudyard Philips came close to the brink of absurdity. He looked to Edgar for some masculine support, despite what he felt about him; but Edgar did nothing more than smile into his drink, as if a witty remark had been written on the bottom of his glass. The spectacle of the apoplectic and self-righteous Sir Peregrine being hotfooted by a twenty-one-year-old flapper had made Edgar Deacon's day; he could have gone to bed without attending a single one of the predeparture parties that were planned for this evening, and slept content.

Now there was more band music from the landing stage and cheering, and the press started beating on the door of Catriona's stateroom with renewed urgency. "Come on, Miss Keys, we're going to miss the morning editions! We've got a train to catch with these pictures!" And so Sir Peregrine bowed to her and kissed her hand with all of the respect that a seadog with all of his thousands of nautical miles and all of his hundreds of empty bottles of Old Haitian rum might justifiably have accorded any pretty young girl with bobbed hair, big breasts, and long legs, and left the stateroom on an even keel.

"He's magnificent," said Catriona, really quite impressed, when he had gone.

Edgar was still squeezing the door closed against a reporter's arm. "Of course he is. It's his job to be magnificent. But he's also the biggest drunk on the seven seas."

"Ah," said Catriona; and it was then that the press at last broke in and rushed to kneel before her with their notebooks and their flashing cameras and their excited questions, as if she were truly a newly crowned queen. Dazzled, she looked at Edgar over the bobbing trilbies and the brilliantined heads, but all he did was raise his glass to her and bow to his new memsahib.

Ten

After the reporters and the photographers had left, Isabelle came into Catriona's stateroom, unsteadier but happier from the effects of two vodka martinis, and from the compliments of a steward who had told her that she had the best legs he had come across since leaving Galway.

"That's what Tony always used to like about me," she said, sitting promptly on the sofa and blinking at Catriona from beneath the black rim of her cooking-pot hat. "My legs."

Edgar had been on the telephone for ten minutes, and at the end of his call he excused himself. "Apparently there's a problem with one of the turbines. Nothing that can't be solved, but I want to take a look. I'll call for you at ten, shall I, just before the reception party starts?"

Catriona went to the door with him. As he put on his hat, she said, "Is there more to you, Mr. Deacon, than meets the eye?"

Edgar looked back at her with a touch of a smile at one corner of his mouth, but his expression was really giving nothing away. "I'm not any more than I seem to be, if that's what you're trying to suggest. You're the queen and I'm your loyal and energetic subject. Also, I have a shipping company to run."

"But where does your sense of style come from? That's unexpected in a businessman."

"My mother's side, I expect. My father was an engineer, my mother was a painter."

"So. You're a Leonardo da Vinci. Engineer and artist."

This time his smile spread wider. "I'd hardly say that. More like an Albert Ballin."

"Who on earth was Albert Ballin?" asked Isabelle, who had been leaning sideways on the sofa so that she could eavesdrop on their conversation.

"The creator of the old Hamburg-America line," said Edgar, without taking his eyes off Catriona.

"He was very rich, Aunt Isabelle, and very dynamic, and quite unscrupulous," Catriona added. "I knew a man in London who had once played cards with him."

Edgar nodded to Catriona in mocking respect. "You're ahead of your years, Miss Keys."

"You're forgetting that I've spent most of the year with actors," she replied.

When Edgar had gone, Catriona rang for the steward to make them some more drinks, and for the maid to lay out her party dress for her and draw her bath.

A steward on a luxury liner like the *Arcadia* virtually became for the duration of the voyage a first-class passenger's personal servant, and before the liner sailed tomorrow morning, Catriona would give him her full instructions for the following four days: when to wake her, when to bring her breakfast, what cocktails to provide and when, what parties and receptions she would be holding in her suite. Her maid she would give complete details of all her clothes, which gowns to lay out, how she liked her bath, how to arrange her dressing table, which shoes to put out.

The steward turned out to be a brisk talkative man with black brilliantined hair as shiny as a painted newel post and the extraordinary gliding walk of someone who has been trying to keep trays of mulligatawny soup on the horizontal for more tilting, rolling, wallowing, and pitching sea miles than he can remember. His name was Trimmer, and he had served on Keys liners for nine years; before that, White Star. Before that, he had been a private in the Boer War, although he had shot nothing more spectacular than a pregnant hartebeest.

The maid was called Alice, after Queen Victoria's great-granddaughter, and was as small and pink-cheeked as a china shepherdess. She had worked in "several houses of note," she kept telling Catriona, "houses where the coals on the fires had to be set in your perfect pyramids, or else they'd make you take them to pieces and start all over again."

"Has madam had a hopportunity to hinspect the vessel?" inquired Trimmer, pouring out Isabelle's third vodka martini with consummate skill.

"Not yet," said Catriona. "The inside of this stateroom is all I've seen so far."

"Well, if I might hexpress my hown hopinion, this vessel is a vision of loveliness," said Trimmer. "I don't think in all of my years hafloat that I hever saw hanything so helegant."

"I'm looking forward to seeing it hall, I mean *all*, for myself." Catriona smiled, and then couldn't stop herself from giggling.

Once Trimmer had closed the door after him, she said to Isabelle, "I can't bear it! By the end of the voyage I'm going to be saying heverything with a haitch hon!"

Isabelle raised her martini. "It's the military, that's what it is. The military always speak like that. It's something to do with making yourself heard on a parade ground."

Alice the maid came through from the bedroom and announced in her tinkly voice that Miss Keys' bath was drawn and that Miss Keys' gown was laid out, and would Miss Keys be requiring the white silk stockings or the dove-grey or the pearl, but respectfully she herself would recommend the pearl, bearing the particular gown in mind.

"Aren't you going to go and get ready?" Catriona asked Isabelle. "I mean, they have given you somewhere to change, haven't they?"

Isabelle's head tilted as if she were already at sea, instead of tied up at Liverpool's landing stage. "Yes, I've been given somewhere to get ready," she said. "A dinky little room with a washstand. But I'm not going yet. There's plenty of time for titivation. Plenty. Tony always says that I spend too long titivating. "For goodness' sake, Belle," he shouts at me, "stop that titivating! You'll titivate yourself stupid, you will!" That's what he shouts at me."

Catriona glanced at Alice, but Alice had been trained in houses of note where the coals were set in perfect pyramids, and so her face registered nothing at Isabelle's outburst, neither approval nor mirth nor condemnation, but instead a kind of beatific preoccupation with life's busy little details.

Although Stanley Keys had been a very prosperous man, and the Keyses had always kept a reasonable array of servants—a chauffeur, a cook, three or four maids, and occasionally a butler—Catriona had never had a maid so completely to herself before, and never a maid who seemed to regard the slightest exertion on Catriona's part to be utterly out of the question. As soon as the bedroom door was closed, Alice began fussily to unfasten Catriona's buttons and to slip down her dress. Then she gently but authoritatively ushered Catriona to the bedroom chaise-lounge so that she could roll down her stockings. She seemed surprised that Catriona wore so little underwear. It was hardly the thing to wear nothing at all under one's cocktail dress but georgette step-ins. But, after all, Alice wasn't used to dizzy young girls from London. Her particular training was in the comprehensive corsetry of rich and gradually widening American ladies; or in the *chemise-pantalons* and voile pyjamas of indolent and fashionable *Italiennes*.

Alice slipped a silver silk peignoir around Catriona's shoulders and led her through to the steamy perfumed bathroom. There, for almost half an hour, Catriona floated and wallowed in constantly replenished hot water, while Alice soaped her all over with pure white scentless French soap, rinsed her, and scoured the hardened skin on her heels (those pretty but shoddily cut shoes of hers!). Then Alice towelled her, led her back to the bedroom, and laid out a manicure table.

"You can open the door now," said Catriona. "I'm sure my aunt's becoming rather tired of sitting out there on her own. And perhaps you could ring for the steward, so that we could have some champagne."

"Yes, Miss Keys," said Alice, and opened the door. There on the sofa, her shoes kicked off, her legs hanging over the chromium sides, her eyes closed and her mouth wide open, lay Isabelle, asleep.

"I think the excitement's got the better of her," said Catriona, doubtfully.

"Is she travelling, Miss Keys?" asked Alice, completely unruffled.

"She's only staying on board tonight, for the reception parties," Catriona told her.

"Well, that's probably just as well. She has the look, I'm sorry to say, of a poor sailor."

"Are you a good sailor, Alice?"

Alice sat down and took Catriona's hand in hers, examining the nails for overgrown cuticles and splits. "Sailing, Miss Keys, is like anything else in life. As long as it is approached with sufficient moral equilibrium, and a certain measure of liver salts, it can be borne."

Catriona watched Alice as she pushed back the softened skin of her cuticles one by one. "I'm intrigued," she said. "What *else* in life can usually be borne with the aid of moral equilibrium and liver salts?"

Alice looked up at her and batted her eyelids once. "*Men,*" she said.

This evening, from ten o'clock until the first strains of dawn, there would be seven parties held all over the *Arcadia* in honour of her builders, her designers, and the men who had financed her (including a tall waxen-faced man in a wing collar from the Government, which had laid out nearly a million pounds for the building of the *Arcadia* on Stanley Key's assurance that in case of war she could immediately be brought into use as a troopship). Catriona, as the new head of Keys Shipping Line, would have to visit all seven parties, from the champagne fountain and seventy-piece orchestra in the main ballroom, to the beer-and-sausages bash that was being thrown in the third-class dining hall for the dockers' representatives and the boilermakers and the suppliers of Bisto gravy browning and cream crackers.

She had chosen a dress that was as original as it was erotic: a thin tracery of make-believe spiderwebs, sparkling with silver thread. A diamond-encrusted spider clung to her left breast, and all the rest of the webs radiated from it. Its French designer, Antoine Claude, had described it as "a gown of shadows and suggestions, and nothing else, except perhaps a sudden unexpected revelation when you are least expecting it!"

Alice lifted the gown over Catriona's head as if she were lifting a cloud of smoke. The fine-textured fabric settled around Catriona's shoulders, and she twirled in front of the mirrors in the bedroom as Alice tried to scuttle around after her and fasten her hooks.

Catriona knew she was in a dream now. She had never seen herself look so startling. Her eyes were made up to make them look even darker and more slanting and more vampish than ever, her hair was glossy and bobbed like a wave of varnish. And the cobweb gown floated around her naked body like a mystery turned magically into a dress—concealing her one moment in layers of grey-on-grey, and then subtly showing the curve of an arm, the pinkish tint of a nipple, even a fleeting triangular shadow of curly hair.

She had always liked to dress to startle. She remembered when she was thirteen, coming downstairs to meet the bow-tied, party-frocked juveniles at her birthday tea with her dress tugged down to bare her shoulders in provocative imitation of Ethel Barrymore. Her father had been furious, but she had never forgotten the stir she had made.

"I must *say*," admitted Alice, in that curious unfinished dialect of the English domestic, "but it's hardly a mourning dress."

"I know that, I know that," said Catriona, turning around and around so that the gown hovered about her in a smoky circle. "But my father wouldn't want me to mourn him, not tonight. He would have been as happy as a sandboy himself if he'd been here."

At a quarter after ten, Edgar came back to Catriona's stateroom in full evening dress. He looked strangely less convincing in tails than he did in his normal business suit, as if he had recently arrived from Ooty hill station in the 1890s, but charming, too. Isabelle had at last been persuaded by Alice to go to her little changing room on E deck, and so Catriona was sitting on her own, smoking, when Edgar arrived.

"I need scarcely tell you that you look ravishing," he said. "If I had wanted to dream up a Queen of the Atlantic in my mind, I couldn't have done better. You're beyond imagination."

Catriona smiled. "I'm just myself, Mr. Deacon."

"Why don't you call me Edgar?"

She drew at her Craven-A and then stubbed it out, still smiling. "I won't call you Edgar, because you're one of the employees of Keys Shipping. I wouldn't want people to think we were too familiar, would you?"

Edgar gave her a small shrug of acceptance, but she could tell that she had annoyed him. They were beginning to test each other's strength now, and Catriona knew that she was going to have to establish her authority quickly, or else he would use her as he had obviously intended to use her, as nothing more than a pretty puppet.

"Are we ready?" asked Catriona. "I think it's time I met everybody, don't you?"

Outside on deck, the outlines of the *Arcadia* had been traced in white necklaces of lights, and her bunting flapped in the warm coastal wind. A band on the quay was playing "The Floral Song," and the landing stage was jammed with glossy black limousines—Humbers and Daimlers and Rolls-Royces. Beyond the docks, the whole of Liverpool sparkled in the summer night.

"I thought you might like to know that we've received a message of congratulation and God-speed from His Majesty," said Edgar as he led Catriona to the doors that would take them to the *Arcadia*'s grand staircase. "He also wished us to accept his deepest sympathies on the death of your Father."

"I should like to see that later, that message," said Catriona.

The promenade decks were packed with local dignitaries in white tie and tails, and their "lady wives" in long gowns and turbans and ostrich feathers. For the moment, however, the guests were all being discreetly held back from the staircase by red velvet ropes. Edgar nodded to the Keys Shipping officer who was politely but decisively heading off anyone who tried to slip down to the Grand Lounge for a surreptitious first taste of the champagne and smoked salmon, and the officer lifted the rope for them.

The loud conversation all around them immediately died away. The rope had been lifted! But for whom? Catriona found herself being stared at by hundreds of pairs of curious eyes; winked at by hundreds of diamonds in scores of necklaces; dazzled by a gross of starched shirtfronts. Then, at the prompting of a Keys officer at the back of the crowd, everybody started to clap, although most of them didn't have the faintest idea why. Catriona smiled and waved, as regally and as sweetly as she could, although underneath her flimsy dress her heart was running an hysterical bicycle race. Two or three flash guns flared, and Catriona paused and turned by the open doorways to give the crowd one last theatrical display of teeth. She loved it, every moment of it. Her adrenaline was high, she felt pretty and bright and full of "It." Now she knew why Nigel never tired of going out onto the stage every night, and twice on Saturdays. To be applauded, to be looked at, to have everybody whispering about you and wondering who you were—it was all too marvellous for words.

Arm-in-arm, Catriona and Edgar Deacon descended the staircase to the Grand Lounge. The staircase came down in a wide asymmetric sweep of semicircular steps, each one cut and polished out of different-coloured marble. On either side of her, as she came down, Catriona could see herself a thousand times over, reflected and reflected again in tall fluted columns of sparkling mirrors.

Then they were in the Grand Lounge itself, and the orchestra struck up first with a fanfare of trumpets, and then with "Pomp and Circumstance." The directors of Keys Shipping were all there, and the man from the Government, and a whole cluster of minor celebrities from sport, theatre, and films. They stood up and clapped enthusiastically as Catriona came across the lounge, and she almost felt like crying.

The Grand Lounge was brilliant. It rose the height of three decks, to an arched glass roof that was a glittering masterpiece of lightness and grace. Supporting the roof were twelve pillars of highly polished chrome, which mirrored every movement of the assembled guests in curves and stripes, and made the whole room flicker with life, like a film. Behind the pillars there were glass-and-chrome tables and chairs, and eleven fountains —naked stainless-steel girls, their arms stretched upwards, with spray surging out all around them to give the impression of undulating waves.

A table was spread with the most lavish buffet that Catriona had ever seen; and behind the table stood a starched rank of waiters and chefs in lofty white hats, ready to serve whatever a guest might wish, from hot country ham to rare roast beef, from hot and cold pigeon to cold smoked duck, from dry Indian curries with fresh *nan* bread and tandoori chicken to slices of pale Scottish smoked salmon. There was crisp-crusted cottage bread, still hot from the *Arcadia*'s bakery; there was cheese from Cheshire and Cheddar from Lancashire; there were huge five-to-sixteen-pound marble pots of caviar embedded in ice; there were fresh wood strawberries and cakes that were monuments in themselves, crammed with cream and nuts and fruits, and laced with kirsch.

The Grand Lounge's shining cocktail bar was as long as an American railroad car, and was ready with more than three hundred bottles of non-vintage champagne, as well as every cocktail imaginable, from a Blue Blazer (fiery whisky poured from one shaker to another) to the gentler tastes of Fish House Punch (rum and peach brandy).

The orchestra quickened its tempo to play "My Girl" and "Get 'Em Again," and Catriona was steered around by Edgar to meet Lord Screpple, who leaned at an alarming angle and looked as if he had been boiled like a lobster; and the Marquis of Henrick, who looked distinctly underdone and had difficulty in catching the attention of the waiters. Then she had to shake hands with every one of the directors and senior management of Keys Shipping, almost every one of whom seemed to have watery eyes and a purple roadmap of Liverpool on his nose, and almost every one of whom pressed her hand between his, pressed it tight, and said how *sorry* he was, love, that Stanley had gone so suddenly to meet his Maker—but still, love, just look at you now, you're a successor and a half, better than a pound and a half of black pudding I'll say—and those watery eyes would strain to penetrate the cobwebs of her dress as if staring alone could melt them away.

"That's a fine lass, Albert. Just like her poor old dad, what? But better-looking, eh?"

"I'll say. Can you take *orders* from a lass, though?"

"Who's talking about orders?"

After the first introductions had been made, Catriona was taken aside by a reporter from *The Times* who had arrived too late for the afternoon's press conference, a vague young man of about thirty-five with a dirty collar and breath that smelled of brandy. He asked her what she thought about Freud and she said she didn't mind his opinions but she wasn't particularly hipped on his taste in suits. The reporter licked his pencil a lot but didn't write anything down.

At ten-thirty, by a sequence of signals as subtle as any of those at a Sotheby's auction, the manager of the first-class restaurant, Mr. Dunstan Oliver, let it be known to the officers upstairs on the promenade deck that they might release the velvet ropes restraining the remainder of the guests, so that they, too, could join the party. The orchestra played "Sons of the Sea" as grandly as if it were the National Anthem, but there was still a rather noisy jostle on the staircase, and the lady wife of one of Liverpool's aldermen put her heel through the hem of her dress. Mr. Oliver, his profile raised like a circular saw, advanced smiling on the jostlers with an equally smiling escort of six headwaiters, and by the sheer intimidating glare of their teeth they quietened the commotion and directed everyone around the Grand Lounge to collect their buffet plates.

Catriona was talking to Lord Hinchcliffe and his daughter Elsie McKay. Miss McKay had been invited as a friend of the *Arcadia*'s interior designer and herself designed interiors of liners for P&O. She wore a slinky butter-yellow gown and a yellow headband, crested by a huge diamond-and-cornelian clasp. "You just watch this mob," she said, in a brittle commentator's voice. "They're going to fall on all that food as if they were starving orphans."

She was right. As the orchestra played selections of Schubert and from the year's most popular West End musical, *Lilac Time*, the guests crowded greedily along the length of the buffet table, elbowing and pushing each other, and leaving the end of the line with plates that were heaped as high as Egyptian pyramids with roast suckling pig, marinated sole, slices of rare beef, caviar and mayonnaise.

The hubbub of conversation, clattering plates, shuffling feet, and clinking glasses made the lounge sound, as Lord Hinchcliffe gloomily remarked, "like the eight-twenty rush hour at Babel railway station."

But to Catriona, the party was sparkling and funny and delightful. Despite the possessive way in which Edgar tried to pilot her through the throng, she managed to attract quite a crowd of sharp young men, one of whom was an outrageously handsome young Californian whose white teeth and white collar gleamed against his suntanned skin, and who made her promise to visit his family's orange groves in Bakersfield "as soon as humanly poss." Another young man, English and very thin, was a lyricist of popular jazz tunes, and just for her he composed on the spot a quirky little fox trot, which he accompanied with two teaspoons.

> My, my, my sweet Catriona,
> No, no, nobody can own her.
> Like a dream
> Or a song,
> You can never
> Hold her long.
> No matter how much tenderness you've shown her.

Apart from the posh young wolves, there were dozens of famous faces. Anybody with even a modest title who lived within driving distance of Liverpool was there; so were such diverse talents as Judge Basil Fuchs, business tycoon and owner of the Boston Braves; Helen Wills, the tennis champion; Princess Lowenstein-Wertheim, the lady aviator; Madge Bellamy, the motion picture star; and Sir Alan and Lady Cobham. Champagne corks were popped like artillery, and the sound of ice being rattled in cocktail shakers was shattering.

Still trailing her escort of attentive young men, Catriona was taken from the Grand Lounge to the first-class dining saloon, where Sir Peregrine Arrowsmith was presiding with undisguised testiness over a party for the *Arcadia*'s designers and engineers, and what he described as "a Mongol horde of advertising agents, licensed victuallers, and fiénds of the popular press." The buffet here was less imposing, although the dining saloon itself was one of the most magnificent interiors that Catriona had ever seen. It was a modernist interpretation of the great hall at Mentmore Towers, the Buckinghamshire home built by Baron Meyer Rothschild, and it was hung with yards of Venetian tapestry and lit by sparkling reproductions of the huge lanterns from the Doge's barge in Venice. All around the upper level of the dining saloon was an open gallery, where guests in evening dress promenaded, drank champagne, and waved to their friends below. A string quintet played Schubert, although a jazz band was waiting in the wings.

"Sir Peregrine," said Catriona, offering her hand.

"Miss Keys," replied Sir Peregrine, taking her hand and kissing it with exaggerated humility.

Edgar remarked, "Quite a jolly party you've got here, Sir Peregrine."

"I suppose the swine have to be fed," said Sir Peregrine.

"Swine?" said Catriona, looking around. "I thought these were the men who designed the *Arcadia*. It doesn't *look* as if she's been designed by swine."

Sir Peregrine cleared his throat uneasily. "Merely a humorous remark, Miss Keys. That's all."

"Oh," said Catriona, coldly. "A joke. Well, as long as the swine themselves don't overhear you."

Edgar tried to smile reassuringly at Sir Peregrine as he ushered Catriona away.

"You don't have to provoke him," he whispered to Catriona as they made their way between the tables. "He's desperate to keep the *Arcadia* as it is."

"I'm just making it clear who's boss," said Catriona.

"To whom? To Sir Peregrine or to me?"

"To both of you."

"Well, all right," said Edgar, clutching her arm more tightly. "But just remember that you have responsibilities as well as privileges."

In quick succession, they visited three more parties. At the reception in the second-class dining room Catriona danced a frantic and hilarious shimmy with the man who had supplied all the *Arcadia*'s sheets and bedspreads, and Edgar watched with humourless appreciation as the crowd of guests clapped in time to every bounce of her breasts under her cobweb dress. Young, vivacious, and unpardonably erotic, he thought. Much more captivating than he could have hoped, and far more enthusiastic about acting as a figurehead for Keys Shipping than he could have imagined. But troublesome. Wilful, aggressive, and unquestionably troublesome.

They had almost finished their tour of the ship's parties and were making their way back along the starboard promenade deck by the open doors of the first-class verandah, when a slim young man in evening dress stepped out in front of them and bowed.

"Good evening, old girl," he said brightly.

Catriona shrieked out loud. "Nigel!" she said. "How marvellous!" She threw her arms around his neck and danced around and around with him, to the amusement of the guests on the deck, who had all eaten quite enough quail now and drunk far too much champagne, but to the suppressed chagrin of Edgar, who hated surprises and wanted everything to be tightly under control, including Catriona.

"What are you *doing* here?" Catriona asked Nigel. "I didn't know you had an invitation. I thought you were in London sulking."

Nigel looked Edgar straight in the eye, although he addressed himself to Catriona. "As a matter of fact, old thing, I didn't actually have a legitimate invitation in the sense that I was actually *invited.* But the chap on the gangplank was a fan of mine. Saw me three times in *The Road to Rome* when we were touring. Said I was red-hot and asked for my autograph."

"This celebration is by invitation only," said Edgar.

"Oh, Mr. Deacon, don't be so stuffy," Catriona protested. "Nigel would have been invited anyway if I'd thought that he'd actually come. But you haven't been introduced. Mr. Deacon, this is Nigel Myers. Nigel, this is Edgar Deacon, the big noise at Keys Shipping. After *me,* of course." She laughed.

Edgar reluctantly shook hands. "I'm familiar with your work, Mr. Myers," he said in a heavy tone.

"Well, if the *Arcadia*'s your work, then I'm familiar with yours, too," said Nigel. "I must say she's a ripping tub."

Edgar momentarily closed his eyes as if to keep whatever feelings were boiling up inside of him well damped down. "Yes," he said, and then, "I suppose you two would like a minute alone together."

"If you don't *mind,* old chap," said Nigel. "Haven't seen the lovely Catriona for four days."

"Well, four days in a long time sometimes," said Edgar. "Can you rejoin us in the Grand Lounge in five minutes, Miss Keys? I want you to make a presentation."

Catriona blew Edgar an impudent kiss. "Of course, Mr. Deacon. Take care now. I'm sure that fat alderman's wife has an eye on you. I'd hate you to be eaten alive before we'd even cast off."

When Edgar had stalked off along the promenade deck, Nigel held out his arms for Catriona and said, "Well? Is this the new you?"

Catriona took his hands and gently squeezed his fingers. "I'm really surprised that you're here," she told him.

"Not half as surprised as I am. Once you'd gone, I thought to myself, That's it; she's gone for good. We're finished. But a chap can always change his mind, can't he?"

"I suppose so."

"Of course he can. Chap's prerogative. But the real question is Can a chap change his girl's mind, too? That's the real question."

Catriona looked at Nigel for a moment or two, and then released his hands. She went to the ship's rail and leaned on it with her arms folded under her breasts, watching the crowds of people who were still milling around on the landing stage. There was the mingled discordant sound of music in the air, music from five or six different bands and orchestras.

"The fact is," said Nigel, joining Catriona at the rail, "the fact is that I have to admit that I love you."

Catriona reached out and touched his arm so lightly that he scarcely felt it.

"I can't *force* you to do anything," said Nigel. "It's not my way, anyhow, to *force* people to do things. I'm not that kind of a chap. But what I'm really asking is, well, is this the sort of life you actually want for yourself? All these steamboats and all these Good and Honest Folk in tweed? It just doesn't seem like you."

"The *Arcadia*'s very glamorous," said Catriona. "Do you know that Douglas Fairbanks and Mary Pickford are joining her tomorrow? And Princess Xenia of Russia? And Sir Alan and Lady Cobham are here tonight."

"You could just as easily meet all of those people in London," said Nigel.

"Not like this," said Catriona. "This is magical. And besides, I'm a celebrity now. The young Queen of the Atlantic liners. Come on, Nigel, *you* know what it's like to be popular. I'm just finding out for the first time."

"Actually, it's very wearing to be popular," said Nigel unconvincingly.

Catriona leaned towards him and nuzzled her head affectionately against his shoulder. "I'm so pleased to see you. Don't let's start bickering."

"You mean that? You're really pleased?"

"Of course I'm pleased, chump."

"Then you'll come back to London with me?"

Catriona stared at him, her lips puckered in a held-back laugh, and shook her head slowly from side to side. "No, Nigel, I can't. But I won't forget you, and I'll always come back to see you if you'll still have me."

Nigel took a shallow breath. "Well," he said, plainly deflated, "I didn't really expect you to say anything else."

Catriona said, "You'll stay for tonight, won't you?"

"What for?"

"There are no trains back to London, not now. It's too late."

"I've got myself a room at the Royal Liverpool Hotel. It's not much. Faces a brick wall, actually. But there wasn't much available, what with this floating fun palace of yours about to depart. However, it'll do."

Catriona hugged him close. "Don't be so silly. You can stay with me. Come and join the party, have some champagne, and then I'll show you my stateroom."

Nigel eased his finger around the side of his stiff white collar. "Do you know something?" he told her. "I think this is the first time that a girl has actually seduced *me,* instead of the other way around. I would say that just about calls for a glass of champagne. Maybe *two* glasses of champagne. Or three."

"Then come and have some."

Inside the Grand Lounge, as they descended the staircase, the orchestra was blaring out "Pretty Soft for You," and the dance floor was whirling with shining evening gowns and black coattails. Catriona saw Edgar standing dark-countenanced among the directors of Keys Shipping, making no secret of his displeasure at Nigel's gatecrashing.

"Bit of a grim cove, that Edgar Deacon," remarked Nigel. "Want a dance before he rushes you off again?"

Nigel, despite his affected manners, was a strong and immaculate dancer. He took Catriona around the beautifully sprung dance floor as if he were carrying her through a field of summer flags, around and around, with their distorted reflections teasing and dazzling them from the lounge's gleaming pillars. She closed her eyes and listened to the music and the laughter, and somehow now that Nigel was here it all seemed like a fantasy, as if the only reality in the world were she and he dancing.

She remembered (dizzily) drinking more champagne. She also remembered making a presentation of a silver-plated model of the *Arcadia* to some distant cousin of the King who had no chin whatsoever and ears like a woodland elf. She remembered dancing with the Lord Mayor, and with two or three fat and perspiring directors, whose bellies bounced against her like overinflated footballs. But most of all she remembered climbing the staircase from the Grand Lounge to the rippling applause of everybody there, and then walking arm in arm with Nigel along the first-class promenade deck as the early-morning sun outlined the dark Gothic towers of the Royal Liver Friendly Society and the Liverpool Pier Head, and sparkled on the Mersey as if gold sequins had been stitched onto every wave.

In her stateroom, Trimmer had left her a small tray with ice and seltzer on it and a fresh white gardenia. "Anti-acid for the hangover, flowers for the soul," said Nigel. "What an imaginative steward you have." In the bedroom, Alice had turned down the bed, both sides. "And your maid has an excellent intelligence network," Nigel added.

They locked the doors, and then Nigel put some sweet low jazz music on the gramophone. He took Catriona in his arms, kissed her, and unhooked the delicate catches of her dress. It fell away from her as softly as it had fallen onto her.

"Perhaps this is what I really missed," he whispered. "A chance to say goodbye to you the same way I said hello."

His right hand cupped the heaviness of her breast, and her nipple crinkled and rose the palest pink between his fingers. He tugged at it gently between his finger and his thumb. He kissed her again and again, and the tip of his tongue touched every one of her teeth, as if he needed to feel every intimate part of her before he lost her forever.

Underneath his black evening trousers he was rearing hard and unmistakable. He peeled off his tailcoat, loosened his diamond cufflinks, wreched open the buttons of his white vest, tugged free his necktie. Soon he was naked except for his white silk drawers.

The gramophone record came to an end and *hiss-*clicked, *hiss-*clicked, while the early sunlight began to illuminate the bedroom like a modern cathedral, all white drapes and lemonwood and frosted glass. But as she lay back on the sheets, still wearing her rolled-down stockings and her dancing slippers, but otherwise completely naked, it was Nigel who filled Catriona's consciousness, and Nigel alone.

Nigel meant security: that little London love nest for two. Nigel meant fun and freedom, but also closeness and friendliness and under-standing, and waking up in the morning to find that someone you feel really fond of is lying asleep next to you. Catriona was brave and often arrogant, but not so brave or arrogant that she didn't miss Nigel's arms around her, or the simple days of making him cinnamon toast in that kitchen in Royal Hospital Road. She knew those days had inevitably passed; but this morning in her stateroom aboard the *Arcadia* she clung to them one last time.

Her eyes were closed as Nigel kissed her neck and her breasts, and his tongue ran up the curves inside her thighs. She caressed and squeezed his bony muscular shoulders and ruffled his wavy hair; and while she caressed him his tongue found every crevice of her and explored it both lovingly and provocatively. Something happened to her like a box Brownie closing its shutter in a moment of utter darkness.

Then he was astride her, and she reached up for him. He was pushing into her, forcefully but not roughly, and with an irresistible rhythm that made her feel as if the inside of her body was effervescent. It seemed to go on and on, but not to last. He shuddered, and she held him tighter, the way you hold someone tighter when something has gone wrong, what's the matter, come tighter, come closer. But the tightness and the closeness were only her last desperate effort to cling on to him, knowing that once he had climaxed she would have to lose him.

"Nigel," she said. The word rose like a smokering, and faded across the silent bedroom.

They lay side by side for almost an hour. They didn't say much. Then, without prompting, Nigel got up and dressed. Catriona stayed where she was, in bed, afraid to get up in case that made him leave all the more quickly.

"Have a safe journey, old thing," he told her. "Look me up when you get back. That's if you still want to."

Catriona's eyes were clustered with tears. She let out a long wavering breath, and then said unhappily, "I won't forget you. You know that, don't you?"

"Chin up, toots," he said, smiling.

"You could come, you know," she blurted out. "I could find you a stateroom, and you could come along, too. My God, I'm the head of the whole shipping line. I can take along anyone I want to."

"Sorry," said Nigel. "It's back on the boards tonight. I only got away yesterday by pleading double pneumonia."

"But you don't have to go. It's only a play."

"My darling," said Nigel, "I said exactly the same thing to you. 'You don't have to go. It's only a shipping line.' But you knew that you had to, just as I know that *I've* got to. It's sad, and I'm going to miss you like hell, but it's the stuff that real life is made of."

The tears rolled down her cheeks. "How do *you* know what real life is made of? You're only an actor. Half the time you don't know what's real and what isn't."

Nigel took a clean linen handkerchief out of his coat pocket, shook it open, and wiped Catriona's eyes, as gently as he would have wiped a child's eyes. "You're probably right," he told her. "But the trouble is that I simply can't come with you, and you're not making it any easier for me to leave."

There was a sharp knock at the stateroom door. Trimmer's voice said, "Hit's breakfast, Miss Keys."

"All right," called Catriona in a blotted sort of a voice.

Nigel said, "Do you want me to hide?"

She shook her head. "Don't be ridiculous. Come in, Trimmer."

Trimmer entered the stateroom straight-backed, wheeling a trolley that was draped in napkins. From underneath the trolley he produced a bed tray, which he set up over Catriona, and which he proceeded to lay with an embroidered linen tablecloth, a silver vase containing a huge and fragrant Belle Blonde rose, silver knives and forks, a linen napkin, and then a plate of minced spring lamb and pickled walnuts, as well as tea and brandied marmalade and toast.

Nigel stood stock-still during this procedure, as if he were waiting upstage in Act Two of *Emperor Jones.* Trimmer passed him by as if he did not exist, the discreet and tactful servant. Catriona glanced at Nigel, but Nigel did not look back at her. Nigel was not actually hiding, but he was definitely playing the part of the unwelcome guest who had no lines to speak for at least another seven pages.

Just as neatly, however, Trimmer whipped away the ashtray and notepad from a small onyx-topped table beside the bed, snapped out a circular linen cloth, and set the table with knives, forks, tea, and another breakfast; and he added, since Nigel was a gentleman, a copy of *The Times,* sharply folded.

Nigel reached into his tailcoat, took out his wallet, and without changing the utter anonymity of his expression handed Trimmer a pound. Trimmer bowed his head to Catriona, and said, "Henjoy your breakfast, Miss Keys. Helevenses in the Palm Court later." Then he retreated from the stateroom and closed the door behind him.

Nigel and Catriona looked at each other and burst out laughing. "He's wonderful," said Nigel, lifting up his tails so that he could sit on the side of the bed and eat his breakfast. "The day we marry and set ourselves up in a country mansion, I promise you that I'll hire him as butler."

Catriona was smelling her rose. "That's not a proposal, is it?" she asked him. Her voice was touched with sharpness.

Nigel reached into the breast pocket of his coat, took something out, and tossed it on to the cream-coloured bedcover.

"I was going to," he said. "But I've seen for myself that it won't work. Well, it was going to be my ploy for getting you back."

Catriona reached across the bedcover and picked up a diamond ring. It was only a small one, the kind you could buy in a chain jeweller's for less than twenty-five pounds. She examined it carefully, and the feeling of sadness inside her was almost painful, but somehow liberating as well. By proposing, Nigel had tied up all the doubts and anxieties and unanswered questions of their affair into one single question, a question which a single answer could decide.

When she answered, he nodded, as if he couldn't have expected her to say anything else; and he picked the ring out of her fingers like a man plucking a forget-me-not.

Eleven

During the morning, while Catriona slept, the celebrities began to arrive. A sleek black Rolls-Royce with silk blinds at the windows brought Douglas Fairbanks and Mary Pickford from Lime Street Station, and a beige Rolls-Royce with a chocolate touring roof brought Princess Xenia.

The newspapers, as usual, had been given the full passenger list, and the boarding ramps were crowded with photographers in wide-brimmed hats. Douglas Fairbanks told reporters that he considered it "a great thrill" to sail on the *Arcadia* on her maiden voyage, and that she looked like "a swell boat." Miss Pickford, in dark glasses, was feeling tired.

Claude Graham-White came storming onto the ship with five porters struggling behind him with the oddest collection of brown paper bags and tartan shooting sacks and tattered valises. And there were plenty of other famous people for the press to harass: Dame Clara Butt, who was accompanied by a yapping circus of seven small hairy dogs, each of which was named after a different colour of the rainbow—Red, Orange, Yellow, Green, et cetera—and each of which wore an appropriate ribbon to identify it; Madge Bellamy, in a glamorous silk dress of powder-blue, and a powder-blue mink stole to match; Jack Dempsey, in a bad mood and a blue suit with loud stripes; and almost last, when the *Arcadia* had already let out her long farewell whistle to the Port of Liverpool and thrashed the waters of the Mersey into a yellowish foam with her four four-bladed screws, Mark Beeney, the young and eligible owner of American TransAtlantic. The reporter from the *Daily Mirror* managed to ask Mark Beeney why he was sailing on the maiden voyage of a luxury liner that was inevitably going to put the best of his own American TransAtlantic fleet in the shade.

Mark Beeney grinned as he stepped on board and said, "You don't think Caesar tried to lick Cleopatra without checking her barge out first, do you?" Like everybody else in England on Tuesday, June 17th, 1924, he had read in his morning paper about "Catriona Keys, the Flapper Queen of the Seas."

At 11:00 A.M., the walkways and gangplanks were taken away, the ship's rails were closed, and the mooring lines were let go. Passengers cheered and waved and sang as the Liverpool Municipal Brass Band played "God Save the King" and "For England, Home and Beauty" and hundreds of coloured paper streamers were thrown from the boat decks and the promenade decks onto the landing stage below. Two hundred red, white, and blue gas balloons were let go and flooded eastwards over Liverpool.

On the third-class deck, the collar of his brown tweed jacket turned up, a cigarette burning untasted in his mouth, Harry Pakenow watched the landing stage slowly move away from him and the last paper streamers break and trail across the river. Beside him, almost apoplectic with excitement and grief, a middle-aged man in a cheap overcoat was waving goodbye to somebody on the landing stage, somebody dear who had to stay behind. A pretty girl in a cloche hat was standing with her hands over her mouth, crying loudly and without shame. Harry thought to himself, You only get sorrow like this in third class; the rich can afford to take their loved ones with them, or come back as often as they wish.

He was wrong, although he had no way of knowing it. In her first-class suite, Mademoiselle Louise Narron, the opera singer, was sobbing into the pillow of the bed which she would share with no one. She had left behind in England the well-known cellist Raymond Walters, who was sitting at his home in Greenwich at that very moment with his wife and two small children, trying to concentrate on a recording of Dvorak's cello concerto while thinking about the *Arcadia* slowly moving away from the Liverpool landing stage.

Harry Pakenow may have been scornful about upper-class unhappiness, but grief was just as vivid on promenade deck A as it was on lower deck E.

Catriona opened her eyes to feel the ship shuddering beneath her. Then she sat up, unsure for a moment if she was in London dreaming that she was on board ship, or on board ship dreaming that she was in London.

"My God," she said to herself, "it's actually going, and they haven't told me!"

She scrambled out of bed and reached for her peignoir. Then she went to the porthole and looked out. Liverpool was already a grey and shimmering mirage of itself, and a wide stretch of churned-up water now separated the *Arcadia* and the landing stage. As if to confirm to Catriona that the liner was really on her way, a dozen tugs let out a chorus of excited whoop-whoops, and the *Aquitania*, which was moored a little further along the pierhead, gave a bellowing *bon voyage* which echoed as far as Bootle and Blundellsands. Janice Bignor heard it faintly as she waited by the bus stop on her way to work, her eyes still blurred from crying, Harry's crumpled letter in her purse.

There was a knock at Catriona's stateroom door, and Alice came in with fresh towels.

"The ship's leaving!" Catriona told her. "Why didn't somebody wake me up?"

Alice fussily arranged the towels in the bathroom and turned on the faucets. "The young gentleman said not to, Miss Keys. He said that nobody was to disturb you on any account at all, not until the ship had sailed."

"Nigel? But why?"

"He said something about not wanting to give you the chance to change your mind. Something about everybody having to go their own way. Well, it wasn't for me to argue."

"No," said Catriona. Then, more slowly, "No, it wasn't. You were right not to wake me. Besides, I've got a hangover like a herd of elephants."

Alice made a show of laying out a pair of blue silk step-ins on the end of the bed. She plainly didn't approve of young girls tripping around with no underwear. Catriona was just about to tell her to put a record on the gramophone when there was another knock on the sitting-room door.

"It's Mr. Philips, miss," called Alice, "the first officer. Ought I to tell him to come back later?"

Catriona tightened the sash of her peignoir. "Yes, could you? No—don't worry. Ask him in. And can you please tell Trimmer to come down and make me a drink."

"A drink, miss? Are you sure you're up to it?"

"Of course I'm not up to it," said Catriona. "But if I don't have one now, I'll never be able to touch another drink as long as I live. Come in, Mr. Philips! Excuse everything. I'm still not sure if I survived last night's party or not."

Rudyard Philips, the first officer, was a broad-shouldered, short-legged man of forty-one, with a large handsome head that looked as if it had been hewn out of Bath stone and then left in a field to weather for a century or two. He had short fair hair—"short-back-and-sides" the barbers called it—and fair bushy eyebrows and a fleshy nose that was deeply creased at the tip.

Being so broad, and having that slightly bandy stance of a man who has been standing on tilting decks ever since he was fifteen years old, Rudyard Philips could never wear a uniform smartly. His jacket was as wide as it was long, and his braided trousers seemed to crease in at least eleven places. Nigel would probably have dismissed him with a remark like "Broad shoulders are the indisputable sign of a small willy," but Rudyard Philips had a strong masculinity about him that had attracted many unaccompanied lady passengers to book on the ships which he commanded time and time again.

"Miss Keys," said Rudyard Philips, taking off his cap. His accent sounded slightly Welsh. "I only came by to present you with my compliments."

"I didn't see you at any of the parties last night, did I?" asked Catriona.

"I was officer of the watch, Miss Keys."

"And they didn't even send up a glass of champagne for you? That's a bit thick."

Mr. Philips looked around for somewhere to put down his cap. He laid it at last on the arm of the sofa. "Officers of the watch are not allowed to tipple, Miss Keys. Obvious reasons."

"I don't see why not. The ship wasn't *going* anywhere."

"All the same, Miss Keys. Someone has to keep a clear head."

Catriona sat down and took out a cigarette. Rudyard Philips stepped forward with a gold Dunhill lighter and lit it for her.

"Do you *mind* acting as first officer, instead of captain?" she asked him through the smoke.

Rudyard Philips shrugged. "I was either going to act as first officer or stay at home."

"And you didn't want to stay at home?"

He didn't answer that. He smiled tartly and briefly to show that he had heard her, but that was all. He looked around the stateroom, noting the flowers and the plumped-up cushions on the sofa and the wine cooler. As first officer, it was part of his personal responsibility to take care of the first-class passengers and to make sure that they never had any reason to irritate the captain with complaints about rattling chests of drawers, or champagne that didn't arrive when it was ordered, or noisy private parties in next-door cabins.

Catriona watched him, and smoked, and then said, "Sir Peregrine was blowing his top about you yesterday."

"Blowing his top?" asked Rudyard Philips. "I can't believe that."

"Can't you? He seemed very steamed up indeed. He seemed to think that if you had half a chance you might do something rash, just to make him look silly."

Rudyard Philips took a long time to reply. Then he said, "I believe he can easily manage to look silly without any extra help from me."

"You don't *really* think that," teased Catriona. "Or do you?"

Slowly Rudyard Philips circled around the stateroom until he was standing only a few feet behind Catriona with his arms folded and his face as inscrutable as a terra-cotta jug. Catriona felt that if she were to unbutton his uniform jacket, she would discover that his chest was absolutely white. Only his face would have been exposed to years of wind and salt and seawater. The rest of his body, under his uniform, would be as pale as that of a prisoner serving a life sentence.

"I usually keep my opinions of Sir Peregrine to myself," he said. "If you work for Keys Shipping, it's wiser."

"You don't get on with him, then?"

"That's not what I said."

"But if you have opinions about Sir Peregrine, they must be either adverse or favourable. Which are yours? Sir Peregrine's opinions about you are definitely adverse."

"Yes?"

"Oh, certainly. Sir Peregrine seems to think that if there was an emergency you might put your ambition first and the safety of the *Arcadia* second."

Rudyard Philips tried a smile, but failed. "And you believe him?"

"I don't know. I don't think so. I don't think you'd have the *je-ne-sais-quoi.*"

There was a difficult silence. Catriona watched Rudyard Philips through the smoke of her cigarette and kept on smiling. There was something so awkward and uncomplicated about him that she couldn't resist a naughty and almost uncontrollable urge to tease him. It was like prodding a bull with a sharp stick just to watch it toss its head in frustration and ripple its brutish muscles.

"You're not stirring the pot a little, are you, Miss Keys?" Rudyard

Philips asked her.

"I could be," said Catriona.

"There's no need," Rudyard Philips told her. "Sir Peregrine's a fine commodore and a good captain. Don't make any mistakes about that. The passengers think the world of him."

"He is a boozer, though?"

"I didn't say that. And, in fact, I'd rather *you* didn't either, with all due respect."

"Oh," said Catriona, pretending to be chastened. "I'm really very sorry. It was just that after what Sir Peregrine said about *you*, I imagined that you might feel the same sort of way about *him.*"

"He's the captain of this vessel, Miss Keys. Between us, we have the largest and the most expensive luxury liner in the whole world to take care of."

"I know that. But you don't get on with him very well, do you?"

"He's not a particularly easy man to get on with, Miss Keys. But that's just part of the job. Few great sea captains are very amenable."

Catriona drew long and leisurely on her cigarette. Then she said, "Supposing the ship was in terrible danger, Mr. Philips, and Sir Peregrine was blotto. What would you do?"

"Miss Keys—"

"*Supposing,* Mr. Philips."

Rudyard Philips rubbed at the back of his neck. "Well, the situation's completely hypothetical. But the maritime laws governing that kind of emergency are quite specific. There's even a law which tells you what to do if all your passengers decide to drink seawater and go insane."

"You're *very* cagey." Catriona smiled.

"You're the mistress of this shipping line, Miss Keys. Sir Peregrine's the commodore. I don't know how else you expect me to behave."

"I don't know either, Mr. Philips," said Catriona. "I really don't know. Do you?"

What Rudyard Philips had failed to grasp, of course, was that Catriona wasn't in the least bit interested in how loyal he might be to Sir Peregrine, or whether he might run the *Arcadia* onto the nearest shoal of rocks just to show the commodore up for a blundering drunkard. She was simply playing that silly, merciless question-and-answer game that she used to play with her theatrical friends in London. What would you do if you caught your sister in bed with a blackie? How would you feel if you caught your best friend stealing from your purse? Would you ever sleep with an Old Wykehamist (*Answer:* No-oo-o—they *invariably* smell.)

Catriona was only provoking Rudyard Philips the way that she and Nigel and Bunny Smythe had all provoked each other on those hungover Sunday mornings in Chelsea, mornings of gin slings and mah-jongg and "Tiger Rag" on the gramophone.

"I'm afraid you're going to have to excuse me," said Rudyard Philips. "I have to do the rounds of all the cabin-class staterooms by noon. Welcome the paying customers aboard, that kind of thing."

Catriona stood up and walked across the room trailing smoke behind her. Beneath her feet, the liner was already beginning to roll very slightly, and the vase of orchids on the sideboard was vibrating with a hollow rattle. Some ocean liners vibrated so violently that their stewards could only fill the wineglasses half full, in case the wine jumped out on the table.

"Are you married, Mr. Philips?" Catriona asked him.

Rudyard Philips slowly raised his eyes. By instinct or by accident, Catriona had touched on his most sensitive emotional toothache. In a curiously congested voice he said, "Yes. Well, yes."

"Couldn't your wife have come with you? Some of the officers' wives have."

"Yes, I—But, no, she couldn't. She has the two youngsters to look after. She's Chinese, you know. Well, you wouldn't have known that. I met her in Hong Kong, on shore leave from the old HMS *Superb*. She lives in Runcorn now, with my sister's family. Her real Chinese name is Surprise-Bloom Flower, but I usually call her Toy."

"Surprise-Bloom Flower? That's pretty."

Rudyard Philips gave an odd brass-band sort of laugh. "Silly names, these Chinese."

Catriona said, "Are you happy, Mr. Philips?"

He frowned at her, unsure of what she was actually asking him. But he found it difficult to hold her gaze for long. "I'm content with my commission, thank you," he said, rather stolidly. "I won't pretend that I wasn't disappointed that I didn't get the *Arcadia* for myself. But, well, she is the new company flagship, and I suppose it was only right that she should go to Sir Peregrine."

"You seem rather down, Mr. Philips, that's all," said Catriona.

Rudyard Philips' face betrayed a fleeting wince, a jumbled expression of something overwhelmingly painful; but then he managed a smile, and said, "Everything's very well, thank you, Miss Keys. And I really must be going. Perhaps you'd care for a guided tour of the ship after luncheon? You really ought to see what a fine oceangoing lady you've inherited from your father."

"I'd like that," said Catriona, and then, "Mr. Philips?"

Rudyard Philips by now had already collected his cap and was backing out of the stateroom. "Miss Keys?"

She was trying to say that she was sorry, that she hadn't meant to upset him, but the words remained unspoken in her mouth like tough half-chewed beef that couldn't be swallowed. Instead she said, "Half past two would be perfect."

Alice, coming out of the bathroom with an emerald-green Turkish towel, said "I've drawn your bath, Miss Keys."

Catriona stood where she was, finishing her cigarette, while Alice waited. She felt really quite rotten for what she had said to Rudyard Philips, although she wasn't exactly sure why. She had upset him, of that she was certain; but whether it was because of the impertinent question that she had asked him, or whether it was because the very mention of Sir Peregrine was enough to make him feel as if his uniform was crowded with itching powder, or whether it was because he was going through a difficult time at home, she just couldn't be sure. Did she really care? Well, perhaps not. He was only a ship's officer, after all, and although Trimmer had said that on his own ships he was very popular with the ladies, especially the Americans, he seemed to Catriona to be pretty dull. The only trouble was, he had somehow made her feel guilty and cruel, and she didn't like feeling guilty and cruel one bit.

As she went into the bathroom and loosened her sash, she wondered if that was why Nigel hadn't come along with her—because she was too young and merciless. A tease. And yet she couldn't help herself. Teasing amused her, and more important, it was really the only way you could find out the truth about people. It didn't mean that she didn't love people, either.

Stepping into the bath, she caught the aroma of this morning's lovemaking between her thighs. Surreptitiously, like a shoplifter, while Alice was busy setting out the soap and the loofah, she cupped her hand down there, and then lifted her fingers to her nostrils so that she could breathe in that mingled musky smell of Nigel. She found it ridiculously arousing.

She closed her eyes while Alice soaped her with magnolia-scented soap—firm slippery fingers massaging her shoulders and her breasts. Then she stood up again, holding on to the art-deco handrail, while Alice meticulously washed away Nigel's last memory. The bathwater sloshed a little as the liner changed course across Liverpool Bay.

After the bath, she sat in the bedroom while Alice combed her hair, sipping at a very cold gin fizz and feeling that flat let-down feeling she always got when she nearly managed a climax but not quite. She wondered how she had ever grown up so outspoken and so unlovable.

Twelve

Rudyard Philips had gone straight to the officers' promenade deck on the port side of the boat deck next to the gymnasium and lit up a cigarette, Wills Gold Flake. He had drawn the coarse tobacco smoke deep into his lungs, held it, and then exhaled it into the wind with all the fierceness of a fire eater. He felt steadier now, although he was still trembling. His breakfast of sausages and fried eggs and grilled tomatoes was lying half digested in the whisky he had drunk when he came off watch in the early hours of the morning. He felt like vomiting; but with several first-class passengers already strolling on the adjacent deck, that was the last thing he could allow himself to do. Contrary to company literature, ships' officers were quite often seasick, but never in front of the passengers.

The *Arcadia* was making her stately way across Liverpool Bay, leaving her home port behind her in the shining haze of a summer day and sailing parallel to the north coast of Wales. In a little while she would be passing Prestatyn, and then skirting Anglesey on her route across the Irish Sea to Dublin. There were still crowds of yachts and steamboats and pleasure craft all around her, their crews waving handkerchiefs and cheering and taking photographs with box Brownies, and the holiday mood was infecting everyone. From the Palm Court on the first-class promenade deck, where some of the mid-morning strollers had already paused for champagne, ham sandwiches, eight different varieties of English cheese, celery, olives, and Bath Oliver biscuits, came the warbling of a jazz clarinet, and the strumming of a hot banjo; and the voices of the steerage could be heard against the breeze, singing that old American comic song "Under the Anheuser Bush."

The *Arcadia*'s maiden voyage was to be a four-day party, and each night was to be crowned by balls and banquets. But for Rudyard Philips it was an oceangoing wake, a celebration of the death of his marriage. He had learned three days before the *Arcadia* was due to sail that his wife Toy had a lover, and that she was thinking of leaving him.

He couldn't blame her, he supposed. He was usually away for weeks on end, leaving her with the full responsibility of looking after Matthew and Janet. She was alone in a strange suburb, a delicate and educated Chinese girl in a terrace of English redbrick villas, with nobody to talk to but surly shopkeepers and Rudyard's sister, who was friendly, yes—friendly to the point of frenzy—but no company at all with her endless chatter about knitting patterns and coal prices and neighbourhood scandals for a girl who liked poetry and serene landscapes and flying kites.

There was no chance that Toy could have kept Laurence a secret for very long. Nobody had secrets in Warrington Avenue, especially when the secret was a vigorous, lean, long-haired university professor with a red Austin Chummy tourer and a multicoloured scarf that must have been twenty feet long. Laurence had met Toy at a bus stop in Runcorn one day when it was raining and given her a ride. Then he had started taking her out at weekends, for drives to Chester and Ellesmere Port and once even to Mostyn. They had talked about Lao-tzu and Chuang-tzu and the silk paintings of the Sung dynasty. Then their conversation had turned to the erotic Tao novel Ch'ing P'ing Mei, and at last their conversation had turned to gasps and kisses in the professor's bed-sitting-room in Birkenhead. Matthew and Janet were already calling him Uncle Laurence by the time Rudyard came home on leave before joining the Arcadia's maiden voyage. Toy had cried and asked Rudyard to forgive her. Rudyard, just like a British officer, just like a pompous self-righteous Boys' Own idiot, had punched her and bruised her cheek. He still went hot when he thought about it. To have punched Surprise-Bloom Flower had been nothing less than madness. Because here he was on the promenade deck of the Arcadia, forty-five minutes out of Liverpool, smoking a cigarette and feeling sick, with nobody to go home to.

Meeting Catriona had been just about the last straw. He had expected Stanley Keys' only daughter to be strong; but he had also expected her to be plain and practical, and to talk to him about bollards and windlasses, and wear beige Fair Isle cardigans. Instead, she had turned out to be waspish and perfumed and slanty-eyed, and to have that intense femininity about her that had first attracted him to Surprise-Bloom Flower. Catriona Keys had both stimulated and humiliated him, and he wasn't sure whether he felt angrier with her than he did with himself; it was a close-run thing.

Just then, one of the stewards came out on the promenade deck, a gingery-haired fairy called McNulty. He shrieked against the wind, "Mr. Philips, sir! Mr. Philips, sir! Problems!"

Rudyard tossed his cigarette over the rail and went back inside. McNulty was hot and excited and smelled of lavender water, and he stood much closer to Rudyard than he needed to. "It's Mademoiselle Narron, sir. The opera-singer lady. She's locked herself in her stateroom and she's sobbing fit to bust. Mr. Willowby's worried she's going to do something drastic."

"You've got your passkey, haven't you?" Rudyard demanded.

"Mademoiselle's jammed the lock somehow. Don't know how, sir.

We've tried everything."

Rudyard hurried down the first-class staircase, beaming reassuringly to the passengers with whom he almost collided on the way. Then he was half running down the long maroon-carpeted corridor, holding the peak of his cap to stop it falling off. On either side of him, in eurhythmic poses, naked girls cast out of stainless steel were holding up frosted-glass lamps, their eyes closed in twentieth-century ecstasy. Through half-open stateroom doors, he glimpsed mink coats laid out on beds; and tailcoats being shaken out for the evening. The whole length of this corridor was stuffy with French perfumes and expensive colognes, and with that inimitable aroma of real leather and real fur and real vicuna that always seems to accompany the very wealthy, a laconic haze of authenticity.

Mademoiselle Narron's stateroom was at the very end of the corridor, underneath the wheelhouse. Monty Willowby the purser was there, as well as Dick Charles the fourth officer, two stewards, and one of the first-class maids, Iris.

"Ah, Mr. Philips," said Monty Willowby. "Glad you could come so promptly. Seems like a case of the artistic hystericals, unless I'm mistaken. You wouldn't have remembered Mr. Caruso, on the *Eximious,* would you? Quite vocal, he got. Crying, and singing '*Vesti la giubba.*' We had to break down the door and give him cold tea with comfrey in it."

"We're not breaking down *this* door," said Rudyard. "Not if we can help it."

"I've t-t-tried p-p-pleading with her, s-s-sir," put in Dick Charles.

Rudyard tried to imagine Dick Charles pleading with anybody, even with Jesus, and didn't find the thought particularly inspiring. Not that Dick was lacking in any of the other qualities that made an excellent fourth officer. He was clever, confident, and responsible. He was good with children, especially first-class children. It was just that his interminable stutter tried everybody's patience to the utmost. In Monty Willowby's words, "You could drink fourpence worth of Guinness and eat a sixpenny ham sandwich in between 'w' and 'would you like some luncheon?' "

Monty Willowby, of course, was a species unto himself. The purser on a huge luxury liner like the *Arcadia* was as near to being an emperor as it was possible to be without actually owning India. He was in charge of the entire corps of stewards and stewardesses, and of everything social, recreational, and financial. He sat on the summit of a busy pyramid of tips, backhanders, *pourboires,* bets, and out-and-out bribes. When a wealthy passenger gave him a sizeable gratuity to ensure special and prompt attention, Monty Willowby in turn would tip the bedroom steward concerned, and the bedroom steward in *his* turn would tip the chambermaids and the pantrymen, and the pantrymen would tip the chefs. In most good travel guides that year, 1924, it was suggested to first-class passengers on front-rank liners like the *Arcadia* and the *Mauretania* that they should calculate on spending a sum equal to at least five per cent of their total fare on tips. Bedroom stewards should be tipped the most; dining stewards sixpence less.

But whatever was paid out, whether it was a shilling for setting out deck chairs or threepence for carving an extra slice of rare roast beef, Monty Willowby would collect his tithe. He was stout, loud, and authoritative, with fiery red cheeks that looked hot to the touch, and a moustache like an explosion in a horsehair sofa. He had served as a sergeant-major at Ypres and Passchendaele, and shot eleven Boche. He proudly claimed that his wife Violet had the fattest bottom in the North of England. "My Yorkshire mare," he called her. If he made less than £750 in tips and bribes on a one-way trip to New York, he considered that times were thin. That was his pet phrase. "Times is thin, Mr. Philips. Times is very thin."

Now, however, with the greatest diva of the decade sobbing and locked irremovably in her stateroom, Monty Willowby's times were more awkward than thin. Shouting through the keyhole in a stentorian voice had brought no results; nor had the promise of complimentary champagne and free Floris chocolates. After bullying and bribery, Monty Willowby had nothing left in his diplomatic quiver except to call for an officer. That was why he had sent for Rudyard Philips. "Officers is paid to impress the passengers. That's what officers is paid for. It don't matter a shit if they can't sail a duck in a bathtub, as long as they impress."

"McNulty tells me you've tried the passkey," said Rudyard.

"Without avail, sir" Monty Willowby nodded. "I think as how she's crammed up the keyhole with pieces of writing paper."

Rudyard listened at the door. When Monty Willowby tried to speak again, he raised his hand to silence him. From inside the stateroom he could hear faint whimpers of anguish, interrupted by an occasional cough. He hoped to God that Mademoiselle Narron wasn't taking sleeping tablets, or anything hysterical like that. But she certainly didn't sound as if she were gargling for the good of her vocal cords, or practising her Caruso sob.

"Go and break out a fire axe," Rudyard told one of the stewards. "I don't want to smash down the door, but I may be obliged to."

Dick Charles said, "I p-p-peeped in through the p-p-p-porthole, b-b-but she'd p-p-p—she'd p-p-p-p—she'd p-p-p-p—"

Everybody waited in high tension as Dick Charles stood staring at them, his tongue poised on the tip of his teeth, his whole being concentrated on pronouncing that one unutterable "p." He was fourth officer, so none of the stewards could think of interrupting him, and Rudyard was far too sympathetic to finish his sentence.

"Pulled down the blind," said Dick Charles quite suddenly, as if sentences like that rolled off his tongue all the time. Monty Willowby puffed out his cheeks in relief.

Rudyard knocked loudly at Mademoiselle Narron's door. "Mademoiselle Narron! Mademoiselle Narron! Can you hear me, Mademoiselle Narron?"

There were renewed sobs, immediately followed by a peculiar gagging sound.

"Mademoiselle Narron! It's Mr. Philips, the first officer! Are you in difficulty? Mademoiselle Narron!"

"Go away!" shrieked the diva. "I wish only to die!"

Rudyard looked at Monty Willowby and both of them pulled their mouths down. "What did I tell you?" said Monty. "The artistic hystericals, in full flight. There's always one of them. Last trip I did on the *Excellent*, we had an Italian juggler who threw himself into the sea with his pockets full of cutlery, to help him sink."

"That's enough, Mr. Willowby," said Rudyard. He was on his knees in front of the door now with his Swiss Army penknife. With one of the thinner blades, he was poking at the lock, trying to extricate the crumpled-up pieces of paper which Mademoiselle Narron had forced into it.

"Go away!" called Mademoiselle Narron, even more histrionically. "I want to be alone with myself! I wish only death!"

McNulty was quite disappointed when Rudyard managed to push the paper out and quickly thrust the key in the lock. He had been looking forward to swinging at Mademoiselle Narron's maple-veneered door with the fire axe. Rudyard slammed the door wide and there on her chaise longue was the celebrated dramatic soprano, frighteningly upright, far taller than any of them had expected, in an astonishing Wagnerian costume of silvered drapery. Her bare wrists were held out in front of her, and both of them were slashed, so that her dark blood was dripping onto the crimson lake carpet, red on red.

She stood up, her eyes wide and wild. She was nearly six feet tall, and on top of her red frizzy hair she wore a high silver headdress with silver-painted ferns and silver sleigh bells on it, so that she appeared even taller. Her costume was the one she had worn as Freia in *The Rhinegold*, and she wore it now as she had worn it at the Metropolitan during the season of 1922, with one white gigantic breast exposed. That one breast alone, thought Rudyard, as he stood in front of the towering Mademoiselle Narron feeling absurdly short and intimidated, that one breast alone is *bigger than my head*.

It was then that Mademoiselle Narron swayed, her headdress jingling, and collapsed. Rudyard tried to catch her and support her, but she must have weighed 170 pounds, and she toppled him over as well.

"Mr. Willowby, go and find Dr. Fields!" Rudyard ordered, struggling under Mademoiselle Narron's weight. "McNulty, give me a hand here. Mr. Charles, tear up that tablecloth for bandages!"

Between them, they lifted the soprano onto the blood-spattered chaise longue, and tied up her wrists with strips of Irish linen. The cuts were only superficial; Mademoiselle Narron hadn't succeeded in slicing into any of the larger veins. Rudyard picked up a gory Gillette razor blade and handed it to McNulty.

"Let's get her into bed," said Rudyard. "Iris, would you raise the blinds please? I'd like some light on the subject."

Mademoiselle Narron's suite was decorated to represent "Sweetness," with walls lined in pink moiré silk, and pink marble furniture. Her bed was French, painted pink and white, with carved cupids and bows across the headboard. For a woman so large, the decor seemed incongruously fussy and pretty, and for a woman who had tried to slash her wrists, cupids and hearts seemed ironic. But when Iris had wrestled off her headdress and they had managed between them to cover her up with her pink and white silk counterpane, Mademoiselle Narron lay there with her eyes closed and her red pre-Raphaelite hair spread out on the pink satin pillow, and Rudyard with surprise realised that she was an extremely handsome woman. She had a firm square opera singer's jaw, but good cheekbones and a long straight nose. Her lips, which she had painted the same pink as the walls, were curved and full.

Monty Willowby came back with Dr. Fields. A ship's doctor for Keys Shipping for over fifteen years, Dr. Fields still retained his Harley Street hauteur and wore grey morning coats and grey silk neckties with gates-ajar collars. He sat down on the edge of the diva's bed and examined her through his half-glasses as if he couldn't decide whether to take Mademoiselle's temperature or recite Charles Lamb on convalescence. He had been known to do either, or both. "Sickness enlarges the dimensions of one's self to oneself," he would say.

"She tried to kill herself," said Rudyard helpfully.

"Hmm," said Dr. Fields. "Not very successfully, even by operatic standards. Opera singers make very poor suicides, you know. Did you know that? Similarly, trawlermen. Don't ask me why. Are you awake, my dear Mademoiselle Narron?"

Mademoiselle Narron's eyes flickered, and then opened. They were a pale translucent green, but very expressive and intense.

"I passed out," she said. "What happened?"

Dr. Field raised one of her bloody wrists so that she could see it. "I fear that you attempted to diminish your enjoyment of this voyage by cutting your wrists."

The diva nodded slowly. "Yes," she said. "I wished for death. It was oblivion I wanted."

"Oblivion? Well." Dr. Field sniffed. "If it was oblivion you wanted, I could have prescribed it for you. At least my kind of oblivion is only temporary. 'And if I drink oblivion of a day, So shorten I the stature of my soul.' George Meredith that was. Rotten writer. Couldn't stand the man. Would you like some pills to help you calm yourself down?"

"I don't think so," said Mademoiselle Narron. "I think"—she raised both her wrists and stared at them—"I think I will not try this again."

"Well, that's capital," said Dr. Fields. "I'll send up the nurse to tidy up your dressings. But just remember, if there's anything at all I can do, I'm always on call to assist. So is the ship's chaplain, Mr. Porrit. Strange chap, though, bit of a fundamentalist. If I were you, I'd give the hospital a call first, as a rule, before the chapel."

Rudyard stayed by Mademoiselle's bedside after everyone had left. Their only chaperone was Iris, who was doing her best to scrub the soprano's blood out of the carpet. Mademoiselle Narron closed her eyes for a while as the sunlight moved gradually across the bedroom, and for a minute or two she slept. But then she opened her eyes again and Rudyard was still there.

"You can leave me now," she said softly. "I think I have learned my lesson. I was acting, you see, acting a part. But my suicide was only acting, too."

"You felt upset about something, though," said Rudyard.

Mademoiselle Narron smiled wanly.

"Someone you had to leave behind?" asked Rudyard.

She nodded.

Rudyard stood up and paced across the bedroom to the porthole. Outside, the sea was sparkling like smashed glass.

"I had to leave someone behind, too," he said, with his back to her. His throat felt unexpectedly dry.

"Someone you loved?" she asked him.

"That's right. Someone I loved. Someone I thought would always love me. But, well . . . that wasn't to be."

"You couldn't have stayed behind, to mend your love with her?"

"And miss this voyage? Not a chance. Besides, I don't think there's anything left to mend. You can't put a broken teapot back together again if you don't have the pieces, can you?"

Mademoiselle Narron said, "I'm sorry. Your heart must hurt like mine."

Rudyard looked down at his gold-braided cap. "I shouldn't have told you," he said. "You're here to enjoy yourself, not listen to problems. But if there's anything I can do—well, you know. I just want you to know that I understand."

"You're a sad man," said Mademoiselle Narron.

"Only when I'm off duty," Rudyard told her, attempting a smile.

"You know something," she said. "I had to leave behind in England a man I thought would stay with me forever. But he went back to his wife and his children; and all of a sudden the dream that I thought was going to last for the rest of my life was vanished forever. I wake up in the morning now and I feel pain. Do you know that pain? I never thought that you could suffer real physical pain from losing someone."

Rudyard checked his watch. "I'm sorry," he said, "I'm very late already. If there's anything more you need, your bedroom steward will help you. But I'll come back later."

Mademoiselle Narron reached out her hand. "Why don't we help each other, you and I?" she said. "Just for the duration of this voyage, no longer. We are both sharing a ship, and sharing a heartache."

Rudyard hesitated for a moment, and then came across and took Mademoiselle Narron's hand. He squeezed it gently and said, "All right. If that's what you wish. If you'll have me."

"It's what I wish," she said softly.

Iris was standing in the doorway watching them. When Rudyard noticed that she was there, he put on his cap, saluted Mademoiselle Narron, and left the stateroom.

Mademoiselle Narron looked down at her freshly bandaged wrists and sighed. Now she would be able to wear so few of her beautiful evening gowns. She thought of Raymond. Raymond's hawklike profile, with that stray piece of grey hair that fell over his forehead when he played his cello. She thought of Raymond's kisses, Raymond's musical lovemaking. But she thought, too, of that ugly last scene in his friend's rented flat in Kensington, and how he had deserted her, walked off, in spite of every-thing that he had promised.

She began to sing, very softly, the part of Elvira from *I Puritani*, and in the next room Iris raised her head like a curious starling to listen.

Thirteen

Catriona couldn't think why, but Edgar Deacon seemed almost reluctant for her to meet Mark Beeney. Of course—since Mark and Catriona were sitting opposite each other at Sir Peregrine's table for the first luncheon of the *Arcadia*'s maiden voyage—they could scarcely have remained stran-gers. But Edgar seemed to go very tight-lipped and testy when he intro-duced them, and for most of the luncheon he tormented his food as if he bore a personal grudge against it, and scarcely spoke a word to the vivacious young movie actress who sat next to him and gushed on and on about Rudie Valentino and D. W. Griffith, and how D. W. had promised her that if he ever decided to remake *Broken Blossoms* he would definitely, but definitely, find a part for her.

Catriona and Mark Beeney sat and watched each other at first like two people who know they have always been destined to meet, and who scarcely need to say anything. All around them, the first-class dining lounge glittered with electric chandeliers, rows and rows of them, and each row was reflected a dozen times in the tall gilt-frame mirrors which were hung the whole 270-foot length of the room. It was like the dining room of an eighteenth-century French palace, with tall palms and canaries in cages and the ten-piece orchestra playing Mozart. The tables were laid with heavy silver plate provided by the same company who had furnished the cutlery for the *Titanic*, the Goldsmiths & Silversmiths Company of Regent Street, in London. Each table was decorated with a massive solid-silver centrepiece of mermaids and fish plunging through an engraved ocean.

For this first luncheon, Catriona wore a simple sleeveless dress of Chinese blue, and a brooch of pearls and diamonds. Her bobbed hair was circled by a blue headband. Her shoes were pale blue satin, and even her stockings were the colour of sea and sky and short circuits. Mark Beeney, in his beautifully tailored grey suit from Wetzel of New York, and his silk necktie from Henry Poole of London, sat and looked at her and thought she was perfectly stunning.

Marcia Conroy had been separated from Mark and was sitting further along Sir Peregrine's table next to Douglas Fairbanks. Although Mr. Fairbanks was waving his arms around and being his usual witty and anecdotal self, telling everybody a very long story about the time he had knocked himself unconscious while leaping off a balcony, without insurance, of course, Marcia was looking decidedly uncomfortable and irritated, and she kept glaring at Mark to catch his attention.

"I saw your press," Mark told Catriona as the stewards came around with steaming tureens of real turtle soup.

Catriona blushed. "The Flapper Queen of the Seas?" she asked him.

"That's right. You're not embarrassed, are you? I thought it was cute. But I did expect a genuine flapper. Instead, there's you."

"You don't think I'm a flapper?"

"Of course not. How could the daughter of Stanley Keys ever be a flapper? Besides, you don't even *look* like a flapper, or act like a flapper. You're not even a jazz baby. You're just what they say you are, Queen of the Atlantic."

Catriona said, "I think you're flattering me on purpose."

"Of course I am. I never flatter anybody by accident."

"I think you have something in mind is what I meant."

"An ulterior motive?" asked Mark. He declined the amontillado sherry that the steward offered him for his turtle soup.

"That's right," said Catriona. "Yes, sherry for me, please."

Mark sipped his soup. "It's not up to Savoy standard, but it's okay."

"Do you want me to send it back?" asked Catriona. "I can, you know."

"Listen," he told her, "I can take care of myself. You may own this shipping line, but I have a shipping line, too."

"Does that make us enemies, or associates?"

Mark tore off a piece of fresh-baked bread and chewed it. "It makes us equal, that's all. Whether you want to be friendly or not, that's up to you."

"What makes you think I shouldn't be friendly? Don't I look friendly?"

Mark shrugged. "I don't know. I haven't got as far as that yet. Right now, I'm still bowled over by how pretty you look."

"You're being very American, you know," said Catriona. "A bit too snappy for your own good."

"You can give as sharp as you get," said Mark, without looking up. "You're a rare girl. You know that?"

"Rare?" asked Catriona, more cautiously this time.

Mark raised his eyes. "Yes," he said. "Rare. To be strong and beautiful and understanding all at once, that's rare."

Catriona paused, silent for a long time. The dining lounge was clattering with the castanet sound of soup spoons. Then she said, "You don't know if I'm understanding or not."

Mark grinned. "You must be to have answered that way."

Catriona glanced along the table at Marcia. "Your friend has been trying to catch your attention ever since you sat down. Don't you think you ought to wave at her at least?"

"Oh, sure," said Mark, and leaned over to give Marcia a little finger wave down the rows of empty soup plates. Marcia mouthed something, but Mark cupped his hand around his ear, and mouthed back, *Can't hear you. Talk to you later.* Marcia huffed in irritation and gave up.

"Is she your secretary?" asked Catriona.

"Marcia? Oh, no. Marcia's my nemesis."

"What does that mean?"

"It means that one day, whether I like it or not, Marcia will hold the key to my entire fate."

"Do you really believe that?" Catriona smiled.

Mark made a *moue.* "Maybe. I don't know. I think everyone has a nemesis. Sometimes it's a person. Other times, it's a thing. The *Titanic* had a nemesis in the shape of an iceberg."

"You shouldn't say that." said Catriona. The idea of it made her feel cold, and she glanced across at Sir Peregrine for reassurance. If the captain was calmly finishing his soup, then everything must be all right.

"You're not scared, are you?" asked Mark, amused. "You think it could happen again? You think it could happen just because I happened to mention it? You're not superstitious, are you?"

"Yes," said Catriona. "Have you ever met a girl who isn't?"

Mark pressed his fingers to his forehead and pretended to spend a long time thinking. Then he said, "No, you're right. I haven't."

"Did it take that long to remember all the girls you've been out with?" Catriona asked him. "Were there really that many girls?"

"Of course," Mark told her. "I'm rich, I'm good-looking. You think I sit home all evening listening to Barney Google?"

"I'm glad to discover you're self-effacing as well," said Catriona.

Mark laughed out loud, leaning back in his chair, but as he leaned back, Marcia caught his eye again, caustically, and his face remoulded itself instantly to Serious. "You see what I mean by nemesis?" he asked Catriona under his breath. He finished his turtle soup in silence.

Edgar Deacon said dourly, "I hope you're enjoying yourself so far, Mr. Beeney."

"Oh, sure," said Mark. "The *Arcadia*'s a beautiful vessel, and no doubt about it. As a matter of fact, Miss Keys, I very much envy you. I wish she were mine."

"I don't think she's for sale," said Catriona, but she wasn't so slow that she didn't catch the displeased exchange of glances between Mark and Edgar Deacon. But she smiled, in the kind of Queen of the Atlantic way which she knew would please Edgar Deacon, and held her tongue.

Now the ship's orchestra played Viennese waltzes, and the soup plates were gathered up with a systematic clattering. Fresh plates and fresh cutlery were laid, and the stewards brought round transparently thin slices of Prague ham. Sir Peregrine began to tell his guests, in tedious and impeccable accents, like someone in the MCC clubroom describing an entire cricket match, over by over, about the time when the *Aurora* had been hired for a round trip to Florida, for the birthday party of a Chicago beef baron's daughter and how five guests had fallen overboard and been swept away by the currents. The beef baron had asked for a discount of $250 for each swept-away passenger, plus a refund for two dozen bottles of Mumm's Cordon Rouge which had been shattered in the storm.

Douglas Fairbanks, far too loudly, explained how he had been accidentally swept up in the rigging of a pirate ship during a rehearsal, and become inextricably entangled there. He had missed lunch with his agent, but "that didn't matter—I would rather have spent the rest of the week stuck up that mast than five minutes with that miserable cuss."

Mark Beeney said to Catriona, "My hobbies are horseback riding, hunting, sailing, chess, skiing, and beautiful girls. What are yours?"

Catriona said, "Mystic experiences."

"What do you call a mystic experience?" asked Mark.

"Falling in love. Having a revelation. Watching the sun rise."

"When was the last time you did any of those things?"

"I watched the sun rise this morning. I had a revelation when my father died."

"What was the revelation? What did you see?"

Catriona laid down her knife. "I saw myself. My real self, I mean. The self I'd been hiding. Once my father had gone, you see, I realised that I wasn't so very different from him, after all. That's why I'm here, instead of back in London."

"You're really going to take an active interest in Keys Shipping?"

"Why shouldn't I?"

"Shipping is such a hell of a risky business these days."

"Shipping always was."

"Well, sure," said Mark, "but you're a pretty young girl of twenty-one with the whole of your life ahead of you. Why the hell should you want to spend your life in stuffy offices running a shipping line?"

"Why the hell should *you* want to spend your life in stuffy offices running a shipping line?"

"I'm different. I'm a man. Besides, I'm ten years older than you. I've sown all the wild oats I'm ever going to sow."

"You mean to tell me you're a has-been already? You disappoint me."

Mark held his wineglass while the steward poured him more Perrier-Jouet champagne. "I disappoint myself. I own one of the fastest and most efficient fleets of passenger liners in the world, and yet I don't own anything like the *Arcadia*. I have dozens of pretty girlfriends, and yet I don't have anyone like you."

Edgar Deacon heard that last remark, and stared at Catriona from under his beetling eyebrows like an irascible bishop. Catriona gave him an uncertain and not wholly reassuring smile in return. She couldn't be wholly reassuring, because she wasn't wholly reassured. Mark Beeney was too handsome and too confident and too ebullient to be resisted for very long. She couldn't dislike him if she tried. His hair was curly and his teeth were white, and even his arrogance about girls was strangely innocent and disarming.

"I'm being taken on a tour of the *Arcadia* after lunch," said Catriona. "Perhaps you and your nemesis would like to come."

"*I'll* come for sure." Mark Beeney smiled. "But I believe my nemesis has an appointment in the beauty salon."

After the ham, the stewards served chicken Kiev with wild rice and fresh asparagus, and followed up with raspberries and cream, button mushrooms on toast, cheese, and crackers. Mr. Willowby came over to the captain's table during the dessert to kiss Catriona's hand and bow to several of the passengers he already knew. Douglas Fairbanks insisted on slapping Mr. Willowby on the back, which Mr. Willowby clearly found unpleasant in the extreme.

"Your luncheon met up to your expectations?" Monty Willowby asked Catriona.

"It was marvellous, thank you, Mr. Willowby."

"Thank you, Miss Keys. There's even better to come."

Mark admitted, "This was excellent, Mr. Willowby. If I can persuade my staff to do half as well, then I think I'll be well on my way."

"Mr. Beeney is too kind," said Mr. Willowby. He gave the impression that he didn't care in the slightest if anybody was kind to him or not.

"You have to buy so much food," said Catriona.

Mr. Willowby nodded, with considerable pleasure. "On this maiden voyage alone, we have 195 pounds of truffled pâté-de-foie-gras on board, 500 pounds of Scotch smoked salmon, half a long ton of fresh asparagus, 250 pounds of fresh-picked strawberries, as well as 250 pounds of the very best grey Malossol caviar. We also stock eighteen different French champagnes; sixty-one vintage wines from Château Branaire-Ducru in the Médoc to Château Haut-Bailly in Graves; thirty different varieties of cigar; and sixteen different ales and lager beers. In case of particular demands, we are also carrying frozen stocks of venison, woodcock, quail, duck, and hare."

"I shan't starve, then," said Mark, his eyes on Catriona.

"I doubt it, sir," said Monty Willowby with self-satisfaction, "and I must say that those American gentlemen who have been inhibited in their home country by the Volstead Act, and by dietary fanaticism, have all found the abundance of our larders to be most reassuring."

"They are," said Mark, "most reassuring."

"Tea is at four, sir," Monty Willowby reminded him. "Dinner is at eight. Supper will be set out in the first-class smoking room at eleven. Early breakfast is available from five-thirty. But if at any time you feel peckish, sir, don't hesitate to let my stewards know. A plate of deviled beef bones and cottage fried potatoes never goes amiss, sir, does it?"

Mark looked pointedly at Monty Willowby's protuberant belly, straining at his beige hunting vest and the gold chain of his Albert watch. "No," he remarked, "apparently not."

For a half-hour after lunch, Catriona went out onto the first-class promenade deck in a white summer coat and a white peekaboo hat to take the breeze. Mark Beeney was strolling arm-in-arm with Marcia Conroy, and he raised his straw boater to her as she passed. Once they had gone by, Catriona could hear them furiously arguing. "Well, what did you want me to do, high-hat her?" Mark protested. Catriona smiled to herself and went to the varnished rail, where she gazed seventy feet down the sheer wall of the *Arcadia*'s side to the frothing green Irish Sea below.

It was almost two o'clock. In an hour, they would be lowering her father into his grave at the Church of St. Christopher, in Formby. The sadness and the regret she felt were almost bottomless, like the deepest reaches of the ocean. But none of her anguish could bring him back, not even to the moment when he had let out his last breath, nor to the second when he had paused at the foot of the stairs and asked Dottie for his Food of Life. The breath he had breathed and the words he had spoken had been heard, and faded, and gone. She hoped desperately that her father was happy, if it was still possible for him to be happy; and for her own sake she hoped that he understood how much she loved him.

Edgar Deacon came up in white ducks and a navy-blue yachting blazer with red stripes. He rested his bony dark-haired wrists on the rail beside her and pretended to stare at the dazzling sea for a while.

"You and Mark Beeney got on well together, then?" he asked.

"We shouldn't have done?"

"Of course you should. I'm glad that you did. You shouldn't forget that he's the competition, though. Nor how much he covets this ship."

"Is that so terrible?"

"My dear, he cares for nothing but his own interests. He would happily see Keys go bankrupt, if it meant that he could have the *Arcadia* for himself. He's quite unscrupulous."

"He's nice. I like him."

"Of course you like him. But he's far harder than he looks. He's not just an oceangoing cake eater. He's one of the brightest young businessmen in America."

"I can't really believe that he wants to see us go out of business."

Edgar turned and leaned his back against the rail. He watched Mark Beeney and Marcia Conroy as they briefly appeared on the far side of the promenade deck, and then as they disappeared again behind the raised glass roof that covered the first-class lounge.

"If it meant that he could acquire the *Arcadia* cheaply, he wouldn't give twopence if our whole work force had to go on the dole. He's a young sheik, Miss Keys, that's all; and the *Arcadia* would be a fine jewel for him to set in his puggaree."

Catriona stared down at the foam as it endlessly unravelled from the ship's glossy black hull and spread out across the surface of the ocean. Only a few feet away from the rail, silent gulls kept pace with the *Arcadia*'s progress, occasionally fluttering and diving for small fish that had been churned up by the liner's giant screws. The ship had passed the shelter of the north Welsh coast now, and the southwest wind had freshened up. Catriona wound her scarf around her hat and turned up the collar of her coat, so that all anyone could see of her was her pretty nose.

"The way Mark Beeney looks at it," went on Edgar, "American TransAtlantic ranks fourth, both in carrying capacity and the prestige of his fleet. His fleet makes money, certainly, but it lacks glamour; and these days glamour is what the cabin-class business is all about. If he could buy the *Arcadia,* he would easily rank third, and he would also have all the swank he's been looking for."

"He's been talking to you about it?" asked Catriona.

Edgar stood straight and self-consciously adjusted his yachting cap. "He's been dropping hints about the *Arcadia* for months, both to me and to your father."

"I mean recently. You were exchanging intimate looks at the luncheon table as if you were secret lovers."

"He did call me before we left Liverpool, yes."

"He made an offer?"

Edgar shook his head. "He just wanted to know if we were interested in selling, that's all. A tentative inquiry. But I doubt if he could go above three million pounds."

"So what do you think about it?"

"I don't think anything about it, other than what I told you last week. We're technically bankrupt, and any offer that might pay off our debts has to be considered. It grieves me considerably to think of having to sell the Keys fleet out of the family, but so far it strikes me as the only reasonable alternative. Three million might keep us going for a little while longer, but then we would have lost the *Arcadia* forever."

"And that's why I shouldn't allow myself to be sweet-talked by Mark Beeney?" asked Catriona, a little irked.

"Let me just say this," said Edgar. "Mark Beeney is very attractive to women, and he has a way with him. For your own sake, for *all* of our sakes, for the sake of those families in Liverpool, you'd be better to keep a relatively cool distance."

Catriona turned to Edgar and peered at him from under the shadow of her peekaboo hat. "You're not just the tiniest bit jealous, are you?" she asked. "I mean, as well as being so businesslike and concerned for those families in Liverpool?"

Edgar gave her a complicated little smile. "I am simply trying to discharge my duty to your late father's company in the way that he would have wished me to," he said. He cleared his throat and then turned away.

Just then, Mark Beeney came across the deck. He grinned and lifted his hat and took Catriona's hand.

"Miss Keys," he said, cheerfully. "I *thought* it was you under that hat. You have the most attractive smeller on the whole deck. Mr. Deacon, how are you?"

Edgar gave a noncommittal nod. "Bearing up, thank you, Mr. Beeney."

"It's almost two-thirty," said Mark Beeney. "The lovely Marcia has gone to the beauty salon to get herself dolled up for tonight's festivities. Didn't we have a date for a tour of the ship?"

"Of course," said Catriona, taking Mark Beeney's arm. "Look, here's Mr. Philips now. Our guide. You'll excuse us, Mr. Deacon?"

"Please," said Edgar, overpolitely. "It's your ship."

Rudyard Philips came up looking surprisingly pink, as if something had just shocked or embarrassed him. In fact Mademoiselle Narron had taken his arm only ten minutes ago as he left the first-class dining lounge and jostled him into a corner, deliberately or accidentally thrusting one of her mighty thighs between his. He hadn't quite been sure what she had been trying to do, and perhaps she hadn't been, either, because nothing had ensued but an awkward tussle and a salvo of "excuse-mes" and "I beg-your-pardons." Blushing, she said that the sway of the ship had made her lose her balance. Could she see him later? With other passengers watching, he had tipped his cap and said, "Assuredly." It had sounded rather old-fashioned but it had been the first word he could think of. The slight cuts on Mademoiselle Narron's wrists had been concealed by three or four large diamond bracelets, and a long-sleeved purple dress by Dior.

"Mr. Beeney is coming with us," announced Catriona as Rudyard came up and saluted her.

"How nice," said Rudyard, and shook hands. Further along the deck, in the Palm Lounge, the band was playing "There's Yes Yes in Your Eyes." In Edgar Deacon's eyes, as he watched Catriona and Mark and Rudyard make their way along to the first-class stairway, there was nothing but disturbance. A thunderstorm in the making.

Fourteen

A half-hour before the coastline of Ireland came into view, Harry Pakenow was sitting on the end of a crowded bench on shelter deck C, trying to compose a letter to Janice. In the note that he had left her on the kitchen table in Bootle he had been blunt to the point of cruelty. But he knew that if he had written what he truly felt for her, he would have found it five times more painful to go. When the *Arcadia* had sailed clear of Liverpool Bay, and the long hazy shores of England had finally merged into the sea, Harry had understood with a deep wave of unexpected grief how much he had actually loved Janice, and how much he was going to miss her. He had faced out to sea with tears clinging to the lenses of his spectacles, and his throat so tight with unhappiness that he could scarcely swallow.

Now he tried to write down what he had always failed to tell her, but it was more difficult than he could have imagined. "I love you" wasn't enough. What he needed was some way of expressing his gratitude for every one of her silly little jokes, and her childish kisses, and every plate of black pudding and bacon she had brought him. What could he tell her about those rainy Sunday walks through the cobbled streets of Bootle? What could he tell her about the evening she had danced the Charleston naked in the bedroom, little breasts bouncing, bead necklace swinging, bare toes stubbing on the threadbare rug?

Ordinary Janice Bignor. England was crowded with girls like Janice Bignor. Yet in her very ordinariness she had been cute and trusting and more lovable than Harry could have told anyone, ever.

He wrote, ". . . never in my whole life . . ." but the wind snapped down the corner of his page, as if it didn't want him to attempt any more. Next to him on the hard varnished bench a grossly fat Estonian woman with a worn-out carpetbag on her lap was steadfastly devouring a whole salami sausage as if it were an act of penance. Three Hungarian Jews with beards and long curly *payees* were playing violins and singing. But few of the third-class passengers were as poverty-stricken or as ethnically colourful as they had been in the past, in the days of open immigration. This year's Johnson-Reed Act had cut America's immigration quota, already restricted, down to two per cent of the foreign-born population of the United States according to the census of 1890. The raised rear deck was promenaded not by Poles and Lithuanians but by college students, schoolteachers, priests, shop assistants, and members of the South Wales Glee Club.

Harry, as he sat on deck in his shabby tweed jacket and his tweed cap, his pants tucked into his Fair Isle socks, had the look of a typical steerage passenger. Like everyone else in third class, he had paid forty pounds return Liverpool–New York–Liverpool, although in his case he had only purchased a round-trip ticket as part of his alibi. Like everyone else in third class, he shared a cabin with five others, enjoying the facilities of an upright foldaway washstand, two clean towels a day, and use of the third-class bathrooms at any time at all. There were fifteen different foods on the third-class breakfast menu, including porridge, chopped chicken livers, and kippers. The days when the third-class steward of the *Lusitania* had reported to his head office in consternation that "quite a number of the third-class passengers . . . inquired for sheets for the beds" were long gone.

Standing up against the freshening wind, Harry crammed the pages of his half-written letter into his jacket pocket. He was about to go inside for a drink when, as if in an odd dream, a small figure in a pink dress came sailing through the air from the rail of the first-class promenade deck above him and landed on the white-scrubbed boards. He bent over and picked it up. It was a doll, with blonde ringlets and a rather sulky-looking china face.

Harry squinted up against the sun. Up by the first-class rail was a girl of about twelve or thirteen, in a pink cloche hat and an expensive pink coat with a fur collar. She waved to him, and he lifted the doll up in his hand. "I'll bring it back up to you!" he called.

He went inside to the linoleum-covered stairway that led up to the second-class deck. A fat man was sitting halfway up smoking a pipe and reading *My Golfing Life* by the golf queen Glenna Collett. He shifted his bottom over as Harry came up the stairs, without once taking his eyes off his book. But Harry was just about to step through the open door that would have taken him onto the second-class deck when a snappy little steward with a clipped moustache blocked his way.

"Sorry, mate, you can't come up here. This is second class."

Harry held up the doll. "A little girl dropped this from the first-class deck. I was only going to give it back to her."

"You're not allowed up here, I'm sorry. If you give the doll to me, I'll make sure she gets it."

Harry licked his lips. He felt that familiar breathlessness in his chest, the feeling he had felt when he had stowed the dynamite in Mark Beeney's limousine. And the same feeling he had felt when he had driven that horse-drawn wagon four years ago right up to the corner of Wall Street.

"I'd prefer to give it back personally, if you don't mind," he said. "I'm not going to stay up there, and I'm not going to get in anybody's way. Now, will you let me through?"

"Not a chance," said the steward. "You think those folks in cabin class pay two thousand quid a trip to mix with riffraff like you?"

Harry, furious, grabbed the steward by the lapels of his beige Keys jacket and shook him. "You think you're any better than me, just because you're serving on a second-class deck? What's the matter with you?"

"You let go of me!" panted the steward, frightened. He swung his arms around like a windmill and hit Harry on the shoulder, but both of them were too scared and excited to hurt each other much. They were still shoving and pulling at each other's clothes when Mr. Willowby appeared, a stately vessel in his own right, all watch chain and glittering vest buttons. He was leading by the hand the small pink-coated girl from the first-class deck.

"Anything amiss here, gentlemen?" he asked.

The second-class steward straightened his necktie. Harry, panting with anger, leaned back against the bulkhead, still clutching the doll.

"This bloody madman tried to force his way into second-class," gasped the steward. "He's mad! He shook me about all over the place!"

"Well, perhaps you deserved it," said Mr. Willowby warmly. Then, to Harry, "You *do* realize, squire, that your third-class ticket does not entitle you to access to the second- or first-class accommodation? I mean, you *do* understand that?"

"I wanted to return this doll to the little girl," said Harry breathlessly. "That was all. Nothing more. And I object to being treated like some kind of subhuman species, just because I paid forty pounds for my ticket instead of two thousand pounds."

"The rules, squire, are the rules," said Mr. Willowby. "And much as I sympathise with what you say, there is a rhyme and reason behind the rules. This shipping line aims to satisfy every one of its passengers, from first-class to third; and if we were to let the third-class passengers stray onto the first-class decks, then, well, they might glimpse more than they ought to of first-class life, mightn't they not, squire? And that would hardly leave them satisfied, would it? Not having caviar and private bathrooms, for instance? So the things the third-class can't stretch to, we keep out of their sight, for their own well-being, don't you see?"

Harry slowly took off his spectacles. "Did I hear you right?" he asked incredulously. "Did you actually say what I thought you said?"

But the argument didn't go any further. The little girl in the pink coat was tugging at Mr. Willowby's hand and pointing to the doll. "That's Margaret," she said excitedly. "He's got Margaret."

"Ah, yes," said Mr. Willowby, staring at Harry with one of those official looks that meant *I'll know you again, chum, you just watch it.* "The delightful Margaret who nearly got herself lost at sea." He held out his hand for the doll and said, "Thank you, squire. The little girl's very grateful."

But Harry hunkered down in the doorway on the dividing line between third and second-class and held the doll up so that the little girl could come and get it for herself. Mr. Willowby hesitated for a moment, but then released her hand and let her go.

She was petite and delicate, this little girl, with dark fashionably cut hair and brown eyes that were wide and solemn and almost too large for her fine-boned oval face. She would either grow up plain or stunningly beautiful. But right now she still had that fey flirtatious magic that made some girls of her age seem to know things that they shouldn't; and started men thinking ridiculously forbidden thoughts.

She wore a three-strand pearl necklace and pearl earrings, and her fingernails were manicured and painted. Her pink velvet shoes had probably cost more than Harry had earned in three months with the Mersey Port Authority; and her perfume was light and flowery and eight guineas an ounce.

"Margaret hit her head when she fell," said Harry, gently. "I think you should maybe take her to the ship's infirmary and have them put a plaster on it." He glanced up at Mr. Willowby, who rolled his eyes up in ill-disguised disgust.

The little girl took the doll and clutched it tight. "Thank you for saving her," she said, seriously. She had a strong Texas accent. "I'll ask Mrs. Hall to see that you're rewarded."

"Rewarded?" Harry smiled. "I don't want a reward."

"Well, maybe I could stand you a drink," said the little girl.

"You don't have to do that, either," Harry told her. "I'm just happy to see you and Margaret reunited. Will you tell me your name?"

"Yours first," the little girl demanded.

"No, yours first. You're the one who owes me the favour, remember?"

"Oh. Well, okay then. I'm Lucille Theodora Foster."

Harry took her hand and gently squeezed it. "Good to meet you. My name's Harold Janeck Pakenow. Are you from Texas?"

Lucille nodded, gravely. "My daddy was Winthrop Foster the Third. My mommy was Gala Jones."

Harry attempted an answer but couldn't. If he thought that leaving Janice was a tragedy, this little girl's loss by comparison was cataclysmic. It had been front-page news for almost a week during May, and it was still a hot item in some of the gossip sheets. He said, at last, "I'm sorry. It was dumb of me not to realise."

Winthrop Foster the Third had been one of the richest oilmen in the United States, his fortune challenging the Rockefellers and the Mellons. Last year, 1923, he had sent his beautiful wife Gala Jones, the onetime toast of Broadway, to spend eighteen months in Europe, taking their daughter Lucille with her. Gala was going to visit London, Paris, Vienna, and Rome, buying clothes, jewellery, and whatever antiques might suit the Foster houses in Houston, Chicago, and New York.

In May, however, Winthrop Foster had decided on the spur of the moment to leave the oil business in the hands of his deputies and join his wife and child for a two-week vacation. He had travelled incognito on the *Mauretania* and planned his visit as a surprise. It was a greater surprise for both of them than he could have anticipated. He flung open the double doors of Gala's suite at the Paris Ritz to discover her copulating on the carpet with the famous Italian racing driver Giorgio Manciano.

Manciano had fled through the lobby of the Ritz in his white silk shirttails, but Winthrop Foster, after an initial argument, had appeared to take his wife's faithlessness as a model of stony acceptance. He hadn't beaten her, or even raised his voice to her, and for three days he had escorted her around Paris as if nothing at all were amiss.

On the fourth day, while Lucille stayed in the care of their American maids, Winthrop had taken Gala for a drive in the huge cherry-coloured Hispano-Suiza convertible which he had borrowed for his vacation from

112

King Manuel of Portugal; and he had driven it at eighty miles an hour into the granite base of the statue of Emile Decize, an obscure French politician whose major claim to fame had been the invention of an unworkable tax system. Gala had been smartly guillotined by the Hispano's hood-cover, and Winthrop Foster the Third had died of internal haemhorrage.

So here was their ten-year-old daughter Lucille, a victim of her parents' fierce and unfaithful passions, travelling back to the United States to be cared for by trust funds and attorneys and reluctant relatives. So poised and so sophisticated. A child brought up in the overheated atmosphere of wealth, fashion, and celebrated affairs. A child to whom the aroma of real hide automobile seats and costly perfumes was more familiar than that of cotton candy.

Harry laid a hand on Lucille's shoulder, although he was conscious that Mr. Willowby was growing restless now, and about as short-tempered as the company rules would ever allow him to get.

"I read about your parents," he told her. "I guess you must miss them a whole lot."

"Mrs. Hall said it was fate."

"*Fate?* Is that what she called it? Do you know what that means?"

Lucille said, "Sure I do," but then she frowned in uncertainty.

Harry said softly, "Fate means when something was always going to happen, whether you wanted it to or not. But you know something? People can change their own fate, whichever way they want to. I did when I was your age. I was poor, not like you. My mother had a hard time finding us enough to eat. But when I was your age, I promised myself that my life was never going to be like that."

"You're still poor, though, aren't you?" asked Lucille innocently. "I mean, you're travelling steerage. Daddy used to say that steerage was the cattle market."

Harry wiped his face with his hand. Mr. Willowby said, "Come along, now, Miss Foster," but Harry kept his grip on her shoulder and said, "Money doesn't really matter, you know? It's not money that makes your life happy or unhappy. I'm happier than your daddy was, right? And that's because I know what I am, what kind of a person I am, and I know what my future is going to be. But your daddy and your mommy, they were in control of everything except themselves. They didn't take care of the most important thing in the whole world, which was *themselves.*"

"I think that's enough, squire," said Mr. Willowby, with no pretence at courtesy. He took Lucille's hand and tugged her away. Harry got to his feet and tried to follow, but the thin-moustached steward barred his way with his arm.

"Just remember," Harry called. "Whatever you do from here on in, it's up to you. You take charge of your life. Don't let anyone else try to do it. And that goes for Margaret, too."

"Margaret?" asked Lucille.

"Sure," said Harry. "You and Margaret, you both have to decide for yourselves. And listen, if you want to talk some more, just lean over the rail and whistle."

"That's enough," said the steward roughly, and pushed Harry back with the heels of both hands. Harry, still smiling, all prickly hair and eyeglasses, jabbed the steward with two stiffened fingers, deep into his crotch. The steward exhaled loudly, and then stepped back a pace or two, panting, his face white.

"Never push me, all right?" said Harry, and made his way back down the stairway. The fat man with the pipe moved aside for him again without even lifting his eyes.

"Do you know something?" he said as Harry reached the foot of the stairs. "That Glenna Collett was fantastic. A natural athlete. Yet she was licked by a grandmother—a sixty-year-old grandmother. Can you believe that?"

Harry paused. Then he said, "Yes, I think I can. I mean, today I saw a man trying to return a lost doll to a young girl, and being refused that small pleasure because he was short of 1,980 pounds."

The fat man didn't reply but went back to his book as if it were the greatest revelation since the Book of Mormon. "Bobby Jones would've licked her," he muttered to himself.

Back on the third-class deck, Harry went to the rail and stared for a long time at the sea. Now and then he turned around, shielding his eyes from the sun, to see if Lucille Foster was looking down from the first-class promenade. But there was no sign of her pink cloche hat, nor her pink coat, nor her pale sad face. Whoever Mrs. Hall was, she must have taken her charge further along the deck, out of sight of the riffraff, or inside to her cabin.

He had no idea why he had felt such immediate liking for Lucille. She was wealthy, after all—a child of the fifthy rich. She had blandly referred to the *Arcadia*'s third-class passengers as cattle. But her social attitudes weren't really *her* fault; they were the only attitudes she knew. He supposed that if *he* had been brought up in swanky hotels in fashionable European cities, and never had to worry about money, then he might have grown to think the same way.

Maybe it was her aura of tragedy that moved him to respond to Lucille so immediately. Maybe it was the fact that in the face of a lonely child he had seen something that he had never quite wanted to believe before now: that the rich were human, too.

While he was leaning on the rail, a girl in a turban hat, a short blue skirt, and rolled-down stockings came up to him with an unlit cigarette perched in her fingers. Without a word, Harry took a box of Ship matches out of his pocket, struck one, and cupped his hands to protect the flame from the wind while the girl lit up.

"My name's Philly," the girl said, blowing out smoke. She was quite pretty, but she wore far too much makeup around her eyes, so that they looked like two bright blue marbles dropped into pots of black shoe cream. Even in the afternoon wind Harry could smell her strong perfume.

"Philly from Philly?" he asked her. He couldn't help smiling at her; she was trying so hard to be a Scott Fitzgerald–type "vamp."

"Philomena from the University of Minnesota," she said. She had a cute lisp which belied all her posturing as a campus vamp. "I'm just on my way back from fifty-five days in Europe."

"Good to meet you," said Harry, clasping her hand. "Did you learn anything?"

"I learned how abandoned the Europeans are. And I mean, *abandoned.*"

"Don't you think it's pretty abandoned coming up and asking a strange man for a light for your cigarette?"

Philly blinked. "What's abandoned about that? You're an American, aren't you?"

"I guess I am," said Harry. "My name's Harry, by the way."

"I think I'm tired of Europeans," said Philly. She kept her cigarette dangling between her lips while she took out her powder compact, bent down, and enthusiastically powdered her bare knees. "You can only take so much decadence, if you know what I mean. In fifty-five days, I've had decadence up to here. And I'm gasping for a decent malted milk. Not that I'm stuck on dairy produce, of course. I'd rather have a shot of giggle water any day. That's why we came back on a British ship. At least you can drink on a British ship."

"We?" asked Harry. He took off his spectacles and wiped them on his handkerchief. The salt in the wind kept misting them up.

"Hey, you look much nicer without your cheaters," said Philly with a smile. "Mind you, I've always been a sucker for guys in glasses."

Slightly embarrassed, Harry put them back on again. "You said 'we,'" he repeated.

"Oh, yes—me and my girlfriend Lydia. She's gone back to the cabin right now to throw up. Lydia and the ocean never did get on."

"Poor Lydia."

"Hey," said Philly, "I could use a walk around the deck. Do you want to take me for a walk around the deck?"

Harry shrugged, and then took her arm. "Okay. Which way round do you want to go? Clockwise or anti-clockwise?"

Philly snuggled close to Harry's side as they crossed the shelter deck to the stairway which led up to the stern deck. She giggled, "Did you hear the one about the girl who said to her date, 'Do you consider my legs long?' and do you know what he said? 'Yes,' he said, 'whenever possible.' "

Together they circled around the stern deck while the Red Ensign flapped and rumbled from its mast, and Philly chattered and pranced and told endless collegiate jokes. "Did you hear about the girl who was so dumb she always used to wonder how they got electric light poles to grow in a straight line?"

As they came around the deck for the third time, Harry glanced up at the rail of the first-class promenade, and there stood Lucille Foster in her pink fur-collared coat. She seemed to be searching for him amongst the crowd on the stern; and when she eventually caught sight of him, she gave him a quick and happy little wave. Harry discreetly waved back.

"Who are you waving at?" demanded Philly.

Harry squeezed her hand. "Just a friend," he told her.

Fifteen

They had been shown the kitchens, where the chefs were noisily preparing tonight's banquet of *filet de boeuf Robespierre,* crabs *maître d'hotel,* and *Pigeonneaux royaux au sauce paradis,* amid a pandemonium of steam and whisks and copper saucepans and the relentless bellowing of the black-bearded Monsieur Vincent, chef extraordinary, who had once astounded London society by serving Edward VII and his mistress Lily Langtry with *cuisses de grenouilles* in pink-tinted aspic, a dish which in those days had been considered suggestive to the point of culinary pornography.

Now Rudyard Philips led them with all the informative courtesy of a well-bred ship's officer to the brightly lit shopping gallery, where he pointed out the boutiques of Van Cleef & Arpels, sparkling with diamonds and rubies; of Zoroastra, where lizard and alligator pocketbooks gleamed along side jewel-encrusted evening purses; and of Alciatore, in which absurd and insanely expensive *objets d'art* and adult *jouets* were offered for the amusement of anyone whose tastes ran to onyx rocking horses with sapphires for eyes, or hip flasks which played "The Sheik of Araby" when you unscrewed them, and whose bank balance was near enough bottomless.

Rudyard said, "This shopping gallery is two hundred and ten feet long, and houses thirty different boutiques and agencies. You can buy anything here from a tube of toothpaste to a ranch in Montana."

116

"Thank you," said Mark Beeney. "I already have a ranch in Montana. *And* a tube of toothpaste."

Rudyard Philips managed the suggestion of a smile, but that was all. After his jostle with Mademoiselle Narron outside the dining lounge, he hadn't been feeling at all like himself. His thoughts were as jagged and mixed-up as the bits and pieces in a child's kaleidoscope. He still missed Toy, he knew that much. But the powerful Valkyrie image of Mademoiselle Narron had swelled almost overwhelmingly in his mind, until she blotted out all rational thought. She alarmed him enormously; but at the same time she had a fierce elemental sexuality which disturbed him like nothing had ever disturbed him before. Perhaps he had discovered a sexual quirk in himself that up until now had remained repressed. Perhaps he really preferred his women to be frightening.

Catriona had felt rather sulky. She had tinkered with the spatulas and spoons while Monsieur Vincent had been effusively explaining the delights of Dover sole Montgolfier (a Channel sole, smothered in a sauce of champagne, crab meat, diced shrimp, egg yolks, onions, thyme, butter, and fish stock, cooked in a bag of oiled paper like one of the celebrated air balloons of the Montgolfier brothers). She had felt tired after last night's party and after today's considerable luncheon; and she had also felt the hour of her father's burial approaching, like the impending visit of an unpleasant relative, with nobody around her to understand her sense of loss.

Mark Beeney had been disappointing, too. He was very tall, and solidly built, and even under his blazer she could tell that he was well muscled and physically fit. But during Rudyard Philip's tour of the ship he had seemed far more interested in the *Arcadia*'s catering supplies and stocks of wine and how many miles of steampipes wound their way around the various decks than he had been in Catriona.

He had asked question after question about the *Arcadia*'s construction, her handling, her budget; where her furniture and fittings had come from; how much the carpets cost per square yard; how Lalique had been persuaded to supply all the glassware at two per cent above cost. He was still asking questions as Catriona stopped by the window of Van Cleef & Arpels and looked over the displays of diamond necklaces. She yawned, half out of tiredness and half out of nerves. The clock at the end of the shopping galley said three minutes of three. Ashes to ashes, dust to dust.

She was looking with her eyes only half focused at a necklace of diamonds and rubies when she became aware that Mark was standing right beside her. He had left Rudyard Philips a few feet away, tactfully inspecting the toes of his shoes, and had approached her so quietly that she hadn't heard him.

"It's three o'clock," he said, gently.

She looked up at him, her lips slightly parted, her eyes moist.

"Well?" she said.

"I'm not such a dumb ox that I don't know what's happening at three o'clock today," he told her. "And you're not so tough that you're going to be able to walk around this ship pretending that nothing is wrong."

Catriona said, "I'm not going to cry, if that's what you're thinking."

"Why not? I cried when my father was buried."

"Perhaps I've cried enough already." She was lying, of course, flagrantly, for as the minute hand shuddered to XII the tears were already running down her cheeks.

"Miss Catriona Keys," said Mark Beeney, and held out his arms for her.

She stayed where she was for a moment, trying to be strong. But she couldn't hold the sobs back, couldn't stop the tears, and she leaned her forehead against his shoulder and clung on to him and wept. Mark said nothing, but held her close to him, one hand around her waist, the other stroking the back of her short-bobbed hair.

"I should have been there," she said miserably. "I should have been there."

"He wouldn't have wanted it," said Mark. "If it was a choice between you doing what you're doing now and attending his funeral, then you can bet your bottom dollar he wouldn't have wanted it."

Catriona raised her head. Her eyes were smudged with tears. "I was so mean to him, I can't even tell you."

"I was mean to my daddy, too. But that didn't mean that I didn't love him. He always knew I loved him, just like your daddy always knew the same about you. You don't seriously think he was so stupid he didn't realise how deeply you felt about him? You—a passionate person like you?"

Rudyard Philips took one or two steps nearer and asked politely, "Are you all right, Miss Keys?"

"I'm all right, thank you," said Catriona. "I just felt a little giddy, that's all."

"We could finish the tour tomorrow, if you'd prefer."

Unselfconsciously, she took Mark Beeney's hand. "No, thank you, Mr. Philips. I think I'd prefer to carry on. I know Mr. Beeney would."

"Why don't you take a couple of minutes to fix your eyes," Mark suggested. "There's a rest room right there. We'll wait for you."

Catriona went through the swing door into the pink-lit scented ladies' room. An attendant in a lace-edged apron ran water into the marble basin for her and set out a soft white towel. The shelves were crowded with bottles of French colognes, pots of rouge and foundation and moisturiser, and there was a set of silver-backed hairbrushes and hand mirrors. Catriona sat down on the pink velvet-seated stool and looked at herself in the gold-framed looking glass. The shadows under her high cheekbones made her look beautiful but haunted, the sad Queen of the Atlantic.

"Oh, father," she whispered. The rest-room attendant looked up sharply and said, "Did you want something, Miss Keys?"

Two girls came bustling into the room, spiffily dressed in Dior day suits and smoking with impossibly long cigarette holders. One of them went into one of the cubicles, while the other sat down beside Catriona and began to lavish purple and silver eye shadow on her half-closed eyelids.

"I really haven't made up my mind yet," called the girl from the cubicle, in a marked North Shore accent. "It's either the dark one with the pencil moustache or the ginger-haired one with the muscles."

"Well, I know which one *I'm* stuck on the most," replied the girl next to Catriona. "The young one who stutters. Don't you think that stutter's just the bee's knees?"

There was a short silence, and then the girl from the cubicle said, "Do you think that Wilma was right, about getting pregnant on board ship?"

"Of course she was, silly," replied the other girl, puckering up her lips to apply her vivid red lipstick. "Wilma's had more boys than anyone in the whole class. *Including* Miss Lipschitz."

They both giggled loudly. But then the girl in the cubicle said, "The trouble is, I can't remember which way you have to do it."

"Wilma was *quite* clear about it," said the other girl. "If the ship's pitching, you make sure you do it with your head to port and your feet to starboard. If the ship's rolling, you do it with your head to the pointed end and your feet to the blunt end. That way, the man's—"

The girl hesitated, suddenly aware that Catriona was listening. Catriona blushed and stood up and said, "I'm sorry, I wasn't eavesdropping."

"Well, I don't mind if you do," said the girl with the purple eyelids. "You might learn something."

"That's funny," said Catriona, "I always thought that if you wore a silk scarf around your neck and sneezed four times when it was over, you wouldn't have to worry about anything else."

The girl from the cubicle thought about that for a moment, and then called out, "Are you trying to be cute?"

Outside, Mark Beeney was waiting for her with his hands in his pockets and a self-satisfied look on his face. Rudyard Philips, a few yards away, appeared to be slightly ill. "Is he all right?" Catriona asked Mark as she came across the shopping gallery.

"Search me," said Mark. "I asked him if he felt okay, and he told me yes. Maybe he's sick because he's been told to take you and me on a tour of the ship, instead of fixing himself up with a sheba. The way most of these officers work, the best girls are all cornered by the time they dock at Dublin. Well, with some notable exceptions, of course."

Catriona took his arm. "How do you know I'm not cornered already?"

"I read in the paper you were sweet on some actor. But I don't see the actor on board."

"No, he stayed behind. His name's Nigel Myers. He's in *Daydreams of 1924.*"

"I've seen it. It's pretty good. Didn't he want to come with you?"

"He couldn't," said Catriona. "He was working."

"That's too bad. You miss him?"

Catriona looked up at Mark and realised he was teasing her. "Yes" —she nodded—"a little."

Mark said, "Do you think this would cheer you up? I mean, after your daddy and Nigel and everything?"

Out of his blazer pocket he produced the dazzling diamond necklace that Catriona had been admiring only a few minutes earlier in the window of the Van Cleef & Arpels boutique. It flashed so brilliantly in his hand that she could hardly believe it was real. There were four strands of one-carat diamonds set in twenty-four-carat gold, suspending a centerpiece of twelve three-carat diamonds and a huge cushion-cut ruby.

"You just bought that?" Catriona asked him incredulously.

"I didn't steal it. It's for you. A token of appreciation from the head of one shipping line to another. And also a token of my respect and esteem, and the fact that you're a very beautiful young woman."

"You're insane," said Catriona hotly. For some reason, she felt insulted as well as flattered. Did Mark Beeney really think that all he had to do was wave a $35,000 necklace under her nose for her to swoon at his feet? The next thing she knew, he'd be buying her a Rolls-Royce, simply so that he could make love to her in the back seat.

"You don't like it?" asked Mark, in exaggerated surprise.

"It's absolutely stunning. But what do you expect in return?"

Mark stared at her in disbelief for a second or two, and then burst out laughing. "You think I'm trying to seduce you?" He grinned. "You think I'm so unsubtle that I'd buy you a diamond necklace and then expect you to hop into bed with me? And anyway, it only cost thirty-five thousand."

"I suppose that makes a difference," snapped Catriona, walking quickly along, her arm still linked with Mark's, but jiggling her hips as furiously and uncomfortably as she possibly could.

Mark tugged her to a full stop. A few paces ahead of them, Rudyard Philips kept on striding purposefully forward, until he realised that he was alone. He stopped, turned, and waited for them, trying to appear interested in a window display of Holeproof Hosiery in beige, Airdale orchid, and sunburn.

"I don't know why you're so mad at me," Mark told Catriona. "I'm

120

giving you a gift, that's all. No strings attached, nothing. No corny seduction. It can't do anything to bring your daddy back to you, or give you any kind of comfort at all. But it's the best that I can do."

Catriona looked up at him, and his expression was so earnest that she felt both foolish and unfair. He was, after all, a fabulously rich young man, and a $35,000 necklace could probably be written off as business expenses —especially since it was a gift to the lady figurehead of the Keys Shipping Line. Perhaps, after all, he wasn't trying to get her into bed. But then that made her feel more irritated than ever, because he *ought* to have been. He may have been the high-and-mighty Mark Beeney, the Sheik of the Seas, but she was the Queen of the Atlantic, and he had no right at all to ignore her. She said in exasperation, "I feel like a cigarette."

"Here," said Mark, and offered her a handmade Turkish oval out of a gold case. He lit it for her with a lacquered lighter and watched her with faint amusement as she testily puffed out smoke.

"Will you take the necklace?" he asked her softly. "It would please me a whole lot if you did."

"I think you're very much more devious than you look," said Catriona.

"Devious? I'm the straightest guy in the world. You ask my accountant."

"You've got everything against you. You're too young and you're too good-looking and you're too rich."

"So what? You're in the same boat. Just look at you. You own a quarter share in a shipping line that's even bigger than mine. You make Clara Bow look like a pouting walrus. And you're twenty-one years old. You've got it made."

Catriona, without warning, snatched the diamond necklace out of his hand. "You're so rude that I think I'll take it," she said. But then, much more meltingly, because she was amused and pleased and comforted by Mark and his gift, she said, "And thank you. You've been really kind."

"Do I get a kiss?" asked Mark, smiling, and adjusting his necktie in anticipation.

Catriona, standing on tiptoes, lifted her lips to him and brushed his mouth so lightly that he scarcely knew that he had been kissed at all. It was enough, though. The closeness of her cheek, the warmth of her flowery perfume, and the way her breast had pressed against his arm. He held her wrist as she backed away from him, and said quietly, "Do I get to fasten the necklace, too?"

She held the necklace up to her throat, and then turned her back to him. Mark took the clasp out of her hands and fastened it. He held her shoulders firmly, longer than he needed to. Then he bent forward and kissed the nape of her neck, with that kind of lingering bruised-roses kiss that Hollywood thrived on. Catriona stayed where she was; she didn't want Mark to think that she was either repelled by his kiss or overexcited.

"Do you think we might get on?" asked Rudyard Philips plaintively. "We're getting a little pushed for time, and we still have the bridge to visit."

"Sure," said Mark in a breathy voice. "We can get on."

Catriona touched the cold glittering necklace and glanced at Mark with mischievous warmth.

"Did you read that article in the *Illustrated London News* about flying people across the Atlantic in giant aeroplanes?" asked Mark as they followed Rudyard Philips up the companionway towards the *Arcadia's* bridge.

"Do you really believe that's possible?" Rudyard replied.

"Sure it's possible," Mark asserted. "All you have to do is build an aeroplane that carries enough fuel to fly from coast to coast, and you're in business. They carry the mail by air, don't they, and from what I've heard they regularly bring bootleg liquor in from Canada by aeroplane. Then there's that fellow who flies people from Los Angeles to Reno for quick divorces. If they can do all that, why can't they carry a few dozen people from London to New York?"

At last they reached the bridge, and Rudyard ushered them in. "Do you think anybody would be foolhardy enough to put money into such an enterprise?"

Mark grinned. "I wouldn't. You're never going to be able to persuade your cabin-class traveller people can actually cross the Atlantic without passing out from the lack of roast canvasback duck and marble bathtubs with gold-plated taps."

Sir Peregrine Arrowsmith was on the bridge this afternoon, incongruously but majestically seated in a large Victorian library chair which he had asked Keys Shipping to install for the occasional relief of his sciatica. On the chart table beside him was spread a small cold snack of hare pâté and assorted sandwiches, with a conspicuously large and effervescent glass of mineral water. He rose stiffly as Rudyard Philips brought Catriona and Mark onto the bridge and saluted. He looked rather grey and drawn, but he managed to kiss Catriona's hand and bow with old-fashioned courtesy to Mark.

"I trust you are finding your tour of my little ship entertaining?" He smiled, with a crusty effort at humour. "She's quite a stylish young lady, isn't she?"

"She's very fine, Sir Peregrine," said Mark. "My daddy would have given his only son to take the bridge of a ship like this."

"The very latest equipment," said Sir Peregrine, indicating the rows of softly shining dials, the gyrocompass, the electric telegraph; and the streamlined art-deco wheel. Through the forward windows, Catriona could see the narrow elegant bows of the *Arcadia* cleaving their way through the dappled green Irish Sea, sending up spasmodic plumes of white spray; and far ahead of her, in the distance, a darker line on the horizon that looked like land.

"That's Ireland," Sir Peregrine nodded. "We anchor in Dublin Bay at five and stay until eight o'clock tonight. Taking on mail, you see, and a few more dignitaries. Not my choice, but there you are. When you're only a sea captain, you have to do what your company tells you to do, what?"

Dick Charles was standing by the wheel, and he turned around to frown at Sir Peregrine with such an expression of mock despair that it was all Catriona could do not to laugh.

"Ireland, very odd place," muttered Sir Peregrine. "You can't trust them, you see, the Irish. I played chess once with Andrew Bonar Law, and do you know what he said? 'Peregrine,' he said, 'when the Irish can prove to me beyond any shadow of a doubt that the ten per cent of the population who aren't insane aren't murderously malicious, then they can have their home rule by return of post.' "

Catriona peered into two or three of the *Arcadia*'s softly effulgent dials. "What's this one for?" she asked Dick Charles. She noticed the crewman at the wheel give her that kind of sideways squint with which private soldiers and naval ratings and automobile mechanics always appraise the tastier-looking wives and daughters of what Trimmer would have called "haristocrats and hofficers."

Dick Charles went very pink and said, "That's our wind-speed indicator. Our anemometer. It t-tells us our p-p-p—"

There was a very long pause. Sir Peregrine offered his fourth officer no assistance, but stood lean and dried up and emaciated, like a Bombay duck in full uniform, while Dick Charles opened and closed his mouth and stared at Catriona as if he were about to blow up.

"Precise wind velocity," he said, quite suddenly. "At the moment it's eleven point four. You see there? Quite average for the t-time of—"

He tried hard, but he couldn't find the strength to utter the first "y" of "year," and he withdrew flustered.

"How fast are we going now?" Catriona asked cheerfully, to cover Dick Charles' embarrassment.

"Thirteen and a half knots," said Sir Peregrine. "But we're beginning to slow down. We don't want to cut Ireland in half. At least, some of us don't."

"How fast will we have to sail to win the Blue Riband?" Catriona asked.

Sir Peregrine, rather crossly, cleared his throat and turned away. It was not protocol for a liner captain to admit that he was trying for a record crossing. On the instructions of his company, he would simply sail his vessel at maximum speed, and if by good fortune he happened to outrun every other express liner on the Atlantic, and if by chance the purser happened to have on board a supply of celebratory Blue Ribands which could be tied around the stems of the passengers' champagne glasses when they reached New York, then that, naturally, was a bonus. But a captain never *tried* for a record, and especially not a British captain. That kind of behaviour would rank him as a show-off.

Mark Beeney put Sir. Peregrine out of his discomfiture. "The *Mauretania* has been the fastest liner on the Atlantic since 1907," he told Catriona quietly. "She can hit twenty-seven knots when she's really running, which means anything up to six hundred and fifty miles a day. All the *Arcadia* has to do is beat that. It would be quite a bonus for you if she did, of course. Your bookings would go up, and so would the market value of your ship. So you can see that I wouldn't exactly crack open a bottle of champagne to help you celebrate."

"We should be able to manage it," put in Rudyard Philips stiffly. "We have the very latest steam turbines, capable of more than 85,000 horsepower. God and the weather willing, we should be the toast of the Atlantic by the time we reach New York harbour."

"I'd rather you tempted neither the Almighty nor the elements, Mr. Philips," said Sir Peregrine. "I have enough difficulties as it is, what with Mr. Douglas Fairbanks aboard, and my sciatica."

He settled back in his chair and morosely began to chew at his hare pâté, while Rudyard Philips with tedious efficiency set out to explain to Catriona how the ship's steering system worked, and how she could be handled in rough seas, and how every major function of the massive marine engines could be monitored at a glance. Catriona yawned. Mark, however, was interested in absolutely everything, though his ceaseless technical questions obviously grated on Sir Peregrine's nerves, for the old commodore shifted in his seat and chewed his toast with the steady ferocity of a skua, and didn't stop muttering to himself until they were ready to leave.

But Catriona said sweetly, "Thank you, Sir Peregrine. I'm sorry about your sciatica. It must be dreadful. Thank you for being so kind." And she bent over his chair before the old man could summon up the energy to stand up, and kissed him on the forehead. He sat back again, speechless.

"Now the lower decks and the engine room," said Rudyard Philips. He peered surreptitiously down at his wrist watch and wished this tour were over, so that he could quickly go round to Mademoiselle Narron's stateroom and confront her. Well, it wasn't so much Mademoiselle Narron he needed to confront. It was himself, and all those geysering emotions that Mademoiselle Narron had released in him. He had to talk to her again, talk to her face-to-face, and find out what the hell was happening to him.

"Do you mind if I smoke?" he asked Catriona as they stepped into the electric lift which would take them down to lower deck G on the *Arcadia*'s waterline.

"You can burst into flames if you want to," said Catriona. Corny humour was one of the youthful enthusiasms of 1924. Even a respectable sporting magazine had suggested that mixed foursomes should take care how they played on the "petting green."

"By the way," said Rudyard Philips, pinching out his used match and funnelling smoke from his nostrils, "this is only one of ten electric lifts aboard the *Arcadia*. Each lift is designed in a different motif, according to where it goes. The library lift is lined with bronze and steel bas-reliefs of books, with all their pages flying out. This one, as you can see, has ship's wheels and compasses all over it. And the lift that goes to the swimming pool has mermaids and waves."

"I haven't even seen the swimming pool yet," said Catriona.

Rudyard Philips checked his watch, more for his own benefit than for hers. "There's a ladies-only swim session at five o'clock, if you're interested." Then, unexpectedly, he looked up and said, "That's a pretty wonderful necklace, if you don't mind my saying so."

"All women appreciate diamonds," Mark Beeney grinned. "If there's a woman in your life, give her diamonds. She'll love you forever."

Rudyard gave a dismissive shrug, half-bitter, half-joking. Even if I could afford diamonds, who would I give them to? To Toy, who right at this minute is probably lying in my marriage bed with "Uncle Laurence," relieved that I've gone? Or to Mademoiselle Narron, whose hot and powerful thigh has started such an upsurge of unwelcome and uncontrollable sensations? First officers on Keys Shipping Line were only paid one pound a day, and on one pound a day you couldn't afford anything from Van Cleef & Arpels.

"Are you all right, Mr. Philips?" Catriona asked him. "You look pale."

The lift hummed to a stop, and the doors slid open. The noise of the *Arcadia*'s engines was much louder down here, and there was a penetrating odor of grease and paint and hot steam. "I'm fine, thank you," he said in a dullish sort of voice, as if he were answering a question in a merchant marine examination; and then, nipping out his Gold Flake cigarette and tucking it back into the yellow and gold box, "Shall I lead on?"

He stepped out of the lift and began to walk along the cream-painted corridor. Catriona and Mark both started to follow him, but they collided with each other as they reached the lift doors.

They probably collided on purpose. It was one of those romantic little accidents that are so eye-poppingly obvious that even the people involved in them can't really believe that it actually happened by mistake.

Catriona stepped forward, but then Mark stepped forward and collided with her again; and then, at the third collision, they got it right. Mark held her very quickly and strongly in his arms, and lowered his face towards hers, his lips slightly parted and his eyes as intent as a baseball player who knows that his last pitch has just got to be his best ever.

Catriona said, "This is *mad*. This is just like the pictures." But she gripped the sleeve of his blazer as he held her tighter, and when he kissed her, gently at first, but then harder, and more greedily, she did nothing to resist him. The lift doors closed just as Rudyard Philips was turning around to see why they weren't following him; and then they were borne upwards again with a warm electric hum, alone in their compass-decorated cubicle. Middle deck F, upper deck E, saloon deck D.

Once she was actually in his arms, Catriona found Mark's masculinity to be overwhelming. His body, through the softness of his beautifully cut wool blazer, felt uncompromisingly hard and athletic. His chin was shaved perfectly smooth, and was aromatic with some lemony, grassy cologne. He kissed with a controlled fierceness which she thought, in the first few seconds, would be resistible; but then she found that the inside of her head was echoing with vibrant and unexpected desire, and that the seam of her camisole was adhering damply between her thighs, like the wings of a butterfly caught in a summer storm.

"My God," she said, wrestling his arm away. "Mark."

He stood straight, grinning, a smudge of her Red Neon lipstick on the side of his mouth, quite unabashed by her struggling.

"You know something?" he asked her. "You are the softest, most fragrant, most feminine thing afloat. Do you know what you've done to me?"

She held her arm protectively across her breasts. She could feel her own nipples through the thin blue silk, as tight as buttons. "I don't care what I've done to you."

The doors of the electric lift hummed apart, and there stood two first-class passengers in wide white ducks, smiling at them inanely. Mark said smoothly, "Excuse us," and piloted Catriona out onto the saloon deck. It was teatime now, and the passengers were gravitating towards the Grand Lounge for cucumber sandwiches and Belgian gateaux and hot scones with strawberry preserve and clotted cream. The Arcadia's jazz band was playing "Ain't We Got Fun" among the frondy palms.

"Will you join me for tea?" asked Mark.

Catriona shook her head. "You go and rescue your girlfriend from the beauty parlour. I feel like a cold swim."

Mark lifted his straw boater. "It's been a pleasure."

Catriona couldn't help smiling. "It usually is," she said. "And thank you for the necklace. It's perfect."

"Do you want me to comment on that?" said Mark.

"No," said Catriona, and pressed the lift button to take her back to promenade deck A.

Sixteen

The *Arcadia* dropped her anchors off Dun Laoghaire, south of Dublin Bay, twenty-five minutes earlier than expected. The bay was crowded with dinghies and lighters and pleasure boats, tooting their whistles and letting off firecrackers. The giant liner was three hundred feet too long to be negotiated into Dublin harbour itself, and all her mail and passengers would have to be brought aboard by cutter, but that hadn't discouraged the Irish from giving her a noisy and cheerful welcome.

Sir Peregrine would have preferred not to stop in Ireland at all, but apart from being a political courtesy, the visit had been made imperative by the simple fact that Keys Shipping owed the Eire Credit Bank more than £400,000. Much of the *Arcadia*'s steel plating had been bought with Irish money, on the understanding that she would dock regularly on her way to and from New York at Queenstown or Dublin. Some of the Irish bankers had actually tried to persuade Edgar Deacon to terminate the *Arcadia*'s Atlantic run at Galway, on the west coast of Ireland, where ambitious investors of the 1860s had constructed a huge and lavish hotel in the hope that all transatlantic crossings would depart and arrive at Galway Bay. The hotel still stood, massively out of proportion to the small run-down town which clustered around it, but Edgar Deacon, with the blunt support of Catriona's father, had firmly resisted any suggestion that Keys Shipping might create a precedent and make use of it. "We might as well sail from bloody Oslo," Stanley Keys had growled.

Dick Charles stood by the rail as the Keys cutter, varnished and polished and flapping with celebratory bunting, came bucking and spraying out across the bay. On the *Arcadia*, by way of greeting, the brass section of the ship's orchestra had been mustered on the raised foredeck and were playing "When Irish Eyes Are Smiling" into the gusty breeze. The shadows of cumulus clouds moved across the sea like memories, and in the far distance, over the dappled and densely green hills of Dublin and Wicklow, a half-rainbow rose as if by magic.

There was no seafaring tradition in Dick's family at all, and it always rather surprised him that he had become an officer on an ocean liner. He had been brought up near the sea, in Deal, on the south Kent coast, but his father had been a grocer, and his older brother Robert had gone into the Army catering corps. Dick had been a lonely boy, lonelier because of his impossible stutter, and the two most lasting impressions he carried of his childhood were of sitting on two biscuit tins in the dark hidey hole behind the counter in his father's shop drinking ginger beer out of a stone bottle and reading *Tiger Tim's Weekly;* and of walking out all on his own across the breezy marshes in his galoshes and his mackintosh to look for herons' eggs. The galoshes (which had been Robert's) had been far too big for him, and he had sometimes pretended that he was the giant in the seven-league boots.

Dick had been advised to go to sea by a senile careers master who had smelled strongly of urine, chalk, and bottled India ale, and who had lost all three of his sons in 1909 on the British steamer *Waratah*, which had disappeared on its way from Sydney to London with three hundred people aboard. Perhaps the careers master had seen Dick as a reincarnation of one of his boys. Dick never knew. But he *had* known that he didn't want to be a grocer, and so he had written to Cunard, White Star, and Keys, asking what he had to do to become a ship's officer.

He liked the Atlantic run, because in spite of his stutter and his bashful appearance, he was very sociable, and he always enjoyed the company of giggly young girls with too much champagne in them, and the loud bonhomie of wealthy and overindulgent businessmen. Life on an ocean liner might be artificial—a community of two thousand strangers dancing and drinking and romancing and telling ridiculous lies to each other for four and a half days—but it was a life in which Dick felt important and even glamorous. He wasn't as overtly lustful as most of the officers, who used to line the gangway at the beginning of each voyage, ostensibly to welcome the passengers on board, but in reality to size up their bunk companions for the coming few days. One White Star officer had already described the de luxe Atlantic liners of the early 1920s as "floating fuck-a-toria." But Dick had been through four or five quite seemly little affairs with girls he had met on board, and two of them still wrote to him. One, a dark-haired little co-ed from Creighton University in Omaha, always ended her letters by imprinting a scarlet kiss at the foot of the page.

On this voyage, of course, there were enough pretty and dizzy young flappers to bring even the most carnal of ship's officers to a standstill, or at least down to "slow ahead." There was a party of twenty-six girls from Louisiana State, returning by second class from a tour of Italy, half of whom were still giddy from the romantic attentions of Neapolitan romeos, and the other half of whom (ignored by the Neapolitan romeos) were grimly determined to win the romantic attentions of anyone, just *anyone*, before the *Arcadia* crossed the three-mile limit. There was a female dance troupe from Yonkers, sponsored by Happiness candy, who were on their way back from a tour of American troops in Europe. And there was a breathless, bare-shouldered, eyelid-fluttering, hotly frustrated abundance of businessmen's wives and mistresses, just aching to be taken into a secluded corner and shown the phosphorescence of the *Arcadia*'s wake on a moonlit night in mid-Atlantic.

It was one of these women ("fallow Floras," the chief second-class steward always called them, since they had been ploughed in years gone by, but not recently) who was now brazenly admiring Dick from the promenade deck below the bridge. She was forty years old at least, but she had a delicate fine-boned face that had kept its freshness, and responded well to Exotica night cream. She wore a green cloche hat which matched her eyes, and a ankle-length raccoon coat, which she kept wrapped around herself in a way that suggested she was very warm in there, warm as toast, and wouldn't Dick like to be as warm as that, too? She had a spattering of pale freckles across her nose which gave her the appearance of impish innocence.

When Dick looked quickly in her direction, the woman smiled and gave him a squiggly little wave with her fingers. Dick blushed, and touched the peak of his cap in acknowledgement.

Ralph Peel, the second officer, came up behind Dick from the wheelhouse, his hands clasped behind his back. "Ho ho," he said in a voice as thick as rubbed flake tobacco, "that one's taken a fancy to you. Now you're for it."

"You know h-h-her?" asked Dick.

"Course I do. You should recognise her yourself. Or p'raps you only read the *Boys' Own Paper*."

"Who is she?"

Ralph Peel came to the rail of the boat deck and happily folded his arms over it. He was a short stubby man from Portsmouth, Hampshire, with a face that was always glossy from shaving, and eyebrows that were so dark they looked as if he had pencilled them in with mascara. He prided himself on his sleek hairy chest, and his sleek hairy back, and his very sleek and hairy legs. Sir Peregrine had nicknamed him the Performing Seal.

"That lady," said Ralph Peel, saluting her cheekily, "is Lady Diana FitzPerry."

"You d-d-don't m-mean *the* Lady Diana FitzP—FitzP—"

"The same," Ralph Peel told him with malicious amusement. "The one who was supposed to be riding half of the House of Lords, and a good seven percent of the Conservative Front Bench, while her husband was out in the Sudan trying to build railways for the dervishes."

"B-but she's *w-waving* at me," said Dick.

"So she is. And that's why you're for it. I warn you, Dick my boy, once a lady like that has taken a liking to you, you won't get away without giving her what she wants."

"Oh, d-dear," said Dick.

Ralph nudged him with his elbow. "I don't know what you're worrying about. She's not exactly a spring chicken, I'll grant you. But if half of the peers of the realm like her, and if seven per cent of Stanley Baldwin's lot think she's worth a go round the park, she can't be all that bad. I saw her photo in the *Sunday Pic*. Nice pear-shaped English upperclass lady, I'd say. Plenty to get hold of. You should enjoy yourself. Perhaps she'll teach you how to eat your peas off your knife without dropping them all down your shirtfront. You could do with a bit of class, you could. Now's your chance."

"God," said Dick, "you're absolutely incoh—incoh—"

"Incoherent?"

"Incoh—"

"Incorruptible? Incommunicado? In Korea?"

"Incorrigible," said Dick at last.

"I don't know," Ralph Peel told him. "I just hope they never put you in charge of a ship when we have to make an emergency turn to port. Can you imagine it? 'Hard ap—, hard ap—, hard ap—!' We'd be sitting on the bottom of the sea before you managed to say 'hard a-port!' "

"My speech imp—speech impediment isn't *all* that bad," retorted Dick. "It only gets worse when p-people like you start r-ragging me."

Ralph Peel's smile widened with the contentment of a man who has all the authority he can happily handle, all the drink he ever needs, plenty of good food, a different woman every week, and one pound a day. He was a man without any complexes whatsoever. He smoked, drank, danced with the lady passengers, and had the longest and most preposterous line about the time he had wrestled a shark with his bare hands in the swimming pool of the old *Eximious* (a freak wave having tossed it on board). To him, Dick's callow alarm at the attention he was receiving from the notorious Lady FitzPerry was a good broad joke. Wonderful. He couldn't wait to tell Monty Willowby about it.

"Can't you just picture it?" he said. "Big white wobbly thighs bulging out of shiny silk stockings. It's the real blue-blooded thing, Dick my lad. Education by Roedean, knickers by Harrods, wedding ring by Aspreys. She'll devour you alive and you'll enjoy every bite."

Dick glanced out of the corner of his eyes at the furry Lady FitzPerry, and she was still smiling at him. "I think I've got a heh," he said. Then, "I think I've got a heh," then, "I think I've got a headache."

Ralph Peel slapped him good-naturedly on the back. "You'll get over it," he said. "Or *under* it, eh? Ho-ho."

"I suppose you're already fixed up," said Dick. "Well, you must be. I've never known you not f-fixed up."

"Well, to tell you the truth, I am," admitted Ralph. "A rather tricky little sheba from the University of Somewhere Boring, in the middle of America. Very cute. Blond. Plenty of It." But there are one or two more I've got my eye on. An heiress, one of them. Very tasty."

"That sh-should suit you d-down to the g-ground," said Dick. 'Sh—she's full of 'It' and y-you're full of sh—sh—."

Ralph slapped him on the back again. "Never mind, Dick. You'll get over it one day. Meanwhile, enjoy yourself with Lady FitzPee."

At that moment, Sir Peregrine emerged from the captain's sitting room, which was next to the navigation room. At the same moment, Dick said, "Shit," and Sir Peregrine stared at him as if he were quite mad, and said, "I beg your pardon, Mr. Charles?"

Dick turned maroon with embarrassment. He didn't feel any better when Lady FitzPerry waved at him again, a quick girlish wave, and called, "Coo-ee!"

Sir Peregrine said with statuesque patience, "Do you think it might be advisable for me to go back to my sitting room and come out afresh?"

By now, the Keys cutter from Dublin harbour had come alongside, and its passengers were coming aboard. As it turned out, there were only five of them: Denis O'Hara from the Eire Credit Bank, and his lady wife; Colleen Sullivan, the Irish singer, who had been booked to appear in the long-running *Abie's Irish Rose* on Broadway; the American golfer Jack Andrews; and a very tall fleshy-lipped man of about fifty who wore a broad-brimmed hat and a calf-length summer overcoat, and about whom nothing was announced. He spoke with a distinctive New York accent, that was all anybody could tell.

The newcomers were brought by Monty Willowby up to the boat deck, where Sir Peregrine shook them abstractedly by the hand, and welcomed them aboard, and trusted they would enjoy their voyage on his little ship (Ha, ha), and invited them, with all the charm of a man who is trying to remember where he left his second pair of spectacles to share his table that evening.

Colleen Sullivan, to Sir Peregrine's acute annoyance, then sang a very slow and very Irish interpretation of the original Charleston, flinging her arms out at every high note, and continually tossing her trailing scarf over her shoulder. Jack Andrews, who was spiffily dressed in patterned golfing socks, baggy knickers, and a bow tie, took off his cap and pretended that he was taking a collection for her. "With a voice like that, who needs to sing?" he quipped.

Although nobody noticed him, there was a sixth new passenger: a handsome-looking middle-aged man with chestnut hair that had been allowed to grow rather longer than the fashion of 1924 dictated: that is, it actually covered the tops of his ears. He had appeared to be one of the tweed-jacketed journalists who had accompanied Denis O'Hara and the rest of the Irish passengers out from Dublin harbour. At least, he had carried a bottle of Guinness in one sagging pocket and a dogeared note-book in the other, and in Ireland that was usually sufficient to establish a man's credentials as a member of the press. But when the cutter was untied, and when it was steered back in a foamy semicircle across Dublin Bay with its whistle piping, he was not among the journalists or the photographers or the smartly uniformed crew of the cutter, with their peaked caps as level as the tops of letter boxes and their collars buttoned up to their chins.

He was, in fact, still on board the *Arcadia*. He was folded up, in the words of that week's *Comic Cuts*, like a cheap penknife, in one of the linen cupboards on the first-class cabin deck. The cupboard was smother-ingly warm, to keep the linen well aired, and he was sweating like a cheese. But he preferred the heat and the contortions to the prospect of facing his creditors in Dublin.

His name was Maurice Peace. He had been born in Smackover, in Union County, Arkansas, and he was a one-time prestidigitator, small-arms runner, singer of political songs, slack-wire walker, and meadow violinist. These days, however, he was a full-time gambler.

Seventeen

Catriona was swimming alone in the *Arcadia*'s heated pool while Denis O'Hara and his lady wife were being welcomed aboard. It was peaceful and still in the pool, with only the faintest slopping of the water against the gold mosaic tiles and the distant echo of the brass band; an arched sanctuary of palm trees and marble pillars and mosaic tiers. At the far end of the pool, a bubbling waterfall, lit with orange lights, coursed effusively down seventeen steps before splashing into a kidney-shaped whirl bath; and by the windows, a curved nickel-plated cocktail bar offered cham-pagne or fresh fruit juice to swimmers who had finished swimming, or swimmers who really preferred to stay quite dry and simply show off their new French bathing costumes. It was still very risqué to bare one's upper thighs, after all. Only two years ago, in Chicago, a whole bevy of bathing belles who had dared to swim in short bathing suits had been manhandled into a paddy wagon for alleged indecency and fined.

Catriona's bathing costume was in pink silk, designed by Madeleine Vionnet in a style which she called "La Rose de L'Infante," because of the Spanish roses around the short ruffled skirt. The costume was an unusual combination of the demure and the erotic: the pink silk top clung like a second skin, transparently revealing Catriona's nipples as she bathed, whereas the skirt was as coy as a frill round the leg of a piano. To cover her bobbed hair, Catriona wore a tight pink cap of treated silk, sewn with patterns of seed pearls.

She had asked Edgar Deacon if she should be up on the boat deck to greet the O'Haras, but Edgar had told her that it really wasn't necessary. He didn't want to trouble her with the tedious formalities of shaking hands with an Irish banker and his lady wife; nor a golfer in funny socks; nor a would-be heroine of the Broadway stage. Besides, he preferred to produce her at tonight's banquet as a glamorous and glittering surprise, all dressed up like a fashion plate from *La Gazette du Bon Ton*.

There was another reason. He didn't yet want to have to introduce her to the tall fiftyish man in the long summer overcoat and the broad-brimmed hat. He wanted her to meet him later, in more controllable circumstances, and for a very particular purpose.

As Catriona languidly floated on the surface of the swimming pool, kicking her legs now and then, and looking up dreamily at the bronze-clad arches of the ceiling, she thought of Mark Beeney.

He disturbed her, and attracted her, as he must have attracted almost every girl who came within the radius of his smile. After all, she thought, he's handsome and charming, and any man who gives you a diamond and ruby necklace worth thousands of dollars without asking for more than a peck on the cheek in return must have some sort of style. Yet, there seemed to be very much more to him. He wasn't just an American cake eater with too much money and a gift for undermining a young girl's honour just when she thought she was clinging on to it the tightest. There was a complicated remoteness about him which made her feel as if he had something on his mind apart from necking. He was an interesting man, even a dangerous one. So dangerous that as she circled around the pool she found herself thinking about him as if they were lovers already.

Suddenly she heard the sounds of an argument echoing loudly from the pool's entrance hall. A woman's voice first of all, high and histrionic and very foreign; and then the voice of the steward who was assigned to keep a discreet watch on the doors during ladies' hour to keep away peekers.

"This is quite absurd!" the foreign woman was shrilling. "The pool is practically empty, and how can you say that Sabran is anything but a decoration! He comes with me wherever I go! And if *I* wish to go to the pool in the ladies' hour, then *he* shall come with me to the pool at ladies' hour also!"

Catriona swam to the steps at the shallow end of the pool and climbed out. Alice, who had been sitting on a narrow bentwood chair in the corner reserved for servants, brought her a huge white Turkish towel, and wrapped it around her shoulders. "What's going on?" Catriona asked her.

"It's Baroness Zawisza, Miss Keys. I think she's trying to bring her young man into the swimming bath."

Catriona put her feet up one after the other onto the chair so that Alice could dry them. Then she slipped on her pink silk mules and walked, still wrapped in her towel, to the entrance. Alice followed at a respectable distance behind.

By the door, accompanied by two uniformed maids, one of whom was carrying an incredibly fluffed-up white poodle, stood a tall defiant woman in a floor-length cape of scarlet marocain, a study in bright-red fury and bright-red wool. The cape was trimmed with a plumed collar of brown speckled feathers in which the woman's magnificent Slavic head, white as alabaster, with deep-set black eyes and black hair which had been scraped back and fastened with scarlet combs, nestled like an animated death mask.

Beside the woman, indifferently smoking a Da Capo cigarette, slouched a bony youth in a white silk shirt and voluminous black silk Oxford bags.

"You are completely without imagination!" the baroness was snapping at the poor steward, who by now had turned extremely red. "You are a peasant, not fit to dig out potatoes! Tell him!" she said, suddenly turning to Catriona.

"He's only doing what he was ordered to do," said Catriona gently.

"He was ordered to make a fool of me?" demanded Baroness Zawisza.

"He was ordered to keep men out of the pool during the ladies' hour, that's all," Catriona told her. "You wouldn't want to see him lose his job, would you?"

"I demand to see Sir Peregrine!" cried the baroness dramatically. "I demand! I demand! I demand!"

"I don't think there's any need to disturb the captain," Catriona smiled. She was rather enjoying this. "I'm Catriona Keys, and this whole shipping line belongs to my family. Don't you think I could help you?"

The baroness frowned at Catriona, and then blew out her cheeks, making the feathers of her collar puff up like the tail of an irritated cockerel. "Poof!" she said. "What is it when I have to leave Sabran outside like a pet dog? Even worse than a pet dog. The dog is allowed inside the pool because the dog is a bitch."

"I think you can bring Sabran inside if you want to," Catriona told her. "There's only me in the pool at the moment, and Sabran doesn't look very threatening."

Sabran, who had been slouching against the side of the door, suddenly stood up straight, and stuck out his chin and tried his best to look very *apache*. Catriona touched the steward's arm, and said gently, "If you get any trouble from Mr. Willowby, just refer him to me."

"Yes, Miss Keys." The steward nodded. "And, thank you, Miss Keys."

Followed by her small entourage, Baroness Zawisza swept into the pool, circling around every now and then to show off the beautiful fall of her Worth cape. "We always used to swim on our estates at Wizajny when I was a girl. My father was magnificent, a broad-shouldered hero in blue and white striped wool, diving from the bridge into the lake! He made us all swim, my five brothers, myself, my four sisters. He said to swim is to live forever. Mind you, I think he was a little eccentric about health. He used to believe in electric shocks, for the galvanization of the body and then the two little ones would each have to pick up the bare terminal of an electric battery. How we all jumped! But I don't suppose it did us any harm."

Catriona said, with the slyness that only a pretty young girl half the baroness's age could have got away with, "It seems to have preserved you marvellously."

"Well," replied the baroness, tartly, "just because I can remember Poland before the war, that doesn't actually make me a certifiable antique. Krysia! My cape. I think I'll swim. Sabran, go to the bar and order champagne. I *hate* champagne," she confided to Catriona, "but unless you drink it all the time, and very conspicuously, people begin to suspect your heritage. Such a nuisance. Will you swim with me?"

One of the baroness's maids, a round-faced Polish girl who didn't appear to speak a single word of English, unfastened the rhinestone-decorated clasp at the baroness's neck and released the cape. Underneath, the baroness, who was as slender as a fashion plate, wore a black vee-necked bathing costume trimmed in silver, with daringly loose legs that came halfway down her white thighs like cami-knickers.

Sabrna, on his way to the bar, where a beige-jacketed stewardess in a jaunty cap was on hand to serve cocktails and wines, turned on one Cuban heel and applauded the baroness as she walked with aristocratic stateliness to the shallow end.

The baroness turned out to be a surprisingly good swimmer, propelling herself with effortless grace around the pool, changing smoothly from backstroke to butterfly stroke to a long-legged breaststroke.

"I think that's enough," she said, after ten minutes. "Father always used to say that you shouldn't allow yourself to become waterlogged."

Her maid Krysia brought her a towel and then a loose white Japanese wrap. Catriona, in her own silk robe, followed her to the small circular table by the cocktail bar where Sabran was sulkily sipping his champagne and tossing cashew nuts into his mouth with the aggressive expertise of someone who has spent many hours of his life waiting for rich women.

"Sabran goes to enormous lengths not to look *kept*," said the baroness, waving her fingers vaguely in the gigolo's direction for a cigarette. "He believes that it is against the fundamental laws of nature, or some such nonsense like that. I shouldn't have let him go to see *Her Gilded Cage*, I don't think. But I always say to him, don't I, Sabran, that to be kept is no disgrace, why should it be, and in any case it's very hard not to look kept when you're moody and thin like he is, and walk around everywhere in those ridiculous pants. Can you imagine trying to earn *any* kind of a living in pants like that?"

"You're a she-cat," said Sabran in a thick Gascony accent. He lit two Da Capos at once, puffing them furiously until the tips were aglow like bonfires, and then passed one to Baroness Zawisza.

"I don't really believe that one person can keep another," said Catriona. "Financially, yes, but not emotionally."

The baroness looked at her through the pungent smoke of her cigarette. "You have a love, is that it? A love you have recently parted?"

"I don't know whether we've parted forever."

"Nobody parts forever, my dear, not even when they're dead," said the baroness. "Death is a veil, that's all. That's what my mother used to tell me. In her younger days, before she married my father, she had a lover called Killinkoski, from Finland. He fell through the ice one winter on the lake we call Jezero Mamry, and drowned. But he visited her as a ghost for the rest of her life. Several times, she said, he even made love to her."

"I never hear such bunk," said Sabran.

The baroness smiled indulgently. "Sabran is trying to speak like an American. That's part of the reason we're sailing on the *Arcadia*. He wants to be a motion picture star in Hollywood. Can you imagine? They'll take one look at his pants and scream with laughter."

"These pants are spee-fee," Sabran retorted.

"Oh, my God, isn't he marvellous!" shrieked the baroness. "It's *spiffy*, my gorgeous young hound. *Spee-fee*, can you imagine? Oh, my God, I think I'm going to choke."

Catriona said, "Have you known each other for long? I've never thought of a woman keeping a man before."

"Well, that's because you're still young, my dove," said the baroness, more serious now. "When you're young, you're resilient enough to put up with all the despair and the passions, the ups and downs, the heartbreak and the sheer damned inconvenience. But when you get—well, when you've lived as full a life as I have, in a comparatively *few* number of years, you begin to look for intimacies that are more controllable. And so what better than a young cowboy like Sabran?"

The baroness sipped champagne, sneezed, and then said in a loud whisper, "Besides, he's a marvellous lover. I can't tell you. He sends

136

shivers down my spine. Not that I'd ever tell that, of course. He'd become too arrogant. He's arrogant enough now. Look at him! If he curls his lip any more it'll disappear up his nose."

"Do you love him?" asked Catriona. In normal circumstances, and to the sort of ladies that Catriona had known in London, to ask a question like that right in front of the lover himself would have been unthinkable. But somehow the baroness had made it quite clear that Sabran was her trained animal, that he did what he was told, and that if he argued with her he would be in danger of losing everything.

"Love?" queried the baroness, raising an eyebrow that had been plucked as thin as the edge of a razor blade. "How can I talk of love? I used to know what it was once. Now, I have more doubts than answers."

While she was saying this, the stewardess behind the bar happened to drop a highball glass and smash it. Catriona turned towards the bar to see what was happening, and to her shocked fascination she saw not only the stewardess but what was reflected in the buffed-up nickel steel that formed the curved art-deco counter.

Underneath the small circular table at which they sat, Sabran had quietly slipped off one of his Cuban-heeled shoes and rolled off his sock. He had then lifted his foot and, with his toes, carefully peeled the wet leg of the baroness's swimming costume away from her thigh, baring the moist curls of her vulva. Even as they chatted of love and Finnish ghosts and gigolos, Sabran was steadily thrusting his big toe in and out of the baroness, to the accompaniment of a sticky little noise that was almost completely masked by the bubbling of the fountain and the slapping of ripples in the pool. It was impossible to make out what Sabran was doing in great detail, because of the mistiness of the nickel, but Catriona could see that his toe was disappearing completely; and the hazy impression of wet black satin and white skin was overpoweringly provocative.

Catriona felt a prickling sensation around the scalp and a sense that this conversation had suddenly lost touch with reality. "Love," she said, trying to remember what they had been talking about.

"You are the *right* age for love," replied the baroness, drinking more champagne and never once sparing even a glance for Sabran. "You have exactly the right chemistry—beauty and poise—and just the right measure of faintly soiled innocence. Also, you are still capable of knowing what love really is. One can lose this capability as one grows . . . well, as one learns more. Tell me about your lover."

"I'm not sure of his name," said Catriona.

"You don't even know who he is? Is he so mysterious?"

"No . . . I'm not sure *which* he is."

"Aha, you have left one lover behind, and now you believe that you may have come across another! Well, that is splendid! You must give yourself as you think fit. Love is one reason for giving yourself. Money is another. Still another is to hurt."

"You think I might want to *hurt* a boy, by falling in love with him?" asked Catriona.

"Of course. You're what—nineteen, twenty, twenty-one? That's the age of maximum conceit in a girl, and minimum sentiment. You don't have to look so much like a bewildered waif with me, you know. I now just what you're up to. Ohh, *doucement*, Sabran, for God's sake."

Catriona tried to ignore the baroness's little gasp of pain. She drank her champagne and watched the baroness's dark deep-set eyes as if they were the eyes of an oracle. Perhaps the oracle could tell her what she ought to do about Mark Beeney. Perhaps, on the other hand, the answer was already formed, even before the question had been fully phrased.

"Boys, anyway," said the baroness, "boys are always getting hurt. They enjoy it. There's nothing a boy likes better than a good mope."

"He's a man, really."

"A man? Hmm, I see from your expression that he is. Well, men can be just as easily hurt as boys; but the problem with men is that sometimes they retaliate and hurt you back. Quite desperately, on occasions. When you're least expecting it."

For a moment, Baroness Zawisza closed her eyes, and the sharp lines of her Slavic cheekbones were hectically flushed. She seemed unconscious to everything around her, not for very long, only the time it would have taken to squeeze the bulb of a plate camera, and for the lens to click, and for the photographer to emerge from his cape with the amused announcement that he had taken a candid portrait of her in the middle of a deep but powerfully disciplined orgasm.

"Men," said the baroness, opening her eyes again as if nothing had happened, "men are only interested in three things: automobiles, fighting, and their own semen. In normal circumstances, the simplicity of these interests makes them laughably easy creatures to handle. But sometimes, they get all three interests confused, and that is when you have to be careful of your own self, and your own soul, not to mention your four-thousand-franc dresses."

Catriona was silent for a long time. Not because she was perplexed or depressed, but because the relentless cynicism of Baroness Zawisza's attitude towards men had restored her confidence in herself. That had been partly what was wrong with her relationship with Nigel. She had allowed herself to be carried along in a bright social whirl, all parties and cocktails and silly undergraduate stunts; and the brightness of the whirl had kept her from seeing how shallow and inconsequential her love affair actually was. Nigel had been fun, and she knew that he had loved her, and probably loved her still, but dancing the Charleston on the tabletops in the Trocadero and throwing streamers out of open Austins wasn't exactly the stuff that great romances were made of. In her mind, she was now approaching Mark Beeney as a woman, not as a girl. She tried to think of her own strength, her own willpower, her own independence. This was going to be something fierce and real, one ego clashing with another ego just as strong. This was going to be something fierce and real, one ego clashing with another ego just as strong. This was going to be the kind of passion that burst like a thunderclap, like the passion between Rudolph Valentino and Alla Nazimova.

"A thousand zlotys for your thoughts." The baroness smiled.

Catriona slowly shook her head. "I was only thinking about something that happened a long time ago."

"How long?"

"Two years."

The baroness tightened up her wrap. "Yes," she said, "I suppose, to you, that *would* be a long time ago."

Eighteen

By seven o'clock it had grown prematurely and spectacularly dark. A bank of thundery cumulus had risen from the southwestern hills like the dust of an approaching multitude, and a few minutes before seven a sudden wind had sprung up, damp and warm and smelling of rain. The surface of Dublin Bay had grown grey and restless, and a few of the smaller craft which still bobbed around the sheer black walls of the *Arcadia*'s sides had headed for Dun Laoghaire, or further to the north, to Howth Head.

"The great forces of nature, Mr. Philips," Sir Peregrine said with undisguised irritation. "Damn and blind them."

"Thundery showers *were* forecast, sir," said Rudyard as the first fat drops of rain splattered onto the windows of the wheelhouse.

"Forecast? Forecast? Don't know what the devil *that's* got to do with it. Just because they were forecast doesn't mean I've got to *like* them, does it?"

"No, sir," said Rudyard, trying to be reasonable.

Sir Peregrine took out his watch and peered at it disapprovingly, as if he were in half a mind to throw it out of the wheelhouse window. There was a marine chronometer on the wheelhouse wall, accurate to within thousandths of a second, but Sir Peregrine would only trust his own watch. His papa had given it to him, on the first day he went to sea, from

Harwich. He had never seen his papa again (Hodgkin's Disease), and that memory of his papa, standing on Parkeston Quay in his tall black hat, not smiling, not waving, was the only memory of him that Sir Peregrine had. Why hadn't papa waved? he sometimes thought. He could, at the very least, have waved.

"Are we ready to go, Mr. Philips?" asked Sir Peregrine. "All passengers aboard, all lines clear? Got rid of all those Irish hooligans, have we?"

"We're ready to leave on time, sir," said Rudyard flatly. "Twenty hundred hours precisely."

"Twenty hundred hours," growled Sir Peregrine. "Another hour of lollygagging about, just to please those mad ginger-haired Fenians. I would rather have anchored of Semarang, in the middle of the fever season. At least the bloody Javanese don't go mad on purpose."

"Yes, sir," said Rudyard, with considerable patience. He had knocked at Mademoiselle Narron's stateroom earlier on, but there had been no reply. Perhaps she had been shopping or promenading or taking tea, but whatever it was, he was now going to have to spend six or seven hours more in stifled uncertainty before he would have the time or the opportunity to face her again.

The sky was now so thunderous that Sir Peregrine ordered all the ship's deck lights lit, as well as the decorative lights that outlined the masts and the funnels and the rigging. Somebody on shore must have taken this as a signal that the *Arcadia* was preparing to get under way, because almost instantly there was a distant crackling and popping, and a sparkling array of red and gold fireworks were set off on the shores of Dun Laoghaire.

"Damned fools," complained Sir Peregrine.

The banquet had been arranged for eight-thirty, half an hour after the *Arcadia* left Dublin Bay. In the first-class staterooms, men were already standing with pained expressions on their faces, their arms rigidly by their sides, while stewards with their tongues clenched between their teeth tried to tie their bow ties for them. Enough hot water had been expended on bathing the first-class passengers alone to float a small fishing boat with a draft of seven feet. The air was dense with Isabey perfume and Klida face powder and Pétrole Hahn for those ladies who wanted *l'ondulation* in their hair. There was a feeling of excitement on every level of the entire nine-storey liner, a warmly muted hubbub as more than two thousand people prepared to celebrate their first night at sea together on the world's largest and most lavish ship. Now it would be real sea, too, not just the narrow confines of the Irish Sea and St. George's Channel. When the sun woke them tomorrow morning, after their night of dancing and eating and celebrating, they would be well out into the Atlantic, and the *Arcadia* would be cleaving through the waves at full speed on her way to New York.

Julius Fields, the celebrated American travel writer and bon viveur, wrote in the red alligator-skin notepad which Keys Shipping had supplied gratis to all first-class passengers that "the sibilant sound of 150 wealthy ladies simultaneously slipping their pale and perfumed thighs into 150 pairs of pure silk step-ins by Jeanne Lanvin must have been enough to set a male grasshopper's teeth on edge."

In the Grand Lounge, the stewards were giving the tables a last polish, setting out clean chromium-plated ashtrays, and making sure that everyone would have fresh dishes of cashews, pecans, and pistachios. In the kitchens it was like Hades—noisier and steamier than ever, with Monsieur Vincent close to total explosion, and his chefs clattering away at their ovens with a sound like three hundred suits of armour being thrown down a flight of stairs. In the first-class dining saloon, fresh orchids, trembling with moisture, were being arrayed in silver art-deco vases on every table.

The dinners that were being arranged in the second- and third-class saloons were almost as elaborate. In second, there were sprays of summer flowers from English gardens, and the passengers would feed on oxtail soup, salad, ices, and a choice of roasted suckling pig or beef Wellington. A small jazz band, called for the occasion the Arcadia Syncopated Jass Quintet, would play the latest hits while the second-class passengers dined, and then they would be entertained into the night by the Ted Bagley Sextet. In third, there would be chicken and roast beef and, oddly, Christmas crackers. Business suits and day dresses would, of course, be acceptable in third class. The menu said, "Dress, Informal."

While Sir Peregrine fretted on the bridge, Catriona was in her stateroom getting ready. At seven o'clock on the very dot, Trimmer came in with a silver tray, on which were laid a selection of tiny appetisers, red and black caviar, macadamia nuts, and crisply fried balls of breadcrumbs filled with chilled French cheeses. Trimmer then mixed Catriona a very cold shaker of gin and bitters, which he left on the sideboard for Alice to pour out. "I don't want to hoffend by dodging hin and hout," he explained. Catriona said, "That's hall right," and giggled. Trimmer seemed to take her teasing in good humour.

Catriona felt fizzy with anticipation, and couldn't stop talking. Tonight she was going to wear a silver lace evening dress by Beer, scooped right down to the belt at the front and under the arms, and worn over a silver slip. The dress was sewn with hundreds of rhinestones, and fell to just above the ankles. She would wear silver lace-trimmed slippers with it, huge pearl and diamond hoop earrings, and a headdress of opals, diamonds, and pearls.

She had tried to pretend to herself that she wasn't interested in attracting Mark Beeney tonight—that she was doing nothing more than playing a glamorous and spectacular charade for the benefit of the family and the Keys Shipping Line. But after two gin and bitters the pretence seemed silly. She had always been the most outspoken girl in her class, hadn't she? And her vitriolic directness had been the prime cause of most of her arguments with her father, not to mention those Sunday morning rows she used to have with Nigel, when (hung over, tired, and sexually satiated) she had told him exactly how *effete* he was, and how *hopeless*, and how he would never amount to anything in the West End, and especially not on Broadway. Surely she could be just as direct with herself and admit that Mark Beeney was the most alluring and alarming man she had ever come across. His absurdly good looks were like a whirlpool, drawing her closer and closer, despite every sensible objection she could raise. Yes, he was dangerous. Yes, he was already accompanied by a pretty lady companion. Yes, he was rich, and probably a playboy of the worst kind. Yes, he was a show-off. But, my God, didn't he have *presence!* He gave off the scent of Dangerous Male as if it were a cologne. And no matter how much she protested to herself while she sat in front of her dressing table and touched up the mascara on her eyelashes, she knew that it was not her sensible Little Miss Muffet intellect that was going to decide what she did tonight; it was her incendiary sense of romance and her steeple chasing pulse. Mark had excited her so much simply by kissing her that she had gone back to her stateroom after she had left him and urinated in fits and starts, thinking of nothing but *him.* She hated him already for making her feel so giddy and so uncontrolled, and that was the very best start that any affair could have.

Early diners were already promenading on the first-class deck and peering tentatively around the Grand Lounge for cocktails when Sir Peregrine, in the wheelhouse, received a message from the harbourmaster at Dublin that he could now depart. He was advised, however, to proceed at no more than four knots until he was three miles out from Dun Laoghaire, on account of the large numbers of sightseeing boats and small fishing smacks which were crowding the coastal waters. The harbourmaster added—in Morse code, of course—that he wished the *Arcadia* a calm sea, a glorious trip, and the protection of King Neptune. Sir Peregrine crumpled up the telegraph message and slapped it back into the hand of the wireless operator. "What the devil do they think this is?" he snapped. "Some kind of damned mythical Odyssey? The next thing we know, they'll be telling us to watch out for sirens and to lash ourselves to the funnels with cotton wool in our ears."

Rudyard Philips could see his own face reflected in the dark glass of the wheelhouse window, like a Shakespearean ghost. "Yes, sir," he could watch himself mouthing. He felt as if he wasn't himself at all.

"Well, then, weigh the anchors, and let's get going," said Sir Peregrine tetchily. "Slow ahead for one mile, Mr. Philips, then full ahead. Let's show these Irish barbarians what a modern express liner can do."

"There is a small vessels warning, sir."

"Of course there is. But there won't be anything further than a mile out; and besides, with all these damned lights on, they'll have to be stone blind not to see us coming. The sooner we get clear of Ireland and out into the open channel the better."

"But, with all respect, sir—"

"Don't argue, Mr. Philips. I won't be argued with. On your own ship, you can make whatever mistakes you want. On this ship, you're my first officer, and I don't expect you to argue."

"Very good, sir."

"Very good yourself, Mr. Philips. Now, carry on. I have to finish getting ready for dinner."

The wind was freckled with rain as the *Arcadia*'s immense anchors were lifted from the seabed and hauled on board by electric winches. Slowly, with three majestic blasts on her steam whistle, she moved away from her mooring and began to sail southeastwards into the metallic darkness, a sheer-sided palace of lights.

The effect, in that blackest of summer thunderstorms, was extraordinary, and many of those watching the *Arcadia*'s departure from small dinghies and sailing boats found it difficult to believe that what they were witnessing was real. "It was as if a whole seaside town had suddenly detached itself from the greater bulk of Ireland and moved mysteriously off into the night," wrote the chief correspondent for the *Dublin Examiner*. Another reporter found scribbled in his rain-spotted notebook the following morning, "If I had drunk three more Guinness than I actually had, I might well have piped my eye. If you're the kind of fellow who likes your moments momentous, and your grandeur grand, then the *Arcadia*'s sailing was for you and no mistake."

And another correspondent, for the *Dundalk Courier*, said, "I have seen fairyland, and it works."

Rudyard Philips stood in the wheelhouse looking out over the reaches of the night with his hands clasped resolutely behind his back. As the *Arcadia* sailed clear of the shelter of Dun Laoghaire and out into the Irish Sea once more, he could feel the deck begin the first exploratory dips and rolls of a long ocean voyage, like a young girl stepping out on her first dance. With her four well-balanced four-bladed screws, the *Arcadia* did not vibrate badly, but, on the first leg of their journey Rudyard had already noticed a kind of musical hum, as the decks and the woodwork and the metal fittings all harmonised to the deeper note of the oil-fired turbines.

There were still a few small boats scattered around in the darkness, and one or two of them let off coloured flares, red and white, which sparkled and then died away. Rudyard ordered the helmsman to answer them with a quick whoop on the whistle. The helmsman said, "One mile out, Mr. Philips, sir."

Sir Peregrine was still in his cabin. Rudyard stared out of the window in front of him for a long while, saying nothing; but then he ordered firmly, "Steady as she goes. Four knots." There were still one or two tiny lights bobbing around them, and however speedily Sir Peregrine wanted to escape from Irish waters, Rudyard considered that the Dublin harbourmaster's warning should be taken seriously. He would wait until they were clear of Eire's territorial waters before he ordered full speed.

At that moment, however, the speaking-tube whistle blew, and Rudyard leaned forward to answer it.

"Mr. Philips?" came Sir Peregrine's echoing voice. "I'd be obliged to see you in my quarters."

Rudyard said to the helmsman, "Hold her steady," and left the wheelhouse to walk along to Sir Peregrine's cabin. He knocked at the door and waited until Sir Peregrine irascibly shouted, "Yes? Don't stand there all night!"

Sir Peregrine was dressed in full formal uniform, medals, gold epaulets, and white wing collar. His white hair was combed into shining furrows with brilliantine, and there was a small cut on his left cheekbone from shaving.

"Isn't it time we stopped dawdling, Mr. Philips?" he wanted to know.

"We're not quite clear of the small craft yet, sir," said Rudyard.

Sir Peregrine went to the porthole and peered out. "What small craft? Those? A couple of decrepit herring boats, that's all they are, and they must be three miles away if they're an inch."

"There are others, sir," insisted Rudyard. "They're difficult to see with the rain blowing athwart us like this."

"*They* might be difficult for us to see," replied Sir Peregrine with ill-controlled ire, "but *we*, Mr. Philips, are about as invisible as Harrods at Christmas. We'll have full ahead, please, as I instructed; and any more of this tomfoolery will result in my ordering you off my bridge for the remainder of the voyage, if I make myself clear. Where's Mr. Charles?"

"In the chartroom, sir."

"Very well. Have Mr. Charles take over and get yourself ready for dinner. If you can't sail a ship, at the very least you can make yourself pleasant to the passengers."

"Sir, I—"

Sir Peregrine lifted a bony well-manicured hand. "Enough, thank you, Mr. Philips. Desist."

Rudyard steadied himself with a deep breath. "Yes, sir. Very well, sir. Thank you, sir," he rattled off as if he were reciting a series of Hail Marys for the forgiveness of his insubordination. Sir Peregrine nodded in lemony satisfaction and then said, "Did they bring up my Evian water yet? It's very thirsty work, dressing for dinner."

Rudyard walked through the chartroom to the corridor which led to his cabin. Dick Charles was in there, his feet up on the table, reading a copy of *Pictorial Weekly* (two pence) and drinking tea. "The old man wants you," said Rudyard shortly. Dick put his magazine down and brushed biscuit crumbs from his uniform. "I h-hope he doesn't w-want me to w-welcome the p—the p—the passengers," he said. "I'm terrified I'm going to run into that Lady Diana FitzP— FitzP—"

"I know who you mean," said Rudyard tiredly. "But I shouldn't worry too much. She'll probably be snapped up by the time you get down to dinner."

At that very moment, though, Monty Willowby poked his head through the chartroom door and said, "Mr. Charles? Mr. Peel said you might be interested to know that Lady Diana FitzPerry has specifically requested to sit at your table tonight. Cocktails sharp at eight-thirty, please, gentlemen. Dinner sharp at nine."

Dick Charles stared at his mug of tea unhappily.

"I think the arrer of true love has stuck itself in your heart at last, Mr. Charles." Monty Willowby smiled.

When he had gone, Rudyard said, "Yes, come on, Dick. There must be worse things than being fancied by the hottest go-er in Westminster."

"I suppose so," said Dick without much enthusiasm.

"Think about it as a duty," Rudyard suggested. "Arduous but not unpleasant."

"Hunh!" Dick protested. "It's all r-right for y-you! You're m-married."

Rudyard looked at him quickly and then, more slowly, down at the floor. "Yes," he said, in a small voice. "I suppose you might say that I am."

The awkward silence that followed was interrupted by Monty Willowby, who popped his head in againand said, "Begging your pardon, Mr. Charles, but Mr. Peel told me to say that he has heard how certain talents as practised by Lady Diana FitzPerry could be beneficial for speed impedimenta. If you see what he means, sir."

Rudyard couldn't help laughing. Dick threw his magazine at Monty Willowby with a loud flutter of pages. It fell open on the floor at a saucy photograph of Lois Byrd, of Mack Sennett comedy fame. "How's ths for a bit to eat?" the caption read.

Rudyard went through to the wheelhouse, and passed on Sir Peregrine's instructions for full speed. Now the *Arcadia*'s reciprocating engines began to build up power, with a deep and noticeable drumming sound that gradually awakened the passengers to the fact that they were really on their way, and that they would soon be sailing at more then twenty-six knots. Catriona asked Alice to open one of her portholes, so that she could hear the splashing of the liner's sharp bows as she cut into the choppy water of the Irish Sea. A smell of brine and fuel oil and summer rain blew into the stateroom, and mingled with the perfume.

It would take three or four miles for the *Arcadia* to build up to her full cruising speed, just as it would take over a mile and a half to stop her dead in case of emergency. Even though she was 960 feet long—longer than the Woolworth Building would have been if it were laid on its side —she could pass a given point when she was sailing at twenty knots, from her sharp-bladed bows to the flag on her overhanging stern counter, in a fraction over twenty-nine seconds.

Two miles out from the Irish coast, the *Arcadia* was making only eight or nine knots, but that was still fast for a vessel her size in coastal water. Sir Peregrine had left his cabin now and descended to the Grand Lounge with Edgar Deacon, Percy Fearson, Ralph Peel, and the rest of his officers, where they began to greet the assembling passengers. The ship's orchestra was playing a mildly syncopated version of one of Chopin's mazurkas, while stewards balanced between the guests like jugglers with trays of champagne. The array of evening dresses was spectacular - so spectacular that it looked as if every diamond and ruby and emerald mine had been plundered simply for the decoration of tonight's gowns, and as if every species of exotic bird had been plucked of its plumage. There were stunning creations by Paquin, Doeuillet, Paul Poiret, and Worth, all of them in ravishing colours and fabrics that shimmered in the light from the chandeliers.

"I felt as if the rest of the world had been stripped of everything of value, regardless of how naked and shabby it might have been left, for no other reason than to make this banquet and ball the most dazzling concentration of human wealth and beauty that there had ever been," wrote Julius Briggs. "So, there was no gold left in South Africa? So, birds of Paradise were struggling to fly without their tail feathers? So, a thousand civet cats had been tortured for their perfumed oils? So, art galleries had been stripped, leopards slaughtered, whole mountains demolished for their quartz? Who cared? Tonight, on this enchanted ship, we cared only for tonight."

Nineteen

The beating of the *Arcadia*'s engines might have been loud, and so might the laughter of the passengers and the warbling of the orchestra. But a little more than a mile away, in slanting rain that was now as fine and as drenching as the curtains of wet organza, there was no sound but the sea and the wind and the desolate puttering of an eight-horsepower petrol engine, as a man called Thomas Dennis tried to nurse it through the night.

Thomas Dennis was a scenic photographer from Dundrum Street in Dublin. He was a single man, but this afternoon he had put out to sea in his friend's twenty-one-foot fishing ketch *Drogheda* and taken with him an eleven-year-old boy named Sean Joyce. Sean was the youngest son of his next-door neighbour in Dundrum Street, a carroty-haired widower whose wife had succumbed two years ago to the effects of fourteen pregnancies, and who fervently and equally believed in the vision of St. Theresa and the joys of home-distilled poteen. Although Thomas Dennis was well educated and artistic, a favourite among the womenfolk of Dundrum Street but considered a softie by the men; and although young Sean was obtuse and scruffy and illiterate, better at throwing cobbles at the Guarda than he was at his schoolwork, the two of them, Thomas and Sean, had become the best of friends. They rarely talked to each other. Theirs wasn't the kind of friendship that needed talk. But they were out almost every Sunday after Mass, walking the hills of the seashore, or the banks of the Liffey, with Thomas springing on ahead with his tiny spectacles shining as he peered inquisitively about for scenes that might be suitable for commercial postcards, and Sean stumbling along behind with the tripod and the cape and the heavy No. 1 Conley View Camera.

Today they had gone out to take views of the *Arcadia* as she lay at anchor. With luck, Thomas would be able to sell two or three pictures to the *Dublin Examiner*, or even the *Illustrated London News*. They had photographed the *Arcadia*'s massive sides from all points of the compass, and then eaten five cheese sandwiches each and shared a pint bottle of Guinness. All of Mr. Joyce's children had been brought up on Guinness, it was mother's milk to them, and so Thomas could scarcely object to the boy's thirst for the black porter, even though he was only eleven.

But Thomas had reckoned without the perverse summer currents and the turning tide, and without the Irish efficiency of the petrol engine, which worked "on and off, according," although according to what had never been explained to him. By the time it had grown so violently dark at seven o'clock, they had already drifted and sailed and drifted and floundered four or five miles southeast from Dublin Bay; and it was only now, at twenty after eight, that Thomas Dennis had been able to patch up the fuel-pump line with a piece of rubber cut from his camera bulb and fix an approximate course towards the Irish shoreline south of Dun Laoghaire.

It was a night of tilting seas and unceasing penetrating rain. Sean sat under the *Drogheda*'s makeshift canvas canopy and shivered in his thin sleeveless pullover and his knee-length flannel pants. Thomas, at the tiller, his brown tweed cap as wet and shapeless as a cow flop, his collar turned up, was obliged to keep taking off his spectacles and wiping them dry.

"It's not so far now, Sean," Thomas kept shouting. "I believe I can see the breakers already. You wait and see, we'll be supping hot soup by nine."

When he first glimpsed the lights of the *Arcadia,* he thought (with a jump in his heart of God-be-praised) that they were the lights of Dun Laoghaire. But then they disappeared behind the shifting grey scenery of the waves for a minute or two, and when they reappeared, they were so much closer that he realised they must be moving towards him, rather than him moving towards them.

He wiped his glasses again, and strained his eyes in the misty rain, and at last he worked out that the lights were moving diagonally towards him on his starboard bow, and then he saw the illuminated funnels and decorated masts that told him he was crossing the path of the *Arcadia*.

"There, Sean! Do you see those lights?"

Sean squinted into the rain and then nodded. "Is that shore, Mr. Dennis?"

"It's not the shore, my boy, but it's the next best thing. The *Arcadia!* That's what it is! Can you see her now? She was due to leave her mooring at eight, so she can't have sailed far! And that means we're nearly home and dry! Now look, will you? Isn't that a sight? You won't see a sight like that again!"

Up in the *Arcadia*'s wheelhouse, Dick Charles was glumly wondering what he was going to do about Lady Diana FitzPerry. In the crow's nest, the lookout, Frederick Cowles, was staring sightlessly at the rain and wondering if his wife had started labour yet. He wouldn't have been able to see the *Drogheda* even if he had been looking in her direction; the evening was far too misty, and the *Drogheda* was wallowing in the troughs of the Irish Sea like a wet pig.

Sir Peregrine had been quite right. From a small boat, the *Arcadia* was as easy to see as Harrods at Christmas. But what he had failed to consider was that if you were floundering around in a small boat, with the wind and the rain blowing steadily onto your port bow, and your eight-horsepower engine coughing and stuttering, and if Harrods were to bear down your port bow at more than eleven knots, accelerating all the time, you would be extremely hard put to get out of the way.

It took Thomas Dennis only three minutes after he first caught sight of the *Arcadia* in the distance to realise that she might be on a collision course with the *Drogheda*. During those three minutes, the *Arcadia* advanced on him by more than three times her total length, or half a mile. There was now less than half a mile of sea between them.

Thomas was gradually clutched by a tight and overwhelming breathlessness, the kind of feeling that he could only think of as sheer dread. He said, out loud, "Mother of God," but when Sean looked up at him he found that he could say nothing else at all. There was nothing he *could* have said that could possibly have helped. He knew Sean couldn't swim, because he had once tried to persuade the boy to take a dip at the Black Rock baths. Even though both of them were wearing life jackets, Thomas doubted if a few pieces of crumbly cork and mildewed canvas could save them in a cold choppy sea more than two miles from shore. And there would be very little that cork and canvas could do to protect them from a 53,000-ton express liner that was now bearing down on them so rapidly that even if its captain had seen them, he would have been completely unable either to slow down or to avoid them.

Sean stood up, his hair spiky in the rain. "Look now, she's coming our way, Mr. Dennis!" he cried, in pleasure. "If I call halloo, will they call back? Will they stop for us, Mr. Dennis?"

Thomas opened his mouth in panic and closed it again. The tiny fishing boat dipped and pitched in the water, its engine sounding as ineffective as a wasp in a jelly jar. The tiller seemed to be quite useless, no matter how violently Thomas wrenched it over, and he suddenly thought of a nightmare he had once had of tumbling over a bottomless waterfall.

He heard dance music. He thought, Holy Mother, am I to die to the sound of dance music? Then his whole world seemed to be blotted out by the towering black walls of the *Arcadia* and by the thunder of her engines and by the white spray that leaped up from her bows like shrouded ghosts leaping out of their ploughed-up graves. Sean screamed, a high piping scream like a girl, and then the *Arcadia* burst the *Drogheda* into tiny splinters, demolishing her as thoroughly as if she had been blown up with gelignite.

Up in the Grand Lounge at that very instant Sir Peregrine was kissing the hand of Princess Xenia of Russia. Although the impact of the collision was no greater than that of running through a raft of half-submerged logs or hitting a large buoy, Sir Peregrine was almost physically conscious of a tremor that wasn't right, a tremor that ran through the living hull of his ship and tingled his nerve endings. He lifted his head with an expression of sudden uncertainty.

"Is there anything *wrong*, Sir Peregrine?" Princess Xenia smiled coquettishly. "Did you chip one of your teeth on my rings?"

There was laughter all around them. The orchestra was striking up with a Charleston. Sir Peregrine frowned in the direction of the grand staircase, and said, "No, no, of course not. Nothing at all."

Rudyard Philips, a few feet away, caught the questioning look on Sir Peregrine's face and wondered what Princess Xenia could have said to him to make him appear so distracted. Next to him, slopping champagne out of her glass, a dark-haired girl in a shimmering gold dress was giggling and honking like a goose and saying, "Isn't that a *scream?*"

Right below the girl's wafer-thin French-made sandals, right below the dance floor, down beneath the layers of second- and third-class decks, of galleys and engine-rooms, right beneath the riveted steel plates of the hull itself, Thomas Dennis was being dragged bodily down the whole 960 feet of the *Arcadia*'s keel, battered and jolted and already scraped as raw as a side of beef. He was still alive, and still conscious, and most horrifying of all, he knew what was going to happen to him. He had nearly three-quarters of a minute of being bludgeoned against the hull, nearly three-quarters of a minute of tumbling through the chilling turmoil of the seawater which flowed beneath the *Arcadia*'s black and impassive length, nearly three-quarters of a minute of unspeakable pain. Then, he was going to have to go through the liner's screws.

Princess Xenia took a tiny crouton topped with Malossol caviar and smiled at Sir Peregrine archly. The orchestra's vocalist picked up his megaphone, and began to sing, "'*Carolina, Carolina, at last you're on the map . . . With a new tune, crazy blue tune, with a peculiar snap.'*"

Thomas Dennis, martyred with agony, opened his lungs to scream, and flooded them immediately with freezing brine. Stunned, drowning, frightened more than almost anything else of the darkness and the terrible feeling of all that black weight pressing him down into the sea, he tried to tell his soul to let go, *let go!* let me die before I reach the screws, let me sit with my head resting in the Virgin's lap, let me know peace before I have to face butchery.

There was a quiet knock on the door of Catriona's stateroom. Catriona said, "Alice, there's someone knocking," and at that moment Thomas Dennis' legs were chopped off at the thigh by the whirling blades of the *Arcadia*'s number two direct-driven screw. The rest of his mutilated body was burst open and flung seventy feet away by centrifugal force. Nobody was looking over the *Arcadia*'s stern counter at that time, and even if they had been, it probably would have been too dark for them to see the brief stain of red that touched the foam. Thomas Dennis had left a single veal pie in his meat safe at home in Dundrum Street, and that was to have been his supper.

It was one of the *Arcadia*'s pageboys at Catriona's door, with a celluloid box tied around with pink satin ribbon. "It's for you," said Alice, tipping the boy sixpence and bringing the box across the room. "An orchid." She peered at the card and smiled as she handed it over.

Catriona was almost ready now. She was just trying to decide whether she preferred the silver-and-diamond brooch with the pearls swinging from it like dewdrops, or the pierrot brooch in white gold and white enamel. She said, "Could you bring me another cigarette, please, Alice? I think my nerves are going to get the better of me. I'm so *excited!*"

The orchid, pale violet and still sparkling with moisture, was from Mark Beeney. On the card he had written, "For the girl of every shipowning millionaire's dreams. Respectfully, Mark."

"I think someone's rather stuck on you, Miss Keys," said Alice. "You know what orchids mean, don't you? Undying passion. If a man gives you an orchid, that's a sign that he's never going to let you go as long as he lives. Not until he gets what he wants, anyway."

Catriona untied the ribbon and carefully lifted the fragile flower out of its celluloid box. She held it up to her cheek and made big eyes at herself in the dressing-table mirror. "It's the same colour as my makeup," she said. "It matches exactly. Isn't that perfect?"

Alice was hanging up Catriona's discarded négligé. "Perfect," she agreed, and meant it, particularly since Mark Beeney had given her an envelope with fifty dollars in it to tell him what eye shadow Catriona was going to be wearing that evening.

"Do you really think I ought to wear it?" Catriona asked Alice, pushing aside the stool of her dressing table and standing up.

"Of course you should wear it," said Alice. "It's a compliment. It doesn't necessarily mean that he's trying to make up to you."

"I don't know," said Catriona, twirling around so that her evening gown spun out around her. "I think I shall leave it in a glass of water. Or perhaps I shan't even do that. Perhaps I shall just let it wilt. After all, if I actually wear it, he's going to think that I'm keen on him."

"Aren't you?" asked Alice, busying herself with Catriona's scattered jars of makeup and thinking about her fifty dollars.

"Aren't I what?"

"Aren't you keen on him?"

"Well, of *course* I am. But that isn't the point, is it? I don't want him to think that all he has to do is buy me a diamond and ruby necklace and send me an orchid in a celluloid box and I'm his. That wouldn't do at all. No, I think that *now* is the time for me to be even more remote than ever. I think I shall ignore him all evening. My God, there are thousands of good-looking men on this ship. Well, hundreds. Well, there are *some*. But he has to fight for me. He has to be a knight in armour. Shining and gallant and ready to die at the drop of a hat."

Alice said, almost crossly, "It wouldn't be very grateful of you not to wear it, would it? After all the trouble Mr. Beeney's gone to."

"What trouble? He bought me an orchid from the ship's florist, that's all. He probably didn't even go down there himself. I expect his man bought it."

"But it's *exactly* the right colour."

Catriona picked up the orchid by the stem, and turned it around between her fingers. "Yes," she said, airily. "I wonder how he knew."

There was another knock. Alice answered it, and this time it was Edgar Deacon, in full evening dress, looking dark and grey-haired and rather saturnine.

"Miss Keys," he greeted her, and then, "May I come in?"

"Of course," said Catriona. "You can have a drink if you want to."

"I brought you this," said Edgar, offering her a white lily in a cellophane box tied with a blue ribbon.

"Oh—" Catriona grinned. "I seem to have one of these already. *Une embarrasse des corsages.* Mark Beeney sent me an orchid. Look."

"Oh," said Edgar irritably. "Well, you'll wear *this* one, naturally."

"Why *naturally?*" Catriona teased him. "I'm not sure I like white as much as purple. White is so . . . *sterile.* Don't you think so?"

Edgar reached into his inside pocket and took out his cigarette holder. "As a matter of fact," he said, lighting up, "it isn't from me. It's from somebody else. Somebody who's interested in meeting you and getting to know you."

"Not Jack Dempsey, I hope?" asked Catriona. "I saw him this afternoon on the promenade deck, and he looked so *moody.* I think I'd be afraid to say 'good morning' to him, in case he decided to try out his latest punch on me."

Edgar said, "No, no. Not him. It's . . . well, it's one of the people who came aboard just now from Ireland."

"O'Hara? From the bank?"

"Not exactly, no. Not O'Hara."

"Mr. Deacon," said Catriona, "I think you're being very coy at this particular moment, and I think I want to know why."

"Miss Keys, I am simply trying to be socially correct." There was a note of forced amusement in Edgar's voice, and Catriona knew that she had just managed to get the edge on him. He was abrasive and sly and calculating as an adder, and he wouldn't let her hold her advantage for long. But right at this moment he wanted something from her quite badly, and although she didn't know what it was, she knew that the only way she was going to stay in control of her own destiny was to keep him wanting.

"You're not sounding *sweetly* coy," Catriona retorted. "You're sounding *deviously* coy."

"I'm not sure that I know the difference."

Catriona pursed her lips in a mock-cherubic pout. "I just think that you've got things a lot more planned out than you've been telling me. You've planned my wardrobe, you've planned out every hour of every day. Now I'm supposed to accept a lily from a strange Irishman. Well, I'm not sure that I'm very stuck on lilies. They remind me of death."

"He's not Irish," said Edgar. "His name's George Welterman, of International Mercantile Marine."

"Oh. The people you want to buy up Keys."

"The people I would prefer to buy up Keys if we find that we are obliged to sell it."

"So you don't want me to offend him?"

"I would rather you didn't." Edgar removed his cigarette from its holder and crushed it out in a stainless-steel ashtray which was presided over by a naked stainless-steel nymph. "He's not quite as dashing as Mark Beeney, I'm afraid, but it's very important that he gets a good impression of us. It will be his recommendation that will go to the Morgan bank to raise the finance to buy us out."

Catriona picked up the lily between finger and thumb and twiddled it around. "I don't even know if selling Keys would be the right thing to do."

"Miss Keys, by the time we get to New York, we won't be talking about the right thing or the wrong thing anymore. We'll be talking about the *only* thing. If we can't convince our bankers that we're going to pull through, and especially if we don't win the Blue Riband, then we won't have any more alternatives left open to us; and that is why it is absolutely essential that we keep on the right side of George Welterman."

"I hope you're not using me as bait," said Catriona.

"I'm not sure what you mean."

"Well, you haven't promised him that I'm going to spend all evening with him, have you? The Houri of the Atlantic?"

"I did say that I'd introduce him to you."

"And that means I have to cut Mark Beeney?"

Edgar said a little impatiently, "Nobody said you had to cut him. You simply have to understand that, no matter how handsome he is, he isn't going to do any of us any good. He wants the *Arcadia* alone; and as far as he's concerned the rest of the fleet can go hang. You just think about young Godfrey Colehill when you think about cutting the rug with a chap like Mark Beeney."

"It really isn't fair," Catriona protested.

Edgar said, more gently, "I quite understand how you feel. But remember your father."

"I *am* remembering my father. All he ever did was to spoil my fun."

Edgar let out a laugh like a piece of dry toast. "You know something, my dear?" he asked her. "You're so much like your father I can scarcely believe it. If your father had been a woman, that's exactly what he would have told me, too. Well, it serves me right for underestimating the hereditary Keys character, doesn't it? All fire and charm and melodrama, hot one minute, cold the next, and as stubborn as a stableful of donkeys."

Catriona, who had her arms outstretched as Alice draped her white mink stole around her shoulders, said nothing. Edgar glanced at her and gave a slight and inconsequential shrug, as if to acknowledge that there was nothing else he could do. He picked up the discarded lily.

"I'll go and tell Mr. Welterman that his corsage was unacceptable."

"Not really?" said Catriona.

"Well, of course. If you don't wear it, he's going to ask me why not."

"But he couldn't have expected me to, could he? I've never even met him."

"It was simply a gesture of respect, from one steamship company to another. It wasn't intended to mean anything else."

Catriona turned her head sideways. "Alice," she murmured. "Alice, what shall I do?"

"Wear Mr. Beeney's, Miss Keys, if I were you," Alice murmured back as she straightened out the hem of Catriona's gown.

"Well, no, I don't think I will," said Catriona. "It's all too ridiculous. In fact, I don't think I'll wear *either*. You can tell Mr. Welterman, or whatever his name is, that I have decided not to wear flowers at all tonight. I am not in a floral frame of mind. Alice, you can flush both of them down the loo."

Edgar raised a hand. "If that's the way you feel."

"Yes, it is. That's *exactly* the way I feel. I don't belong to anybody, and that includes you."

"But you'll let me have a dance tonight?" asked Edgar unexpectedly.

Catriona stared at him. For a long, oddly magnetised moment their eyes were held on each other, as if both of them were trying to convey something far more than they could express in polite (or even impolite) conversation. Nigel had once said to Catriona, "There are some things that can only be explained in bed." When Catriona looked at the darkness in Edgar's eyes, she knew exactly what Nigel had meant. Could he really be "one of those," or was there much more to him?

What nobody on board the *Arcadia* knew at that moment, though, was that the tide was gradually washing the brutalised body of Thomas Dennis in to shore, and that, not far away, weeping with shock and desperation, a young boy called Sean Joyce was clinging coldly to a broken spar.

Twenty

The orchestra played "Somebody Loves Me," from George White's *Scandals of 1924*, as Catriona came down the staircase into the Grand Lounge, one upraised hand resting lightly on Edgar's white evening glove. Every one of the first-class passengers turned and applauded (even, with exaggerated fierceness, Marcia Conroy), and Sir Peregrine stepped forward to bow to his glittering new mistress.

"You're looking *marvellous*, Sir Peregrine," she told him, with exaggerated imperiousness. "They should have displayed you at the British Empire Exhibition at Wembley."

Sir Peregrine cleared his throat with a dry little bark. There wasn't any answer to a compliment like that, especially when it came from the heiress of the shipping company which employed him. Stiffly, and with many more sharp tugs at his cuffs than were necessary, he escorted her along an informal receiving line to be introduced to Princess Xenia, to Douglas Fairbanks and Mary Pickford, to Baroness Zawisza ("We've met." She smiled, and Sabran, who was glowering in the background, bared his teeth at her), to Claude Graham-White, and Jack Dempsey (who appeared to have shaken off his sulks and took her hand as gently as if he were picking up a porcelain ornament), to Dame Clara Butt, to Señora Zelmira Paz de Gainza (who smelled powerfully of gardenias and displayed as many diamonds as Tiffany's engagement-ring counter), to Charles Schwab of Bethlehem Steel, and to Mr. O'Hara from the Irish bank.

Then, last of all, Mark Beeney stepped forward. Only a few yards away, Catriona could see Marcia Conroy in a shimmering black evening gown by Jeanne Lanvin, willowy and blond and holding her champagne glass as if she could cheerfully crush it.

"I never saw anyone, *ever*, look as ravishing as you do tonight," said Mark, and kissed her hand.

"Thank you for your orchid," she told him.

"It was a pleasure. I chose it myself."

"Aren't you wondering why I'm not wearing it?"

"No. I didn't think for one moment that you would."

155

"I see," said Catriona, taking a few steps away from him across the floor of the Grand Lounge, and smiling brightly to a very tall woman with ginger hair and a long-sleeved dress in an uncompromising shade of brick-red.

Mark, who was following her at a wary distance, said, "You were flattered that I thought of you, but you didn't want to show that you owed me anything. 'Who does this cowboy think he is, sending me flowers?' That's what you thought. So what did you do? Stick it in a glass of water? Press it in the pages of your diary?"

"I asked my maid to flush it down the loo, actually." Catriona smiled.

"Forgive me, Miss Keys," interrupted Rudyard Philips, stepping forward. Catriona couldn't help noticing how sweaty he was and how agitated, as if he were running a high fever. "I would like you to meet Mademoiselle Louise Narron, the celebrated operatic soprano."

"I'm charmed," said Catriona, touching hands with the tall woman in the brick-red dress. "And what a startling dress."

"I must tell you the truth, Miss Keys," said Mademoiselle Narron in a gush of unexpected familiarity, touching her forehead as if she were singing the part of Sieglinde in the Valkyries, and still maundering around the wooden hut in Act I. "It is not what I chose to wear, but circumstances did not allow me to wear anything else. You are right. It *is* startling. I wish it were not."

Rudyard Philips pulled a tight face that Catriona didn't understand at all. "I'm sorry," she said, quite baffled.

Rudyard said in a congested voice, "Mademoiselle Narron . . . had an accident."

"I cut my wrists," explained Mademoiselle Narron. She raised her hands as if they were still bleeding. "An unhappy association. A stupid moment of despair. But your gallant Mr. Philips here rescued me from myself, and from my own stupidity." She linked arms decisively with Rudyard Philips, who looked as if he were about to pass out from heatstroke. "Everything they say about British officers is true."

Now the orchestra played "I'll See You in My Dreams," and Mark Beeney reached out his hand to Catriona and said, "Dance?"

Edgar, watching Catriona from the side of one of the reflecting pillars, gave her a one-shouldered shrug that seemed to mean, "Go ahead, if you really have to."

Mark danced athletically, but with the noticeably self-conscious precision of someone who has never been a natural dancer, and who has had to spend hour after tedious hour being manhandled around the floor of his dance class by his exasperated instructor. In fact, whenever he took the dance floor, no matter what music was playing, and no matter who his partner was, he could still hear Miss Czestochowski screaming at him, "You haff *niece*, Mr. Beeney! Bend them!"

Catriona was quiet for the first few minutes, enjoying the closeness of Mark, the silkiness of his shirt, and the smell of his cologne. He was so tall, compared to her, that if she looked straight ahead of her, she could see nothing but his white bow tie and his suntanned Adam's-apple.

"Your friend Miss Conroy isn't smiling much," she said, as lightly as she could manage.

"Oh, Miss Conroy," said Mark. "Why, yes. She does look glum. She had some bad news over the ship's telegraph. Her great-great-great-grandfather is dead. And has been for some time."

"You shouldn't make fun of her," said Catriona.

"Who's making fun?"

They danced past Edgar, and Catriona glimpsed for the first time the man called George Welterman. He looked bulky and stiff in his evening clothes, and he held his arms a little way out from his body as if his sleeves were stuffed with handkerchiefs. Catriona smiled momentarily, but closed off the smile as soon as Mark had twirled her out of range.

"I hope that wasn't George Welterman," said Mark, his face expressionless.

"You know him?"

"Of course I know him. He's the chief chiseller at IMM. If they want to acquire something—whatever it is, equipment or stock or securities— out goes George Welterman. In the business, they call him Firesale Welterman, on account of the prices he pays for just about everything. You should be careful. From what I hear, he's got his beady little vulture eyes on Keys."

"What if he has?" said Catriona. "We haven't decided to sell up yet."

"You may not have a choice."

"What's that supposed to mean? I own a quarter of the voting stock, and my mother owns twenty-six per cent. Or at least we *will* do, when everything's been transferred."

"There are plenty of ways of *forcing* you to sell," said Mark, "and you can believe me that George Welterman knows them all. In fact, he probably invented most of them. I don't know whether you're aware of it or not, but IMM already own something like twelve per cent of Keys stock, and if they start offering your shareholders better prices, and if they promise them a more profitable fleet and higher dividends—well, your bankers and your shareholders may ultimately prefer dividends to glamour."

"Edgar seems to believe that if we *do* have to sell, then selling to IMM would be the most practical thing to do. And the most humane."

"The most *humane?* How does he work that out?"

"Well,"—Catriona blushed—"because at least IMM would keep Keys running as a company, and not sell it off bit by bit and put all of our employees out of work."

"You believe that?"

"Is there any reason why I shouldn't?"

"Only that George Welterman is the most unscrupulous character since George Remus. I mean, look at it from his point of view. IMM already operate White Star through a British holding company. What on earth would be the point of duplicating that administration and setting up a separate holding company to run Keys? If I were IMM, I'd simply take the best Keys ships into the White Star fleet and sell off the clunkers to the Greeks, or the Chinese or maybe the Russians."

Catriona danced a quick and complicated little fox-trot step, partly to show off, and partly because Mark made her feel immature and embarrassed. Mark had to double-shuffle to keep up with her.

"How do you know I haven't thought of that already?" she demanded.

"Because if you had, you wouldn't have mentioned the names of humanity and George Welterman in the same breath."

"I think I'm quite capable of handling my own business affairs, thank you."

"I'm sure you are. I'm just giving a word to the wise. Keep your eye on George Welterman, that's all."

"Don't think I won't be. And don't think that I won't be keeping my eye on *you*, too, Mr. Mark Beeney."

Mark steered Catriona around a couple of small-time Hollywood stars who were dancing in place with their faces stretched into impossible smiles for the benefit of the official Keys photographer and his brightly popping flash gun.

"Miss Catriona Keys," said Mark, "I have no designs on you whatsoever. Except that I'd love another dance, when you're free. And maybe the last dance of the evening."

"What about Marcia Conroy?"

"Marcia? I told you. She's only a stenographer. Well, maybe not a stenographer. But a friend, and nothing else. You're worried how cross she's looking? Don't worry. It's only because she forgot to wash in Woodbury's facial soap this morning, and she doesn't have the 'skin you love to touch.' Or maybe it was Listerine she forgot. I don't know. I don't think I care. Do you?"

Catriona didn't answer. The orchestra brought "I'll See You in My Dreams" to a flourishing ending, and the dance was over.

"You'll dance with me again?" asked Mark.

"I don't know," she replied, turning away.

"You don't *know?*" he said in surprise. "Who else is there to dance with? Schwab? Well, all right, Schwab. I suppose that's okay if you want to spend the rest of the evening talking about steel and money and steel and money. Catriona"—he caught her sleeve, tried to hold her back—"Catriona, listen to me. Listen! I think I have a crush on you. In fact, I think I'm smitten. You know what smitten means? It means I've been thinking about you all afternoon. I shouldn't have been. I should have thought about shipping. I should have thought about Marcia. But I didn't. I thought about you. Isn't that crazy?"

Catriona allowed him to pull her back. "Catriona?" he asked her gently.

She still wouldn't look at him. But she said, "All right. The last dance, if you really mean what you say."

He held on to her arm a moment longer. "Jesus," he said, with a voice that seemed to be choked up with frustration and affection, the same way a gutter chokes up with leaves. "Why didn't I meet you when you were sixteen? I could have trained you from the very second it was legal. Do you think that's outrageous of me?"

Catriona gave him a quick, vivid grin. "I don't take training," she said and walked off on her own with almost scandalous independence to rejoin Edgar.

Dick Charles had just handed over control of the *Arcadia* to the fifth officer and had hurriedly changed for the evening into his full-dress uniform, the one with the button missing. As Catriona walked across the Grand Lounge to be introduced to George Welterman, Dick came clattering down the gilded staircase with his head bent downwards, hoping with a kind of panicky hopelessness that Lady Diana FitzPerry wouldn't notice him arriving.

Sir Peregrine, with all the skill of a man who has spent the better part of his life piloting large ships into small harbours (albeit with occasional lapses of accuracy), came across the floor at full steam and intercepted him as he was making for the bar.

"Mr. Charles," he said, dryly. "I have someone here who's been dying to meet you, although God alone knows why."

"Y-yes, sir. Of c-course, sir," Dick stuttered. "I was just getting myself a g-glass of champagne, sir."

"The stewards will bring you your champagne, Mr. Charles," said Sir Peregrine. "Just come along with me."

Dick Charles followed in the wake of his captain with the obedient innocence of a young man who has not yet discovered that life features very few fated encounters, but that when it does, they are almost invariably vicious. It was only when Sir Peregrine stood aside, and tugged Dick around as if he were a ballroom dancer, that Dick understood how neatly and quickly he had been ambushed. Of course, the lady had asked for him by name; and, of course, Sir Peregrine had obliged by bringing him over. Sir Peregrine took a pride in giving his passengers everything they desired, especially when everything they desired was as easy to provide and as dispensable as a junior officer who couldn't even pronounce the word "pepper." He had provided far more complicated pleasures in the past.

"Mr. Charles, how *lovely* to meet you." Lady Diana FitzPerry smiled, and Dick Charles gave a rigid bow, as if the ship's laundry had left the ironing board in the back of his shirt. He couldn't think what to do or what to say; he couldn't even think what to think. His mind felt as empty as a ship's funnel.

"Lady FitzPerry is on her way to the Great Plains," said Sir Peregrine, baring his teeth. "She tells me that she was much taken with that magazine advertisement for motorcars, the one that describes how wonderful it is 'Somewhere West of Laramie.' Is that the one, Lady FitzPerry?"

"You must have seen it," gushed Lady FitzPerry, still holding on to Dick Charles' fingers. "They call it *word magic*, the way it's written. It's all about driving into the red horizon of a Wyoming twilight, with the wind blowing your hair, and a lean rangy cowboy riding beside you."

"It s-sounds p—" began Dick Charles, and then found himself unable to say any more. He stood to attention, his brain as devoid of intelligence as that of a freshly born infant, trapped into silence by his merciless stutter, and with one of London's most notorious femmes fatales pinching his fingers as possessively as a fiddler crab.

Lady FitzPerry glanced at Sir Peregrine uneasily, but Sir Peregrine was beaming as patiently and as affably at Dick Charles as if his fourth officer were carrying on the wittiest of cocktail conversations. In fact, the commodore was enjoying the spectacle of Dick Charles' total social paralysis almost as much as he enjoyed his Elgar records when he was alone in his sitting room.

"Perfectly stunning," said Dick Charles, in quite a different sort of voice.

"Well," put in Sir Peregrine, "I really must circulate. Have you talked to Miss Pickford yet? Charming lady."

Dick Charles and Lady FitzPerry found themselves alone together. Dick Charles hesitantly raised his hand, as if to say, "Cheers, then," but when he looked down he realised he didn't yet have a drink. Instead, he turned the gesture into an abrupt tug at the end of his nose, and then he immediately wished he hadn't.

Lady FitzPerry, close up, had all the style of an upper-class English whore. She was wearing a slim evening gown of gold lace, through which Dick had no trouble at all in seeing the pinky-brown ovals of her nipples, and the curve of her small flattish breasts. Her hips were narrow, but more from dieting than from natural trimness, and her ankles were thicker than they should have been. But she had a devastatingly high-class eroticism about her, and Dick felt that if she hadn't been wearing a silver-beaded apron around her waist, her gown would have shown just about everything she had to offer. She was smothered in diamonds; they clustered around her fingers and clung to her ears and sparkled around her wrists. Dick found himself staring at her full pale pink lips and wondering how many noble penises she had taken between them to earn herself so much fabulous jewellery.

"You *stutter*," said Lady FitzPerry. "I didn't realize."

"It's hard to t-tell from f-far away," Dick told her.

"But it's *awful*," she said. "Have you always had it?"

"As long as I c-can remember."

"Couldn't you be cured? I mean, surely hypnosis is good for stutters? Or acupuncture? Or even mah-jongg? I don't know. It seems so *awful.*"

Dick shrugged. "My mother once t-took me to a pee— to a pee— to a pee—"

"Oh, my God," said Lady FitzPerry. "Is it always like this?"

"Almost always," Dick told her. Then added, "Paediatrician."

"Well," said Lady FitzPerry with a resigned sigh, "it looks as if I'm in for four days of coitus interruptus."

"I beg your pah—" said Dick Charles.

"Never mind, my love." Lady FitzPerry smiled. "We *all* have our crosses to bear. Can you find me some more champagne?"

Dick Charles beckoned to one of the stewards, feeling not unlike a nine-month-old mink who is immediately destined to become the collar of a wealthy society lady's fur coat. The steward came speeding over with a tray of champagne and a lascivious leer that Dick Charles didn't care for at all.

Ralph Peel, the second officer, was doing rather better. He had found an innocent and enthusiastic admirer in Alison Cabot White, a seventeen-year-old Cape Cod heiress with big eyes, buck teeth, and an urgent desire to dispense with her virginity. She *adored* hairy men (having glimpsed, at the age of fifteen, the dark pubic curls which strayed out of the bathing costume of a Hyannis lifeguard), and the sleek sea-lion whorls of hair which emerged from Ralph Peel's stiff white collar were enough to enthral her for the whole evening.

Ralph Peel was telling her, "I went to sea because I was lonely. I thought, The sea's a lonely place, it'll suit me, if you know what I mean. I never thought that I'd meet anyone like you. I suppose if I never thank the sea for anything else, I'll thank it for introducing me to you."

Monty Willowby overheard him as he was passing by, and rolled his eyes up in mock prayer. Monty, looking like a sartorial Humpty-Dumpty in his immaculately pressed full-dress uniform, was on his way to have a quiet word with the bar steward about putting aside one bottle of Perrier-Jouët for every five bottles opened. Normally, Monty expected a lay-away ratio of one to ten, but it was unlikely that the company accountants would miss fifty cases of champagne when more than five hundred would be poured down the privileged throats of the passengers.

Similarly, Monty operated a complicated network of "savings," as he called them, on every level of the nine-story liner, in every class, and in every department. If only one spoonful of Malossol or Beluga caviar were "saved" from every order that was sent from the kitchens to the first-class staterooms, then by the end of the four-day voyage, there would be six ten-ounce jars of caviar which would technically not exist, and which therefore could be sold at premium prices to Monty's friends in the New York restaurant trade. There was one fashionable restaurant on East 49th Street which served its customers almost exclusively with provisions which had been originally intended for the kitchens of White Star, Cunard, and American TransAtlantic—fillet steaks, fresh vegetables, and fine French wines.

The Keys company were quite aware of the extent of Monty Willowby's operations, although no official word was actually spoken about them. The simple truth was that they preferred to have somebody powerful and efficient in charge of the "savings," rather than let the crew and the kitchen staff pillage what they could. On one Keys steamer, the *Elite*, the passengers had been reduced to eating sausages and meat pies after the ship's entire chilled-meat store had been stripped and sold at bargain prices to a wholesale butcher in Sydney, Australia, in the middle of a cruise. Monty Willowby would never have allowed that kind of daylight robbery, nor would he countenance the pilfering of glassware, linen, cutlery, ropes, brass fittings, or hot water bags. His "savings" business was profitable and clean, and he wanted it to stay that way.

As he walked with rotund dignity across the Grand Lounge, however, he was abruptly arrested by a dapper little man with no medal miniatures (hence: no class) but a look about him which immediately gave the impression of money. He was slightly Latin, this man, with a close-clipped moustache, drooping eyelids with long eyelashes, and an expression on his face of permanent amusement, as if he had just thought about something very private but very funny. He was smoking a cigar which Monty recognised at once as a Partagas Flor Special Cabinet No. 7.

"You're Mr. Willowby, aren't you?" asked the man in a flat Michigan accent.

"That's correct, sir. And you must be Mr. Fribourg, of New York, unless I'm badly mistook."

"You know your passenger list, Mr. Willowby."

"It's my job, sir. Everything to your satisfaction, sir?"

"Eminently," said Mr. Fribourg. "In fact, I don't think I've been spoiled so outrageously since I dined at the Men's Café at the Waldorf-Astoria with James A. Patten."

"We're flattered, sir." Monty Willowby nodded. "Now, if there's nothing else . . . ?"

"Just one thing," said Mr. Fribourg. "It strikes me, as a businessman, and as an entrepreneur, that a voyage of such historic importance is sadly lacking in souvenirs."

"Souvenirs?" asked Monty Willowby suspiciously. "Souvenirs" were what some of the Belfast shipfitters called such sentimental memorabilia as three hundredweight of brass stopcocks, or a complete set of mahogany wardrobes.

Mr. Fribourg puffed briefly at his cigar to keep it burning, and then smiled at Monty Willowby with the same close-up candour that dentists radiate when they size up a badly decayed molar.

"You know the kind of thing," he said. "Facecloths with *Arcadia* sewn on them. Cutlery with the company crest."

"There *is* a souvenir shop in the gallery, sir," said Monty. "They do an excellent line in *Arcadia* teaspoons and emblazoned luggage. Not to mention hand-coloured postcards."

"Well, those kinds of things are all very nice," said Mr. Fribourg, resting one hand on Monty's left epaulet and guiding him out of the mainstream of the reception. "But what makes the money is originality. Originality coupled with intimacy."

"I don't get your drift, I'm afraid," said Monty, doubling up his chins to stare uncomfortably down at the nail-polished hand which continued to clutch at his gold-braided shoulder. "And I'm afraid that I'm terrifically pushed for time just at the moment. Perhaps we could talk this over in the morning."

"Come on, now, Mr. Willowby, the moment I saw you I guessed that you were the kind of man who always had his ears open for an interesting deal. I'm talking big money. Thousands of dollars. You think I'm kidding?"

"Not for a moment," Monty told him with a sigh.

"Good," said Mr. Fribourg. "Because this is my idea. You have several hundred famous people aboard this liner, right? Well, you know that better than I do. Each of these people occupies a stateroom, and each of these staterooms has a bathroom which is lavishly equipped with the very latest Crane fittings, right?"

"I'm not sure of the brand," said Monty. "But, yes."

"Well, I happen to know they're Crane fittings, because Crane were the only people who could make them in the right shapes and the right colours. So, these fittings are very desirable. The kind of fittings that nobody would be ashamed to have in his own home. But just think how much *more* desirable they are because they're fitted to the first-class staterooms of the *Arcadia* on her maiden voyage, and because they've been used, *intimately,* by motion picture stars and big financiers and famous sports personalities."

Now Mr. Fribourg's voice dropped to an amused whisper, and he brought Monty so close to him that Monty could smell the brandy and tobacco smoke on his breath. "Think, Mr. Willowby, of *owning* the actual toilet seat that Princess Xenia of Russia—well, the actual toilet seat. Think of being able to say to your dinner guests, 'You see that toilet seat, that toilet seat is the very same toilet seat which Mary Pickford—well, it was fitted in Miss Pickford's bathroom on the maiden voyage of the *Arcadia.*' That's what I am talking about when I say originality and intimacy. It's original, and it's intimate. It's the very next best thing to having that famous personality kiss you. Well, isn't it? It actually means that you, the toilet seat's new owner, can sit where a motion picture star sat. I've even thought of a romantic name for it. Cheek-to-Cheek. Now, isn't that genius?"

Monty Willowby gradually eased himself out of Mr. Fribourg's grasp. It was about as easy as unwinding a particularly tenacious snake from around his neck, and when at last he was able to stand straight again, at a reasonably refreshing distance from Mr. Fribourg's Havana-laden breath, he tugged down his evening coat with relief.

"I think, Mr. Fribourg, that one of us is probably going mad," he said. "And since you are the passenger, and I am paid to be respectful to you, it must be me."

"You don't like the idea?"

"It doesn't matter whether I like it or not. It can't be done. And what's more, I won't *let* it be done. I'm not in the business of unscrewing this vessel's sanitary fittings and auctioning them off to a lot of film fans. I'm the purser."

"I know," said Mr. Fribourg. "I know. But you were also the purser on the *Callipygic*, weren't you, in 1912?"

"What of it?" Monty Willowby demanded.

"What of it? I'll say what of it. The *Callipygic* was sunk in the Straits of Johore, that's what of it, in October of that same year. No loss of life, but a very unfortunate loss of valuable cargo, namely five thousand pounds of opium for the manufacture of laudanum and morphine and suchlike. And yet who was seen in Singapore only a week or two later, looking very prosperous indeed, and in the company of Kim Lim, the opium merchant? It wouldn't have been *you*, by any chance?"

"You're talking dangerous talk, Mr. Fribourg," said Monty Willowby uneasily. "I could have you confined to your stateroom for this."

"And I could have *you* confined to one of His Majesty's prisons, Mr. Willowby. Come on, now, pilferage is pilferage. But there are limits. I could mention two firms of Lloyd's underwriters who would pay dearly to find out what happened to that cargo. Not to mention the directors of Keys Shipping."

Monty Willowby snapped out a clean white handkerchief and pressed it against the side of his neck. "That's the way it is, is it?" he asked, and obviously didn't require an answer. Mr. Fribourg wetted the end of his cigar and kept on smiling.

"Toilet seats, is it?" said Monty Willowby. Mr. Fribourg nodded.

"Well," said Monty Willowby, "I'll have to give it some thought. I can't rush into it without proper preparation. It needs thought. Strategy."

"Don't leave it too long," said Mr. Fribourg smoothly.

"Don't you worry about that," Monty Willowby blustered. "I've got a reputation for extricating myself out of awkward spots."

A deep and sonorous gong announced to the chattering assembly in the Grand Lounge that the banquet was served. Sir Peregrine led Catriona into the first-class dining saloon, followed by Edgar Deacon, with Princess Xenia, and a red-faced Rudyard Philips escorting Mademoiselle Narron. The orchestra played the promenade from Mussorgsky's "Pictures at an Exhibition," as arranged by Ravel, with a clashing surfeit of cymbals and an excessive blaring of trumpets, completely overdoing the grandeur of what was already a colossally grand procession. "The privileged went in two-by-two," reported a feature writer from the *Los Angeles Examiner*, "and your correspondent was inspired by the comforting notion that even if the Lord saw fit to drown the entire Earth during dinner, and left no survivors except those who had booked passage on this vessel, at least the finest of the world's diamonds and the most tempting of its couture gowns would have been saved from the flood."

Mark Beeney took Marcia through to dinner. He said, "You're tense. You're all tensed up. Why are you so tense?"

"Why do you think I'm tense?" Marcia demanded. "You don't think I've noticed how you've been making pilchard's eyes over that Keys girl? It's so *embarrassing.*"

"What's embarrassing? She's a sweet young girl."

"You know damn well what's embarrassing," retorted Marcia. She flashed a synthetic smile at Claude Graham-White, who had found himself in the company of a silver-rinsed lady from Delaware with an ostrich plume in her headband and a diamond necklace that spread over her *poitrine* like a million-dollar child's bib. Whatever Graham-White said to her, she giggled and said, "That's so *English.* It makes my toes curl up just to hear you *say* it that way."

Mark said under his breath, "What you don't seem to understand is that Miss Catriona Keys will shortly inherit a very major stockholding in this shipping company. I need to be friends with her."

"Well, I suppose I've heard worse excuses," said Marcia.

"Marcia, I don't have to *make* excuses. Not to you, nor anybody. I don't know why you've come over so possessive all of a sudden. We've always been chums, haven't we? Why the grand production? You know how I feel about you. Nothing can ever change that."

"You didn't send me an orchid this evening."

"No, I didn't. I sent you a gardenia. What's the difference?"

Marcia made a face. "The difference is that I'm jealous, that's all. There, I've finally managed to spit it out."

Mark stopped, and stared at her in disbelief. "You're jealous? What do you have to be jealous about? Anyway, you're not the jealous type. When was Marcia Conroy, the elegant lady-about-town, the beautiful bitch of the Biarritz set, ever, and I mean *ever*, jealous?"

Marcia closed her eyes for a moment, and then opened them again and looked at Mark with a tiredness that he had never seen in her before. "I've never admitted it to you before, and if you ask me tomorrow I'll probably deny it, even under torture. But the fact is that I've been in love with you ever since I first met you. You don't think I'd drop strawberries and cream down just *anybody's* pants, do you? I'm in love with you. I'm in love with you in a way that I've never been in love with any other man. And that *includes* Woofy Thomas."

She paused and took a steadying breath. Then she said, "And the reason I've never told you before is because I knew that if I did I would lose you. Just like I know that I'm going to lose you now. Well, all I can say is I did try, didn't I? And jolly good luck to Miss Catriona Keys."

"Marcia, she's nothing more than a sweet young girl."

"I know, darling. I can tell by the way your mouth fills up with saliva every time you think of her. You can't wait to bury your face in those huge great bosoms of hers, can you? I should have known you'd go for a girl like her. Half-child and half-mother. Your Freudian susceptibilities are showing. In fact, they're quite naked."

"I don't know what the hell you're talking about."

"Oh, Mark, you don't have to pretend. Not for my sake. If you like her, then go and get her. How can I stop you? But just remember that I'm on this ship, too, and that I don't really enjoy being humiliated in public."

Mark guided her to the captain's table and pulled out her chair for her. "I seem to remember that you invited yourself along on this little bunfight," he told her. "And I also seem to remember what you told me in Venice. You remember that night in Venice, at the Grand Luxe Hotel?"

"You wore grey silk pyjamas."

"And you wore nothing at all."

Marcia hesitated and then sat down, nodding in acknowledgement to Baroness Zawisza, who was sitting opposite in a peacock-blue gown onto which pink pearls had been sewn in trompe-l'oeil circles on each breast. Somehow it was five times as erotic to glimpse the baroness's priceless simulations than it was to see the real authentic articles. Sabran, who wore white pumps and no socks, stood sulkily behind the baroness's chair.

Marcia murmured to Mark, reaching her hand up to touch his cheek, "I told you that night that we were two free-flying creatures, lovers by accident rather than design. Two random snowflakes whirling through the night, sometimes touching, sometimes far away, blown on the wind."

"That's right. That's what you said."

"And you believed me?"

"Why not?"

"If you don't know why not, then you don't know women very well. Good God, Mark, you don't even understand how gorgeous you are. Ronald Colman? He's nothing. You're a beautiful man; so beautiful you're more like some exotic species of animal, rather than a man. Whenever I hold you, it's like holding a lion."

"Marcia," Mark interrupted hastily, conscious that Baroness Zawisza and two or three of the other guests were listening to all of this with undisguised fascination. "Marcia, this isn't the time or the place. Please. Let's discuss it later."

Marcia was unabashed by the amused stares of her table companions. "Perhaps there won't be any later. After all, you seem to have other things in mind."

Mark took Marcia's hand and pressed it to his lips. "You are quite stunning," he told her softly, "in every sense of the word."

Baroness Zawisza laughed out loud and applauded. Mark raised his eyes from Marcia's hand, and for one split second caught Catriona looking at him from her seat next to Sir Peregrine. He had no way of knowing that Catriona had Baroness Zawisza's words on her mind: "Men are interested only in three things: automobiles, fighting, and their own semen."

Catriona had been placed opposite George Welterman and next (on her left) to Douglas Fairbanks. While Douglas Fairbanks dominated the conversation with a long and funny story about Lee De Forest and the problems he had encountered with Phonofilm—the first sound-on-film motion picture, which had been released last year—Catriona had time to study George Welterman more closely. He was a big padded-looking man, with a large horselike head, and yet he wasn't entirely unattractive. His face was deeply cleft with lines, and his hair was a dull alloy grey; but there was a strangely youthful look in his pale blue eyes, as if a twenty-year-old man had been made up with cosmetics and rubber and false eyebrows to play the part of a middle-aged tyrant. He wore only one ring, and that was not on his wedding finger. It was a heavy signet of twenty-four-carat gold with an embossed crest on it.

Douglas Fairbanks, having finished his story, turned to Catriona and raised his glass of champagne. "That's enough about me," he told her. "I think it's time we heard from our beautiful hostess, don't you? We may not have got very far yet, but up until now this voyage has been the most fun I've had in years, and that includes making *The Three Musketeers* in 'twenty-one. I'd like to propose an impromptu toast to Miss Catriona Keys, for being such a brilliant jewel in such a brilliant setting."

"I'll drink to that," said George Welterman and raised his glass, too. He had a slow, precise, and cultured-sounding voice. His blue eyes didn't leave Catriona's face once. "This shipping line has an unfair advantage in my opinion. The world's most beautiful passenger liner, and the world's most beautiful heiress."

Catriona glanced at Edgar and saw that he was watching her keenly but with obvious approval. When George Welterman reached across the white linen tablecloth and touched Catriona's hand, Edgar smiled to himself and took a sip of champagne as buoyantly as if he were congratulating himself.

"You're too flattering," Catriona told George Welterman. She wished very much that Edgar would stop staring and smiling.

George Welterman said, "I never flatter. I'm not in the flattering business. I'm a man of complete exactitude."

"You hear that?" Douglas Fairbanks laughed. "When a man like that tells you you're beautiful, you can lay money on it, you're beautiful. I wish he'd tell *me* that I'm beautiful."

"How do you like Ireland, Mr. Welterman?" asked Catriona in that lofty tone of voice that Nigel always used to call her Queen-Victoria-asking-the-Zulu-King-how-he-liked-whist voice. But George Welterman recognised her attempt to distance him for what it was, and in the same precise way as before said, "You can call me George, if you care to." His eyes were still fixed on her, still unblinking. He gave Catriona the unsettling feeling that he was able to see right through her clothes, perhaps even deeper than that, into her mind. It was like having the leg of her step-ins pulled aside by a cold and inquiring hand, like feeling icy fingers caressing her with detached and calculating intimacy. She looked away to one side, but when she looked back again, George Welterman was still staring at her.

"Very well, then, *George,*" she acknowledged with a polite smile that she allowed to die almost instantly. She couldn't think why he made her feel so very young, and so very clumsy. She was used to being able to captivate almost all of the men and boys she met, simply by being pretty and sharp and bright. But it was going to take more than prettiness, and more than brightness, to cope with George Welterman. It might even take more than her inherited fortune. He had about him an utter hardness which even his precise voice and his friendly table talk couldn't disguise. Anybody who wanted to beat George Welterman at his own game, business or sexual, would have to be equally uncompromising: diamond against diamond.

168

"You went to Ireland on business? Or just for the Guinness?" asked Douglas Fairbanks.

"Personally, I can't think of a single defensible inducement for visiting Ireland at all," put in Sir Peregrine, and then abruptly remembered, like a man jolted by that odd falling sensation just before going to sleep, that he was sitting only one place away from Mr. O'Hara, from the Irish bank. Fortunately, Mr. O'Hara seemed to be engrossed in a conversation about bedding plants with Mrs. John D. Rappermeyer IV, who cultivated rhododendra, and he hadn't heard. Or diplomatically pretended he hadn't.

"I don't have the time to travel for any other reason except business," George Welterman said. "I haven't taken a vacation in twenty years and I'm not sure that I'd take one if it was offered to me. That doesn't mean that I'm blind to my surroundings, though. Whenever I can, I try to take a quick tour of the surrounding countryside. This time I was given the use of an automobile for a few days, and I was able to visit the west coast."

"Very romantic place, the west coast of Ireland," Douglas Fairbanks remarked, brushing up his moustache with his fingertips. "But the precipitation is all hell."

"He means the rain," put in Mary Pickford, who had been half listening to what they were saying.

"I found it . . . rather frightening, in a way," said George Welterman.

"I couldn't imagine *anything* frightening you," Catriona said, archly.

"Oh, I don't mean frightened in the sense that I felt personally threatened. The Irish are very friendly people, perhaps more so to Americans than they are to the English. No, what frightened me was the lack of *will to progress.* It was the acceptance of things as they are, and as they always have been. As long as there are just sufficient potatoes to keep the family alive, and just enough peat to cook them on, and as long as there's a little tea bread on Sundays for when the priest comes to call, and a little whiskey to keep the cold out, they seem to be satisfied. There's no sense of commercial aggression whatsoever. There's no *capitalism,* not in the way that we understand it."

"And it frightens you?" asked Catriona.

"Yes, frankly it does. Capitalism is the essential tool for the general improvement of the human condition, and for the stability of nations."

"It also keeps me in silk socks," said Douglas Fairbanks.

"I'm serious," said George Welterman.

"Well, maybe that's your trouble." Douglas Fairbanks grinned at him.

Catriona said, "Don't you ever take time off, George? Ever? Don't you have a hobby?"

"Does it worry you that I shouldn't?"

"Yes, I suppose it does. If you don't take any time off, how can you ever look at your business with a fresh eye?"

George realigned his place card so that it squared up with his dessert fork. "I'm a self-contained kind of man, I suppose. An internal combustion engine. Everything I need in life is inside of me."

"You can't be that self-contained. Nobody is."

Douglas Fairbanks said, "Were you ever married?"

"No," admitted George. "But once I was in love."

"Only once? Didn't you know that love is the essential tool for the improvement of the human condition, and for the gradual erosion of the bank balance?"

George smiled, but didn't answer directly. Instead, he said, "Her name was Myrtle Greensleeves."

"Myrtle Greensleeves the motion picture actress?" asked Douglas Fairbanks. "Seriously?"

"I told you, I'm always serious." There was no hint of mockery on George Westerman's face, none at all.

"Hey, darling," Douglas Fairbanks called Mary Pickford. "Did you hear that? Our friend here was once in love with Myrtle Greensleeves."

"Oh, *really?*" asked Mary Pickford, her face bright. But then she frowned and said, "But didn't she—"

George Welterman fastidiously arranged his fish knives and forks so that they were all parallel. "Yes," he said. "Idiopathic muscular atrophy. Well, that's what her doctors called it. She wasted away."

"She was so *pretty*," said Mary Pickford. She plainly didn't know what else to say.

"Yes." George Welterman nodded. "She was so pretty, and she was so talented, too, and I suppose that's why I loved her. To some people, almost every love seems like the great love of their life, but Myrtle was truly mine."

"Those are very romantic words," said Catriona without sarcasm.

"Romantic?" asked George Welterman. "I don't think so. I'm not a romantic man, Miss Keys. I'm just describing the way it was."

"I never heard," said Douglas Fairbanks. "Did Myrtle . . . Well, what I'm trying to ask is Whatever happened to her?"

"She's still alive, if that's what you mean. She's in a sanitarium in the Santa Catalina Mountains in Arizona now. You wouldn't recognise her."

"Do you ever go to see her?" asked Catriona.

George shook his head. "She made me promise to stay away. The last time I saw her she was like a skeleton. All she can do is lie on her bed all day and watch her old movies. She watches them over and over. Do you remember *Bitter Roses?* Well, she was making that picture when I first met her. We had a hand in some of the finance. She watches that one all the time."

Now the stewards were hurrying around with terrine of guinea fowl, quenelles of pike, and dove breasts in gin-flavoured aspic. Catriona looked at George Welterman and said, "Let's talk about something else, shall we? I didn't want to upset you."

"I'm not upset," said George. "I simply wanted you to understand that just because a man doesn't take vacations, and just because he sees human tragedy in terms of economic failure, that doesn't mean that he doesn't have a soul."

Douglas Fairbanks said loudly, "Did anyone here ever try to run fifty feet with an orange between his knees?"

Twenty-one

By the time the banquet was over, it was almost midnight, and the *Arcadia* had begun to demonstrate her own distinctive rolling motion for the first time. Actually, it was more of a roll—hesitate—and then a roll back again. Baroness Zawisza said, "This ship is a young virgin, you see . . . she can't make up her mind whether she wants to roll or not."

The seas, in fact, were preternaturally calm, and the *Arcadia* glided through them like an illuminated carnival float being wheeled across a dark and deserted plaza. This was just as well, since a fifteen-course dinner which had included *filets de boeuf Robespierre*, goose stuffed with chestnuts, sweetbreads *á la Toulouse,* and *suprême* of chicken with truffles, was not likely to quell the sensitivities of anyone prone to seasickness. The meal had finished with strawberries, over which Mark Beeney sprinkled pepper. "It's something my daddy taught me," he said. "Pepper brings out the flavour of strawberries like nothing else."

There were several toasts. The loyal toast, to their majesties King George and Queen Mary. A toast to the financiers and the shipbuilders who had made the *Arcadia* possible. A toast to Catriona, and a toast to the *Arcadia* herself. There was applause and laughter, and the orchestra played "Pomp and Circumstance" to swell the breasts of the assembled company so that they matched their swollen stomachs.

Then Sir Peregrine announced one minute's silence in memory of Catriona's father, and sixty tables of first-class passengers stood with their heads bowed while Catriona herself closed her eyes and tried to remember those walks with her father along the dunes at Formby. It was five after midnight now, and the day of his funeral had passed. Tomorrow it would be a week since he had died. Catriona thought how irresistibly true that old cliché was, that time goes on, and leaves the dead behind. She and the *Arcadia* and all of these hundreds of guests had already travelled into Wednesday, June 18th, while her father would be arrested forever at June 11. "They shall grow not old, as we who are left grow old."

In the second-class dining saloon, with its pale veneered panelling and its stainless-steel motifs of mermaids, dinner had finished about a half-hour earlier, and the passengers were waltzing to the music of the Ted Bagley Sextet. The stewards served complimentary brandy (two-star) and complimentary cigars (King Edwards) to the gentlemen; while their lady wives were offered crème-de-menthe and Cadbury's chocolate mints (in comparison to the handmade pralines by Leonidas of Antwerp which were offered to the ladies in first).

Even deeper down in the social layer cake, in the third-class saloon, the air was thick with cigarette smoke and the passengers were dancing a conga. The bar was serving whisky and ginger, port and lemon, and five different brands of bottled beer. But the singing was loud and cheerful, and streamers were unfurled all across the dance floor, and there were funny hats and red papier-mâché noses, and hooters and squeakers for those who had drunk too much to do anything much more than hoot or squeak. In the opinion of the chief third-class steward, it was "a knees-up to remember."

Harry Pakenow had spent most of the dinner talking to a French Communist schoolteacher with a harelip and a photographic memory of the works of Karl Marx. To this schoolteacher, the dictatorship of the proletariat was everything—that, and cassis, and Pont l'Evèque cheese, and his black-haired wife with her greasy forehead and smudged red lipstick. Harry, however, was not in the mood for discussing politics in any depth. Discussion was all very well, but it didn't win revolutions. Only violence won revolutions—swift and committed acts against the capitalist establishment. To what else would the rich pay any attention? But there was nothing Harry could say to this schoolteacher, with all his intense and recitative opinions about the distribution of wealth and the opium of the people—especially when Harry had already committed a political act far more telling than anything this poor man would ever manage in the whole of his active life.

There were thirty sticks of dynamite in the trunk of Mark Beeney's Marmon in the hold below the *Arcadia*'s waterline, and to Harry that was the only political statement it was necessary for him to make. One bomb was worth a million leaflets.

With most of the steerage bumping and winding their way around the dining tables in the conga, Harry went out to shelter deck C and leaned against the rail with a bottle of Worthington and a cigarette.

Although there was a southwesterly breeze blowing across the ship, the night was warm and unusually clear, even for midsummer, and the sky was bedecked with its own jewellery, the stars. To first-time travellers across the Atlantic, it was the sight of the stars at night that was the most breathtaking. They seemed so sparkling and so near that you could almost reach up your hand and feel them prickle against your fingers. And the ocean was so calm that, as the stars set, they were bisected by the horizon before they finally disappeared around the curve of the earth.

Harry leaned his back on the rail and looked up towards the first-class promenade, where young Lucille Foster had stood that afternoon to wave to him. He hoped that when the bomb went off, Lucille would find herself in the care of someone who wouldn't panic, someone who would take her immediately to the lifeboats. There was a high risk, of course, that some of the passengers would drown, but he very much didn't want one of them to be Lucille. He sucked at his cigarette until he was down to the raw hot smoke at the end; then he flicked it over the side.

He heard giggling in the darkness. He didn't take any notice at first, but then Philly came tripping out from the shadow of the electric winch which stood at the side of the deck, tugging along behind her a small blond-headed girl with a button nose and wide brown eyes. "Oh, it's *you*," he said, with half a smile. "And this is your mate Lydia, I suppose."

"Didn't I tell you?" said Philly to Lydia. She was wearing a silver shimmy dress, and as she giggled and wriggled, the silver braid shone like Christmas decorations or the fringes round a birthday cake. "Isn't he *cute?* Lydia, don't you think he's just too *cute?*"

Lydia held out a soft, damp little hand. "I guess he is," she said cheekily, and then burst into uncontrollable giggling again.

"I heard you were seasick," Harry said to Lydia, swigging at his bottle of beer.

"I *was*," said Lydia. "It was too awful. Upchuck, upchuck, upchuck. I thought I was going to die. But I'm much better now. I think it was the meat pasty I ate on the boat train. I don't know what the British put into their pasties. Minced dog, I guess. Well, maybe minced horse. But anyway, everything's hotsy-totsy now."

"You girls should be dancing," said Harry.

"Oh, we don't care for the conga," Philly told him. "We only care for starlight strolls around the deck, you know the kind of thing. I guess you could call us natural romantics."

Lydia said to Harry, "You have a real funny accent, you know?"

"I've been living in England for four years, that's why," Harry explained. He finished his beer and wiped his lips with the back of his sleeve. "It's a Liverpudlian accent, scouse they call it. It rubs off on you without you realising it. Same as their sense of humour. Do you know what they call black people? Smoked Irishmen."

Lydia giggled again. Harry held up his empty bottle and said, "Maybe we ought to write a message and toss it into the sea. Then some poor shipwrecked mariner on a desert island somewhere can swim through reefs and surf and schools of sharks to open it up, and find out what a good time we're having on this voyage."

"Didn't I tell you?" said Philly, rhetorically. "He's absolutely *copacetic*."

"Why don't you go join the party?" Harry told them. "All I'm going to do is watch the stars, drink another bottle of beer, and then go to bed. I don't think I have the same stamina those first-class people do. Maybe it's something to do with the first-class diet. Maybe caviar really *is* better for you than steak and kidney pudding. Or maybe they put something in the third-class beer so that we won't stage a mutiny."

Lydia said, *"Hee-hee-hee-hee,"* as if she were a character in Little Orphan Annie, the new strip cartoon which had just started in the American funny papers. But Philly said, "Why don't you come down to our cabin? We have a bottle of giggle water we bought in Calais, France. Real French grape brandy. We could play rummy and get spifflicated."

"Don't you have anybody else in your cabin?"

"There *was* another girl, Lorna, but she wanted to go share with her friends. They're all in the Penn State ladies' swimming team, or something like that. I guess they want to spend their time chewing the fat about swimming hats, or how to do the backstroke without drowning."

Harry thought for a long moment. What else was he going to do? Drink another bottle of warm beer? Go back to the cabin which he was sharing with two Lithuanian students and a German musician who seemed to carry all of his personal effects around with him in loosely tied brown paper parcels? Return to the dining saloon and dance the conga with all of those sweating choristers and cheap-suited shoe salesmen and lady philosophy students with the curse? He felt inexplicably anti-social, unexpectedly critical of his fellow proletarians. How could they actually hope to overthrow the establishment when they were so easily pleased, when they were happy to dance the conga in a badly ventilated lounge at the very bottom of the passenger decks, while up above them, in halls of glittering mirrors, the rich and the famous swept around to the harmonious sound of a whole orchestra? He took off his spectacles and pinched the bridge of his nose. He could already feel the dull ache of tomorrow's hangover.

"All right," he told Philly and Lydia. "Anything's better than doing the conga."

The three of them linked arms, and made their way across the gently rolling deck. In the corners and shadows, couples were already intertwined, murmuring like doves before dawn; and on one of the hard varnished benches, with his arms around his black-haired wife, the French

Communist schoolteacher was smoking a Caporal and earnestly denouncing Hegel. One man, who looked to Harry like a deserter from the Foreign Legion, stared out at the ocean and whistled a plaintive tune through his broken nose. He had the appearance of someone who has punched a great many people, both men and women, extremely hard, and might easily do so again.

There were four wooden bunks in Philly's cabin, as well as an upright washstand, which folded away when it wasn't in use, and a folding table which could be erected between the two lower bunks on a stiltlike leg. Three large pipes ran from one side of the ceiling to the other, and Philly was sure that one of them came from the second-class bathrooms, because every now and then it gurgled inside and grew very hot. On the cream-painted wall, Lydia had stuck with chewing gum a black and white photograph of a grinning young man with very protruding ears and enormously wide trousers.

"Take off your coat," said Philly. "You might as well make yourself at home." She dug around under the mattress of her bunk and at last produced a half-bottle of pale brandy with the label *Les Trois Mers.* "Here it is," she said, unscrewing it, "although God knows why they call it the Three Mothers."

Lydia kicked off her shoes, hiked up her pale blue satin dress, and sat on the bunk with her legs crossed, like a little blond elf. "I vote we drink the brandy, and then play spin the bottle."

"Who's the guy with the flappy pants?" Harry asked, hanging up his tweed sports coat behind the door.

"Oh, him. Lonnie McBride, one of my boyfriends. Isn't he spiffy?"

"In those pants, and with those ears, he looks like a strong wind might carry him off at any moment."

Lydia giggled. "You don't have to be rude. Well, not *that* rude. You ought to see him dance the black bottom."

Philly took the toothbrushes out of the glasses by the washstand and half filled them with brandy. "*Salut!*" she said, lifting her own glass, clinking it against Harry's, and swallowing a huge mouthful. Then, watery-eyed, gasping, she said in a squeaky voice, "That's how they say cheers in France, did you know?"

Harry sipped his brandy more slowly. He didn't like it very much, but it warmed him more than beer. "At the rate you're drinking it, we should be playing spin the bottle in exactly"—he checked his watch—"three and a half minutes."

"Sit down," Philly told him, and then came and perched herself on his knee, tugging her shimmy dress up until he could see the lace trim around the hem of her knickers. "I just love your cheaters," she said and kissed the lenses of his spectacles, leaving a bright pink imprint of lips on each one. She was warm and she was wearing some cheap flowery perfume that Harry found, in spite of himself, to be unusually arousing. He didn't know if she felt him stirring beneath her, but she kissed him again, and then again, and the second time she kept on kissing him and wouldn't stop. Her tongue wriggled between his lips like a pink baby seal and lapped at his teeth. Gently, but provocatively, he bit it. Philly said breathlessly, "Ow."

"I hope you two don't think you're going to have *all* the fun," complained Lydia. "That's why I suggested spin the bottle. At least it's *fair.*"

"All's fair in love and war," said Philly, greedily kissing Harry again. Brandy and saliva ebbed and flowed from Harry's mouth to Philly's mouth and back again, like the tide.

Bending forward, Lydia reached behind her and unhooked her gown, five hooks, one after the other. Then she struggled it off over her head and threw it across the cabin. With a shriek of laughter, dressed in nothing but her camisole and her rolled-down stockings, she threw herself on Harry and started kissing him and nipping at his ears. Harry shouted, "Ah! That tickles! Get off! That tickles! Lydia, get off!" The three of them collapsed on the floor of the cabin in a struggling heap.

Laughing, protesting, he fought back. But it was a fight that he was too breathless and too tensed up to want to win. In the end, with whoops of triumph, the two girls unbuckled his leather belt (from the store where Janice worked) and dragged his pants off him. His dark red erection was already rearing from the fly in the front of his knee-length cotton undershorts. "Eureka!" cried Philly.

What followed took several hours: until the porthole was filled by first blue light of sunrise, as pale and as sensitive as the flags that grow in the water meadows of Minnesota. It happened, for the most part, silently, like the flickering pictures in a zoetrope, and although it was erotic and sometimes plain dirty, it had a grace of its own which left Harry feeling tranquil and at peace with himself, and even at peace with what he had done, and was about to do. Lydia clambered on to him first, while Philly kissed him and bit him and unbuttoned his shirt. Under the arch of Philly's armpit he saw Lydia pull aside the leg of her camisole, and press his crimson erection against the damp blonde curls of her pubic hair. Then, with her own fingers, she slipped him inside her, and although she was as tight as a duck, she was also warm and wet and irresistible, and he let his head drop back on the rug, his eyes closed, while she bucked herself up and down, panting softly under her breath, a breathy hymn of practical ecstasy. Then Philly was at him, licking away with her furrowed tongue the juices of his struggle with Lydia, probing in places where no woman had ever probed him before, until he didn't know whether to be shocked or delighted. He thought to himself, Who was it who talked about the rigid morality of the working classes? And then Philly was sucking at him so hard that he could scarcely stand the pain of it, the sheer thrill of it, the abandonment of it. There was more: Lydia insinuating herself towards him at four o'clock in the morning, Greenwich Mean Time, the cheeks of her bottom spread wide apart in her own clutching fingers. Philly rousing him yet again and biting at his shoulder as he lay on top of her in a crowded few minutes of sweat and perfume, and what was to prove the last ejaculation that he could manage. And then both of them cramming themselves into the bottom bunk with him, all thighs and breasts and bottoms, while he slept, or attempted to sleep, and the *Arcadia* rolled —hesitated—rolled beneath them.

But they were not alone, of course. They were not the only lovers. As that iris-blue sky was lighting up the windows and the glass roof of the Grand Lounge, Mark Beeney was dancing the last waltz of the evening with Catriona, slowly and elegantly stepping around the floor that was scuffed by dancing shoes and sticky with spilled champagne, amidst empty tables and trailing streamers and crushed flowers.

There was no sign of Marcia Conroy. An hour ago, she had gone back to her stateroom, swallowed three aspirin, and buried herself in her bed, too drunk and too stunned even to cry. Nor was there any sign of George Welterman. Discreetly, after one stiff dance with Catriona, and another with Princess Xenia, he had excused himself and withdrawn to his cabin. He had not gone straight to bed, though. At two-thirty in the morning, he had rung for his steward and asked for a glass of hot malted milk. At four, he had asked for more writing paper. As Mark and Catriona were waltzing around the Grand Lounge together, he was standing by one of the portholes in his stateroom, dressed in a maroon bathrobe, and smoking a cigar in an amber holder. His face appeared to be even more deeply engraved with lines than ever.

Twenty-two

There had been many other encounters during the night: some fateful, some trivial, some downright ludicrous, but all, in their own way, dramatic. The inflated promotional brochures that Keys Shipping had handed out to the passengers of the *Arcadia* had made them quite aware of how much they were making social and maritime history; but all of them wanted to make personal history, too, to do something that they would want to remember for the rest of their lives.

"I remember the time I sailed on the maiden voyage of the *Arcadia;* I met this gorgeously handsome tennis player from Phoenix. We had four days and four nights of absolute heavenly passion. I sometimes wonder what became of him . . . whether he ever won Wimbledon, or anything like that."

"I drank more champagne on that voyage than I ever drank in my whole life, before or since. I had champagne for breakfast, champagne for elevenses, champagne for lunch, champagne for tea. I even washed my teeth in champagne. After we docked in New York, I had a hangover that lasted for two weeks."

"I fell in love on the *Arcadia*. The man I fell in love with was your father. His Christian name was Jack. I forget his other name."

Mr. Joe Kretchmer, the president of the Wisconsin Agricultural Insurance Company, a short, bald, good-humoured man with an hilarious line in Wisconsin Polack stories, fatefully became acquainted with Mr. Duncan Wilkes, a newspaper owner from Anderson, Indiana. Mr. Wilkes was six foot four tall, slow-talking, with blond eyelashes like a large white pig, and fleshy ears that shone scarlet when the sun got behind them. His newspapers were crowded with columns of flower shows, funerals, and small advertisements. "You sell a newspaper to a small community by telling that small community all about itself," he remarked. "If you printed nothing more than the electoral register every week, you'd have a steady guaranteed sale."

Mr. Kretchmer and Mr. Wilkes had very little in common. Mr. Kretchmer loved his wife and his family of five daughters and most of all he loved horses. Mr. Wilkes was an unrepentant misogynist to whom the very word "lingerie" was something vaguely nauseating, and whose natural habitat was the smoking room, and the leather club chair. But both men, Kretchmer and Wilkes, were prodigious eaters.

After Mr. Wilkes had silently supped three plates of turtle soup, and then with an equal lack of commotion munched his way through five pieces of toast liberally spread with hare pâté, and four dove breasts in aspic, Mr. Kretchmer reached across the dining table and tapped him on the back of the hand.

"You'll forgive my saying so, sir, but I do believe I'm looking at a gentleman after my own heart. Or should I say stomach."

Mr. Wilkes swallowed his last forkful of juniper-flavoured dove and wiped his mouth. "I care for my food, sir, if that's what you're saying. My late mother was one of the finest cooks in Madison County, Indiana, which was one of the reasons my late father married her. I was brought up on good food and plenty of it. My late mother's biscuits were like Paradise on a plate, that's what my late father used to say. 'Renata,' he used to say, 'these biscuits are like Paradise on a plate.'"

"Well, sir," said Mr. Kretchmer, "perhaps we ought to make a little wager between us, so that we both take advantage of all of the fine food on this voyage. Supposing I wager that I can eat every single item of every single meal that is served to the passengers between here and New York; and supposing I wager that you cannot."

Quartermaster Oliver Lennox, at the head of the table, said jovially, "That's a wager that you can never win, Mr. Kretchmer. I've seen the menus for this voyage, and you can take my word for it, a man would explode if he ate everything on offer. If you think tonight's banquet is something, wait until you see what we have for you tomorrow. A whole lamb in pastry stuffed with herbs, and breast of woodcock with orange liqueur."

"I'll wager I can eat a serving of everything," said Mr. Wilkes quietly, mopping up his plate with a bread roll. "I was intending to do so, in any event."

"Now, gentlemen," put in Quartermaster Lennox, "we don't want to turn this table into a gambling hell."

"Let them do it," said Lord Willunshaw loudly from the far end of the table. "It's good for chaps to have an enthusiasm in life. Makes a change from all this postwar slackness we've been getting from the coal miners and the civil service, and God knows who else. Let them do it! And I'll put twenty pounds on Mr. Kretchmer."

"Yes, *do* let them," twittered Grace Bunyon, the stage actress. "I just *adore* to see people making pigs of themselves. It reminds me so much of those hysterical royal garden parties."

"Well, I'm not sure that I ought to." The quartermaster frowned.

"Damn it, man, they've paid for their food. You can't stop 'em," said Lord Willunshaw.

"No, well, I suppose I can't," Lennox admitted. "In that case, very well."

Mr. Kretchmer stuck out his hand, and Mr. Wilkes took it and shook it; a pink trotter clasped within a Neanderthal paw. "You're on," said Mr. Wilkes in his quiet, quiet voice; and Grace Bunyon was to say later that she had never heard such a gently threatening voice in her whole life, not even when Herbert Beerbohm Tree played Othello.

Right then, the dining stewards cleared the covers and brought on the sole in Pouilly Fumé, the Spanish mackeral *à l'Arcadia*, and the sweetbreads *à la Toulouse*.

"Would you care for the sole, the mackerel, or the sweetbreads, sir?" the steward asked Joe Kretchmer.

Joe Kretchmer looked Duncan Wilkes straight in the eye and said, "Yes."

Henrietta Chibnall, the daughter of Laurence Chibnall, the English champion show jumper, applauded loudly and squealed, "It's wonderful!

It's too wonderful! They're both going to be *frightfully* sick!"

Another fateful encounter: a mild, amiable-looking man in a noticeably dishevelled dinner suit, his hands in his pockets, sauntered into the men's smoking room after the banquet was over and proceeded to stroll from table to table, nonchalantly but systematically picking up anchovy sandwiches and crackers spread with ripe Stilton cheese as if he hadn't eaten anything at the banquet at all. As a matter of fact, he hadn't, because no place had been set for him. He was Maurice Peace, stowaway and professional gambler, and he had only emerged two hours ago from the steam-heated sanctuary of the first class linen cupboard.

A steward asked him if he would care for a drink. He thought about it for a while, his cheeks crammed up with cheese crackers like a ruminative rabbit, and then he said, "A half-bottle of Pommery and Greno Sec, if you don't mind. And perhaps a Welsh rarebit, with lots of cayenne pepper."

"You'll forgive me if I ask your stateroom number, sir," said the steward. "I don't appear to recognise you."

"Of course you don't recognise me," Maurice smiled. "I'm travelling incognito."

There was a difficult little silence. Then the steward licked his pencil and said, embarrassed, "Your stateroom, sir?"

Maurice leaned towards the steward and whispered, "B-*mmph.*" Then, smartly swivelling around on the worn-down heel of his patent-leather pumps, he raised his arm in cheery greeting to the first man who came through the mahogany swing doors. "My dear fellow! I've been waiting for you!" he cried enthusiastically, and the steward, too concerned about the consequences of annoying a first-class passenger to press the matter of his stateroom number further, scribbled on the order, "B-13," which he happened to know was occupied by Mrs. Archibald Zuckerman, the widow of the recently deceased automobile tyre millionaire. Mrs. Zuckerman handed out five-dollar bills as if they were Salvation Army leaflets, and he was pretty sure that she wouldn't query the price of a half-bottle of champagne.

The man whom Maurice Peace had greeted so robustly was Mark Beeney, returning briefly to the smoking room to look for the cigarette lighter he had left there earlier in the day. He said, "Hello, old boy," in an abstracted way, but he didn't give Maurice the brush-off that someone with fewer friends and acquaintances might have done. For all Mark knew, Maurice might have been a regular American TransAtlantic passenger, and business across the North Atlantic was far too competitive these days to allow any shipowner to say the kind of thing about his customers that William Henry Vanderbilt had once said about his railroad passengers—"The public be damned!"

Maurice Peace said, "A fine dinner, hey? A real fine dinner." The steward, moderately satisfied with Maurice's credentials, left the smoking room to fetch him what he had ordered. Mark Beeney lifted up one or two cushions, peered at the top mantelshelf above the fireplace, and said, "You haven't seen a gold and enamel cigarette lighter, by any chance?"

"Well, no," said Maurice. "But if it's been handed in, then the purser will have it. He's your best bet."

"I guess so," said Mark. Then, "Do I know you?"

Maurice Peace held out his hand, "We met in New York, about three years ago," he lied. "I don't suppose you'd remember me. I'm Maurice Peace."

"Mark Beeney," replied Mark, shaking hands. "Listen, I must say that I'm damned annoyed about that lighter. It had sentimental value, you know? I'm not usually one for losing things, either. Only money."

"You're a gambling man?" asked Maurice hopefully.

"I believe in luck, if that's what you mean," Mark told him.

"You're bidding in the ship's pool?"

"Of course. There isn't any chance at all that the owner of American TransAtlantic isn't going to bet on the distance the Keys flagship can travel in a day. No chance at all. Do you know what time they're bidding?"

"In about a half-hour, I gather," said Maurice. The time and location of the ship's pool was one of the few reliable facts he did have to hand, having accosted one of the smoking-room stewards almost as soon as he had managed to struggle out of the linen closet. This was because more money rode on the outcome of the ship's pool than almost any other gambling event aboard, with the exception of some very humourless and long-running card schools, and some notably eccentric wagers. The ship's pool was the nightly auction of twelve potentially winning numbers, and it was conducted in the smoking room by the officers of the ship and a celebrity auctioneer, picked from the passengers. The numbers were determined by the first officer, and represented a field of ten estimated mileages for the next day's steaming, plus "low field" and "high field." If the *Arcadia* was running at twenty-six knots, she could reasonably be expected to sail 624 nautical miles in twenty-four hours, from noon to noon, and therefore the numbers 619 through 629 would be auctioned —with "high field" to cover the possibility of the shipping company ordering extra speed and "low field" to take care of any possible engine breakdowns or bad weather. When there was a particularly persuasive auctioneer in charge of the proceedings, the pool could frequently exceed £1,000, which in 1924 was worth almost $5,000. For $7,000, you could buy a brand-new custom-built Pierce-Arrow two-seater runabout.

"Well, I'd better get back to the dancing," said Mark. "Maybe I'll see you later."

"You want a private wager on the mileage?" asked Maurice.

Mark, halfway through the smoking-room door, turned and looked back at Maurice narrowly. He was quite sure he *had* seen him before, but the time and the place completely escaped him. Mind you, Maurice Peace had one of those featureless faces that you could never really remember and never actually forget. He had short mouse-brown hair, parted in the centre—but then so did millions of other men. He had brown neutral eyes, and a nose with a slight bump at the bridge. His mouth was soft and pale and undistinctive, except for a thin clipped moustache along the upper lip, And yet so many men wore thin clipped moustaches, particularly since the release of *The Thief of Baghdad.*

"Okay, I'll make you a private wager," said Mark. "How about a hundred dollars?"

"Make it five," said Maurice. He had £120 in his left spatterdash, enough for one big personal wager like this, and for a small opening stake in a poker game.

"We don't know the numbers yet," Mark replied.

"What does that matter? Whatever number you buy in the ship's pool, high or low, I'll bet you five hundred dollars that it's at least three miles fewer."

Mark smiled. He had been deliciously conscious all evening of the harmonic vibration of the *Arcadia*'s reciprocating engines, and the humming of her turbines, and he knew that she was running smoothly and quickly. He wanted this ship for himself, and any criticism of the headway she was making was almost like hearing from his lawyers that a girl he was dating had a reputation for being too "fast." Maurice Peace didn't know it, but he had instinctively given Mark Beeney the one challenge that he couldn't refuse. That was the way Maurice Peace made his precarious living, however: by the seat of his unpaid-for trousers, and by his supernatural sensitivity to all those perverse prides and private weaknesses which led men to lay down good money, in any currency, simply to prove themselves right.

"Very well," Mark said. "Make it five hundred. I'll have pleasure in collecting it from you."

Maurice Peace took another sandwich, and pushed it into his mouth. Somehow Mark couldn't take his eyes off him; he felt in some inexplicable fashion that this man was to have an eerie and significant hand in his destiny, or had already done so in the past. What had Marcia said at Brown's Hotel about a shiver coming over her, like cold water?

"I'm trying to place where I've met you before," Mark told Maurice. "A speak, maybe, in New York? The Marlboro Club, on Sixty-first? The Tree, on Fifty-fifth?"

Maurice Peace shrugged and shook his head. "I've been in Ireland for the summer. The flat racing, you know. Good horseback racing in Ireland, the best. What the Irish don't know about horses you could tell your sister Sue in a two-cent telegram."

"You came aboard at Dublin?" Mark frowned.

Maurice took two more sandwiches, one in each hand, and bit at them alternately. "A thirsty fish, the anchovy," he said in a noncommittal voice. Mark said slowly, "Yes . . . I guess it is," and went back to the Grand Lounge for the after-dinner dancing. The swing door swung behind him.

Then, on the curving staircase leading up onto the promenade deck from the first-class lounge, there was an encounter between Rudyard Philips and Mademoiselle Narron. Mademoiselle Narron had changed out of her red gown because she had felt the first twinges of a migraine headache coming on. Red made her migraines worse. Now she wore a low-scooped gown by Martial et Armand in turquoise crêpe du Maroc, trimmed with gold thread. Between the stately freckled custards of her breasts lay a green-and-gold enamelled pendant, one of the last gifts she had received from Raymond Walters before Raymond had decided to put his wife and his cello before the uncertainties of operatic passion. (How Raymond had loved her once, though! How he had gripped the girdle of fat that surmounted her hips, and squeezed it with all the speechless appreciation of a man who had once stood for two and a half hours in front of Rubens' "Arrival of Marie de Medici" in the Louvre, completely missing his lunch.)

Rudyard said, "Mademoiselle, we ought to talk, you and I. I mean —we really ought to get things straight between us. It seems that we've rather got off on the wrong foot."

"The wrong foot?" Louise Narron asked him. It was an English idiom which, inexplicably, she had never heard before. She looked down at her green slippers and then back at Rudyard, frowning in bewilderment.

Rudyard took her arm and shepherded her upstairs to the foyer. "The thing is," he told her, "I may have given you the wrong impression."

"I see," she said thoughtfully. "In what way?"

"Well," said Rudyard, "you asked me if I would help you. And, I said yes, I would."

"And you no longer wish to do so?"

"Not at all. That's not what I'm saying at all. I *do* wish to help you, very much. It's just that I'm not sure you took what I said the right way."

"A misunderstanding, you mean? *Une mésintelligence?*"

Rudyard clasped his hands together, but then realized that he looked and felt like an Anglican priest and dropped them immediately down to his sides. One of his housemasters at school had always called him "the Reverend Philips" because of his unctuous mannerisms. He said, "Quite frankly, I'm in just as much of a mess as you are. I don't think I'm really going to be very much help."

"You told me. You had to leave someone behind in England whom you loved. But that is fate, isn't it? We cannot help fate."

Rudyard guided Mademoiselle Narron to the window. In the glass, their reflections stared back at them with dark secrecy, two supercilious ghosts who could cynically and magically float in the night. Rudyard could smell Mademoiselle Narron's perfume, and the closeness of her statuesque body made him feel strangely feverish and uncertain of what he was going to say.

"Perhaps it's better if we look for our *own* answers," he said. "I think, if I were to try to help you, and if you were to try to help me . . . well, I'm afraid that there might be an entanglement."

"Des complications? Mais pourquoi? Je veux vous calmer. Rein plus."

"Well, I know," said Rudyard. "The trouble is, I think I might be rather inclined to take your solicitude for something else . . . for affection, for instance."

"Why not?" demanded Mademoiselle Narron. "Is affection such a sin? How can one person help another without affection?"

Rudyard rubbed his forehead. "I don't know. I'm afraid I'm rather confused."

Mademoiselle Narron laid one mighty arm around his shoulders. In her green evening shoes she was at least an inch taller than he was, and apart from confusing him, she made him feel indescribably puny. Perhaps, when it came down to it, that was exactly what attracted him towards her with such irresistible strength. Perhaps, at this moment, he needed nothing more than a muscular Earth Mother, *die herrschende Erdemutter,* to help him to overcome his bitter sense of loss about Toy and to reinflate his collapsed self-confidence. The only problem was, he was afraid of Mademoiselle Narron, and even more afraid of what he felt for her. We can all admire the Niagara Falls, but very few of us actually want to go over them in a barrel.

"Of course you are confused," Mademoiselle Narron told him. "I am confused, too. It is desperately confusing to be rejected. But all I hope is that in our confusion we can cling to each other, and give each other comfort."

"I don't know," said Rudyard. He took out a cigarette, tapped it on his thumbnail, and lit it, blowing the smoke out of the side of his mouth so that it wouldn't go into Mademoiselle Narron's face. "I think that it's better if we don't go on meeting each other. Better for both of us."

Beneath their feet, the *Arcadia*'s deck was rolling—hesitating—and rolling again. There was a sense of time and destiny passing in the night. Whether the portents of astrology were true or not, the vivid stars wheeled wonderfully above the *Arcadia*'s line of passage, and the separate fates of her passengers were changed with each rising and setting star.

Rudyard said, "I'm married, you know."

"Of course you are," said Mademoiselle Narron. "I saw your wedding band. But marriage is all nonsense, don't you think, when you come down

184

to it?"

"You've been talking to some of our American passengers, haven't you?"

Mademoiselle Narron curled the ends of her gingery hair around her fingers. "What of it? They are mostly very sharp, very witty. They call Sir Peregrine *le grand fromage.*"

"*Le grand fromage?* You mean the big cheese?" Rudyard couldn't help laughing.

"There." Mademoiselle Narron smiled. "I amused you. I cannot be *so* bad for you."

Rudyard, still grinning, breathed out smoke. "No, mademoiselle, I don't think that you are. Perhaps you are just what I need."

"Then you will accept my invitation to come to my stateroom for coffee and liqueurs?"

"That should be *my* line," said Rudyard.

Mademoiselle Narron twirled around the promenade deck with surprising lightness and style, her toes pointed like a prima ballerina's. "It doesn't matter who seduces whom," she sang. "If there is affection and honesty, then who cares?"

"You're seducing me?"

Mademoiselle Narron stopped in mid-pirouette. "Of course. Do you think that we can really help each other if we don't make love?"

Rudyard felt the *Arcadia* dip and roll, nosing into new currents. It was one-fifteen in the morning, and she was passing the Fastnet Rock, on the southern tip of Ireland, before heading out into open ocean. From here to New York there was nothing but seawater. For a moment Rudyard turned away, not angrily or temperamentally, but only to hold on to the rail and let the deep thrumming of 50,000 horsepower vibrate through his fingers and his bones and his soul. This was a ship with the power and the grace of a classic racehorse. This was a ship that should have been his.

"You'll come?" asked Mademoiselle Narron.

A steward passed between them with a half-bottle of Pommery champagne and a Welsh rarebit on a silver tray. Rudyard waited until the steward was out of earshot before he said, "Louise? You don't mind if I call you Louise?"

"You'll come?"

Rudyard nodded, not speaking in case the heavens heard him committing himself. He was still under the same skies as Toy, after all; and he could still picture quite clearly the gentle flatness of her Chinese face, and her tiny dark-nippled breasts, and that childlike mound of Venus on which no hairs grew. He could still remember her saying, "Heaven and earth are not ruthful; to them, the ten thousand things are but as straw dogs." She had been quoting Lao-Tzu's *Tao-te-ching.* Rudyard hadn't understood a word of it, not a single word. But, while he was here on this brightly lit promenade deck with Louise Narron, Toy was probably sleeping with her lover Laurence, and not dreaming of Rudyard even for a moment. May be that was justification enough for anything.

"You'll forgive my hesitation," he said. "It isn't meant as an insult."

"I am not in any position to forgive you," replied Mademoiselle Narron. "I cannot give you absolution, Rudyard, any more than I am seeking absolution in return. I am simply seeking reassurance and comfort."

Rudyard said, "Yes, well," and crushed his cigarette out underfoot. If Sir Peregrine had seen him drop a lighted cigarette on the deck, it would have meant a ten-minute lecture; and he would never have done it aboard his own *Aurora*. But tonight was different. Tonight was a night when the rules didn't count. At least they didn't count if you were brave enough not to want them to.

Once inside her stateroom, Mademoiselle Narron closed the door behind them and pranced across the room to the cocktail cabinet. "I can offer you a cocktail they invented for me in Rome in 1921, for the opening of *L'Incoronazione di Poppea*. I was Poppea, of course. I was wonderful that season! My voice had wings! The cocktail is called Poppea, after the part I played. Can you guess what's in it? Peach brandy and gin, flamed with sugar."

"I'll just have a Scotch, if you've got some."

"A Scotch? That's a drink for those who want oblivion, not fun."

Rudyard loosened his bow tie and took off his dinner jacket. "Perhaps I can find one when I'm not in pursuit of the other."

"Well," said Mademoiselle Narron teasingly, "it depends which one you are pursuing and which one you hope to find! There will be no oblivion with me, I can assure you. Raymond always used to say—well, it doesn't matter what Raymond always used to say. He will never say it again. Not to me. But I am not a passive woman, you know. It has never been my nature to take life recumbently."

Rudyard, a little uneasily, watched Mademoiselle Narron pour him almost half a glass of straight Scotch whisky. "That's—that's quite enough," he advised her. "I'm officer of the watch at four A.M. I can't afford to have a hangover."

"If you can afford to follow your heart, you can afford anything. Do you know who said that?"

Rudyard took his drink. "I'm not sure that I do. Was it Oscar Wilde?"

Mademoiselle Narron was blithely setting fire to a jiggerful of gin and sugar. She watched the blue flames spit and crackle for a moment, then tipped the blazing spirits into a chilled pink glass of peach brandy. "Oscar Wilde would never have said anything so ridiculously romantic. It was Raymond. He said it one day when we were walking on the South Downs.

If only I had known then that he would leave me."

"Don't you think there's any chance at all that he might change his mind?" asked Rudyard.

She shook her head. "I saw his face when he told me it was all over. It is worse sometimes for the person who is leaving than for the person who is left. Such pain on poor Raymond's face!" She sipped her cocktail, and then spread herself out on her sofa. "Do you want to kiss me?" she asked.

Rudyard said, "I beg your pardon?"

"Do you want to kiss me? You can kiss me, if you like."

"Mademoiselle Narron—Louise—"

She ran her hand through her wild gingery hair and threw back her head. "Oh, how much I like Englishmen! Always so cold, always so polite! Don't you know how much that drives me crazy, that coldness? It inflames me! I say to you, 'Kiss me! please kiss me!' A Frenchman would have been lying beside me in the blinking of an eye, in an instant, plastering me with kisses! But you say, 'I beg your pardon?' so polite, so stand-office!"

"*Offish*, actually," corrected Rudyard, grateful to have the opportunity to change the subject.

"What? What did you say?" questioned Mademoiselle Narron.

"It's not stand-*office*. It's stand-*offish*. 'Ish' is an English ending that means 'sort of.' As, for instance, in 'greenish.' "

" 'Greenish?' What is 'greenish?' Like 'Greenish Mean Time'?"

Rudyard perched himself on the arm of one of the chairs. "If you were feeling seasick, *mal-de-mer*, and if your cheeks were looking rather green, I'd say, 'My dear Louise, you look a bit greenish.' Or, it's like 'peckish' meaning hungry."

"Ah," said Mademoiselle Narron, nodding in comprehension. "And also like 'radish'?"

"Well," said Rudyard, with an abrupt laugh. But then he realised that Mademoiselle Narron's attention was fixed exclusively on his face, and that she was devouring him alive with her eyes. "Well," he said, less confidently, "sort of. Yes, sort of like radish."

"But you still have not kissed me," she protested, her voice throaty. "You have taught me 'ish.' But you can teach me 'ish' from the other side of the room. You cant teach me 'ish' by letter. To kiss me, you will have to come closer."

"Louise—"

"*Aaah!*" she shrieked, a perfect middle A. "Come closer! Oh, you're so cold! Even Raymond was never as cold! It thrills me! Don't you see what you're doing to me? You're so cruel!"

With a melodramatic flourish, like a tragic heroine quaffing poison in the last act of a Wagnerian opera, she drained down her gin and brandy cocktail. Then she swung her arm and lobbed the empty glass across the stateroom. It landed unbroken in a half-open desk drawer. Rudyard stared at her in utter surprise as if she had thrown it so accurately on purpose.

"I am a woman on fire!" Mademoiselle Narron declaimed. "I am a woman on fire and you are a pillar of ice! How can I melt you unless I embrace you?"

She rose to her feet and she was as red and as inexorable as a column of erupting lava rising from Mount Etna. Fiercely she jerked off her evening gloves and hurled them to the floor. Then she tugged open the buttons of her evening gown and wrestled it off over her head. While she was temporarily blinded inside her upraised gown, Rudyard said, "Louise, I'm not sure that this is really the way to—"

"What did you say?" she cried in a muffled voice.

Rudyard stood up. It seemed inappropriate to be sitting cross-legged on the edge of an armchair while Mademoiselle Narron was struggling so enthusiastically out of her clothes. It made him feel even more like the Reverend Philips than ever. He put down his whisky glass, but then he picked it up again and drank the whole lot down in one swallow. For some peculiar reason he began to think of the time when he had been selected to go in to bat for the school cricket team when they were seventy-five for six wickets against Dulwich College, and when only an heroic batting effort could possibly have saved them.

"Listen, Louise," he began. "I can't say that you don't attract me. You do, like the devil. You're a remarkable woman."

She didn't give him the chance to say any more. She emerged flushed from her tangled evening gown and tossed it onto the sofa. "I knew you were tender from the moment you first looked at me," she said. *"That* one, my heart sang! *That* one, he is for me! Balm to the spirit, comfort for the soul!"

Dressed in nothing more than her pink underslip, beneath which her huge breasts bounced in a complicated two-step, and in pink silk stockings, over the top of which her heavy white thighs wobbled in rhythmical accompaniment, Louise Narron advanced across the crimson rug with her arms open wide for Rudyard to embrace her. Rudyard stared at her for one giddy moment: at her wide green eyes, at her irrepressible red hair, at her pink pouting lips which wanted nothing more than to suck and nuzzle at his unprotected flesh. And he thought, God, I'm scared.

He could have funked it, of course, with a quick salute and a hurried good night. He could have pushed her away. He could even have pretended to faint. But then how could he have endured the rest of the voyage, seeing her four or five times a day on the promenade deck, and at dinner? He would have ended up slinking around his own ship like a fugitive.

Besides, although he was frightened by her, she *did* excite him. She made his brains feel as if they were effervescing in champagne, and the blood between his legs boil like giblet gravy. And it was his fear of her, as much as anything, that electrified him.

He said, "Louise, we ought to—" but then she grasped his face in her hands and kissed him soundly on the lips.

He wondered if this was what it was like when you drowned. Louise Narron's mouth was clamped so tightly to his that he was unable to breathe, and after the first thirty seconds the room seemed to go dark and the stars appeared to come out. He thought of Toy, and about the silly cricket match against Dulwich, but he also found it impossible to ignore the huge bosoms that were squashed against his mess jacket, and the Amazonian thigh that was working its way up between his knees. Then he felt the greedy fingers that were twisting open his buttons, and the grasping hand that was forcing its way into his trousers, and he understood with considerable clarity and also with some relief that he was being raped.

As for Louise Narron herself, her disappointment and her hurt both needed quenching so thoroughly and so urgently that she was not ashamed of what she was doing. Usually, in spite of her operatic physique, she was a shy and very feminine woman. Coquettish sometimes. For Raymond had always taken the initiative when they had made love together, and Raymond had always treated her as if she were a gentle and sensitive creature, a butterfly or a bird. He had adored her sheer fleshiness, of course. That had been the stuff of his desire for her. He had loved to enfold his penis in the rolls of her stomach or between her breasts. But he had always treated her fat as if it were ethereal, as if it were nothing more substantial than the billows in a Rubens painting,and he had always given her wings. Except on that last day, when the ethereal had suddenly been exposed as being heavily corporeal; and Louise Narron had discovered that she could no longer fly.

Raymond had been the latest and the most painful in a lifetime of rejections. Louise's parents had been rigid bourgeoisie, and puritanically suspicious of anything theatrical. Her father, a magistrates' clerk, had once tanned her for singing a trill on the Sabbath. Her mother had disapproved of everything she did, and had thrown two terms of school crochet work on the fire because Louise had been "too proud" about it. Only the efforts of a sympathetic Ursuline sister at the convent where she was educated had allowed Louise to carry on with music lessons; and even when she was chosen to sing with the Metropolitan Opera Company her parents had refused to attend, because her opening performance was in *Le Nozze di Figaro,* and her mother had once been annoyed by an Italian lodger.

Her success in opera had been meteoric. Her voice, in the words of the opera critic for *Le Figaro,* was like "the core of the sun." But in her private life there had been one disastrous affair after another. Guido Carlo, the operatic producer; Charles Feldman, the producer; and then

Raymond. Perhaps her lovers, mistaking her success on the stage for supreme confidence, and her statuesque body for a dominant personality, had always expected her to take the initiative. Perhaps, contrarily, she had needed them too much. Whatever it was, she was determined to be aggressive with Rudyard. She was determined that she would never wait again by a telephone that never rang, or in a dingy hotel room for somebody else's husband who never showed up.

She pinned Rudyard down on the silky quilt of her bed while she forced him to penetrate her. She gripped his wrists and clung on to them as if she were riding a Scott motorcycle, and jostled her ample buttocks onto his midriff until he had pierced the very deepest crevice of her. His face was ruddily tanned as far as his collar: the rest of him was white, apart from the two tanned gloves of his hands. He coughed and went crimson as he filled her, far too promptly, with semen. Then she rolled over and lay on the bed staring at the ceiling, while he hopped and struggled into his mess trousers.

He didn't feel guilty, of course, that he hadn't satisfied her. In 1924 it was still unusual for men to realise that women needed to reach a climax quite as regularly as men. The word "orgasm" was not in public currency. As long as a chap got it over with, well, that was all right; and if the woman liked it too, well, that was a bonus.

"You're disappointed," said Louise.

"Of course not," Rudyard told her, flicking one end of his bow tie over the other and tightening it up. "That was wonderful."

"No, it wasn't," said Louise. "It was sad. Sad, and useless."

Rudyard knew that she was right. But he couldn't understand what had gone wrong. As a matter of fact, he couldn't understand why it had happened at all. He finished tying his tie.

Louise sat up. Between her parted thighs, white fluid dripped slowly out of ginger hair, as slowly as glue, or honey. She thought of the morning that Raymond had once sat naked on a Czechoslovakian bentwood chair and played Mozart on his cello. Sad, sweet, throatsome music that had made her openly cry. She had left a single tear running down the window that overlooked Kensington Gore and the Albert Hall.

"Well, perhaps we should try again, when I have had fewer Poppea cocktails," said Louise. "Or then again, perhaps not."

Rudyard said, "I'm sorry. I don't know what to say."

"Why should you say anything? It was just as much my fault as yours."

Rudyard buttoned up his suspenders, and then pushed his arms into the sleeves of his mess jacket. "Let's talk tomorrow," he said.

"Yes," she said. She was still sitting on the bed when Rudyard left the stateroom and closed the door behind him as quietly as if he were closing a safe which contained a guilty secret.

Only a few minutes after Rudyard had left Louise Narron's state-room, the wireless officer—Willis the Wireless, as he was unfailingly nicknamed—knocked respectfully at the door of Sir Peregrine's sitting room. Sir Peregrine was listening to Elgar on his gramophone and twiddling his stockinged toes in time to the music. "What is it?" he demanded. He was drinking mineral water with a slice of lemon in. it and nibbling at cashew nuts. He always felt hungry in the early hours of the morning, and he had been known on several occasions to make his way down to a ship's pantry in his dressing gown, to pilfer a slice of game pie or some of the hot rolls that the night shift were making in the bakery.

"Message from the harbourmaster at Dublin, sir," said the wireless officer.

"Well? What do the bloody Irish want now?"

Willis the Wireless had only been seconded to the *Arcadia* at the last moment, and he was unused to captains as grand and as elevated as Sir Peregrine Arrowsmith. What was even more unnerving, he had taken the wireless message himself, and he knew what was in it. All he could find the courage to do was to hold out the message in a trembling hand until Sir Peregrine snatched it from him, and then to stand to attention, his eyes fixed on the oil painting above the fireplace of RMS *Shannon* in an Atlantic swell. Sir Peregrine's sitting room was panelled in oak and spread with Indian carpets, like a Pall Mall club in miniature. The interior designers had originally suggested "a functional studio," but Sir Peregrine had adamantly refused to have anything to do with it. "Too damned German," he had declared.

Chewing cashews, Sir Peregrine unfolded the message and read it. Halfway through, he stopped chewing. In the quick block letters of a wireless operator's hand were written the words "Irish fishing vessel has rescued eleven-year-old boy Sean Joyce, survivor of wreck of fishing smack *Drogheda*, out of Dublin. Boy claims *Drogheda* was run down by *Arcadia* at high speed and sunk. Search continues for Thomas Dennis, hirer of boat, feared drowned."

"What's this nonsense?" asked Sir Peregrine fiercely, holding up the message as he chased the last few fragments of nut around the insides of his cheeks with the tip of his tongue. "When did this arrive?"

"Just arrived, sir," said Willis. "Just arrived this minute."

"Well, what does it mean?" demanded Sir Peregrine. "What does it all mean? An eleven-year-old boy says I ran him down? What kind of damned nonsense is that?"

"I don't know, sir," said Willis unhappily.

"I don't *expect* you to know; don't worry about that," blustered Sir Peregrine. "Every single damned wireless message the Irish send out is either incomprehensible or reprehensible. Generally both. I'm asking you *rhetorically*, if you know what it means. In other words, I'm *asking* you, but I know the answer already, and the answer is humbug, that's what the answer is. Hum-bloody-bug."

He circled his sitting room as if he were chasing a bluebottle. Then he stopped and stiffly handed the message back to the wireless operator and snapped, "Send a message to the Dublin harbourmaster. What's his name? O'Shaughnessy or some other damned barbaric nonsense. Ask him what the damned hell he means by this message. Ask him what the damned *hell* he's going on about. Put it politely, of course. Say, "*Arcadia* in no known collision. Kindly furnish details. And may the whole of Ireland sink into the sea without a trace." No, leave out that last sentence, damn it."

Back in the wireless room, Willis the Wireless donned his headphones and hurriedly began to send back to Dublin the message that the *Arcadia* knew nothing of any collision with the *Drogheda,* and would Dublin please furnish further information. He was still tapping away at his key when Rudyard Philips looked in at the door, looking tired and anxious and still adjusting his bow tie.

"Anything up?" he asked, offering the wireless officer a cigarette.

Willis declined the cigarette with a wave of his hand and continued tapping out Morse.

"What's wrong?" Rudyard repeated. In reply, Willis pushed across the original message from Dublin harbour. Rudyard picked it up and read it carefully.

"My God," he said. "We've killed someone."

The wireless officer took off his headphones and laid them on the table. "I don't know yet, sir. That's the only information we've received."

"What did Sir Peregrine say about it? I mean, he's seen it, of course?"

"Oh, yes, sir, I took it straight round to his sitting room. He took it very bad, sir. Said it was nonsense."

Rudyard said, "Very well," and walked quickly along the deck to the door of Sir Peregrine's quarters. He tightened his bow tie, and knocked.

"Oh, it's you," said Sir Peregrine. He was ready for bed now, in royal blue silk pyjamas, with the Keys company crest embroidered on the pocket in gold braid.

"I've just seen the message from Dublin, Sir Peregrine," said Rudyard.

"As well you might." Sir Peregrine nodded. "More damned madness, that's all I can say. The whole damned country's populated by thieves and lunatics. Now they're claiming we've run over one of their sightseeing vessels. Madness."

"We did leave Irish waters at an unusually high speed," Rudyard reminded him.

"Unusually high speed, Mr. Philips?" asked Sir Peregrine. "What do you mean by that?"

"I mean we were steaming full ahead, sir, when we were still within the three-mile limit; and we *had* been warned of the presence of small craft. Also, the visibility wasn't particularly good."

Sir Peregrine stared at him glassily. "If that is so, Mr. Philips, then I would like to know who was on the bridge at that time."

"I was, sir. Acting under your specific instructions."

"What?" said Sir Peregrine. "What instructions? To steam out of Irish waters like a bat out of hell? Did I specifically instruct you to do that? To proceed at full speed without paying any attention whatsoever to the presence of small craft? Did you hear me say that?"

"Not in so many words, sir."

"Then what? What were these specific instructions that led you to believe you could run down anyone you liked, willy-nilly?"

"You said slow ahead for one mile, sir, and then full ahead. You said we should show those Irish barbarians what a modern express liner could do."

Sir Peregrine clasped the back of his library chair, and his fingertips dug into it as if he were gripping an Irishman's neck. "In that case, Mr. Philips, I believe you misheard me. I believe we have a misunderstanding here, and that's putting it charitably. I don't know how things were run on the *Aurora*, God help her, before she went into dry dock; but I don't want them run like that on *this* vessel. I specifically told you slow ahead for three miles, and to pay particular attention to small vessels."

"I have to disagree with you, sir. You clearly said slow ahead for one mile, and when I continued to sail slow ahead as a precaution, you criticised me for disobeying your orders. The impression you gave me was that you wanted to vacate Irish territorial waters as quickly as humanly possible."

"*Impression?*" screamed Sir Peregrine. Spit flew from his lips, and he stalked around the library chair and confronted Rudyard from only six inches away. "*Impression?* You're the captain of your own ship, Mr. Philips, and you talk about sailing the world's largest passenger liner on an *impression?*"

Rudyard said dully, "We've had a collision, Sir Peregrine. A man may have drowned. All you're trying to do is lay the blame on me instead of on yourself, where you know it belongs."

Sir Peregrine turned away. "I see," he said. "You're reduced to snivelling now, are you, and blind accusations? Is that it? You won't accept the responsibility of your own foolhardy actions? Is that it? Is that what you're trying to tell me?"

"You gave me clear orders to sail slow ahead for one mile, and then to sail full ahead thereafter," repeated Rudyard.

"Rubbish!" Sir Peregrine exposulated. "Rubbish and double rubbish!

How dare you suggest that I could do such a thing! You pathetic, spineless, lukewarm, chattering sea creature! How dare you! I order you confined to your quarters until further notice!"

Rudyard took a deep, unsteady breath. "You've been waiting for this, haven't you? You've been waiting for any opportunity to get me out of your way. Well, you can do your worst, but I can remember your orders to the last letter. If someone's drowned, then it's your responsibility, and however much you bluster and fuss, I'm going to make damn sure that you get just what you deserve. You're a puffed-up, ridiculous incompetent, and it's about time this company realised it. You no more deserve to captain a ship like the *Arcadia* than Captain Bligh deserved to command the *Bounty*."

Sir Peregrine stood upright and still, as white and as brittle as a fossil of himself might be if it were excavated from the chalk cliffs of England in some far and unrealised future.

"You are confined to your quarters," he repeated. "Mr. Peel will take over your duties until further notice."

Rudyard was shaking with wrath and nerves. When he spoke, his voice wavered uncontrollably. But he managed to say, "You've made a serious mistake, Sir Peregrine. This isn't any ordinary voyage by any means. It's the *Arcadia*'s maiden voyage, and the slightest mishap will be investigated with ten times the ordinary amount of rigour. What's more, Mr. Edgar Deacon is aboard; and so is Mr. Fearson, and so is Miss Catriona Keys. They will want to know what has happened in the utmost detail."

"And you will tell them, I suppose?"

"It's my duty."

"I forbid you."

"You can't forbid me to do anything."

"I forbid you! Go to your quarters! You're under arrest!"

"You're a madman," Rudyard told Sir Peregrine. "You're a complete and utter madman."

"And you, Mr. Philips, are worse," retorted Sir Peregrine. "You, Mr. Philips, are a bore."

Twenty-three

Halfway through the last waltz, Catriona had known already that she was in love. She hadn't meant to be, not so drowningly, not so helplessly. She had thought that the affection she still felt for Nigel might have saved her from being swept away, a life belt to which she could cling when Mark Beeney's sheer masculinity threatened to overwhelm her. But as the orchestra played a torrential version of "Over the Waves" waltz, and as Mark danced her slowly and elegantly around the floor of the Grand Lounge, she leaned her head against his starched white shirtfront and allowed him to hold her close. She didn't care about Nigel anymore; her feelings wouldn't let her. Neither did she care about Marcia, whom she saw leaving the lounge with a face—as her father would have put it—"as cheerful as a cracked dinner plate."

Mark said, "You tried to fight me, didn't you?"

"Fight you?" she murmured. "What do you mean?"

"You wouldn't wear my orchid. You're not even wearing my diamonds."

She looked away. "There were too many rubies. They wouldn't have gone with my gown."

"Nonsense. You were fighting me. And I'm glad that you did."

"Glad? I don't know why."

"Of course I'm glad," Mark told her. "If you hadn't tried to fight me, I wouldn't have thought that you cared. I would have thought that you were playing with me—teasing me just for fun. But you weren't. You were serious. That's why you fought. And that's why I'm even more pleased now that I've won."

Catriona raised her head. "Who says you've won?"

Mark grinned ingenuously. "I do. You're not going to snatch my victory away from me are you, at the last crucial moment?"

She said nothing but pretended to admire the reflecting pillars as they danced past. Then she leaned her head against him again and whispered, "I think you're the bee's knees. You know I do. It's not even worth denying it."

"Are you sorry you flushed away my orchid?"

She laughed. "No. Pleased. Anything to teach you not to be so arrogant."

The orchestra brought "Over the Waves" to a tired close, and Mark and Catriona applauded. Mark looked at his watch. "It's almost too late to go to bed," he told Catriona.

"Almost," she said. Her heart, after she had spoken, expanded inside her chest like one of those mud bubbles in a New Zealand geyser, and then collapsed again. She couldn't have said anything more suggestive if she had sat down and thought about it all week. She took Mark's hand, as if to reassure him that she really wasn't as fast as all that, and that she still needed his guidance and protection. For an instant, she was frightened that she might have put him off.

"My stateroom or yours?" he asked her abruptly. Then he smiled, and she knew that everything was perfect. The morning sun was shining, the ship was running fast and smooth, and she was intoxicated with champagne and affection.

"Yours," she whispered. "I own a quarter share of this ship, or at least I will do, and so far I've only seen the inside of two staterooms. Mine's 'Wind.' What's yours?"

" 'Moon,' " he whispered back. "Come along, I'll show you. Just let me order another bottle of champagne before we go. I'm developing a taste for your Perrier-Jouët."

"I'll be drunk," Catriona murmured, close to his ear. "I'll be totally helpless." She felt warm and giggly and completely feminine, and when he kissed her forehead and her cheek and the bridge of her nose, she could feel that she was already ready for him. Hadn't she been ready for him the moment he had first kissed her? Hadn't she fet that tingling urgency the very first time he had touched her hand? Moist as the opening buds of a horse-chestnut tree.

She had fallen for him. She knew it, although she also knew that she was probably being very silly. He was rich, vain, and unquestionably the most scandalous womaniser on both sides of the Atlantic, not to mention right in the middle of it. Hadn't he carelessly jilted Marcia Conroy right in front of everybody—the very girl he had brought along as his companion?

Still, the worst she could suffer would be a broken heart; and after the constant niceness of Nigel, she had something of a hunger for the agonies and the delights of a passionate romance. She felt a need for danger, an almost self-destructive desire to hurl herself right in front of an emotional express.

Mark unlocked the door of his stateroom and guided Catriona inside. All the table lamps were lit, and John Crombey was sitting at Mark's bureau, immaculately dressed in white tie and tails, poring through pages and pages of company accounts.

"Good morning, John," said Mark loudly.

196

"Oh." John blinked. "Good morning." He glanced up at Catriona and began to shuffle his papers into a tidy stack. "I was hoping we could have an early meeting on the Cleveland problem."

"Well, sure," Mark told him, tiredly peeling off his tailcoat. "But it depends what you mean by early. As far as I'm concerned, it's still late."

"I was hoping now."

"I'm sorry, old buddy. You're going to have to hope again."

John Crombey sighed, and then stood up, swaying a little with the hesitant roll of the *Arcadia*'s decks. "We're losing a whole lot of money on that Cleveland loading operation," he said sharply. "Twenty, maybe thirty thousand. We're going to have to revise our ideas from the basement upwards."

"Let's talk about it later, shall we?" said Mark.

"Okay," agreed John Crombey. "I think I could do with a couple hours' sleep in any case."

When John Crombey had left and closed the door behind himself three times, Mark tugged off his patent-leather evening pumps and walked across to the bar in his stockinged feet. Catriona untied the straps of her shoes, too, and arranged herself on the curving half-moon-shaped sofa.

"Champagne?" Mark asked her. She nodded.

Mark's staterooms were as lavishly decorated as her own; only the style was far more masculine. The theme of "Moon" was expressed in silvered leather chairs, a midnight-blue-carpet that was sprinkled with galaxies of hand-woven stars, and walls that were panelled in brushed steel and white enamel. On the bureau stood a white ceramic statuette of "Her Highness, the Moon" by François-Louis Schmied, a naked girl with a cloak that curved like the moon and a headdress of stars.

"You know that your Mr. Deacon heartily disapproves of us being together," said Mark, bringing over two tall tulip glasses brimming with cold champagne. He sat down beside her, unbuttoning his white vest.

"I don't blame him," Catriona replied. "He's quite sure that you're going to inveigle me into selling the *Arcadia* to American TransAtlantic."

"And you don't think that I might have exactly that intention?"

"If you do, you won't get much joy out of me. I haven't got the slightest intention of selling anything to *anybody* at the moment. I'm enjoying myself too much."

Mark touched the fine crystal rim of his champagne glass against hers. "I'll drink to that," he said. "But just bear in mind that you won't enjoy yourself too much if Keys goes bankrupt."

"Who says it's going to?" Catriona replied, with mock sharpness.

Mark smiled. "Come on, Catriona, it's common knowledge in the shipping business. Everybody knows that Keys is hanging on by its fingernails. You don't think I haven't noticed all those merchant bankers and financiers on board? The smoking room was like a creditors' meeting when they auctioned the ship's pool last night. If you ask me, most of them were bidding because they believed it was the only chance they were ever going to get of recouping some of their investment."

Catriona sat up straight. "You don't have to be cheesy about it."

"Who's being cheesy? I'm being realistic. You may own twenty-five per cent of a major shipping line, kiddo, but the banks own *you*. Didn't you notice that O'Hara fellow, from the Eire Credit Bank? Every time anybody took a second helping of caviar he winced. He was working out just how much it was all going to cost him, spoonful by spoonful."

Catriona felt suddenly bothered, and hot. She knew that Mark was right, but she didn't want to talk about it, especially now, and especially to him. The whole fun of meeting Mark Beeney had been that they both owned shipping lines, and that she had been able to believe that she was at least his equal (if not his better, since the *Arcadia* looked as if she was going to be such a success). But now—whether he was doing it intentionally or not—Mark was casually picking away at Catriona's glamour. There wasn't much ritz in being Queen of the Atlantic if her realm was seen to be irrevocably in hock.

She climbed off the half-moon sofa and went across to the porthole. Mark watched her, quietly sipping his champagne, as she drew back the star-sewn drapes and stared out at the morning sunshine. The Atlantic was sparkling so brightly that it brought tears to her eyes; but even after she had let the curtains fall back, she didn't turn around.

"You're here for the same reason as George Welterman, then?" Catriona asked.

"I'm not sure I understand you."

"You're here for the pickings? You're here to buy up what's left of my father's ambitions?"

"I'm here to enjoy myself, that's all. But obviously I'm interested if I can do a deal."

Catriona turned on him. "Thirty-five thousand dollars for a necklace? An orchid before dinner? Soft talk and late dancing? Is that what you call doing a deal?"

Mark grinned. "Not personally. I'd just call it being romantic."

"Have you made a bid for the *Arcadia* since my father died?"

"Listen, Catriona, this conversation is getting way off beam. I didn't bring you back here to talk business."

"Oh, I see. You just brought me back here to soften me up."

"I brought you back here because I think you're beautiful, and unusual, and attractive; and you have a whole lot more sex appeal than any other shipping line owner I know."

"So that's it. No credit, no liquidity, but plenty of sex appeal." She felt so furious now that she banged her champagne glass down on the white-topped table next to her and folded her arms tightly. It was a gesture not only of trying to hold in her anger but also of closing herself against Mark. "I knew I was being stupid when I first let you kiss me. Now I *know* I was being stupid."

"Catriona, please," Mark appealed to her. "You're getting yourself upset over nothing. I'm not softening you up. Nothing like it. I like you, and I want to be with you, and that's all there is to it."

"You still haven't answered my question, though, have you?"

"*What* question?"

"You still haven't told me if you made a bid for the *Arcadia* after my father died."

Mark stood up and walked across to Catriona with one hand deep in his pants pocket and the other held guardedly in front of his mouth. He looked at her for a long while, his eyes careful and thoughtful and a little hurt. His mother-of-pearl collar stud had come loose, and his collar was sticking out sideways, so that he looked like a very wealthy urchin, a street Arab who had unexpectedly come into money. She was resisting him as fiercely as she could; but she still couldn't deny to herself that he was madly arousing.

"What if I *had* made a bid?" he asked her. A crescent of shuddering sunlight danced on the side of his face, the bright reflection from a crystal ashtray in the shape of a half-moon. "Would that *really* make any difference?"

Catriona gave him a look of utter simplicity. She was pale from tiredness, but the darkness under her slanted eyes gave them the fashionable lambency of a desert princess's eyes, as if they were staring at Mark over a yashmak. Mark, for his part, had to concede to himself that if a man liked ravishingly pretty girls with high cheekbones and well-shaped jaws, and that shapely kind of figure that was halfway between the forbidden delights of puppy fat and the elegant leanness of the mid-twenties, then Catriona was as irresistible as cocaine or champagne or kisses in the first light of a summer morning at sea.

"I didn't mean to upset you with all that talk about bankruptcy," he said. "I guess I'm just plain clumsy when it comes to mixing business with pleasure."

"You did make a bid, though, didn't you?"

"Well, was it so *wrong* that I made a bid? I was doing what anybody else in my position would have done. Nothing more. I was thinking about my company's future, that's all. Trying to expand and progress."

"I'm not criticising your business acumen," Catriona retorted, very quietly but also very vehemently. "And, believe me, I don't think you're clumsy at mixing business with pleasure at all. You seem to have managed to make an offer both for me *and* my father's ship in one go. I can't say that you're not clever, or that you haven't got a good eye for a bargain.

The trouble is, I can't say that you're a particularly lovable kind of person, either."

"Catriona, will you give me a chance?" Mark retorted. "I made the offer for the *Arcadia* because the ship is beautiful, and because American TransAtlantic sorely needs an elegant flagship. I called Edgar Deacon on the day your father died. In fact, I called him as soon as I got the news. I realise that may sound ghoulish to you, but I very much wanted to get my bid in first. I offered four million pounds in cash. The offer still stands, although I'd like to have some kind of an answer by the time the *Arcadia* reaches New York. I'm surprised that Edgar didn't tell you about it."

"Perhaps he didn't think your offer was worth considering," said Catriona tartly.

"Nonsense. With four million pounds, he can make an appreciable payment to all of your creditors, and refit two or three more of your ships, and keep Keys going as a moderately profitable family business. At least that's the way John Crombey has assessed it."

"What on earth do you think Keys Shipping would be without the *Arcadia*? The *Arcadia* was my father's dream."

Mark smiled and shook his head. "Sometimes when people dream they lose touch with reality. I'm not decrying what your father did. You only have to *look* at this ship to see what he did, and what he was capable of doing. The man was a genius, and a visionary. But there are mouths to be fed, not the least of which is yours. And, one way or another, you're going to have to sell. Either the *Arcadia* alone or the whole damn fleet."

"And of course you'd prefer it if we sold the *Arcadia* to you?"

"Naturally. I haven't made any secret out of it."

"But you think that if you seduce me you'll have twenty-five per cent of the voting stock in your favour right from the beginning?"

Mark reached out his hands for her, but she tugged herself away. "Listen," he snapped at her, "if you think I've been making love to you just because I happen to want the *Arcadia*, then you're doing me a serious injustice. I mean, *personally*. The two things are entirely separate and distinct. I wouldn't even insult your intelligence trying to cajole you into selling me the world's most expensive ocean liner by making time with you? What kind of a rat do you think I am?"

"I don't know," said Catriona cuttingly. "But whatever you are, you're not being very decent about it."

"I don't *believe* this," said Mark. "I don't believe what you're saying to me! You really think that I'm trying to flatter the *Arcadia* out of you? You really think that?"

Catriona looked away and didn't answer. The truth was that she wasn't at all sure whether Mark had actually been trying to seduce her into selling him the *Arcadia* or not. If he *had* been planning on using her to undermine Edgar and the rest of the Keys board of directors, why had he started talking about business so openly and ingenuously as soon as they got back to his stateroom? Why hadn't he done nothing more than feed her with a surfeit of brut champagne, devious flattery, and gentle kisses, and wait until she was swooningly in love with him before suggesting that she should use her shareholding to pressure the Keys board into selling their flagship to American TransAtlantic? He was either being dazzlingly clever or numbingly stupid, and she couldn't decide which. The trouble was, Mark was so wholesome and so handsome, and his teeth were so startlingly white, that it required a particularly sustained and strenuous kind of anger for *anyone*, lt alone a pretty young girl, to feel betrayed by him for very long.

"Maybe we're both tired," said Mark. "Maybe we should call it a night and talk again tomorrow."

"I don't know what there is to talk about," said Catriona.

"There's us, isn't there? Or am I deluding myself?"

"Us?" she said with a sideways smile. "The rich shipping line owner and the poor shipping line owner?"

Mark shook his head. "Not at all. Two people who happened to meet on a maiden voyage, Mark Beeney and Catriona Keys."

"Well," she said heavily, "we'll see."

"You *will* talk to me, won't you?" he insisted. "You won't just leave me hanging?"

"No," she said, more gently, "I won't just leave you hanging."

She crossed the stateroom and picked up her shoes. She felt as if her throat had been tightly bandaged and she could scarcely find it in herself to speak. "Thank you for the champagne," she said, going to the door.

Mark said, "You haven't even drunk it. Why don't you stay and drink it? You might as well. They won't be serving breakfast for another hour."

"A quarter of this ship is mine. I can get breakfast whenever I want to. And I'm sure *you* can, too, with your charm."

"Catriona—"

She closed her eyes. She didn't want to hear any more, not at the moment. She just wanted a chance to go back to her own stateroom and look at herself in her own looking glass and cry to herself in the privacy of her own bed. Whatever Mark said now, she wouldn't be able to believe him. She wouldn't even be able to delude herself that he was telling the truth. The night's romance had melted like spun sugar in the heat of the morning sun, and suddenly all the sparkle had gone.

"I'll see you later, perhaps," she said, and went to the door. Mark came over and opened it for her.

"I want very much for you to believe me," he told her. "I know how you're feeling now, and I'm sorry I upset you. I guess I'm just another damned crass American businessman at heart. Marcia always told me that it showed from a mile away, because of the pointed lapels on my dinner jackets."

"I didn't notice them," whispered Catriona. "Maybe, if I had, I would have been more careful."

Mark licked his lips as if they were very dry. "I'm going to say something now that I've only said once in my life before," he said. "It doesn't come easy and I'm not sure that it's going to sound just as unconvincing to you as everything else I've been saying—"

"Mark—"

"No, please, let me finish. I don't want you to walk out of this door without realising that I've fallen in love with you."

Catriona swallowed. She felt as if she had dreamed all this before, as if her real life and her imaginary life had suddenly and unexpectedly converged. She could even remember the starry pattern on the carpet from some long-ago dream; and as the *Arcadia* rolle din the Atlantic swell, she thought to herself, That was why I felt in my dreams as if the whole world was tilting from side to side. Or, it could have been nothing more than tiredness, and too much champagne, and déjà-vu.

"Did you hear what I said?" asked Mark.

Catriona said, "Yes, I heard you."

"Do you believe me?"

She blinked at him. "Didn't you think I would?"

He grinned and shrugged, not sure how to answer that. Then he said, "You sure you won't come back and finish your champagne? I'm going to be very drunk if I empty that bottle all on my ownsome."

Catriona said, "You could always pour it into the sea. You might impress some lovely young mermaid."

Mark said, "I'll see you later, then. Sleep well."

"Yes," replied Catriona. "You too."

Ten minutes later, up on the bridge deck, outside the open door of his sitting room, Sir Peregrine saw Mark Beeney emerge onto the first-class promenade in his shirtsleeves and his stockinged feet, carrying a bottle of champagne. The commodore watched in bewilderment as Mark leaned out over the rail and emptied a splattering stream of champagne into the ocean. Then Mark went inside again.

Sir Peregrine stared at the deserted deck for a long time. Then he looked down at the china cocoa mug he was holding tightly in both hands. He could see the early morning sky reflected in it, and the dark outline of his captain's cap. He drained the mug to the bottom, and then pulled out a large white pocket handkerchief to dab at his lips.

He wondered if that damned pompous Philips would notice how strong his breath smelled if he just had one more. He certainly felt he needed it, if only to reassure himself that Philips was an incompetent idiot, and that if anybody had been run down and drowned by the *Arcadia* it was plainly and unquestionably Philips' fault. Philips had been on the bridge at the time. Philips was responsible. A captain could hardly be expected to be in fifty-two different places at once, could he? And if his orders were flouted—if a 53,000-ton ocean liner were piloted as recklessly as if it were a speedboat—then how could he possibly be blamed?

He opened the cupboard in his sitting room and took out the bottle of white Haitian rum. It was already a third empty. He unscrewed the cap and filled the cocoa mug to the halfway mark. Just this one, and no more.

He stood in the centre of the room drinking and thinking. He wondered briefly why that fellow Mark Beeney had emptied a bottle of champagne into the sea. Damned eccentric, some of these Americans. Damned rum lot altogether.

There was a rapping at his door. He called suspiciously, "Yes?" But it was only the wireless officer Willis with a message from the Meteorological Office.

"Well, what does it say?" demanded Sir Peregrine. "Read it to me."

"It says there's a possibility of severe weather in the early hours of tomorrow morning, sir. All that hurricane activity that was reported in the West Indies before we left—well, one of the most violent hurricanes has veered northeast at latitude twenty-seven degrees, sir, and it appears to have gathered forward speed. Could be rather a nasty one."

"I see," said Sir Peregrine.

He remained where he was, his eyes fixed for no reason at all on the brass cabin hook which was used to hold back his sitting-room door. At the moment it was loose, and it swung slowly backwards and forwards like a shining question mark.

"Are you all right, sir?" asked the wireless officer.

Sir Peregrine raised his head. "Mm?" he queried.

"I was wondering if you were quite yourself, sir."

"Ah, *were* you," said Sir Peregrine. "And if I were not myself, who did you suppose I might be?"

Twenty-four

At three minutes after seven on the morning of Wednesday, June 18th, the officer on the bridge was Ralph Peel. He was looking particularly sleek and pleased with himself this morning, although there was a slight puffiness around his eyes which attested to a night of champagne, more champagne, and several hours of strenuous copulation with Alison Cabot White, the Cape Cod heiress, who was gripped with what was now an even more deeply rooted penchant for hairy men. God, she had tugged at Ralph Peel's hairy back until he had bellowed out loud and woken up her mother! But it hadn't been the first time he had been obliged to nip smartly into a clothes closet in a first-class stateroom, and it probably wouldn't be the last. He had enjoyed himself thoroughly, and to prove it he kept whistling "Scotland the Brave" over and over until the helmsman was heartily sick of it.

Rudyard Philips was still in his quarters, not at all sure whether he was actually under arrest or not. He had called Mr. Deacon four times on the ship's internal telephone, but Edgar had taken his phone off the hook, and Rudyard's calls had been rewarded with nothing more than the monotonous beeping of the busy signal. Rudyard paced up and down the maroon carpet—seven feet one way, six feet the other. Then he sat down on the end of his mahogany bunk and lit a cigarette, blowing the smoke up to the cream-painted ceiling. He felt fretful and anxious, and yet he wasn't certain whether he had any cause to feel fretful and anxious or not. Sir Peregrine had told him he was under arrest, but there was nobody at his door to ensure that he stayed in his cabin. Louise Narron had seemed gravely disappointed with his lovemaking, but he had managed it, hadn't he? He had proved to her that she aroused him. So why had there been so much uncertainty about whether they were going to continue their affair or not?

In exasperation, he called Percy Fearson's number. The telephone rang for almost two minutes before it was picked up, and Mr. Fearson's strong northeastern accent said, "Yes? What do you want?"

"Mr. Fearson? It's Rudyard Philips. I hope I haven't woken you up."

"You can hope all you like, lad. You have. Well, what is it?"

"I seem to be under arrest, Mr. Fearson."

"Under *arrest?* Did I hear you quite right? What are you talking about?"

Rudyard rubbed his left eye with a nicotine-stained finger, and it stung. "It's Sir Peregrine, sir. He's accusing me of running down a small boat and drowning one of the occupants. He says I'm under arrest, confined to my billet, sir."

"Running down a small boat? I don't know what the devil you're on about, lad. *What* small boat? We haven't run down any small boats, have we?"

"Sir Peregrine may not have told you, sir, but we have. A fishing vessel called the *Drogheda,* a couple of miles out of Dublin Bay."

"That's ridiculous. We would have known. We would have felt it."

"Not necessarily, sir. The *Arcadia* is an extremely large ship. Very

204

few people on the *Titanic* knew that they'd struck an iceberg until she started to founder. We could cut through an average-sized fishing vessel like an axe through Derby cheese."

Mr. Fearson said thoughtfully, "I see. When did we first find out about this?"

"Early this morning, Mr. Fearson. They sent us a wireless message from Dublin. That's when Sir Peregrine ordered me to go back to my billet and to consider myself under arrest."

"It was your fault, then, this accident, was it?"

"Not at all, sir, although that's what Sir Peregrine's claiming."

"Why should he claim such a thing when it isn't true?"

Rudyard said, "I don't know, sir. I don't want to appear disloyal. I was actually on the bridge at the time it was supposed to have happened, but we were steaming full ahead, on Sir Peregrine's specific orders, when in my own opinion we should have been going ahead far more slowly. The Dublin harbourmaster had already warned us to look out for small sightseeing boats. But Sir Peregrine told me not to worry, and to build up full speed as soon as possible."

"You realise what you're saying," said Mr. Fearson seriously.

"Yes, Mr. Fearson, I do. And that's why I've woken you up."

"Well, lad, I think I'm glad that you did."

"What shall I do, sir?"

"Stay where you are for the time being. If Sir Peregrine's ordered you to be confined to your cabin, then that's where you'd best stay put. But believe me, I'm going around to talk to Mr. Deacon now, and then we'll most likely have a talk with Sir Peregrine."

"Thank you, sir."

"Don't thank me till we've found out what's happened, and who's to blame. I can tell you that Mr. Deacon, for one, is going to explode. There's a lot hangs on this voyage, lad, and if the slightest whit goes wrong . . . well, there's going to be hell to pay. Hell."

Rudyard took a deep breath. "I'll await your call, sir."

"Like as not you will," said Mr. Fearson, matter-of-factly, and put the telephone down.

At three minutes past seven, Catriona was sitting at her dressing table, her chin in her hands, staring at her tear-blotched eyes in the mirror. A little way behind her, Alice was laying out her cream crepe-de-chine dress for the morning, along with her shoes, stockings, and silk slip (she never *quite* knew if she ought to put out panties, it depended so much on Catriona's mood). In the sitting room, Trimmer was laying out the breakfast that Catriona had asked for: grilled grapefruit, toast, black coffee, and a glass of chilled apricot juice. He was humming "Gimme a Little Kiss."

"They're always the same, these shipboard romances," said Alice as she collected up Catriona's discarded evening gown. "They always end in tears."

"This *isn't* a shipboard romance," said Catriona.

"It's a romance, and it's on board a ship, so what else can it be?"

"It's a clash of personalities, that's what it is. And apart from that, it's a complete and utter swizz."

"He told you he loved you," Alice reminded her. Alice adored a good shipboard romance, especially between the wealthier and more illustrious passengers. It was something she could tell her mother about, when she got back to Runcorn. Her mother would sit with her feet in her sheepskin footwarmer, cupping her hands around her mug of Bovril, and listen with doddering relish to Alice's stories about the glittering improprieties of the famous.

"Of *course* he told me he loved me," Catriona retorted. "The silly thing is, he actually does. Or at least, I *think* he does."

"Well, then," said Alice.

Catrion took a Craven-A out of the cigarette box on the dressing table. "It's no use saying 'well, then,' " she retorted. "He loves me, yes, but the trouble is that he loves the *Arcadia* even more. He's a shipowner. He adores ships, the bigger and the more glamorous the better. How can a mere girl measure up to a fashionable ocean liner?"

"You mustn't upset yourself, Miss Keys," said Alice, with the syrupy sympathy of the personal servant.

"I'm not upsetting myself. It's everybody else who's upsetting *me.*"

Trimmer knocked at her bedroom door, his face lifted as rigidly as a Zeppelin spotter towards the northeast corner of the stateroom, so that he wouldn't be guilty of glimpsing Catriona in her crimson satin deshabille. "Your breakfast his ready, Miss Keys. Hit's hall laid hout. Hand a copy of the ship's newspaper, halso."

In common with most large Atlantic liners, the *Arcadia* was to produce her own daily newspaper, offering tidbits of gossip about her celebrity passengers, glowing articles about the competence of her crew, and a crossword to while away those tiresome twenty-minute gaps between meals. Crosswords were a hot passion in 1924—so hot that a Chicago housewife had complained to the press that she was "a crossword widow," and that a New York man had been arrested for refusing to leave a restaurant after four hours of struggling to complete a crossword there. The Baltimore and Ohio Railroad provided dictionaries in each car for cross-word-puzzle addicts; and if you were really obsessed, you could buy a tiny dictionary to strap to your wrist. The *Arcadia*'s crossword wasn't noticeably sophisticated. It offered clues like "Kind words don't butter them" and "Propels ship and fastens wood."

Catriona sat down to her breakfast feeling unhappy beyond description. Her toast tasted like face flannels, and she could hardly bring herself to choke down even a mouthful of coffee. Her apricot juice, which had been laboriously squeezed by one of the *Arcadia*'s chefs from eight fresh apricots, she didn't even touch.

Perhaps she had misjudged Mark altogether. After all, if he had really wanted the *Arcadia* more than he had wanted her, why he had even bothered to tell her that he loved her? Perhaps she was being more suspicious of herself than she was of him. Perhaps she was being as stubborn and as unforgiving as her father had been. Whatever anyone had said to her father, he had always needed concrete proof before he was prepared to believe it. He had never taken anything on trust, not even Catriona's assurances that she was happy and normal and well, and that her wildness didn't involve anything more than a few late-night dinner dances, a few too many gin and bitters, a giggly striptease on a pleasure boat that had been beating its way up the Thames, and regular but faithful fornication in Nigel's bed. Catriona's father had always been prepared to think the worst of her, and maybe that was why she was now prepared to think the worst of Mark Beeney. And yet: Mark *had* made an offer for the *Arcadia*, £4 million in cash, and there was no question that to gain Catriona's support and friendship wwould be his quickest route to settle the deal, right under Edgar Deacon's disapproving nose.

Trimmer, who was flapping at a few toast crumbs with his napkin, said, "Hanything helse, Miss Keys?"

"No thank you, Trimmer. This will be fine."

"Residue, Miss Keys?"

"I beg your pardon?"

"I beg *your* pardon, Miss Keys. 'Residue' was the word which one of my hofficers used to use to describe an 'angover. I was wondering hif you might be suffering the same problem. Hor similar, you understand."

"Well," said Catriona, "sort of."

"Hin that case, miss, might I make so bold as to hoffer you my patent remedy for 'angovers? Trimmer's Terror, my hofficers used to call hit, but hit halways produces the most hinstant heffects."

Catriona couldn't help smiling. "Hall right," she said. "Let's have a taste of Trimmer's Terror."

Trimmer marched himself punctiliously to the cocktail cabinet, where he made a great exhibition of opening doors, taking out spoons, and arranging glasses. He poured into a tall Lalique glass a measure of Russian pepper-flavoured vodka, then stirred in a beaten raw egg, a liberal squeeze of lemon juice, and finally, for good measure, a quick dose of Tabasco sauce.

"Does it really work?" asked Catriona cautiously as Trimmer presented it to her on a circular silver tray.

"They used to drink it in the Royal Flying Corps, Miss Keys, whenever they was called hupon to fly hover the henemy trenches hafter an 'eavy night on the Château Lafite."

Catriona took the glass, and sniffed it. "No wonder there were so many casualties," she said.

"Right down the 'atch, miss," Trimmer urged her.

Catriona hesitated for a moment, and then swallowed her glassful of Trimmer's Terror in three gagging gulps. It was like drinking blazing frog spawn, if such a thing were conceivable. She lay back on the sofa and gasped for breath, her eyes springing with tears, and her stomach gurgling and burning. For a whole minute the world seemed to be splintered and spotted with pain and pepper.

"I hope you haven't done her a mischief, you and your patent remedies," said Alice, bustling into the sitting room with clean towels over her arm.

Catriona sat up. "I think," she said, swallowing and reswallowing, "I think that I'm going to be all right. I *think*."

"What did I tell you," said Trimmer with self-satisfaction. "Nothing like it hafter an 'eavy night."

Catriona was just about to creep into her bed for two or three hours' sleep, and Alice was already unscrewing the thick green frosted-glass jars of night cream, when there was a knock at the stateroom door. Trimmer answered it, and from the bedroom Catriona could hear the clipped consonants and rounded vowels of a young and well-bred Englishman.

"Who is it, Trimmer?" she called.

"Begging your pardon, Miss Keys, hit's a gentleman. 'Ere's 'is card. 'E wonders hif 'e might be allowed a minute's conversation."

"Well . . ." Catriona frowned. She read the card, crisply engraved with copperplate script. *Mr. Philip Carter-Helm, 3 Pont Street, London SW1.*

"I don't know him, do I?" she asked. "Tell him I'll see him later."

"'E says 'e's a friend hof Mr. Beeney's, miss; hand that 'e halso 'appened to be han hacquaintance hof your respected late father."

"Oh," said Catriona. She hesitated for a moment and glanced across at Alice, seeking approval. Alice, who didn't like to be committed to giving her approval for anything, in case she was blamed afterwards, was industriously plumping up cushions. A friend of Mark Beeney's? thought Catriona. Perhaps Mark was trying to say that he was sorry, in which case Catriona would quite properly be able to forgive him.

Alice said, "You must do as you wish, miss. Far be it from me."

"All right, then, Trimmer," said Catriona. "Why don't you show him in? But only for a moment, please. I'm hideously tired."

Trimmer opened the door and Philip Carter-Helm stepped in, a little reticently, holding his hat in front of him like a small steering wheel. "Miss Keys," he said. "You must think me terribly ill-mannered."

"Well, this is hardly the time, if you know what I mean."

"I appreciate that," Philip Carter-Helm agreed. Catriona turned away, with what she hoped was an imperious look of disregard; but she had to admit to herself that Philip Carter-Helm was really rather attracive, if you fancied wholesome-looking chaps like Tom Merry, from the *Magnet*. There was also something inexplicably familiar about him, although she couldn't even begin to think what it was. She had certainly never met him before, not even at the Arts Ball.

Philip said, "I can only claim a very recent friendship with Mark Beeney, I'm afraid. But he did ask me if I could sort of have a chat with you."

"Was he too retiring to come and do his own chatting?" asked Catriona.

"Well, no, but he's afraid that he's been rather misunderstood."

"I see," said Catriona. Cold as Cleopatra. Modern and aggressive as Isadora Duncan.

"He wants you to know that his feelings towards you are completely separate form his desire to buy the *Arcadia.*"

"All right," replied Catriona airily. "I'm quite prepared to believe him, although it really won't make any difference at all, since the *Arcadia* happens *not* to be for sale. Not to Mark Beeney, anyway."

Philip said, "Oh," and looked around the stateroom as if he had mislaid something. Alice said, "Whenever sir happens to be ready," but at the same instant Philip blurted out, "Do you think that's a terribly good idea?"

"Do I think *what's* a terribly good idea?"

"Not to consider Mark Beeney as a possible buyer for the *Arcadia.*"

"What does it have to do with you?" Catriona demanded. "I don't want to sell her at all, as a matter of fact. It all depends on how successful this voyage turns out to be. That, and a few financial matters, but I can't see that any of them are any affair of yours."

"I'm sorry. I didn't mean to speak out of turn. But in the shipping business, the state of Keys affairs is pretty much common knowledge. Besides, I *did* know your father."

"Thousands of people knew my father."

"Of course. But I always liked to think that there was a special little spark of recognition between us. Like minds, don't you know."

"So you're in ships, too?" Catriona asked him, not frantically interested if he was or not. As a matter of fact he was getting to be rather a bore, and she felt tired and vexed.

"Marine insurance, tedious stuff like that," said Philip.

"Well, in that case, you couldn't have been much of a like mind; not with the father *I* knew. He could never abide anything tedious. Any more than I can. It's hereditary, I suppose."

"I'm sorry if I'm boring you. But Mark did ask me to come and explain how he felt. And I do feel myself that you could do very much worse than sell the *Arcadia* to American TransAtlantic. For one thing, they'll certainly look after her."

"Did Mark send you to explain why he behaved like a copper-bottomed cad, or did he send you to persuade me to sell him the *Arcadia?*" Catriona inquired. "That was exactly what I was trying to tell him: that he doesn't know the difference between business and pleasure. If you ask me, I think he keeps his heart pressed flat in his bank book."

"Please," said Philip. He looked for somewhere to put his hat; he couldn't find one, and so hung on to it. "I'm really not making a very good job of this. What I feel about the *Arcadia* is entirely my own opinion. I really feel that if your father had been given the choice—either of selling off the whole shipping line or simply of selling off its biggest asset and its biggest liability, the *Arcadia*—well, I believe that he would have gritted his teeth and sold the *Arcadia*. Better to keep the business in the family. You'll never get half as much as the shipping line's really worth, not if you sell it outright. Think of the goodwill Keys have built up over the years; think of the shipping contracts."

"For your information," Catriona retorted, "our managing director has looked into the figures *more* than thoroughly, and he happens to believe that if we have to sell, an outright sale would be best. And whatever *you* feel about what my father would or wouldn't have done, *I* happen to know that he cared about the people who worked for him more than anything else, and I also happen to know that he wouldn't have sold the *Arcadia* to Mark Beeney, because if he had, the rest of the shipping line would have collapsed and half of Liverpool would have been joining the dole queue."

Philip Carter-Helm was about to say something sharp in reply, but he stopped himself and bowed his head and said, "I'm sorry. This is very impertinent of me, and tiresome, too. You're right, of course, in a way. It would be very difficult to keep Keys going, just on the proceeds from selling the *Arcadia*. Even four million doesn't go frightfully far these days, not in the shipping business. You'd have to struggle very hard to keep your head above water; and that wouldn't really be your sort of style, would it?"

"Is Mark expecting a reply of some sort?" asked Catriona.

"Well, I don't know. If you see fit to send him one."

Catriona was beginning to feel very tired again, and nauseous. The *Arcadia* kept rolling and plunging, not violently, but with unsettling persistence.

"I don't know," said Catriona. "Perhaps he doesn't deserve a reply. On the other hand, perhaps he does."

"I think he'll be pleased just to know that you're not angry with him," suggested Philip.

"Angry? No, I'm not angry. *Peeved*, perhaps. I don't know. Not even that. I suppose he meant well. Why don't you just tell him that every-thing's jake, and leave it at that."

"Everything's jake?"

"That's the message."

Philip Carter-Helm stood where he was. Catriona said. "That's all, goodbye," but Philip blushed and swallowed and looked embarrassed.

"I *was* supposed to give you a kiss."

"A kiss?"

"From Mark, that is."

"What kind of lover sends kisses by proxy?"

"A shy one, I suppose."

"There's nothing shy about Mark Beeney," said Catriona.

"Not normally. But from what I gather, he's not normally repentant, either."

Repentant. Hmm. Catriona rather liked the sound of that. She could almost picture Mark in a monk's habit, lashing his own back and groaning with remorseful agony.

"All right," she said. "If you think he's truly repentant."

Philip cleared his throat behind his fist, and then stepped forward and kissed Catriona quickly on the cheek. It was a brief brotherly kiss.

Catriona looked up at him. There was something about his eyes which she found curiously disturbing, as if there were somebody she knew looking out from behind an unfamiliar mask.

"You don't—?" she began, but the question wouldn't form itself in her mind.

"Thank you for putting up with me," said Philip. "Perhaps you'll give me the pleasure of a dance sometime during the voyage. Then I can make up for being so boorish."

"Don't mench," said Catriona, being deliberately flapperish.

After Philip Carter-Helm had left, Edgar came into the sitting room and closed the door. He looked a little grey, but his bow tie was still immaculate, and his patent-leather shoes gleamed like two wet sharks.

"Who was that?" he wanted to know.

"A friend of Mark Beeney's. Nobody special. Yawns incarnate, if you must know."

Edgar took out a cigarette and offered one to Catriona. She shook her head, but then she changed her mind and took one. Edgar lit it for her with a steady white-cuffed hand.

"You know that I don't particularly approve of the way in which you've been encouraging Mark Beeney. I thought I'd made it abundantly clear before the voyage started that he has nothing to offer us, only difficulties. He's a personable young man, of course. But he's only inter-ested in American TransAtlantic, and his own amusement. Not in you; nor in the future of Keys Shipping."

"Well, well. You don't approve," said Catriona.

"I don't really think you know what you're letting yourself in for. Nor the company."

"Don't I?"

Edgar said to Trimmer, "Pour me a pink gin, will you?" Then, to Catriona, "Just because I confided in you when you first came back from London, just because I made it clear that Keys was in financial difficulty, that doesn't actually mean that I expect you to involve yourself actively in the running of the company. I'm the managing director, and that happens to be *my* job."

"You're worried that I might sell the *Arcadia* behind your back, just because I happen to like Mark Beeney?"

"Well, of course not; and in any case, you couldn't. You have only a quarter of the common stock, and that is not enough to be a deciding factor in itself. Besides—"

Catriona raised an eyebrow. She wished very much at that moment that Edgar would go away and stop nagging her. Why did everybody want to talk business all the darn time? She decided to give him as long as it took them both to smoke their cigarettes; and then to ask him to go. She liked Mark; she liked dancing; and quite frankly all this shipping talk sent her scatty.

"Besides what?" she asked.

"You're going to be a sensible girl, that's all," said Edgar. He tried a smile. It didn't quite fit, so he tried another. "You've seen what grave responsibilities we have. You know what IMM are offering us. I personally feel mortified that we have to think of selling to anyone, but I know where my duties lie, and I believe that you do, too. I believe in—what shall we call it?—the natural sagacity of the younger generation"

"Oh, bunk," said Catriona. "You don't think that I'm going to want to sell the *Arcadia* to Mark Beeney just because we've been dancing all evening?"

"You're a modern girl," said Edgar tightly, and a little cryptically.

Catriona smoked for a while, long exaggerated puffs, then abruptly crushed her cigarette out. This was all a pose. She was tired and hungover, and all she wanted to do was crawl into her bed, close her eyes, and sleep until it wsa evening again.

"You don't really think we'll have to sell Keys, do you?" she asked. "Have you talked to Mr. Whatsit of the Irish Bank? Surely *he's* impressed."

"He's not unimpressed," Edgar agreed, with caution. "On the other hand, he's like all our investors. All of our creditors, rather. He'd prefer to wait and see."

"Do you think we're going to take the Blue Riband?"

"God willing. Sir Peregrine tells me the engines are running like honey. And all due to that new injection valve your father developed. A very great man, your father, in all respects."

Catriona said, "Do you really think that there's any chance of keeping Keys in the family?"

"To be honest, Miss Keys, I don't know. I fear that too many creditors will press us too soon. Success has its drawbacks as well as its advantages, don't y'know. If they begin to think that we're back in the money, then we're going to be inundated with bills from hotels and meat wholesalers and vintners and fuel suppliers; and we won't be able to meet even half of them."

"How much has George Welterman offered us?"

"For the whole fleet? Eighteen million pounds."

"That doesn't seem like very much. The *Arcadia* alone is worth four."

"I doubt if we'll get a better offer, or any other offer at all. The Keys fleet is prestigious, certainly, but most of its vessels are already out of date."

"Oh, *I* don't know," said Catriona hotly. "The whole thing makes my head go round."

Edgar looked at her carefully. She couldn't quite understand his look. It was clear and correct on the surface, and yet because of its meticulousness it was also mysterious. Perhaps she hadn't known enough Anglo-Indians to be able to penetrate the mental regime of the Raj, in which life had been a never-ending seating arrangement.

"I'll let you get your feet up," said Edgar. (That was Raj talk, too: officers and their lady wives put their feet up; enlisted men got their heads down.) "And, really, if I were you, I wouldn't concern yourself too much with friend Beeney."

"I won't stop being nice to him, if that's what you mean."

"I'm not asking you to. I'm simply saying that it would be of some assistance if you could be equally nice to George Welterman. Well, maybe not equally. But nearly equally. He's a very sensitive individual."

"So he told us. He had a very sad love affair with Myrtle Greensleeves."

"Oh, yes, *that*," said Edgar, with unexpected impatience. "But, in any case, I'd appreciate it if you would do your best to make him feel welcome, even if you can't make him feel loved."

"Miss Keys," said Alice. "Time for your night creams now."

"All right, Alice," Catriona told her. "And thank you, Mr. Deacon. I'm sure that I'm much the wiser. And I won't interfere in business. Not too much, anyway."

"I'm glad we've reached an understanding," said Edgar, and then slowly drained his glass of pink gin to the bottom. He opened his mouth just a little wider so that the cocktail onions could roll in.

The telephone rang. Trimmer picked it up and said, "Miss Keys' cabin?" Then, "Mr. Deacon, sir, it's for you. Mr. Fearson."

Still munching onions, Edgar took the telephone and said, "Percy? What's going on?"

Catriona had already gone through to her bedroom and closed the door as Percy Fearson explained about the *Drogheda*, and Rudyard Philips' arrest. That was why she didn't see him snap his fingers preemptorily at Trimmer for another pink gin and sit down on the end of the sofa with his face as grey as the North Atlantic in winter.

Twenty-five

At twenty-one minutes past seven in the morning of Wednesday, June 18th, a number of things were happening simultaneously aboard the *Arcadia:* Edgar Deacon and Percy Fearson were grimly making their way to Sir Peregrine's quarters to confront him with their discovery that the *Arcadia* had run down the *Drogheda;* the wireless officer was jotting down a message from Dublin that the mangled remains of Mr. Thomas Dennis had been recovered by a shrimp boat from Dublin Bay; Catriona, in a mask of Swiss face creams that cost over $95 the one-ounce jar, at a time when you could buy a refrigerator for $87.50 or a radio for $37.25, was slowly closing her eyes in sleep; Harry Pakenow, scratching himself, was coming out on deck to take some early-morning air; and all over the *Arcadia* the cabin stewards and dining stewards and smoking-room stewards were hurrying to set tables and trays with silver cutlery, fold up clean linen napkins, and set out hundreds and hundreds of plates and coffee cups and jars of marmalade for breakfast.

In the kitchens, the underchef was supervising the frying of hundreds of rashers of prime English bacon, the whisking of scores of eggs, the devilling of huge casseroles of beef bones, and the wholesale squeezing of oranges and grapefruit and tangerines. Tea was being brewed in six varieties, from Darjeeling to Lapsang-Souchong. There were also three different coffees—Colombian, Kenyan, or a dark-roasted Continental. Breakfast included cornflakes and Post Toasties for those who wanted cereals, or kedgeree with fresh buttered haddock for those who wanted a taste of the English country house. There were West Country pork sausages, Loch Fyne kippers, and cured hams. For those who had really developed an appetite during the night's festivities, there was the crowning breakfast speciality of roast Norfolk gosling, served with quince jelly and cinnamon toast.

Below the waterline, the ship's laundry was a scalding purgatory of steam and shouting and the churning of electric washing machines, as the mountains of linen that had been soiled at last night's banquet were cleaned and pressed: over 150 tablecloths, more than 1,100 linen napkins, as well as scores of aprons, chefs' hats, shirts, collars, and white jackets.

In the bakery, the day shift, in their tall white confectioners' hats, were already starting on the fancy pastries for the afternoon's tea (the night shift, a more lowly caste, baked the rolls and the loaves). In the cold rooms, huge carcasses were being swung out on hooks, ready for butchery for this evening's banquet. Electric vacuum cleaners growled up and down the endless carpeted corridors.

The *Arcadia* was a small town afloat on the Atlantic Ocean, and as the day began she bustled with all the necessary activities of a small town. Her lifts rose and sank, her cisterns filled and flushed, her pipes flowed with steam-heated water. It had been pointed out that when the *Titanic* sank, the magnitude of her loss in human and social terms had been equal to the utter disappearance in the space of just three hours of a community the size of Middleport, New York, or Bradford-on-Avon, in England. The *Arcadia* was even larger than the *Titanic,* and apart from her elite human cargo she carried millions of dollars' worth of valuable cargo and precious jewels. The money spent on insurance premiums for the ship and her passengers alone was marginally higher than the annual municipal budget of Plainfield, New Jersey.

Harry Pakenow, in a grey and white work shirt and a cotton jacket, sat on one of the varnished benches on the after poop deck, smoking a cigarette and thinking with intense steadiness of the moment when he would trigger his bomb.

The enormity of what he was planning to do was becoming increasingly vivid to him now that he had been sailing on the *Arcadia* for a day and had already become acquainted with the ship and some of its passengers. When he had bombed Wall Street, it had all been different. He had planned for weeks, but when the moment for the explosion had actually arrived, it had been nothing but a clatter of horse hooves, a quick jostling through the crowds on the sidewalk of Broad Street, and then a teeth-jolting bang. He had hardly known the locality, and he had known none of the people he had killed. But by the time he came to sink the *Arcadia,* he would know her as well as he knew Bootle, or Mersey Docks; and he would certainly know Philly and Lydia, if nobody else.

Earlier this morning he had been brought a cup of tea and two digestive biscuits in his cabin by the third-class steward, but he wasn't sure if he felt like any breakfast. The *Arcadia* was rolling and wallowing much more heavily now, and Harry had already seen four or five passengers emerge from their accommodation with their faces the particular hue of overcooked veal.

A steward went past with a tray which smelled of greasy broth and said, "Anything you want, mate?"

Harry shook his head.

"Stiffening up a bit," the steward said cheerfully, nodding towards the cumulus clouds which were stacking up on the southwestern horizon. "In for a vomity afternoon, I shouldn't be surprised."

"You don't have to sound so cheerful about it," said Harry. He was beginning to wonder if he ought to have smoked this cigarette or not.

The steward caught his balance. "Seasickness," he said, "there's nothing like it. Good for the system. Clears you out like nobody's business. Do you know what they used to do at Bantry Bay in Ireland? They used to offer you a sail around the bay for sixpence, and if you didn't throw up by the time you came back, they gave you your money back. Guaranteed, it was. Just the thing after too much drink or a greasy lunch."

"I'm glad you told me that," said Harry.

"Well, that's nothing," said the steward. "I was on the *Aurora* once in mid-winter, crossing from Boston to Southampton. Rough, I couldn't describe it. We thought we'd have to turn back to America. Everybody was so sick we had to roll the carpets up. That's the nice thing about a maiden voyage like this one. The cabins don't smell of sick already."

"Will you please go away," Harry told him, "and take that broth with you?"

"Only making conversation," said the steward cheerfully, and disappeared inside.

It was not only the rolling of the ship that made Harry feel so bad, although he prayed that just for five minutes, just for *one* minute, she would stop tilting first to one side, hesitating, and then tilting back the other way again. Just long enough to get my equilibrium back. Just long enough for me to remember which is horizontal and which isn't. It was also the butterflies in his stomach that afflicted him: the nervous janglings of anticipation at what he had committed himself to do.

I am going to blow this whole damned ship up, he thought. All this massive pride, all this overblown vanity, all this ill-gotten and grotesquely flaunted money. It will sink to the bottom of the sea and *then* we'll see who the bosses are. But, my God, what an act. What a commitment.

A small polite voice beside him said, "Are you feeling all right?"

He looked around, and there stood Lucille Foster, in a pale lilac cloche hat and a pale lilac morning dress with silver and gold braiding.

"I saw you from the first-class deck," she said, "and I thought you looked rather ill."

Harry smiled down at her, amused. "I think it's the way this ship

216

keeps leaning one way, and then leaning the other," he said.

"But that's the whole *fun* of ships," Lucille enthused, sitting down beside him. "If they don't roll around, they're not worth going on. You ought to sail on the *Berengaria*. She rolls just wonderfully."

"Well, I suppose it seems wonderful if you're used to it," Harry told her. "This is only my second time."

"They have Dammert treatment in first class," Lucille said.

"Dammert treatment? What's that?"

"I don't know, but you have to breathe it in. Mommy used to have it all the time, even when it was smooth. It settles your ears. That's what makes you feel sick, you know, your ears."

"You're very knowledgeable for a very young lady."

"I'm eleven in August. That's not young."

"Well, no, I guess it isn't, especially if you're used to being ten."

Lucille looked out across the ocean for a while, and then she said, "I was very upset, you know, at the way they treated you yesterday. Mommy wouldn't have stood for it. She said you ought to be polite to absolutely *everybody*, no matter how poor or unfortunate they are."

"Your mommy sounds like an understanding lady."

"She was. Daddy was madly in love with her."

"I was sorry to hear about them dying," said Harry. "Well, I wasn't sorry at the time. To me, your daddy and mommy were just rich people you read about in the newspapers. But now I've met you, I suppose I can understand that they were real people, too. You didn't deserve anything to happen to you like that."

"Mrs. Hall says it was very romantic. She said they had a romantic destiny."

"Who's Mrs. Hall?"

"She's the lady I'm travelling with. She's Uncle Robert's housekeeper. She's very sweet, but a little old-fashioned when it comes to things like boys and staying up late and dancing."

"You have boyfriends?" asked Harry.

"I used to, in Paris. There was a French boy called Armand Lautier. He was twelve, and *very* suave. Sometimes Mommy would let me ask him around for dinner and give us champagne. She said there was nothing like young love. Of course, we weren't actually in love. I mean, we were just friends. But I let Armand kiss me once, in the bedroom."

"Did you enjoy it?"

"I don't know . . . it was pretty *wet*. But it wasn't *wholly* unpleasant."

Harry laughed. "You're quite a young lady, do you know that?"

"It's only because I have a privileged background. It *does* make a difference, you know, when your folks have pots of money, and you're given a good sound education. I had five tutors in Paris, can you believe that? *And* a lady who taught me deportment, and not to say keen."

"Well," said Harry, "that's really keen."

From the first-class deck above them, the spiralling breeze wafted down the sound of piano music as an early breakfast was served to those passengers who had decided that they were too hungover and too hungry to be able to stay in their beds any longer; or those who were hoping that a plateful of good solid food would suppress their seasickness; or those who had decided after so much dancing and drinking and fornicating that it really wasn't worth going to bed at all. Mr. Joe Kretchmer and Mr. Duncan Wilkes were there, of course, both with their plates heaped high with eggs, bacon, cold pheasant, and kedgeree. Neither of them appeared to be tucking into his food with any exceptional gusto, and Mr. Kretchmer looked noticeably grey, but they both ate with determination and doggedness, their jaws chewing in time to the piano player's laconic version of "Blue Morning (Now You've Left Me Feeling Blue)" and there was no question of either of them surrendering.

"It must be strange not to be rich," Lucille remarked to Harry.

"Strange?" asked Harry. "Well, I suppose it is. But if all the money in the world were shared out more fairly, then nobody would know what it was like to be rich, and nobody would know what it was like to be really poor. People wouldn't be drinking champagne and eating caviar, but then people wouldn't be starving, either."

Lucille said, "Do you really believe that?"

"Of course. Don't you?"

"Well," said Lucille, thoughtfully, "I don't like the idea of people starving, but the world would be terribly dull if all the money were to be shared out equally. Daddy always used to say that charity was nonsense, except as a tax loss. He could afford to buy every man, woman, and child in the whole of the United States one good meal, with meat and vegetables and Jell-O to follow—but only once. Then he would be quite bankrupt. And what good could he do to anybody once he was bankrupt?"

"That," said Harry, "is an age-old capitalist fallacy. Nobody's asking the rich to buy one free meal for every man, woman, and child in the world. All we're asking them to do is pay their workers more reasonably, share out their profits more equably, and recognise that all human beings are equal."

Lucille was silent for a minute or two. The cloud bank that had been building up on the southwestern horizon was now looming high above the *Arcadia*'s masts, and the wind had freshened to Force Three, so that the brownish oil smoke from the funnels was billowing and twisting away to the northeast, like a chiffon scarf being shaken at a stranger's funeral. The sea began to seethe softly, and the deck heaved and pivoted, lifted and then suddenly dropped, leaving Harry's stomach seven or eight feet up in the air.

"Are you a *Communist?*" asked Lucille intently. "You are, aren't

218

you? Mommy's friend Pascal used to talk like you. He said that one day everybody in the whole world would wear the same clothes and live in the same houses and earn exactly the same amount of money every week. He used to make Mommy laugh."

"Why's that?"

"She used to think being a Communist was flying in the face of human nature. She used to say that even if everybody earned exactly the same amount of money to begin with, one day someone would pay her some of their money just to see her act or dance or hear her sing. Then, when she had finished acting or dancing or singing, she would be richer than they were."

Harry gave a wry grin. "I would have liked to have known your mommy. I think she and I could have had some rare arguments."

Lucille said, "Can I ask you a question?"

"Of course."

"Are you frightened of something?"

He turned and looked at her narrowly. "Frightened? What makes you ask that?"

"I don't know. I just think that you're frightened, or worried, or something like that. I can see it in your eyes. Mommy could see things in people's eyes. She once told a friend of ours that he looked sick, and by the end of the year he had died of cancer."

Harry took out another cigarette and tapped it on his thumbnail. His stomach rose and fell, but he swallowed hard and managed to keep it where it was, on the end of his oesophagus. He wondered fleetingly how Philly and Lydia were feeling, especially after all that cheap brandy.

"You're not frightened that we're going to sink, are you?" asked Lucille.

"Of course not. It would take an Act of God to sink this ship."

"You're a Communist. Communists don't believe in God. At least Pascal didn't. He still bought me a white Bible for my confirmation, though. He knew it would please Daddy. Daddy was a revivalist. He loved Aimée Semple McPherson. He said she was God's messenger."

"Well, maybe she is," said Harry, lighting up his cigarette, his hands cupped against the wind.

Lucille said, "Do you think we ought to be friends, you and I?"

Harry leaned back. "Yes," he said, "I do. Don't ask me why. But I do."

"All right, then," said Lucille. "Because you're my friend, here's a five spot to buy yourself a drink."

She opened her lilac purse, and took out a five-dollar bill, which had been meticulously folded into a tiny square. She unfolded it and held it out.

"I can't take that," said Harry.

"But you must. You saved Margaret."

"I didn't save Margaret for any other reason except I didn't want you to lose your doll."

"But you're a Communist. You believe in rich people sharing what they have with poor people. This is all I've got left from my allowance, and I want to share it with you."

Harry closed his hand over hers, so that she kept the bill tight within her grasp. "Listen," he said, "I really don't want it. I don't want to hurt your feelings, but I don't want it."

Lucille frowned at him. "You're not really a real Communist then, are you?"

"Perhaps I'm not."

"But you can't be! Communists are supposed to be unscrupulous. *You're* not unscrupulous. Not a bit of it."

Harry smoked his cigarette and looked at Lucille through narrowed eyes. "Maybe you rich people *do* have an edge on us, after all," he said. "Maybe you're all psychic."

"Psychic? What does that mean?"

"It means knowing what goes on in other people's heads."

Lucille thought about that, and then said suddenly, "You're not going to do anything *silly*, are you?"

Twenty-six

At six minutes to eight, as Lucille Foster climbed the companionway to the first-class deck and returned to the anxious custody of Mrs. Hall, several other things were happening aboard the *Arcadia*. Maurice Peace, in the first-class smoking room, was dramatically laying down a straight flush in front of a small poker school of wealthy American and German businessmen, thereby beating the full house of Mr. Hubert Hubbard, who owned most of Minneapolis (if not St. Paul) and thereby collecting nearly $11,500 in winnings. Douglas Fairbanks, in his stateroom decorated on the theme of "Music," groaned and grumbled momentarily in his sleep, before burying his face in the pillow again. Baroness Zawisza, in her stateroom decorated on the theme of "Passion," lay back on her bed with her rose and green Bellina chemise drawn up around her white and ample thighs, dreaming of spring days in Dziwnow, on the Pomeranian Bay, while Sabran lapped at her dark-haired vulva with the elegant persistence of a young cat. Rudyard Philips tried to telephone Percy Fearson again, but without success. He bit his nails. And Monty Willowby was in the bathroom of Princess Xenia's stateroom with a screwdriver, struggling to remove the original mahogany lavatory seat and replace it with a cheaper seat which he had taken from one of the third-class washrooms.

Oddest of all, though, Dick Charles was gradually opening his eyes in his own narrow berth and attempting to remember what had happened to him during the night. He had been quite sure that he would wake up next to Lady Diana FitzPerry, and yet here he was in his own quarters, with his mess uniform hung neatly on a hanger, his cap perched on top of his washstand, and a stunning hangover that would have brought a fully grown ox to its knees. Jerkily, he sat up, gripping the varnished wooden side rail of his bunk for support, and tried to focus on the square-faced Smith's alarm clock on the shelf over his desk. He sank back into his bunk with relief. He wasn't due on duty for another hour yet, thank God. He actually said it out loud: "Thank God."

But how had he got here? And where was Lady Diana? And all of those extraordinary pranks that had gone on during the night—had they really happened, or had he simply been dreaming, or drunk, or temporarily insane?

He could remember Lady Diana insisting that he come to her stateroom for a nightcap. Both of them had drunk a considerable quantity of champagne already, and their progress along the blue-carpeted corridor of the first-class accommodation had been characterised by an intermittent series of sudden rushes from one side of the corridor to the other, and a lot of giggling. Once, Lady Diana had actually fallen over and lain on her back, kicking her legs like a schoolgirl and shrieking upper-class shrieks at the top of her voice. It was probably a good thing that the rest of the first-class passengers had been equally incapable, or else there might have been a nasty scene.

At last they had reached her stateroom (theme: "Gold"), and there she had thrown off her evening slippers, demonstratively unfastened her gown, and leaped around and around until her gown had eventually fallen to her ankles. She had tossed it carelessly across the room and Dick had caught it in mid-air. "You're a gentleman," she had slurred, "and an oshifer."

Naked, ribby, and ridiculously well bred, she had thrown her arms around Dick and smothered him in so many kisses that he had gasped for breath. "This is the moment of truth!" she had declared. "So, open the champagne, and we'll drink to the moment of truth!"

They had drunk, in Mumm's, to the moment of truth.

"This is also the moment of reckoning!" Lady Diana had cried. "Let us drink to the moment of reckoning!"

They had drunk to the moment of reckoning. In Mumm's.

Then they had drunk to the Decline and Fall of the Roman Empire; to the late Gilbert John Elliot-Murray-Kynynmound, 4th Earl of Minto; to the Lancashire Fusiliers, *all* of them; and to the Atherstone Hunt.

Dick Charles had almost forgotten his stutter by the time Lady Diana FitzPerry had dragged him by the wrist to her bed (a gilded four-poster in the Egyptian style, with a gold-threaded counterpane). In fact, he had forgotten who he was, or why he was here, and he had been barely capable of anything that could reasonably have been interpreted as stiffness. There had been a half-hour interlude of juicy but inconsequential coupling, after which Lady Diana had suggested a light middle-of-the-night snack of cream cheese and soused herring. They had eaten, and then drunk chilled Polish vodka, and then returned hastily to bed, where Lady Diana had ridden him so mercilessly that he had cried out, "S-stop it! *P-please!*" until she had forced him into ejaculating with such violence that it was almost painful.

Later, with a glazed but direct stare, she had shaken him by the shoulder and said, "Have you ever played Corkies?"

Dick had been almost asleep, his mouth hanging open against the pillow. He had moved his head from side to side to indicate that he hadn't.

"That's why I like soused herring so much," she had said. "It gives me wind so that I can play Corkies."

Dick had closed his eyes. In the darkness of his drunkenness, he had prayed for equilibrium, and for sleep. God, bring me sleep. Or at the very least, bring me a glass of mineral water and four aspirin.

But there she had been again, shaking his shoulder. "If you've never played Corkies, you've never lived. You're not falling asleep on me, are you?"

"Nmph," Dick had assured her.

She had bounced out of bed and walked through to the living room. Dick had phased in and out of sleep at least three times before she had returned. She had peeled back his right eyelid with the ball of her thumb, and in her left hand held up two champagne corks. "You see these? Corks! These are what we use to play Corkies. It's really wonderful! The Master of the Rolls taught it to me. Or was it the Lord Chancellor? I forget which. One of these dear old legal boys, anyway."

Dick had pulled at his face with his fingers to wake himself up a little. Then, his head sagging and his brain spinning around and around like a ship's propeller, he had propped himself up on his elbow and tried to focus on what Lady Diana was doing.

"It needs *wind*, of course," she had been chattering. "It's no use at all without wind, but then dear Lord What's-his-name always had such dreadful wind. You can't sit on the Woolsack all day or whatever it is without suffering from *some* flatulence, can you?"

Dick had stared at her in silent desperation. "No," he had told her, in a voice like that of someone agreeing to have his dog put down.

Lady Diana had climbed onto the gilded counterpane on all fours, with her wide bottom cocked into the air and her elbows spread like a chicken. "All we need is a champagne cork . . . and *only* a champagne cork will do, mind you . . . and a little cold cream . . . and then . . . *ahh* . . ."

Dick had frowned at her intently. "Now what happens?" he had asked her.

"Well, *you're* supposed to do it as well. It's a kind of game. The person who shoots the cork the furthest is the winner."

"W-what do they w-win?"

"Well, I don't know. What do you think they *ought* to win?"

"I d-don't know."

Nothing had happened for almost five minutes. Lady Diana had remained in her peculiar crouching position, her bottom still raised, an expression on her face that could only be described as the Considerable Inconvenience of St. Theresa. But then, without warning, there was a ripping kind of a noise, and the champagne cork popped across the bedroom and landed somewhere on the white merino rug.

"There!" Lady Diana had clapped. "A good four-footer, at least!"

Dick Charles had sat up straight. He had suddenly caught sight of his face in the mirror on the dressing table, and he had never seen himself looking so drawn or so perplexed. "Four-footer?" he had queried.

"One of the best I've ever done!" cried Lady Diana. "Do you want to try? I bet you could beat me, if you really put your mind to it! Try for a five-footer, at least!"

The rest of the morning had been a jumbled collection of laughter, rolling on the bed, and strange disconnected conversations. He could remember Lady Diana recounting in some detail a picnic she had once attended, with the Greys, who had been relatives of the Viceroy of India, or some such; and how the Hon. Arabelle Timmons had shown the assembled company what unusual tricks could be accomplished with hard-boiled eggs. All this talk of the landed classes being pillars of England's morality was rot. Utter rot. They were the most licentious assembly of people on God's earth, and what lusts they were unable to satisfy on horseback, they promptly extinguished in the loins of the nearest maid-servant, like plunging a red-hot poker into a bucket of water. Then . . . Lady Diana had discussed at length the comparative merits of dukes and baronets, and how the baronets that she knew, although they were largely not as energetic as the dukes, were largely *larger*. This conclusion provoked gales of laughter, and a lot of ankle thrashing, and it took several large drafts of champagne to settle Lady Diana down again.

The extraordinary thing was that Dick couldn't remember, even impressionistically, how the morning had ended. He could vaguely recall pouring another drink for them both, but after that, hardly anything at all, except perhaps, a remote argument about champagne corks and cold cream. He had been nuzzling up to Lady Diana's naked side, he could remember that, and laughing about something silly.

But then *nothing*—except waking up in his own quarters with a crashing hangover.

He went to the washstand, fumbled it open, and filled up the basin with tepid water, which he splashed into his face in an ineffectual attempt to revive himself. In the oval mirror on top of the washstand, he looked like a photograph of a death mask by Madame Tussaud. God knows what Sir Peregrine would say when he turned up on the bridge for duty. "Need the padre, do you, Number Four?" he would say, in that stiff buzzardlike croak of his. "Expecting to get a free burial at sea?"

"N-no, sir," Dick said to his reflection in the mirror.

He dressed slowly, and with increasing thoughtfulness. Surely, a woman like Lady Diana could have had her pick of any one of twenty aristocratic young men who were travelling on the *Arcadia.* There were two peers of the realm on board, too, so why not them? Instead she had chosen him, Fourth Officer Dick Charles, for no reason that seemed to make any sense. Well, he knew he was moderately good-looking, and that in spite of his stutter he was quite a personable young man. He could row quite well, and he didn't drop his aitches. He even ate his fish with two forks instead of a fish knife, which among young ocean liner officers these days was one of those refinements of etiquette which had almost completely died out. He could speak French, bad Cantonese, and a smattering of Portuguese. Still, why had Lady Diana so carnivorously picked on *him*, when there was such an abundance of upper-class prey for her to snatch? And if she was the kind of woman who enjoyed slumming, well, there were scores of well-sculpted young men in steerage—much lower class and much better looking.

He opened three drawers in his locker before he found a clean pair of underpants and a short-sleeved undervest. He tugged them on uncomfortably, as if they belonged to someone else. Then he pulled on a pair of calf-length navy-blue socks and fastened them with sock suspenders. It was then that he rang for his steward to bring him a pot of treacly black coffee, three aspirin, and a corned-beef sandwich spread a quarter of an inch thick with hot English mustard.

At the same moment that Dick Charles' steward poked his ginger short-back-and-sides around the cabin door and said, "Ready for brekker, sir?" Edgar Deacon was round on the far side of the boat deck rapping at Sir Peregrine's quarters. Percy Fearson stood beside him, grim and stocky-shouldered, his hair standing on end in the morning wind.

Sir Peregrine's voice called, "Come," with a slight thickening of phlegm, and this was followed by a noisy throat clearing.

Edgar opened the door and stepped inside. It was hot in the commodore's sitting room, with that particular stifling heat that you only came across on ocean liners, smelling of baked paint, fuel oil, and stuffed upholstery. Edgar said, "Good morning, Sir Peregrine," with the flat carefulness of a man who cannot trust himself to hold back his temper. "You slept well?"

At this unexpectedly solicitous remark, Sir Peregrine lifted his skeletal head and stared at Edgar with one eye open and one eye tightly closed, as if he were finding it difficult to focus. "Well, Mr. Deacon," he said, "you too?"

Sir Peregrine was sitting in his armchair, which he had dragged to the middle of his sitting room, with all the stiffness of an elderly and unpopular monarch. He was still wearing his crested bathrobe and his leather slippers, and his reading spectacles were suspended by a thin chain that had tangled itself around one of his ears. He had been reading *Vanity Fair,* and the book was now spread open over the arm of his chair, like a ridge tile, to keep his place. He had reached chapter thirteen, and he had been relishing Thackeray's comment that "whenever he met a great man he grovelled before him, and my-lorded him, as only a free-born Briton can do." The sarcasm, of course, was quite lost on Sir Peregrine, who quite seriously believed that he himself was a great man, and that grovelling from both his crew and his passengers was what he rightly and properly deserved.

The problem was that since the war, it wasn't easy to get people to grovel. The war had made the hoi-polloi too cocky, too damned "equal." Take this overbearing office-*wallah* Edgar Deacon, as a gross example. A professional bloody nuisance of the first water.

He misjudged Edgar, of course, and badly. Edgar saw the tragedy of Sir Peregrine's career with great clarity, and it was often painful for Edgar to watch. There was almost a Shakespearean quality about the way in which this hollow-looking man dragged himself down all the years of his life, hideously burdened by his huge sense of pomp, and by an heroic vision of himself which few of his friends or his subordinates shared.

Edgar said, "I'm told that you ordered Mr. Philips to confine himself to his quarters." He stood with one hand thrust into his trousers pocket and the other hand pressed against his neck, as if he had a boil or a wasp sting.

"I have ordered Mr. Philips to consider himself under close arrest, if that's what you're getting at," replied Sir Peregrine.

"Would it be too impertinent of me to ask why?"

Sir Peregrine cleared his throat again. "I am the master of this vessel, Mr. Deacon. As such, I have both a right and a duty to do whatever may be legally necessary to protect the ship herself, her crew, her cargo, and her passengers."

"And you considered it legally necessary to confine Mr. Philips to his quarters?"

"You're questioning my authority?" asked Sir Peregrine, with a sudden burst of fierceness. "Is that it?" He continued to squint at Edgar with his one moist eye, his lips tightly drawn together like the sewn-together lips of a shrunken head from the Upper Amazon, his neck stringy and red. But despite his gizzardly show of outrage, Edgar wasn't at all sure how angry the commodore truly was. Sir Peregrine didn't really seem to be concentrating on what they were talking about at all. His attention seemed to be stealing off somewhere else, to some remembered time and place where Edgar and Percy Fearson were unable to follow.

"We simply want to know what's up," put in Percy Fearson. "Mr. Philips rang me this morning and gave me his side of the story. Now I think we ought to hear yours. Fair does, after all."

"Well," said Sir Peregrine remotely, "and what does Mr. Philips say about me?"

"He says he's still completely loyal to you, if that's any consolation," said Percy Fearson.

"I don't think it *is* a consolation, thank you," said Sir Peregrine.

"Well, whether it is or whether it isn't, locking a man up is a serious matter. He's a captain in his own right, you know. A respected officer of the line. So that's why we need to know what's going on, and urgent. We don't want no scandals on this voyage. None of your Sunday paper headlines, 'Mutiny on the *Arcadia*,' or whatever."

"You won't get any scandal," said Sir Peregrine with a wonky smile. "And I can assure you that whatever Mr. Philips says, he has only been confined to his quarters for a small misunderstanding over the chain of command. An example to his brother officers, that's all. It's unpleasant, I'll grant you. But occasionally one is obliged to take certain disciplinary steps."

Edgar was twirling the model gyroscope on Sir Peregrine's sitting-room table. Quite calmly, without looking up, he said, "Mr. Philips seems to feel that his arrest has something to do with our running down a fishing smack called the *Drogheda.*"

"What?" snapped Sir Peregrine. His manner reminded Edgar of a retired lieutenant-general he had once known, in Murree, who had fought out the Battle of the Somme again and again on his croquet lawn, requisitioning his guests' tea cakes to form the German lines, and clambering breathlessly out of his ha-ha in a tweed deerstalker to represent going "over the top."

"According to Mr. Philips, we ran down a fishing smack," Edgar repeated. "He says that we were running out of Irish waters at full speed ahead, in poor visibility, and we sank it without anyone on board knowing

226

that we'd hit it. A man is missing, feared drowned."

"Well," said Sir Peregrine, "that's quite correct."

"How long have you known?" asked Edgar.

"The message reached us just a few hours ago."

"A few hours ago? And you didn't think to inform me?"

"I was awaiting confirmation. You know what the Irish are like. Full of—you know, wild stories."

"We receive a message telling us that we've run down a fishing smack and drowned one of its occupants and you can seriously dismiss that as a wild story?"

Sir Peregrine pronounced each word of his reply with exaggerated care, but he still managed to invest it with a certain shabby dignity. "I have commanded the bridges of some of the greatest ocean liners of my day, Mr. Deacon. When you were still a boy in knee britches, I was crossing the North Atlantic as the master of the *Aurora*, the *Eximious*, and the *Lustrous;* through storm, accident, and blizzard. The message from Ireland was unconfirmed, and therefore I sought confirmation. The last thing I wanted to do, especially when there was no immediate danger to the safety of the *Arcadia*, was to spread exactly the kind of alarm and hysteria to which you are now demonstrating yourself to be prone."

He rose from his armchair, knocking his book onto the floor. "Mr. Philips was on the bridge at the time of the incident. I shall expect him to make a full report. It appears to me that the reason for the collision was that Mr. Philips was disobeying my specific instruction to make way with *such expediency as may be safe.* Perhaps it went to his head, taking command of such a powerful vessel for the very first time. Perhaps he thought to prove that I was too old and cautious for such a commission. But the outcome was that the *Arcadia* was sailing far too fast for the prevailing visibility, and for the waters she was in, and there was a tragic accident."

"Mr. Philips says just the opposite," put in Percy Fearson. "Mr. Philips claims it was you who told him to make full ahead, against the warnings of the Irish authorities, and against his own better advice."

"Mr. Philips was on the bridge," replied Sir Peregrine. "Although I must always take ultimate responsibility for anything that happens aboard this ship, Mr. Philips was on the bridge. That means that the piloting of the *Arcadia* at the time of the incident was *his* responsibility. If visibility was poor, he should have slowed down. Can you really imagine *any* captain, even the most reckless, ordering full speed without having any regard to the weather or the surrounding seas? No, gentlemen. If you are looking for a culprit, I'm afraid you will have to look to Mr. Philips. Regrettable, but there you are. A fine young captain gone to the dogs, I'm afraid."

Percy Fearson breathed to Edgar, "I do hear that Mr. Philips has been having a little trouble at home. You know, domestic problems. Wife went off with somebody else."

Edgar gave the gyroscope one final spin. It hummed around like a top, tilting from one side to the other in its gimbals as the *Arcadia* rolled from port to starboard, hesitated, and then rolled back again.

"All right, Sir Peregrine," he said at last. "But remember this: In future I want to hear *every* message of any importance that reaches us by wireless. I should have known about this incident the minute you received the news yourself. You may be a legendary sea captain, but you're not a businessman, and you're not a banker, and you have very little expertise in public relations."

Sir Peregrine said, "I shall judge the suitability of passing on any wireless messages to you strictly according to the contents of each message, as and when it arrives."

"Just make sure that your definition of suitability concurs with mine," said Edgar. Then, "Come on, Percy, I think it's time we found ourselves some breakfast."

They left Sir Peregrine's quarters and closed the door behind them. Percy Fearson said, "Is that it? Is that all you're going to do?"

"Do you really think that I'd let that old goat speak to me like that without taking it further?" said Edgar. "If we received a warning from the Irish authorities, then the wireless officer took it down at the time, and the helmsman must have been aware of it, too. Who was on the helm when we left Dun Laoghaire?"

"Bunyan, I believe."

"Then before we eat, let's go and find Bunyan."

Bunyan had just woken up after six hours' sleep. His tiny cabin smelled of sweat and beer. There was a photograph on the wall of a terraced house in Manchester, and a cheesecake picture of Anna Q. Nilsson. Bunyan sat on the edge of his bunk in large trousers and a stained white undershirt, alternately blinking and sniffing.

"What we need to know is precisely what warning the Irish port authority gave to Sir Peregrine when the *Arcadia* left Dun Laoghaire," said Edgar, as warmly as he could.

Bunyan sniffed and blinked. "Well, sir, they said there was small vessels in the vicinity."

"And?"

"And, we had to proceed slowly for at least one mile, sir."

"Are you sure that's what they said?"

Bunyan nodded.

"And so that's what you did?"

"Yes, sir. Sir Peregrine said slow ahead for one mile, then full ahead."

"Full ahead after one mile, regardless?"

"Not regardless, sir. Full ahead after one mile, should it be safe, sir."

Edgar glanced at Percy Fearson. Then he said to Bunyan, "You'd swear to this in a court of law?"

Bunyan nodded and blinked.

"Very well, then," said Edgar, and left the cabin.

Outside, Percy Fearson said, "What do you think?"

"I don't know what I think," Edgar replied. "Well, I *do* really. I think he's been nobbled."

"You're serious?"

"It only takes five pounds to change a man's mind, Percy. That, and the promise of promotion in a year or two."

"We've still the wireless officer to talk to," said Percy.

Edgar checked his watch. "All right," he said. "Let's see what that message said for ourselves."

They went up to the telegraph room. The wireless officer who had been on duty the night the *Arcadia* left Dun Laoghaire was off duty, but the second wireless officer, a nervous young man with a large pimple on the end of his nose, hastily produced the wireless messages for the night in question.

Edgar went through the messages one by one, quickly and coldly. The second wireless officer watched him with a stare as fixed as a parrot. At last Edgar said, "Here it is. Harbourmaster Dun Laoghaire to *Arcadia*. You may now proceed. We wish you calm sea, a voyage crowned by glorious success, and something illegible about King Neptune. You are advised of the presence of small sightseeing craft, and requested not to make full speed for one mile."

He held the message up to the light. Then, for comparison, he held up the next message, a telegraph from London for Mr. Charles Schwab. He said, "*This* message was written with a blunt pencil, the next message with a sharp pencil. The message *before* it was written with a sharp pencil. So why is this message different?"

The second wireless officer looked at Edgar balefully. Then he pushed forward a small glass jar containing more than a dozen different pencils. "This is our pencil jar, sir. Some of them are sharp and some of them are blunt."

Edgar stared back at him, then collated the messages and replaced them neatly on the desk.

"Penny for 'em," said Percy Fearson as they went down the companionway to the Orchid Lounge for breakfast.

"I don't know what to think," said Edgar. "It doesn't sound like Philips, handling a ship so recklessly. He's not the type. But if you say he's been having wife trouble . . . well, maybe he wanted to try to outshine Sir Peregrine, to bolster his own morale. Chaps do the oddest things when they have wife trouble. Or maybe he just wasn't paying attention."

"The lookout couldn't have seen the *Drogheda* either. And there's not often the lookout doesn't pay attention."

They walked into the pale mauve Orchid Lounge, where gilded basketwork chairs were arranged beside trellises of silk artificial flowers. A waitress in a mauve pillbox hat topped with a gold tassel showed them to a table in the corner. "Enjoy your breakfast, Mr. Deacon. You too, Mr. Fearson," she said, making big movie-actress eyes at Edgar and coquettishly jiggling the fringes of her skirt as she walked away.

"Have Monty Willowby speak to that girl," Edgar said irritably. "The last thing our cabin-class passengers want is a flirtatious breakfast."

Percy Fearson opened the breakfast menu and studied it with a great show of earnestness. "I don't know whether to have the Belgian waffles or the coddled eggs," he remarked. "Perhaps I ought to have both."

In his sitting room, Sir Peregrine was pouring out the last of *his* breakfast. He held the empty rum bottle upside down for almost a minute, waiting for the last hesitant drop to fall into his beaker. Then he sighed and set the bottle back on top of the sideboard. One dead, how many more to go? He knew that he wouldn't be able to resist drinking again, now that he'd started. He had a pounding headache, and breath so strong that pigeons could have perched on it.

Still, for a man of his character, what did a few drinks matter? There were plenty of great men in history who had been fond of the sherbet. He wouldn't be surprised if the King himself didn't gargle once or twice in Napoleon brandy before retiring, or even after rising.

Drink helped a man's vision. It steadied his temper, collected his thoughts and enabled him to see things shipshape and sharp. And those were qualities you couldn't even claim for a woman.

Ah, a woman, he thought. What I could have been with a woman. And for a brief moment, before he lifted his last mug of rum to his lips, he remembered a sweet Edwardian profile, and Lily Langtry curls, and a voice that now spoke from nowhere but his memory.

On the deck below, Catriona slept. She dreamed of dancing and of running down one claustrophobic passageway after another, looking anxiously for Mark. She dreamed that Mark's lips were close to her ear and whispered, "I will love you for money."

And as the morning passed, the *Arcadia* began to plunge and toss like a wild pony as she forced her bows into an ocean that was already beginning to grow tumultuous and dark.

Twenty-seven

Catriona arrived in the Grand Lounge five minutes later for the fashion show. It was not that she actually felt *sick;* it was just that the cup of tea she had drunk after Alice had awakened her seemed to be tilting from side to side inside her with every roll the *Arcadia* rolled.

The decks were very lively now, and there was a waiting list of white-faced cabin-class passengers for Dammert treatment, oxygen and atropine, to settle the inner ear. Those who had fox-trotted and fornicated and drunk champagne until dawn were being punished the most severely, victims of what Second Officer Ralph Peel called "Atlantic justice." The prettiest flappers and the smartest sheiks were now hanging over the basins in their cabins, their eyes like freshly opened clams and their hair sticking up like Willy and Wally.

The stewards, of course, were courteous and soothing, and brought beef tea and stomach settlers with expressions on their faces that could only be compared with fifteenth-century Italian saints. When they met each other in the kitchens and the linen stores, however, they passed on gleeful gossip about the discomfiture of their wealthy and celebrated charges; and the greatest mirth of all was aroused by the vivid description that Jack Dempsey's steward gave of the wonder boxer groaning out loud and promising God that he would never fight again. "Lord, Lord, I'll never t'row anudder punch, never!"

Catriona had never suffered badly from motion sickness. She had ridden happily and hilariously on every helter-skelter and whirling caterpillar at the seaside fun fairs to which Nigel had taken her. But even so, the sky outside the Grand Lounge was now ominously stormy, and the *Arcadia* was making her way through the waves with a peculiar sideways dance, since the sea was running from the southwest and her helmsman was steering her on a northwesterly course. And as Catriona crossed the floor of the lounge to be greeted by Edgar Deacon and by Monsieur Victor Delain, of the *Gazette du Bon Ton,* who was organising the fashion parade, she felt an extraordinary sensation of unreality as the deck tilted uphill, paused, and then tilted downhill again.

Just behind Edgar stood George Welterman. He watched Catriona trying to stagger as elegantly as she could towards them, but his expression remained strangely rubbery and unformed, like an empty hot-water bag. Only Percy Fearson stepped forward to give Catriona his hand and steady her.

"There aren't many people here yet," remarked Catriona, looking around. A long roll of maroon carpet had been laid down across the centre of the lounge, and it was lined on either side by two rows of little gilt chairs. But so far fewer than a third of the chairs were occupied, and fewer than half of the ladies who occupied them were smiling. Every now and then, one of them would get up, carefully set down on her seat the tasselled notepad and silver pencil supplied by Keys Shipping, and hurry biliously away to the Ladies'.

"It is just my luck," said Monsieur Delain. "I organise the most splendid of fashion shows outside France, and what is my reward? A storm, and everybody sick. Even my best mannequin is sick."

"I suppose we'd better start," said Edgar tiredly. The *Arcadia*'s social director, a normally breezy man called Eric Coleman, was standing on the other side of the lounge with a far away look, absentmindedly chewing the edge of his clipboard. "Eric!" called Edgar, and when he had caught the social director's attention, he mouthed the word "start."

Catriona had been looking for Mark Beeney, or for Marcia, but there was no sign of them. Instead, George Welterman stepped forward and loomed close to her and said, "Would you do me the honour of sitting next to me?"

Catriona glanced at Edgar. Nobody else would have known what the blank look on Edgar's face was actually supposed to convey, but Catriona did. It meant, Be nice to George Welterman, if you please. It meant, Everything's at risk; not just Keys Shipping itself but your family fortune, too, and all of your gorgeous salon dresses and your ritzy South African diamonds. It meant, I didn't make you Queen of the Atlantic for nothing.

"Of course, Mr. Welterman," said Catriona. "The honour is all mine."

"I did ask you to call me George."

Catriona smiled a bright, false smile. "Oh, of course. I'm so sorry. George it is, then."

George Welterman propelled her with the respectful tips of his fingers to one of the little gilt chairs.

"You don't suffer from seasickness?" she asked him as she sat down. He shook his head. "Seasickness is all in the imagination."

"And you don't have any imagination?"

He lowered his broad bottom onto the inadequate seat. "You're teasing me," he told her, with no sign of humour, but equably enough to show that he wasn't upset. "Well," he said, "you're a young girl."

"Does that give me a special dispensation to tease you?" Catriona asked him.

"No," he replied. "But it means that I can forgive you more quickly."

"What makes you think that I *want* to be forgiven?"

George Welterman reached into the cuff of his expensive grey morning suit and pulled out a cream-coloured handkerchief. He dabbed at the sides of his mouth and then patted his forehead. "You really don't like me?" he asked.

"I didn't say that."

"You said nearly as much. If you don't think it's worth asking my forgiveness for teasing me, then you don't think much of me at all."

Catriona stared at him. Through the middle-aged ambiguity of his face, those disconcertingly youthful eyes stared back at her. He wanted something from her, but she couldn't decide what. Not affection. Not passion. Perhaps it was nothing more than approval. Yet why should such a wealthy and domineering man want the approval of a pretty flapper of twenty-one?

"You seem rather . . . *heavy,* that's all," said Catriona. "You don't seem to be the kind of man who likes to depend on people. Not for anything."

"You don't think I ever depended on Myrtle?"

"Myrtle? I don't know. How could I possibly judge?"

"Well, I'll tell you," said George Welterman, crossing his legs, "I *did* depend on Myrtle. I depended on Myrtle for my future happiness. Of course it wasn't her fault that she let me down."

"She had muscular dystrophy and you accuse her of letting you down?"

George Welterman waved his big hand dismissively. "I didn't mean it like that. I loved her. As a matter of fact, she looked a whole lot like you do now. That day I first met her, out on the movie lot . . . she shone like the sun. You have that quality. That shine. You also have Myrtle's sharpness. She could be sharp, you know. She had a temper, too. I knew her so mad one evening that she ripped her evening gown apart"—he made a pulling-apart gesture with his fists—"a Chanel gown that cost me nearly a thousand dollars."

Catriona didn't say anything. Instead, she looked at George Welterman narrowly. He was bulky and strong, and you could tell as soon as you came close to him that he had influence. His shirt cuffs were so starched, and his gold cufflinks were so expensive and yet so hideous, and he smelled so distinctively of masculine sweat and old-fashioned barber-shop shaving lotions, that he couldn't have been anything else but a self-made business mogul. A Big Cheese par excellence.

It was their very ugliness, their very awkwardness, that made men like George Welterman attractive to women. Better-looking men could never understand how any woman could find them even remotely interesting, let alone put up with their brutishness and their ill-temper and their crude sentimental maunderings. But women understood. Women knew what it was about men like George Welterman that made them irresistible. It was their lumpy bodies, their demanding sexuality, and their knotted-up personalities. There was nothing a woman could find more intriguing than a man with a grudge, or a problem, or a psychological complex, especially when he wanted very little more from her than money, unconditional sympathy, and the occasional grunting bout in bed. Not that any woman, no matter how intrigued she was, could ever unravel the complexities of George Welterman's mind. She could never understand his peevish day-to-day complaints, his blinded sense of right and wrong, or his inverted interpretation of human happiness. She would try, of course. Often passionately, usually desperately, but always unsuccessfully. Myrtle Greensleeves had tried, but she had failed, too. Because George Welterman believed that nobody in the world could ever be happy unless they lived the way *he* lived, and accepted capitalism without question, like he did. Yet he himself was never happy.

This was the paradox about George Welterman which Catriona was already finding interesting, and which compelled her to listen to what he had to say, even though her instincts were jangling warnings to her with every word that he spoke, and every suggestion that he came up with. Then there was his uncompromising ugliness, which stirred up extraordinary thoughts inside her, like: I wonder what he looks like naked. I wonder how it would *feel* to be assaulted by such a grotesque man. To be utterly sullied by someone so lumpish.

George Welterman said, "The next time I see Myrtle will be at her funeral. Can you imagine that? Well, I guess you can. You've just lost your father, haven't you?"

"Don't you ever write to her or telephone her?" Catriona asked.

"I write to her every day."

"Does she write back?"

George Welterman glanced at her. "Why is it that women have such a knack for asking exactly the right question?"

"You mean she doesn't?"

George Welterman lowered his head. "No," he said. "Never."

"Do you tell her you love her?" asked Catriona.

"I tell her everything. Where I'm going, what I'm doing, what I'm thinking about. Myrtle is the only person in the whole world to whom I reveal myself completely; and she never answers."

Catriona said, "You don't seem embarrassed to tell people about it."

"Why should I be?"

"I don't know. It all seems rather personal to me, and yet it was almost the first thing you talked about when we were sitting down at dinner last night."

George Welterman shrugged, but didn't say anything.

234

"Do you want people to feel sorry for you?" asked Catriona.

"People?" queried George Welterman.

"Oh, I'm sorry if I misunderstood," said Catriona with pursed lips. "Do you want *me* to feel sorry for you?"

"You're a very exceptional young lady," said George Welterman. "You have the ability to understand people, as well as your beauty."

"It was something I inherited from my father. Our only blind spot was we could never understand each other."

George Welterman said, "Would you have cocktails with me later, in my cabin? You can bring your maid, of course, if you want a chaperone."

"Would I need to be chaperoned?"

"It depends how much of a stickler you are for appearances."

"Oh, I'm always a stickler for appearances."

A string quintet from the ship's orchestra struck up with a cranky little piece by Debussy called "Le Chanson de Bilitis," and the sparse audience began to applaud.

George Welterman said, "At six, then? Would that suit you?"

"Six-oh-three," said Catriona teasingly.

George Welterman stared at her for a moment, his eyes unreadable, and then nodded.

The far end of the Grand Lounge had been curtained off with scalloped gold curtains, which were illuminated in green and red, like the proscenium of an Eve Leo picture palace. Eve Leo was the wife of Mr. Fox of Fox Pictures, and she had already set a worldwide trend by decorating her husband's movie theatres like princely palaces, with epic murals, gilded columns, glittering chandeliers—every imaginable architectural style and sumptuous sensation piled one on top of the other.

Monsieur Delain emerged from the curtains and clapped his hands for attention. "Lords, ladies, gentlemen. Today I was to have presented for you the latest and most *secret* Paris styles for the fall and for the winter, a preview of several famous collections. Alas, the ocean has not been kind to us, and three of my mannequins are suffering mal de mer." (At the very mention of seasickness, even in a foreign language, yet another lady rose from her little gilt chair and tilted off to the Ladies') "But with the facilities I have left," continued Monsieur Delain, "I will do my best to please your eye, and to entertain you. The music, please."

It was the most extraordinary fashion show that Catriona had ever attended, although she hadn't attended many. Gorgeously gowned in daring new creations by the cream of Paris designers, five leggy and elegant girls attempted to parade up and down a floor that kept rising and falling and leaning from side to side. One minute they would be toiling up a one-in-six hill, the next they would be tottering on their tiny high-heeled slippers down a slope that was steep enough to launch lifeboats.

As the *Arcadia* rolled, one girl lost her balance and sat down very hard in the lap of Dame Clara Butt, who promptly swallowed the mint imperial she had been surreptitiously sucking and almost choked.

The dresses, though, were fabulous, and could be bought for fabulous prices. Catriona adored a sleeveless dress by Doeuillet of black muslin printed with red and yellow flowers, with a wraparound front which swept all the way down to the very low waistline, where it was fastened in a scarflike knot. She also made a note of a violet crepe day dress by Lelong, with a three-tiered skirt trimmed with scarlet ribbon, and a plaquet of red ribbon down the bodice. Neither gown would cost less than £700.

The most stunning dress of the show, though, was unquestionably a black lace evening dress by Doucet, exquisitely fragile, with an overdress with tight sleeves which flared out at the elbow like wilting convolvulus flowers. It was trimmed with diamonds, and its sash was fastened with a silver and garnet buckle.

"You like it?" asked George Welterman as Catriona applauded.

"It's exquisite," said Catriona. "I *love* it."

"Then it's yours," said George Welterman. He picked up his silver propelling pencil between his sausagelike fingers and asked, "Who's the designer?"

"Doucet. But you can't possibly buy it for me."

George Welterman wrote down "Doosay." Then he looked at Catriona without smiling at all. "If you really hadn't wanted me to buy it for you, you wouldn't have told me the name of the designer before you refused it."

"So! You're just as hep to human nature as I am," said Catriona.

"I certainly am." George Welterman nodded. "And three times as experienced."

"I suppose when you've bought it for me you'll want to see me wearing it?"

"Of course."

Catriona made what she thought was her world-weary-femme-fatale face. Nigel had always thought that it made her look like someone at a party whose eyes had been caught half closed in a Kodak flash photograph. Sexy, but goofy. She said, "It just goes to show, doesn't it? No matter how sophisticated he is, every man comes out with the same old lines."

"So what?" said George Welterman quite roughly. "You have a special objection to lines?"

"Hoary old lines like 'I want to see you wearing it,' yes."

"Well," said George Welterman after a moment's thought, "how about a different kind of line?"

"Such as?"

"Such as, will you approve the selling-up of Keys Shipping to IMM?"

"Not *that* again. I've had enough of that to last me a lifetime. You all seem so frantic about it."

"Frantic?"

"Well, nobody ever seems to talk about anything else. It's really too dreary for words."

George Welterman said, "I apologise. We must all seem like very tedious old men to you. But, of course, the future of Keys Shipping is extremely important to very many people in the shipping business; and you, young lady, by an accident of heredity and fate, have a very important part to play in its destiny."

"Edgar said I wasn't to meddle in business affairs," said Catriona. "Oh, look, look at that beautiful ottoman."

George Welterman had half turned to look at the sleek black Martial et Armand three-piece before he realised that he wasn't really interested, and he turned back to Catriona.

"Do you know what I'm offering you for Keys?" he asked her.

"I think so."

"Well, whether you understand anything about shipping or not, you have to recognise that it's an excellent offer. More than excellent. It would solve all of your problems, not to mention a few of mine."

"You don't look like a man with problems, Mr. Welterman."

"George, please. But of course I have problems. Many White Star ships are growing elderly and need replacing. Many White Star routes are running at a loss. If I were able to buy up Keys, I would be able to modernise our fleet overnight, and also cut down on many of our more unprofitable routes, where Keys and White Star are running competitive services for too few passengers and too little freight. These are modern times, Miss Keys. We can no longer afford the luxuries of the Edwardian era, when liners used to sail with only twenty passengers aboard and nearly two hundred staff to take care of them."

Catriona said, "Did you know my father?"

"Of course. Everybody in shipping knew your father."

"But did you know him well?"

George Welterman eyed Catriona cautiously. "As well as anyone, I suppose. We once sailed up the Irrawaddy together."

"And do you think that he would have sold out everything to IMM, just because the company was finding things difficult?"

"I think you're misunderstanding the situation, Miss Keys. If your father had still been alive today, then the difficulties which you are facing would not have existed. Perhaps if your father had had a son, who could have taken over the company and rallied the confidence of the banks and the stockholders . . . But, sadly, the problem which Keys Shipping faces is that your father had only one child, and that child is a girl."

"You're trying to say that the company is going to have to be sold because of *me?*" Catriona felt empty, and shocked. It simply hadn't occurred to her before that Keys Shipping was in jeopardy because the company's creditors had no faith whatsoever in a young woman's ability to be able to keep the company going. And, in a way, she felt that she had let herself down, too, by acting so nonchalant and flippant and half-baked and forgetting that she could have shown Edgar and Percy Fearson and all of the company's creditors that she was seriously interested in keeping the family business running.

George Welterman tugged at his sharp white cuffs. "Your poor father's luck was always a little like that. And it was the same to the very end, wasn't it? He built this wonderful ship with every ounce of energy he could muster, not to mention credit. And he never even got to see it sail. He should be with us now, you know. Such a tragedy."

Catriona said, "I only want to do my best."

"Of course you do, my dear." George Welterman smiled. "I know that."

"But I'm still not sure that selling out is the right thing to do. Philip Carter-Helm said that it could be possible to sell only the *Arcadia*—I mean, not that I *want* to sell her—but he said that she should raise enough money to keep the rest of the line going."

"Who's Philip Carter-Helm?" asked George Welterman suspiciously.

"Well, I don't know, really. But he's a friend of Mark Beeney."

"And he said that you could sell the *Arcadia* alone—I presume to Mark Beeney?"

"Oh, of course. I mean, he did make it clear that he was Mark Beeney's friend."

"He said that you could sell the *Arcadia* alone, and make sufficient profit to keep the rest of the fleet afloat?"

Catriona nodded.

George Welterman slowly shook his head. "No, no, my dear. You can see what he's trying to do, but it won't ever wash. I've been through the Keys accounts for the past five years, and believe me there isn't any way in which four million pounds could give the company sufficient working capital to revive its fortunes. Not without your father at the helm, that is. He did it once: when the *Arcadia* was first planned. He was very short of capital then, but he was able to drum up enough to lay down the keel, and every plate that was riveted into place afterwards gave the banks more confidence, and the stockholders more tolerance. An exceptional man, your father. But you won't see the like of him again. He was one of the old school."

He paused, picking his teeth with the edge of his fingernail. Then he asked, "By the way, what does he do, this Philip Carter-what's-his-name?"

"I don't really know," Catriona confessed. "I think he's in marine insurance."

"Probably a salesman, if you ask me," commented George Welterman. He had worried out the offending shred of meat, and now he was inspecting it closely on the end of his finger. "Some of them do nothing but sail continuously from one side of the Atlantic to the other, selling life insurance to passengers. Well, they have a captive audience, after all; and everybody feels a little vulnerable when they're at sea."

"He didn't *seem* like a salesman," Catriona remarked.

"They're the best kind," said George Welterman.

Catriona watched a mannequin hurrying down the steeply angled runner in a tartan afternoon coat by Drecoll, but she hardly noticed the style or the cut. "My father cared so much for the people who worked for him," she said. "If you do buy Keys, you will look after them, won't you?"

George Welterman laid a hand on her arm and leaned so close that she could smell his Euthymol toothpaste. "I have already explained to Edgar Deacon that IMM would regard the acquisition of Keys as a sacred trust. A trust to preserve your father's dream of what this shipping line should always have been, and a trust to protect all the thousands of people who depend on Keys for their livelihood. We know what it would do to Liverpool and Formby if Keys were to close; and that's partly why we're making our offer. A collapse in the shipping business wouldn't do any of us any good."

"Then what would I have to do?" asked Catriona. "To show that I approved of the sale?"

George Welterman beamed like a man who has just taken a mouthful of gritty spinach. "All you have to do is tell Edgar. Edgar will know what to do."

"And you really think that there's no chance of Keys being able to survive on its own? Supposing we take the Blue Riband? Supposing the *Arcadia* is booked up all winter?"

George Welterman shook his head in what he intended to be a gesture of avuncular kindness. "I'm sorry. I've been through the accounts and I just don't see it."

The *Arcadia* was rolling very badly now, and there were scarcely any ladies left in the fashion show audience. A last lone mannequin struggled up and down the heaving floor, showing off a honeycomb-patterned Molyneux cape, but then Monsieur Delain fought his way out of the curtains and announced that the parade was over. There was a smattering of applause, and the string quintet struck up a doleful version of "For He's a Jolly Good Fellow."

Edgar came up and leaned over Catriona's chair. He gave her a tight humourless beam. "Fruitful, was it?" he asked her.

"Mostly banana oil, if that's what you mean," she retorted. "Banana oil" was a fashionable alternative to "bunk."

George Welterman suddenly, unexpectedly, let out a loud laugh and gripped Edgar by the wrist. Catriona could tell by the expression on Edgar's face that the grip actually hurt.

Twenty-eight

During the fashion show, Mark Beeney and Marcia Conroy were having a screaming match in Marcia's stateroom.

Mark had knocked at Marcia's door to explain about the previous night, to tell her that he hadn't taken Catriona to bed, that he wasn't serious about her, and that he hadn't meant to humiliate Marcia so openly. The truth was that he hadn't heard from Catriona all morning, that he hadn't dared to send Philip Carter-Helm around to her stateroom again, and that he was pretty certain that their flirtation was over. He still had a crush on Catriona. There was something about her which made his blood race around like two bees in a buggy. But he had to face up to facts —and the facts were that Catriona didn't appear to have responded to Philip playing Cupid, nor to Alice's highly paid assurances that Mark Beeney was the most desirable man on board, and Mark's father had always told him that it was no good flogging a dead horse, even if it was only two feet away from the winning post.

Marcia was puffy-eyed and pale. She smoked a pink cocktail cigarette as furiously as if she were falling behind in a cigarette smoking race, and tried to look everywhere except at Mark. Her stateroom was decorated in the style of "Spring," with a mural of orange grass and black silhouetted poplars, and she complemented the theme by wearing a white crepe-de-chine teddy with ruffled pink straps and bows.

"Thank God you didn't do that to me in London," she said. "Every gossip columnist in Fleet Street would have *crucified* me. 'The girl Mark Beeney jilted.' I can see it now."

Mark leaned against the bureau, in pleated white sailing pants and a beautifully cut blazer with gold buttons. At his neck was a loosely tied silk cravat, which lent him the appearance of a slightly piratical college rowing buff. "Marcia," he said, "I'm sorry. I got carried away."

"Well, don't let me stop you, old thing. Far be it from me to come between an American shipping magnate and his puppy-fat floozy."

240

"She's not a floozy, and you know she isn't. The whole point is that she's going to inherit a quarter share in Keys Shipping, including this ship; and I very badly want this ship."

"So you're prepared to snuffle around her like a sex-starved truffle hound, is that it?"

"Listen, Marcia, I have my business to think about."

"Your business, but not the dignity of the girl you invited to come to New York with you? Is that it?"

Mark jabbed a finger at her. "I didn't invite you. You invited yourself."

"So you keep reminding me. *Just* in case I forget that I'm not wanted on voyage."

"You invited yourself because you had some damn-fool premonition. Well, the way you're going on, and the way that ridiculous Keys girl is going on, I hope the damn premonition comes true."

"Oh," crowed Marcia, "so that's why you've come crawling back! She doesn't want you! The plump little heiress isn't interested! Well, that serves you damn well right. You cabin-class cowboy."

"Who the hell are you calling a cowboy?" Mark demanded. "Who came tapping on my door like some second-class whore when I was in London? Don't talk to me about crawling!"

"You boorish shit!" screamed Marcia. "Every day I offer up a prayer of thanks that I never agreed to marry you!"

"I never asked you! And I never would!"

"Oh, so your memory's failing you as well as your talent for picking up fat little girls? Just remember that evening in Brussels! Was that or was that not a proposal of marriage? And did I or did I not turn you down?"

Mark took a deep breath through both nostrils. He paused. Then he said, "We'd both had too much wine. And too many *moules marinières.*"

Marcia clapped her hand against her forehead as if it were a cold compress. "Do you know something, Mark," she said, in a quieter and a more regretful voice, "you really don't have the first idea about how to make a girl feel better."

"I'm not trying to make you feel better," Mark told her. "I'm trying to tell you that I'm sorry I embarrassed you. You can either accept my apology or kick me out of the door. It's up to you. But—well, I hope you say that you forgive me."

Marcia sucked tightly at her cigarette, and then crushed it out in the stainless-steel ashtray. "I suppose it would be pretty frightful for you to have nobody to sleep with for the next two days."

"That isn't what I mean and you know it."

"Do I?"

Mark couldn't help grinning. "Well, maybe I do. But right now I can't think of anyone I'd rather sleep with than you."

"Even if your podgy heroine changes her mind?"

Mark ran his hand through his curly hair in exasperation. "Will you stop calling her names? She's a nice girl."

"She's *large.*"

"She has an ample bust, that's all. You're only jealous."

"Not very *modern,* are they, ample busts? Ample busts were what my grannies used to have. Busts and bustles, and peacock feathers in their hats. Anyway, Freud says you're looking for a mother figure if you go for girls with large bosoms."

"Marcia—" Mark protested.

Marcia swung her long legs off the sofa and stood up. "All right," she said, "I'm being jealous. I'm not usually. But somehow this is all different. When we're on land, I can catch the next train, or hire a limousine and disappear, and never have to see the girl you sleep with next. What the eye can't see, the heart can't grieve over. I love you. You're a beautiful creature. But I know that I can never own you, and that's why sometimes I have to pretend."

Mark lowered his head, and then looked up at Marcia from under V-shaped eyebrows. "Do you want a drink?" he asked her.

She nodded. "There's some Perrier-Jouët in the icebox."

While Mark untwisted the wire on the champagne cork, Marcia opened her cigarette case and took out another cigarette, yellow this time, and lit it. "I suppose I've spoiled everything," she said. "Now you'll be afraid even to talk to me, in case I try to snare you."

"It hasn't occurred to you that I'm very fond of you, too?"

"Fond? That's a carefully chosen word. You can be fond of dogs, or children, or Black Forest *gâteau.*"

Mark filled two Lalique glasses with vintage champagne. "Are you asking me to prove it to you?"

"Love can't be proved, Mark. Love can only be established. One act of sex means nothing."

"How about this?" said Mark, and produced from the breast pocket of his jacket an emerald and diamond necklet—a simply designed rectangle which flashed with thirty-eight half-carat diamonds and a rare Brazilian emerald of absolutely flawless cut. He held it out to Marcia on the palm of his hand, and when she hesitated, he cocked his head inquisitively sideways, as if he were asking her why she should even think of holding back.

"You're *bribing* me," she said in a thick whisper.

"I'm saying I'm sorry. Is this such an immoral way of saying sorry?"

She turned away. She sucked tearfully at her cigarette. "I don't know," she said. Then, turning back to him, "You've done it again, haven't you? You've caught me completely off guard. God, you're a cowboy, and no mistake."

"I'm not asking you to go to bed with me."

"You don't have to *ask* me, do you?"

The emerald flashed with gaudy green fire in Mark's outstretched hand. "It's beautiful," said Marcia. "And for all I know, you might have bought it for her."

"Do you really need to know?"

She shook her head. There were sparkling tears on her eyelashes. She held out both hands, cupped, the yellow cigarette still burning between her fingers, and Mark nonchalantly allowed the diamond and emerald necklet to pour out of his hand into hers. She held it up, and her face was prickled by hundreds of reflected sparks of light. The necklet felt warm and slippery, as real diamonds do, the smoothness of silk, the utter hardness of human emotion.

Mark stepped forward and lowered one strap of Marcia's teddy. "I'd like to see you wearing it," he said. "Shall I put it on for you?"

She held up the necklet between fingers and thumbs. "You're such a bastard," she said.

Mark took her cigarette away from her and stubbed it out. Then he lowered the second strap of her teddy and slipped the shiny crepe-de-chine free from her breasts. He leaned forward and kissed her bare throat and bit at the lobes of her ears. He sensually rolled her nipples until they crinkled up tight. With a smooth sweep of his hand down her bare back, he slid down her teddy to her waist so that she could step out of it. She huddled up to him like a naked orphan, clutching the lapels of his blazer, her breasts touching his cold gold buttons, her moist public hair pressed against the sharply creased leg of his white yachting pants. They kissed voraciously.

Later, Marcia lay back on the spring-green quilt of her curtained bed, surrounded by flower-patterned pillows and carved daffodils, while Mark caressed and kissed her and made her feel as if she were suffocating from suppressed passion. She closed her eyes, and concentrated on the deep erotic sensation that was tensing the muscles of her thighs and making her vagina tight with pleasure.

"You know that I shall never forgive you for this," she whispered, her eyes still tightly closed. All she could see was darkness, figured with scarlet designs. All she could feel was that nervy, trembling tautness that made her want to clench her thighs together.

Yet Mark, with both hands, spread her thighs wide apart and carefully draped the diamond and emerald necklet in her blond pubic hair, which she always kept closely trimmed with nail scissors. The emerald itself he laid with his fingers between her opened lips, vivid green on vivid pink.

"You wear it like a queen," he told her with a crooked grin. His dark eyes were sparkling with delight. His shoulders were so suntanned that Marcia's fingers looked in contrast as if they had been fashioned by Michelangelo out of flawless white Carrara marble.

They made love in absolute silence. The *Arcadia* rolled and swayed and dropped beneath Marcia's bed, but somehow it only added to the rhythm of their joyful and friendly copulation. Afterwards, Mark went through to the sitting room to pour them more champagne and to light them a cigarette each, one turquoise and one black.

"You still want her, don't you?" asked Marcia, sitting up in bed, her small breasts squashed against the quilt.

"Who?"

"You know damned well *who*. Miss Catriona Keys. The puppy-fat flapper of 1924. You won't rest until you've thoroughly dishonoured her."

"You think that going to bed with me is dishonouring?"

"I think that going to bed with you is delightful. But that's another story altogether. We aren't talking about the same thing."

Mark lay back on the large pillows, smoking his black Russian cigarette. His suntan was cut sharply in half by the white outline of his thigh-length shorts and by his white feet. Absentmindedly, the way men do, he played with his softened penis, unconscious of how Marcia was watching him. It was so different from the gentle long-fingernailed way in which she touched him. He squeezed it and rolled it, and stroked the dark dividing line between his balls with his middle finger, quite innocently, thinking of nothing else but how relaxed he was, and how much he enjoyed lying here next to Marcia while the *Arcadia* plunged herself into a summer storm.

Marcia said, with a faint hint of regret, "I could watch you all day."

"All day every day?" asked Mark.

Marcia said, "You're not *that* fascinating," and couldn't understand it when Mark bust out laughing.

Twenty-nine

It was against the rules of their contest that either of them should make way for more food by deliberately inducing vomiting; although, after a testy argument, it was agreed that seasickness, being involuntary, was allowable. And so it was that at ten minutes past eleven, after a breakfast

244

of Wiltshire bacon rashers, scrambled eggs, cold pheasant, a brace of kippers, smoked ham, toast, deviled beef bones, smoked chipped beef in cream, and roast Norfolk gosling, Mr. Joe Kretchmer and Mr. Duncan Wilkes were already sitting in the first-class smoking room, each with a large whisky and soda, while the stewards brought them ham sandwiches, cheese, giant black olives, and platefuls of mushrooms on toast.

They had started their eating marathon as mild friends. But it had only taken last night's dinner and this morning's breakfast, accompanied by an unpleasantly tilting deck, to reduce their relationship to determined grumpiness. They had said good morning to each other but very little else. Most of the communication that was necessary between them was carried on by their self-appointed lady seconds: Henrietta Chibnall, for Mr. Kretchmer, because she believed that he was going to be most wonderfully sick; and Grace Bunyon, the actress, for Mr. Wilkes, because she thought that he had the look of a classical hero about him, like Hercules. She was particularly taken by the blond hair which grew out of his ears.

The rest of the passengers watched with guarded amusement as the bald-headed Mr. Kretchmer picked up a large ham sandwich and established his first crescent-shaped bite in it. Mr. Wilkes ate an olive first, fastidiously spitting the pip into his hand.

"That's just the stone, I hope, Mr. Wilkes?" asked Henrietta Chibnall. "You're not palming anything you shouldn't?"

Mr. Wilkes opened his hand to reveal the well-chewed olive pip. His face was a picture of testy misogyny. "That's all right, Mr. Wilkes," said Henrietta brightly. "One olive down and nine to go."

With his natural instinct for a contest, Maurice Peace sidled into the smoking room and stood by the door with his hands in his pockets watching the two men stuffing their mouths with food. "Not another eating competition?" he remarked to nobody in particular.

"I'm afraid so," said the tall man standing next to him. "On every voyage some American tries to get more than his money's worth by choking down absolutely everything on the menu. It wouldn't surprise me if one of them kills himself."

"You're a doctor?" asked Maurice Peace.

"I'm the _Arcadia_'s doctor, Dr. Cumberland Fields," the tall man replied.

"Oh, how do you do. Pleased to make your acquaintance," said Maurice Peace. "My great-uncle used to be a doctor, in the Civil War. He says he sawed seven legs off at Chancellorsville. Confederates, of course."

Dr. Fields, in his grey suit and his old-fashioned upright collar, gave Maurice Peace a distant smile. Being British, he didn't have the slightest idea why Maurice had said "Confederates," or even why he had said "of course", but it was company policy to humour passengers in all things, and so he automatically smiled.

"You don't think there's really any danger, do you?" Maurice asked him.

Dr. Fields blinked. "I beg your pardon. Any danger of what?"

"Any danger of what you said. Of one of those fellows killing himself."

"Well, the human body is an extraordinary machine," said Dr. Fields. "It will tolerate all kinds of reckless abuse, including the sudden ingestion of large quantities of rich food. But that tall fellow, Mr. Wilkes I believe his name is, I'm not so sure about his constitutional ability to be able to survive such eating."

"You're not?" asked Maurice, interested.

"He has the florid appearance of a man who suffers from high blood pressure, and possibly heart disease. He could be committing suicide—albeit by the most luxurious means available."

"Hmm," said Maurice.

"I really think the captain ought to persuade them to give this contest up," said Dr. Fields. "It's really frightfully offensive, if nothing else. I mean, one can hardly describe the sight of a ham sandwich being forcibly crammed into a fellow's mouth as *aesthetic*, can one?"

"Noo," Maurice agreed. But his mind was already working on the possibilities of opening a book on the two marathon eaters, and in the light of Dr. Fields' expert assessment of Mr. Duncan Wilkes' state of health, there was a very reasonable chance of cleaning up quite a few thousand pounds. Very reasonable indeed.

It didn't occur to Maurice that there could be anything ghoulish in betting on the likelihood of Mr. Duncan Wilkes' sudden demise from overeating. It wasn't as if he himself had incited either contestant to test his intestinal tract so challengingly. Maurice was simply a better on odds, a gambler on likely outcomes. He never saw himself as a participant in everyday life, only as an interested outsider. After all, he was the only first-class passenger on board who didn't have a ticket. "I feel like a ghost," he had once told an almost insensible wino as they sat side by side on the painted horses of a deserted steam carousel in Paragould, Arkansas, while dawn appeared behind the tulip trees.

He elbowed his way through the small circle of passengers, and laid his hand with a flourish on Mr. Kretchmer's shoulder. Then he turned his head this way and that, to make sure that his gesture had caught everybody's attention, and said, "Ladies and gentlemen, not forgetting any peers of the British realm, if there are any present, I protest at the way this contest is being carried on! Protest most vigorously!"

Mr. Kretchmer looked at him, his cheeks bulging with ham sandwich. "What's wrong?" he wanted to know. He blew out a few crumbs of bread, and Grace Bunyon snapped out loudly, "No cheating, Mr.

246

Kretchmer!"

Maurice ignored Mr. Kretchmer's question and said in the staccato style of a fairground barker, "No contest between two such sporting gentlemen as these should be carried on without the rest of the passengers being given the opportunity to back their favourite! A sporting bet is part of the great tradition of Anglo-Saxon life, and I *deplore* the fact that a tournament as unusual and as exciting as this one is being allowed to take place without an official book being opened! I expect that several of you have already made private bets. But I propose to open the official *Arcadia* eating contest book, and I invite you to place your wagers with me and support your own particular fancy."

There was laughter and applause. Somebody called out, "I bet they're both as sick as parrots before tomorrow lunchtime!" But Maurice raised his hands for silence and said, "I'll be opening the book in five minutes, by the bar. Those of an adventurous disposition are welcome to join me. I might even permit them to stand me a drink."

There was more laughter, but Maurice was quite serious as he withdrew towards the bar and rummaged through his pockets for pencil and paper and stray dollar bills. As he went, he beckoned to a young steward called Minchin, a Newcastle boy with a shiny black cowlick and the build of an undernourished jockey. "Yes, sir?" asked Minchin.

"Here's twenty-five dollars," he said, pushing a crumpled-up ball of greenbacks into Minchin's uniform pocket. He glanced over Minchin's narrow epauletted shoulder to make sure that nobody was watching. "I want you to spread the intelligence that Mr. Kretchmer is suffering from the worst duodenal ulcers since Napoleon, and that the only reason he's travelling to New York is to see an ulcer expert. Pass it around that he's only supposed to drink milk, and that if he touches anything stronger than barley water he's probably going to pop off before we're in sight of the Statue of Liberty."

"Is that *true*, sir?" asked Minchin worriedly. "I was going to bet on him myself."

"True?" asked Maurice. "What does it matter to you if it's true? You've just earned yourself twenty-five dollars, and there's more where that came from, if you do a good job."

Minchin stared at Maurice for a long time, like an anxious ferret. Maurice said, "Well? What's the matter?"

"My father said I was never to tell lies, sir."

"Did he now? Did he say anything about advantageous exaggeration?"

"I don't know, sir. He didn't mention it by name."

"I suppose you wouldn't like to send him a telegraph and ask his opinion?"

"He's deceased, sir."

"Ah," said Maurice. "There's the proof of it. Telling the truth gets you nowhere at all but the crypt. Edgar Allan Poe said that. Or was it Ambrose Bierce? Who knows? Well, who cares? But run along now and earn your money, and we'll discuss the moral philosophy of it later."

Maurice went to the bar and ordered himself a drink. Then he turned around and watched in satisfaction as young Minchin went from passenger to passenger, politely enquiring if they wanted another cocktail, oh, and by the way, did they know that Mr. Kretchmer was suffering from chronic duodenal ulcers? By the time the first bettors approached Maurice with their big white fluttering five-pound notes, the favourite was already a foregone conclusion, although Maurice took a particular pleasure in remarking that Mr. Kretchmer looked in *very* good health, didn't they think? and relishing the twitchy, sidelong answers he received in reply. Oh, yes, excellent health.

When all the passengers had laid their bets, he had gathered in £ 725 for Mr. Wilkes and £35 for Mr. Kretchmer. If Mr. Wilkes collapsed in mid-marathon, as Dr. Fields had suggested he might, then Maurice would be better off by £550. And so far he had only taken bets in the smoking room. There were still plenty of suckers in the Palm Lounge and the Orchid Lounge and around the swimming pool.

But there was one more errand that Maurice had to run before he could gather in any more stake money. Last night, when Princess Xenia of Russia had graciously consented to auction off the ship's pool, Mark Beeney had successfully bid for ticket number 627. Although the weather was getting up, and it was unlikely that the *Arcadia* would be able to exceed the official estimated mileage of 623, Maurice still didn't want to take any unnecessary risks. Gambling was gambling, but folly was folly. And in Maurice's opinion, it was folly not to do everything within one's power to make sure that the right cards came up, and that the right horses came in, and that the right ball stopped in the right slot. Besides, he was still low on ready money, and he needed very much more if he was going to stake himself for another night's heavy stud.

Whistling to himself, Maurice went up in the electric lift to the boat deck, and made his way along to the purser's office. The varnished door was half ajar, but all the same he knocked politely before he stuck his head around to see if anyone was in.

He caught Monty Willowby in the extraordinary act of trying to conceal a lavatory seat under his mess jacket. The problem was, the mess jacket was cut very tight, and Monty Willowby was very portly, and the seat was one of the larger mahogany variety, complete with gilt-embossed cover.

"Oh," said Maurice, in perplexity. "I hope I'm not intruding."

Monty Willowby looked down at the lavatory seat as if he had never seen it before, and then tossed it noisily down in a corner of his office.

"Just testing it," he said with a loud attempt at nonchalance. "Had some complaints about them. You know, sharp edges cutting into tender legs. *Yours* all right, is it, sir?"

Maurice frowned at Monty Willowby, and then at the lavatory seat, and then back at Monty Willowby. "All right?" he enquired.

"No sharp edges, is what I was getting at."

"Oh, no. Nothing like that. No sharp edges. Smooth as a baby's bottom."

Maurice was about to say something else but then he changed his mind. Monty Willowby wasn't listening anyway. He sat down at his desk like a slowly deflating observation balloon, fold by fold, billow by billow, and stared at the heaps of paper in front of him in baffled resignation. Usually he kept a neatly regimented desk, but now he was half buried in bills of lading, wireless messages, timetables, schedules, and passenger rosters.

"It's too much, you know," he said, mostly to himself. "It's more than a body can cope with."

Ever since Mr. Fribourg had approached him last night with his preposterous blackmailing demand to collect as many celebrity toilet seats as he could, Monty Willowby's carefully organised existence had gone utterly haywire. Twenty minutes in a first-class bathroom unscrewing the seat was twenty minutes wasted out of an already hectic day. He'd already had complaints from Mr. Peel that he hadn't made himself conspicuous enough to the passengers at breakfast. "Big chap like you, Monty, don't know how you manage to make yourself so scarce."

The trouble was, Mr. Fribourg had badly frightened him. Those medical supplies which he had spirited off the *Callipygic* in 1912 had netted him more than £14,500, and that was at 1912 prices. They would probably be worth twice as much today. He had arranged the fraud, he had seriously believed, for the finest of all possible motives. His mother, Mrs. Enid Willowby, a gentle and tender soul who had ruined her health bringing up eight sons and two daughters in a damp villa in Penge, in South London, had been advised by her family doctor to seek a drier climate, or die. With the proceeds from the *Callipygic* cargo, Monty had bought her a house in Tangier, and arranged for the services of a European physician and a Moorish maid, and even for a Daimler motorcar. Monty's reward had been that his mother had flourished and become one of Tangier's most notable English eccentrics, sending her servants every evening to feed all the stray cats in the Medina with fish heads and horse meat. She hadn't been particularly grateful to Monty. In fact, she made a point of visiting friends in Fes whenever he was able to get shore leave in Tangier. But Monty supposed that children, like parents, should never expect any thanks. He just sometimes wished that his mother would pop off and leave him her house. She was eighty-six, after all, and enough was enough.

The *Callipygic* had been a very sizeable theft, however: even bigger than Monty had expected, and it was still remembered in marine insurance circles with considerable wrath. If it ever got out that Monty had been responsible for it, he would probably end up in Pentonville. No—not probably. Certainly. Ten years and no remission, and nothing to look forward to on his release but poverty and doss houses.

That was why—absurd as Mr. Fribourg's scheme appeared to be—Monty was still industriously unscrewing toilet seats.

Maurice said in his blandest voice, "I don't know whether I ought to report this or not, but I've just seen a boat."

Monty raised his head. "A boat? I beg your pardon? A *boat?*"

"That's right," said Maurice, trying to sound like an enthusiastic but hopelessly naïve amateur. "About five minutes ago, off the left side. At least, it looked like a boat."

"What kind of a boat? A fishing boat? Something like that?"

"Well, no. Not really. More of a lifeboat."

"A lifeboat? Was there anyone in it?"

"I don't know." Maurice shrugged. "I really couldn't see. It's pretty wild out there, after all. It was just a lifeboat, with a couple of oars sticking out of it."

Monty stood up and scrabbled through the papers on his desk to find his telephone. He cranked the dial, and then said, "Bridge? Is that you, Mr. Peel?" To Maurice, he said, "Don't go away."

"I won't." Maurice smiled.

"Mr. Peel?" said Monty. "It's Mr. Willowby. I have a passenger here who says he saw a lifeboat adrift off the port bow. About five minutes ago, he says. That's right. No, he couldn't see; but he says there were oars visible. That's it. Yes. I'll bring him up to the bridge."

The chances of locating a single drifting lifeboat in a sea that was rising all around them now like the black slate roofs of Victorian churches were almost nil. But the code of the seaways was quite clear: survivors were to be sought for, no matter how remote the chances of finding them might be. And that was why Sir Peregrine testily ordered the *Arcadia* to be turned off to port in a wide circular sweep that would take her back on her course by five or six nautical miles. The lookouts aloft were told to keep an extra-sharp watch; and the promenade decks were crowded with passengers in raincoats and yellow oilskins, all glad of a little ocean drama to help them forget their seasickness.

Maurice Peace, of course, didn't bother to look. Instead, he went to the first-class cocktail bar and began gathering in more bets for the Wilkes-Kretchmer eating contest. He had already assured the outcome of the ship's pool for today, and won himself $500 from Mark Beeney, and so he was feeling quite pleased with himself—pleased enough to order a mimosa for his elevenses, and to put it on Mark Beeney's tab.

Beeney, he was sure, would be good for quite a few thousand dollars more.

Thirty

At one o'clock, after an hour and a half of futile wallowing in the wild seas, Ralph Peel ordered the *Arcadia* to resume her course. The wind had now risen to gale force, and the ship was rolling more than twenty degrees from one side to the other. Only the bravest and the sickest of the passengers remained outside, while the wind screamed in the wires, and thousands of gallons of green water thundered onto the foredeck. The noise was devastating, like a hundred Alpine avalanches all at once, accompanied by the shrieking and keening of a cathedral full of professional mourners.

Despite the storm, however, luncheon was being laid out as usual. In the first-class dining lounge there was supposed to be a special lunch in honour of the *Arcadia*'s designers and engineers, although most of the honoured guests were still huddled in their cabins, their faces buried in their pillows, praying that their designs and their engineering would stand up to a Force Ten gale. The first-class stewards hurried up and down the sloping carpets of the dining lounge with the surefootedness of goats, expertly fitting the edges of the tables with mahogany "fiddles"—those raised flaps which were supposed to prevent a passenger's meal from sliding into his lap in rough weather.

Catriona had gone back to her stateroom to change for luncheon. The great grey waves she could see through her porthole were now twenty or thirty feet high, which was well on the way to what the commodore of the Cunard Line had described as "a precipitous sea." Waves that were eight to twelve feet high were only "rough." Alice made her lie down for a while, with a cold flannel on her forehead, while Trimmer brought her a glass of iced champagne.

"I never thought a huge ship like this would roll about so much," she said. She was beginning to feel distinctly queasy.

"A few hextra tons don't make no difference to han hocean," said Trimmer.

"No," said Catriona. "Apparently they don't."

By one o'clock, however, she felt well enough to put on a royal-blue Poiret day dress with a floppy white embroidered collar, and accompany Edgar into luncheon. Edgar was noticeably quiet, and the unusual pallor of his cheeks made his dark chin seem even darker, as if he hadn't shaved this morning.

To assemble in that glittering dining lounge, and to sit at tables for lunch while the entire room leaned twenty-five degrees one way and then twenty-five degrees the other, was for most of the *Arcadia*'s first-class passengers an experience they would remember all their lives. It was quite useless trying to keep one's cutlery to oneself. Every time the ship rolled, all the knives and forks and spoons would shower noisily down to one end of the table, and then shower back again when she rolled the other way. Wineglasses were held in special compartments to prevent them from tipping over; but all the same they could only be a third filled. All the chairs and tables, of course, were securely anchored to the floor.

Mark Beeney appeared a few minutes before the soup was served, with Marcia Conroy on his arm. He caught Catriona's eye for a moment before he sat down, and gave her a quick, questioning smile. She tried to smile back, but her mouth wouldn't respond in time. When she turned away, she saw Edgar looking at her with undisguised thoughtfulness.

"Are you feeling sick?" she asked him.

"Perhaps," he replied, rather cryptically.

Next to her, Douglas Fairbanks said, "It's all in the mind. You should just pretend that you're sitting down to lunch at your favourite restaurant. Forget that the table's tilting from side to side. Tilt with it." Mary Pickford retorted, "You always say that everything's in the mind. Well, maybe it is. But the trouble with all this rolling about is that it's in the stomach as well."

A bread roll, half-broken, tumbled down the table between them, bounced off the fiddle, and dropped onto the floor. Catriona looked up the table to see where it had come from and saw Baroness Zawisza with her butter knife raised, her empty hand still cupped in the shape of her escaped bap.

"Well played, Baroness," remarked Douglas Fairbanks, winking at Catriona.

In accordance with that unshakeable perversity which characterises almost every meal that is served at sea, the first course which was brought out at this storm-tilted luncheon was fresh asparagus soup. It would have been quite easy for the head chef to change the menu to pickled herrings, or smoked trout, or pressed chicken with brandy sauce, all of which would have been far more manageable in a precipitous sea. But that would have meant compromising the standards of a first-class restaurant for the sake of the weather; and Monsieur Vincent would never allow *anything* short of complete capsize to interfere with the quality and the variety of the food he offered. This, despite the fact that the kitchen floors were already awash with soup.

Pairs of stewards manhandled huge white china tureens from table to table as if they were clowns in a German circus. One of the stewards would attempt to ladle while the other did his best to keep the tureen level. Every now and then, the *Arcadia* would give an extra curtsey, and the soup stewards would all have to totter off sideways, helplessly following the weighty inertia of two gallons of fresh asparagus soup in a desperate attempt to prevent a catastrophic spillage.

At first, everybody was alarmed. But when their soup bowls had been quarter filled with soup, and they had each managed to rescue a spoon from the sliding shoals of cutlery, their concern subsided and the absurdity of their predicament began to tickle them. Soup went everywhere. It poured off the ends of the tables; it splashed down the fronts of ladies' day dresses; it emptied itself out of one bowl into the bowl next to it. Mark Beeney even managed to pour a spoonful of soup over his left shoulder, which left both Marcia and Catriona helpless with laughter. Only Edgar wasn't amused. When he had tried for the fifth time to pursue the small pale green semicircle of soup in his plate and missed it, he slammed down his spoon and sat with his arms folded and his face like a pre-Columbian ritual mask. Catriona said, "Don't worry, Mr. Deacon. I'll tell them not to serve you any gravy with the next course."

After the soup, Marcia excused herself, and with the help of a steward, she tottered off to the ladies' room. Catriona stayed where she was, finishing her bread roll and trying not to look either at Mark or at George Welterman, who was sitting right down at the far end of the table with Dame Clara Butt. But Mark stared at her all the time, his arms folded on top of the fiddle, one of his shoulders slightly higher than the other where he had stuffed a linen napkin under his jacket to prevent the soup soaking through to his silk shirt.

"Catriona," he said, so quietly that at first she wasn't quite sure that he had actually spoken to her. She looked up, not at Mark but at George Welterman, who was also watching her. George must have possessed extra-sensitive ears, because he nodded, as if to say, It's okay, answer him.

She turned to Mark and managed a smile. "I'm not angry with you," she said.

Mary Pickford said, "Angry? Who's angry with whom? Catriona, are you angry with Mark? Is that it? Why, I just adore a quarrel. Douglas, *do* listen, they're quarrelling."

"I'm trying to drink this fucking soup," Douglas Fairbanks complained.

Mark said, "Can we meet later? Talk, maybe?"

Catriona shrugged. She knew that she had Mark exactly where she wanted him, and that the more offhand she was the more enthusiastically he would chase her. But, actually, she didn't feel like being offhand with him. The anger she had felt last night, when she had thought that he was only wooing her for the sake of buying up the *Arcadia*, had largely subsided. He *was* a businessman, after all. And he *was* amazingly handsome. The kind of man who was more handsome in the flesh than he was in her imagination.

"What about Marcia?" asked Catriona. "Won't she be angry?"

"Oh, Douglas, *do* listen to this, this is marvellous," enthused Mary Pickford.

"For Christ's sake, it's none of your business," protested Douglas Fairbanks. "You don't have any right to listen."

"It's so *romantic,*" Mary Pickford told him. "What other excuse do I need?"

"I don't know," Douglas Fairbanks told her. "Did you make an offer for the motion picture rights yet?"

"Marcia understands," Mark lied. "She knows the way I feel about you."

"She *says* she understands," said Catriona. "But does she?"

"Do you want to ask her?"

"No. I wouldn't be so cruel."

"Then believe me. And join me for dinner at eight o'clock this evening."

Catriona glanced at Edgar. On Edgar's face there was a positive no. She looked further, towards George Welterman. On George Welterman's face there was an odd, stony watchfulness.

"You must go to dinner with Marcia," she told Mark in an imperative whisper. Mark could hardly hear her because the stewards were briskly clearing away the soup plates. "But you could meet me for supper at ten o'clock, after the theatre show. You know where my stateroom is."

"Boy, is that *romantic,*" said Mary Pickford.

Douglas Fairbanks winced. "I wish you wouldn't say 'boy.' Do you know what it sounds like, when you say 'boy'? It's nearly as bad as saying 'gee.' "

"Why shouldn't I say 'gee' if I want to? I make more money than you do."

"You want to bet?"

Marcia returned from the ladies' room looking paler but steadier. She sat down next to Mark with a wan smile. Mark kissed her cheek and there wasn't a lady on the table who didn't think, *Judas.* Except for Catriona, of course, who knew that she desired him more than she had ever desired Nigel. Nigel had been a lover and a chum. Mark was too good-looking and too tempestuous to be anything but a lover and a competitor, and lovers who were competitors were the best kind. It was the men she had to fight for who always aroused her the most.

The stewards served out the next course: blinis with sour cream and fresh Malossol caviar. The blinis were supposed to be served with Polish vodka, in diminutive Wielkopolski glasses, but the steward who was bringing all the glasses into the dining lounge on a large kidney-shaped tray was fatally deceived by the *Arcadia's* hesitation on the peak of each roll, and attempted to cross an open stretch of floor just as the ship began to roll back again. A hundred glasses smashed, to the delighted and slightly hysterical applause of the cabin-class diners.

It was just as the essence of black mushrooms *au Chablis* was being served that the first of the crises occurred. The fifth officer, Derek Holdsworth, balanced his way into the first-class dining lounge with his white cap wedged under his arm, and whispered with obvious urgency into Dick Charles' ear. Dick Charles whispered back at him, and then abruptly sprang to his feet. A more experienced officer, of course, would have smoothly excused himself and left without causing a commotion. But Dick Charles was both inexperienced and overexcited, especially after this morning's games of Corkies with Lady Diana FitzPerry. He flapped his hands for silence, and then he announced, "My lords, ladies, and gentlemen. An emer— an emergency has arisen. It apuh— it apuh— it appears that a young g-girl has become trapped in the rigging. She may be in d-danger of duh— she may be in danger of duh— she may be in danger of drowning. So I must leave you at once, and d-do what I can to rescue her."

Crumpling up his napkin and throwing it onto the table, Dick Charles followed Derek Holdsworth to the staircase.

It took a few seconds for Dick Charles' announcement to register in the further corners of the dining lounge. But then, with one noisy accord, as if they had just received the news of the declaration of another war, or the sudden death of Mae Murray, the first-class company rose from their seats and followed him up the staircase to the boat deck.

"What on earth's up?" demanded Edgar.

Mark Beeney, coming across and taking Catriona's arm, said quietly, "It sounds like you've got trouble."

For a moment, Catriona was jostled away from Mark by excited passengers, all pearls and fringes and beaded headbands, but then suddenly Philip Carter-Helm appeared, and politely but very firmly held back two overexcited French ladies so that Catriona could make her way through.

"Thank you," she said.

Philip smiled that disturbing smile of his. He was handsome, all right, but for some reason she couldn't find him attractive. Perhaps it was because he seemed to be so smug. He always gave her the impression that he knew something which she didn't.

"I wouldn't go up on deck, if I were you," said Philip. "It's jolly wild out there."

Mark came up behind Catriona and took her arm again. "Philip," he acknowledged him.

"I was advising Miss Keys not go up on deck," said Philip.

Mark grinned. "I think you'll find that Miss Keys has a mind of her own. She's not always right, but she's always determined."

Catriona said, quite kindly, "I do think that I can look after myself, thank you, Mr. Carter-Helm."

Charles Schwab, the American steel billionaire, stood aside to let Catriona pass him on the sloping stairs. "I have to tell you, Miss Keys, this is just about the most exciting maiden voyage I was ever on. Just *marvellous*. Is this a stunt, too, this drowning child? You really know how to keep your passengers entertained."

Although the first-class passengers were now crowding the grand staircase, and chattering in anticipation, the dining-room stewards politely but adamantly refused to permit them out on deck. It was too wild out there, and the last thing Sir Peregrine wanted was to lose some expensive socialite over the side. White Star officials still shuddered when they thought of Colonel Astor and Mr. Benjamin Guggenheim going down in the *Titanic*, and that had been more than twelve years ago now. Collectively, the passengers on board the *Arcadia* were worth more than 450 million dollars, and Keys were very anxious to keep them all on board.

Catriona found Edgar by the double doors that led out onto the boat deck. He was struggling into a yellow oilskin and black galoshes. "What's going on out there?" she demanded over the hubbub of excited passengers.

"A little girl went out to see the storm," Edgar shouted back. "Derek Holdsworth says she was almost swept overboard, but she got herself caught up in one of the electric cranes. That's all I know. Apparently they can't reach her."

"I'm coming out too," Catriona insisted.

"You can't! The sea's running all over the decks!"

"I'm coming!" Catriona shouted. "It's my ship and I'm coming!"

Mark Beeney put his arm around Catriona and said to Edgar, "It's okay. I'll come out too and take care of her."

Edgar snapped up the buttons of his oilskin, his face bland and unexpressive. Then he said, "All right. Steward, help them into their waterproofs will you?" With that, he nodded to Derek Holdsworth to open the door for him, and he stepped out with his head bent into the howling wind.

"Ladies and gentlemen, *please!*" called out Percy Fearson from the side of the foyer. "The weather's too rough for any of you to go out on deck! Please carry on with your luncheon! There isn't anything you can do except finish your meal! We'll keep you informed of everything that happens!"

Douglas Fairbanks elbowed his way forward. "Miss Keys," he said. "I understand that a young girl is caught up in the rigging somehow. Well, I insist that I come out to help. Swinging around in the rigging is my forte, after all."

Catriona didn't really look her best at that moment. The steward had given her an ankle-length yellow oilskin with sleeves that reached her knees, and a pair of rubber galoshes that were so huge she could scarcely take a step in them. Mark, with a large yellow sou'wester pulled over his eyes, looked as if he were posing for an advertisement for Compass brand sardines.

Catriona looked towards Percy Fearson and said, "Do you think it's all right if Mr. Fairbanks comes?"

"I should reckon it's all right," said Percy Fearson. "Seeing as how he clambered around in *The Thief of Baghdad*."

"You saw that picture?" asked Douglas Fairbanks with a flashing grin. "Did you like it?"

Marcia had now realised that Mark was going out on deck with Catriona. She tried to stagger towards them through the crowded foyer, but George Welterman held her arm. "You heard what they said," he told her. "We should just go back and finish our luncheon."

"But Mark's going outside."

"He's an experienced sailor. He won't get into any trouble."

"Not with the sea, maybe."

"You mean you're concerned about Mark and that Keys girl?" asked George. "Well, perhaps you have cause to be. But it's her ship he wants, not her affections."

Marcia gave him a quick, uncomprehending glance. "Her *ship?*" she asked. Then she turned away and began to clamber back down the staircase, gripping the handrail to help her balance. Most of the rest of the passengers began to follow her and resume their meal.

Derek Holdsworth opened the doors for Mark and Catriona, and helped them out onto the boat deck. The wind and the spray hit Catriona in the face like a bucketful of crushed ice. She staggered and slipped, and Mark had to catch her arm and guide her across to the handrail.

"Can you manage?" yelled Derek Holdsworth. "I'll be along in a minute with Mr. Fairbanks. The girl's on the starboard crane on the promenade deck."

"All right," Mark shouted back.

It had been one thing to look out of her cabin porthole and watch the heaving waves from the luxurious security of her silken bed; but even the nauseating rolling of the dining saloon had not prepared Catriona for the sheer thunderous drama of what was outside. The huge liner was driving her bows into walls of water that were twenty or thirty feet high, and pitching up columns of spray that seemed to hang above the foredecks for minutes at a time before they collapsed onto the boards with a rattle like gunfire. The wind was almost overwhelming, and Catriona had to gasp for breath as she and Mark clutched and staggered their way back along to the second-class promenade, and to the rail which overlooked promenade deck A.

Edgar was already there, with Second Officer Ralph Peel and Fourth Officer Dick Charles. On the promenade deck below, six or seven of the crew were paying out a reel of line in preparation for an attempt to lasso the overhanging jib of the starboard electric crane.

"What's going on?" shouted Mark. "Where's the girl? I don't see her."

Edgar gripped his shoulder and pointed towards the very apex of the crane's jib. Catriona peered through the slanting spray, and at last caught sight of her. A pale-faced bedraggled figure in pink, clinging to the slippery metal.

"How the hell did she get up there?" asked Mark.

"Search me," said Ralph Peel. "But she was lucky she was spotted at all."

"Can't one of your men climb up the crane and carry her down?"

"In this sea? Not without a line. That's what we're doing now. Trying to throw a line over the jib so that someone can go up there and slide the girl down on the rope."

"What's her name?" asked Catriona. "Are her parents on board? How could anyone let her go out in a storm like this?"

Ralph Peel wiped spray from his face with the back of his hand: The wind and the sea were so noisy that they could scarcely hear each other shouting. And all the time the *Arcadia* was plunging and rolling and bucking her way through the ocean with the ferocity of an untamed mare.

"Her name's Lucille Foster. She's the daughter of Winthrop Foster the Third and Gala Jones. Those two who smashed themselves up in that motor accident in Paris. She's on her way back to America with a guardian, Mrs. Hall; but Mrs. Hall is down in her stateroom flat out from seasickness. So *she's* not much help."

At last Douglas Fairbanks appeared, wrapped up in shiny black oilskins, with a sou'wester that was two sizes too small for him. "I can't compliment your costume department," he told Catriona. "Now where's this girl?"

"Up there, right at the end of that crane jib," said Ralph Peel. "We're trying to throw a line over the jib and make it faster, so that someone can climb up there and lower her down."

"How did she get way up there in the first place?" Douglas Fairbanks wanted to know.

"That's the same question I asked," said Mark.

"And *why*, in a storm like this?" added Douglas Fairbanks.

"Have you tried talking to her?" said Catriona.

"We tried, miss," said Ralph Peel. "She didn't answer, though; and I don't even think she can hear us."

"Have you thought of lowering the crane's own hook, instead of trying to throw a line around it?" Douglas Fairbanks wanted to know.

"That was the first thing we thought of, sir. But that's a nasty hook on there, very heavy and we didn't want that swinging around the deck in a Force Tenner. Quite apart from which, it looks like the young girl's got her hand right up in the pulleys. If we tried to operate the crane, we'd probably end up injuring her. Tearing her arm off, or worse."

"I just don't understand how she managed to get up there," Douglas Fairbanks repeated.

"She could have shinned, sir," said Ralph Peel. "It's not impossible, especially for a youngster."

On their tenth or eleventh attempt, the crewmen at last managed to throw their line so that it snaked up over the crane's jib and swung down to the deck below. One of them immediately snatched at the other end and made it fast. It was prevented from sliding down the sloping arm of the crane by the protruding pully mechanism, but that was all that held it. It would take a brave man to climb up there in a sixty-mph wind.

"Volunteers?" screamed Ralph Peel into the gale. Almost immediately, one of the crewmen, a ginger-haired youngster called Stokes, seized hold of the wet rope and began pulling himself up it, monkey fashion.

"That's it, lad! Keep at it!" shouted Ralph Peel, although it was doubtful if Stokes could hear him. The rope spun around and around, and several times Stokes was forced to cling tight and stay where he was as the tilting of the *Arcadia*'s deck left him hanging over the side, seventy feet above the threshing ocean. To lose his grip and plunge into a sea like that would mean immediate drowning, or crushing against the side of the ship.

Catriona borrowed Derek Holdsworth's spray-speckled binoculars, and peered at Lucille Foster through the driving wind. The girl appeared to be calm, almost thoughtful, as she clung to the end of the jib. She wasn't even looking down at her would-be rescuers. Instead, with her hair stuck in pre-Raphaelite waves to her forehead, she was staring at some dark point in the distance. The moment, perhaps, when her father's Hispano-Suiza had collided with the base of that statue. Her mother's last second of life: "Winthrop, what *are* you doing?"

Stokes was halfway up the rope now, but the wind was gusting worse than ever, and there was no doubt that the seas were growing more calamitous every minute. Although Catriona didn't know it, luncheon in the first-class dining saloon had already been abandoned, and an heroic attempt by the second-class stewards to bring hot beef tea and chicken pies to the second-class passengers had been temporarily called off after a boiling urn had rolled the whole length of the corridor. Down in tthe lower levels of the ship, among the third-class passengers, there was something of a storm party going on, as seventy or eighty of the hardier beer drinkers among them clung around the bar and did their best to empty it of brown ale. Harry Pakenow was among them, although he was staying on lemonade. Half an hour after lunch, he had been monstrously sick over the side of shelter deck C, sicker than he could ever remember in his whole life. In the third-class recreation room, the upright piano broke loose from the screws that were holding it to the deck and rumbled across the room like a miniature express train, smashing its way clean through the starboard wall and ending up in the gentlemen's washroom with a resonant Wagnerian bang. In the second-class pantry, the door of a crockery cupboard swung open unnoticed, and on the ship's next roll, two hundred china cups and saucers came gushing off the top two shelves and shattered on the floor.

"What the hell's Sir Peregrine up to," Ralph Peel muttered to himself. "Waves like this, he ought to be taking them aslant."

Now Stokes was waving from his perch halfway up the rope that he couldn't cling on any longer, and that he was going to have to come down. He slid jerkily back to the deck, burning his hands as he went; but it had been a courageous try, and his shipmates clapped him on the back as he dropped onto the slippery boards. He gave Ralph Peel the thumbs-up.

The pitching of the *Arcadia*'s bows was so severe that seawater was crashing onto the foredeck and sluicing along her promenades like a seething tidal bore. Most of the passengers, seasick and battered, had returned to their cabins, although Maurice Peace was still running a poker game in the smoking lounge, and Mr. Wilkes and Mr. Kretchmer were sitting side by side in basketwork chairs in the Orchid Lounge, munching their way through sandwiches and fruitcake, which was all their steward had been able to bring them. Neither had yet been seasick, and this was probably because their stomachs were so full that they were incapable of even the slightest regurgitative spasm. In the Grand Lounge, the ship's pianist sat with his tails hanging tidily over his piano stool while he played a saucy little selection from Charles Gulliver's revue *The Whirl of the World,* currently showing at the London Palladium with Lorna and Toots Pounds.

As the rolling and pitching grew worse, Mademoiselle Narron burst out of her stateroom in a state of histrionic fright and made her way whimpering and warbling up to the officers' quarters. The electric lifts were not operating, so she climbed the stairs in her fright-white négligée with all the wide-eyed drama of Lady Macbeth. Outside, on the boat deck, she was instantly drenched by nearly half a hundredweight of cold seawater, but she struggled on to Rudyard Philips' cabin and knocked loudly at the door.

Rudyard, who had been sitting fretfully on his bunk, jumped up and opened the door at once. "Louise!" he said. "My dear Louise, you shouldn't be here! Look at you, you're soaked!"

Mademoiselle Narron collapsed heavily and wetly into Rudyard's arms, obliging him to take three quick steps backwards to keep his balance. He kicked the cabin door shut with his foot, and then he manhandled Mademoiselle Narron as gently as he could manage onto his bunk. When he leaned over to loosen her négligée, however, she seized his face between her hands and pressed him forcefully against her huge slippery bosoms.

"Rudyard! I'm so frightened! We're going to sink!"

Rudyard took hold of her wrists and firmly released her grip. "Louise, listen to me, we are *not* going to sink. That's nonsense! No ocean liner has been sunk by heavy seas in the whole of this century, nor will it be. We can ship thousands of gallons of water before we're at any risk. The *Carmania* heeled over fifty degrees once, so that her lifeboats were broken to pieces, but she stayed afloat. And so will the *Arcadia.*"

"But I'm so *frightened!* I didn't know what else to do but come to you."

"You shouldn't be here at all. I'm in enough trouble as it is."

"You're in trouble? What for?"

Rudyard went to his washstand, took out two tumblers, and poured each of them a brandy. "That's all I've got, I'm afraid," he told her, "but it may help to settle your stomach. The truth is, my dear, I'm under arrest. Confined to my quarters until further notice."

"Confined to your quarters? What have you done? How can they arrest you?"

"The captain has the power to arrest anyone he chooses. In this particular case, he chose to arrest me. He says that I'm responsible for an accident we had when we left Irish territorial waters. We ran down a small boat, and killed someone."

"*This* ship? The *Arcadia?*"

Rudyard nodded. "You wouldn't have noticed. The boat was too small. But I was on the bridge at the time, and so I'm being held responsible."

"That is terrible. You are a good sailor, *n'est-ce-pas?*"

Rudyard looked down at his drink. "I suppose so. I always used to think so. I'm not much good at anything else."

"How can you say that?" Louise demanded, sitting up on the bed. Her red hair stuck to her cheeks and her shoulders like fronds of Japanese seaweed. Her pink nipples showed through the thin wet cotton of her négligée, and her cheeks were flushed both with brandy and determination. "How can you say that you are no good at anything else?"

"I'm not much of a Romeo, am I?" Rudyard asked her, without raising his eyes. He couldn't bring himself to use the word "lover." "And I didn't do much of a job when it came to keeping my wife."

"You were at sea. It wasn't your fault your wife left you. What else could you do?"

"Oh, come on now," said Rudyard, bracing himself against the washstand as the *Arcadia* heeled off to starboard. It was like dropping in a lift, except that your stomach never quite caught up with the rest of you. In a moment or two you would be rising up again, passing your stomach on its way down, and just as your stomach came scrabbling up to meet you, down you would drop yet again. In the next cabin, through the thin partition wall, Rudyard had heard Derek Holdsworth being catastrophically ill, and he didn't feel particularly chipper himself.

Mademoiselle Narron said, "It was my fault, what happened to us when we made love. I expected too much."

"That doesn't make me feel very much better. In any case, don't let's talk about it, if you don't mind."

"But I have been thinking about it so much! You need someone who is going to bring you out. At the moment, everything you do is so tight, so restricted. You never express yourself. Perhaps you are afraid to. Perhaps you think that people will ridicule you if you burst out and do everything that you have always wanted. Look at me, though. All the time I am making such a fool of myself! Pretending to kill myself! Falling all over you like some lady from an opera! But even if people laugh at me, who cares? At least I do what I want. At least I live my life with fullness and with passion. But you? In your mind, you are so reserved! That is why our lovemaking was such a disaster!"

"Oh," said Rudyard, sourly. "I didn't know you thought it was a disaster. Sorry I thought I could satisfy you. Very unprovoked of me, I'm sure."

Louise lurched across the cabin and took his hand. She had lost one of her slippers on the boat deck, and so she limped as well as lurched. But there was an expression of such friendliness and sympathy on her face that she looked almost beatific. Behind her raggedy red hair, a discreet halo should have shone.

"I have been so uncaring to you," she said. "Here I am, accusing you of not giving yourself to me, and I never even thought about giving myself to you. If you do not think it terrible of me, I will show you how to make love in the way that I like to make love. I will show you how to make me cry with pleasure. Please, don't be offended. I am not criticising your virility, only your upbringing, and the way your stuffy English schools have led you to think. What happens in love does not happen inside here," she said, pressing her fingers to his forehead, "it happens outside of you, everywhere," and here she swept her arms in a wide dramatic circle, knocking Rudyard's shaving mug onto the floor.

Rudyard turned his face away, and took out a cigarette. He tapped it on his thumbnail. "I don't know," he replied, with the cigarette waggling between his lips. "I don't know whether I've got the inclination any more. I've got too much on my mind. Being arrested, well, it's not exactly a joke."

"What better to occupy your mind than making love?" enthused Louise and reached out for him with both hands. "Through making love, you can forget about everything, and anything."

At that instant, however, the *Arcadia* bucked and tilted so violently that both of them were thrown sideways to the floor. And even though Louise screamed loud and long at the top of her operatic voice, Rudyard heard a deep rending noise, followed by a thunderous crash, and then the steady gushing of hundreds of gallons of seawater as they seethed from the foredeck to the poop deck and cascaded back out into the ocean.

"What's happening?" shrieked Louise. "We're sinking! I know it!"

"It's all right!" Rudyard insisted, snatching for the rail at the side of his bunk to steady himself. "We're just steaming head-on into a series of deep troughs, that's all."

But the *Arcadia* rose again and rolled, and then dropped into the next trough like a demolished building. Again there was a tearing of metal and a discordant twanging of snapped wires, and that thirsty sucking seething sound of the sea. God, thought Rudyard, as he clutched Mademoiselle Narron close to him, both of them kneeling on his cabin floor like waifs, if we don't turn aslant to this storm, we're going to founder. Why the hell doesn't Sir Peregrine turn her aslant?

The *Arcadia* was now rearing and dropping in a thunderous seesaw motion; and when she plunged her bows into the next trough, her screws actually rose clear of the water for a moment. Her front superstructure was badly damaged, and she had lost nearly eighty feet of railing on the port side. But still she forged straight ahead on course, taking the waves directly on her bows. Down in third-class, where the ventilation was less effective, and the cabins were more crowded, vomit was running down the gangways in a brown and acrid tide, so that even those who hadn't felt nauseous before began to throw up. All through the nine-storey ship there were shouts of despair and sickness, and the clatter of falling crockery and spoons.

In the Grand Lounge, the pianist turned wearily to selections from Ivor Novello's new revue *Puppets!* But by now, only one elderly industrialist was listening to him, an old man of eighty-seven with a face like a dry chamois leather. He had crossed the Atlantic so many times before that he had lost count, and was never ill.

Out by the after rail of the boat deck, Douglas Fairbanks was preparing to climb out onto the jib of the electric crane to rescue Lucille

Foster. A line had been fastened around his waist, and Ralph Peel had screamed at him above the wind and the spray that he should come back down at once if he got into difficulties. "Your fan club will crucify us if we lose you over the side! So will your studio! *And* your insurance company!"

Mark had tried to persuade Catriona to go back inside, but she had refused, so he made her stand in the shelter of the second-class entrance and hold on tight to the handrail. "Now stay there!" he shouted at her. "Because if you go overboard, I'm going to have to go after you, and I'm wet enough already!"

She looked under his yellow waterproof hat at his spray-splashed face. His expression was very straight, very college-boy, and very sincere, and she believed him. If she was swept off the ship, he *would* dive after her, even though it would probably mean a quick and violent drowning for both of them. Greater love hath no man, she thought. But she didn't particularly want to put it to the test.

Mark turned away, and half skidded, half staggered across to the rail of the promenade. Douglas Fairbanks was now standing on the rail itself, ready to swing over to the crane on a line which had been fixed for him by the crewmen on the deck below. "Who's got a camera?" he shouted, balancing himself by twisting one foot between the railings. "Quick—a camera! You don't think I'm going to let this go unrecorded!"

Someone, considerately, had brought a Kodak camera and a flash attachment. Douglas Fairbanks struck an heroic pose on the rail, one hand on the line and the other hand raised like Robin Hood, or the Thief of Baghdad, or Zorro; and the flash gun popped loudly in the howling wind. Then he launched himself from the rail, slid right down the rope to the promenade deck below, rolled over in a heap of yellow oilskins, and screamed out, "Shit! I've wrenched my goddamned ankle!"

The flash camera popped again, and he yelled out, "Not *now,* you stupid bastard! You print that piture and I'll kill you!"

Catriona, defying Mark's instructions, came over to the rail. Mark turned to her and raised one eyebrow. "Pretty hopeless, huh? And the sea's getting worse. How do we get her down now?"

"She climbed up there by herself, perhaps she can climb down by herself," suggested Catriona.

"That's ridiculous," said Mark. "If she was able to climb down, she would have."

"Perhaps she wouldn't. Perhaps she wants to stay up there."

"You're talking through the back of your head, if you'll pardon the expression. Why should she want to stay up there? Why should she want to go up there in the first place?"

"I don't know. But her father and mother were only just killed in a car accident, weren't they? When you're shocked and you're grieving, your mind can work in some funny ways."

Mark gave her a look which meant, Well, *you* should know; although he wasn't so insensitive that he said it out loud.

"Maybe you're right," he told her. "In which case, what can we do?"

"I don't know. Perhaps her guardian could help. Mrs. Hall, wasn't it?"

Just then, however, Monty Willowby appeared on deck in a soaking wet pea jacket and a waterproof hat that looked as if it had been designed to prevent the wearer from being deluged by incontinent elephants. "Mr. Peel, sir!" he shouted. "I've just heard what's happening up here!"

"Well, there's nothing you can do!" yelled Ralph Peel. "You might just as well go belowdecks!"

Monty leaned close to the second officer's ear and shouted, "There's a fellow down in the steerage, sir! It seems that he's made a friend of the girl! I wonder if it might be a good idea to bring him up here, see if he can talk her into coming down!"

Ralph Peel squinted up through the spray at the small pink-dressed figure clinging to the jib of the crane. A wet rose petal stuck to a naked branch. "We can't get up there after her," he agreed. "Perhaps it's worth a try."

The *Arcadia* slammed headlong into the next towering wave, and spray from the bows hurtled as far back as the first-class staircase, amid-ships. Ralph Peel slipped, and then gripped the rail. "You go and find this fellow from downstairs," he ordered Monty. "I think I need to talk to Sir Peregrine!"

Then, as Monty waddled down the second-class staircase, Ralph bellowed at Mark, "You keep an eye on things, Mr. Beeney! I'll be back directly! We'll never get that girl down if we keep on hitting these troughs head-on."

Mark gave him a mock salute and held Catriona tighter around the waist. Even through their wet and squeaking oilskins, she could feel the firmness of his muscular hip and the strength of his arm. It didn't seem to matter to her now if he wanted to buy up Keys Shipping or not. She wasn't a child, after all, was she, who was going to be taken in by a smile and a kiss and an extravagant necklace? She wasn't some romantic shopgirl who was going to be impressed by orchids, and champagne. Although . . . and she thought this with a sudden shudder of wistfulness, wouldn't it sometimes be quite nice if she were?

Thirty-one

Sir Peregrine was in the wheelhouse, standing stiff and relentlessly upright in spite of the *Arcadia*'s chaotic pitching and rolling, his eyes fixed on a horizon which it was impossible to see through the salt-caked glass of the windows. The helmsman was gripping the ship's wheel close to his chest, as if he were Moses offering up his only precious son to the Lord. It was here, in this dim and greenly illuminated grotto, that battle was done with whatever seas that God thought it pertinent to whip up.

Ralph Peel struggled in through the doorway, as slick as a seal, and then shut out the wind and the rain and the shrieking of the wires behind him. He stamped his feet on the sisal matting to shake the worst of the wet off him. Then he pulled off his sou'wester and crossed the wheelhouse to where Sir Peregrine was standing with such dignity and resolution.

"Mr. Peel?" asked Sir Peregrine, without even turning to look at him. He scratched at the tip of his aquiline nose with his fingertip, as if he couldn't decide whether to pick it or not. When Ralph said nothing, he looked around at last and said, "Mr. Peel?"

"With all due respect, Sir Peregrine, is there some way you can steer aslant to the waves, forty-five degrees, so that we don't pitch so violently? We're having a lot of trouble getting that young girl down from the crane, and the pitching isn't helping one bit."

Sir Peregrine cleared his throat. "We are making way as expeditiously as possible, Mr. Peel. We have nearly two hours to make up, after that wild goose chase, looking for that so-called drifting lifeboat. We have . . . well, nearly two hours to make up. So we're making full ahead. As fast as possible, and without wavering from our charted course."

Ralph Peel glanced towards the helmsman, but the helmsman was too preoccupied with the next gathering wall of water to worry about anything but keeping the *Arcadia* steady.

"With all due respect, sir," said Ralph Peel, "this doesn't make sense. Almost every passenger on board is sick as a dog, sir; and we've got a young lady stuck up a crane. Apart from that, it looks like we've torn away half of the front superstructure, rails and all."

Sir Peregrine swayed slightly, but by some miraculous balancing mechanism within his cochlear duct, he managed to stay upright. Ralph,

266

however, was obliged to grab for the brass rail around the side of the wheelhouse with both hairy hands. There was another cannonlike roar of seawater; and when the *Arcadia*'s bows emerged yet again, like a surfacing shark, Ralph could see through the salty window that one of her knight-heads had been torn away.

"Sir Peregrine, this is insane! You're breaking the ship to pieces!"

Sir Peregrine stared at him beadily, and for the first time it occurred to Ralph Peel that the commodore was drunk. Not just drunk, but so overwhelmed by the effects of Haitian rum that he was acting out an existence which, when he sobered up, he would never even remember. He was in a fantasy world of his own, where the ocean raged at captains and their liners like a great grey monster, but could always be tamed, where boatswains' whistles forever blew a high-pitched accolade to the greatest heroes of the sea. His gilded destiny may have been denied to him by Rudyard Philip's miserable and grisly accident, but now he would live it out in the only realm where it could still be lived, within his mind. It was full ahead to New York, full ahead to champagne and cheers, full ahead to a blue riband and a place in English history books: "During the early 1920s, several liner captains made their mark on maritime legend. Perhaps the most illustrious of these was Sir Peregrine Arrowsmith, of Keys Shipping, whose . . ."

Sir Peregrine staggered and clutched Ralph's sleeve. "We must, uh —we have to make all speed."

"Sir," insisted Ralph, "we *have* to change course. It's imperative."

"No, no," said Sir Peregrine, tugging at Ralph's sleeve even more fiercely. "Won't hear of it. Can't be done. You make sure we're— well, you know what to do. You're a good man. Excellent second officer. Hairy, I suppose. Rather hairy. Not many chaps as hairy as you. But, well, you know what the Bible says about Esau and Isaac. Esau was a hairy chap, wasn't he? But no reason why he shouldn't have been promoted, all in good time."

"Sir Peregrine," said Ralph, quietly but very intently, "we have to steer a different course. We can't go on ramming these forty-footers head-on."

Sir Peregrine stood upright and tugged at the knot of his necktie. "You're wrong," he said. "You're *wrong*. And . . . you're not only wrong, you're insubordinate. I arrest you. You're confined to your quarters. There now, what do you make of that? Go on, off you go."

"Sir Peregrine—"

"Don't bother me now! I'm busy! You're under arrest and that's all there is to it! Now clear off my bridge before I have you kicked off!"

Ralph hesitated for a moment, breathing as deeply as an organ pump. Then, with the bandy-legged walk of a man who has been negotiating angled decks for most of his life, he crossed the wheelhouse, tugged on his sou'wester, and opened the door. The spray lashed against the veneered woodwork, and the wind blew up a shower of charts.

"You're in trouble now, Commodore!" Ralph shouted. "You're really in trouble now! I'm going straight to Mr. Deacon!"

"Give him my dearest regards!" Sir Peregrine called back. "And shut that damned door!"

Ralph Peel struggled along the gusty deck to Rudyard Philips' quarters, and banged loudly on the door with his fist. Rudyard answered the door almost immediately, but would only open it two or three inches. He looked white and bedraggled, and from inside his cabin there blew a strong smell of cigarette smoke. Ralph hardly ever smoked; he thought it was bad for the performance.

"I've just been up to the bridge!" Ralph shouted. "Sir Peregrine's pissed as a parrot! He won't change course for anything! He's already smashed half the foredeck superstructure, and if this sea gets any worse, he's going to start buckling the plates!"

"Have you told Edgar Deacon?" Rudyard screamed back.

"I'm just going now! But you're the first officer! Get up there and make sure he doesn't drown the whole damn lot of us!"

"I'm under arrest!" said Rudyard. "Confined to quarters!"

"So am I! But what the hell difference does it make? He's so drunk he doesn't know what he's doing!"

Rudyard bit his lips. "I don't know!" he said, against the wind. "I'm in enough trouble as it is!"

Suddenly the cabin door was tugged wider apart, and Mademoiselle Narron appeared in her wet négligée. Rudyard was shocked. It was strictly contrary to Keys regulations for a ship's officer "to entertain or to harbour a passenger, of either sex, in his personal accommodation." But Ralph Peel didn't even blink, except to shake the spray from his eyelashes. As far as he was concerned, the "no harbouring" regulation had been written solely for the moral guidance of junior officers straight out of college, or to spare the embarrassment of senior officers who were too geriatric to entice anything up to their bunks that could reasonably be described as tasty.

"The captain is *drunk?*" she asked in horror.

"Very," said Ralph Peel. "We could tap off his breath and use it to run the boilers."

Louise Narron threw her arm around Rudyard and clutched him tight. Rudyard looked helplessly at Ralph, like an explorer who had been mistaken for her long-lost offspring by an affectionate mother orang-utan. "My darling," said Louise, "this is your moment! This is the time when you can show me what a hero you are! We are sinking! You hear what Mr. Peel says! You must go up to the bridge and take over the ship! You must!"

"All right," said Rudyard desperately. "All right, if that's what I have to do! All *right!*" He reached for his cap, which was swinging on a hook on the back of the door, and tugged it on to his head.

"My God, you're beautiful!" cried Mademoiselle Narron. "So stoical! But underneath, so full of courage! The English hero!"

Soberly, Rudyard told her, "Louise, you'd better go back to your stateroom. Borrow my coat, it's in the wardrobe there. And take care down the stairs. I'll come down later and tell you what's happened."

"I can't wait here?"

Rudyard shook his head. "It's better if you go back to your cabin. Call your stewardess and ask her for a hot drink. Something with rum in, to calm you down."

"Kiss me," she demanded.

Rudyard glanced at Ralph. Ralph was waiting by the door with a wide wet grin on his face. "Go on, kiss her, if it makes her happy," Ralph cajoled him. Rudyard gave her a quick, unsatisfying peck.

Once they were outside on deck, Ralph said, "That's a fair-sized beauty you've got there. Tits like tugboats. You been through it yet?"

"Don't be so damned vulgar," Rudyard snapped. He raised his collar against the wind.

"No offence meant, I'm sure," Ralph told him, and punched him affectionately and knowingly on the upper arm. "Opera singer, isn't she? Plenty of lung power, eh? "Whoa-ho-ho-ho whoa-ho-ho'!" He gave a coarse imitation of an operatic trill.

"Just go and get Edgar Deacon," Rudyard instructed him. "The sooner the company takes charge of this damned mess the better."

"I'm off," Ralph assured him, and went.

Rudyard was left on the boat deck on his own, the spray rising all around him in clattering white towers, the wind screeching through the rigging in an endless and hair-raising lament. His head was boiling with fear and indecision, but also with an extraordinary compulsion to show Louise Narron that he was worthy of her melodramatic expectations. Because now, quite suddenly, he could understand the key to his failure wtth Toy, the reason why he had so disastrously disappointed every woman who had ever loved him, and himself as well. He had the looks of a hero. That short, clear-eyed bearing of Captain Scott. He had the uniform of a hero. But when it came to heroic acts, either marine or sexual, he had never known what to do. Nobody at school had ever told him what was required of him, on board or in bed. One of his French masters, staring out of the window at the quad, had said, "When it comes to *les jolies mademoiselles* . . . well, it's all a question of *panache.*" Yet it was only now, under the chivvying and bludgeoning of Louise Narron, that he thought he understood what *panache* actually was, and how seriously he had lacked it.

Panache was letting Louise Narron beat him, and then beating her back. *Panache* was telling Toy that she was his, and nobody else's, and somehow arranging for her to sail on the *Arcadia* with him, away from Laurence. *Panache* was taking control of the *Arcadia* in the middle of this catastrophic storm, and proving his seamanship and his style.

He fought his way forward and slammed open the door of the wheelhouse. Sir Peregrine was sitting down now, and unsteadily attempting to light his pipe. The helmsman was doggedly holding the liner's course dead ahead, even though he was blinded by the salt on the windows, and obviously seasick. Dick Charles was there, too—on Sir Peregrine's instructions—but all he was doing was clinging on to the handrail and looking miserable.

Rudyard banged the wheelhouse door shut behind him, brushed the spray from his shoulders, and approached Sir Peregrine in three short steps. Sir Peregrine said, with a wry twitch of his lips, "You're confined to your quarters, Mr. Philips. Or am I mistaken?"

"Not mistaken, sir," said Rudyard. "Not in that matter, anyway."

"Aha," replied Sir Peregrine, turning sideways in his seat and sucking noisily at his meerschaum. "So I am to take it that I am mistaken in some other respect?"

"Your course, sir. You have to alter your course."

"Mr. Peel thought that, too. Would it be naïve of me to think that Mr. Peel has put you up to this?"

"I have not been put up to anything by anybody, sir. But we must change course, or the *Arcadia* will be seriously damaged."

Sir Peregrine took his pipe from his mouth and peered at it closely, as if he found it difficult to focus. "Well, Mr. Philips, that's your opinion. But my opinion is that unless we face these waves head-on, we're liable to lose a great deal more than a few feet of railing."

"Sir Peregrine—"

The captain stared at him beadily. "You are under arrest, Mr. Philips, for your wanton handling of this steamer when she left Irish territorial waters. Simply by coming up here to the wheelhouse, you have committed an act of insubordination which could lead to your dismissal from the company. Well, because you're a good sailor, and because you have the *Aurora* to look after, and because I'm not a vindictive man, I'll forget this intrusion, and try to accept it in the spirit in which I hope it was intended. But unless you confine yourself to your quarters at once, and stop this interfering in my management of the ship, I shall have to make a full report on your conduct and recommend your dismissal."

"You're drunk," said Rudyard. "Look at you—you're drunk!"

Sir Peregrine put down his pipe. "When drunk," he said, "I am still ten times more proficient at handling a ship than you are when you're sober. Now get out of here before you make a greater fool of yourself than

270

you already have."

Rudyard stood his ground, his hands by his sides, his brain chasing itself under his short-back-and-sides like a mad dog.

"I'm taking over command, sir," he said.

Sir Peregrine struck a match and passed it backwards and forwards over his Three Nuns tobacco. At last the leaf lit up, and he began to puff bright blue smoke out of the side of his mouth with a noisy smacking sound.

"Sorry," he said to Rudyard, shaking out his match. "Did you say something?"

Rudyard found that he was shaking. He didn't want to shake. He didn't even think that he was frightened. But he suddenly realised what an impossible situation he was in. Louise Narron had seemed to make it a requirement of their continuing affair that he should stalk forward to the wheelhouse and prove himself a hero. What was more, he knew that if he couldn't impress Louise Narron, he would never be able to win back Toy. Yet, as a captain in his own right, and the first officer on board the *Arcadia*, he knew that the price of his heroism could well be the finish of his entire seagoing career. To announce to Sir Peregrine that "I'm taking over command, sir," was a *prima facie* act of mutiny, for which he could be liable to criminal charges, and even hanging. The *Arcadia*, after all, was a small but elegant fragment of the British Isles, and for him to usurp Sir Peregrine's authority was verging on treason against His Majesty. There would be leading articles in *The Daily Telegraph*, his family would be humiliated and if he wasn't executed, he would be fined, and imprisoned and ruined.

Rudyard was a straightforward man, not good at subtleties, but he was subtle enough to realise that Sir Peregrine's deafness was feigned, and that by asking, "Did you say something?" he was actually giving Rudyard just one more chance to step back from the yawning chasm of imprisonment and disgrace. And if he was prepared to give a chap that kind of a chance, then maybe he wasn't such a bad old stick after all. And maybe he wasn't wrong about the course on which the *Arcadia* was heading. Was Rudyard so sure that a forty-five-degree slant to the direct onslaught of the waves would *really* save the ship from foundering?

There was a long pause, during which Sir Peregrine calmly continued to smoke his pipe. But Dick Charles, from the other side of the wheelhouse, pulled a contorted face at Rudyard and shook his head mechanically from side to side, as if to say, *Please*, for your own sake, don't risk it.

It was then that the wheelhouse door opened again, and Edgar Deacon stepped in, accompanied by Ralph Peel. Both of them were white-faced and dripping with seawater. Edgar took off his sou'wester and slapped it against his coat. He glanced at Rudyard briefly, but then, without any preliminaries, stepped straight up to Sir Peregrine's chair and demanded, "What's going on? Mr. Peel tells me you're steering a dangerous course."

Sir Peregrine did Edgar the courtesy of taking his pipe out of his mouth. But he fastidiously licked his lips before he replied, "Mr. Peel is an officer of comparatively little experience. Most of his commissions have been on vessels of 20,000 tons or less. His idea of what constitutes a dangerous course in a 50,000-ton liner differs considerably from mine. And that is all."

"The front railings have been ripped away. We've lost all kinds of spars and rigging, even the company flag."

Sir Peregrine said, "Yes. You're quite right. But I would rather sustain two or three hundred pounds' worth of superficial damage than lose the entire vessel while steering on an ill-considered course, wouldn't you? To steer aslant to this particular storm would not only lose us several hours' steaming time, but it would unquestionably expose us to the risk of swamping. The wind, as you might have noticed, is variable, and many of the worst waves have been taking us on our port quarter. That means that if we steer to starboard, we stand the risk of taking a wave broadside on, and foundering. So, I have made the decision to keep to our course, and make the best time possible, regardless of the temporary discomfort to our passengers."

He paused, so that he could draw on his pipe and keep it going. "If you are concerned about the company colours," he said, "I have two or three spare flags in my locker. Along with the Jolly Roger, of course," he added, with heavy sarcasm.

Edgar said tersely, "You really believe that a slantwise course would be more dangerous to the *Arcadia* than the course we're heading on now?"

Sir Peregrine nodded. And puffed. And then puffed again.

Edgar turned to Rudyard Philips. "Mr. Philips, what's your opinion? Would it be wiser for us to steer aslant to this storm, or not?"

Rudyard hesitated. He was waiting for Sir Peregrine to look round at him—maybe to wink, or at the least to give him a confiding nod. But he should have known better. Sir Peregrine remained in his chair, sending up intermittent smoke signals, like a red Indian in a Saturday matinee cowboy picture communicating the message that "I am imperturbable." The *Arcadia* collided with another cliff of solid seawater and groaned aloud. Edgar, for all his businesslike dignity, had to cling on to the rail that ran around the wheelhouse, just as tenaciously as Dick Charles.

Rudyard avoided Ralph Peel's intent stare. He said, too quietly for anyone to hear, "This is probably the best course."

"What?" demanded Edgar.

"I said"—and here Rudyard lifted his head so that he was looking directly at Ralph Peel—"I said that this is probably the best course. The course on which we're heading at the moment."

Ralph Peel wiped his mouth with his hand; and then, not knowing what to do or say, propped his fists on his hips and blew out his cheeks in frustration.

Edgar said, "You're sure we won't suffer anything more than superficial damage, Sir Peregrine? The sort of damage that we can repair before we reach New York?"

"Weather permitting," concurred Sir Peregrine.

"And you agree?" Edgar asked Rudyard.

Rudyard, feeling hot and nauseous, nodded his assent.

"Well, then, Mr. Peel," said Edgar, "it seems, to say the least, that you were acting overzealously. If the captain is convinced that he is handling the vessel in the best possible way, and his first officer agrees with him, then there isn't a great deal more that we can say, is there? Except that I'm going to need your help in getting the Foster girl down from that crane, and that I'm going to take a pretty dim view of this incident once we've outrun this storm."

"Don't worry, Mr. Deacon," said Sir Peregrine in a tired and slightly patronising tone, "I'm sure that I can deal with Mr. Peel in the appropriate fashion when the time comes."

Ralph Peel was about to say something but changed his mind and pulled his sou'wester onto his head with such fury that he snapped the clasp. "Permission to carry on, sir?" he asked Sir Peregrine sharply; but without the slightest trace of irony or temper. He was a good enough officer to know when he had lost a battle both of politics and rank.

Rudyard continued to stare at the wheelhouse door long after Ralph and Edgar had pushed their way back out into the storm again. He believed that he had done the right thing; and yet how had the right thing proved to be so wrong? How could he go back to Louise and tell her that he had decided not to wrest the wheel out of Sir Peregrine's hands after all? That instead he had agreed with Sir Peregrine that he *was* steering the right course?

How could he tell Louise that he had betrayed a brother officer in front of the *Arcadia*'s owners, and that his mealy-mouthed agreement with Sir Peregrine would probably lead to Ralph Peel's dismissal?

Sir Peregrine fished under his chair and produced a bottle of white Haitian rum. "Drink, Mr. Philips?" he asked. "Just a little celebratory snifter?"

Rudyard said, "No." And then, more clearly, "No, I won't, thank you, Commodore. I don't usually drink on duty."

"Please yourself," said Sir Peregrine, and swigged a whole mouthful of rum straight from the neck of the bottle.

"Your very good health," he said cruelly.

Thirty-two

Monty Willowby found Harry Pakenow in the corner of the third-class bar, still nursing his glass of lemonade, his face as grey as a crumpled-up copy of the *Daily Mirror*. Beside him, her cheek resting on the sticky surface of the table, snoring harshly, was a cheap and pretty young college girl, with blotted lipstick. It was Philly, exhausted by seasickness and French brandy and a whole night of enthusiastic sex. She was dreaming that her next-door neighbour from back home in Minnesota, bald and fifty-five, was scooping vanilla ice cream between her naked thighs. She often had dreams like that.

Harry, however, was dreaming of nothing. He was beyond seasickness, beyond exhaustion, beyond the class struggle and the international rights of the oppressed proletariat. He was staring at a framed photograph of Their Majesties on the opposite bulkhead, and waiting for the voyage to end. By whatever gods to whom it was necessary for a Marxist revolutionary to pray, please let it end.

"Hullo, it's Mr. Pakemoff, isn't it?" said Monty, trying to be cheery. "Enjoying the ups and the downs, are we? Having a sociable time?"

Harry adjusted his spectacles and frowned at Monty blearily. "Oh, great," he said, in an accent that was far more Liverpudlian than New Jersey. "I can't remember when I've ever liked throwing up quite so much. Really great."

Six or seven third-class passengers were crowded around the bar singing intermittent choruses of "Yesh, Shir, That'sh My Baby" in that strangled off-key warbling of the hopelessly drunk. One of them, with the collar of his green tweed jacket turned up, was trying to tell the others what his wife had said when they had bought their new three-piece sitting-room suite on "easy payments"—which was the latest and most popular way for working-class people to furnish their homes.

"She said—do you know what she said—she said, 'Do you know something, Wally? Only two more payments and the furniture's ours. Then we can throw it out and get some new stuff'!"

Nobody laughed much. Everybody had heard the joke before on the wireless. They had also heard the one about the new parents who had been paying their doctor's bill on the "never-never." "Only one more payment, dear, and baby belongs to us!"

Monty said to Harry Pakenow, "Do you mind if I sit down, squire? You see, I've got a bit of a problem."

"What's that? Piles?" asked Harry expressionlessly.

Monty managed a twitchy little smile. "We had a bit of a misunderstanding, you and me, the other day. Over that doll business."

"Oh. Misunderstanding, was it?"

"Well," grunted Monty, easing himself down on the settle next to Harry, and tugging at his cuffs, "the truth is that I have to stick to company regulations, even when I don't particularly feel they're necessary. One rule for everybody, don't you know? Otherwise, there'd be chaos."

"You told me. Regulations like, keep the champagne and the caviar out of sight of the steerage, or they might start to get restless, and take over the ship."

"Well, squire, just my little joke," said Monty. "But the truth is, we need a bit of help."

"*You* need help from *me?*" asked Harry, running his hand through his prickly hair.

"Not me personally, you understand," Monty told him. "But it's that little girl Lucille Foster. She's stuck up a crane, you see, and she won't come down."

"She's stuck up a what?"

"A crane. You know the ones I mean. The ones we use for winching stuff on board. It seems like she climbed up, for some reason or another, and now she won't come down. And in this kind of weather, we can't reach her."

"Has she said why she's up there?" asked Harry, concerned, but still confused by his sickness.

Monty shook his jowls. "Too windy. Can't hear. Besides, I don't think she'd tell us in any case."

"Well," said Harry, "what do you want *me* to do?"

"You've made a friend of her, haven't you? Saved her doll, and all that. And didn't I see you talking to her just this morning on the after poop deck?"

"We've talked, yes," admitted Harry. "But that's about all. I don't know whether she thinks that I'm a friend of hers or not. All she wanted to do this morning was pay me a fiver for rescuing Margaret, and ask me what my politics were. I think she finds poor people like me to be a curiosity."

"But you'll come and help us to get her down?"

"I suppose I'll have to."

"No *suppose* about it, squire. If we don't get her down soon, she's going to *fall* down. She might have fallen down already, while you're sitting her discussing it and making up your mind."

Harry rubbed his unshaven chin. He hadn't been back to his cabin to wash or change since the German salesman in the bunk below had vomited porridge and half-chewed bratwurst all over his own chest. Harry thought that his own seasickness was disgusting enough. Other people's was stunning. It was only during a storm at sea that you realised that there had to be limits to human comradeship, even for enthusiastic Communists.

"We'd better hurry, then," he said, and squeezed out from behind the table.

"Your young lady's all right?" asked Monty, nodding at Philly.

"Oh, sure," said Harry. "She just had a little bit too much of everything."

Monty buttoned up his coat and pulled a face. "Don't know what's the matter with young girls today. Wasn't like that in my day, and I can tell you that for nothing. In my day, a chap at least had to *ask*."

"Times change," muttered Harry, and then said, "Which way?"

"Up the stairs, I'm afraid. Lifts aren't used in bad weather, in case they jam."

They reached the second-class promenade deck, where a steward bustled Harry into a black oilskin and a black waterproof hat. Then Monty Willowby pushed him out through the door into the storm, and across to the rail where Derek Holdsworth, Mark Beeney, and Catriona, were all trying to shout and wave encouragement to Lucille.

Harry was completely unprepared for the noise and the violence of the sea. He stood for a moment rigidly clutching the rail, the brim of his hat lowered against the splattering spray, his shoulders hunched against the wind. He had never seen nature in such a catastrophic temper, and for the first time in his life he actually felt frightened. It was the feeling of helplessness that alarmed him so much: the feeling that, no matter how important and historical he considered himself to be, the wind and the sea would pluck him off the *Arcadia*'s deck and drown him just as contemptuously as anyone else.

"Is this the man?" Mark Beeney yelled at Monty Willowby.

"That's right, Mr. Beeney, sir! Mr. Pakemoff!"

"Pakenow!" Harry shouted out.

"*What?*" asked Mark.

"Never mind," said Harry. "Where's the girl?"

Mark gripped his shoulder and pointed to the far end of the crane's jib. "You see her?" Harry stared and blinked and then nodded.

Mark shouted, "We have to coax her down to the lower end of the jib. We should be able to reach her then."

Harry was conscious of someone else standing beside him, and turned around. It was a tall girl in wet oilskins and boots. Even through the wind

276

and the spray he could catch that faint whiff of expensive perfume that means money, and heaps of it. Under her drooping sou'wester the girl was remarkably pretty, with slightly slanted eyes and a full-lipped mouth. It took a very rare beauty to be able to look feminine and desirable in an oversized oilskin.

"Tell her we understand how she's feeling," said the girl. "Tell her she mustn't give up."

Harry looked questioningly at Mark, who said, "Oh, this is Miss Keys. Catriona, this is Mr. Pakemoff."

"I'm glad you could come up," said Catriona in her clipped London accent. "We don't know how much longer she can hold on."

"You're Miss Keys of Keys Shipping?" asked Harry.

Catriona nodded.

"Right, then," said Harry. He couldn't think what else to say, especially to such young and exalted capitalists as these. He knew Mark Beeney, of course; he had seen his photograph in the newspaper dozens of times. But the few pictures he had seen of Catriona hadn't prepared him for anyone so pretty and alluring. He felt suddenly shabby and out of place, and he wished he had been able to shave. And yet, damn it, why should he? He was just as good as either of these two; and whatever monuments to selfish wealth they could build up, he could just as readily tear down again.

"Can you get me a loud-hailer, please," he asked, wiping rain and snot away from his face with the back of his hand.

"A loud-hailer, Mr. Holdsworth!" called Mark Beeney.

Catriona said, quite sharply, "How did you manage to get to know someone like Lucille Foster?"

"Is it so surprising that I should have done?" asked Harry. Then he shrugged, and said, "Yes, well, I suppose it is. Different walks of life, and all that."

"Mr. Willowby said something about you saving her doll."

"That's right. It, er—well, it blew off the deck. I caught it and brought it back to her, that's all. Well, I tried to bring it back, but you know what the rules are. I wasn't allowed past the third-class entrance. No cross-fertilisation, by order."

Catriona looked at him carefully. He was good-looking in a scruffy, boyish way, and he reminded her of some of the young actors she had met when she was living with Nigel. Awkward, sarcastic, talented young men in their early twenties; already bitter about the unfairness of a world which seemed to be indifferent to their abilities, and yet still energetic enough to keep on railing against it, and keep on trying. Harry Pakenow hadn't yet reached the brink of the waterfall, where aggressive bitterness tips over into unrelieved defeat.

She thought she rather liked him. In those spray-speckled glasses, he looked studious and cute. The kind of boy you take home to meet your parents and who makes a tremendous hit with your mother, although your father doesn't care for the potatoes in his socks and the way he refers so disparagingly to Stanley Baldwin.

"Hey, Catriona, look!" shouted Mark. "The girl's waving! Look, she's waving!"

Everybody looked up towards the jib of the crane, shielding their eyes against the wind. And sure enough, like the flapping arm of a rag doll, Lucille Foster's arm was waving slowly backwards and forwards. Over the doleful moaning of the wires, Catriona could hear the word *"Harry,"* and then again, still faint, but more distinctive than before, *"Harry."*

"Harry?" she asked Harry. "Is that your name?"

Harry swallowed. For some ridiculous reason, he felt suddenly drowned in sentimental feelings. He wiped his nose again, and cleared his throat, and then gave Lucille a wave with both of his arms, and shouted, in a voice which caught in the middle, *"Lucille! It's me! Come down!"*

Lucille kept on waving, and then they heard the snatched-away word *"Can't."* And then, *"Can't come down."*

Harry turned to Catriona. "She's stuck up there," he said seriously. "Someone's going to have to climb right up there and get her."

Derek Holdsworth arrived with the loud-hailer. Mark said, "Mr. Pakemoff here says the girl's stuck. We're going to have to climb up and get her loose."

"Pakenow," said Harry.

Mark said, "What?"

Derek Holdsworth looked unhappy. "I was hoping she could climb down by herself," he said. He had a thin triangular face, and a large nose, under which a small moustache clung like a smudge of coal dust. He could have been a very young Eugene O'Neill. He certainly shared O'Neill's intense and worried expressions.

Harry took off his sou'wester. His spiky hair was already wet, and stuck to his scalp. "The sooner we get started, the sooner we'll get her down," he said. "That line you've tied round the lower end of the jib there, can you get the other end up here, onto this deck?"

"Well, sure," said Mark. "But we've already tried to swing across to the crane from here. In fact, it was Douglas Fairbanks who tried, and if Douglas Fairbanks can't do it—"

Harry sniffed and took off his glasses. "Do you think you could just, you know, do it?" he asked.

Mark stared at him and then at Catriona and then at Derek Holdsworth. "All right," he said, "if that's what you want. Mr. Holdsworth?"

"If that's what he wants." Derek Holdsworth shrugged.

"By the way," said Harry, lifting up his oilskin so that he could wipe his spectacles on his trousers. "The name is Pakenow, pronounced Pak-ehnov. All right? Not Pack 'em off."

"Sure," said Mark, distractedly. He was used to dealing with employees.

The line which Douglas Fairbanks had used for his ill-fated attempt to swing across to the crane's upright was hurled up from the deck below to the second-class promenade. Harry told Derek Holdsworth to lash it fast to the railing; and then without any posing or delays, he climbed over the railing and started to monkey-swing, hand over hand, from the promenade to the crane.

Several times, the *Arcadia* heeled over so violently that he had to hold on tight, and wait until the roll was over. But it took him less than a minute to reach the crane, and once he was there, he fastened his legs around its wet steel upright, waited for a moment to catch his breath, and then started to climb up to the joint where the jib connected with the main pillar. Catriona watched him in fascination. It seemed as if his determination that something had to be done to rescue Lucille Foster had completely overcome the fact that it was impossible. He hadn't even asked how they had tried to rescue her before. He didn't need to learn by anybody else's mistakes.

Soon Harry was astride the jib, and working his way up to the pulleys where Lucille was crouching. He was soaked, and he was sweating, but as he shuffled his way up the twenty-degree angle of the precarious jib, he felt more determined and more excited than he had for years. And there, clinging to the tip of the crane, drenched in spray, shivering with cold, was this unhappy little rich girl who hadn't been able to befriend anybody on board the *Arcadia* except him. It took him about ten minutes to climb right up to her. She was wet and bedraggled, and her lips were mackerel-blue with cold. When he reached out for her, and grasped her chilly little hand, she shuddered and shook and burst into tears.

"Lucille," he shouted, in the gentlest shout he could manage. "Lucille, I love you."

She sobbed and she shivered and she couldn't stop. Harry hadn't seen a face so vulnerable, a face so injured, since the funeral of a labour leader in Queens, in 1919, when the dead man's daughter had knelt by his coffin and silently expended her grief in half an hour of tears. Grief, dammit, was classless. Because this girl Lucille, who was richer than anybody he had ever known, richer than all hell, was as desolate and as lonesome as that labour leader's daughter, and younger, too. And for the first time in his life, Harry began to wonder what the hell it all meant, all this class struggle, all this bombastic oppression, and all this talk of revolution. The repudiation of both capitalism and Communism was right here, to be caught in the open palm of an understanding hand. The answer to them both was tears.

"Lucille," said Harry, clutching her tight. "What the hell are you doing up here?"

"I climbed," she bleated.

"In a storm like this, you climbed?"

"It wasn't so bad when I first climbed up. But then it got worse, and I was frightened."

"I'm not surprised," said Harry. "I'm frightened now. Do you see that sea out there? That's rough!"

"I wanted to die," said Lucille, miserably. "I was going to throw myself off into the ocean."

"Are you really as sad as all that?"

Lucille's shoulders, in Harry's arms, seemed as frail and bony as an injured bird's. "I don't know," she said. "I thought that if Mommy and Daddy were in Heaven, I could join them. I can't bear being left behind."

Harry said, "Lucille, there isn't any Heaven. Your mommy and daddy are gone. They lived their lives, they enjoyed themselves, and they loved each other. But now they're gone. Do you see what I'm getting at? That's why we don't want you to throw yourself into the ocean, because then you'd be gone too, and you wouldn't have lived even half the life your mommy lived, would you?"

Lucille said, "I'm so unhappy."

"Of course you're unhappy," Harry told her. "You've lost your mommy and your daddy, and that's absolutely the unhappiest thing that could have happened to you. But what do you think your mommy would have said if she could have seen you now? 'Lucille' she would have said, 'come down off that ridiculous crane at once!' Your mommy loved you, Lucille. Your mommy was Gala Jones, and she was famous. She wouldn't want you to die, not for anything. How is anybody ever going to remember how beautiful and how nice she was, if you don't stay alive to tell them?"

There was a long silence between them, two or three minutes. Lucille clutched Harry tight, and the spray blew around them as they sat on their precarious perch, like flecks of snow. Harry thought of the words he had read in Bootle Public Library, one rainy afternoon when Janice had gone to see her mother. "And we forget because we must, and not because we will." He didn't know who had written them. Someone who had been obliged to cling to the realities of real life, like he had.

"Are you going to come down now, chuck?" Harry asked Lucille, in that soft encouraging tone that fathers in Liverpool could use with their daughters.

Lucille said, "My dress is caught in the wires."

Thirty-three

Towards evening, the seas began to subside, and the gale-force wind began to blow itself out. At half past seven, the skies to the southwest cleared, and the passengers of the *Arcadia* were treated to a summer sunset on the scale of the Last Judgement—dazzling cords of light that played on a sparkling grey sea, and mountainous banks of cloud that were gorged with crimson, purple, and smoky gold, and topped with cream. In the smoking room, where he had lost something very close to £600 in large white fivers to Maurice Peace during the course of the storm, Sir Terence Harding-Crump stood by the porthole observing this glory for almost five minutes before remarking, "You think they'd tone it down a bit. This is a British ship, you know."

Maurice Peace, his mouth chockful of club sandwich, scooped in £ 250 more, and said, "You're right, Sir Terence. It's in very squalid taste. God was supposed to be an Englishman, not a Broadway set designer." Then he smiled benignly at the gentleman opposite, whom he had now fleeced for the sixth successive game. But Maurice never cheated. Well, not very often.

The gentleman opposite was one of those odd coves who always stirred up a whirlwind of rumour on voyages like these. He was very tall, and he habitually wore perniciously small sunglasses and a white silk scarf around the lower part of his face. His large head was topped by a dense thatch of peppery hair, a toupee so blatantly false, right down to the canvas backing which showed through the parting, that Baroness Zawisza had concluded that it could not possibly be worn by a man who was actually bald. "It is a *disguise*," she had declaimed, "not a cosmetic improvement. If a man were bald, and had to wear a toupee like that, he would *die* of embarrassment." The rest of the first-class lady passengers had at first supposed that the man was a ruined Russian prince, travelling incognito. But Princess Xenia soon scotched that idea. She knew *all* the Russian princes, especially the ruined ones, and even behind those menacing spectacles he was nobody that she could place. Then the ladies had wondered if he were a celebrated motion picture star, hideously burned in an accident in Europe, travelling back to Hollywood for plastic surgery. Yet all the most famous motion-picture stars seemed to be accounted for.

Douglas Fairbanks was on board, and hobbling bravely about with a bandaged ankle. Rudolph Valentino was filming *The Eagle.* John Barrymore, the Great Profile, was taking a vacation in Honolulu. And whoever it was under that thatch, it wasn't Charles Farrell or John Gilbert. Perhaps the mystery man was a great millionaire, returning to the United States after a tragic love affair. On the other hand, perhaps he wasn't.

What made him even more mystifying was his voice, which could only be heard indistinctly through his silk scarf. Was he American, or British? Perhaps he was a German, trying to elude the military police, who wanted him for grotesque war crimes. Perhaps he was Baron von Richthofen himself, the Red Baron, who was supposed to have been shot down in 1918.

But all anyone could determine for certain was that he was travelling alone and that he always dined alone. He ordered a nightly trolley of entrecôte steak or poached halibut to be wheeled to his stateroom, which was one of the most expensive on board, and designed on a theme of "Joy" —which meant that he ate his steak amidst a great many frosted glass sculptures of naked girls with their arms flung up in the air. He emerged only after dark, to sit in the smoking room in his bizarre disguise, and play cards, usually for stakes of £600 to £700. Not too much, but not sneezing money, either.

Maurice shuffled the cards and beamed, "Another hand?"

The gentleman opposite shook his head slowly from side to side. "I think not," he said hoarsely. "She'll kill me if I lose any more."

"Ah, so there's a she?" said Maurice, quite affably, not obviously prying.

"It was a figure of speech. I was talking about fate."

"Ah, *fate*," said Maurice, in the manner of a man who knows all about fate, the same way that other men have become familiar with prostitutes or loan sharks. "Well, fate's a peculiar mistress, wouldn't you say so?"

"I suppose so. There are more peculiar things."

Maurice kept on shuffling. The cards flowed from one hand to the other in a ceaseless flickering flow, and he never looked at them once. "Well, then," he said, "that's an interesting point of view. What could be more peculiar than fate?"

"Mr. Wheatley's housing scheme," said the gentleman opposite.

Maurice snapped the cards into a single immaculate deck and laid them face-down on the table. "I'm afraid you've lost me there, sir. What's Mr. Wheatley's housing scheme, when it answers?"

"It's a proposal, currently suggested by the British Government, that local authorities should build houses for the poor at a cost to the taxpayer and to the ratepayer of £240 each. Well, it's scandalous nonsense, of course."

"I see," said Maurice. "Parliamentarian, are you? Is that it?"

The tall man sighed and lowered his head, so that Maurice had a generous view of his canvas-backed toupee. "It's all very difficult," he said, in a voice which was distinctly English. "This is not really my sort of style at all."

"Maybe another game will cheer you up," said Maurice, shuffling the cards yet again, so that they flowed out of one delicate white-fingered hand into the other like Chinese paper snakes. Maurice's hands could have been the hands of a watchmaker, or a Baldovinetti cherub. Gentle, soft, sure, with perfectly manicured nails. Not effeminate, but immaculate. The hands of an expert gambler, a man who has spent most of his waking life in dim West Coast saloons and smoky New York speaks and chemin-de-fer pits all over the civilised world; a man who scarcely sees daylight from one Christmas to the next. Maurice could tell stories about poker games in Zurich that had gone on for nearly a week, about outrageous bets in France on the speed of Burgundian snails, and that last riotous night of legal gambling in Nevada, on October 1st, 1910, when he had won $17,630 on a single hand of faro, and had his left nostril bitten by a woman in a fruit-laden hat.

He had contrived all of his adult life to be on the scene of as many of the most historic, gilded, and richly profitable gambling events to which it was possible for one man to travel. He would bet on anything anywhere, from Epsom to Longchamps, from Hong Kong to Reno, provided the company was the classiest and the stakes were high. He was not a "Gentleman Jim"—one of those spuriously elegant gamblers with pomaded hair and ostentatious cufflinks. He was a plain workingman. But he was one of the best.

The tall man in the toupee watched Maurice shuffling for a while, and then pushed back his chair. "Yes, I think I'll pass, if you don't mind. You don't mind if I pass? Four hundred pounds is quite enough to lose in one storm."

"Suit yourself," said Maurice.

"I only wish that I could," replied the man in the toupee. He looked suddenly disconsolate, like a scarecrow with no crows to scare. "But it seems to me that my life these days has very little to do with suiting myself. I have served others for so long that most of the people around me have forgotten that I might have a few modest needs of my own. At least, *she* seems to have forgotten."

Maurice Peace grinned at him. It was rightly said of Maurice that he had the kind of face you thought you knew already, even when you were meeting him for the first time, but which you could never quite remember once he'd gone. Even his name seemed to fade from people's memories, like the print on a box of cereal that had been left too long in a grocery store window.

"*I'll* give you another game, old boy," put in Sir Terence Harding-Crump, producing a crinkly sheaf of ten-pound notes from his grey Savile Row jacket. "Perhaps I can win back on calm seas everything that I lost when it was rough. And, besides, I believe I feel lucky again."

Completely ignoring Sir Terence, Maurice asked the man in the toupee, "Who's *she?* The *she* who seems to have forgotten?"

"She? Did I say she?" The man quite openly adjusted his toupee so that it covered more of his forehead, and tugged at his silk scarf. "Well, yes, she."

It didn't seem as if the man was going to explain himself any further and Maurice certainly wasn't going to press him. He was much more interested in the contents of the man's wallet than in the murky secrets of his private life, although his extraordinarily inept disguise was most intriguing. The curious thing about it was that, as a disguise, it actually worked, because nobody could decide who he was. But then, it was possible that nobody knew who he was anyway, with or without his false hair and his raffish silk scarf.

Sir Terence said, "Ready, Mr. Peace?"

"Oh, sure," said Maurice, a little abstractedly, and blocked the cards into a neat stack again.

"I think I'll have a drink," said the man in the toupee.

"A drink to forget, or a drink to cheer you up?" Sir Terence guffawed. At Harrow, his nickname had been Chortler.

"A drink to the successful outcome of this voyage," the man in the toupee said dolefully. "And perhaps a drink to Their Majesties, for good measure."

"Try the king-size martini if you're not going to play any more cards," suggested Maurice, with that same sly grin. "It's a house special. Six ounces of freezing-cold gin over ice. A real belter. Mr. Ernie Byfield invented it at the Pump Room in Chicago, because he thought it would encourage his diners to spend more money on extravagant food."

"And did it?" asked Sir Terence, picking up his cards and fanning them out in his hand.

Maurice dispassionately looked at the natural nine which he had dealt himself. "Not a chance," he replied. "The staff were carrying the guests out to the taxi rank before dinner had even started."

The smoking-room steward came over with his silver tray balanced on his fingertips and took their order. Maurice, as usual, asked for club soda. Sir Terence wanted a dressed crab sandwich to keep him going until dinner.

"Do you have something riding on this voyage?" Maurice asked the man in the toupee in an offhand tone.

"I beg your pardon?"

"You said you wanted to drink to the successful outcome of this voyage. That led me to suppose that you might have something tied up in it. A stake in the shipping company, something like that."

The man said, "Yes, well, I suppose you could put it that way."

"Keys are a bit wobbly on the Stock Exchange," said Sir Terence. "If I were you, I'd order *two* of those martinis."

"Oh, I'm not a stockholder," said the man in the toupee. "More of a beneficiary."

"Curiouser and curiouser," Sir Terence said to himself.

Maurice was silent for a while, as he concentrated on his game. Then he said, "Did I ever see you in Monte Carlo?"

The man in the toupee lifted his head up. "Possibly," he said, although he didn't sound very sure of himself. "But, of course, you wouldn't have recognised me. I mean, I wouldn't have been dressed like this."

"Why *are* you dressed like that? All the ladies seem to think that you're a famous film star suffering from leprosy. Well, I don't know about the leprosy, but you're not a famous film star, are you?"

There was a lengthy pause. The man picked up a pencil that had been left on the table, and then set it down again. "No," he said, "I'm not."

"You're British?"

The man nodded.

"And you're not a leper?"

The man shook his head.

Maurice turned to Sir Terence, who was lighting up a Sobranie cigarette with a gold lighter by Terra Nova of Italy. "It's all very mystifying," he said. "Here we have a British gentleman who is not suffering from leprosy travelling in a patently obvious disguise. He may be a Parliamentarian of some kind, because he seems to be worried about a welfare housing programme. He plays cards as if he were something of a regular gambler, and yet he plays them cautiously. His caution appears somehow to be connected with an unknown female whom he calls "she." Now, is that a puzzle or is that a puzzle?"

"I agree," said Sir Terence. "It's a puzzle." Then, "Damn," as Maurice beat him yet again.

"He's not a Government minister," said Maurice. "A Government minister couldn't get away from his office for long enough to cross the Atlantic dressed as a failed cellist. Besides, he expressed an anti-Government sentiment earlier on. Nor is he a senior civil servant. Senior civil servants don't usually go to Monte Carlo to gamble, and this chap has admitted that I might have seen him there."

The tall man in the toupee listened to all this with great moroseness, his arms folded on the card table. But behind his tiny dark glasses, his eyes were obviously following the soft sleight-of-hand of Maurice Peace's dealing, and the way the cards seemed to fly in and out of their suits at Maurice's unconcsious command. He said nothing, though. Gave nothing away. If they wanted to find out who he was, and why he was here, they were going to have to do it by themselves.

The smoking-room steward arrived with their refreshments. The king-size martini manifested itself in a chilled tulip-shaped glass of magnificent proportions; while Sir Terence's crab sandwich was served on a silver plate that was decorated with cracked crab claws, piped mayonnaise, and flowers that were cut from radishes and tomatoes. It was impossible to order even a humble bacon sandwich on board the *Arcadia* without it being served up as though it were an exotic dish from one of the world's finest restaurants. Maurice's club sandwich had been a ziggurat of freshly roasted turkey, Derbyshire cheese, iceberg lettuce, Polish tomatoes, and West Country ham; and it had taken him nearly two hours to eat it.

"Their Majesties," said the tall man in the toupee, rising from his chair and lifting his martini glass.

Sir Terence rose too, and out of respect for the *Arcadia*'s nationality, so did Maurice.

"You know something funny," said Sir Terence as they sat down again. "I used to know a chap out in Singapore who was an absolute devil for the wives of any officer who was more than one rank above his. I think it was his own quiet way of mocking the Army without getting himself into serious trouble. Randy bugger, and no mistake. The wives used to call him Half-Hard Horace. Well, one night out at Selarang Park, which was where most of the brass used to stay—"

The tall man in the toupee belched loudly. "I beg your pardon," he said. Then he sat back in his chair and examined his empty martini glass from a greater distance, as if he were longsighted. "I beg your pardon," he repeated.

Maurice looked at Sir Terence and raised a questioning eyebrow. Sir Terence shrugged. Through the porthole of the smoking room, the evening sun shone as if it were being painted for the cover of a children's annual for 1925.

It was almost time to dress for dinner, and the orchestra could be heard in the background playing a smooth preprandial melody.

"Steward," called the tall man in the toupee. "I believe I'll have another of those martinis."

"I regret that they're limited to one to a passenger, sir."

"I see. Well, bring one for my friend here, and if he doesn't want it, I'll drink it for him."

Maurice took a ten-pound note off the table and gave it to the steward. "Bring the gentleman what he wants, okay? I'll make sure that he doesn't throw himself overboard, or anything picturesque like that."

The steward palmed the money as deftly as Maurice had been dealing cards. "Very good, sir," he said, with that distant rabbitlike stare that is acquired through years of pocketing tips.

Thirty-four

As soon as the storm subsided, Monty Willowby gave instructions for the *Arcadia* to be cleaned and disinfected, from the boat deck down to the waterline. It was an Augean task, involving the sluicing of hundreds of acres of corridors and dining rooms, the drying out of scores of rugs, and the remaking of more than a thousand bunks and beds. Broken plates and glasses had to be swept up, baths and basins scoured out, lavatories cleaned, and carpets (where anyone had been blessed with sufficient foresight to have them rolled up) replaced and fastened down.

Stewards went from cabin to cabin with tea, coffee, seltzer, and sandwiches. Any passenger who still felt chronically sick was wrapped in a blanket and ushered solicitously to the ship's hospital, which was directly over the swimming pool. Monty Willowby ordered the ship's printing press to run off 2,000 "storm certificates," which would be filled in with each passenger's name and presented as a souvenir of their experience. It had, after all, been the worst summer storm for four years.

Towards the cocktail hour, the ship began to return to normal. Welders and carpenters were out on the foredeck in a flurry of windblown sparks, patching up the damage to the railings and the knightheads. Stewards were busily laying the tables for dinner and unfastening the fiddles which had kept the lunchtime cutlery in place. The chandeliers were glittering, and all the palms in the Palm Court had been restored to their upright positions. The kitchens began to clatter, and to fill their lungs again with the aroma of *ris de veau Brillat-Savarin*, *châteaubriand clouté aux truffes*, and *la mousseline de grenouilles au Riesling*—a delicate mousse of frogs' legs in Austrian wine.

Nonetheless, the *Arcadia* had been christened in her first rough sea, and she would no longer smell so aromatically of fresh paint and new varnish and musky wood veneers. Like all of her sister steamers on the North Atlantic route, she would now be haunted by the lingering smell of seasickness. It was unavoidable; it was as much a part of sailing across to America as the fancy-dress ball on the last night afloat, or the first sight of the Statue of Liberty.

Sir Peregrine left the bridge to Derek Holdsworth and retired to his cabin, where he sat for an hour in silent meditation before ordering his steward to run him a bath, seventy-one degrees Fahrenheit exactly, and to bring him a fresh bottle of Haitian rum. He was now catastrophically drunk, but he also felt calmer and more resolved about himself than he had for months. Perhaps the world had failed to recognise his greatness. Perhaps Mavis had failed to recognise his love. But destiny, after all, could rise above such disappointments. Destiny would bear him in her arms, and ensure that when the golden rolls of history were written, his name would shine in its deservèd place. That was the way he pronounced the word in his mind: deservèd.

Lucille Foster was asleep, drugged with codeine, in the ship's hospital; while Mrs. Hall, in a brown dress, waited by her bedside with an expression of martyrdom. Mrs. Hall had been brought up in martyred circumstances. Her father had been a loss adjuster and a fanatical believer in St. Sebastian. Her mother had been one of the few ugly daughters from a large and wealthy family from Back Bay, Boston. Now she was responsible for the safe passage across the Atlantic of the hysterically bereaved daughter of one of the world's most glamorous corpses. It was all too much.

Harry Pakenow had found himself to be a hero. Dazed, drenched and shivering like a greyhound, he had been wrapped in a large plaid blanket and taken by two cheerful stewards to Catriona's stateroom, where he had been given a steaming and cologne-perfumed bath by one of the stewards. He had then been dressed in well-pressed flannels and a warm shirt, and invited up to the Orchid Lounge for a drink. Edgar had shaken his hand and given him a company check for twenty pounds, and Catriona had asked him to join her for a glass of champagne.

Catriona thought that all of this fuss was absolutely marvellous, especially since it gave her the chance to play out her role of Queen of the Atlantic. She hadn't had so much fun since the opening night of *The Mask and the Face* at the Criterion, when Frank Cellier had got gloriously drunk and told her he loved her, and Athene Seyler had attempted to dance the can-can. She adored Harry's bemusement: the way he sat so awkwardly on his chair and blinked through his pigeon-fancier's spectacles at all the fluffy mink stoles and the clinging satin dresses and the sparkling diamonds. She was reminded of her childhood in Formby, when she was five or six, and perfumed ladies had come into her bedroom to bestow vermouth-flavoured kisses on her and feed her with chocolates and trifle. That had been "before the War," when summers had been longer and more idyllic, and ladies had worn skirts that swept the grass. But the *Titanic* had sunk when Catriona was nine; and when she was eleven, War had been declared; so that "before the War" was only a heavenly memory of childhood, a blurred fantasy both of her own memory and of her

Mother's nostalgia.

She said to Harry, "You were very brave."

He held his champagne glass in both hands, uncertain of how much to drink, and how quickly. "I didn't see what else I could do," he replied. "She couldn't get down by herself."

"Nobody else managed to do it," Catriona told him.

"No, well. It was pretty wild out there, wasn't it?"

Catriona watched him for a while. He sipped his champagne, and then cleared his throat.

"You're not embarrassed, are you?" she asked him.

"A bit," he admitted.

"You've nothing to be embarrassed about. You're the man of the hour."

Harry looked around, and then pulled a face. "I'm not used to nobs, that's all."

"Oh, *nobs* are we?" teased Catriona.

Harry gave her a shy grin. "Well, you know what I mean. First class. It's a different world, isn't it? Different people."

"You really think so?"

Harry didn't answer. But he swallowed another mouthful of champagne and nodded.

Catriona said, "Supposing I said you could travel first class for the rest of the voyage?"

"Pardon?" He looked at her in alarm.

"There's no need to jump up in the air. I think you've deserved it. I can't give you a medal. The least I can do is let you travel the rest of the way in luxury."

"Well," said Harry breathlessly. "No, I don't think I can. I mean, you know, thanks, but no."

"We can lend you a dinner jacket, if that's what you're worried about."

A dinner jacket? thought Harry. She thinks I'm worried about a dinner jacket? All I'm worried about is blowing the bottom out of this ship and sinking everyone and everything in it.

"I'd rather—Well, I'd rather stay in third, if you don't mind," he told her.

At that moment, Edgar came up. He looked at his pocket watch and snapped it shut with an audible click. "Don't you have a cocktail appointment, Miss Keys?"

"All in good time, Mr. Deacon," said Catriona. "By the way, I've been trying to persuade our hero here to travel for the rest of the voyage in cabin class."

Edgar grasped Harry's shoulder and smiled. "Of course you must. I wouldn't hear of anything else. I think we have one spare stateroom on the bridge deck. I'll make sure that the purser arranges it right away."

"Listen, I really appreciate it," said Harry. He was feeling cornered now, trapped by everybody's upper-class geniality and suffocated by Chanel perfume and that overheated atmosphere of furs and silks and diamonds. "I appreciate it very much, but no. I paid for a third-class ticket, and I guess you could say that I'm sort of a third-class person."

"Of course you're not," said Catriona. "What's third class about rescuing a girl from a crane in the middle of a storm?"

Edgar said, with a slight hint of tension in his voice, "Miss Keys, your appointment."

"Oh, yes," said Catriona. Then, to Harry, "You'll have to excuse me. I have to change for a private meeting. But do promise me that you're going to travel first. Promise me."

Harry looked down at the expensive Indian carpet on the floor, and then wiped his mouth with the back of his hand. Catriona stood up and regarded him with gentle amusement. Then she bent forward and kissed him on the forehead. He jerked his head up as if he had been burnt.

"Oh." Catriona smiled with mock-coyness. "I didn't mean to startle you. I just thought the hero deserved a kiss from the management. After all, if this were a French ship, they would have kissed you on both cheeks."

"You're lucky it's not a Greek ship, squire," said Monty Willowby. Even his struggles with the first-class toilet seats had not completely squashed his sense of humour. "Did I hear you wanted that suite on the bridge deck, Mr. Deacon? Not the best, I'm afraid. But much more spacious than third. A bath of your own. A double bed. And hot cocoa before you go to sleep at night, with two sugars."

"I really don't want to cause any trouble," said Harry. He was feeling panicky now, and almost asthmatically breathless. He wondered if he were actually allergic to rich people.

"No trouble at all, squire," said Monty genially. He laid one podgy arm around Harry's shoulders—a familiarity which he never would have allowed himself with a genuine first-class passenger—and said, "Take the opportunity while you've got it. You won't be able to do it again. Once in a lifetime, for a fellow like you, travelling first class. You can tell your grandchildren about it."

Harry stared back at him, wide-eyed behind his spectacles. There seemed to be no way out but to say yes. All of these people were so dominant, so confident, and so relaxed in these intimidatingly opulent surroundings. The only way to escape them was to do whatever they wanted.

"All right," he whispered. "That's great."

Monty bent towards him and said, "Speak up, squire. Didn't catch you." But all Harry could do was lick his lips in consternation and wonder if they would bring him some more champagne.

Thirty-five

Catriona was on her way back to her stateroom when she collided with Philip Carter-Helm. He was hurrying along the corridor with his hands thrust in his pockets, and his bow tie was untied.

"Oh! Hallo," said Catriona.

Philip inclined his head. "I say. Here I am, galloping along like a prize ass."

Catriona smiled. "You don't have to talk like an old Etonian for my benefit."

"I'm sorry?"

"I know you come from the North. I heard it in your voice the first time you came around to tell me that Mark Beeney was sorry."

"Oh." Philip grinned. "In that case."

"You're in a hurry," Catriona remarked.

"Well, yes. Expecting a message from the wireless room, as a matter of fact."

"Where do you come from?" asked Catriona.

"What? My cabin."

"I mean, where in the North do you come from?"

"Oh. Cheshire."

"Not far away from me, then."

"No."

Catriona smiled at him. For some reason she couldn't understand, she felt quite relaxed with him, as if it wasn't particularly important to make polite conversation. She said, "Have I met you somewhere? I seem to recognise your face."

"Not unless you go to the Crown and Anchor at Holborn bars."

"Well, no, I've never been there. Are you staying in New York, or are you going on?"

"Oh, I'm staying in New York. In fact, I'm coming right back, on the next ship. This is a sort of a joyride, really."

"No business? Marine insurance, wasn't it?"

Philip laughed politely. "Yes, that's it, what a memory, hey? No, not much business. Well, some family business, but that's all."

"You've got relations in New York?"

He paused for a second which seemed oddly significant. "I hope so," he said.

They began to walk together down the corridor, Philip going back the way that he had come.

"You know something," he said, "I think it's quite incredible, the effect that one's relatives can have on one's life, whether one knows them very well or not."

"I'm not sure that I follow you," said Catriona.

Philip raised a hand. "Look at this ship, for instance. Your father built this ship, didn't he? What an extraordinary achievement. And what an effect it's had on your life. Yet, really, you didn't know him particularly well, did you?"

"Not really."

Philip stopped where he was, his hands in his pockets. "From everything I perceived about him when I met him, and from everything that people told me about him, your father was a remarkable man. Very strong, very determined. But mysterious, too, in a way; although I suppose that everybody, once they're dead, becomes mysterious. There are always so many unanswered questions, so much tantalising information which is taken to the grave. My God, if only we could interrogate the dead for one last time before they went."

Catriona said, "I'm not sure that I like this conversation."

Philip stared at her, and then blinked himself back to his senses. "Oh. I'm sorry. I do tend to get carried away sometimes. I didn't mean to say anything in bad taste. I'm sorry. Did I upset you?"

"No, you didn't. Well, a little. But never mind."

Philip frowned along the corridor. "I suppose I'd better go and get my messages."

"Yes." said Catriona.

"I wish—" he began, then checked himself.

"You wish what?" asked Catriona.

"It's nothing, really. I suppose I'm rather a dreamer."

"A dreamer? What do you mean?"

"Well, sometimes I wish that life could have turned out different. Especially in the light of what one has managed to learn, as time goes by."

"Do you always speak in riddles?" Catriona smiled.

"That wasn't *supposed* to be a riddle."

"Perhaps it wasn't," said Catriona. "Perhaps it was more of an answer without a question." She was beginning to like Philip Carter-Helm, not because of what he was saying, which was all quite foxing, but simply because he was warm, relaxed company. And, quite unusually for a good-looking man, he wasn't trying to make a pass at her.

"Who are you?" she asked him, without really meaning to.

"Who *am* I?" he replied. He paused, made a face, shrugged, and

292

then said, "Who is anybody? I'm all kinds of things. A marine insurance assessor. An amateur fisherman. A chess player. My father's son, and my sister's brother. Oh, and I'm quite good at croquet."

Catriona said slowly, "You told me the other day that I'd do well to sell the *Arcadia* to Mark Beeney; if I had to sell her at all."

"Yes." He nodded, a little more cautiously.

"Well, tell me something. Why did you say that? You don't have any personal interest in it, do you?"

"Hm," he said, as if he were disinclined to answer.

"Well?" she pressed him.

"Well," he said. "I think I'd rather wait and see."

They said their goodbyes outside the door of Catriona's stateroom. Alice was hovering menacingly inside; and when Philip caught sight of her, he waved and coughed and retreated quickly.

"Rather *untidy* young gentleman," said Alice as Catriona came in.

"Untidy?"

"Didn't bother to tie up his necktie, did he? A gentleman always does up his necktie, in front of a lady. That's unless they're particular friends."

Catriona turned and looked back at the door, which had just closed behind her. "I don't know," she said, "Perhaps we *are* particular friends."

Thirty-six

Dinner, because of the storm, had been put back to nine o'clock. In his cabin, Rudyard Philips was unhappily dressing in front of his mirror, reasonably sure that his support of Sir Peregrine had assured his release from arrest, but also sure that neither Ralph Peel nor Louise Narron would ever speak to him again.

Like the well-intentioned brother in the Grimm's fairy story who had mistakenly taken the left-hand fork in the road which led through the enchanted forest, Rudyard felt as if everything he had said and done since Toy had left him had been perplexingly and paradoxically wrong. He knew that he should have stood by Ralph, and denounced Sir Peregrine's navigation through the storm. He knew that he should have seized the wheel, and proved himself a hero to Louise. But he also knew that Sir Peregrine, no matter how drunk he had been, had probably been steering the right course, and the fact that the *Arcadia* had weathered the waves with nothing more than superficial damage to her foredeck had proved the old soak to be right.

The ironic part about it was that Rudyard would receive no commendations from Sir Peregrine to compensate him for losing Ralph Peel's comradeship and Louise Narron's affection. He had, after all, been showing no more loyalty than the commodore would normally have expected of him. He only hoped he was right in assuming that Sir Peregrine would allow him to leave his cabin and attend dinner.

Well, he thought, tying up his bow tie and staring at himself in the looking glass, he would never see Louise again once this voyage was over. Nor would he be likely to serve with Ralph Peel any more. The *Aurora* would be out of dry dock by the time he returned to Liverpool, and he would have his usual command back.

Perhaps he should reconcile himself to the fact that he was always going to be second best—that he could never have what he really wanted, whether it was a ship or a woman. Perhaps if he lowered his sights and lived out his life as good old dependable Rudyard Philips, then all these vicious conflicts of loyalty would come to an end. He was lucky to have the *Aurora*, wasn't he? And there was never any shortage of eligible young women on board ship. He would find somebody some day. Somebody plain, and likeable.

There was a knock at his cabin door. He took a cigarette out of his cigarette case, and said, "Come in." It was a messenger boy with an envelope, ship's stationery, with his name "Mr. R. Philips" written on the front in oblique blue handwriting. He tipped the boy sixpence and tore the letter open with his thumb.

It read, "My darling Ruddy . . . I have been visited by your brother officer Mr. Peel who told me everything that happened on the bridge. He told me that you had no choice, and that I should not feel badly about you, because he himself bears no grudge, and would have done the same in your dilemma as you did. In any case I think you have shown me that no woman can live her life alone, according to her own rules and nobody else's. . . . You are a gentle man whose simple affection and constant honour are an example to me. I was prepared to think only the worst of you, because I had been so badly hurt by my previous affair, when I should only have been thinking the best. Forgive me, Louise."

Rudyard laid the letter carefully on the edge of his bureau, and lit his cigarette. He watched the letter through narrowed eyes as he smoked, as if he wanted to make sure that it was real, and that it wasn't going to burst into flames or shrink away to ashes.

Then he found that he had to clear his throat and press his eyes with the tips of his fingers, because he was crying.

Thirty-seven

It was while Catriona was dressing for her cocktail appointment with George Welterman that Trimmer remembered where he had first seen Philip Carter-Helm. He waited, of course, until she was dressed; and he expressed his aspirate admiration for the way she looked, in her casual Patou gown of white crepe de Maroc, almost ankle-length, but bare-shouldered, with thin white straps. He particularly admired her headband, too, with a white silk rosette on it, and hanging ribbons. But while he was serving her a single strong gin and bitters, and lighting her up a small black Dutch cigar, he said, uncertainly, "That gentleman what was 'ere this morning, miss."

"Yes?" asked Catriona. She tilted up her chin while Alice sprayed her with perfume. The gramophone played "Hit Me in the Nose Blues," with a sleazy, shuffling, late-night kind of rhythm.

"Well, miss, 'e did say as 'ow 'e used to be han hacquaintance hof your father's, hif I'm not mistaken."

"That's right. What of it?"

"I was trying to think what hof it myself, miss; and then this arver I remembered has 'ow I seen your father haccompanied by a young man not dissimilar to Mr. Carter-'Elm when I was chauffeuring your father just habout three year hago; honly then, hof course, Mr. Carter-'Elm was considerably younger-looking."

"Where was this?" asked Catriona. She splayed out her fingers, and inspected her nails.

"Hin Formby, miss, when they was first discussing the plans for the *Arcadia*. I 'ad to drive them to Liverpool, and they was talking about it nineteen to the dozen, 'ow the money was going to be raised, 'ow they were going to lay the keel. I remember it so much because they 'ad a hargument. 'Ammer and tongs."

"Philip Carter-Helm had a hargument—I mean an argument—with my father?"

"That's right, miss, as I remember it."

"But what did they *argue* about? Come on, Trimmer, you can't leave me in suspenders."

Trimmer tried to look as if nothing short of white-hot pincers could drag such a confidence out of him.

"Oh, come along, Trimmer," said Catriona. She blew cigar smoke impatiently, and felt very Gloria Swanson. "Nobody blames chauffeurs for listening. Especially now that my father's dead."

"Well, miss, I believe they was discussing a ship that used to belong to Keys in them days, the *Orange*."

"The *Orange* sank, didn't it?"

"Yes, miss. About two weeks hafter Mr. Carter-Helm and Mr. Keys 'ad such a bull-and-cow habout it. Mr. Carter-'Elm was saying something habout hinsurance, and 'ow nobody would hallow it; and your poor father was 'ollering back hat 'im and telling 'im not to speak like that, 'ow dare 'e. Hexpediency, that's the word your father kept using, hover and hover. *Hexpediency*."

Catriona waited for Trimmer to say something else, to explain what her father's argument with Philip Carter-Helm was all about. But Trimmer simply stood there, the light from the chandelier shining off his polished black hair, and waited to be dismissed.

"That's all?" asked Catriona.

"'Fraid so, miss. Hafter that we was in something of a haltercation with a homnibus, and I didn't 'ear the remainder."

"Well," said Catriona, "I suppose that's something. The *Orange* sank off India somewhere, didn't it?"

"That's it, miss. Gulf of Khambhat. All 'ands saved, luckily. But a sad thing to lose 'er. Lovely ship, one of the best we 'ad."

"I thought we was lost ourselves, that storm we had today," said Alice. "I really thought the Lord had called me at last."

Catriona held up a pair of diamond and sapphire earrings, one to each earlobe, to see how they looked. "My father designed this ship, Alice. You don't think one potty little storm could sink it, do you?"

"Oh, of course not, miss. I didn't actually allow as it would."

Trimmer, who had now returned to the cocktail bar to buff up the glasses, said, "I think Miss Keys is 'aving you hon toast, Alice."

Catriona pouted out her lips. She liked the way she looked in the mirror. Definitely Gloria Swanson. She just wished the storm hadn't given her such a headache.

Trimmer said, "Hit was quite a blow, miss, hall the same. Never known a blow so bad, not hin the summer."

"Perhaps God sent it to remind us that we shouldn't be so vain," said Catriona.

"Well, 'oo can tell, miss? 'E moves hin very hinscrutable ways."

Catriona was almost ready when Edgar knocked at the door, with yet another reminder that she had a cocktail appointment with George Welterman. "All right," she said snappily; but before he could close the door, she called, "Mr. Deacon?"

"Miss Keys?"

She hesitated, and then came across the room and said, "Can I ask you something?"

His eyes were like those of a rabbit, not frightened, but utterly impenetrable, either out of great knowledge or out of massive ignorance, both of which are equally threatening.

"I, um—" said Catriona, and then realised that both Trimmer and Alice were listening intently, even though they were both devoting enormous energy to shining glasses and to tidying up her cosmetics. "Let's talk out on deck. I'd like some fresh air."

Edgar took her arm and escorted her out onto the first-class promenade deck. The wind was still brisk, but there was a cheery seaside friendliness about the ocean, and the flags and bunting clapped in endless and enthusiastic applause.

"Have you seen a young chap called Carter-Helm?" Catriona asked Edgar.

Edgar looked at her intently. "I believe so," he said. "Fresh-faced, is he? Quite personable?"

"That's the man. Have you ever met him before?"

Edgar shook his head. "I don't believe so. Should I have done?"

"Well, I don't know. But he told me himself that he was a friend of my father's; and just now Trimmer told me that my father and Philip Carter-Helm had a tremendous argument about something or other about three years ago, when he was driving them both into Liverpool."

Edgar looked perplexed. "Did Trimmer say what the argument might have been about?"

"The *Orange*, as far as he knows. And something about insurance. But this was about two weeks before the *Orange* sank."

Edgar burst out laughing, but his laughter was so yapping and high that Catriona couldn't believe for a moment that he was at all amused.

She said, "What on earth's the matter?"

"It's just funny, that's all. It's just the type of gossip that Trimmer revels in. You mustn't take any notice at all. Scuttlebutt they call it on board ship."

"I just thought it was peculiar, that's all."

"My dear, I don't suppose for a moment that it was Philip Carter-Helm at all. Trimmer's half blind these days, anyway. He ought to wear spectacles, except he's too proud. Had an Indian clerk like that once, in Calcutta. We used to call him Andha, that's Hindu for someone who can't see his nose in front of his face."

"It seems odd that Trimmer should have made it up."

"Oh, I don't know," said Edgar with forced joviality. "Servants are always trying to impress. It's not a serious vice. But, well, you should take what they say with a pinch of salt."

Catriona said, "My gosh, it's nearly a quarter to seven. I was supposed to meet George Welterman at six-thirty. I'd better go back and get Alice."

"Alice?"

"Well, to chaperone me."

Edgar waved his hand dismissively. "You won't need Alice. George is a perfect gentleman. At least, from what I've seen of him."

"Are you sure?"

"Why?" Edgar laughed. "You're not frightened, are you?"

"No, of course not. But you seem to think this is all so important; I want to do the right thing."

"You'll be doing the right thing if you simply make George feel that you and everybody else at Keys thinks he's a wonderful chap. Or at least a half-wonderful chap. I'm afraid he's one of these people who needs flattery as well as persuasion. He's already put in his offer, of course; but he would quite enjoy seeing us dance for our supper while we're about it."

Catriona narrowed her eyes and scrutinised Edgar as if she were an elderly lady on her first jury service.

"I always thought I knew who you were," she told him. "Now, I'm beginning to wonder if you're someone else altogether."

"I was your father's friend, if that's what you mean. I still am."

"No, I didn't mean that," said Catriona.

"Then what?"

"I mean you seem rather *frantic* about this sale to IMM. Not calm and collected at all. Couldn't we string them along a bit, make *them* dance, instead of us? That's if they want us so badly."

Edgar shrugged and looked away, as if he were already thinking about something else. "It's business, I'm afraid. There are other considerations, apart from money. Obligations, contracts, that kind of thing. Now that your father's gone—"

Catriona said, rather archly, "Now that my father's gone, *I'm* here."

"Well, of course. But in a more decorative capacity, shall we say."

"I don't think twenty-five per cent of the voting stock is *entirely* decorative, do you? At least, nobody else seems to think so. I'm beginning to wonder whether all you men are clustering around me for my stunning looks or my ravishing shares."

"Miss Keys, really," Edgar protested, almost primly, as if she had accused him of behaving indecently in front of a lady.

"I just hope you're not selling out to IMM because you don't want Keys to be managed by women, that's all."

"My dear Miss Keys, there isn't any question at all that the board doubts your sincerity, or your devotion to your father's memory. But running a shipping line in Liverpool is not like organising a *thé dansant* in South Kensington, especially when to all intents and purposes that

298

shipping line is already bankrupt."

Catriona turned her face to the wind. "Very well," she said. She tried to sound both offended and forgiving at the same time; because in spite of everything she didn't want to fall out with Edgar, or upset him too much. "But I do reserve the right to see what I can get out of George Welterman. Perhaps I can get more than eighteen million pounds, just by being decorative."

"Hmph," returned Edgar, unimpressed.

He escorted her down to A deck, however, where they happened to bump into Dick Charles. Edgar inclined his head to Catriona in a reserved little gesture of respect, and said to Dick, "Will you please take Miss Keys to Mr. Welterman's cabin, Mr. Charles, and also present him with my regards."

"V-v-v— certainly, Mr. Deacon."

Catriona, as they walked together along the corridor, couldn't help thinking that Dick Charles looked extremely white.

"Are you all right, Mr. Charles?" she asked him. "You're not ill, or anything?"

"N-no, Miss Keys. Tremendous f-form. F-first class."

"Well, I hope you don't think that I'm being rude, but you don't look first class. You look rather pale."

"J-just a couple of things on my mind, Miss Keys. N-nothing to get worried about."

"You can always talk to me, you know, if there's something upsetting you."

Dick Charles saluted her. "V-very k-kind of you, Miss K-keys."

He led her to the door of George Welterman's stateroom. Perhaps he wasn't a very good sailor, thought Catriona. After all, the crew were just as susceptible to seasickness as the passengers. She couldn't have guessed for a moment that his problem centred entirely around Lady Diana FitzPerry, and the corks of Perrier-Jouët champagne, and Pond's cold cream.

George Welterman opened the door of his stateroom himself. The theme of the apartment was "Mount Olympus," and the walls were decorated with friezes of Roman gods, all with marcelled hairstyles and pointed beards, with sheaves of lightning bolts in their quivers.

George Welterman himself had all the dignity and darkness of Zeus. He was wrapped in a black and silver quilted robe, with an ostentatious silver cravat around his neck. Beneath the lower hem of his robe, Catriona could see the cuffs of his evening trousers, with silver-grey stockings and black silk slippers. Smoke from his cigarette drifted raggedly across the room towards the ventilator grille.

"Is this your chaperone?" he asked Catriona, nodding towards Dick Charles.

"No," she said. "Mr. Charles was just leaving."

"Mr. D-deacon sends you his f— sends you his f— sends you his felicitations, sir."

"So." George smiled when Dick Charles had left. "You decided it was safe to come alone." He tapped his cigarette in a stainless-steel ashtray.

"Is there any reason why I shouldn't have done?"

He made a self-deprecatory face, and bent forward to kiss her hand with dry lips. "There *have* been women," he said, "who have been afraid of being alone with me."

"Afraid? I can't think why. You're rather a teddy bear."

George let out a small explosion of amusement. "A teddy bear? That's the first time any woman has called me a teddy bear. Well, perhaps you'll learn otherwise."

"You intend to show me your claws?"

"Maybe. But let me pour you a drink first."

"All right," said Catriona, turning away from him. "Gin and bitters. The way they make it in the crush bar at the Court."

"I can't say that I've ever been to the Court."

"You didn't see *The Farmer's Wife?* Well, perhaps you wouldn't have done, would you, being in Ireland. But you *should* have done. It was hilarious."

"You're quite a theatre person, aren't you?" asked George, opening up the black lacquered cocktail cabinet.

"I lived with an actor."

"I know," said George. He smiled in self-satisfaction as he half filled a modern Lausitzer glass with Gordon's gin. "Your father didn't approve of that, did he?"

"Is that anything to you?"

George shrugged. "It's nothing to me. Not morally. If a girl wants to live a slightly disreputable life, hanging around with actors, living in sin, that's no concern of mine."

Catriona flushed. "I don't think I'm enamoured of the *tone* of this conversation. I didn't accept your invitation so that you could make cheesy remarks about my private life. Anyway, I know dozens of perfectly reputable girls who live with their boyfriends. Well, quite a few, anyway."

George came across with her drink and held it up for her. "I'm not being critical. Don't get me wrong. It's just a little difficult for old fogies like me to get used to the modern age, that's all. When I was first stepping out with girls, remember, it was pretty scandalous if they smoked, even in private. You smoke anywhere you feel like it. And some of those clothes you wear—well, they're pretty scandalous, even for today. You're a new kind of girl, and it takes a while for people like me to get used to the idea."

He sat on the largest chair in the room, a huge Olympian throne, without offering her a seat. He sipped his drink and then said, "Another thing that throws me off balance is your interest in business—coupled with the fact that you own so much of Keys Shipping. In my day, girls left business to the men. What did a girl know about buying and selling? It wasn't their world. A girl's world was all dances and tea parties and strawberries and cream."

"You have a very over romanticised notion of the female sex," Catriona told him, sitting down on the end of a deep black velvet sofa. "At least, you have a very romanticised notion of the girls in London. I can't speak for Cheltenham or Oxford or anywhere else. I expect the girls there are still as fresh and goody-goody as you'd like to imagine them. Dances and tea parties and frocks down to their ankles. And *all* virgins."

George drank and smoked and nodded reflectively. "I suppose they are. Well, I *know* they are. It's the same in America, in all the proper middle-class suburbs. Well-painted homes, shiny new Packards, and daughters who never listened to nigger music and walk down the aisle with their hymens intact. It has to be that way. That's what makes capitalism strong."

"I'm not sure that I follow you," said Catriona. "What makes capitalism strong? The well-painted houses or the intact hymens?"

George looked at her. She could tell that he was slightly surprised that a girl could say the word "hymens" out loud, even a sophisticated flapper like her.

"Well," he said, in a slow voice, "you have to remember that a country which bases its strength on capitalism needs a stable base, a middle class of moderately well off professional people who not only desire the products that capitalist industries offer them but have the money and the credit to pay for them, and are satisfied with what they've got when they've got it—although not *too* satisfied not to hanker after next year's model. And the way to keep this middle-class base secure is to fix the prices of everything they want, from a spanking new automobile to a college education for their kids, at exactly the right level, so that they can *just* afford them if they're thrifty, and if they work hard, but never have too much money left over. It's that exact income-to-desire ratio that keeps a capitalist system functioning, and expanding. It has to be finely tuned. If people have too much free cash, they suddenly realise that they don't have to work so hard, and that they can afford booze and gambling and messing around with women not their wives. Homes break up, efficiency at work starts to suffer, moral codes crumble, people start asking awkward political questions. The economy loses its whole meaning and its whole momentum. Happiness in a capitalist system is always having not quite enough. That's why I believe in well-painted homes and intact hymens and non-union labour, and why I think that short skirts and jazz and bootleg liquor are the first signs of America's coming financial collapse."

"You drink liquor yourself. And you've invited a girl in a short skirt not your wife into your stateroom, alone, for cocktails."

"I'm different, my dear; just like most of the cabin-class passengers on this luxury tub of yours are different. We all have sufficient money to be both publicly moral and privately licentious at the same time. Not many middle-class folk can afford such extravagance."

Catriona sipped her cold gin and then said, "What do you think of me, really?"

"What do I *think* of you?" George repeated.

"I get the distinct feeling that you're trying to say something to me, or *about* me, and I'm not sure what it is. I don't know whether you disapprove of me because you think I'm a flapper, and because I drink gin and smoke cigarettes, and have love affairs with men—which I can assure you is *quite* usual, these days, especially if he's somebody you care for— or whether you're simply saying that you're a little old-fashioned and you haven't quite got the hang of me yet. Or whether you're saying—"

George raised his hand and shook it quickly, to tell her that she shouldn't say any more. "You're a social phenomenon, that's what I think of you," he said. "At least, you're *part* of a social phenomenon. And if I appear to be talking my way around the bushes to get to the trees, it's only because I'm like a hunter who doesn't really understand the nature of the animal which he is stalking. When Edgar told me about you . . . Well, I knew your father, and I expected something different."

"A virgin."

"I didn't mean that. I see you're going to tease me with that for the rest of the voyage. I meant, I expected a girl who was going to be more conventional. Less free, less outspoken. Less worldly, but perhaps more practical, the way Northern girls usually are."

"You thought I was going to wear glasses and sensible tweed suits and be able to train red setters with one hand, while baking leek and lamb pudding with the other?"

George smiled and then laughed. Then, more because she wanted to make him move out of his chair than because she actually wanted one, Catriona asked him, "Would you light me a cigarette, please?"

He opened a silver box of Abdullas and brought it over. He watched her with that same curious young/old expression as she took one and held it between her lips. She had a disturbing feeling that he found the gesture erotic. Nigel had once told her about a German friend of his who would pay ten pounds just to watch a woman, naked except for black silk stockings, sit on a bentwood chair and smoke a cigarette. And Welterman was a German sort of a name.

"Have you thought any more about my offer to buy up the Keys fleet?" asked George, lighting Catriona's cigarette.

"Not really. There's no rush, is there? Not that *I'm* aware of."

"You understand that I would quite like to be able to know that I can count on your support."

Catriona smoked for a while without answering. George Welterman disturbed her even more than Edgar. At least she was sure that whatever games Edgar was playing, he had the best interests of Keys Shipping at heart, and the interests of all those poor families in Liverpool who depended on Keys so much for a living. But George was enticing her out like a deep-sea fisherman who had hooked the hair of a mermaid, out into the cold waters of real risk, both personal and financial. And the question was Did he want this particular mermaid for her alluring human form, or did he want her because he could sell her tail for $2.50 the pound in the best fishmonger's? She couldn't tell; and despite the extraordinary frankness with which he spoke of love and sex and Myrtle Greensleeves, George wasn't giving any clues away at all. He had been angling these waters all his life, and they were his own chilly territory. Catriona began to feel the first palpitations of inexperience, even fright.

"I'm still not sure that we ought to sell," she said. "Edgar advises it, but honestly I don't know whether it would be such a good thing or not. Especially in such a hurry. I know that my father wouldn't have sold. Not the whole fleet, anyway."

"I dislike to have to remind you that your father is no longer with us," said George Welterman. "You really have very little choice, you know. And since mine is the only realistic offer—"

"It just seems like an indecent rush to me, that's all. Father's barely been buried, and yet everything he ever worked for is already being auctioned off."

"I'm afraid that business does have its indecent moments," said George. "And it is not a world for women. I was genuinely surprised when I learned that your father had left so large a stockholding to you."

"Perhaps he knew that I'd take care of it."

"My dear Catriona." George smiled, and he didn't need to say any more to communicate his contempt for the idea of a twenty-one-year-old girl dabbling in shipping.

Catriona said, "You don't have to patronise me, you know. I'll bet that I can shimmy better than you can."

"Oh, no doubt."

"Supposing I *won't* agree to sell?" Catriona asked him. She watched his eyes, but they scarcely even flickered.

"You'll probably be outvoted by your fellow stockholders. I know that your mother is keen to sell; she wants the financial security. And the banks appear to recognise the benefits of Keys being taken under the wing of International Mercantile Marine."

"Then you don't need to worry what I think, do you?"

"I prefer unanimity." George smiled. "It's better for the company's public appearance. Keys needs to engender all the confidence it can as a shipping line."

"Well, I don't know," said Catriona. "I just want to wait and see what happens when we get to New York."

"Very little will happen, my dear, believe me, except that you probably won't be able to afford to bring the *Arcadia* back to England again; and if you don't pay some of the outstanding accounts that Keys has in America, you may very well find that this glorious vessel is impounded until you can make some offers to settle your debts. Now, that would be *very* dismal, wouldn't it? And what would you do about it, shimmy for pennies in Battery Park?"

"You don't have to be insulting," snapped Catriona.

"The truth is always painful, isn't it?" George smiled. "I'm sorry, my pet, but you asked for it."

"No wonder Myrtle Greensleeves never writes back to you," said Catriona.

George stared at her for a very long moment; and in that moment Catriona realised that she had upset him beyond all reason. "*What?*" he demanded; and his voice barked like a half-brick thrown against the wall of an empty alley.

"I'm sorry, but you asked for it, too. You can't bully women the same way you bully your business colleagues. And when you're on somebody's ship, as a guest, I would have thought it was pretty rotten manners to behave as if you owned the place. You may do soon, but you don't yet."

"Do you want me to ruin you?" George rumbled. "I could, you know."

"I'd like to see you try."

"You wouldn't be worth it," said George, trying to control his sudden temper. He reached for the silver cigarette box, took out another cigarette, and then laid it back on the table whose top was inlaid with variegated marble portraits of the classic Roman gods.

"Is that what you think?" asked Catriona in a high-pitched voice. "Is that what you really thought of Miss Greensleeves?" She felt more confident now, now that she had been able to tug at his most sensitive nerve. Not too confident, he was a man with a convoluted and difficult personality, and even as he began to curb his anger she could sense him working out another approach, another ploy, another less troublesome way to reel this mermaid in. He made her feel exactly her age—grown-up, pretty, and confident. Soemtimes brazen, often clever. But only twenty-one, with all the dangerous inexperience of someone who has only been an adult for two or three years. Old enough to say sharp and witty things. Too young to understand the devastating effect they might have.

In the company of older people, Catriona sometimes felt that she was almost a star—adorable, flirty, and fun. But at other times she felt

304

that she wasn't really a very nice person at all. She hoped, uncertainly, that George, Edgar, and Mark Beeney didn't talk about her behind her back as if she were an exhibitionist brat. But how could you be nicer and still be treated as if you were an adult? And if you were a beautiful-looking girl, the kind of girl whom middle-aged theatrical producers had watched out of unblinking and acquisitive eyes as you were dancing across the stage of the Gaiety at the opening night party for *Our Nell*, your bare knees flickering on their irises like an erotic French nickelodeon, your breasts bouncing against the thin eau-de-Nil silk of your frock and at the same time hammering on the tautened valves of their hearts, how could you ever *afford* to be nice?

She hadn't yet discovered the fine balances between teasing and tempting, between wit and cheek. She hadn't even discovered herself: not as a lover or an heiress or a friend. But she knew a little. Her father had been both free with her and yet strict. He had allowed her to find how wide and busy the world could be, and yet reminded her of its restrictions and its conventions. And perhaps the fact that Nigel had been her only lover—in that theatrical back-stage tumble where stars might easily take four men to their dressing rooms at once, and chorus girls had it standing up behind the flats—perhaps that was the truest example of how caring and sympathetic her father's guidance had been.

They had done very little but shout at each other, she and her father. But she was gradually beginning to realise how strongly she had cared for her. It took the devious and manipulative attentions of a man like George Welterman to show her; and she felt like whispering a thank you to her father, along with the message "I miss you."

George said, "You mustn't think that I'm a bully."

"I don't," said Catriona. "And it wouldn't make any difference even if you were. I'm not the kind of girl who allows herself to be bullied."

"Well, I said you were a smart girl. And you are. You're *smart.*"

"I think I'm rather callow, if you must know. If I were *really* smart, I'd be able to work out a way to tell you what you could do with your offer. Stick it up your jumper."

George Welterman threw himself back in his chair, jauntily crossed his legs, and laughed. "I like you," he said. "I really, truly, like you. How's your drink?"

"I won't have another one, thank you."

"Come on. You can manage the other half."

"No. I had too much of a hangover this morning. In any case, they'll be serving dinner soon."

"We ought to celebrate," said George. "The beginning of a marvellous business relationship. Welterman and Keys, I can see it now."

"Don't you think you'd better get down to writing to Myrtle?"

"Aha—" George grinned—"you can get me once but you can't get me twice. You'll learn that, as time goes by. One-Time Welterman, the man you can only trick but once. No, Myrtle can wait. Myrtle won't answer my letter anyway. Whereas you . . ."

He stood up again, both hands in his pockets, and leaned forward to stare at her.

". . . you remind me so much of the way she used to be. So much. You can really unsettle me sometimes. Do you know that? I look at you and I see Myrtle. Same profile. Same kind of provocative look. Shyness and pertness, all mixed up. Do you know who else you remind me of? Miss Austin, Texas. This year's Miss Austin, Texas. Same figure, just like an angel. I wired Miss Austin for an appointment when I saw the photographs, but, well, it wasn't to be. A previous commitment, she told me."

"George," said Catriona. "I think I have to go now."

"Oh, come on. We've settled our business. Patched up our differences. Have one more little snifter before you go."

"Well . . . I shouldn't."

"Who *says* you shouldn't? Let me tell you, you *should!* It relaxes the inhibitions. And there is no reason whatever why you should be feeling inhibited, is there?"

Catriona finished her cigarette and stubbed it out. George said, "One more little one, huh?"

It was the way he raised one eyebrow and rubbed his hands together that put her off. He looked suddenly grotesque—ingratiating and yet boorish at the same time. She found her shoes, slipped them on, and stood up. "No," she said. "I have to get ready for dinner. But thanks, anyway. If thanks is the word."

With one loping step forward, George suddenly snatched at Catriona's arm. Catriona, however, twisted herself away; and for a moment the two of them stood staring at each other, both of them surprised— George at his own behavior, and Catriona at the swiftness of her own reaction. It had been as quick as a well-rehearsed wrestling move, and if someone else had been in the room, and half turned away at the crucial moment, they may not even have noticed that anything had happened.

"Ah," said George, "so you're as much of a tease as I thought you were. They have a name for girls like you in the States."

"They have a name for men like you the whole world over."

"Catriona, you're getting me wrong."

"I don't think so, George. I think you're getting *me* wrong. I think you've badly misunderstood what this phenomenon you think I'm a part of is all about. Young girls may be freer these days, but we're not all straight out of *The Beautiful and Damned.* My God, you're being so damned *middle-aged!*"

"You vamp," said George, in a soft, critical snarl.

"Oh, don't you just wish I was? A siren gliding into your life with slicked-back hair and dark eyes and half a gallon of Nights of Allah splashed over my shoulders. But, my dear George, we may have petting parties, we free and immoral young things, and we may have love affairs, but we have them only amongst our own immoral young selves. The *last* person I want to coax into the back of a struggle buggy is a wheezing old marine financier who's probably going to get his corset laces tangled up with the convertible top."

"Well," breathed George, "you're really something of a bitch, aren't you?"

"Perhaps you're right," Catriona retorted. "Perhaps I *am* a bitch. But then perhaps you should get it through your head that you're talking to someone who behaves the way they do in *spite* of people like you—not because of you. You and your whole stuffy, cheesy, pompous generation. You know what Scott Fitzgerald called it, the way young people feel today? 'One vast juvenile intrigue.' And it's *true*, that's exactly what it is. The young against the old. If my mother knew how young I was when I first kissed a boy, she'd probably fall over with her legs in the air. She still thinks that I'm going to shrivel up like an Egyptian mummy before I'm thirty because I've been living with a man without even being engaged to him. It mortified her! It scandalised her! But it's all part of young people fighting against old people. It's *modern*. And you know something else that Scott Fitzgerald says? 'At eighteen our convictions are hills from which we look; at forty-five they are caves in which we hide.' "

George was noisily pouring himself another highball. "I'm glad you're well acquainted with the holy scrolls of the most tawdry and illiterate young American writer being published today."

"Of course I am. Didn't you ever have heroes? People you believed in?"

"The only people I ever believed in were William McKinley, J. Pierpoint Morgan, and Mark Hanna."

"Oh, yes? And what did *they* have to say for themselves?"

"Mark Hanna uttered the great truth that anyone who has any experience of public life knows that they never owe the public anything. And Morgan pointed out the greater truth that men don't go into business for their health."

"*You* obviously don't. Not the way you've been trying to do business with *me*. Any more of that pawing and you'll have a heart seizure."

"What the hell do you mean, *pawing?*" George roared. Really roared, with his neck veins bulging, and his fist clenched so tightly around the stem of his highball glass that Catriona was sure it was going to snap.

"This is still my father's ship, Mr. Welterman," Catriona replied. Her heart was tumbling over and over, cake and circuses, but she managed to keep her voice quite level, and as cool as she could. "And on my father's ship, I expect to be treated with respect. Even by you."

George circled cagily around the room, his fingers drumming on chairbacks, tabletops, bureau lids. *Drrrp, drrrp, drrrrp.* He was breathing with the regular heaves of a long-distance swimmer, and his whole body was crammed with emotional tension.

"You're such a hypocrite," Catriona told him; and she was pleased by the assured, throaty way her voice came out. "You speak to me as if I'm a delinquent shopgirl. You talk about moral codes, and the middle class, and you give me all that applesauce about capitalism. *God,* you're a hypocrite! All you can think about is how to rake more money together, and how to get your hand up my dress at the same time. Moral codes? The only moral codes you live by are getting rich and taking as many dumb Doras to bed as you can fit in between telephone calls."

George abruptly stopped his pacing and stared across the room at Catriona as if he had decided something important.

"I'm going to show you something," he said.

"Well, I'm not interested," Catriona told him. "I'm leaving."

"*Wait!*" George bellowed at her; and in two or three violent wrenches, he pulled his quilted wrap down, and tore away his cravat, and bared his body from the waist up.

Catriona, who had been starting towards the door, stopped in shock. George Welterman was well-built for a man of his age, and a little underexercised, a little overweight, but it was not his physique which stopped Catriona so abruptly. It was the pattern of crimson and twisted burns which were emblazoned on his naked chest; a pattern which, as he turned towards her, formed itself into a single word and a single device, all fashioned from skin that had been shrivelled up like the umbilical cord of a three-day baby. She could not even begin to imagine what agony George must have endured to scar his body so deeply and irrevocably with a heart, and with letters three inches high that spelled out the name MYRTLE.

"Is this the kind of thing that you find on the chest of a hypocrite?" George panted. His forehead was glassy with sweat. Tributaries of sweat ran from his shaggy armpits. His belly swelled in and out as he breathed.

Catriona said, "George, I can't stay here any longer." Her voice was as uncontrolled as if she were speaking into a high wind.

George tugged off the robe that was bunched around his waist and threw it aside. Then, with quick jerks, he loosened his belt and kicked off his slippers.

"You think you have a right to go?" he asked her. "You think you have a right to insult me that way and then walk out? You call this floating stewpot of flatulent egotists *your ship?* Respect you want? On *your* ship? I'll tell you who owns this ship, Catriona, my darling. Mr. O'Hara owns this ship, and the National Marine Bank, and a hundred other creditors. My company, IMM, is one of them. So when you get high and fancy with me, when you talk about respect, just remember that this is *our* ship, my pet, not yours, and that the only respect we'll give you is the respect you deserve. You bitch."

Catriona felt as if she couldn't breathe. She thought, My God, *I can't breathe.* And in that breathless moment, George took two savage strides forward and gripped her wrist and yanked her arm around behind her back so hard that she screamed. With his free hand, he seized the thin straps of her white cocktail dress and tugged them off her shoulder, tearing her white silk underslip away with it. There was a flash of bare breast, of pink nipple, before Catriona twisted herself around and pulled her wrist free and scrambled onto the black velvet sofa.

George caught her frock, ripping it wide open at the back. Then, with a second lunge, his strong bare forearm was across her throat, and he was heaving her back against him, arching her spine, and forcing her head up.

"You're chok—" she tried to scream, but he clamped his hand over her mouth. She tried to bite at his fingers with her teeth, but he pulled her arm around behind her again, so far up her back that her fingers touched her bobbed hair, and the pain was so sharp that all she could do was squeeze her eyes tight shut and gurgle. The only thought in her mind was *He's killing me. He's killing me. He's killing me!*

But then she felt her arm released; and his hand fumbled under her skirt and reached up for the elastic of her step-ins. She felt the silk pulled away in three ferocious tugs; and then George forced her face forward into the cushions of the sofa, and tore away the last few shreds of her underthings.

"God!" she screamed, her voice muffled by the suffocating velvet pillows. "God, get off me!"

His penis was so hard it felt as if it had a bone in it. He forced it into her in an unstoppable thrust. He was a big, ugly, and powerful man. He went right up inside her until she jumped with the nervous shock of it. She screamed again, but then he leaned heavily on top of her back and forced his fingers between her teeth again. She bit him this time. She felt his flesh crunch, and she could taste his blood in her mouth. But he stayed on top of her, pushing himself into her in deep, irregular thrusts.

"You bitch," he grunted. "You bitch. You sleazy, immoral bitch."

She could scarcely hear him. There was a metallic singing noise in her ears, and she was choking for air. And all the time, he was bludgeoning her with his thighs, pushing his erection so far into her that she trembled like a storm-shocked racehorse. She thought, *He's killing me. I'm going to die.*

He shouted something; and then suddenly it was all over. He released her and rolled heavily off the sofa onto the floor, where he sat wheezing and panting, his reddened lust dying away in his lap.

"My God," he said. "Myrtle. Myrtle, my God."

Catriona, sobbing in spite of the fact that she didn't even want to sob, didn't want to show him how much he had hurt her, how humiliated and sullied and filthy she felt, climbed shakily onto her feet. She pulled down the hem of her dress, and then pressed her fingers to her lips to feel how bruised they were.

She couldn't speak. Her throat felt as if it had been squeezed tight and would never open again.

George reached for his robe and wrapped himself up in it. Then he went across to the table, picked up his drink, and finished it in two swallows.

"You want one?" he asked her. Then, "No, I guess you probably don't."

"I'm going," said Catriona. The voice didn't sound like hers at all. Maybe she had only said it inside her head. She walked towards the door, colliding with a side table as she went. George moved across and barred her way.

"I suppose you expect an apology," he said. His eyes were puffy, and he seemed to be having difficulty focusing on her.

"I just want to get out of here," whispered Catriona.

"And then what?"

"And then I'm going to go to Sir Peregrine Arrowsmith and have you locked up. That's all."

"You realise that if you try to do that, I'll ruin you."

"I think you've already succeeded in doing that."

"Well, now," said George, keeping a firm grip on the door handle, "don't you think you'd better consider your choices carefully before you go rushing out of here?"

Catriona stared at him in disbelief. "You've just raped me!" she shrieked at him. "Now you're talking about *choices?* Let me get *out* of here!"

"I can't let you go, Catriona. Not until you promise that what happened is going to stay our secret. You get that? Our own personal secret, just you and me. A little romantic episode that nobody needs to know about."

"Romantic? Romantic! You must be out of your mind. You're a mental case. Now, let me go." She was babbling, half whispering, half screaming. All she could think about was this dark and threatening man blocking her way. This man who had already hurt her more than she could bear to think about, and who now might hurt her again. Even kill her this time.

"I've got to get out," she told him. And then, crying, her mouth turned down in despair and shock, "I've got to get out!"

"I can't let you out, Catriona. Not until you promise. And don't forget our little deal, either. We have a deal going, remember?"

Catriona pressed her hand against her mouth. The ship was rolling beneath her feet and she was sure she was going to be sick.

"I can't let you out," George repeated.

It was then that the door was suddenly pushed open from the outside, with all the momentum given to it by someone who has been striding along a corridor at top speed and opens a door without breaking stride. Miraculously, it was Mark. He took one step into the room and then stared at both George and Catriona in utter blankness. The door banged against the sideboard behind him, and then slowly swung shut again on its rising butts.

"Catriona? What the hell's going on here?" Mark asked her. "George? What's happened?"

Catriona said, "Oh, Mark. Oh, God," and then crumpled.

Thirty-eight

She dreamed that she was sailing across a strange glassy sea, in an extraordinary woven coracle, with the wind blowing against her face. She could hear singing, high-pitched and distant, and flute music. She turned and Mark Beeney was standing close behind her, his face slightly inflated as if he had been drowned for a long time.

"The *Orange*," someone whispered.

She said, "What?" through glutinous lips, but she knew that she was alone.

The *Orange*. This time the whisper was silent. But suddenly there was a surge of fear; and a feeling that the sea was sliding in through torn-open bulkheads, and a terrible knowledge that the world was going down beneath her feet.

She heard someone arguing. She heard her father's voice, again and again, saying *No. No, lad. No.* But both she and her father knew that arguing was useless, and that the *Orange* would sink, however much they protested. Or perhaps he wasn't protesting. Perhaps he was only pretending to protest. Because when she looked across the room, he was smiling in smug satisfaction and swinging his half-hunter as if he were intent on hypnotising her.

Thirty-nine

Edgar came to see her in her stateroom after dinner. Dr. Fields had given her a sedative and ordered her to rest for the remainder of the evening. She hadn't told Dr. Fields what had really happened, only that she had felt faint after drinking a large gin and bitters, and collapsed. Whether Dr. Fields had believed her or not, she couldn't tell. He had sat at her bedside in his grandfatherly coat and gates-ajar collar, looking at her shrewdly for almost a minute, not saying a word. Then, when he was leaving, he had said, "If there is anything else you need—or anything else you wish to tell me—don't hesitate to call. I shall drop by later tonight and see how you feel."

She had slept, fitfully and nervously, for about an hour. Edgar had been in twice to see her when she was asleep and stood at the foot of the bed with Alice beside him, an unreadable expression on his face.

The truth was, Edgar was now seriously worried. George Welterman had gone much too far, damn him. He had behaved, characteristically, as if the whole world and everyone in it had been provided for his own private profit and amusement. Only Myrtle Greensleeves had escaped him, by contracting muscular dystrophy, and George had never been able to forgive her for that. But he had gone much too far by assaulting Catriona Keys, and the consequences for Keys Shipping and for Edgar's own future could be catastrophic.

Although Edgar would never have admitted it to anyone, it also cut painfully deep that George Welterman had soiled the only heterosexual erotic fantasy that Edgar had ever harboured.

Edgar had watched Catriona grow from childhood into pretty adolescence, and from pretty adolescence into remarkable young womanhood. He had always considered her to be somebody special in his life; not because he had ever believed that he could have her, nor that he and she could ever be suited, but simply because she was lively and young and modern, and because she was one of the most attractive girls he had ever known. Edgar had thought to himself, with wry acceptance, that if a man who has devoted himself year after year to hard and ambitious toil on the engineering side of a large shipping line, and to the insistent demands of the pocket watch in his vest pocket, and honouring his friends—if a man like that can't have just one secret dream, one blurred and arousing illusion of the boss's twenty-one-year-old daughter—well, then, why had God ever granted us the gift of imagination?

He had known all along that Catriona was at risk from George Welterman; but he had never believed that George would be so boorish and crass actually to attack her. From now on, the whole complicated bluff and double bluff that Edgar was trying to juggle on board the *Arcadia* was going to be far more difficult to bring off. And if he didn't bring it off, Keys would collapse into bankruptcy and scandal, and Edgar would probably end up in prison, or worse.

He said to Catriona quietly, taking her hand, "I'm sorry."

She looked at him from underneath drugged eyelids. "Sorry? What for?"

"For what happened. For you. For George."

She gave him a half-smile. "It's too late now, isn't it, for saying sorry."

"Yes," he said. He glanced up at Alice, who was standing guard only a few feet away, on the other side of the bed. "Yes, I suppose it is."

Alice insisted, "You won't upset her, will you, Mr. Deacon? Dr. Fields said she had to stay quiet."

Edgar gave Alice a grimace that was supposed to have been an understanding grin. "You mustn't blame George too severely," he told Catriona, even though the words were dog's dirt in his mouth. "He's had a difficult life, when it comes to women. He's had to put up with all kinds of pressures. I suppose sometimes they just have to burst out."

"Poor George," said Catriona in a trembling voice.

"Well, not *poor* George," said Edgar hurriedly. "But misguided George. Reckless George. Maybe even stupid George."

Catriona said, "You're going to lock him up, aren't you?"

Edgar stared at her for a moment or two, with that bland Edwardian E. M. Forster face, then breathed in deeply through both nostrils and looked up towards the ceiling.

"You're going to do something?" asked Catriona. "He attacked me. I thought he was going to murder me."

"He wouldn't have done that. George is—well, he's bottled up sometimes. Arrogant. He loses his temper. But not—well, he's not homicidal. He wouldn't hurt you. Not really."

Catriona stared at him, her sheets drawn across her breasts like Sheridan's Tilburina, stark mad in white satin. "How can you say that?" she quavered at him. "He raped me, and almost choked me to death. You're making it sound as if he did nothing more than—God—mildly insult me or something. *Mr. Deacon, he raped me!*"

She sat upright in her bed, her face white with outrage and shock. Edgar lowered his eyes in desperate embarrassment. Until now, Edgar had always seemed to her to be bossy and punctilious, determined to keep her in her place; but she had always thought that he would protect her. She had always thought that if she were threatened or cornered or pursued by some intolerable wolf, that he would immediately step in.

Instead, Edgar seemed to have delivered her to George Welterman, unsuspecting and unprotected; and now that she had suffered the humiliating consequences of George Welterman's twisted ideas about love and passion, he didn't even appear to care. She started to cry, large silent tears, not so much because of what George Welterman had done to her, but because she suddenly felt deserted by someone she had believed to be on her side.

Edgar had been an extension somehow of her father's masculine protection. Her father had charged him with taking care of her. But now that Edgar had failed in his charge, the last vestige of her father's care and influence had vanished, and she felt a sense of loss that was sharper than any she had ever felt before.

"Sir Peregrine will support me," she said. "Sir Peregrine will have him locked up."

Edgar shook his head. "Sir Peregrine is an employee, Catriona. He has to do what he's told."

"It's Miss Keys to you," Catriona reminded him, as acidly as she could.

Edgar drew up a chair and sat down beside the bed. "Listen, Miss Keys," he said quietly, "I feel as angry and as bitter about what George Welterman did as you do. I feel responsible, too. I should never have let you go to see him without a chaperone. But, well . . . you didn't, and the result was that George went berserk. He's hard and disciplined when it comes to business, don't y'know, but he has this feeling that everybody and everything rightfully belongs to him, and that they're his for the taking. He's like a Roman emperor, Nero or Caligula."

"But you're going to do *nothing?*" asked Catriona. "You're going to let him get away with raping your wonderful Queen of the Atlantic? Do you really think that little of me? That it doesn't matter if some brutish lunatic beats me around and does the worst thing to me that any man can do to any woman? Doesn't it *matter?*"

Edgar unsteadily wiped his mouth with his hand. "There are two important considerations here, Miss Keys. But I'll tell you what. If you think them over carefully, and at the end of the day you still want to have George Welterman locked up, then, very well, I'll have him locked up. I'll have a police escort waiting for him in New York, and I'll have him formally charged with assault and rape."

Catriona said, "What considerations? What culd be more important than my personal choice not to give myself to George Welterman?"

Edgar said, "The first consideration is Keys Shipping. The success of doing any sort of a deal with IMM depends very much on George Welterman personally. Few of the other influential directors at White Star are as interested in acquiring the Keys fleet as he is. And, of course, if we make a complaint against him, and have him arrested . . . Well, it troubles me, what he's done. It troubles me deeply. But I think this is one of those occasions when we must think of the poor men and women at home who are depending on us so much."

"What's the second consideration?"

"The second consideration is you. Your reputation, your family's reputation, and the reputation of your company. The fact of the matter is that you went to George Welterman's cabin alone, without a chaperone, and many judges and juries would interpret that as a sexual invitation."

"You're not serious."

"Oh, I'm serious. And they'd think that, even before George Welterman's lawyers started suggesting that you behaved towards him in a provocative fashion, and that you deliberately enticed him. George would make sure that his case was heard in front of the kind of country-bumpkin jury who love to be scandalised by vamps and flappers and petting parties. They'd hold up all those newspaper headlines calling you the Flapper of the Seas. They'd bring in evidence to show that you'd been living in sin with an actor. They'd produce photographs of your flimsiest dresses, and witnesses who would say that you were flirting with every man on board. Didn't Mark Beeney give you a necklace? What for? they would ask. For nothing? Or are you in the habit of giving your favours to wealthy men in return for jewellery and furs and champagne? You wouldn't stand a chance."

Catriona rested back on her pillows. She looked at Alice, but Alice was staring glumly at nothing at all. In a throaty voice Catriona said, "You've worked it all out, then?"

"I'm just telling you what to expect if you press charges."

"What I mean is, you've worked it all out from the very beginning. You've made me appear to be a certain type of girl, solely for the purpose of wooing George Welterman. George Welterman adores girls like me. They remind him of Myrtle Greensleeves. I should have realised how much when he brought up her name that very first time at dinner. "I was in love once," he said, and all the time he was looking at me. I was bait, wasn't I, Edgar? I was the poor unsuspecting innocent, and you were my pimp."

She pronounced the word "pimp" with such distaste that Edgar involuntarily sat back, shocked. He blurted, "You can believe me, Miss Keys, if only I'd suspected for one moment, I'd have—"

Catriona turned her head away. "It's too late now, isn't it, for excuses? It's even too late for revenge, if a jury's going to think that I'm a cheap sheba, whether George raped me or not. I think you'd just better get out of here."

"Miss Keys, believe me—"

"I believe you," said Catriona, and the painful part about it was that she did. "Now, leave me alone."

Edgar stood up. Alice said to him quietly, "It's best if you do, sir. She's not herself at the moment."

Edgar, with uncoordinated movements, pushed back his chair and left the stateroom. On the way out, he passed Trimmer, who said nothing to him at all, and when Edgar attempted a brief smile of greeting, found an invisible speck on one of the glasses he was polishing and devoted all of his attention to that.

Forty

George Welterman sat in his bath with a flannel soaked in cold water draped over his face, so that he looked like a mummy from some forgotten Egyptian tomb, or a man posing for his own life mask. In his dressing room, his valet busied himself laying out his formal dinner suit, his boiled shirt, his starched collars, and his silky socks. The valet had asked no questions when George had asked him to draw a second bath and to lay out a second dinner suit only two hours after George had washed himself in the first bath and dressed himself in the pants and shirt of the first dinner outfit. It was not that the valet was blindly obedient. It was simply that he could smell the perfume in the sitting room, and that he had noted the disarray of the cushions on the sofa, and that he knew George Welterman for what he was. A pig who walked on his hind legs.

George himself felt very little. Tired, perhaps. Drained both of bodily humours and of that quirky irritation which afflicted him whenever he came close to girls like Catriona. But he was confident of his right to take whatever pleasures came to hand, and he certainly felt no guilt. Rather, he still felt irked by Catriona's refusal to indulge him. He didn't like girls to refuse. It was neither necessary nor normal. All girls liked money and power, especially when they were coupled with masculine brutishness. Girls who fought back were both rare and odd, in his opinion.

Perhaps she was one of *those*, he thought, behind the cold mould of his face flannel. A daughter of Sappho.

He was still idly reflecting on these matters when he heard the bathroom door close. He said through his flannel, "Duncan?"

There was no reply. He peeled off the flannel, and said again, "Duncan?"

Then he became aware of the dark tall figure standing just beside him and he turned his head. It was Mark Beeney, dressed immaculately in white tie and tails, his tanned face quite serious and composed.

"I'm bathing," said George. He was suddenly conscious of his reddened genitals, floating in the soapy water.

"That makes no difference to me," said Mark.

"Duncan!" shouted George. "Duncan, where the hell are you?"

"Duncan is temporarily deaf," said Mark in a quiet voice.

"What the hell are you talking about?" demanded George. "Duncan! Duncan! I want you here right this minute!"

There was no answer. The bathwater, agitated by George's shouting, slopped into silence, and then formed a still and scummy meniscus. George looked up at Mark and said hoarsely, "What do you want?"

"What do you *think* I want?"

"For Christ's sake," George spluttered. "How the hell should I know?"

Mark was taking off his tailcoat. He hung it on the hook behind the door. He smoothed back his curly hair with both hands, and then he smiled. "If you can't guess, George, then I don't believe there's any hope for you, either in this world, or the next."

"You touch me," warned George, "and every damned IMM lawyer in New York will have your hide off. I'm telling you now."

"Touch you?" asked Mark, rolling up his white shirtsleeves. "I wish I didn't have to."

"I'm telling you—" George began, but then Mark seized his iron-grey hair in one strong hand and pushed him under the bathwater with such violence that gallons of water were sprayed over the sides of the tub and across the floor.

Mark held him there, under the surface, by gripping his hair. Beneath the thrashing surface, George's eyes were wide open, his mouth aghast, as he struggled to break free from Mark's powerful hold and breathe in some air. But Mark wouldn't let him go, even when he reached out of the water and tore at Mark's arms with his fingernails, bruising and lacerating him in his panic to escape.

It must have been more than a minute before Mark released him. He came crashing out of the bathwater, coughing and shrieking for air, while Mark stood beside him and watched him with an expression of utter disgust.

At last George lifted himself out of the tub, still coughing, strings of phlegm and water hanging from his lips, and found himself a towel.

"You bastard," he managed to choke out. "You're going to pay for this like you wouldn't believe."

"You animal," said Mark.

George reached for the door handle, but Mark's temper blew like a pressure valve. He punched George in the kidneys, and then in the side of the head, just next to his left ear. George staggered, slipped on the wet tiled floor, and then fell, jarring his back. He lay against the bathroom wall, his face screwed up in pain, his forehead already swelling into a cherry-coloured bruise.

"I'm going to tell you once and once only," said Mark. "If you get within twenty feet of Catriona Keys from now on, if you even pick up the phone and try to talk to her, then I'll wring your neck. I'm not kidding you, George, I'll kill you."

"You were born in the wrong century." George coughed. "You should have been one of the Knights of the Round Table. Charging around, rescuing damsels in distress. You damned idiot."

Mark rolled down his sleeves, fastened his cufflinks, and then took down his tailcoat from the peg behind the door. "I'm not kidding you, George," he repeated.

George said, "All right, I believe you. Now, will you please help me up? I think you've broken my back."

Forty-one

At dinner that evening, it was announced with regret that Miss Catriona Keys was "indisposed, from seasickness." There was no reason for any of the first-class passengers to doubt the truth of the story, since fewer than two-thirds of them had found the stomach to turn up for what had been advertised in the ship's newspaper as "a gastronomic celebration in the French style." Even to those who had summoned up the strength to dress in evening gowns and tailcoats, the prospect of sitting down to a menu which included *la feuillete de queues d'écrevisses, le soufflé de truite au homard*, and *côte de boeuf St. Christophe au fleurie à la moelle*, was almost more than their equilibrium could stand. Especially since the *Arcadia* was still rolling, less violently, but still distinctly, through that humped and glassy-looking ocean that so often follows a storm. Many passengers had only to be *reminded* that they were on board ship to feel

318

distinctly unwell.

Mark Beeney escorted Marcia Conroy in to dinner. George Welterman did not appear until *le rissole de foie gras Perigourdine,* and even then was unusually quiet. Still, that didn't matter. Douglas Fairbanks was doing most of the talking, describing with cheerful self-deprecation how he had twisted his ankle. He didn't mind telling his fellow passengers the truth, as long as the press headlined his injury as the result of an "heroic attempt to rescue a doomed young heiress."

Maurice Peace was there, at Rudyard Philips' table, eating with the amiable relentlessness of the born freeloader. Baroness Zawisza had been through a fierce argument with her gigolo Sabran after the storm, and so now she was eating alone, with exhibitionistic sparseness, leaving her crayfish tails untouched, and her goose-liver rissole nothing but nibbled, in the hope that Sabran would see how much she was suffering. At the same time, however, she was raising and lowering her finely plucked eyebrows at Claude Graham-White, who was sitting opposite. She didn't realise that Claude Graham-White was attempting to remember the whole of "The English Flag" by Kipling ("What should they know of England, who only England know?") as a means of neutralising her blatant eroticism.

Lady Diana FitzPerry was sitting at Dick Charles' table, and she didn't take her eyes away from him for a single moment, even when she was sipping her *crème de tortue blonde d'Alexandre Duma,* based on a speciality served at Maxim's, in Paris. Dick Charles, however, was reassured by her attention, rather than disturbed, and he managed to join in the conversation at the table with only a few random stutters. He had been alarmed and confused by her sexual sophistication at first, but now that it was evening again and the storm had subsided, he suddenly began to feel rather warm and rather blasé about their whole peculiar night of love, and even to think about Corkies as something he might like to try again.

The extraordinary man in the toupee was also sitting at Dick Charles' table, at the far end, although he said nothing to any of his fellow diners, and sucked at his turtle soup so noisily that the lady next to him was finally constrained to say to the steward, "Do you mind taking this gentleman's soup away? I can't hear the orchestra."

Nobody saw the quick looks that the man in the toupee gave to Lady Diana; or, if they did, they kept it to themselves. They were looks not so much of flirtation, or even of curiosity. They were the half-interested glances of someone who is already aware what is going on and simply wants to keep himself abreast of events. But Lady Diana was obviously his sole preoccupation, because he fended off any attempts at engaging him in conversation with a one-word answer and a shake of the head.

The centrepiece of the evening, however, was the continuing contest between Mr. Joe Kretchmer and Mr. Duncan Wilkes. After a light tea of cucumber sandwiches, potted shrimps, scones, fruit cake, and cream-filled meringues, they were now addressing themselves to the entire Wednesday-evening dinner menu; turtle soup, goose-liver rissole, trout soufflé, and beef and everything, washed down with Riquewihr, Tain-L'Hermitage, La Chapelle-de-Guinchay, and (with the soufflé aux fraises) a bottle of Philipponnat champagne.

Both men (to the completely undisguised delight of Maurice Peace) were sweating like hogs, and crimson in the face, and Duncan Wilkes in particular seemed to be finding it increasingly difficult to push each forkful of food into his mouth. He chewed each piece endlessly, frequently covering his mouth with his hand as he belched, and he drank bottle after bottle of Perrier water to aid his digestion. The thought that both of them would rise from three hours of dinner, only to be faced within twenty minutes by a supper of devilled kidneys, calves' brains in black butter, toasted Cheshire cheese, grilled mushrooms, ices, and fresh fruit, was almost more than Maurice could relish. He had taken nearly £4,000 in wagers, and was hoping to clear at least half of that as profit.

Sir Peregrine had taken Dame Clara Butt into dinner, and appeared to be in top form—witty, courteous, and full of scandalous little anecdotes about some of the famous and infamous people who had travelled on his ships. He claimed that he had once surprised Lord Curzon very early one morning on the first-class promenade deck attempting to ride a one-wheeled cycle. He also claimed that one very eminent statesman (whose name he refused to divulge) had missed his way back to his cabin after a particularly bibulous dinner, and had climbed into bed with the elephantine wife of the German ambassador in New York. He had only discovered his mistake when he awoke the next morning, but the ambassador's wife had been far from upset about it. "I only just managed to escape with my dignity intact," the statesman had told Sir Peregrine. "I also learned the meaning of *Achtung!*"

Harry Pakenow, in a dinner suit that was only one size too large, had been placed next to Monty Willowby, so that the purser could take care of him. He was beginning to enjoy himself, in spite of his convictions. His cabin was small, but very plush, with its own bath and a small curtained bed instead of a bunk. At first he had considered that he would be betraying the proletariat if he accepted the hospitality of the rich; but then he had thought, I'm going to sink them all soon, why not soak them for all I can get out of them?

What was more, everybody was being so *nice* to him. Gentlemen passengers had come up and shaken his hand and congratulated him, and some of the younger girls had fluttered their eyelashes and patted their bobbed hair and giggled at him so flirtatiously that he had blushed. Harry had expected to be patronised, but he wasn't. Everybody talked to him as if he were one of the chaps. At least, it seemed to him as if they did. What he didn't understand was that everybody in cabin class was used to being pleasant to their servants (especially *these* days, when a cook could cost £240 a year) and that he was actually being treated as if he were a chauffeur who had rescued the children of some titled family out of a runaway dogcart.

To Monty's discomfort, Mr. Fribourg had also contrived to sit at his table, and just after the soup he leaned over and murmured, "How are the seats coming along?"

Monty glanced uncomfortably around at his guests. "I have five," he said, quickly raising the fingers of one pudgy hand.

"Five? I need at least fifteen."

"It's not easy," said Monty. "I tried to get Sir Alan Cobham's this morning, but he was sitting at the time."

"It has to be fifteen. For fifteen famous seats, I could make a fortune."

"For God's sake, Fribourg, this whole thing is ridiculous. Why not buy the seats at a plumber's and just pretend they've been sat on by famous people?"

Fribourg stared at Monty for a long time, as if this idea hadn't even occurred to him. Then he shook his head quickly, and said, "No. You think I want to be caught for fraud? I'm an honest man."

The orchestra was playing soothing selections from *Tonight's the Night.* The huge chandeliers sparkled and glittered. As the soup was finished, the dining-room stewards hurried between the tables gathering the plates. And all the while the *Arcadia*'s turbines thrummed through her superstructure as she forged ahead through the evening Atlantic at nearly twenty-eight knots.

In second class, they were eating asparagus soup and beef Wellington, and listening to a solo lady singer in a fringed frock whose soprano version of "Under the Laburnums" was compared by the sixth officer, a cynical young man called Spratt, to "the strangling of geese by an inexpert foraging detail from the Salvation Army."

In third class, it was tomato soup, liver pâté, and roast chicken with lemon stuffing and peas. The topic of conversation at nearly every table was Harry Pakenow, whose rescue of Lucille Foster had elevated him so abruptly to the upper decks. Not just to second class, under whose rubber revolving heels the steerage lived and dined, but to first class, whose kid-soled dancing pumps beat a soft and superior tattoo on the ceilings one storey above. Philly, however, did not miss Harry for longer than an hour or two. Soon she was making eyes at a young physics teacher from Bangs, Texas, who wore a brown and yellow checked three-piece suit and ate everything that was put in front of him. Whatever Philly said, he answered "Yes'm" and "No'm."

Upstairs, in the first-class dining lounge, as the stewards were clearing away the glass dessert dishes with a clatter that sounded like Tibetan monastery wind chimes, Edgar Deacon crossed over to Rudyard Philips' table, where George Welterman was sitting, and leaned over George's chair.

"Is everything all right?" he asked, quietly.

George screwed up his napkin in his left hand. "No, Edgar, everything is not all right."

He turned around, so that Edgar could see his raging red bruise. "This," he said, "was courtesy of Mark Beeney."

"Beeney did that?" It was as much as Edgar could do to conceal his pleasure.

"You bet Beeney did it. He forced his way into my stateroom, paid my valet fifty dollars to look in the other direction, then he half drowned me in my own bathtub and beat me up."

"I don't know what to say, old man," said Edgar.

"Well, don't say anything," George told him. "Just put that jumped-up young ape behind bars."

"You're not lodging a complaint for assault, surely?" asked Edgar.

"You want me to lodge a complaint that he was blowing kisses at me?"

"Please," said Edgar, involuntarily colouring at the idea of men blowing kisses to each other. "You have to understand that if you lodge a formal complaint against Mark Beeney, then it's all going to come out about Miss Keys."

"Miss Keys? That harlot! And that's another bone I've got to pick with you, Edgar. I thought you told me she was a flapper. A real hot young sheba, that's what you said. Jesus, it was like trying to get it off with a mountain goat. I've got bruises all over me."

"Perhaps this isn't the time to discuss it," said Edgar, glancing up at the interested faces of the other diners. "Let's talk later in my cabin. Maybe a bottle of Hine will help you to see things a little more calmly."

"I'm calm," gritted George. "On my mother's grave, I'm calm. But don't you or Miss Keys ever try anything like that again. Because Keys Shipping would look pretty sick without IMM's support, don't you agree? And Miss Keys herself would look pretty sick if I got some of my friends from the yellow papers onto her. 'Heiress importunes rich passengers for sake of saving her shipping line.' How about that? The whore of the high seas."

Edgar, still smiling, said, "I think you'd better withdraw that remark, George."

"I'm not withdrawing anything. Either like it, or stuff it in your ear. Now, will Miss Keys back up an outright sale to IMM, or what?"

Edgar said, "Nobody is backing anything. Not until you withdraw

322

that remark you just made about Miss Keys."

"What are you?" George demanded. "Another one of those knights in armour?"

"You're supposed to be a gentleman, George," said Edgar. "Even when my back's against the wall, even when I don't have a single card left to play, I still expect the people with whom I deal to be gentlemen."

"Forget it, then," said George. "Forget the whole damned deal. Let's just see how Keys can make out without IMM."

"*George,*" said Edgar firmly, and he knew that he didn't have to say anything else. It wasn't in George's interest to let Keys go, and George was only indulging himself in some bad-tempered bluffing. George himself was quite aware that the time wasn't right for that kind of endgame either, and he allowed his temper to expire, and his head to sink back between his bulky shoulders like the head of a falling pressure valve.

"Very well," he said. "I'm sorry I called her a whore. But, believe me, it's a pity for her that she didn't behave like one. We could have had this deal almost sewn up by now."

"Is that all you expect?" Edgar asked him. "That the people around you should behave like whores?"

George looked back at Edgar with those strange old/young eyes. "When I'm paying, yes," he said.

Edgar stood up straight. He looked very correct and Anglo-Indian. There were a hundred things he could have said. But saying what one wanted to say was nothing at all to do with good business. Instead, he laid a hand on George's shoulder and told him wryly, "I'll make sure you're not too disappointed in us."

There was a sharp, impatient knocking on the captain's table. It was Sir Peregrine, who had risen to make a speech. Rudyard Philips, at the next table, allowed his hand to close at last over the hand of Louise Narron, who was sitting beside him, and she gave him in return the kind of look that a white houri might have given an Arabian sheik in one of those softly pornographic Victorian paintings entitled "The Prize of the Hhareem." Whatever George Welterman thought, real affection was still possible, even in the advanced age of 1924, and there were still people who would go to bed with each other for no other reason than for love.

Sir Peregrine tugged down his white vest, and then let his arms drop down by his sides. He spoke in a clear, carrying voice—a voice that could be (and had been) heard between two vessels at sea without the aid of a loud-hailer—and everybody in the long sparkling dining lounge could understand every word. The only trouble was, they couldn't quite understand what the words meant when they were put together.

"My lords, ladies, and gentlemen . . . today is an auspicious day for all of us, despite the fact that we are at sea. Today is the first day of Ascot, and you will be delighted to know that the storm which afflicted us so ferociously earlier in the day blew itself out . . . and that Ascot opened in a gay blaze of sunshine."

There was a brief, embarrassed spatter of applause, and Rudyard Philips said, in a voice which he hoped sounded hearty, "Bravo!" Ralph Peel, at the next table, turned away in disgust. He didn't bear a grudge against Rudyard for standing up for Sir Peregreine, but he didn't want to hear any more of it.

Sir Peregrine acknowledged this applause by lowering his head and staring at his half-eaten strawberry soufflé for nearly a minute. Then—just when everybody was beginning to get restless—he snapped his head up again and announced, "I have heard on the ship's wireless that Scullion, belonging to Mr. G. Hardy, won the Ascot Stakes, by two lengths from Keror. I think we should all be tremendously pleased. For what reason . . . well, I think each of us can make his own mind up. Or her own mind up. Or its, in the case of a horse.

"Furthermore, I have learned from Sir Edwin Lutyens, the well-known architect, and a frequent traveller on Keys vessels, that his daughter Ursula is engaged to marry Viscount Ridley. This news also came by wireless, and I'm sure that each and every one of you is as thrilled and as . . . well, as thrilled as I am. Simply thrilled."

Rudyard was worried now. He squeezed Louise's hand just once, and then released it. He heard someone in the dining lounge say quite distinctly, "He's drunk. The fellow's quite drunk."

Sir Peregrine suddenly said, "To sail . . . as indeed we are sailing now . . . on the maiden voyage of one of the world's most . . ." He paused, searching for an adjective. "Most . . . *auspicious* . . . ocean liners, a veritable Venus of the waves . . . that indeed is a privilege both for myself as captain and indeed for every one of you who has been lucky enough . . . or indeed privileged enough . . ."

"He's paralytic," someone else whispered loudly.

An anxious murmuring rippled up and down the dining lounge. Sir Peregrine looked around and half raised his arm, as if the murmuring were caused by a wasp which he could swat. But then a woman's voice said, "I can't believe it. He's actually drunk. He can't even talk properly."

Rudyard got up from his seat, and quickly crossed the aisle to Sir Peregrine's table. He grasped Sir Peregrine's elbow and steadied him, smiling as he did so to all the guests who were staring at him in such surprise and anxiety.

"Mr. Philips," said Sir Peregrine, "what the devil are you doing? I'm addressing the passengers. Kindly return to your seat at once."

"Sir, you're not well," Rudyard insisted. "Why don't you come back to your quarters with me and lie down for a while."

"Lie down? Lie *down?* Are you mad? I'm giving a speech. I can't lie down."

324

"It's all right, Sir Peregrine. You've said everything you needed to say. Now, why don't you let me help you get back to your quarters."

Sir Peregrine indignantly wrenched his arm away and stood up straight, his eyes bright with indignation. "Mr. Philips, sir, I'll have you know that I am completely in control of my faculties, and that you have committed a serious breach of company and maritime discipline. Besides, I thought you were supposed to be under arrest, in your cabin."

"Sir Peregrine, please," Rudyard begged him.

But he didn't have to beg any more. Sir Peregrine's face suddenly turned a hideous mauve, and he opened and closed his mouth like a fish behind glass. Before Rudyard could save him, he toppled over backwards and fell into his strawberry soufflé, and then onto the floor. He lay there twitching and quivering for a moment, and then lay still.

"Go down to the second-class dining lounge and bring Dr. Fields up," Rudyard ordered one of the stewards. "Quickly, now! Tell him the captain's had a heart seizure!"

Forty-two

Rudyard's diagnosis, as it turned out, was not entirely accurate. According to Dr. Fields, the commodore had suffered an attack of apoplexy—the rupture of a blood vessel in the brain—brought on by drinking three bottles of Haitian rum one after the other, and by the unusual tension in his cerebral arteries caused by the excitement of arguing with Rudyard.

"You need not blame yourself, Mr. Philips," he said. "The commodore was well overdue for something like this."

"Will he die?" asked Rudyard.

Dr. Fields was rummaging in one of his coat pockets for something. "Die? Well, he may. In fact it's quite likely. He's a very sick man indeed."

Rudyard looked over Dr. Field's shoulder, through the half-open door of Sir Peregrine's bedroom, where the commodore was lying on his bed, his face reposed, but oddly cream-coloured, as if it had been carved out of cold semolina, except for two flushed spots on his cheeks, like blobs of raspberry jam.

"He's in a coma," said Fields. "It's quite common after an apoplectic attack. He may gradually recover from it, or he may die within a few hours. There is very little that any doctor can do."

"If he recovers . . . ?" asked Rudyard.

Dr. Fields was an experienced ship's doctor, and nobody's fool. "If he recovers, Mr. Philips, he will probably be paralysed down his right side. I can tell that already by lifting his arms and his legs and seeing how they fall. He won't be able to resume his duties for months, if at all. I doubt if he will ever command the Keys fleet again, or the *Arcadia*."

Rudyard stared at Dr. Fields and swallowed so loudly that he was sure that Dr. Fields had heard him. If Sir Peregrine was unable to command the *Arcadia* again, that meant simply that Rudyard, as the next most senior Keys officer, would take over. He had won, after all. Sir Peregrine had toppled himself, in the greatest act of poetic justice that Rudyard had ever heard of. Rudyard looked around Sir Peregrine's sitting room and thought to himself, This is going to be mine. Where that picture of the *Shannon* hangs, there I shall hang the Chinese watercolour that Toy gave me on our first anniversary, birds on a summer evening. And over there, on that bureau, I can set out my photographs of Matthew and Janet.

Dr. Fields said, "Sir Peregrine isn't a bad man, you know. He's pompous, of course, but then I think that he has a right to be. The saddest thing of all is that he wanted to be a great liner captain, of the same stature as Sir James Charles, and somehow that lustre always seemed to escape him. I hope, when you command this ship, that you will remember him occasionally and with some charity."

"That's a very old-fashioned speech." Rudyard smiled at him.

"Loyalty and respect are old-fashioned values," said Dr. Fields. "Why do you think I wear a wing collar? Not out of affectation, but to remind myself that there was once a time when people treated each other according to certain codes of courtesy."

"Well, yes," said Rudyard uncomfortably. "I suppose I'd better get to the bridge."

"It's all yours, Mr. Philips," Dr. Fields told him.

Forty-three

A drama of a different kind took place an hour or two later in the first-class smoking lounge. There, the ship's wealthier gamblers had assembled to bid for numbers in the ship's pool, and also to hear the results of the previous twenty-four hours' sailing. The room was dense with cigar and cigarette smoke, gusty with laughter, and heady with that second-night-at-sea feeling when you know that land has been left far behind you, and your destination is still far ahead of you, and that you can kick up your heels and do whatever you damn well please for the next two and a half days.

Maurice Peace was there, of course, with a club sandwich and a pack of cards, quietly eating while he relieved the tall man in the toupee of forty-five pounds at poker. Mark Beeney was sitting on a leather sofa by the mock-Tudor fireplace with Marcia, his tie loose and his tan rather reddened by champagne. Marcia herself was wearing a contented, provocative smile, lots of scarlet lipstick and a clinging green satin dress which did very little more than emphasise, *en vert*, that she was naked underneath. She had been quite determined this evening that Catriona wouldn't outdo her; although her pleasure at the announcement that Catriona was "indisposed" had been enormous. For one whole evening, she had no competition from the twenty-one-year-old queen of puppy fat. For one whole evening, she could have Mark all to herself.

Philip Carter-Helm was smoking a Passing Clouds and lying back in a club armchair watching the smoke rings rise to the ceiling. Douglas Fairbanks, his bandaged leg propped on a footstool, was telling yet another enthralled circle of passengers about his exploits during the storm. From the way he told it, he had been the only person on the whole ship, and the odd thing was that nobody interrupted him to say that, excuse me, but *I* went through the storm, too.

Rudyard Philips made a brief and rather formal appearance, with Mademoiselle Narron on his arm, and gave only guarded answers to those passengers who asked after Sir Peregrine's health. "He was overtired, after the storm," he replied, his mouth opening and closing like a money box. "He hadn't slept for twenty-six hours."

Louise Narron, in an extraordinary turquoise organza gown which came down in tiers like an ornamental fountain, looked as happy and as carefree as any woman who has deliberately decided to fall in love. Whenever Rudyard spoke, whatever he said, she smiled at him admiringly, and pursed her lips as if she felt like kissing him.

Jack Dempsey was asleep in one of the corner armchairs, his lips vibrating with every breath. Since he had exhibitionistically loped twenty times around the promenade deck that evening, to demonstrate how fit he was, and then skipped for quarter of an hour to "The Darktown Strutters' Ball" on his Victrola, it was hardly surprising that he had dropped off as soon as dinner was over; although his appetite would probably arouse him in time for supper.

Dame Clara Butt was not in the smoking lounge. She detested smoke and gambling and raucous noise, and so she had retired to her cabin, where her maid was massaging her large white buttocks with Lanes'

Emulsion. If the painter Ingres had been on board (which he couldn't have been, since he had been quite dead for fifty-seven years), but if he *had* been on board, he would have painted Dame Clara in this position for all posterity to admire, and called the painting "Venus and Thetis."

Now Baroness Zawisza rose, to exaggerated applause, to the small auctioneer's rostrum which had been set up for the bidding, and looked beautifully and a little tiredly all around her, so that Sabran would be able to see how wan she was, and how exquisite. Sabran, in fact, was playing rummy with Maurice Peace, and rapidly losing both his temper and all the spending money that the baroness had given him for the entire voyage.

"Tonight's auction will be the most exciting," said the baroness, in her melodious Polish accent. "We have been tossed hither and thither by a summer storm, we have clung on for our dear lives. We are lucky to have covered any nautical miles at all, and not to be lying under the ocean, conversing with the haddocks. So, without further preamble, I will tear open this envelope and tell you how many miles the *Arcadia* travelled in her first full twenty-four hours of sailing . . . and the answer is 622!"

There was a falsetto cry of delight from Lady FitzPerry. "I've won! That's mine! Six-two-two! Isn't that *wonderful!*"

There was more applause, and a few appreciative noises from the gentlemen as Lady FitzPerry came up to the rostrum in her flowing Drecoll organdie dress, under which her small breasts jumped up and down like a pair of boisterous lambs. Maurice Peace, who was still playing rummy with Sabran, glanced momentarily up at Mark Beeney and smiled. He was, after all, five hundred pounds better off, quite apart from the cash which he was taking from Sabran.

When he had finished the hand, he excused himself and crossed the smoking lounge to the sofa where Mark and Marcia were sitting.

"Well," he said, with his placid and anonymous smile, "it seems as if the *Arcadia* didn't quite manage it."

Mark reached into his inside pocket, and counted out five £100 notes, which he folded and handed over to Maurice Peace without comment. Maurice, who had been born suspicious of the flavour of his mother's milk, counted each note before tucking them away into his wallet. "You want to bet on tomorrow's distance?" he asked. "Fair weather all the way, from what the officers tell me."

Mark looked up at him for a moment or two, and then pointed a finger at him. "I *know* you, don't I?" he said.

Maurice shrugged. "No reason why you should."

"I've seen you before, I'm sure of it. Did you ever travel on the *Melusine,* of the American TransAtlantic line?"

"I know the *Melusine,*" said Maurice ambiguously.

"Well, I think I know you," replied Mark. "You're a gambling man, aren't you? One of our professional passengers, to put it politely."

"You're not *obliged* to bet with me, Mr. Beeney," said Maurice affably.

"I'm sure I saw you aboard the *Melusine* the last time I sailed on her to Rio de Janeiro," Mark told him. "A great many of our passengers lost a great deal of money on the gaming tables on that trip; and it wouldn't surprise me at all if most of it was lost on your account."

"You know how it is." Maurice smiled. "Memory sometimes plays odd tricks on you."

"Not half so odd as some of the tricks that *you* play, I'll bet."

Maurice turned to Marcia and gave her an avuncular beam. "This young man of yours is a stylist, and no mistake. Has he promised to marry you yet?"

"Not yet," said Marcia, more piquantly than Mark would have liked.

"Maybe he hasn't had his fill of thrills yet," said Maurice. "So how about it, Mr. Beeney? One more bet, on tomorrow's distance? Name your odds."

Marcia said, "You don't have to bet with him, Mark. He's a professional. You'll only be throwing your money away."

"Now then, Miss Conroy," said Maurice, "you shouldn't interrupt a gentleman when he's betting; nor when he's praying; nor when he's making water. That's what my old grandmother told my mother, in any case. She said, What does anybody want with a man who's busted, damned to eternal hellfire, or who's got wet feet?"

Marcia raised her elegantly plucked eyebrows and couldn't think what to say in reply. She wasn't used to American folk humour. But Mark raised his hand, as if he were pledging allegiance to the flag, and said seriously, "I'll tell you what we'll do. We'll each pick a mileage for the next twenty-four hours; and whoever is nearer to the real mileage will be the winner. From you I expect as a stake a sizeable portion of the winnings you've taken so far. Would five thousand pounds sound acceptable?"

Maurice was taken aback. "Five thousand pounds?" he asked Mark, lifting his cupped hand to his right ear, as if he hadn't heard properly. "Pounds, did I hear you say, or dollars?"

"Pounds," said Mark with a tight smile.

"But that's my whole living," protested Maurice. "If I step off this steamer with scarcely any money, then what will have been the point of my travelling on her at all?"

"She will have taken you home from Ireland," said Mark. "She will have fed you and cared for you, and washed your shirts. And considering you probably didn't pay your fare to begin with, that's not to be sneezed at."

Maurice expostulated, "Are you trying to suggest that I'm *stowing away?* Now there's an old-fashioned idea for you. Jim Hawkins on board the *Arcadia.*"

"It doesn't matter to me," said Mark. "It's not my ship. At least not yet. I'm more interested in taking your money from you."

"Well, of course you are," said Maurice. "And I shan't deprive you of the opportunity. It's a great risk, of course, but it's a fair one. All I want to know is What can you put up in return? It has to be something pretty spectacular. Bonds, notes, something of that kind. After all"—and he said this with an unusual hint of concern—"you may be depriving me of my living."

For the first time, Mark saw a flaw in Maurice Peace's calm and enigmatic facade. The revelation was only brief—nothing more than a twitch at the corner of his ceaseless smile—but it was enough to show Mark that Maurice was growing a little too old and a little too cautious for big-time bets. Maurice was still a master of poker and rummy, and he could probably continue to make a respectable living out of cards for the next twenty years, or until he died. But to stake almost the entire gambling proceeds from the richest ocean voyage in postwar years on one single number—well, that was something different. That required a particular variety of nerve which Maurice Peace might no longer possess.

Maurice had seen for himself what happened to old men when they lost their edge. He had seen Jack "The Spot" McLinton lose the seaside house he had built for his retirement on the single turn of a wheel of fortune. He had seen Walter Lillard carried dead from the Red Onion in Nevada, shot by an outraged opponent who had caught him using a Kepplinger holdout mechanism. And he had seen himself, in the glittering French mirrors of the *Arcadia,* a man past middle life who was still making a living out of kings and aces and jacks.

"I'll tell you what I'll bet you in return," said Mark slowly, putting his arm around Marcia's bare shoulders, "I'll bet you my automobile."

"Your *automobile?*" asked Maurice suspiciously.

"That's right," said Mark. "It's a Marmon, 125-horsepower, only ten months old, and it's garaged in the hold right now, so you can inspect it if you want to. I think it cost $25,000 all told, or thereabouts. It has a cream kid interior, a cocktail cabinet, a gold-washed radiator, and all the gadgets you could wish for."

"*Mark,*" interrupted Marcia, in horror. "That's your new car. You can't possibly bet that. Not that beautiful, beautiful car."

"No, no, he's right," retorted Maurice. "He's asking me to give up all of my profits. It's only fair play that he should give up something that means as much to him in return. Money wouldn't mean anything to him, now would it? What's five thousand pounds to a man like Mark Beeney? Nothing at all! Write out a cheque, add a few noughts, he wouldn't even miss it. But a very special motorcar: now, that's something different. To lose that motorcar would hurt. And the whole point of this bet is that, if you lose it, it has to *hurt*. Am I right, Mr. Beeney?"

"Yes." Mark nodded. "It has to hurt."

Maurice kept on smiling and cracked all the knuckles of his left hand one by one. "I should like a look, of course, at what I'm getting."

"You're very confident that you're going to win," said Mark.

"I always win," Maurice told him. "Just as you said, I'm one of your professional passengers."

At that moment, Harry Pakenow suddenly appeared, as if he had sprung up from a trap in the middle of a pantomime. His hair was sticking straight up and he was chewing a stick of celery.

"Mr. Pakemoff," said Mark with well-simulated warmth. "I hope you're enjoying yourself."

"Pakenow," Harry corrected him. "But, yes, I think I am. I think I've discovered champagne."

"Fatal," said Maurice. "Take my advice, my boy, and stick to club soda. Champagne is the elixir of idiots."

"Well, you're probably right." Harry grinned, his eyes crescent-shaped behind his small wire-rimmed glasses. "But I've enjoyed it all the same. Did I hear you talking about Mr. Beeney's Marmon?"

Mark gave Harry a small, irritated look—a look which Marcia recognised from those times when their lovemaking had been interrupted by telephone calls. His Marmon was one of his most prized personal possessions, and he hardly ever talked about it, even to her. She knew how much it must have cost him to stake it against Maurice Peace's profits. It was rare, one of a kind, and if he lost it to Maurice Peace he would never have the heart to order another one the same. Marcia wondered if he would feel even half as distracted if he lost *her*.

"Mr. Beeney's Marmon has become the subject of a bet," said Maurice Peace. "We are each going to estimate how many nautical miles the *Arcadia* will be able to cover during the twenty-four hours which commenced at noon today; and whoever bets the nearer figure will be the winner. My stake is, er, money. Mr. Beeney's stake is his Marmon motor-car, which even as we speak is waiting for me in this stately vessel's hold."

Harry Pakenow uneasily rubbed the back of his neck. "I thought I heard you saying that you wanted to look it over," he said to Maurice.

"Indeed you did," Maurice enthused. "You don't make a bet without seeing the colour of your competitor's money, now do you?"

"Well, I suppose you don't," said Harry, with a sort of laugh that was more like a series of painful hiccups. "But, you know . . . a Marmon's a Marmon."

"Oh, I see," replied Maurice, taking hold of Harry's arm. "A Marmon's a Marmon, is it? Well, tell me, Mr. Pakenow, just how many Marmons have you had the pleasure of owning?"

Harry tried to twist himself away, but Maurice wouldn't release him.

At last Harry held still and admitted, "None, actually."

Maurice raised his head high and beamed. "*None*, the boy says. Well, how about a Packard, or a Stutz, or a Pierce-Arrow? None of those, either?"

"No," said Harry. "I've never owned a motorcar, as a matter of fact. I've never had the money."

"Well, that's a pity," said Maurice Peace. "I thought for a moment there, from what you said, that you were an expert on Marmons, and I was going to ask you to venture down to the hold with me and give me your considered opinion on what Mr. Beeney's stake was worth."

"You're really going to inspect it?" asked Harry.

"My dear boy, of course I'm going to inspect it. I'm going to give it the most thorough inspection that any automobile has ever been subject to. I'm going to jump up and down on the seats, to make sure the springs are intact. I'm going to poke about under the hood. I'm going to sniff the cognac in the cocktail cabinet. I'm going to fondle the leather to make sure that each seat came from the same herd of animals."

"The silver door handles were made by Buccellati, and the picnic basket was supplied by Abercrombie and Fitch," put in Mark. "I expect you want to check that all the teacups are intact."

"Of course," said Maurice, and then let out a short, staccato laugh. "Do you know something," he said, "I've always wanted a ritzy motorcar. Never in my life have I ever owned a really ritzy motorcar. I had a flivver a couple of years ago. I won it in a poker game in Elizabeth, New Jersey. But when the tyres wore out, I sold it to a pet-store owner in Queens for five dollars, to keep his hamsters in. A hamster hotel! I've never owned an automobile since."

"Well, now's your chance," said Mark. He extended his hand, and Maurice shook it. "I bet six hundred thirty miles. What's your estimate?"

"Six hundred and thirty miles." Maurice beamed. "She'll never do it. I'll give you six ten."

"Are you really going to inspect the car?" asked Harry anxiously.

Maurice said, "Of course. I'm looking forward to it."

"I'm not sure that passengers are allowed to go down in the holds during the voyage," Harry told him.

"Oh, I'm sure I can find a way," Maurice told him. "Besides, what's it to you? Eat your celery and mind your own business."

Harry said, "Listen, Mr. Beeney here has accepted the bet without expecting to see any of your winnings in ready money. Why should you want to check out his car?"

"Because I'm a naturally suspicious man, my dear boy, and because I love to inhale the scent of pure luxury. There are certain aromas which every man must breathe into his nostrils at least once during his lifetime if he wants to claim to St. Peter that he has lived at all. The smell of freshly casseroled partridge; the smell of a new pair of Gamba ballet shoes; the smell of *morilles* soaking in hot water; the smell of Latakia tobacco snuff; the smell of the petticoats of a young girl the morning after her coming-out party."

Marcia couldn't help laughing. "You're quite a character, Mr. Peace, if you don't mind my saying so."

"My love, we are at sea," said Maurice. "And the enchantment of being at sea is that one may be exactly what one wishes to be. To sail in a luxury liner is a dream—a dream from which one will only awake when her prow nudges the pier."

Harry Pakenow was now very agitated. He knew that he was over-reacting, but he was too intoxicated to be able to stop himself. His fear of Maurice Peace opening the trunk of Mark Beeney's Marmon and discovering his thirty sticks of dynamite took him like a kind of seizure, a spasm of panic that made him wince and tremble as if he had suddenly developed acute malaria. It was not that he was afraid of arrest. He was quite reconciled, and always had been, to the idea that he might have to serve a long jail sentence for what he was doing—or even be hanged. Plenty of other young Marxists had been martyrs to the cause of over-throwing world capitalism—shot, electrocuted, and strangled by judicial ropes. Harry always used to say at his revolutionary meetings that every mink coat and every chinchilla beret was matted with the blood of America's young activists. No, what he was most afraid of was failure, of having to stand on board the *Arcadia* as she arrived in New York. He had already sent coded letters to all of his friends in America warning them of the *Arcadia*'s impending sabotage, and to have to face them and say that he had been foiled by a middle-aged gambler in a food-stained dinner jacket —well, that was unthinkable.

"Are you all right, Mr. Pakenow?" asked Marcia kindly. "You've gone very pale."

"Too much champagne, that's the trouble," said Maurice. "Come on, my friend, sit down and put your head between your legs, and I'll have the steward bring you a strong cup of Bovril. Steward!"

"It's—quite—out—of—the—question—to—inspect," quavered Harry. His teeth chattered, and perspiration ran down the sides of his face. Maurice Peace ushered him over to a leather club chair and pushed him gently into a sitting position.

"You'll be all right, old man. It's delayed shock, probably, from that gallant rescue of yours. Ah, steward. Will you bring this gentleman a cup of hot Bovril, please? He's feeling a little out of sorts."

Just then, like a dark cloud passing over the sun, George Welterman appeared, his forehead still bruised, his eyes as unpleasant in their aspect as a rained-off picnic. He was holding a large balloon glass of Denis Mounie cognac, which he swilled around and around in his hand. "Something wrong?" he asked Maurice, although his stare was reserved for Mark Beeney.

"Only a slight case of inexperience with the giggle water," said Maurice.

"You mustn't," Harry insisted. "You can't—"

"You mustn't?" inquired George. "You mustn't what?"

"He's spifflicated, that's all," said Maurice. "He's got this notion into his head that I mustn't look at Mr. Beeney's motorcar, and for some screwy reason it's got him all excited."

"Why should you *want* to look at Mr. Beeney's motorcar?" George asked, swilling his brandy around.

"Because I'm going to win it, that's why," Maurice told him. "Mr. Beeney has bet that the *Arcadia* will cover six hundred and thirty nautical miles by tomorrow noon. I have bet him, in return, that she won't make better than six hundred and ten. If Mr. Beeney loses, he will have to give me his motorcar."

"Well, well. From what I hear, that's a very special piece of automobile. Didn't I read a piece about it in *Popular Finance?*"

"And *Collier's,*" put in Mark. "They ran a whole spread on it."

George Welterman took that remark as an invitation to step a little closer. He stood over Mark and Marcia for a moment or two, one hand in his pocket the other cupping his brandy glass, and as Maurice said later, "You could almost hear the snakes hissing in his brain."

"That sounds like a bet that I'd enjoy a share of," George said to Mark after a while. "In fact, there's nothing I'd like better than to take that automobile off your hands."

"What would you want with a twenty-five-thousand-dollar Marmon with silver handles?" Marcia asked him.

"Oh, nothing." George smiled. "But I'd take considerable pleasure in running it into a solid concrete wall."

"You know something," said Maurice, "you're a Philistine."

George ignored him. He sipped his cognac and watched Mark with those disturbing eyes of his, and said, "I'll bet that the *Arcadia* manages *more* than six hundred and thirty miles. At least five miles more."

"That means she's going to have to average twenty-six and a half knots all the way," said Mark.

"She's easily capable of it," said George.

"Well, I don't think you stand much of a chance," commented Maurice.

"That's what the family doctor said when I was born. But I survived, and flourished."

"Is that what you call it?"

George couldn't resist a grin. He liked being insulted. It showed him that he was getting under people's skin. In a peculiar way, it was a substitute for being liked. If he couldn't be adorable, at least he could be irritating.

"What are you going to put up in return?" Maurice Peace wanted to know. "I've already staked five thousand pounds. It has to be something that makes your pips squeak."

George didn't take his eyes off Mark Beeney once. Even those passengers who hadn't caught the gist of their conversation could sense at once the cat's-fur charge of electricity that had been generated by their mutual dislike. Mark, to George, was everything for which he felt utter contempt in modern business: smooth, good-looking, image-conscious, *nouveau riche.* "Ballet dancers" was how he usually described young men like Mark. In return, Mark found George Welterman crass and insensitive and bullying. They would have hated each other even if they hadn't been rivals in business.

"Mr. Peace," said George, still watching Mark intently, "I don't really have anything to offer which would interest you, except money. So, if you win, I'll offer you five thousand pounds, to match your stake. Is that acceptable?"

"What if Mr. Beeney wins?"

"If Mr. Beeney wins, I'll withdraw my offer for Keys Shipping; let them sink or swim, and give Mr. Beeney the opportunity to buy up the *Arcadia.* That's what you want, isn't it, Mr. Beeney?"

"Can you afford to do that?" Mark asked narrowly. "What the hell will the people at IMM have to say if you withdraw?"

George said, "They'll just have to live with it, and so will I. But I'm not going to have to withdraw. As usual, I'm going to win."

"So you bet six hundred and thirty-five?" said Maurice, taking out the telltale stub of pencil that always identifies a gambler.

"Do we shake hands on it?" asked George.

Mark hesitated for a moment and then held out his hand. "Mr. Welterman, I think you have yourself a bet."

Maurice glanced up from his notepad. He suddenly realised that this contest had very little to do with him at all. In the guise of a simple wager, the two most powerful men on the *Arcadia* had at last faced up to each other in a silent, intent contest. There was much more than a motorcar or a business deal involved in this bet; there was masculine pride, ferocious honour, and reputation.

Maurice asked, "Are you coming down to the hold to inspect the automobile with me, Mr. Welterman?"

George thought about it and then said, "No, I don't think that will be necessary. I know just how much attention and money Mr. Beeney has lavished on it: engine tuned by Wolf Barnato personally; upholstery handstitched in France. I read all about it in the magazines. Besides, I think I'd rather wait until I can sit behind the wheel and call it mine."

"Well . . . I guess you've got a point there," said Maurice. "No point in ogling it until its yours. Or *mine*, as the case may be."

Harry raised his spiky head and said in a bewildered voice, "You're not going to look it over?"

"I don't think so," Maurice told him. "We're going to wait until we've won it. We've only got twelve hours to wait before noon tomorrow, in any case. Then we'll know."

"Twelve hours," Harry repeated.

Maurice bent over him, his hands on his knees, and looked worriedly into his face. "Are you sure you're feeling all right, my dear boy? Maybe you should lie down."

But Harry shook his head and irritably pushed away the cup of Bovril that the steward had just brought him on a tray. Now, because of the ridiculous whims of these wealthy gamblers, he was faced with the prospect of setting off his bomb in mid-Atlantic or not at all. There was no choice left to him. The *Arcadia* was going to have to go down in deep water, and that would mean that she would undoubtedly take hundreds of her passengers with her. His act of revolutionary war had been forced on him before he was ready, and he was going to have to carry it out almost at once, without hesitation and without mercy.

He took off his spectacles and blinked at the blur of faces and black and white dinner suits. He almost wished that he knew how to pray.

Forty-four

At one o'clock in the morning, out on the smooth reaches of the summer Atlantic, Rudyard Philips became Louise Narron's lover for the second occasion. This time, however, everything was different. This time, her cries were like those of a warbling vireo, sometimes throaty and slurred, sometimes high-pitched and excited. This time, her hips rose up to meet him with strength and urgency, and she clasped his head between her hands and pressed it between her huge breasts until her cleavage was as humid with his panting breath as a hothouse at Kew. This time she struggled and cried, and even sang, and when they were finished, she refused to release him, refused to let him leave her, and held him on top of her white cushiony body for what seemed like hours.

"I was such a fool," she whispered. "I saw only my own sorrow, my own right to be loved. I forgot that you needed to be loved as well. I wanted a hero from the opera to stride onto the stage of my life and sweep me away in his arms. Why is he so *hesitant?* I thought. Why is he so *anxious?* But you needed rescue too, my love. You too were hurt and bewildered and unsure. Also, I realised after the storm that to act like a hero, simply for the sake of it, is to act like a clown. All the names engraved on the world's monuments are the names of idiots."

"I will have to get back to the bridge shortly," said Rudyard.

"But you'll come back before dawn?"

"I'll try."

She kissed his forehead, his eyes, and the wings of his nose. "You have that wonderful English melancholy. Do you think that we will always love each other as much as we do tonight?"

"Well, I suppose so. I mean, yes, of course."

"You don't have to wait until tomorrow, you know. There doesn't have to be any formality between lovers. You don't even have to wait for a ring."

Rudyard lifted himself up and looked at her in the Atlantic moonlight. Beneath them, the bed creaked and vibrated like a living beast, as the *Arcadia*'s turbines drummed at full speed. She was making twenty-seven and a half knots now, and the foam from her bows glittered and sparkled with phosphorescence.

Louise Narron's eyes glistened as brightly as the spray. Her red hair was spread out all around her on the pillow. Her skin was as white as nougat. Rudyard had the disturbing feeling that he had somehow been enlisted into a theatrical romance of Louise's own creation, except that the lines he was expected to speak next were going to commit him for real, and for life. She was, wasn't she, directing him to say that he would marry her?

"Isn't it strange," said Louise. "Two people, lonely and rejected and afraid, how they can find each other in this way? How they can discover that they wish to spend all of eternity together, as lovers and as passionate friends?"

Rudyard said, in a voice which would have been more suitable for addressing a Boy Scout church parade, "You said last time that it was sad and useless. Our lovemaking, I mean. I can't understand how you've managed to change your mind so dramatically."

"Can't you, my love? Well . . . perhaps last time I was looking for too much. Perhaps I was looking for the wrong thing. More than likely, I had drunk too many Poppea cocktails, and they always make me vexatious, even though I adore them. They would make St. Ursula vexatious! There now, I've blasphemed for you. Can't you see that I would do *anything* for you? Forever and ever?"

"I'm still married, you know," said Rudyard.

"Of course you are. But to what? To memories? Your marriage has burned to ashes. You must make sure that you use those ashes to fertilise the seeds of your new life, and your new love."

"Louise—"

She reared up, her breasts jouncing, and threw back her head. Then, to Rudyard's horror, she sang a high C, so loud and so long that the chandelier began to ring.

"Louise! Please!" he shouted. There was a thunderous knocking from the adjacent stateroom. The last thing that a first-class passenger on the *Arcadia* wanted was to be woken up in the small hours of the morning by a shrill blast from *Tannhäuser*.

"Tell me you adore me," she said. There were jewels of perspiration on her upper lip.

"I," he said, "adore you."

"Tell me you love me."

"I love you."

"Kiss me."

He kissed her. Her perspiration tasted like seawater.

"Promise me that you will love me for all eternity." She pronounced it in a very French way—"éternité." Somehow, pronounced like that, it sounded even more eternal than plain old English eternity.

Rudyard hesitated. A great weight constricted his chest. He found it extremely difficult to speak, as if he had eaten his third dry digestive biscuit in succession. Then, in a gabble, he managed to blurt out, "I-promise-to-love-you-for-all-eternity."

She kissed him, and then pulled him back onto the pillow beside her. "You have such beauty," she said. She raised her left arm towards the porthole, through which they could see the solitary moon rising and dipping as the *Arcadia* rolled. She extended her wedding-band finger so that it eclipsed the moon, and then she whispered, "The moon can be our ring for now. Now that you have promised."

Rudyard hesitantly kissed her neck. Then he reached across and cupped her weighty left bosom in his hand. He did, in fact, love her. At least he was infatuated by her. She was trembling and weak, and yet domineering at the same time. She could gasp at the thrusting of his loins, as submissive as a dizzy young girl; and yet she could also make him say whatever she wanted him to say, against his will. She smelled of flowers. Sweet williams, he thought, from his garden.

His hand strayed across the pillowy continent of her stomach, until his fingers found themselves ambushed in damp fur.

"I love your melancholy," she whispered, staring at the ceiling.

Forty-five

Although it was one o'clock in the morning, Mark knocked at the door of Catriona's stateroom; and when Alice answered, he asked if she was awake, and if he could see her. Marcia had gone on ahead to slip into silk pyjamas, refresh her makeup, and spray herself with perfume. She imagined that Mark, too, was getting himself ready, and collecting a bottle of cold Perrier-Jouët for them to crack.

Alice said, "She's awake, but I don't know whether she'll want a visitor. She's been having nightmares, you know."

Mark passed a sharply folded five-pound note through the gap in the door. "Tell her that it'll do her good to talk to somebody friendly."

Alice stared at the money for a moment; and then, by that extraordinary sleight-of-hand in which all domestics of the 1920s were expert, caused it to vanish from Mark's fingers and reappear in the pocket of her frilly apron. "I'll try, Mr. Beeney," she said. "I can but try."

After a minute or two she came back and beckoned him inside. "She's feeling much better. Dr. Fields came around about an hour ago and said she's recovered from the worst of the shock. A monster, that man, I can't tell you. But I heard what you did later, and I'm very gratified."

"You heard?" Mark smiled.

Alice made a pushing-down gesture with her hands, miming the way Mark had submerged George Welterman in his own bathtub. "The bath," she said. "Drowning was too good for him, if you ask my opinion."

She led Mark across the sitting room to the bedroom. Catriona was propped up on three frilly pillows, looking pale but relaxed. She wore a pair of pleated georgette pyjamas in pale rose, with Brussels lace panelling over the bust, and tight wrist-length lace sleeves. She had been drinking cocoa and reading a copy of *Elite Styles*. When Mark came in she smiled and patted the bed to show him that he should sit close to her.

"I don't know what I would have done without you," she said. "I think he would have murdered me."

"How are you feeling?" he asked her, taking her hand with all the directness of a longtime friend.

"I'm tired," she told him. "I still feel bruised. But I don't think I feel as hysterical as I did before."

"Is Mr. Deacon going to press any charges?"

"I don't know," she said. "It's really up to me."

"But Mr. Deacon has suggested you shouldn't make too much of a fuss, in case IMM change their minds about doing a deal with you. Is that it?"

Catriona nodded.

"I thought that might happen," said Mark. "And the trouble is that Mr. Deacon is probably quite right. That's why I took the trouble to pay George Welterman a little visit of my own."

"I know," said Catriona. "Alice told me. From what his valet said, you almost drowned him, and then punched him so hard that he couldn't hear in his left ear for half an hour."

"He deserves worse. But he's a very influential man, as well as a very unscrupulous one."

"I can't even think about him without feeling nauseous." Catriona shivered.

Mark said, "You could get your own back, of course."

"I don't even know whether I want to."

"You could hold out against selling Keys to IMM."

"And sell the *Arcadia* to you, instead? God, you're as unscrupulous as he is."

"I'm sorry," said Mark. "I didn't mean to sound as if I was exploiting your feelings."

"Well, aren't you? Isn't everybody?"

Mark held her hand between his. "Believe it or not, I care about you. In fact, I care about you very much."

Catriona said nothing. She felt jagged and wretched, like a china-headed doll that was coming apart at the seams.

Mark said, "Whatever Edgar tells you, not all of your fellow stockholders want to sell out to IMM. If you were to vote against a sale to George Welterman, then you'd probably find that you had just about enough backing to prevent it, at least for the time being."

"But Edgar keeps telling me that we *have* to. If we don't, we'll go bankrupt, and everybody who works for Keys will be thrown out of a job. Believe me, Mark, he showed me a family down by the docks, and the way they have to live, you wouldn't believe it. I couldn't be responsible for making their lives any *more* poverty-stricken. If I did that, do you think I'd ever be able to go back to my father's grave and lay flowers on it?"

"A flapper with a social conscience," said Mark, gently teasing her.

"A person who happens to care about other people, that's all," Catriona retorted.

"Really?"

Catriona said, "I'm twenty-one, Mark, that's all. I want to behave like twenty-one. I want to enjoy everything that there is to enjoy. But that doesn't mean that I have to be completely callous, does it?"

Mark stood up. "You remember that young chap I sent round to see you? Philip Carter-Helm?"

"Yes. What about him? I thought he was rather stodgy."

"Hm," said Mark, "he's not nearly as stodgy as he first appears. In fact he knows a great deal more about Keys Shipping than I do; and I even suspect that he knows a great deal more about it than *you* do."

"He used to know my father; or so he says."

"I was talking to him in London," said Mark. "He explained quite carefully how the common stock in Keys Shipping is apportioned. The way it works out at the moment, those stockholders likely to vote in favour of selling out to IMM number fifty-one percent. Those who are likely to vote against selling out to IMM number twenty-four per cent. That, of course, is without counting in your own twenty-five per cent on either side.

"If you decided to go along with Edgar and the rest of the board, then obviously the vote would be overwhelmingly in favour of the sale to IMM. But if you *didn't*—well, there are one or two waverers in the yes lobby. Mr. Fearson for one. He doesn't like IMM one little bit; and there's no doubt at all that if they bought up Keys he'd be out of a job. And your Aunt Isabelle is something of an unknown quantity."

"How do you know all this?" asked Catriona.

"I have to confess that I was told most of it by Philip Carter-Helm. He's quite encyclopaedic when it comes to the subject of Keys Shipping. He knows your gross annual turnover, the amount of freight, and the number of passengers you carried, as well as their classes and their destinations; the names of all of your agents abroad; how many ships you own; and where they all are. You name it, he knows it."

"He doesn't make a very good Cupid, though. Too dull."

"Well, I'm sorry about that. I thought you were mad at me for mixing business with pleasure."

"I was."

"And I'm sorry. I didn't mean to make you mad. The trouble is, we don't have very much time. When the *Arcadia* arrives in New York, Edgar's got to have some kind of a financial deal wrapped up, at least tentatively; because otherwise Keys may never be able to get her out of harbour again, and you can imagine what *that* will do for your reputation. I don't know how many return bookings you have already, but I should imagine you're almost sold out. Can you imagine the consequences of having to turn all those people away?"

Catriona closed her eyes for a long moment, and then opened them again and looked at Mark with tiredness and resignation.

"I know what the problem is," said Mark. "The problem is that you don't think you can trust me. What's going through your head right at this particular instant is: Mark Beeney wants the *Arcadia*, and he'll do anything and say anything to get it. Whereas *you*, of course, are worried about the chances of the family business surviving on its own, and all those unfortunate poverty-stricken people who work for Keys back in Liverpool."

Catriona was about to say something, but Mark raised his hand. "Hear me out, that's all. International Mercantile Marine took over the Blue Funnel Line three years ago. Maybe you don't remember the Blue Funnel Line. It wasn't much: a little family business about a sixth of the size of Keys, mainly carrying livestock and groundnuts between Galveston and Pensacola and New York. A few business passengers, not too many. But IMM dismantled that shipping line in six months. It sold off all the ships it didn't want for breaking, or to shipping companies in Japan and China; and it sacked all the staff and sold off all the warehouses. By the end of a year, you wouldn't have known that Blue Funnel Line had ever existed."

"But Edgar said that IMM had promised to keep Keys together," Catriona protested. She didn't really feel like arguing; but Mark seemed to be so insistent on having it all out, in explaining his motives, and excusing his lack of sensitivity.

"What do you think a promise from George Welterman is worth?" asked Mark. "The kind of man who can attack a woman when there's nothing she can do to defend her honour . . . you believe a man like that?"

"I don't know. I really don't. I don't actually want to talk about it anymore."

Mark said, "You really believe that I was trying to seduce you so that you wold sell me the *Arcadia*? You really believe that?"

Catriona looked away. She suddenly felt embarrassed. "It crossed my mind; of course it did."

"Well, why don't you ask me? Straight and direct?"

She looked quickly and directly into those clear and overserious eyes of his. "Well?" she asked. "Did you?"

"You want me to tell you a romantic lie, or the naked truth?"

"I've always preferred the naked truth."

"Well, if that's what you want . . . I first approached you because I thought you were stunningly pretty, and because I wanted to get to know you."

"And you don't want the *Arcadia* at all?"

"Of course I want the *Arcadia*. I want both of you. You personally, and the ship. It's only my eagerness, yes, and maybe my clumsiness, too, that allowed the two to get themselves mixed up."

"You really think—" began Catriona.

Mark shushed her. "Dr. Fields said you had to rest. *Rest*, he said, okay?"

"You don't have any heart at all, do you?" Catriona asked him. She knew she shouldn't have invited him in, especially now when she was feeling so touchy. Why couldn't he say the right thing just once, whether it was the truth or not? All he seemed to do was upset her. He was worse than George Welterman; worse because he was just as hypocritical, and eight times as good-looking, and because George Welterman had raped her and Mark Beeney hadn't.

Alice had already laid down her crochet and was looking at Mark, sizing him up, in case any forcible chaperone work was called for. In her time, Alice had protected dozens of ladies and less-than-ladies from dozens of ardent gentlemen, many of whom had been far larger and far more persistent than Mark, and a great deal drunker. It was partly a question of persuading them that they would be doing the honourable thing by saying good night and leaving, and partly a question of jabbing them very hard in the arse with her crochet hooks.

But Mark, leaning forward, took both of Catriona's hands between his and said quietly, "Perhaps it's just infatuation. I hope it isn't, because it feels so good that I want it to last. You have to understand that what I said yesterday about loving you . . . I meant it. But it doesn't change things, in the sense that I can allow myself to give up trying to buy the *Arcadia.* It can't, and I'd be screwy if I pretended it could. I want you, and I want your ship. But I don't intend to exploit either need in order to satisfy the other. If you can't love me the way I love you, but you want to sell me the *Arcadia* . . . well, I suppose I'll have the consolation prize, at least. If you love me, and you *don't* want to sell me the *Arcadia* . . . I'll have to accept that, too, although a great deal more gladly."

"And if I don't love you, and I don't want to sell you the *Arcadia,* either?" asked Catriona in a soft whisper.

Mark looked down at the embroidered counterpane, still clasping her hand between his. His diamond-studded Jaeger-le-Coultre wristwatch was ticking away the seconds to one-thirty in the morning.

"I'm not sure," he said. "Nothing like this has ever happened to me before. I believe in whirlwind romances, sure. But is this a romance? I mean, in the ordinary sense? I don't know. I can't explain how I feel. I'm used to talking in terms of preferred stock and tonnage and bills of lading. How can you use that kind of language to say that you've met someone you shouldn't really get involved with, for all sorts of the very best reasons, and yet you only have to look at her and you can't resist her?"

He raised his eyes. The glow from the futuristic Marianne Brandt bedside lamps outlined his tanned and angular cheekbones by lighting up the tiny blond hairs on them. Catriona felt like reaching up and touching them, but Mark still held her hands fast together, as if she were a prisoner of his passionate indecision—a hostage to the feelings which disturbed him so deeply.

"I felt so responsible for what happened to you today," he said. "I should have stepped on George Welterman's hands the first minute he tried to climb on board."

"It doesn't alter the way you feel about me?"

"Do you think it should?"

"You understand what he did to me, don't you?" asked Catriona. She was trying to keep her voice level, but it wasn't easy.

Mark released her hands at last. She wasn't sure what the significance of this sudden letting-go might be; but he said, in a sentence that was made up of small chopped-up phrases, "I've known George for years, and I should have realised right from the start what he was trying to do."

Catriona said, "You're screwy."

He smiled. "Of course I'm screwy. I'm screwy about you."

"You're screwy to be screwy about me."

"Well, maybe. But I can't help it."

"Oh, nerts."

"You don't believe me? You don't believe what I'd do for you?"

"I don't believe that anyone can fall in love so quickly. Nobody except me."

Mark grinned, a wide grin that was full of sparkling white teeth. "You love me too? You and your ship, or just you?"

"Just me. You can leave my ship out of this."

"But you don't mind anymore that I *want* the *Arcadia*?"

Catriona shook her head. Mark was making her feel quite intoxicated now, with all this talk of love. She suddenly thought, it's absurd, but I do love him. I loved him the very first moment I looked at him. And now he loves me, too. And there's nothing to worry about but love, love, love.

"Wait," said Mark, unexpectedly serious. "You do realise that this could be nothing more than one of those infamous shipboard romances? You know what they say in those Keys advertisements about taking a girl down to the rail, and showing her the wake of the ship glistening in the moonlight, as if that was all you were going to show her?"

Catriona frowned. "You're right. We should probably call the whole thing off before it gets too hot. Besides, it's late. Good night, Mr. Beeney. So nice of you to enquire after my health."

Alice suddenly put in, "Excuse me just a moment, Miss Keys. I think I forgot to switch off the gramophone," and she put down her crochet and bustled into the sitting room. Closing the door behind her, of course.

"Dear Alice," said Catriona. "She's strict, but she's understanding."

In the lamplight, with her bobbed hair shining, she looked to Mark like somebody magical: half human and half enchanted. It was probably nothing more than her dark, slightly slanted eyes, or the curve of her forehead. How can anybody describe the subtle shades and elusive lines that make one girl beautiful? There were similarities in Catriona's face to Marcia's, and to all of the girls that Mark had found especially attractive. But to him, Catriona had everything that made a girl irresistible, and even if she had been George Welterman's sister, he would have fallen in love with her right from the start.

He bent his head towards her, his lips parted, and for a moment they looked at each other from only three inches apart. The hovering anticipation of a kiss, thought Catriona, is equal to at least half the total pleasure of the whole experience. Gradually, as if she were falling asleep, she closed her eyes, and then Mark touched her lips with his, delicately at first, as softly as if he were trying to bite snow, and then more insistently, tasting the sweet greasiness of her lipstick again and again. She uttered something, but neither of them knew what it was. It was simply a sound of love.

His tongue tip ran the length of her closed mouth, and then gently thrust forward, parting her lips, encountering her teeth and the tip of her own tongue. He licked her upper incisors, feeling the white square shape of them, and then he ran his tongue around her top teeth from the back to the front, and deep into the back again.

For a moment, their tongues wrestled in a welter of shared saliva. Then Mark's rigid tongue licked Catriona's tongue into curling submission, circling around it, thrusting beneath it, and teasing the membrane that joined it to the floor of her mouth. Her tongue retreated shyly, while he provoked it and played with it.

Catriona opened her eyes for a moment and she could see the side of Mark's forehead and his short, well-brushed curls. She reached up with her hand and stroked the back of his neck, around his stiff starched collar, and then the curve around his ears. He was so appealing, so masculine, that she could almost have eaten him. Sunk her teeth into those golden-brown muscles and devoured him whole.

The kiss, after whole minutes, was over. Mark sat up straight, staring at her, unable to take his eyes off her, any more than she was able to take her eyes off him.

"Well," he said. "Miss Catriona Keys."

"Mr. Mark Beeney," she answered him.

"Where do we go from here?" he asked her.

"Do you really want to go *anywhere?*"

"Not just now. But what about tomorrow? And what about the day after tomorrow? And Saturday, when we reach New York?"

She reached out her arm, tightly encased in exquisite lace, and touched his shoulder. At that moment Alice, who wasn't taking any chances with Catriona when it came to young gentlemen, returned with a fresh skein of cotton.

"You're feeling all right, Miss Keys? Not too tired?"

"Alice, I'm feeling wonderful."

"Well, that's as may be. But remember what the doctor said. And don't let yourself get carried away. You had a nasty shock. You haven't felt the worst of it yet."

"I know," said Catriona.

Mark said, "I ought to be going. I don't want to tire you out."

"You'll come and have breakfast with me tomorrow?"

"Of course I will, if you think you'll be up to it."

"I think so," said Catriona. She smiled at him, because she couldn't help smiling at him. "I seem to have a new lease of life all of a sudden. I can't think why."

"You'll take care, won't you?" he told her. "George may have hurt you more than you realise."

"I'll get my own back on him yet," said Catriona. "Don't you worry about that."

"You won't be the first person who's wanted to. I just hope you're the first person who succeeds."

Catriona said, "By the way, how's Sir Peregrine? Have you heard any more news? Edgar told me what happened at dinner."

"Nothing so far," said Mark. "They're saying that he was probably overtired, after the first night and the storm and everything. According to the purser, he's resting."

"Mark," she said, as he stood up and straightened his coattails.

"What is it?"

"I don't know," she said. "It isn't really anything."

He waited where he was. He knew she had something important to tell him. In the end, in a strained voice, she said, "You will give me some time, won't you?"

"For what?"

"For everything. To think."

"Sure," he said and leaned forward and kissed her again.

Alice said, "It's time you took a rest, Miss Keys. You've had enough excitement for one evening. Come on, if you want to get up tomorrow —"

Catriona said, "Yes. I suppose I'd better." She felt more tired than she could ever remember. She smiled at Mark and settled down amongst her pillows, and the last thing she heard was the soft sound he made as he snicked the door lock closed in the sitting room.

Forty-six

Marcia said, "Where have you been? You haven't even changed. And where's the champagne?"

Mark looked down at his empty hands. "Did I say something about champagne?"

"Well, no. Not exactly. But one *assumed*."

"Oh," said Mark. He closed the door of the stateroom behind him. The theme of the sitting room was "Spring," but it was stifling enough in there to be midsummer. Marcia was curled up on the sofa with her long cigarette holder and a tall glass of seltzer, dressed in short-sleeved pyjamas of very pale green silk, with a laurel-green collar and piping.

"I don't know where your mind *is* these days," said Marcia. "You wander around as if you're half asleep."

"Marcia, I have a thousand things on my mind. Not the least of which is you."

"And what are the other nine hundred and ninety-nine? Miss Catriona Keys, Miss Catriona Keys, Miss Catriona Keys, and so on, I suppose?"

"Will you forget about Miss Keys?"

"Only when you do."

Mark loosened his necktie and sat down in a green velvet armchair with varnished wickerwork sides. "You're being possessive again," he told her.

"Is that such a sin? Is it even so surprising, when you've just given me a diamond and emerald necklace and told me how much you adore me?"

Mark rubbed his eyes with his finger and thumb. "I'll call the steward," he said. "Do you really want champagne, or would you rather have coffee?"

"Coffee?"

Mark blearily checked his wristwatch. "It *is* nearly two in the morning. They'll be serving breakfast soon."

"Look," said Marcia, "if you want to go to bed, don't let me stop you. If my company makes you yawn, I'd hate to keep you."

"Stop being so damned unsure of yourself," Mark told her.

"Me? Unsure of myself? My dear Mark! I'm not unsure of myself, and I never have been. What I'm really unsure about is you. Do you really love me, or are you just playing?"

"Playing?" he asked her.

"Yes, my dear, playing. The same way you play with money, and the same way you play with ships. You've never had anything to do with anything that's real, have you? Not real struggle, or real love, or real disappointment. Even that beloved car of yours is only a fantasy. No wonder you're prepared to gamble it away. It never really existed at all, did it, except as a figment of your imagination. Now that it's real you don't even know if you want it or not. Well, I'm beginning to wonder if that's all that I've turned out to be. A dream girl who has come inconveniently true. A fantasy woman who has turned out to be a human being, much to your embarrassment. How discomfiting for you, to have to fulfil obligations and promises to someone you thought was nothing more than a pretty illusion inside of your head!"

"You're drunk," said Mark. "I'll order coffee."

"My God, if it could only be as simple as that," said Marcia. "If only I could be sure that you loved me, just by sobering up!"

Mark said, "Marcia, you're talking gibberish. You know what I feel about you."

"That's the trouble," she said. "That's the whole trouble."

"I don't know why you even came on this voyage," he told her. "You've done nothing but throw one jealous fit after another. And for no reason."

"I suppose Miss Catriona Keys isn't a reason?"

"What the hell does it matter if she is?"

"Well, is she?" Marcia demanded.

"Is she what?"

"A reason? Don't you even listen to me when I'm screaming at you?"

"For God's sake, pull yourself together," said Mark. "The more jealous you get, the uglier you look."

Marcia threw her glass of seltzer across the room. It smashed against the stainless-steel edge of a side table, and the contents fizzed across the carpet. "That's it, you bastard," she snapped. "You can take your diamonds back and your promises back and you can choke on them, for all I care!"

Mark stood up and raised both of his hands. "Marcia," he said, "you're just acting crazy, that's all. Too much to drink. Too much dancing. Too much of everything."

Marcia stared at him with eyes as blue as cornflowers. "I came on this voyage because I was worried about you. I had a premonition that you were going to drown. It was so strong! I could almost feel the coldness of the sea."

Mark was silent. He lowered his hands.

Marcia said, "I came because I care about you desperately. Even if you and I aren't going to stay together, I still want to know that you're safe. I still want to know that you're happy."

Somehow, the impeccable English upper-class accent in which Marcia spoke these words made them seem all the more telling to Mark, and all the more poignant. An accent so crystalline was usually associated with confidence and self-assurance and inherited success. Instead, it was now being used to enunciate despair and uncertainty, and to express a longing that could never be fulfilled.

In spite of all of the diamonds, in spite of all of the champagne, in spite of all of the kisses, Marcia had been sensitive enough to understand that Mark didn't really, truly love her.

Mark said, softly, "I didn't ever intend to deceive you, you know. I never held out promises that I wasn't going to deliver."

Marcia's eyes were filling with tears. "You didn't have to," she said. "You, yourself, are the promise."

"I do love you, you know," he told her.

She looked up. Her voice came out as a brave, tearful gasp. "Yes," she said, "I know. It's wonderful, isn't it? Wonderful, how many different varieties of love there are. There are as many different varieties of love as there are candies in a sweetshop. I think you and I had the kind that tastes very, very sweet while it lasts, but melts away before you realise it's gone. Fondants, isn't that it? Strawberry fondants. It's a pity we didn't have the barley sugar. It doesn't taste so sweet, but it lasts almost forever."

She was crying quite openly now, the tears streaking dark marks on her pale silk pyjamas. Mark sat down beside her and held her shoulders, but she refused to allow him to draw her close to him.

"I know you went to see Catriona Keys just now," she sobbed. "My stewardess saw you outside her cabin."

"She was sick," said Mark. He hadn't told Marcia that George Welterman had raped Catriona. Mark and Alice and Edgar were the only ones who knew, although Dr. Fields had probably guessed. Dr. Fields had once told a young assistant of his that "medical complaints on board ship are caused seventy-five per cent by nausea and twenty-five per cent by libido"—so if Catriona's condition hadn't shown any symptoms of the first, it had almost certainly been attributable to the second.

"So sick that you had to visit her at one o'clock in the morning, for over half an hour?" Marcia demanded.

"What do you think?" Mark asked. "You think that I went to bed with her?"

"I don't know what to think. I know that I was waiting for you to come with a bottle of champagne, and that I was expecting you to make love to me. But, well, obviously you had something more important to do."

"Marcia, you're not being fair."

"Why should I be? Why do I have to be fair? Are you fair to me? Have you ever been? What does fairness have to do with it?"

Mark let her go. He thought for a moment and then stood up. "Listen," he said, "I'll come around again in the morning."

"Oh. You're going. So that's your answer, is it?"

"Marcia, if I were you, I'd order the giant pot of black coffee, drink all of it, and then go to bed."

"Oh, to hell with your coffee."

"Okay," said Mark. "I'm going. I'll be back in the morning, when you've come back to your senses. But right now, I don't particularly like your company and I don't particularly enjoy what you're saying to me. You can't bludgeon people into loving you, Marcia. It has to come naturally, if it's going to come at all."

"Brother," said Marcia, bitterly, "you just spoke a mouthful."

Mark turned, and walked across to the door.

"You don't have to give me any parting thoughts," said Marcia. "Just, you know"—and she flapped her hand at him—"be on your way."

Mark hesitated for a moment or two, then opened the door, went straight out, and closed it quietly behind him.

He didn't stay to listen to the painful sobbing that he could hear through the stateroom door. Instead, he took out a cigarette, lit it with a quick snap of his lighter, and strode with a serious face back to his cabin.

Forty-seven

Rudyard opened the door of the wheelhouse and stepped in, carrying a Coronation mug full of sweet cocoa. Dick Charles was already there, his face lit an unnatural green by the lights from the ship's instruments. Through the darkness of the windows in front of them, Rudyard and Dick and the helmsman could see their own reflections suspended in the night, as if their own ghosts were tirelessly following them across the Atlantic to remind them, in Shakespearean fashion, of their own mortality.

"Good evening, sir," said Dick smartly, with scarcely the trace of a stutter.

"Good evening, Mr. Charles," Rudyard replied, and set his cocoa down on the ledge beneath the windows. "Everything quiet?"

"Everything s-steady, sir. The wind's dropped to f-four knots, and w-we're m-making just over the twenty-eight."

"Think she can go faster?"

"P-p-possibly, sir. But Mr. Deacon said to keep her under twenty-eight and a half. He d-doesn't want to b-blow her up the fir—, the first time out."

Rudyard smiled. "She won't blow. She's unburstable. And smooth? Look at that skin on my cocoa. Not a ripple. She makes the *Aurora* seem like a motorbus."

There was a momentary pause while Rudyard leaned over to check their compass heading. Then Dick said, "Have you seen Sir P-peregrine recently, Mr. Philips?"

"I spoke to Dr. Fields just before I came up here."

"Is there any imp-provement?"

Rudyard shook his head. "He's still in a deep sleep. Dr. Fields thinks he may sleep for another twelve hours yet. But there isn't any doubt that he's going to be paralysed."

Dick Charles didn't say it, but the way he looked at Rudyard and then glanced out towards the prow of the ship, where it was cutting a white arrowhead of foam into the darkness of the sea, that look left the thought that Well, so you got what you wanted after all, fluttering between them like invisible signal flags.

"He's a grand old chap, Sir Peh—Sir Peregrine," said Dick. "One of the grand old men."

"That's right," said Rudyard. It suddenly occurred to him that Dick Charles didn't like him at all. Dick hadn't appeared to like Sir Peregrine much when Sir Peregrine was still in charge. But his resentment of Rudyard—for no reason that Rudyard could think of—seemed by comparison to be quite open and undisguised.

"I suppose they'll g-give the *Aurora* to Ralph Peel," Dick suggested.

"I don't know," said Rudyard. "So far, nobody's given anything to anyone. Sir Peregrine is still the commodore of the fleet, and still captain of the *Arcadia.*"

"But if he's p-paralysed . . ."

"If he's paralysed, then it's up to Mr. Deacon and the rest of the board to decide what to do. Not to me."

Dick thought about that and then said, "G-good. I'm g-glad we've got that s-straight."

Rudyard looked at him oddly. But Dick Charles only grinned and then picked up his waterproof jacket. "I'll go off d-duty now, Mr. Philips, if it's all the s-same to you."

"Very well. Could you ask Mr. Peel to spare me a moment, if he's in the wardroom?"

"Y-yes, sir."

Dick Charles left, and Rudyard was left staring out at his own phantom face. It had never crossed his mind before that he might not be very popular, and the feeling was both disconcerting and depressing. He picked up his cocoa, spooned out the crinkly brown milk skin, and ate it. Then he sipped the scalding-hot drink, and wished that he had a digestive biscuit to eat with it.

The helmsman, a short beefy man with cheeks that looked as if they had been peppered with birdshot, said, "Very tranquil sea now, Mr. Philips. We've made up a good twenty miles already."

Rudyard nodded without speaking. But then he thought that his silence might be interpreted as aloofness, so he turned, and said, "Yes. Very good. We might take the Blue Riband yet."

"Oo, wouldn't talk of it, sir," said the helmsman, sucking in his breath admonishingly. "Sir Peregrine won't have talk of the Blue Riband on the bridge. Says he don't hold with Blue Ribands. Just to get there at premium speed, with premium safety, that's what he says."

Rudyard was tempted to remind the helmsman of the numerous occasions on which vessels commanded by Sir Peregrine had arrived in port with sizeable dents in them, and half of their superstructure missing. But the commodore's sudden stroke appeared to have stirred among the officers and crew a nostalgic feeling of loyalty for the old man, and all his sins seemed to have been mysteriously absolved. Perhaps the days of Sir Peregrine would be remembered as a Golden Age, after all.

The door opened again, and Willis the Wireless came in with a telegraph message. "It's for you, Mr. Philips, personal and confidential."

"Where's it from?"

Willis looked uncomfortable. "Well, from Liverpool, sir."

Rudyard opened the message and read it. For the sake of transmission through the open airwaves, it had been written in very plain and unemotional words. But Rudyard could easily guess what pain and uncertainty had gone into it, and when he had read it once he had to lower his hand and take a deep breath to steady himself.

It said, "Parting incident forgotten. Laurence has now left. Hoping you will return. But can you consider job on land. Absences too difficult. Please reply soon. Mrs. Philips."

"Did you want to send a reply, sir?" asked Willis in a quiet and diplomatic voice.

Rudyard raised the message again and quickly scanned it. Then he said, "Let me think about it. You'll still be on duty for an hour or so?"

"You're sure, sir?"

"Yes, Mr. Willis. I'm sure."

"Very good, sir."

After Willis had gone, Rudyard slowly crumpled the message up in his hand and thrust it into his uniform pocket. So, quite unexpectedly, Toy had decided she wanted him back. But at what a *time,* and under what conditions! "Can you consider job on land?" she had asked, at the very moment when command of the *Arcadia* was within his grasp. "Can you consider job on land?" when he was standing on the bridge of the world's fastest and largest liner—over a sixth of a mile of harmonious machinery and power. A floating city of more than a thousand people of which he was the despotic leader.

"Hoping you will return," she had written, too—only twenty minutes after he left the rumpled bed of Louise Narron, and had almost managed to reconcile himself to the idea that he would seek a divorce from Toy and marry the opera singer as soon as possible. As he had dressed, he had even imagined himself at grand premières at the Metropolitan and La Scala, proudly squiring the star herself, with flash guns popping and champagne cascading, and flowers showering down on them from every balcony and box.

And now this quiet restrained message from Toy. "Parting incident forgotten." She meant *forgiven,* but obviously hadn't wanted to say anything in a wireless message which made him look as if he had done something that needed forgiveness. "Can you consider job on land?"

He looked across at the helmsman but the helmsman was concentrating on his compass. The *Arcadia* was dead on course, thrusting through the summer night in one long surge of accurate horsepower. Her running lights shone like stars caught in the branches of a moving forest. Her funnels exhaled dark breath. She was magical and luxurious and she was almost his, if only he could convince himself that he loved her more than Toy.

How could he phrase his reply? "Land job impossible sorry"? No, there was not need for him to apologise. He was soon to command one of the greatest ships on earth. Better to say something proud, and stern like "I am married to the North Atlantic. Goodbye." Yes, that was it. He picked up his intercom, and said, "Mr. Willis, I want to send a telegraph. Yes, now."

Forty-eight

Sir Peregrine suddenly said, "Mavis, where did you leave my pipe?"

He opened his eyes. He looked up at Dr. Fields and frowned. "Mavis?" he asked.

"It's Dr. Fields, Sir Peregrine. There's nobody called Mavis here."

"Ah," said Sir Peregrine. His jaw slackened slightly. "I could have sworn I was talking to Mavis." Then, with another frown, "Are you *sure* Mavis isn't here?"

"Only me, sir, at the moment, and Nurse Queensland."

"Nurse . . . ??"

"Queensland, sir. You must remember Nurse Queensland?"

"Ah," breathed Sir Peregrine. "Yes . . .."

"You've been very ill, I'm afraid," said Dr. Fields. He took out his clinical thermometer and shook the mercury down with two or three flicks of his wrist. "You were very lucky it wasn't fatal."

"Fatal? But I've just been to tea with . . . the Borages, was it? Where have I just been?"

"You haven't been anywhere, Sir Peregrine. You've been lying here in your bed unconscious."

"I could have sworn . . . " said Sir Peregrine. "I could have sworn that I was talking to that fellow Borage. He said something about Black Prince strawberries. He was trying to bring some on early, under glass. Didn't you hear him? He was only . . . just over there . . . somewhere . . ."

Dr. Field sat down on the edge of Sir Peregrine's bed. "You've had a stroke," he said soberly. "A burst blood vessel in the brain. You were very fortunate that it didn't kill you at once."

Gently he took the commodore's wrist, and peered down at his pocket watch. "Your pulse is well over a hundred," he said. "You're going to have to take things very easy from now on." He leaned forward and tucked the thermometer under Sir Peregrine's tongue. "Don't bite it. It's the only one I've got."

Sir Peregrine frowned around him in bewilderment as Dr. Fields waited for the mercury to rise. As soon as the thermometer was taken out of his mouth, he said, "I can't understand why Mavis isn't here."

354

"Perhaps she went out," said Dr. Fields, as kindly as he could. Sir Peregrine was rolling his eyes from side to side, and he was obviously distressed.

"Out?" asked Sir Peregrine. "But *where?* Why should she have gone out?"

"I don't expect she's gone for long," Dr. Fields told him. "Just to powder her nose, perhaps. Or to get some fresh air."

"But I was sure that . . . "

"Yes? You were sure that what?"

"I don't know," said Sir Peregrine. His face folded up like Rudyard's message. "I'm not sure what I was sure of. I'm not at all sure."

Dr. Fields stroked the back of the old man's hand. It was veined, weatherbeaten, speckled with liver spots. On the wedding-ring finger was a ring engraved with the crest of the Keys Shipping Line. Dr. Fields said, "Who's Mavis?"

"Mavis?" retorted Sir Peregrine, staring at him. "You don't know your own sister? Well, that's nonsense, Borage. Tripe. That's what it is. Tripe. Now, where has she hidden herself? Playing games, is she? I've been looking for her all afternoon. You can't possibly say that she's . . . "

The old man suddenly let his head drop back, so that he was staring at the ceiling of the sitting room above him. Curved panels of mahogany, beaded and polished. A modern reproduction of Nelson's quarters on the *Victory.* He tried to focus, but then he gave up and lay back with his eyes watering and his face grey with desperation. "I don't understand," he said, as if he were pleading with someone. "I don't understand this at all. You said she was going to be here. I wrote. Look, my letter's still there, by the clock. She must have seen it. Surely she read it. Surely she read it. I don't understand why she's—"

He was silent for almost a minute, panting softly and licking his lips. Then he whispered, "My dear Mavis, I am not a man who is accustomed to begging. I have never begged anything from anyone in my life. But, now, please hear me out. Without you, Mavis, my existence will have very little meaning. Why should I worry if the sun rises, Mavis, if I can no longer expect to see you during the day? Why should I bother to eat and drink, to keep myself alive, if I can never be with you? Mavis—"

He gagged and choked on phlegm. Dr. Fields lifted his head up, and called Nurse Queensland to bring him a glass of water. Nurse Queensland was there in a moment, a bustle of starch. She was one of the nurses of the old school. Trained at Barts. Served in field hospitals on the Somme. A red face, a nose that looked like a fire-alarm button, and a bust as broad and white and crisp as the Slessor Glacier.

"He's delirious," said Dr. Fields. "He keeps talking to someone called Mavis."

Nurse Queensland said, "I saw boys like that at Passchendaele, just before they died. Talking to their sweethearts back home just as if they could see them standing right there in front of them. Perhaps some of them could. When you've been through a war like the last one, you believe in the supernatural."

"At least there won't be any more wars like that one," said Dr. Fields. He had himself served for a year on a troopship in the Mediterranean, and he had seen eighteen-year-old boys go through agonies that not even he could understand, after years of medical practice. How do you cope with boys who haven't even lived yet, but whose arms have gone, whose faces have gone, whose sex has been reduced to gristle? He let Sir Peregrine's head fall back on the pillow, and stood up. The old man was breathing more evenly now. His eyes were closed, and to all appearances he was deep in a dreamless sleep.

"You ought to have a rest now, Dr. Fields," said Nurse Queensland. "Don't you worry about the commodore. I'll take care of him."

Dr. Fields looked down at Sir Peregrine and nodded. "Very well, Nurse. I am sure you can manage. There's one thing, though. If he should talk of Mavis . . . well, don't disillusion him. Tell him that she should be back with him very shortly, and that he mustn't worry about her."

Nurse Queensland said, "Poor old chap. He's probably been worrying about his Mavis all his life; if he could only have told anyone about it."

"Yes," said Dr. Fields. "That's usually the way."

Forty-nine

Dick Charles had arranged to meet Lady Diana at two o'clock in the morning, after he came off duty. But because Rudyard had relieved him a few minutes early, he was able to change and wash his face and make his way down to her stateroom by a quarter of two. He cleared his throat, adjusted his blue silk necktie, and knocked. He smelled rather strongly of a German cologne he had bought two years ago in Hamburg.

He had been thinking about Lady Diana all day, except when the storm had demanded his full attention. At first he had been confused. Then, when he had begun to understand what they had been doing together, and all the Freudian implications of it, he had been seriously frightened. After the storm, though, he had begun to think of her again, and his fright had turned slowly to curiosity, and then to a peculiar kind of renewed desire.

He was breathless and jumpy as he waited outside Lady Diana's door, and he kept glancing nervously up and down the corridor to make sure that nobody was watching him. Ships at night were full of wanderers. People who felt sick, and who found their cabins claustrophobic. People who couldn't sleep because of the endless drumming of the turbines. People who were surreptitiously visiting or returning from beds that were not their own. In third, they called such wanderers "the glass-o'-waterers," because even if they were caught outside some pretty girl's cabin with their pyjama pants around their ankles, they would explain that they had left their own berths for "a glass-o'-water."

Quite abruptly, Lady Diana's door was opened. But instead of Lady Diana, in her revealing silk négligée, a very tall man stood there, and by the way his collar was flapping and his trouser fly was gaping open, it was plain that he had only half finished dressing.

"Yes?" the man demanded in a sharp upper-class accent.

"Buh-buh-buh- I-I— buh—" stammered Dick.

"Well?" the man wanted to know. "What do you want?"

"I, uh, I, uh, I was j-just making certain that everyone was cuh— was cuh— was comfortable."

"At two o'clock in the morning? My dear chap, if they're not comfortable by two o'clock in the morning, they're never going to be comfortable. Good night."

But before he could close the door, Lady Diana called out, "Who's that? That isn't Dicky, is it?"

"Oh," said the tall man, taken aback. "Are you Dicky?"

"W-well, I'm D-dick," said Dick.

"Ah," said the tall man, in the manner of someone who has just been told that they have dropped their hammer through the conservatory roof. "So you're Dick. Or *Dicky*. Well—ah—that puts a different—ah—complexion on things. *What?*"

The last *"what?"* was so explosive and so interrogative that Dick thought he had actually been asked something. "Er, yes," he answered. It was a response that was strictly in accordance with the Keys Shipping Line Handbook of Passenger Service. "If you have any doubt about a question that a passenger has put to you, always answer yes and then ascertain *afterwards* whether whatever it is that he has requested is either possible or practicable. This rule does not apply, of course, to questions relating to dangerous, revolutionary, unpatriotic, immoral, offensive, or religious matters. "Dick had always wondered what he would say if a passenger asked him, "Is there a God?"

Lady Diana appeared, in a pale blue concoction of flowing silk and frothing lace. She was drinking something bright blue in a martini glass. There was a maraschino cherry in it which looked mauve.

"My darling Dick, you must come in. You're early."

For a moment, the tall man completely blocked the doorway, but when Lady Diana prodded his arm with one of her long fingernails and said, "Come on, now, dear," he reluctantly stepped back and let Dick past. Dick gave him a smile which he hoped was cheerful, but which was actually horribly distempered (as he saw when he glanced at the mirrors over the mock fireplace).

"You must meet, er, *Walter*," Lady Diana gushed. "He's my chiropractor. Aren't you, Walter? I don't know how I could survive without him. That's why he's coming to America with me. I never know when I might need him, night or day. Once my neck gave way when I was at the ballet. Just gave way! All I could do was stare down into my lap. Fortunately it was *Swan Lake* and I detest *Swan Lake*. I keep expecting one of the *corps de ballet* to lay an egg."

"Walter" was buttoning up his trousers and fastening his cufflinks. He looked extremely disgruntled.

"He has to change, you know, into his white uniform, don't you, Walter?" explained Lady Diana. "That's why he's somewhat, well, *déshabillé*." Rather impatiently, she added, "Hurry up, now, Walter. It doesn't take all night just to do up your cufflinks, does it?"

"No, madam," said 'Walter, in a voice as heavy as West Indian treacle being poured into a bowl of junket. "Whatever you say, madam."

"People are so *sarcastic* these days," said Lady Diana twitchily. "Don't you find them so? Even people you don't expect to be sarcastic, like policemen. Do you know what a policeman said to me the other day, by St. James's Park?"

"No," said Walter. "What?"

Dick glanced uncomfortably across at the "chiropractor" and then back to Lady Diana.

"I think I've c-come at an aw, at an aw, at an awkward moment," he said. He replaced his cap on his head and tugged the peak to straighten it.

"You're not *going!*" cried Lady Diana. "But why? You don't think that Walter and I were—well, you don't think that Walter and I—"

"I just think I've c-come at an," said Dick. And then, while both Lady Diana and "Walter" stared at him with furrowed and melodramatic expressions, he said, "awkward moment."

Lady Diana hesitated for a second or two, trying to decide whether to storm off into her bedroom, burst into tears, or fling herself down on the couch in frustration and despair. It didn't take her long to decide to fling herself down on the couch in frustration and despair.

"You're like all the rest of them, aren't you, Dick? A reputation counts for so much. You believe what people have told you about me, rather than what you've seen for yourself. Well, if that's the way you want it, who cares? I've still got the rest of the night to get drunk. Perhaps I'll throw myself off the ship."

"You c-can't d-do that," said Dick.

"And why not?"

"It's against c-company regulations. No d-diving off the side. No j-jettisoning of r-rubbish."

"So that's what I am? Rubbish? Rubbish that can't even throw itself away because of company regulations? Walter, I feel a twinge coming on. Walter, stand near me!"

"Walter" sighed, and took one or two reluctant steps in Lady Diana's direction. She threw him a poisonous little sidelong glance as he continued to wrestle with his collar stud. "God, you can't even trust your own chiropodist."

"I thought he was a chiropractor," said Dick. He felt stifled by something that could have been nasal congestion, but felt more like jealousy.

"My dear, they're *almost* the same thing," said Lady Diana distractedly. "But really, if you want to go, go. I don't care what you think of me."

"As a m-matter of fact I think very huh, very huh, very highly of you," said Dick.

"*Highly?*" asked "Walter," as if it were one of those fashionable new slang words like "darb."

"Yes, Walter," said Lady Diana. "Some people do. Poor Dicky, have I misjudged you? Have I been mean?"

"W-when I t-talked about the rubbish, I was only quoting a r-regulation," Dick told her. He took off his cap again and tucked it under his arm. "I didn't mean to suh, to suh, to suggest that—"

"Walter" grimaced as he inserted his last stud and reached for his necktie. "That's all settled, then, is it?" he asked Lady Diana. "I can go now?"

"Yes, dear, I suppose so," said Lady Diana. "I'll see you tomorrow, shall I, for the usual treatment?"

"Hmph," said "Walter." He shook on his jacket, arranged his triangular white display of handkerchief in his breast pocket, and then marched out of the cabin without even saying goodbye.

"Extraordinary chap," remarked Dick as the door closed behind him.

"Yes," agreed Lady Diana in a tired voice. "I like to think so."

Dick sat down on the corner of the couch, his cap on his knees. "How long have you had t-treatment from him?"

"Treatment? Oh, years. Years and years and years. Would you mix me another Boopa-Doopa, there's a good boy."

Dick took her glass and went to the cocktail cabinet. He sniffed at

359

the dregs of what she had been drinking, and frowned at himself in the pink-tinted mirror at the back of the cabinet, engraved with leaves. "I'm n-not entirely s-sure what a Boo, what a Boo—"

"Ice, gin, blue curacao, bitters, and a cherry, my pet."

"Sounds absolutely revolting."

"Well, it is. But to drink anything at two o'clock in the morning is revolting, so why not go the whole hog?"

"L-listen," said Dick, as he stirred up a Boopa-Doopa with a swizzle stick, and mixed himself a very strong in and French, "I w-want you to know that what happened last n-night was—w-well, it wasn't my n-normal sort of thing."

"I would never have guessed," Lady Diana told him. "You're an absolute natural."

"B-but it c-can't lead anywhere," said Dick. "I m-mean, once we've got to New York . . . "

"Do you *want* it to lead anywhere?" asked Lady Diana. She sounded surprised.

"It depends what you mean by l-lead," said Dick uncertainly. He gave her his amateur version of a Boopa-Doopa, which she peered at closely, sipped once, and then put down carefully on her small side table, as if it were a mixture of Pepto-Bismol and hemlock.

"You don't want us to be *lovers*, do you?" asked Lady Diana. "I mean, we *can't* be lovers."

"I thought perhaps we were already," Dick told her. "If that wasn't acting like luh, like luh, like lovers, what we did last night, well . . . "

She leaned forward and kissed him on the nose. "You're so sweet! Your incoherence excites me beyond all bounds! A stuttering swain!"

"You d-don't have to be rude about it."

"But I *do*, my darling. You have to learn to live with it! After all, you'll be living with it long after we've waved goodbye."

"I'm not sure I *want* to w-wave goodbye."

Lady Diana's eyes widened. "You're not—*stuck* on me, are you?"

Dick looked down at his cap badge. "A little," he admitted.

"But after this morning, I couldn't possibly imagine that you'd take me seriously."

"I d-didn't, at fir— At first," said Dick. He swallowed a large mouthful of gin and wiped his mouth with the back of his fingers. "But you're n-not like the others, are you?"

"I'm sorry, dear," said Lady Diana. "I was only half listening. I'm not like the other what?"

"W-well, the other women."

"Oh, I see. And that's why you acted so jealous when you came in?"

"J-jealous?"

"*Aren't* you jealous?"

"I suppose I am."

"God, I can't stand jealous men. What on earth gives you, a stuttering steamship officer, the right to be jealous of me? I've been adored by earls, by princes, by peers. I've even been proposed to by a nizam. Do you know what a nizam is?"

"Some k-kind of Indian chappie, I should think."

"My God. You're so *ignorant*. How could I take you to Ascot?"

"Ascot's g-going to be over by the t-t-time we g-get back to—"

Lady Diana held on to his protuberant ears and kissed him all over his face—dozens of little kisses, like forget-me-nots, so that he could scarcely breathe.

"Oh, Dicky, you're such a wonderful sort! But don't take me too seriously. I've seen too much, and loved too much, and all I want is a few days of fun. Life's so short on fun these days, don't you think so? And this is my chance, four days on the good ship *Arcadia*. Wooed and seduced by the wonderful Dicky Charles."

Dick clinked the ice in his gin and French and looked abashed. "It's nice of you to say so," he said.

Lady Diana lifted her drink, peered at it dubiously, and then put it down again. "I *was* going to say that I'll drink to that," she said, more to herself than to Dick.

"W-well, *I'll* drink to it," said Dick, and tipped back his gin and French in one long swallow.

Lady Diana stood up, reached behind her, and released the thin ribbon which held her négligée together. She only had to shake her shoulders once and it dropped down to her hips, revealing her long dimpled back, with the pattern of moles on the left shoulder blade, just where Dick remembered them from last night.

Lady Diana had told him that the moles were in the pattern of Sagittarius, her birth sign. The outlook for Sagittarians for 1924 was *an unexpected windfall from an official quarter.* Lady Diana had taken this as a good omen, although she had refused to tell Dick why. "Women must keep their mysteries," she had said, turning away.

Dick, in spite of himself, and in spite of his tiredness, found that he was aroused. He put down his gin glass next to her scarcely touched Boopa-Doopa and stood up. He approached Lady Diana from behind and laid his hands on her shoulders. He kissed her hair, and then her cheek. She smelled of something so exquisite and so expensive that both his heart and his pay cheque began to tremble. She was so small, and so erotic! He could think of nothing else but her upraised hindquarters, her cheeky smiles, and the sexual games she had played with him.

He said, "I may stutter sometimes, you know. But that duh, that duh, that doesn't make me any less of a man."

"I know," said Lady Diana simply, letting down the front of her négligée so that her small breast was bared to the lamplight. "But you mustn't ever forget that you don't own me. Not a bit of me. Not even one toenail, when it's clipped off. Not even one hair, if it falls out. You don't even own the waft of my French knickers, when I toss them into the laundry basket."

Dick kissed the side of her neck and licked inside her ear. "You c-can be d-dashed c-cruel sometimes, c-can't you?" he said.

"Of course," she said. "And don't you adore it?"

She turned around and seized the buckle of his pants. With three quick jerks, one to the left, one to the right, one to the left, she unfastened his belt, and then her hand ran deftly down his fly buttons as if she were shelling peas. His redness bobbed up out of his woollen underpants, and he thought to himself, in delight and fright, "It's happening again! So quickly, and it's happening again!"

And he didn't once think of "Walter," back in his own cabin, who was fitting on his toupee and putting on his small dark glasses, and preparing himself for an early breakfast as the *Arcadia*'s mystery man.

He was too involved in sighing, as he anointed Lady Diana's insides.

Fifty

Breakfast on Thursday morning was an especially grand affair. The first-class dining lounge had been festooned with garlands of roses, which had been specially prepared before the voyage by the royal florists in London and stored in pink tissue in the *Arcadia*'s cold room, behind the bacon sides and legs of lamb.

The lounge was sparkling with nine o'clock sunshine, and fragrant with the scent of pink and white floribunda. Twelve pretty young girls in Greek tunics with roses in their hair flittered between the tables in a free-form interpretation of music from Ravel's ballet *Daphnis and Chloe*, while stewards carried out shining chafing dishes that were heaped with glistening yellow mountains of freshly scrambled eggs, crisply fried bacon, fried whitebait, curried kidneys, brains in black butter, and shoals of brown varnished Loch Fyne kippers.

Champagne was served, and so was Dragon Smoke tea from south-western China, and Costa Rican coffee. The table linen was all pink damask, and every table was strewn with white roses. Everyone had dressed up for breakfast, the gentlemen in white flannel blazers and white ducks, and the ladies in a variety of pink and white frocks of silk and laon and crepe de chine. "The whole lounge had the appearance of being in a *froth,*" wrote the society editor of the newly established newsmagazine *Time.*

Mark was waiting for Catriona at a small circular table in the corner of the lounge opposite the orchestra. As she made her entrance, he stood up, his tan looking darker than ever against his perfectly cut blazer. The crest of American TransAtlantic was embroidered in red and gold on his breast pocket.

Catriona, a little pale, was escorted in by Edgar Deacon. She had chosen to wear not pink or white, although it had been requested that all first-class passengers should do so, but a mauve crepe dress with flowing sleeves, a black feather belt, and a skirt that was formed of layers of triangular drapes of pleated fabric. She also wore a matching cloche hat, in mauve, with one long ribbon which reached down as far as her hem.

"You look just a little bit more than perfect," said Mark, reaching out and taking her hand. There was a bustle of conversation as people around them noticed the way they greeted each other.

"And you look just a little bit like Rudolph Valentino on a yachting holiday." Catriona smiled.

"That's a compliment?" Mark asked Edgar. But Edgar refrained from smiling or from answering. George Welterman was sitting only two tables away, talking in a loud voice to Charles Schwab, and Edgar didn't want to look as if last night's crisis had disturbed him.

"Enjoy your breakfast," Edgar told Catriona, pushing in her chair for her. "I must go and have a word with Mr. Philips."

Rudyard Philips, in his white cruising uniform, was sitting in the captain's chair recounting his story about the mixed-up shoes on the *Aurora* (Grand Duchess Marie, America's ranking Russian exile, had found a pair of men's tennis shoes, size ten, outside her door in the morning instead of her silver evening slippers, size four, and had illustrated her displeasure to the captain by wearing them in to dinner).

Edgar leaned over and said quietly, "I'm sorry to interrupt you, Mr. Philips. But a quick word in your ear."

Rudyard excused himself, and followed Edgar outside to the anteroom, where they stood in a corner by a large overhanging *Helzine soleirolii,* or baby tears.

"You seem to be filling in for Sir Peregrine very adequately," said Edgar.

"Thank you," said Rudyard. "I am a master in my own right, of course."

Edgar nodded. "I've spoken to Dr. Fields again," he said. "Sir Peregrine isn't likely to regain the use of his right arm, it seems, nor his right leg—not without months and possibly years of treatment."

"I see," said Rudyard.

Edgar laid a hand on Rudyard's gold-braided shoulder. "We have to face up to the fact that this is the end, as far as Sir Peregrine's seagoing career is concerned, although he may probably wish to stay with Keys as an adviser. We're going to need a new master for the *Arcadia*, and a new fleet commodore."

"Yes," Rudyard replied. He was standing as straight-backed as he could.

"Obviously you're hankering to get back to the *Aurora*," Edgar went on, "but under the circumstances the board is going to have to ask you to take over as captain of the *Arcadia* for the rest of this voyage, and also for the return run to Liverpool. After that—well, it's no secret that the future of the company is in the balance."

"Taking command of the *Arcadia* is scarcely a hardship, Mr. Deacon." Rudyard smiled. "And didn't I understand you to say that IMM have guaranteed the jobs of all of our officers and crew?"

"As far as economically possible, they have," said Edgar. "But what I really want you to understand is that it may be two or three months before we can find a suitable replacement for Sir Peregrine, and even when we've found him, he's going to have to spend quite a few weeks familiarising himself with the ship. So you may be away from the *Aurora* for some time."

Rudyard felt as if his stomach had dropped down one of the *Arcadia* 's lift shafts. He could see himself in one of the engraved mirrors on the other side of the anteroom, and his mouth had opened. He looked like a bystander in a news photograph of a serious accident. The serious accident, however, had happened to him.

"You're, er, happy with that arrangement?" asked Edgar, a little puzzled by Rudyard's silence. His voice was very clipped, very office-*wallah*."

"I sort of took it for granted that *I* was next in seniority," Rudyard told him, trying hard not to sound desperate. "After Sir Peregrine, I mean."

"Yes?" said Edgar, obviously expecting him to say more.

"Well, I assumed that if anything were to happen to Sir Peregrine . . . I mean, I didn't think that anything like *this* would happen . . . but if he retired . . . or decided he wanted a shorebound billet rather than an ocean going job . . . well, I assumed that I would take over the *Arcadia*."

"You *are* taking over," said Edgar.

"But only temporarily," Rudyard told him.

"Yes," said Edgar.

"But why? I thought I was the natural successor. I've had enough years at sea, damn it. I'm experienced enough."

Edgar put his arm further around Rudyard's shoulders and spoke to him in a clipped, fatherly tone. "We know that, Mr. Philips. We're aware of your record, and how long you've been serving the company, don't y'know. But the thing is, when it comes to making a choice for commodore, you have to think of the way the shipping company is going to appear in the eyes of the travelling public. Do you understand what I'm saying? We need somebody for commodore who is not only experienced but *looks* experienced. A weathered seadog, if you like. A man with presence, and dignity, and age."

"You don't think I have dignity?"

"Mr. Philips, that's not what I'm saying at all. I'm simply saying that we now have to look for a commodore who fits the public's idea of what a commodore should be."

"You're passing me over because I haven't got a grey beard?"

"Of course not. And, in any case, you're not being passed over. You're still captain of our second-most luxurious steamship. You can't sneeze at the *Aurora.*"

"The *Aurora* is not the *Arcadia,* Mr. Deacon, and you damn well know it. The *Aurora* is old, underpowered, and she has about as much elegance as the Liver Building."

"I've always thought of the Liver Building as rather dramatic," said Edgar.

"It may well be," Rudyard retorted, "but you wouldn't want to put to sea in it, would you?"

"Mr. Philips, I think you're exaggerating," said Edgar. "The position is that if Keys remains independent, the board will shortly choose a new commodore, and that in the meantime you are to be captain of the *Arcadia.* That is all."

"I don't think you quite understand," said Rudyard. He was so hot now with anger and fear and disappointment that he was sweating into his tight white collar like an attendant in a Turkish bath. "I've been counting on this promotion."

"Counting?" asked Edgar, cocking his head to one side. "I'm sorry?"

"I've been *counting* on it," Rudyard repeated, but he couldn't bring himself to say how much. His humiliation was agonising enough without having to admit to Edgar that only an hour ago he had sent a wireless message back to Toy, telling her that under no circumstances could he consider a career on land, and that he had found new happiness with another woman. Whether this woman was Louise Narron, or whether she was the *Arcadia,* even Rudyard himself had not quite been sure. But one thing was now certain: he wasn't going to get the *Arcadia,* even if his happiness depended on it.

"You shouldn't be too disappointed," Edgar was saying, although Rudyard was scarcely listening to him now. "If Keys is bought up by

IMM, you'll no doubt get the chance to command IMM ships, as well. Perhaps the *Mauretania.*"

Rudyard said abruptly, "I'd better get back to the passengers."

"Listen," said Edgar, "you didn't really believe that—well, you didn't think that you were automatically going to take over as commodore, did you? Because nobody ever said anything about that in writing. You weren't given that specific promise."

"No," said Rudyard. "Nobody gave me that specific promise."

Edgar looked relieved. "You'd better get back to your passengers then."

Rudyard returned to the dining lounge with two spots of high colour on his cheeks. The steward drew out his chair for him, and he sat down. He began to eat his bacon and sausage links with quick, mechanical gestures, nodding and smiling now and then at the passengers who sat opposite him. One of these was Baroness Zawisza, who this morning was in excellent spirits. Sabran had lost his last cent last night to Maurice Peace, and in an attempt to win just a little of his money back, he had given Maurice a note for five hundred pounds. He had lost all of that, too; and so he had been presented with no alternative but to return to the baroness and ask her to meet his debt. The baroness had gladly written him a cheque; but had demanded in return a whole night of slavish services, including one of her favourite delights, which was to be made love to while she was asleep. Or mostly asleep, anyway.

Baroness Zawisza said to Rudyard, "You're looking thoughtful, Captain. You were going to tell us about the time that you lost your propellers off the island of Crete."

Rudyard said, "I've just learned that I am not going to take over the *Arcadia* permanently."

It was unforgivable to share a company confidence with a passenger. But Rudyard was so mortified by what Edgar had said that the had to tell someone, and that someone couldn't be any other member of the ship's complement, and it especially couldn't be Louise Narron. He could see Louise's flaming red hair between Jack Dempsey and George Welterman, and he felt like throwing back his chair, stalking across the dining lounge, and strangling her.

Baroness Zawisza said, "You must be very disappointed."

"I'm—" began Rudyard loudly, but then, more softly, "I'm quite disappointed, yes. She's a marvellous vessel, you see. Quite unlike anything else on the Atlantic today, and that includes the *Mauretania.*"

Sabran, sitting next to the baroness, lit up a cigarette, took two or three sulky puffs at it, and then crushed it out into his kippers. Baroness Zawisza patted the poor boy's wrist, and said to Rudyard, "We all have our problems, you know. Once I was riding on the banks of the Wrka, and I met an old peasant who had fallen down under the weight of a load

366

of firewood. I wet his lips with Château Lynch-Bages as he lay there on the ground, and fed him a small piece of smoked quail. Then I rode on my way."

"He must have been very consoled," said Rudyard.

Sabran said, "Wee-meen! They are completely without mercy!"

Maurice Peace was thoroughly enjoying his breakfast. He sat with his napkin tucked into his collar, munching his way through bacon and whitebait, and alternately sipping coffee and soda. He had made a healthy profit from last night's cards, and the only possible cloud on his horizon was the fact that there were no clouds on the horizon. The day was clear and calm, and the *Arcadia* was making good time. He was wondering whether the best start to his morning might be to set fire to a few oily rags and push them down a ventilator shaft, so that the ship would have to slow down for a fire drill.

At the very far end of the lounge, however, Joe Kretchmer and Duncan Wilkes were in serious difficulties. They sat facing each other, divided only by their dogged rivalry and by seventeen different platefuls of breakfast, including plovers' eggs and pickled head cheese. Duncan Wilkes had nearly given up at the sight of more brains. He had only just managed to gag down two of them last night. Now, here they were again, fried crisp on the outside, and swimming in black butter, with capers.

Henrietta Chibnall, Mr. Kretchmer's second, was growing bored and rather nauseated by the whole affair. Mr. Kretchmer had not yet been spectacularly sick, as she had hoped, and she was growing increasingly sensitive to his grunts and puffs of abdominal exertion, not to mention the grease which kept running down his chin, and which it was her duty to mop up.

Grace Bunyon on the other hand had almost completely fallen in love with Duncan Wilkes, although she was concerned that by the end of the voyage, he would be far too fat to be good for anything, let alone romance. But she bravely mopped his sweating forehead for him, and quoted Shakespeare to give him encouragement. What she didn't know was that Duncan Wilkes, within the orderly caverns of his mind, had decided that his heart was probably not going to be capable of withstanding this constant feasting, and that by the time the *Arcadia* docked in New York he would be dead.

The prospect did not alarm him. Throughout his life, as he had built up his small newspaper empire, he had always learned to abide by the decision that he had taken, whether they were good decisions or bad ones. He had decided, wisely or foolishly, to compete with Joe Kretchmer in an eating contest, and he was prepared to die rather than to give in. He believed quite firmly in a Victorian Heaven, in which gentle angels in long nightgowns flew about amongst the clouds with feathered wings; and in which the righteous and the perservering were allowed to sit at God's table, irradiated by the sort of warm tangerine-coloured light you see on summer evenings in the Midwest.

He would miss the crabmeat *crêpes louise* at the Chicago Pump Room; and he would miss his St. Bernard named Flong (after the pâpier-maché moulds in which hot metal was poured to make plates for his newspaper's rotary presses). But, on the whole, he was content to go out eating.

Maurice Peace, with his uncanny nose for anything that smelled like a loser, watched Duncan Wilkes and noted his silent internal resignation with relish. He had seen too much death in the name of a good bet to feel sentimental about it.

Mark Beeney, who had ordered nothing more for breakfast than a pink grapefruit, three pieces of toast, and a bottle of Mme Bollinger's finest champagne, glanced across at the Wilkes-Kretchmer table and grinned. "How those two manage it, I just don't know. I doubt if they'll ever want to eat again."

Catriona said, "Mr. Deacon says it's good for publicity. Particularly since Mr. Wilkes owns his own newspapers."

The steward came around, and Catriona ordered eggs Benedict and coffee.

"You're feeling better?" asked Mark.

"I think so. Dr. Fields gave me some sleeping pills, and I think that I'm over it now. But I don't know how *he's* got the nerve just to sit there as if nothing had happened," she said, nodding towards George Welterman.

"That's George Welterman's style. You'll just have to grin and bear it. He's the original thick-skinned gorilla."

"Did you know he had a burn across his chest?" said Catriona. "It's terrible. Really deep, livid scars. He must have done it himself. It spells out the name Myrtle."

"He's screwy," said Mark. It was obvious that he didn't really want to talk abou t George Welterman; and that, for Catriona, was a quietly reassuring sign of his affection for her. A man who really loves you doesn't want to discuss any of the other men you've known. He has an interest in trying to pretend that he's the first. The first to buy you jewels, the first to give you your taste for Bollinger champagne. The first to love you so that the stars seem to burst above your bed.

Catriona laid her hand on the pink tablecloth, among the white roses, and Mark laid his darkly tanned hand on top of hers.

"I feel as if I don't have anything to give you," she said, in a quiet voice. "I feel as if George Welterman took it all away from me."

"That's nonsense," said Mark. "I can understand it, but it's nonsense."

"You really think so?" asked Catriona. The steward arrived with a silver coffeepot and poured her a cup of coffee.

Mark leaned forward and spoke to Catriona confidentially. "George Welterman didn't take anything from you. All he did was to destroy his own dignity."

Catriona would have loved to be able to believe him. But the shock of being attacked by George Welterman had abated, only to leave her with a terrible sensation of emptiness. She felt warm towards Mark. She hoped that she could trust him. But somehow the warmth had very little oxygen to sustain it, within that emptiness; and the trust had nothing to lean on. She seemed to have been betrayed by so many more people than George Welterman alone. She seemed to have been betrayed by everyone who allowed a man to do what he wanted with a girl, and then advised her that to complain about it would be more trouble than it was worth. Life and Business have to go on, Catriona. Don't rock the boat for the sake of an inconsequential rape. And, anyway, how can you ever *prove* that it was a rape? The way girls dress these days . . . the way they behave in Scott Fitzherald novels . . . why, you were lucky to be raped by somebody who was white and middle-aged and respectable.

You were lucky it wasn't somebody from steerage!

Mark said, "I'm opening my mouth and putting my foot in it, aren't I?"

Catriona nodded. Quite suddenly she was near to tears.

"I'm sorry," he said, withdrawing his hand. "I shouldn't have been so insensitive. I guess I deserve a kick in the head."

"You're not insensitive," said Catriona. "It's just that—well, what happened—it's going to take me a little while to get over it."

"I know," said Mark. "I feel like a failure for not killing him."

"You would have killed him?" asked Catriona.

"I felt like it. I even opened my desk drawer and took out my gun and loaded it. But killing George Welterman wouldn't have solved any problems. It would only make them worse. The genius of men like George is that they make themselves so obnoxious when they're alive that you know damn well they're going to be absolutely intolerable when they're dead."

"I suppose you're right," said Catriona. "But thank you for thinking of it. He's such a toad."

Mark said, "Don't thank me too much. My motives were pretty selfish, too. In fact *very* selfish. I didn't particularly want to be sent to prison, not when I had the chance of spending more time with you."

"You're banana-oiling again."

"Not a bit of it." Mark smiled. "In fact, there was something I wanted to ask you. Something serious."

"How serious?" asked Catriona. The steward had just brought her eggs, and set them in front of her. She looked up at Mark and in that moment, when she saw his face, she knew what he was going to ask her. *God*, she thought, he's desperately handsome. In that white flannel blazer, with that curly hair of his, he looks absolutely the bee's knees. And I know that I'm pretty, and I know what he's going to ask me, but please God don't let him ask me. It's too soon after George; and it's too soon after Nigel; and it's too soon for me. I've only just begun to discover that what I thought was sophistication was only confidence, the sheer confidence of being twenty-one; and I've only just discovered that there's a whole complicated unknown world going on out there, and that too many people are expecting me to understand what it's all about, when I don't.

Mark said, "You're not ready for this, are you?"

"For what?" she asked him, breathlessly.

"I can see it in your face. I'm sorry. I think I've made a fool of myself."

"Tell me," she insisted.

He shook his head. "Forget I said anything. Let's just talk about business."

"I don't want to talk about business. I want to know what you were going to say."

"I was going to say—" began Mark, but then he shook his head again, and made a production out of spreading his toast with Oxford marmalade.

"If you don't tell me, I shall do something drastic," said Catriona. "Like *scream*."

Mark looked up from his toast and smiled. "I'd rather you didn't scream," he said. "Too many people have hangovers around here. What I was going to say was that I don't want this voyage to be the last I see of you. In fact, I'd like you to get off the *Arcadia* when she docks in New York and spend a week or two with me in Boston. You could take Alice along as your chaperone."

More seriously, Mark said, "I'm stuck on you, Catriona, if you want to know the truth. It sounds too sudden. It sounds absurd. It probably sounds like a whole lot of applesauce. But that's the way I feel. I love you. You're the cat's miaow."

Catriona hesitated for a moment, but then she touched his hand again, and said, "What happened last night—"

Mark made a face. "To some people, what happened last night may make a difference. I don't know. It doesn't to me. I know what George Welterman is like and I know that it wasn't your fault. I just hope that you can forgive me for not getting there earlier."

Catriona said, "You'll have to give me some time to think."

"I know. Well—maybe I shouldn't have asked you at all. I didn't want you to get the wrong idea."

"How could I possibly get the wrong idea about you?" asked Catriona.

"Well—"

"You said you love me. I believe you. All I have to think about is what I'm going to do about it."

Mark raised his hands as if he were being stuck up in a bank robbery. "You've got me, Miss Keys, just any way you want me. But let me know soon, won't you?"

As Catriona leaned across the table to kiss his cheek, Mark lifted his eyes for just a fraction of a second and saw Marcia Conroy appear in the doorway of the dining lounge, dressed in pink and white. Marcia's face was open and expectant for a moment, until she caught sight of Mark and Catriona together. It was too late to do anything; too late to pretend. So Mark reached up and held Catriona's cheek with his fingertips, delaying the kiss, and that was in spite of the murmur of gossip all around them, and in spite of the fact that Marcia had turned around and stormed angrily away, pushing aside a steward carrying a tray of cocktails, and tearing away a whole green tendril of baby tears from the anteroom.

Life on an ocean liner thrives on gossip and society scandal, and everybody saw what had happened, even if they didn't understand the full implications of it. Only one first-class passenger wasn't there as a witness, because he felt that he had something far more important to do. Harry Pakenow had returned to third class.

Fifty-one

Harry had already tried once that morning to gain access to the after hold, next to the ship's laundry and immediately beneath the swimming pool, where the motorcars were stored during the voyage. The hold was below the waterline, and the only door was marked NO ENTRY WATERTIGHT DOOR. He had asked one of the crew if it was possible for him to see inside, but the crewman had shaken his head and said that it was more than his life was worth to let a passenger into the hold. "Just supposing she rolled, and you got yourself crushed to death," the seaman had said. "What the 'ell would I do then?"

The purser had a key, the seaman had told him. If the purser said it was all right for him to take a look, then it was all right for him to take a look, but otherwise no.

It simply hadn't occurred to Harry that he would find it almost impossible to get into the motorcar hold. He stood for a long while in the passageway outside the hold, his hand held over his mouth, looking like a character from a Mack Sennett house party in his borrowed morning suit with rumpled trousers and sausage-tight vest. It was just his luck that the one man who could give him admission to the hold was the one man aboard the Arcadia whom he disliked the most, and who was least likely to assist him. What would a third-class passenger like you want with all those first-class motors, squire? he would ask. No good ogling *them*, squire. You'll never be able to afford even *one*. You'll never be able to afford even one *wheel* off one of them.

That was why Harry went back to the steerage deck and looked for Philly and Lydia.

It was breakfast time in the third-class dining room. The passengers sat at long tables covered with red and white gingham cloths, while the stewards served them with a choice of fruit juices, bacon, eggs, porridge, kippers, and toast. For an extra threepence you could have a meatball, or *koteleti;* and for sixpence you could have black pudding, baked beans, and fried potatoes. The surcharges were not company policy, but the stewards and the chefs made a regular practice of offering the steerage a few little extra tidbits at reasonable prices. If any of the teachers or students of Polish immigrants had been able to afford it, they could have had glasses of champagne at three shillings the glass, or poached turbot (damaged during serving, but otherwise perfect) for two and two pence.

Most of the third class, however, were travelling on a tightly restricted budget, and those who had few extra shillings to spend were either too embarrassed to eat a plateful of black pudding and potatoes in front of those who only had a small kipper in oatmeal, or preferred to save their money for tonight's beer.

Harry bumped into Philly just as she was cooming out of the women's room with her nose and her knees powdered, and her lipstick freshly painted. She was wearing a short emerald-green frock and a cheap green feathery hat.

"Harry!" she said, "I thought you were travelling with the nobs now."

"Well, I'm supposed to be," Harry told her. "But the trouble is that I need some help."

"Help?" said Philly, suspiciously, lifting up one leg so that she could adjust her rolled-down stockings.

"It's nothing difficult," said Harry. "It's just that it's slightly shady. Do you know what I mean?"

"*Shady?*" asked Philly.

"Ssh," Harry told her, sealing his lips with his finger. "The fact is, I'm something of a bootlegger. I'm trying to ship some contraband liquor into New York. I was given a contract to supply a speak called Hoyle's Homelike Club on Second Avenue. They're a top-class place, and they asked me for some good Scotch whisky and London gin."

"Well, so?" asked Philly. Like most American college students, she was unimpressed by hooch, or the men who dealt in it. Hooch was a way of life.

"Well, the fact is that one of the fellows in first class is a contraband agent. I wouldn't have known about him unless they'd let me go up there. He's had a tip-off from someone in Liverpool that I hid the liquor in one of the automobiles which is parked in the hold, and when we dock at New York he's going to be waiting beside that car to arrest me."

"Is it really beautiful in first class?" asked Philly irrelevantly.

"It's wonderful," said Harry impatiently.

"But is it *really* beautiful?"

"It's the bee's knees. But, please, will you help me?"

"You're worried because some cop is going to be waiting by some car to pull you in? Well, you're ridiculous. You shouldn't. All you have to do is walk straight off the ship, and leave the cop to wait by that car until his beard grows. How can he ever prove it's yours?"

Harry took Philly's arm. "Philly," he said, "you don't understand. I spent all of my money on that liquor. Everything I made in three years of hard work is invested in it. If I can't hide it, and sell it in New York, then I'm going to be down on my backside again. Nothing between me and the sidewalk except a red cotton patch."

"But what can *I* do?" asked Philly.

"It's very easy," said Harry. "All you have to do is distract the purser while I slip into his office and borrow his key."

"Distract?" asked Philly suspiciously.

"You know what I mean. Act all vampish. Seduce him."

Philly wrinkled up her nose. She was one of the free and rebellious young jazz babies, one of the dancers in the dark, but she didn't like her morals to be taken for granted. She wasn't what her grandmother would have called "a scarlet harlet."

Harry took out a cigarette. "There's a century in it for you, if we pull it off. How does that sound?"

"A hundred?"

"You're hearing me."

Philly said, "Well, okay. But only for *distracting*, right? Nothing else. I'm not losing my *purity* for a lousy hundred."

"Your purity?" asked Harry. "What do you think we were doing the other night, washing out our smalls and singing spirituals?"

"We didn't do *anything*," said Philly. "Just because a girl plays arond a bit, that doesn't have to mean that she's *deflowered*, does it? I had a good time, that's all. You can't blame a girl for having a good time. But

I'll still go to the altar pure. That's when I *do* go to the altar."

"So you'll tell your fiancé you're a *virgin?*"

"Of course I will."

"So what's it eventually going to take to deflower you?" Harry asked. "Dynamite?"

Almost immediately, he wished he hadn't said that. It was the kind of circumstantial evidence that juries adored, especially since the yellow press had made everybody, house wives and roof painters and janitors alike into shrewd legal experts. "Anarchist talked of dynamite before luxury liner blast." Mind you, he thought,—it was doubtful if anybody would survive the sudden sinking of the *Arcadia*, himself included. If he ever appeared in any kind of court, it would probably be in Purgatory.

Philly pouted. "You don't really care for me at all, do you? You're the kind that just uses a girl, then throws her away like a cigarette butt. Dynamite, indeed. The nerve!"

"I'm sorry," said Harry, blinking behind his spectacles. "I didn't mean to be sarcastic."

"You're really sure you can pay me a hundred?"

Harry nodded. "As soon as I get paid for the liquor. If you give me your address, I'll mail you a certified cheque."

"Well . . . it would help with schoolbooks."

He took her hands, and squeezed them. "You're terrific. I knew you'd understand."

They went up in the lift to the bridge deck. Philly was nervous about entering the exclusive and perfumed domain of the cabin-class passengers, but Harry put his arm around her waist and reassured her. "I'm a hero. They'll let me do anything."

He led her along to Monty Willowby's office. Monty (although they couldn't have known it) had just returned from an unsuccessful foray to Baron Zawisza's stateroom in an attempt to unscrew her lavatory seat. To his chagrin, he had been interrupted by Krysia, her maid, who had returned to the stateroom to fetch the baroness her freshwater pearl earrings (the baroness often changed her jewels four or five times a day). Monty had blustered out the excuse to Krysia that he was checking a complaint about noises in the plumbing, and rapidly left, his round stomach bobbing up and down like a beachball at an English seaside resort. He wasn't in a very good humour when Harry knocked at his door.

"Ah, our gallant hero," he said, snappily. "Not at breakfast? Grand breakfast this morning. Something worth dressing up for."

"Um, I was just wondering if it would be possible for me to take this young lady into breakfast," said Harry.

Monty said, "What? This young lady? From steerage, is she?"

"I do think the company prefer to call it third class these days?" Harry told him.

Monty glanced at him with an expression that plainly meant Don't get clever with me, squire. You may be a hero, but you're steerage, and if I want to call you steerage, then I will.

Out loud, though, he said, "I don't think that's going to be possible, squire, on account of the catering arrangements."

"Oh, I'm sure they'll have enough bacon and eggs to go round," said Harry. "She doesn't eat much, do you, love?"

Philly tittered. Harry thought, God, I told you to be vampish, not squirm and giggle around like a nine-year-old.

Monty said, "It's a question of seating, squire. And timing. And it's a question of *dress*, too. First-class ladies were asked this morning to dress in white or pink, to suite the decor. White or pink. Whereas this young lady—he looked Philly up and down, eyeing the cheap emerald frock and bedraggled feather hat, as if she had worn them on purpose to offend him —"well this young lady is in *green*. Very distinctly *green*."

Harry was looking around the office for keys. He wasn't sure, but he thought he could glimpse a varnished wooden key board on the wall of the small office at the back, where the ship's safe and deposit boxes were kept. He could see the gleam of metal through the crack in the door, and what looked like part of a name tag.

"Green?" he said to Monty Willowby. "Well, I can tell you something. If there's one thing this young lady *isn't*, it's green."

Either Monty didn't see the humour in this remark, or else he didn't want to. He picked up a heap of papers, shuffled them noisily, and then looked up at Harry and Philly as if he couldn't understand why they were still there.

"It's not on, you know, squire. I'm sorry. It's not me, nor the management. *We* wouldn't object. It's the other passengers. They don't pay first-class fares to sit next to third-class people."

Philly, trying to be coquettish, said, "Couldn't you make a teentsy-weentsy exception, just for me?"

Monty shook his jowls in a treble negative.

Philly perched herself on the edge of Monty's desk, so that her skirt, already scandalously short by the standards of 1924, rose above her knees and revealed several pale inches of inner thigh. "You're such a cutie," she said, and let out a high-pitched giggle. "If I thought you weren't already surrounded by adoring women, do you know what I'd do?"

Monty stared up her skirt with eyes as suspicious as a hermit crab's. "I don't know," he said, "What would you do?"

"Why, I'd smothher you all over with kisses." Philly giggled and leaned forrward to stick a large bow-shaped kiss of fresh sticky lipstick on Monty's forehead.

Monty looked up at her, startled. The kiss seemed to have awakened him, like the Frog Prince. "You can't do that, miss," he said, clamping his hand over his forehead in horror.

"What do you mean, I can't? I just did!"

Monty said, "Listen, this is all very well. But rules are rules. And it doesn't matter what you do—"

Philly giggled again, hopped down from the table, and immediately sat herself in Monty's lap. "You're so sweet!" she told him, plinking the tip of his nose with her fingertips. "How come you have to worry about regulations, a sweet guy like you?"

Monty tried to wrestle her off his lap without actually touching her anywhere embarrassing. But all she did was cling around his neck, kick her legs in the air, and shriek with laughter. Harry, meanwhile, smiling and nodding with as much innocence and dumbness as he could manage, side stepped his way around to the back of Monty's chair, towards the open door of the inner office. As Philly plastered Monty's cheeks with another kiss, and another, he quickly glanced behind him and saw that the ship's keys were indeed all hanging there, scores of them, and each one labelled.

"Miss, please!" exploded Monty. "Listen, please! Listen, get off!"

"She's quite incorrigible, Mr. Willowby, isn't she?" said Harry, in his slyest, most cretinous-sounding Bootle accent. "Can't do a thing with her."

But Monty, at last, gripped hold of both of Philly's wrists and managed to prize them free from his neck. He stood up, and she rolled off his lap onto the floor, where she sprawled with her skirt right up to her frilly pink step-ins. With an exaggerated expression of stage chivalry, Monty averted his eyes while she collected herself.

"Well *you're* a flat tyre," compalined Philly.

"I may well be just what you say I am, miss," said Monty. "But I'm afraid I've got far too much on my plate taking care of this ship and her passengers, not to mention the stewards and the stewardesses and God knows what else, and I simply can't—"

Monty suddenly turned and stared at Harry. Harry had been just about to shuffle himself sideways into the inner office, so that he could get a better look at the key board. Monty didn't say anything, but the look on his face was enough. You keep out, squire. Harry had to grin, and retreat towards the main cabin door like a schoolboy who has been caught near a greenhouse with a catapult in his hand.

Harry tried to appear nonchalant, but he was sweating with muscular tension. It was ten o'clock already, and if he couldn't get into that cargo hold by noon, the chances were high that Maruice Peace or George Welterman would discover his sticks of dynamite, and the *Arcadia* would sail into New York as smugly and as elegantly as she had left Liverpool, a floating triumph for decadence and oppression. Admittedly, Harry had learned some surprising new things about the rich since he had been

376

travelling in first class. They had appeared to him for the first time to be almost as human, and easily as idiosyncratic, and often as comradely, as any of the workers he had known. They were, despite their wealth, no more than people. But he knew tha the couldn't allow his political ideals to be compromised by his personal susceptibility to first-class comfort and to individual gestures of friendship and generosity. No matter how pleasant the rich may be, they upheld a society which Harry believed to be criminal. The ark of Mammon, her passengers and crew, would have to go to the bottom.

"I, er—I suppose that absolutely means I can't take this young lady into breakfast?" Harry asked.

"Sorry, squire," Monty told him. "Just not possible. Now, if you'll please excuse me . . . "

There was a moment of hiatus, a moment in which all three of them were posed in a tableau, as if waiting for fate or fortune to supply them with their next line. And fate, or fortune, did. Because Dick Charles suddenly appeared at the door, his face white, and said, "Mr. Willowby! Wanted urgently forward!"

"What's wrong?" asked Monty.

"C-can't tell you," stuttered Dick. "But quick! On the duh, on the duh, on the double, Mr. Deacon said."

Monty clenched his teeth at Harry and Philly and said, "You'll excuse me." Then he was off along the deck, waddling after Dick Charles like the walrus following the carpenter.

Harry spread his hands. "For one time in my life, I've actually had some luck," he said. "He's gone, and he's left his office open. I'm beginning to feel there might be a God up there after all."

Philly was busy adjusting her lipstick, screwing up her nose at herself in the mirror of her powder compact. "What a toad! If I'd known how ugly he was, I wouldn't even have agreed to do it! But you won't forget my hundred, will you?"

"Fifty."

"Fifty? What kind of bunk is that? You said a hundred."

"I said a hundred if it worked. It didn't work. It's only an accident he's gone off now and left the place unattended. You're lucky to get fifty."

"If you don't give me a hundred I'll scream rape."

"Go ahead, scream rape."

"All right. Rape!"

"That wasn't loud enough." said Harry. He was scanning the key board now, his fingers touching each hook in turn, looking for the label which read after cargo hold.

"What do you mean, that wasn't loud enough?" demanded Philly.

"You heard me," said Harry. Laundry, library, linen store (1st); linen store (2nd); linen store (3rd).

"How about this, then? Rape! I say, rape!"

"Louder," Harry urged her.

"Okay, smart buns. *Rape!*"

Claude Graham-White, who happened to have been passing the purser's office on his way forward, put his head through the door, and said, "I say, is everything all right?"

Philly said indignantly, "No, everything is *not* all right. This man's raping me."

Claude Graham-White looked first at Philly, with her fists planted indignantly on her hips, and then across into the inner office at Harry, who had his back to both of them.

"I don't like to split hairs," he said, "but that gentleman is standing eight feet away from you with his back turned. I rather fail to see how he can be—well, interfering with you in any way."

"Take my word for it," said Philly. "He's interfering with me."

"But how?"

"He said he'd pay me a hundred and now he says only fifty."

"Well," said Claude Graham-White, "I'm afraid I can scarcely intrude on a commercial transaction. Not really my business."

"Are you trying to suggest," squawked Philly. But Harry interrupted her by saying, "All right. A hundred. Now, just keep quiet."

Claude Graham-White went off, slightly bewildered, to his cabin. He had eaten one too many bloaters and felt a desire to return to his room and meditate on the meaning of digestion. Philly said, "Huh!" and crossed her arms as emphatically as she knew how. She felt cheated, although she wasn't quite sure why. It was probably because Monty Willowby had denied her entrance to the first-class dining lounge for breakfast, and despite the fact that Harry hadn't really intended to take her there at all, she had been made to feel distinctly steerage.

But Harry was more interested in the ship's keys. At last, he found a label which identified the long key which depended from the hook beneath it as belonging to the after carriage hold. He said to Philly, "Carriage? Do you think they could have used 'carriage' as a fancy word for 'automobile'?"

"How should I know?"

Harry bit his lip. Then he said, "I don't know. I suppose I'll just have to risk it," and he lifted the key off its hook. He also took the key which opened the door of the after cargo hold, just in case.

"Right," said Harry, ushering Philly out of the purser's cabin, and onto the deck. "You go back to the third-class deck. I'll see what I can do with these keys."

"But you won't forget the money? You won't go back on your promise? A hundred?"

Harry kissed her cheek. "A hundred it is. Just as soon as I sell my liquor. Now, you take the forward lift. I'll go down the stairs."

Harry was so intent on what he was doing that he didn't notice the strange feverish atmosphere on the deck. He collided with one or two passengers hurrying forward, and said, "Pardon me," because even after four years he still wasn't English enough to say, *"Excuse me,"* in that particularly frosty tone that the English used; but he didn't stop long enough to realise that anything unusual was happening.

He reached the first-class stairway and made his way down to the entrance to the first-class lounge. From there, he walked quickly along the corridor aft to the double doors which led down to the first-class cabin deck. Then down again, and again, and again, and again, until at least he reached the orlop deck, and jogged along to the door of the hold where the automobiles were stored. Gasping for breath, he tried the key, in the lock and it turned smoothly. He opened the heavy door and swung it forward with a deep feeling of relief. In his anxiety about finding the key, he had almost forgotten the magnitude of what he was about to do, or the danger to himself.

The hold was lit only by a dim row of inspection lamps on the bulkheads. It echoed to the deep drumming of the *Arcadia*'s turbines, and it smelled of heavy grease and automobile polish. Harry closed the door behind him and cautiously crossed the metal floor to the first row of automobiles—seven Rolls-Royces, all shining as if they were strange religious trophies being ferried from one land to another. Then another row of Pierce-Arrows and Austro-Daimlers.

It took him nearly ten minutes to locate Mark Beeney's Marmon. It was parked right against the rivet-studded wall of the ship's side, and for Harry that was perfect. The explosion would have maximum effect, so close to the plates of the hull, and would probably blast the ship open so wide that nobody would be able to staunch the flow of seawater in time. The *Arcadia* would sink to the bottom of the Atlantic like a brick.

Dennis had been right; it wasn't difficult to open the Marmon's trunk. All Harry needed was a short length of bent wire and a wide-bladed screwdriver (which he had found conveniently lying on the dashboard of a nearby Minerva Laundaulet). There was an odd springing noise, and the trunk dropped down flat, banging loudly on to its hinges. Alarmed by the bang, Harry crouched where he was for almost half a minute, listening. But the hold was silent, except for the vibration of the ship's engines. Harry sniffed. His nose always used to run when he was excited.

He took the clock which regulated his bomb out of the Marmon's trunk, and peered at it carefully in the lamplight. Then he wound it up, turn by turn, until the spring was as tight as it could go. He set it for twelve o'clock noon. He was just about to put it back when he heard a sound a little way away from him, a scuffling sound, like a football. He quickly raised his head and froze.

For almost a minute, there was nothing. But then he heard a high-pitched sneeze, and he gradually stood up, the bomb's clock mechanism still held in his hand. His chest was constricted with fear, and his heart seemed to be running and tumbling at three times its normal rate.

"Who's there?" he said, hoarsely.

There was another long, aching silence. Then hesitantly, one foot in front of the other, Lucille Foster appeared from behind the rear mud-guard of a Rolls-Royce, dressed in a yellow summer frock and wearing a white straw hat with yellow flowers around it.

"Lucille?" asked Harry. "What are you doing down here?"

Lucille didn't appear to be at all abashed. "I was just coming out from breakfast with Mrs. Hall I saw you running off down the stairs and I went after you."

"But why?"

"I don't know," she said. "You look peculiar, that's all. I thought you might need me."

"You should still be in bed."

"I'm all right now. Honestly. Even Dr. Fields said I was all right. I was only suffering from shock."

"But won't Mrs. Hall be looking for you? She'll be worried."

Lucille came closer and stood demurely with her white-gloved hands in front of her, dangling a small yellow purse with a gold clasp. "Of course she'll be looking for me. But that's not the point. The point is, I came to see what was the matter with you."

"There's nothing the matter with me."

"Then what are you doing with that clock?"

"Clock?"

"The one you're holding in your hand."

"Ah, *this* clock. Well, this clock—this clock is a *present.*"

"A present? For whom? Is it someone's birthday?"

"Sort of. One of the people I met in first-class last night . . . well, he was so generous to me. I decided to make him a gift."

"But why are you putting it in his car?"

Harry couldn't think why Lucille was asking him all these appalling questions. But then he thought, calm down, she's only a child. She's just curious. She likes me, she feels indebted to me. Naturally she wants to know what I'm doing in such blatantly odd circumstances. She's not trying to trick me or trap me. At least I hope to hell that she isn't.

"I, er—well, I was embarrassed," said Harry.

"Why were you embarrassed?"

"Well, it's a pretty cheap clock. I couldn't afford anything else. I didn't have the nerve to give it to him face to face. So I decided to hide it in the trunk of his car, and write a note on it saying thanks. He might keep it, he might decide to throw it away. But at least he won't have the embarrassment of having to pretend that he likes it . . . and that's what would happen if I gave it to him in person."

Lucille smiled. "For a Communist, you know, you're a very considerate person."

"Well, that's what Communism is all about. Being considerate to other people. At least, that's what it's *ideally* all about. It doesn't often seem that way."

"That's because you're only considerate to poor people. You don't think that wealthy people might have feelings as well."

"You're wrong," said Harry. "I believe that everybody has feelings."

"Mother would have said that you're deceiving yourself."

"Maybe she would. Everybody deceives themselves sometimes. Some people deceive themselves pretty much all of the time."

Lucille came forward and took Harry's arm. She looked up at him and her eyes were as clear and as confident as two flawless sapphires. "You don't deceive me, you know," she told him. "Not for a single minute."

He was uncomfortably conscious of the timing mechanism ticking away in his hand. "I don't?" he asked her.

"Not for a single minute," she said, shaking her head. "I knew when I first met you that you were the sort of person who could never hurt anybody. Mother used to know lots of men who hurt her. She was always saying, 'Oh, Friedrich, you have hurt me so badly.' Or, 'Oh, Jean, what you have done to me.' But you're not that type of man. I know you're not. Otherwise you wouldn't have climbed all the way up that crane and rescued me."

Harry looked away. "Well," he said, "I only did that because I like you."

"You would have done it for anybody. You're one of those very, very, very kind people. I know you are."

Harry looked at Lucille for a long speechless moment. She was smiling at him with such brightness and trust that he could scarcely speak. She always acted so sophisticatedl she talked and walked and behaved with all the blasé manners of the rich; and yet beneath her act she was utterly innocent, utterly uncritical of him, and she had invested in him all of her confidence, and so much of her affection. Perhaps such trust in the world and the people in it was the greatest gift that the rich could give to their children; a gift which the workers could never afford. Freedom from fear, freedom from want, and freedom from uncertainty. Always to feel safe, always to feel content, and always to be quite sure of the future—what a child's mind couldn't do if it was blessed with those three reassurances right from the beginning! Most working-class children could never hope to raise their minds above the plain relentless demands of having to earn their own living.

The thought gave Harry a sharp taste in his mouth, of defeat and regret, and of bitter jealousy. Yet he was so touched by Lucille's obvious trust in him that he was brought, by surprise, to the very brink of changing his mind about sinking the *Arcadia*.

"You're not unhappy about something, are you, not *still?*" asked Lucille.

Harry shook his head. "No. You couldn't call it unhappy."

"I am fond of you, you know."

"Yes, I'm beginning to realise that."

"When I was stuck up that crane, I didn't want anybody but you. Not anybody. Especially not Mrs. Hall."

"No, I know you didn't. And I'm flattered. I'm pleased, too."

Lucille looked around. "Are you going to stay down here, or are you going to come upstairs for elevenses? There's going to be a Punch-and-Judy for the children."

"Punch-and-Judy? I haven't seen a Punch-and-Judy for years."

"This is going to be a super one. With music."

Harry said, "Why don't you go on ahead of me? I won't be a minute. I just have to wrap up this clock nicely, and write a note, and close up the car's trunk."

"This is Mr. Beeney's car, isn't it?"

"You know it?"

"Of course. It's been in all the magazines. Was it Mr. Beeney who was so nice to you?"

Harry nodded.

"What if I tell Mr. Beeney that you've hidden a present in his car?"

"No, you mustn't do that. This is supposed to be a surprise."

"But what if I do?"

"Then I'll put you over my knee and spank you."

Lucille laughed brightly. "You'll have to catch me first!"

She ran round behind a large green Daimler. Harry dodged after her, around the other way. But she guessed what he was doing, and skipped across to the next row of cars. It was only because he quickly doubled back on himself and crept the length of a beige Pierce-Arrow, his head bent so that she wouldn't see him coming, that he was able to creep up behind her and catch her. "Got you!" He grinned.

He held her with his one free hand. She didn't try enough to struggle, but instead raised her own hand so that it rested gently on his. She said, in a soft and reflective voice, "Sometimes I have dreams that it's the end of the world."

"What do you mean by that?" He could hear the ticking of the clock, with less than two hours to run.

She smiled. "I don't know. I suppose I'm being silly."

Then she suddenly pulled free from him and danced away between the cars, laughing a clear bell-like laugh. Harry tried to chase her, but he collided with the rear wing of a Rolls-Royce, and his timing clock was knocked from his hand and onto the metal-plated deck.

He picked the clock up, terrified that it might have stopped. But when he put it to his ear, the ticking was as strong as before.

"You haven't broken it?" asked Lucille.

"No, it's still going."

"You really *would* have been embarrassed if you'd given it to him, and it didn't even *go!*"

"Yes," said Harry. Then, "Yes, I guess I would."

"Are you coming up for elevenses?" asked Lucille.

"Yes. Just give me a minute or two. I'll see you by the Palm Court."

"All right. And just remember I love you!"

Harry stood where he was, beside the Rolls-Royce, his timing clock in his hand, as Lucille danced away across the automobile hold, and waved to him at the door. When she had gone, he looked down at the clock and it said twenty after ten. *Just remember I love you,* she had said. A little girl who was already richer than he could ever dream of being. *Just remember I love you.*

He walked back to Mark Beeney's Marmon, and knelt down beside the open trunk. Quickly, expressionlessly, he wired up the timing clock and tucked it back into the trunk beside the sticks of dynamite.

He closed the trunk, and then he wedged the end of the screwdriver into the lock so that it would be almost impossible to open, even if somebody did come down here before twelve and attempt to check over the car.

Then he walked quickly back to the door of the hold, closed it, and locked it. The *Arcadia* is doomed, he thought. Nothing can save her now. In a few hours, she'll be down where she belongs, beside the *Titanic.* And that's the way all of these vainglorious barges should go, until the capitalists stop building them, and give their wealth away to the people who really deserve it.

Fifty-two

The excitement on the upper promenade decks which Harry had failed to notice as he descended to the automobile hold was caused by a frantic report that a first-class passenger, a lady, had been seen to leap off the rail of the boat deck into the sea.

She had been spotted by only two passengers, a retired brigadier and his wife who never took breakfast, because they believed it was bad for the liver. They had seen her climb up onto the rail, her white négligée flapping in the Atlantic breeze, and then dive with arms outstretched, a seagull, a flying crucifixion, into the boiling foam of the ship's wake. They had immediately rushed to the bridge and announced, "Lady overboard!"

All the time that Harry had been working on his timing clock, although he hadn't realised it, the *Arcadia* had been turning in a fast 180-degree turn, while passengers crowded the rails in an attempt to catch sight of the lady's body in the water. The rumour went flying around that it was a high-society suicide, and newspaper reporters scoured the passenger lists and drank even more whisky and water than usual as they tried frantically to guess who it could be.

Sir Peregrine was informed of what was happening, but he only said, "I see. Perhaps you'd better tell Mother."

Edgar went immediately to the wheelhouse, where he was joined after a few minutes by Catriona and Mark Beeney.

"What's happening?" asked Catriona. "I heard that somebody's gone overboard."

Rudyard Philips said, "It's not confirmed yet. But Brigadier Repson says he saw her jump off the rail of the boat deck."

"Did he have any idea who it was?" asked Mark.

Edgar shook his head. "He can't see too well, at a distance. But it was a lady, he said, in a white nightgown."

"Can't you assemble the passengers for a roll call?" asked Mark.

"We will later, if we can't find her and we have to call off the search. But just at the moment, I'd prefer it if every single passenger was keeping a lookout for her. It's surprising what some people can see. Things that even a trained sailor might miss."

Mark said, "It couldn't have been that French opera-singer lady, could it? She tried to commit suicide right at the beginning of the voyage."

Rudyard, without turning around, said, "That thought did occur to me, too, Mr. Beeney, but I called her and checked. It appears that she's much happier now, and that she's lost all of her suicidal tendencies."

"Well, nothing like the love of a good man," remarked Edgar obliquely.

Rudyard answered this comment with a small, sour smile.

There was nothing more they could do in the wheelhouse, so Mark and Catriona went outside and joined the other passengers who were craning and bobbing their heads around for a first sight of the lost lady in white. Their chances of seeing her, however, were millions to one. There was a strong current running, and a fresh mid-morning wind was getting up. If the seventy-five-foot drop to the ocean from the rail of the boat deck hadn't concussed the lady and drowned her, she would probably have gone under from tiredness and exposure by now. At any time of the year, the North Atlantic has never been recommended for its swimming conditions.

"I hope to God it's only a mistake," said Catriona.

"Whatever it is," Mark told her, "I just pray that they get a move on. I've got a large bet riding on today's mileage."

Catriona was shocked. "Some poor woman's life is at risk, and all you can think about is your stupid bet?"

"You're not going to succeed in making me feel guilty about it," said Mark. "Anybody who dives off the boat deck does it because they want to kill themselves. If that's the case, why don't we all just go on our merry way and leave the poor woman alone? If you're really set on suicide, which she must have been, then the last thing that you want to happen is for someone to come and rescue you."

Just then, with the perfect timing of true fate, a steward handed Mark a sheet of writing paper on a silver tray. "Only received this a minute ago, sir, from the ship's post office." Mark tipped him a half-crown, and then tore open the letter with his thumb. It read:

My darling Mark, as you read this I shall already be looking down on you from Heaven, if there is such a place! I haven't always been very sensible. I know that, and I haven't always been good to you and to other people. But I hope that you will forgive me for having loved you so dearly, and for losing heart at last when it became quite clear that you would never be completely mine. You mustn't feel guilty for what I have decided to do. It is my own choice entirely, and it is the way that I prefer to seek my oblivion, rather than pining for the rest of my life like the old lady in the Listerine mouthwash advertisement who still cannot work out why her fiancé cancelled their wedding, all those years ago. You see? I still have a sense of humour, my darling. And a sense of proportion, too, for I know that you will never really love me, although I cannot for the life of me think why. Just promise me this: that you will think of me now and again, and perhaps drop a wreath into the Atlantic at this spot whenever you cross it. Yours hopelessly, Marcia.

Mark took only the flicker of an eye to understand what the letter meant. His cheek muscles tensed and twitched, and as he folded the letter up and tucked it back into its envelope, he looked a terrible shade of beige, as if his suntan was nothing more than a blotchy foundation cream.

"Mark—" said Catriona, taking his arm.

He held up the envelope. "It's Marcia," he said. "It's Marcia who jumped overboard. She's drowned herself, and all because of me."

He folded up, like a marionette with cheap wooden hinges, and sat down hard on one of the promenade-deck benches. "I can't believe it," he said. "She always said that she loved me. But I never thought that she really meant it. It was all just like a play. I never once dreamed—"

Catriona sat down beside him. She felt desperately sorry for him; but at the same time she couldn't help thinking that the only serious rival she believed she had for Mark's affections had now suddenly disappeared. God, was she a witch for thinking that?

She said, "It couldn't have been *all* your fault. She must have been a bit strange in the head, too. Some people do the most peculiar things, and all because they're just a little unbalanced."

"Unbalanced?" said Mark, bitterly. He opened the letter again and passed it to her, so that she could read it. "I suppose you could call that unbalanced, but it seems pretty calm and rational to me."

Catriona touched his sleeve. "I'm sorry," she said. "I didn't mean to say that—"

He made a face. "It doesn't matter. It's a shock, that's all. We'd better go up to the wheelhouse and tell Mr. Philips who it is."

There was a new arrival in the wheelhouse, and when she saw him, Catriona instinctively backed out of the door again and remained outside on the deck while Mark spoke to Rudyard Philips. It was George Welterman, in a yellow straw skimmer, and a blazer striped with red and black. He looked moody and irritable, and from the expression on Edgar's face, Catriona could guess that he had been giving everybody at Keys a difficult time.

Rudyard came to the wheelhouse door. "I've just told Mr. Beeney that we're doing our best to find the young lady," he told Catriona confidentially. "But I have warned him that the chances of us locating her are very slim."

"He owns his own ships," said Catriona. "He must know that as well as you do."

Mark glanced towards her from inside the wheelhouse. There was an expression on his face which told her that he might have known it, but perhaps, at this moment, he wasn't yet ready to believe it.

"I'm sorry," said Catriona. "It's been a terrible shock."

George Welterman said loudly, "Mr. Philips! How many miles are we going to sail back?"

"Until we find the girl," put in Edgar. "Or at least until we're quite positive that she must have been lost."

George drummed his fingers on the varnished woodwork in a testy, spasmodic rhythm. "You realise you're going to lose all possible chance of winning the Blue Riband? This is the second time we've had to turn back."

"The Blue Riband is secondary to the safety of this ship and her passengers, Mr. Welterman," said Rudyard.

"Well, well," said George, "speaking like a commodore already, are we?"

Catriona, who had caught most of this conversation, suddenly found herself saying in a clear voice, "Mr. Welterman!"

George slowly swivelled his head towards her, his eyes bland but childishly threatening, Catriona hadn't looked at him face-to-face since he had assaulted her, and she had forgotten already how eerie those eyes could be. Her throat felt tight, and she became suddenly sensitive to the *Arcadia*'s hesitant, nervous rolling.

"Mr. Welterman," Catriona repeated, "I would prefer it if you addressed any comments you may have about the officers of this ship to the management, and not directly to the officers themselves. Now, will you kindly leave the bridge. It is out of bounds to all but invited passengers during the hours of daylight, and out of bounds to *all* passengers during emergencies."

George Welterman said, "You're joking, of course, Miss Keys. I'm the European director of International Mercantile Marine."

"This ship is registered in Liverpool in the name of the Keys Shipping Line, and I am telling you to get off the bridge," said Catriona. Her voice sounded as brittle and sharp as a broken sliver of glass, although inside herself she was very close to angry tears.

George glanced uneasily at Edgar Deacon. But Edgar remained expressionless, neither confirming Catriona's instruction nor countermanding it. He did, however, take one neat step back, like a man who anticipates a fight brewing and doesn't want to be caught in the line of fire.

George let out an explosion of amusement that was more of a whinny than a laugh. "It's preposterous, of course! Edgar? Tell her it's preposterous."

But now Rudyard stepped forward. "I'm afraid Miss Keys is right, sir. The company regulations are quite clear. You'll have to leave the bridge."

There was a hideous moment when George Welterman's face went through as many contortions as a melting waxwork. Then he said with threatening softness, "Very well. If that's the way you people want to play it. But I warn you—*I warn you*—this won't be forgotten."

Catriona said, "We won't forget it either, Mr. Welterman." At that moment, she hated him more than anybody she had ever hated in her life. In fact, she hadn't hated anybody at all until she had met him. And yet, the curious thing was, he had gone through agony so that he could bear on his chest the name of the woman he had loved.

He raised his straw skimmer as he left the wheelhouse and gave Catriona a sarcastic nod of his head. "I'll see you at luncheon, Miss Keys?"

he inquired, but she turned her face away.

It was Douglas Fairbanks who first saw Marcia in the ocean, thereby completely redeeming himself for his fluffed rescue of Lucille Foster. He let out a great *Thief of Baghdad*–style whoop and cried, "There, Captain! There she is! Just off to starboard?"

Without hesitation, Rudyard, tersely, said, "Full astern all," although it would still take the *Arcadia* nearly a mile of seaway to come to a complete stop. Then, as the cheers and shouts of the passengers rose all around him, Rudyard went out onto the bridge deck and stood with both hands on the railing to see for himself where his one lost passenger was.

"She's floating!" somebody shouted. Then the distinctive voice of Baroness Zawisza cried out, "She's not *floating*, you idiot! She's *swimming!*"

And miraculously enough, on the glassy swell of the ocean (through a sea which, if you were on board the *Arcadia*, looked almost preposterously flat, and yet which, if you were trying to swim in it, looked like the Himalayan mountains in ceaseless motion) there was Marcia Conroy in a clinging white négligée, the Ophelia of the *Arcadia*, doing a slow but entirely competent sidestroke.

"My God," said Mark, right next to Catriona. "My God, she's alive!" He looked at Catriona and he obviously didn't know whether to cheer or to cry.

Rudyard called to Dick Charles, "Lower nets to starboard! Then lower a boat! And double quick?"

It was a remarkable sight, on that mid-morning in June, in mid-ocean: the largest ocean liner in the world drawing slowly to a stop within a hundred yards of a single woman in white splashing her way through the waves as if she were exercising at her local swimming baths.

"She never told me she could swim," said Mark in amazement. "I mean, not as well as *that.*"

Catriona held his hand, happy that Marcia was still alive, but guilty, too, because of the way she had felt only half an hour before, when she had first learned that Marcia was missing. She couldn't stop the tears that filled her eyes and she had to wipe them with her fingers. Mark noticed, but then he was on the verge of crying, too.

Soon the huge ocean liner was drifting slowly within fifty yards of the spot where Marcia was floundering her way through the sea. None of the passengers could yet be sure that she had seen the ship, because she hadn't looked up from the water or acknowledged their arrival in any way at all. But they cheered frantically, and waved their hats, and several well-meaning men threw down life jackets and deck chairs, until the chief steward managed to persuade them that a blow on the head from a deck chair could succeed in drowning Miss Conroy where the Atlantic Ocean had failed.

The lifeboat was still being winched down when Rudyard Philips did an extraordinary thing. He suddenly tossed aside his cap, loosened his necktie, and unbuttoned his uniform.

"Mr. Philips?" asked Edgar.

But Rudyard didn't reply. Instead, he bent down to take off his shoes, which he kicked back into the wheelhouse. Then he quickly unbuttoned his shirt.

"Mr. Philips, you're not thinking of diving in after her?" said Edgar. "Mr. Philips, that's the most ridiculous—"

It was too late. With a face set as straight as a bust of Liszt, Rudyard climbed the rail, balanced for a moment with his toes right on the edge of the highly varnished wood, and then swallow-dived the entire seventy feet down into the sea.

There was a cry of surprise and delight from everybody on the starboard side of the ship as Rudyard arched gracefully through the air, and then hit the water with a clean splash of spray. It was a perfect dive, like a diagram out of *Chums* on "How to Swallow-Dive." Everybody clapped as he emerged and started swimming strongly towards Marcia, and even Jack Dempsey cheered.

Rudyard reached Marcia in two or three minutes. The sea was freezing, and she was on the point of total exhaustion. Her sodden clothes, which like Ophelia's robes were "heavy with their drink," were about to drag her under. As Rudyard pulled her head back into the classic life-saving position, she gargled, and cried out, "Sidestroke medal!"

Rudyard told her breathlessly, "Relax," and began propelling both of them backwards towards the ship. The lifeboat had now been launched and, with Ralph Peel at the prow, was being rowed rapidly towards them. The chilly salt waves splashed over Rudyard's face, and he choked and spat to stop himself from swallowing too much brine.

There was more applause as Marcia was lifted dripping from the sea, and held up in Ralph Peel's arms, the rescued maiden. The news photographs of the event, most of the journalists reckoned, would have to be judiciously retouched, since Marcia's négligée, when wet, was almost completely transparent. But what a humdinger of a story! "Beautiful British Debutante Rescued After Mid-Atlantic Plunge." And they would always have a set of uncensored prints for themselves. The man from the *Daily News* was already hogging the wireless room, his brown leather golf brogue wedged against the door, transmitting his story to New York; while the society correspondent of the *New York Daily Graphic* was fretting outside on the boat deck, just in front of the lady from the *Los Angeles Examiner*, Marjorie Driscoll, whose story, headlined "Desperation Dive of Star-Crossed Society Sylph," would earn her the sobriquet of "sob sister of 1924."

But none of these eager newshounds were there to see the real high tragedy of the rescue. None of them saw Rudyard Philips release his hands from the side of the lifeboat and vanish beneath the surface. In fact, it was two or three minutes before anybody realised he was missing, and by then it was far too late.

Rudyard hadn't known what he was going to do until he saw Marcia Conroy in the water. But then, as if he had been visited by a divine revelation, it had all seemed perfectly clear. Suddenly, he could choose honour instead of ignominy; glory instead of demotion. Marcia was his passenger, she was his personal responsibility, and so as the captain of the *Arcadia* he was duty bound by all the rules of the sea to save her. That was the way to solve everything: to die in the course of his duty. That was the way to be remembered forever as the captain of the ship which he would never be appointed to command. Wouldn't Toy be sorry that she had deserted him for Laurence? And what tears Louise Narron would weep for him! Sir Peregrine, even Sir Peregrine in his paralysed dotage, would remember him with fondness and regret; and Ralph Peel would forgive him for taking the old man's side during the storm.

He would be better off drowned. It would be better for himself, and better for everyone who knew him. He felt as if his very existence had been preventing other people from living their lives happily, and so the only answer was to cease to exist. That was why he had tossed aside his cap, unbuttoned his uniform, unlaced his shoes, and dived into the ocean. He hadn't done it to rescue Marcia (although he was obliged to, because she was his alibi); but to breathe in as much briny seawater as he could and let his cold weighted lungs sink him to the bottom of the ocean.

Rudyard's last impressions were of the sea slapping against the side of the lifeboat; of Ralph Peel kneeling forward to lift Marcia out of the water. He could hear cheering, but somehow it seemed strangely distant, like the cheering of a football crowd six or seven streets away. He thought, They're cheering for me. That's the way to die. At sea, under a sunny sky, to the sound of applause. Then he slowly opened his hands so that he sank away from the lifeboat and allowed himself to drop just below the surface of the waves.

He heard the booming of the ship's turbines, amplified through the water; he heard the metallic tinkling of bubbles. Then he exhaled, every ounce of breath that he could, and breathed in the Atlantic. It was one of the strongest acts of will of his whole life, to inhale seawater, but he did it until his lungs were flooded. He sank down, his brain already dying from oxygen starvation, and he turned as he sank, as if he were flying in slow-motion through the criss-cross sunlight of a dream, and then down into darkness, where no living man could go, and where his face took on a greyish pallor because the sunlight could no longer penetrate. He descended through a silvery shoal of herring, and then deeper still, where it was cold beyond imagination, and where the fish took on forms that were only appropriate in nightmares.

In the pocket of his trousers was the wireless message from Toy, which he would take right to the bottom with him.

Louise Narron, on the first-class promenade deck, was the first to realize that Rudyard had disappeared. She cried out, *"Où est* Rudyard? Where is Mr. Philips? Mr. Peel! Where is Mr. Philips?"

The sailors in the lifeboat looked all around them, and then at each other. "Not in the boat, sir!" one of them told Ralph Peel. Angrily, Ralph Peel shouted back, "Then where the hell is he? Rudyard! Where the hell has he got to!"

They rowed around the *Arcadia* for more than a half-hour, while George Welterman stood alone on the foredeck in his red and black striped blazer, watching them with simmering impatience. It was 11:20 now, and unless the *Arcadia* made at least thirteen miles more progress on her course before twelve noon, he was going to lose his bet. Maurice Peace, who had bet a lower figure than the bridge's estimate, sat in a deck chair eating a banana and meditating on the generosity of fate. He had always wanted a luxury automobile, and now as long as the *Arcadia* remained stationary, it seemed as if he was going to get one. He hadn't even been obliged to resort to the paraffin-soaked rags in his blue canvas holdall. He handed his empty banana skin to a passing steward, and tipped the man £1.

At 11:28, George Welterman lost his patience altogether. He came up to the bridge, where Ralph Peel was now in charge, and demanded, "Mr. Peel! We must now be on our way! Some of us have appointments to keep in New York!"

"We'll make up most of the time, sir," said Ralph. "Just at this moment we're searching for our first officer."

"Can't you understand that he's *drowned?*"

"It appears that way, sir, but we are simply carrying out a routine search, according to the rules."

"Well, damn the rules, Mr. Peel. That man has obviously been lost. An idiot could see that. We have to get under way."

Ralph Peel turned and looked George Welterman up and down. There was nothing tactful or compromising about Ralph when it came to dealing with obstreperous passengers; he saved all his hairy charm for pretty young heiresses and flirtatious dancers. Men passengers were nothing but a nuisance, to be carried for commercial reasons only.

"I am the second officer on this vessel, sir, and just at this moment I am in command."

"Get me Mr. Deacon," George ordered.

"I'm afraid you'll have to find him yourself, sir. I'm directing a search for a missing member of the crew."

"Get me Mr. Deacon, damn you!" George screamed at him. *"Who the hell do you think you're talking to?"*

Ralph was completely unimpressed. As Dick Charles said later, "He didn't even turn one of his sixteen million hairs." He simply said to George, "If you have any complaint, sir, the normal procedure is to write to the shipping line in Liverpool or New York. The normal procedure is not to shriek like a baboon."

George, furious as he was, realised that he wasn't going to get very far with Ralph. So he stormed along the boat deck to the lift and descended, muttering and cursing to himself, to A deck, where he stalked down the corridor to Edgar's stateroom with such ferocity that several people turned to stare at him after he had passed them by. He beat on Edgar's door with his fist, and then pushed it open.

Edgar was sitting with Percy Fearson, urgently discussing who they were going to appoint in place of Sir Peregrine. As George Welterman came in, he stood up.

"George! You don't look too pleased with life."

"I am not," said George, throwing his straw skimmer across the room, and then planting his fists on his hips. "This ship has delayed long enough. I want you to order your officers to get her under way, and I mean now."

"As a matter of fact," said Percy Fearson, "we're searching for a missing crew member. We'll be under way in five or ten minutes."

"Do you think I don't *know* that?" George snapped back at him. "But if we're going to move at all, we're going to have to make another thirteen miles at least by twelve o'clock, or you and I and Keys Shipping are in a whole lot of hot water."

"I don't understand," said Edgar.

"It's very simple," George told him. "I made a bet last night with Mark Beeney that this ship could make six hundred and thirty-five miles today, by noon. At least thirteen miles more. So far, she's covered just a few yards under six hundred and twenty-two."

Edgar put down the papers he was holding and stood up. "Am I hearing you correctly, George? You want us to abandon the search for Rudyard Philips because you have a *bet?*"

George lifted his head defiantly. "It's not just an ordinary bet, Edgar. There's a great deal at stake. Keys Shipping included."

Percy Fearson glanced at Edgar anxiously.

"You've bet Keys Shipping?" asked Henry.

"In a manner of speaking, yes. I've bet that if the *Arcadia* doesn't cover six hundred and thirty-five miles today, I'll withdraw my offer for Keys. In fact, I've guaranteed it."

"You can't gamble something like that!" Edgar exclaimed. "We *already* have draft agreements!"

392

George shrugged. "Agreements are only made to be broken. Why do you think we have lawyers?"

"This is impossible," said Edgar. He was clearly very angry. "We have only a half-hour to make thirteen miles from a dead stop. We'll never do it. We don't even have enough steam up to reach full speed."

"Either you make up those thirteen miles, or everything's off," said George.

"You're talking through your hat," said Edgar. "You're just as committed to this sale as we are."

"Nonetheless, that was the bet I made."

"But of all the damn-fool things to do!" Edgar protested.

George went to the porthole and stared out at the ocean. The sunlight turned his face into a dusty white death mask. "Perhaps I *wanted* to lose. Perhaps I wanted to see you ruined. I don't think anything would give me greater pleasure than to see you buried at last under the collapsing pillars of your own worm-eaten empire."

"But everything we've arranged—"

George gave a slow, disinterested shrug. "You still have a lot to learn, don't you Edgar; in spite of your sharp Anglo-Indian manners. You're a good man, though. Not quite in my class, but good. What you lack in spontaneity I believe you make up for in acumen."

Edgar glanced up at the clock. "I don't think there's any hope of us making thirteen miles by noon."

"Well . . . in that case the only way to protect the sale is for you to make no headway at all. Another passenger has put in a low-field bet of six hundred and twenty; and it would be better for him to win, rather than Mark Beeney. With him, I have bet only five thousand pounds. I shall expect you to underwrite that sum personally, of course, if I lose it. But wouldn't you rather lose five thousand pounds than the whole of this deal?"

It was then that the deep throbbing of the ship's engines began to reverberate through the decks again.

"Well?" asked George.

Edgar said, "I can't delay her any longer; we'll never take the Blue Riband if I do. I've asked Mr. Peel to circle the area once more, and then we're going to be on our way," said Edgar.

"It depends which is the more important to you," said George.

Percy Fearson took his pipe out of the pocket of his Harris Tweed jacket and said, "This fairly turns my lights over, this does. I always said that I hadn't got the stomach for business, and believe me I don't. Not when it comes to dirty little squabbles like this. You bet the whole caboodle, did you, Mr. Welterman? And now you come crying for help when it looks as if you're going to lose. By heck. That's all I can say. My old father would have taken his belt to you."

But Edgar said, "Quiet, Percy, We're not here to talk about the rights or the wrongs of it."

George went to the cocktail cabinet and helped himself to a large Coon Hollow bourbon. "You people should be running church outings," he said sourly, "not a luxury shipping line. Look at you. You're so much in debt your bank has to order red ink by the tanker. You're paddling around the middle of the Atlantic with a ship worth ten million pounds and a passenger list worth two hundred times that amount, and what are you doing? Looking for one man who was dumb enough to jump into the sea when he didn't even have to, and who must have drowned a half-hour ago."

The Cartier enamel clock on the wall of Edgar's stateroom said 11:32. Edgar put his hands into his pockets and then said, We're going to continue to search for Mr. Philips for another ten minutes, George, and then we're going on. On this shipping line, human life comes before anything. Money, schedules, anything. If we lose the shipping line because we tried to find someone lost at sea, then that's the way it'll have to be."

"More fool you," said George, swallowing his drink in one gulp and picking up his hat.

"I have a suggestion, though," said Edgar, quietly. "It could be officially announced that the *Arcadia* has managed to run six hundred and thirty-five miles today; and we could then make every effort to catch up that extra five miles during tomorrow's sailing. We haven't yet taken her as fast as she can possibly go. We still have six thousand horsepower in reserve, over and above our registered horsepower. That's my estimate, anyway. So you could still win your bet."

Percy Fearson looked up, his face scandalised. George Welterman paused as he was about to place his straw skimmer on his head. Then he nodded and left the stateroom without a word.

Fifty-three

Marcia had been lifted aboard, wrapped in a blanket, and then carried in Mark's arms down to the ship's hospital, where Dr. Fields and his nurses had already prepared a bed for her in a private room. Catriona followed a little way behind in her mauve Doucet dress, escorted by Dick Charles.

Behind her came a shouting collection of American journalists and photographers, and a herd of curious passengers. Monty Willowby appeared from the direction of the forward staterooms with a large brown-paper parcel under his arm (Sir Gerald and Lady Burnutt's lavatory seat, which he had feverishly unscrewed during Marcia's rescue) and he succeeded in diverting the press and the passengers so that Marcia could be borne safely to her bed. Marcia's stewardess, Ada, was already there with a clean nightgown of turquoise silk, and she shooed Mark into the hospital anteroom while Marcia was bathed and changed.

The anteroom was plain and painted in cream. On the wall was a single Georges Barbier print, mostly orange, of two nude ladies pouting at two pouting doves. Catriona took a cigarette out of her small silver case, and Mark came across and lit it.

For two or three minutes, Catriona smoked in silence. Then she said, "Is this going to change anything?"

Mark said, "Why should it?"

"Oh, don't be so naïve," she told him. "She tried to kill herself, and all because of you."

Mark shrugged. "We'd argued. But I didn't have any idea that she felt so rejected."

"You must have told her about us."

"I didn't, as a matter of fact."

"You should have done, just to be fair."

"That's what *she* told me," complained Mark. He took out a cigarette himself and stuck it in the corner of his mouth. "I had to be *fair*, she said. Well—what's fair? I ask you? *I* don't know what's fair. Is it fair that I've fallen in love with you, and out of love with her? Is it fair that I've fallen in love with you, and yet I still want to buy the *Arcadia*? Tell me what's fair, and I'll do it. I don't *know* what's fair."

"Oh, for God's sake," said Catriona. "You don't have to be so petulant about it."

"Petulant?" he exclaimed. But then he banged his fist on his own forehead and nodded and grinned and said, "All right. I'm being petulant. It's inherited. In Boston, they call us the Petulant Beeneys."

Catriona said, "I'm just concerned that you're going to feel responsible for her now, in case she tries to kill herself again."

"Of course I feel responsible."

"So responsible that she's going to come between us?"

"Of course not."

Catriona blew out smoke. "You say of course not. But if you *feel* responsible, then you're going to have to act accordingly, aren't you? In a responsible way. And the only way to fulfil your responsibility, and to prevent Miss Conroy from leaping off this ship again, is to tell her that you've loved her all the time, and that you still love her. 'Sorry about

Catriona, she was just a mistake.' "

Mark said, "Why do girls always have to make life so damned complicated?"

"We *don't* make it complicated." Catriona told him. "It's simply that we can face up to things, which men can't. You don't have anything more complicated to do than make up your mind whether you want to stay with Marcia or come with me."

"You make yourself sound so hardboiled," said Mark. "I think *I'm* hardboiled. In business I'm hardboiled. But you—*whoo!*"

Catriona came and sat down beside him. She touched the back of his wrist, her fingertip circling around and around. "There's nothing hardboiled about facing up to what you are and what you want out of your life," she said, gently. "It's honesty, that's all. I inherited it from my father and I had to use it against my father when I first went to London. I knew what I wanted, even though I was only seventeen. I wanted to be free. I wanted to discover what life was really like outside Formby, and I did. Perhaps it was scandalous. Well, it was scandalous. None of my friends ever managed to do it, and most of them are still living at home with their parents even now. But I found a man who loved me, and I learned about love, and I don't think that's too hardboiled, do you?"

Mark looked at her seriously, and then down at her circling finger. His cigarette was still unlit. "I don't think I've ever had the opportunity to go after love like that," he said.

"You make it sound like a bear in the woods, which you can either hunt or leave alone."

"Well, isn't it?"

"Sometimes. And sometimes it springs up on you and attacks you when you're least suspecting it."

"Like when?"

"Like the moment I first saw you."

"I don't believe you fell in love with me then," Mark smiled. He kissed her forehead, and then her cheek, and then her lips. "Nobody falls in love like that."

"Prove it."

It was then that Dr. Fields appeared, with his stethoscope hanging around his neck, and set his black leather bag down on the table. He thoughtfully sucked a shred of breakfast bacon out from between his false teeth, and then he said, "Well . . . I've made a thorough examination."

"Is she all right?" asked Mark.

"She's as well as one might reasonably expect her to be. She has severe bruising, from jumping into the water from such a height. She is also suffering from shock, from exposure to cold seawater, and from complete exhaustion. But, well, none of those conditions is difficult to treat. If she has plenty of rest, and plenty of affectionate company, she should recover by the time we reach New York."

Mark said, "Did she tell you why she'd jumped?"

Dr. Fields looked at him narrowly and then nodded. "She did explain it to me, yes."

"And?"

"And nothing," said Dr. Fields. "What do you expect me to tell you? That you shouldn't jilt young ladies when you're as rich and as good-looking as you are, in case they kill themselves? It's a risk that some people have to take. Not a risk that *I've* ever been fortunate enough to have to run. But a risk, nonetheless, which can have tragic consequences for everybody concerned."

"So what do you suggest?" asked Mark.

Dr. Fields coughed. "If you like, you could try being more consider-ate towards her for a while, provided you don't raise her expectations beyond what you're prepared to give her. Don't tell her that you love her if you don't. Don't promise to marry her, or anything foolish like that. It might help her to come out of her depression now, but it would kill her later on when she found out that you didn't mean it. Be her friend, that's all I can say. She deserves at least that much."

Mark said, "Can I see her?"

"For a short while, yes. But I want her to sleep."

They went into the room where Marcia was lying. The shade had been drawn down over the porthole so that the sunlight was dimmed. There was a vase of pink silk peonies on the table, and on the wall a soothing pink and grey landscape. Marcia's head was wrapped in snowy white bandages, and the hand that lay on the plum-coloured blanket was bruised and scratched. She looked up at Mark and Catriona with eyes that were already drooping from the effects of sedatives.

"Mark?" she whispered.

He drew a chair across. Catriona sat on the end of the bed. "I'm here," he said. "How are you feeling?"

"Unreal," she slurred. "I'm not sure if I'm dead or if I'm alive."

"You're alive, believe me. I didn't know you could swim like that."

"Was I really swimming? I can't think why. I thought drowning would be easy. But once I was in the water, I kept thinking, Swim. I could hear my old games mistress calling out, *Swim, gel, swim!* And so I swam."

Catriona said, "You were lucky somebody saw you. There were only two or three people out on deck."

"Lucky?" said Marcia. She turned towards Catriona for the first time. "Well, I suppose I am, if you can call it lucky to survive when you've lost everything you've ever wanted."

"I'm sorry," Catriona told her. "I wasn't trying to crow."

"You don't have to apologise," said Marcia. "It isn't your fault that Mark loves you more than me. It's just the way of the world, isn't it?"

Mark held Marcia's hand. "Don't even think about it. Just get yourself well first."

Marcia gave him a fleeting, regretful smile. She kept closing her eyes for longer and longer intervals each time, and it was obvious that she was almost asleep.

"That officer who saved me," she whispered. "Is he all right?"

Mark looked towards Catriona. Catriona said, "He's quite well, as far as I know."

"He said something strange to me . . . when he reached me. . . . Do you know what he said?"

Catriona shook her head, but then realised that Marcia couldn't focus on her any longer, and said, "No. What did he say?"

"He said, "You were quite right, this is the way to go.". . . I couldn't think what he meant."

She slept, her mouth slightly open. She stirred for a moment and said, "Mark . . . it can't be true that you're . . ." And then she slept again. After two or three minutes, Mark and Catriona got up and went out of the room on tiptoe.

Dr. Fields was in the anteroom making neat illegible notes with a tortoiseshell Waterman pen. Mark told him, "She's sleeping now." Catriona gently linked her arm with Mark's, and Mark covered her hand with his own. The way they were standing, they could have been a bride and groom standing before a registrar. Dr. Fields screwed the cap on his pen and looked up at them.

"Well," he said, "it's always very difficult to say anything about an attempted suicide, particularly to those most closely involved. One has to work out for oneself how responsible one should be for the welfare of others. Are you, Mr. Beeney, responsible for Miss Conroy's life because you courted her and then rejected her? Are you your sister's keeper, as it were? These are difficult questions, hard to answer."

Mark said, "Do you really think she'll try it again?"

"That's impossible for me to judge," said Dr. Fields. "She's chronically depressed about your abandoning her. It appears from what she told me that you never made her any romantic pledges; but that she had always assumed from your conduct towards her that one day you might ask her to marry you."

"I'm afraid that's an assumption that I did nothing to foster," said Mark. "I never promised to marry her and I never would. I don't think for a moment that we'd be suited."

"You couldn't even carry on your relationship at—shall we say the same distance as before?"

"I don't think so. Not since I've met Miss Keys."

Dr. Fields stood up, and with the air of a stage magician, produced from his breast pocket a white handkerchief the size of a small bedsheet.

He blew his nose two or three times, and then folded it back again.

"There's nothing more that we can do, then, except to keep her under supervision, to feed her with sedatives, and to make sure that even if she feels unwanted as a prospective wife, she doesn't feel unloved as an individual human being. It's asking a lot of both of you, I know. But in your own different ways—as far as one person can ever be responsible for the health and safety of another—you owe her at least the opportunity to live."

Afterwards, Mark took Catriona up to the Orchid Lounge, where he ordered for himself a large Peter Dawson on ice, and for Catriona a Bollinger mimosa. They sat silently for quite a while, until Catriona said, "You're thinking about jilting me, aren't you?"

He looked up quickly. "Of course not. What gave you that idea?"

"It would be easier, wouldn't it? You wouldn't have to feel guilty about Marcia anymore. And you wouldn't have to feel guilty about me, either. If there's one thing I've learned about you, it's quite simply that you don't know how to mix business with romance."

Mark leaned back in his mauve wickerwork chair. "I wish you'd tell me the secret."

"There isn't any secret. Not as far as I can make out, anyway. It just seems to me that if you want to do business, you have to do business, and that if you want to make love, you have to make love. But you can't do both. Business has a hopelessly brutalising effect on love, and love has a hopelessly confusing effect on business."

Mark took out his cigarette case. "I guess I can't argue with that. You've just had the experience firsthand, after all."

Catriona gazed at him for a moment, trying to find the courage to say what she had planned to say next. She was the Queen of the Atlantic, and when you were a queen, you had royal pride. You had personal pride, too. Pride that made it a matter of importance that men never jilted you —*you* always jilted them. Even men you really cared about, the way that Catriona had grown in the past two days to care about Mark.

At last she managed to say, "I think we'd better call this off, you and I. I think we're going to end up hurting everybody, including ourselves and perhaps our businesses as well."

Mark frowned at her. "Are you serious?" Then, looking at her more closely, he said, "You're serious."

She prayed that she wasn't going to cry. She could feel her mouth tightening as she tried to suppress the ache in her throat. In a voice that sounded almost like a ventriloquist's doll, she said, "It's no use, Mark. It isn't going to bring us anything but heartache. Let's just pretend we never met."

Over in the corner of the Orchid Lounge, the ship's pianist began to play romantic and nondescript tunes, like "Days of Desire" and

"Moonlight Promenade." They were silly songs, written for banal singers, but somehow Catriona thought of the words of "Moonlight Promenade" and the tears slipped from her eyes like liquid mercury running through her fingers.

> It was one of those nights
> When my heart took flight,
> And when the moon arose it lit the roses round my pathway,
> And when I walked with you,
> I found it oh so hard
> To tell you this must be our final promenade.

Mark took her hand, grasped it tight. "Catriona," he told her. "Catriona, listen to me. How many times in my life do you think I've fallen in love? I mean, *really* fallen in love, as if I've been struck by lightning. The answer is twice. Once, when I was twenty, I fell in love with a girl who used to pose for *Broadway Magazine* calendars. Her name was Eunice, and my mother hated her. And the other time was you. But between Eunice and you, there hasn't been anybody. Flirtations maybe. Affairs. But nobody who's hit me over the head the way you have."

"What about Marcia?" Catriona asked, wiping her eyes.

"As far as Marcia's concerned, I'm going to do just what the doctor asked me to do. Be friendly, make her feel wanted. But I'm not going to make any promises. The only promises I'm going to make are to you."

> And when I walked with you,
> I counted every yard,
> For this was our last moonlight promenade.

Catriona said, "I love you." And then, *"Damn* it!"

"You'll come with me to Boston?"

"I haven't made up my mind yet."

"Then make it up."

Catriona hesitated for a moment, but then she thought, What on *earth* am I hesitating for? It's all happened like a whirlwind, but who cares? When you find the man you really love, that's the way it happens. You fly together like two magnets, and from then on you're stuck.

"All right," she said with a slow smile. "I'll come. As long as you're sure that I can bring Alice."

"You can bring fifty Alices."

Mark glanced up at the clock. It was two minutes of twelve. "I have to run now," he said. "I have a meeting with John Crombey, and then I have some wireless messages to dictate. But let's take a walk after luncheon; and why don't you let me escort you to the fancy-dress ball

400

tonight?"

"I was going to go with Mr. Philips," said Catriona. The thought was suddenly sad and strong. Edgar had told her that it would be excellent for passenger morale if she appeared at the fancy-dress ball on Rudyard Philips' arm. Now Rudyard Philips was lost, presumed drowned; and although Catriona could only remember him as a short, rather pugnacious man with a rather abrupt way of speaking—a stickler for shipboard etiquette, rather diffident and difficult to talk to—she was still regretful, because he was one of her officers and he had died in the course of his duty. Her father would have been upset, and so was she.

Mark said, "I've lost some good friends at sea, including my father. The sad thing is, you can't even bury them."

"I don't suppose Mr. Philips would have minded," said Catriona. "He did tell me that the sea was everything he had."

"In that case," said Mark, "I guess he wouldn't have minded too much. I don't suppose my father would, either. But my mother used to say that it wasn't the same, throwing a wreath on the sea. Not the same as placing it on a headstone."

Catriona said gently, "I'll see you at three, in the Palm Court."

It was twelve o'clock exactly.

Fifty-four

At noon, on board the Keys liner *Arcadia,* in mid-Atlantic, several crucial events took place.

The most crucial event was the spring in Harry Pakenow's time clock, displaced by less than one-sixteenth of an inch when he dropped it on to the deck of the automobile hold, failed to activate the sear which was supposed to fire the primer which would detonate his thirty sticks of dynamite.

Twelve o'clock came and went, and the *Arcadia,* having abandoned at last her search for the body of Rudyard Philips, was swiftly and majestically building up speed again as she sailed towards the golden western horizon, her bows glittering with spray, her slanted funnels streaming out plumes of smoke, a picture postcard of a luxury 1920s liner making her way across the ocean to New York. To take the passengers' mind off the tragedy, Ralph Peel had ordered complimentary champagne for everyone in cabin class, free sherry in second and a bottle of ale apiece in third. Fox trot music blew across the first-class decks in the lunchtime breeze, and gradually the party atmosphere began to revive, especially in anticipation of today's celebration lunch and tonight's fancy-dress ball.

There was some excitement, too, at the prospect of Mr. Joe Kretchmer and Mr. Duncan Wilkes meeting each other over luncheon, because both of them had been seen to falter during elevenses, especially when the smoking-lounge steward had brought them *le snac du jour,* which had been a hot Gruyère fondue of plovers' eggs, Dublin Bay prawns, spiced cubes of pork, and diced marrow. Maurice Peace had been predicting that today's lunchtime confrontation would probably decide the winner of the eating contest, and he had been taking hundreds of pounds in extra bets. Interest in the contest, which had flagged during the past few meals because it had seemed as if the competitors would do nothing more spectacular for the rest of the voyage than slowly masticate their way through forty-three different dishes a day, was suddenly and generally revived.

Another crucial event was that Sir Peregrine sat up in his berth and announced to Nurse Queensland that he was perfectly well and that she had better bring him his trousers, unless she wanted to be instantly dismissed. Nurse Queensland called for Dr. Fields, but Dr. Fields was busy with Lady Cressworthy, who had been complaining about pains in the small of her back particularly after last night's after-dinner tango. By the time Dr. Fields had examined Lady Cressworthy and discovered a row of purple contusions which appeared to have been inflicted by the bones of a spectacularly tight corset, Sir Peregrine had struggled into his uniform and limped out of the cabin up to the bridge. "I am perfectly well, madam," he had told Nurse Queensland, flapping at her with his good arm. "I am in the rudest possible health. But if you don't stop your fussing, I shall be even ruder."

He swung himself scissor-legged into the wheelhouse, and announced to a startled Ralph Peel that he was resuming command of the *Arcadia,* both operationally and socially. If he was still limping by tonight, then hang it all, he would appear at the fancy-dress ball dressed up as Long John Silver. Mr. Peel was to correct the *Arcadia's* course by one and a half degrees to port, and what the devil was he doing running the ship at twenty-nine knots? Were they in a *race?* If so, with whom? Dignity and safety came before speed. And Mr. Peel, once he had carried out his orders, was to return to his quarters and have another shave. Sir Peregrine did not care for officers on the bridge who looked like lemurs.

"You can call my steward and tell him to bring me a large glass of Russian tea with a spoonful of maple syrup in it, and two aspirin tablets. What's the latest from Ascot?" Because of the time difference as they crossed the ocean, the early afternoon races had already been run.

"Mrs. Jeffrey's Dinkie won by a neck from the King's horse Weathervane in the Royal Hunt Cup, sir."

"*Mrs. Jeffrey?* You mean to tell me that the Royal Hunt Cup was won by a *woman?*"

"Yes, sir," said Ralph. Then, seeing how displeased the commodore was, he added, "I'm afraid so, sir."

"What else?" demanded Sir Peregrine.

"Sansovino won the Prince of Wales stakes."

"Well, thank God for *that*. Where's Mr. Deacon?"

"I'll have him sent up to the bridge, sir."

"No, no, don't bother. Where's Mr. Philips?"

There was an awkward silence. The helmsman glanced uncomfortably at Ralph Peel; but then, when he saw that Sir Peregrine was frowning at him ferociously, he snapped his eyes straight ahead again.

"You haven't been told, sir?" asked Ralph.

"Told? Told what?"

"About Mr. Philips, sir. I would have assumed that Dr. Fields would have told you."

Sir Peregrine reached out for the back of the captain's chair with his left arm and gripped it to support himself. "*What* would you have assumed that Dr. Fields would have told me?"

"I'm not sure I ought to say, sir. I don't want to cause you another stroke. Perhaps you ought to ask Dr. Fields, sir, with respect."

"If this intelligence about Mr. Philips is so shocking that it strikes me down for good, then all I can say is that there are worse ways to go. One *could* die at the annual dinner of the Shipwrecked Mariners Society, during one of Gerald Maude's awful speeches."

"Well, sir," said Ralph Peel. "I'm sorry to be the first to tell you that Mr. Philips is dead. He was drowned about an hour ago, trying to rescue a passenger who went overboard."

Sir Peregrine stared at Ralph Peel with his mouth slightly open and his tongue tucked in his cheek. Then he said, "Drowned?"

"Yes, sir."

"I see. Well . . . that's most regrettable. That's really quite tragic. The poor fellow never quite managed to get things right, did he? What with running down that Irishman off Dun Laoghaire, and all that strange business during the storm. Which reminds me. I thought you were supposed to be confined to your quarters for insubordination."

"I, er—well, I *was*, sir. But Mr. Deacon said that—"

"Deacon, yes." Sir Peregrine nodded. Then, "Have you found Mr. Philips' body yet? Made a search, I suppose?"

"Yes, sir. But no sign of him. He must have gone down like a sack of coal."

"I see. Sack of coal. That sounds like him. Sort of thing Philips would do. Was the passenger rescued?"

"Yes, sir. Miss Marcia Conroy, travelling with Mr. Mark Beeney."

At that moment the door to the wheelhouse opened and George Welterman appeared. "Mr. Peel?" he said harshly. "We've slowed down! Now why the devil have we slowed down?"

Sir Peregrine turned around, and it was only then that George Welterman realised he was there. He blinked and coughed loudly, but he seemed to be incapable of speech.

Sir Peregrine said, "Did my ears deceive me, sir, or did you just address an inquiry to my third officer about the vessel's forward speed?"

George wasn't put off for very long. "Mr. Deacon promised that he was going to run the ship as fast as possible to make up for lost time," he blustered. "He promised me that personally."

"Oh, did he?" said Sir Peregrine. In spite of his weak and dangling arm, he looked the picture of nautical elegance. "Well, I regret that as captain of the *Arcadia* I have just countermanded that instruction, and I promise you, equally personally, that if you attempt to barge into this wheelhouse again, or anywhere else on this ship which is out of bounds to passengers, then I will have you locked up in your stateroom until we reach New York, for your own safety, of course. I may even instruct your steward to forget to bring you your meals."

Without waiting for an answer, Sir Peregrine turned his back on George Welterman and addressed himself to the Atlantic chart that was spread out on the navigation table. George was congested with fury; but his temper had already done him enough harm on this voyage, and he controlled himself with an effort of will that made his neck swell over his collar like pink raspberry sponge bulging over the top of a white ramekin.

When George had marched off along the boat deck, Sir Peregrine said to Ralph Peel, "If that man ever speaks to you again on any subject apart from women, fishing, or the price of a weekend in Ostend, you may feign total deafness."

"Yes, sir," said Ralph, rather shaken.

The brass ship's chronometer read twelve noon.

Henry Pakenow was on the forward boat deck. He stayed as near to number one lifeboat as he could, smoking nervously and waiting for the dull internal thunder that would tell him that his dynamite had gone off. He had seen Lucille in the Palm Court during elevenses, although he had been unable to join her because Mrs. Hall had made quite sure that she and her young charge shared a table for two, in the corner. Since then, Harry had tried to keep his eye on Lucille wherever she strolled, but it wasn't easy to follow her around without appearing to be bothersome, and a few minutes before twelve Mrs. Hall had ushered her inside to dress for luncheon. There was little that Harry could do except pray that somebody would have the sense to put a life jacket on her and lead her to the boats.

At one minute to twelve, the Palm Court orchestra was playing "Can You Toddle Like a Tiger Toddles?" which Harry considered to be a suitable requiem for the most insensitive, hedonistic, and spendthrift generation ever. The Great War had taught them nothing: but this would. Just as the sinking of the *Titanic* had irrevocably crippled the Edwardian principles of wealth and class, so the sinking of the *Arcadia* would help to destroy the fatuous speeded-up world of champagne and jazz and privileged young sheiks. They would know for certain that they couldn't dance on the graves of working-class heroes any longer.

Twelve. The gilded clock in the great first-class stairway began to chime *Gregorius*. Harry gripped the rail and waited for the explosion. When a whole minute passed and it didn't come, he wasn't actually surprised. The clock that Dennis had built into the timing mechanism had only cost one-and-eleven, from Bumfrey's, in Runcorn High Street. Communist revolutionaries couldn't afford chronometers. But as time passed and the *Arcadia* continued to sail unharmed into the midday sunlight, her wires humming like a Gregorian choir as the wind blew through them, Harry began to wonder if something might have gone wrong. He stepped quickly across the boat deck to where the fifth officer, Derek Holdsworth, was chatting sociably with the Hon. Constance Pruitt, and said, "Do you know what the time is, please? My watch seems to have stopped."

Derek Holdsworth took out his pocket watch and said, "Five minutes past twelve exactly, Mr. Pakemoff."

The Hon. Constance Pruitt, a very pretty brunette whose prettiness was somehow majestically enhanced by her squinting eyes, said, "I hope you're enjoying yourself, Mr. Pakemoff. Wasn't that rescue exciting? And that poor officer! I cried when I heard!"

"Pakenow," Harry corrected her. Then he stared at her as if she were one of those dotty girls whom long-suffering aunts take out for the day from mental institutions, so that they can all sit tight-lipped in a tearoom and be suitably mortified by the poor creature's loud, peculiar conversation, and the way she drops meringue on her kilt.

Constance Pruitt wasn't to know that Harry couldn't even begin to comprehend the idea of *enjoying* himself, or of being excited by Marcia's rescue, not in these crucial minutes while he was waiting for his bomb to go off.

Derek Holdsworth, alert to the oddness of the moment, said, "You'll be looking forward to luncheon, I expect, Mr. Pak-*enow*. It's a special luncheon in honour of our Irish investors. I understand we'll be serving brill, flamed in Irish whiskey."

But without a word, Harry turned around and hurried aft towards the staircase. Halfway there, however, he thought, Supposing the bomb goes off when I'm below decks? I won't stand a chance. Maybe I should wait four or five more minutes. The Hon. Constance Pruitt was watching him as he suddenly paused, and she turned to Derek Holdsworth and remarked, "They're very *strange*, aren't they, the working class? I've never really seen them close up before. Oh, except for the servants, of course. They seem to be so *agitated* by something these days. Daddy says it's because they've forgotten their place. It was the war, he says. Everybody forgot their place."

"I think Mr. Pakenow's a reasonable enough sort," said Derek Holdsworth. Then, "Good afternoon, Lady Musset. Good afternoon, Mrs. Chalk-Herbert."

Three minutes passed. Four. Two gentlemen in white flannels passed either side of Harry as they promenaded around the boat deck, as if he were nothing more than an ill-sited davit. One of them was saying, "It just goes to show you that the whole idea of *pluck* isn't dead yet, by any means." They must have been talking about Rudyard Philips.

Harry knew now that his bomb wasn't going to work. More slowly, he made his way to the grand staircase and descended to the first-class lounge. One of the stewards came up to him with a luncheon menu tucked under his arm and said, "A cocktail, sir, before luncheon?"

"I, er, no, thank you," Harry told him. Then, "I've lost my way, actually. Can you direct me to the nearest lift?"

There was only one thing to be done. To go straight down to the automobile hold and set off the dynamite himself, by hand.

While Harry was making up his mind to detonate his bomb by himself, Dick Charles was hurrying along the corridor to Lady Diana FitzPerry's stateroom with a spray of irises and gladioli, and a box of Charbonnel et Walker's *marzipan gingembres* with paper-lace ruffles all over it, and a paper swan on top.

Dick was in a state of high excitement. Last night had been outrageous, ferocious, hilarious, and at times even frightening. But it had persuaded him beyond any doubt that a lady like Lady Diana was exactly the woman he needed. She had the breeding of a prize borzoi bitch, the wealth of a minor sultana, the etiquette of a lady-in-waiting, the language of a sailor, and the vaginal grip (and here he had to borrow the phrase that Ralph Peel used so often) of a drowning woman clinging to an HB pencil.

Dick knocked hurriedly at Lady Diana's door. Then he straightened his necktie, wiped the perspiration from his forehead with the back of his hand, polished up his shoes against the side of his trousers, cleared his throat, and waited.

There was no reply.

He knocked again; and this time as he knocked the door eased open a little way. Somebody had closed the door, but had obviously forgotten that the lock had been held back on the latch. Dick hesitated, but then

406

pushed the door open and stepped into Lady Diana's living room. Flowers in one hand, candy box in the other, and that little sprig of hair that stuck up on the crown of his head plastered down with water. He said, "Hullo?" and then he listened.

He heard panting. It certainly *sounded* like panting. Then he heard tiny cries of pleasure. "Oh, my darling. Oh, my darling. Oh, deeper, *deeper!* Oh, my absolute darling!"

He looked down at his flowers and his candy and suddenly he felt completely ridiculous. How could he have imagined that a lady like Diana FitzPerry, a lady who had been pleasured by some of the most celebrated and eminent men in England, a lady who had been taught to blow champagne corks out of her bottom by the Lord Chancellor himself—how could he ever have imagined that a lady like that could have seen him as anything more than a momentary plaything?

He wasn't going to rush into her bedroom and surprise her *in flagrante delicto*. He was too shy and too sensitive for that. Instead, he quietly laid his flowers and his candy on the sofa, and then went across to the bureau and wrote in pencil on a pad of the *Arcadia* notepaper, "My dearest Diana, It appears that I have been foolish. Nonetheless you may be sure that I will conduct myself for the remainder of the voyage with extreme decorum. Regards, Dick."

Next door, in the bedroom, he heard Lady Diana squealing in passion, and her feet bicycling madly against the sheets. He waited for a moment longer, but then he quietly left and closed the door behind him.

It was only when he was halfway along the corridor, next to a magnificent gold fire extinguisher with the coat-of-arms of Keys Shipping on it, that he let out a loud and awkward sob.

Harry, meanwhile, had reached the orlop deck, and was half walking, half running towards the door of the automobile hold. He opened it up with the key which he had lifted from Monty Willowby's board, and then quickly crossed the deck between the lines of cars until he reached Mark Beeney's Marmon. The screwdriver which he had wedged into the lock was still protruding from it, and so Harry gripped hold of it and tried to pull it out.

He strained and sweated, clenching his teeth, but he had driven the screwdriver into the lock too far. He tried waggling it from side to side, but after two or three waggles, the blade of the screwdriver snapped off, and the lock was irreparably jammed.

He stood by the car, panting loudly. There was nothing he could do. If he couldn't open the trunk, he couldn't detonate the dynamite. He began to realise with an extraordinary mixture of frustration and relief that he had actually failed. He hadn't been able to sink the *Arcadia* after all. And even though she would arrive in New York harbour as the floating embodiment of everything he detested in modern society, at least Lucille

Foster would be quite safe, and so would Philly and Lydia, and so would all of those third-class passengers who had sung and danced in the saloon with him, and those first-class passengers who had treated him with friendship and generosity when they might have treated him as if he were something swept up from steerage.

He tried prizing open the Marmon's trunk just once more, but his heart wasn't in it, and he gave up. There would have to be another way, another time. Perhaps when the *Arcadia* was in dry dock in Liverpool. He knew plenty of the lads in the maintenance yards. Any one of them would help him to slip into the dock with six or seven hundred pounds of dynamite.

The thought of returning to Liverpool quite cheered him. He had old friends in New York, old political comrades, and old schoolfriends. But it had been years since he had seen them, and who knew how much they might have changed. Besides, he was beginning, quite unexpectedly, to miss Janice. The thought that he would still be alive to sail back and see her was suddenly very appealing. He would knock on the door and surprise her, and then what a reunion they would have. Fish and chips in the *Echo*, two or three bottles of Newcastle Brown, and the bedsprings wouldn't stop complaining all afternoon.

Harry walked across the deck of the automobile hold, his footsteps echoing against the steel sides of the ship. He had almost reached the door when he became aware that Derek Holdsworth and two seamen were waiting for him, at ease, their hands neatly clasped behind their backs.

"I'm afraid you're in serious trouble, old man," said Derek Holdsworth.

"Trouble? What kind of trouble?" Harry asked him. He glanced towards one of the blue-jumpered seamen for support, but the seaman did nothing except to give him a pursed-up little grin.

"This part of the ship is quite out of bounds to passengers. You're trespassing. Apart from that, you were seen by myself and these two men to be attempting to break into one of the automobiles here. I'm afraid to say that we're going to have to confine you to your cabin until we reach New York, and then report what you've been doing to the police.'

"The New York police?" asked Harry. "But this is a British ship. The New York Police don't have any jurisdiction on board a British ship."

"You're an American citizen, aren't you? Or so Mr. Willowby tells me, having examined your passport. An illegal act committed on board ship by an American citizen is subject to US law."

"I wasn't doing anything. I was only looking at the cars."

"How did you get in here?"

"The door was open. I just walked in."

Derek Holdsworth said, almost casually, "Johnson, Pettigrew, will you search him for me, please?"

Harry took a step back. "If I was a first-class passenger, you wouldn't talk to me that way."

"Well, perhaps not." Derek Holdsworth smiled. "But you're *not* a first-class passenger, are you? You're not even a second-class passenger. And so I think I shall address you as I damn well please."

"Listen," said Harry, "all I was doing was looking at the cars."

"You'd like me to think that was *all* you were doing?"

"Go see for yourself," said Harry. "I haven't touched anything. Not a thing."

One of the seamen was examining the Marmon. At last, his suspicion was aroused by the scratches on the paintwork around the lock of the trunk where Harry had been trying to force it open, and he called out, "Here, Mr. Holdsworth. I believe I've found it."

Derek Holdsworth prodded Harry along in front of him until they reached the Marmon. "Well," he said, "Mr. Beeney's car, hey? There's gratitude for you. You give a fellow a first-class cabin, and all the trimmings of first-class luxury, and what does he do for you? He tries to steal more, that's what he does for you. Can't be satisfied with what he's got, oh no, not now that he's got a taste for it. And that's the trouble with working-class people today. You make them think that they deserve two days' annual holiday by the seaside, and by God, they'll go on it. You make them think that they deserve higher wages, and by God they'll demand a *right* to higher wages—which is all nonsense of course, because the minute you pay people more you have to charge more for the things they want to buy."

"Is this a lecture or what?" asked Harry.

"Can't get it budged, sir," said one of the seamen, referring to the trunk of Mark's car. "It looks like he's been tampering around with the lock."

"Is that true?" Derek Holdsworth asked Harry. "Were you actually trying to force this car's boot open?"

Harry nudged his spectacles back onto his nose with the back of his hand. "Do you think I'd tell you, even if I had?"

"Well, old man, you'd better come up with *some* kind of an explanation," said Derek Holdsworth. "Because if you haven't got a sufficiently plausible reason for being here, and trying to burglarise other people's property, then I'm afraid that I'm going to take you straight to the captain, and have you locked up in your quarters until we get to New York."

"I never went near that automobile," said Harry.

"We saw you," said the fatter of the two seamen.

"If you saw me, you ought to go to work in the moving pictures," Harry retorted. "The studios are crying out for people with good imaginations."

The seaman quickly glanced across at Derek Holdsworth, to make sure that he wasn't close enough to hear what they were saying, and then he murmured, "Have you got friends in the moving pictures? In Hollywood? I always wanted to work in the films. I used to act once, in rep. Dewsbury repertory company, in Yorkshire. They always used to say I was one of their best actors. Falstaff, I played. With cushions under my jumper, of course."

Harry stared at him. "Why don't you go and boil your head?" he suggested, and Derek Holdsworth heard that.

"All right, that settles it," he said. "We're going to the captain. Johnson, take Mr. Pakenow's arm, will you?"

Harry tried to pull his arm away, but the thinner seaman held it tight, and together they walked across the hold to the door.

It was at the door that Harry broke down. It came on him unexpectedly, as if someone had hit him over the head. And, in a way, they had. He had suddenly experienced a terrible revelation: that the capitalists and their way of life could never be defeated, that it was futile even to expect that they could. No matter how many bombs he let off, no matter how many luxury liners he sank, he would never make any impression on them. Their resources were beyond imagination. Their belief in the rightness of their system was unassailable. It had been one thing to *imagine* how rich people lived, which was all he had been able to do before he set off the bomb on Wall Street. But now he had seen it for himself at first hand. He had seen the silver cutlery and the sparkling jewels and the brocade upholstery. He had tasted the meals of prime meat and exotic fish and rare wine. He knew now that the rich would never let it go, this way of life, and that they would never share it. It would be hopeless to delude himself that they would. You might be able to bomb a man into changing his religion, but you could never bomb him into losing his taste for oyster loaf and canvasback duck. You could never bomb him out of a preference for New & Lingwood shirts, or Huntsman suits. The very *richness* of the rich had overwhelmed him, and he knew that he hadn't even experienced a fraction of it. He had talked to people in Bootle who lived with a family of five in two rooms, and ate bread-and-scrape six nights out of seven, and yet here were these cabin-class passengers wondering out loud if they ought to spend the summer at their Long Island house, or in their apartments in Paris. How could you even *begin* to terrorise people who lived like this?

It was caviar which had stunned him most. To see one woman spread onto a fragment of toast a spoonful of greyish eggs which cost the equivalent of two families' meals for two days, and eat it without a qualm, that was more than Harry had been able to understand.

As it was his inability to understand, and his failure to set off his bomb, and his shameful relief that he was going to survive to go back to

Janice which finally dropped him to his knees. He clutched the leg of Derek Holdsworth's uniform trousers, and wept like a small child.

Derek Holdsworth was extremely embarrassed. It was one thing to frog-march a chappie up to the captain. It was quite another thing to have the chappie clinging to your leg. He had only followed Harry down here because the Hon. Constance Pruitt had been watching the fellow, and had suddenly suggested that he might be up to something shady.

"Look here," he said, "I'm sure you weren't *actually* trying to break into that car, were you?"

Harry was paralysed with grief. He could do nothing but cry and pant for breath. His whole life was folding up inside him like the bellows of a cheap camera.

Derek Holdsworth said to the fatter seaman, "He didn't actually *steal* anything, did he? And there wasn't any damage?"

"Few scratches on the paint, sir."

"Well, that's nothing. Perhaps we've overdone it a bit. Chap is a hero, after all. You know. Saved that girl, and so forth."

He bent forward and said loudly in Harry's ear, "All right, old man. We've decided to let you go. Do you understand me? We're going to let you go. Now, all you have to do is go back to your cabin and behave yourself, and we won't say any more about it. How's that? Okay?"

Harry sat back against the cream-painted wall of the corridor. He took off his spectacles and wiped them on his tie. He felt completely devastated and ashamed. The worst thing was, he was guilty of everything that Derek Holdsworth had accused him of, and worse. If he had been able to break back into the trunk of Mark Beeney's car, he would have sunk the ship and Derek Holdsworth with it.

Derek Holdsworth held out his hand. "Come on, old man. Up you get."

Harry hesitated for a moment, then reached out his own hand and allowed Derek to lift him to his feet. He wound his glasses back around his ears, and then gave an unhealthy-looking grin.

"Thank you," he said hoarsely. "I don't know what for. But, thank you."

Derek Holdsworth watched him stumble off towards the companion-way and wondered if he had done the right thing.

"Most extraordinary," he said to Johnson. "You can never quite tell with these chappies, can you? Hero one minute, dunce the next. Can't be too uncharitable, though. Chap probably went to a frightful school."

In his quarters at that moment, Dick Charles was splashing his face with cold water to disguise the fact that he had been crying. He patted his eyes with a towel, and then stared at himself in the small mirror on his bureau. My God, he thought, look at you. You're acting like a boy of fourteen. Jealous, stupid, and ridiculous. If you were half the grown-up man that Ralph Peel is, you would have gone to bed with Lady Diana, enjoyed yourself, and left it at that. But oh no, *you* have to get infatuated, You have to go along with Charbonnel et Walker chocolates, and flowers, when all the lady wanted was a hard five minutes in bed, and a hard smack across the bottom if she talked back. But when will you ever *learn?* You're a ship's officer. Ship's officers can have any eligible girl they want, just by snapping their fingers. Kings of the floating fuck-a-toria, that's what they are.

And yet, as he began to change for luncheon, into the neatly pressed uniform that his steward had laid out for him, Dick still felt miserably sad and wished that he hadn't written that note to Lady Diana, and wished, above all, that he hadn't arrived at her stateroom until ten minutes later, or better still, ten minutes earlier.

"D-d-diana," he lamented to himself in the mirror.

At a quarter after twelve, on the inquiry of Maurice Peace, Second Officer Ralph Peel announced that during the twelve hours preceding noon, the *Arcadia* had officially covered 636 nautical miles.

"Are you *sure?*" Maurice asked him, stunned. "In spite of the fact that we turned back and spent an hour looking for that drowned officer?"

"That's what it says here," said Ralph, and handed Maurice the small sheet of paper on which the navigator had written "636.02 naut. miles."

Maurice glanced across the smoking lounge at George Welterman, who was standing not far away with a whisky in his hand. George Welterman saw him looking and gave him a long, slow wink.

"Well, congratulations," Maurice told him a few minutes later as they met in the corridor on their way to luncheon. "It looks like you've got yourself a new car."

George stopped and wagged a finger. "You mustn't think of it that way. *I* don't. I have two cars already, not that I drive. Only chauffeurs and mechanics drive."

"So how *do* you think of it?" asked Maurice.

"I think of it," said George, "as having got my revenge on Mark Beeney."

"You gamble for *revenge?*" said Maurice.

George turned his head and eyed him narrowly. "Don't you?" he asked.

Maurice said, "No, never. I never gamble for any reason at all."

"But you must get *something* out of it, or you wouldn't do it."

"Wouldn't I?" said Maurice. "I'll tell you something, George—you don't object if I call you George—I gamble because it's the only thing I ever knew how to do, and the only thing I'm ever likely to know how to do. Can you see me farming fifty acres of land in Iowa? Or picking oranges in California? I've done those things, but they're not what I do. What

412

I do is gamble. Not for revenge. Not for profit. Not for anything, except one thing: I gamble because there's nothing else for me to do."

"You're bullshitting me," George told him.

Maurice couldn't bring himself to smile at all. "Would I bullshit a seasoned campaigner like you?"

"I expect so," said George.

They went into luncheon. The lounge had been decorated for the amusement of Keys' Irish bankers with green satin shamrocks and white lilies; and the orchestra, dressed in green tailcoats and high green hats with buckled hatbands, were playing "Killarney" and "What Do You Think of O'Hooligan?"

"I sometimes wonder how the Irish can bear this kind of thing," said George Welterman sourly.

"No sign of Mark Beeney," remarked Maurice.

"Well, that's good," said George. "I can't wait to tell him the news myself."

"Do you have any money on that pair of eaters?" asked Maurice. "I reckon that one or the other of them is going to keel over today."

George shook his head. "Contests for the sake of contests don't interest me, Mr. Peace. I'm only interested in contests that have some crushing result."

"Like taking Mark Beeney's beloved Marmon away from him, so that you can drive it into a brick wall?"

George slapped Maurice's back. "You've got it."

"Like taking five thousand pounds from me, too, I suppose?"

George nodded with malicious happiness.

"Now you've got the car, you couldn't perhaps see your way clear to — Well, no, perhaps not."

"No," agreed George. "Perhaps not. But as a consolation prize, I'll let you come down to the hold and look the car over."

The chief steward came up to them and nodded his head respectfully. "Gentlemen . . . you wish to be seated for luncheon?"

"I have an invitation to join the captain's table today," said George.

The steward's smile stayed fixed to his face, but the welcome in his eyes died away. "Ah, Mr. Welterman, I'm sorry. It appears that there has been some mistake."

"Mistake? What are you talking about?"

"I regret the captain's table is a little *overbooked*. You are to sit at Mr. Charles' table today."

George Welterman's face was thunderous. "Who gave you that instruction?" he demanded.

"Sir Peregrine Arrowsmith, sir. I'm sorry."

George was plainly finding it almost impossible to contain his rage. He took one long deep breath that filled his lungs, and held it. Then he said in a voice that was shaky but controlled, "You may take a message to Sir Peregrine for me. You may tell him that I am going to sit at his table whether he likes it or not. You may also tell him that when White Star take over this ship, I will do everything I can to find him a room in the home for retired seafarers. And that will be in spite of the fact that he hasn't had the courtesy to find a place for me."

The chief steward was white-faced. "Please wait a moment, sir," he said and hurried off.

Maurice Peace said with quiet satisfaction, "Do you ever get the feeling that you're not too popular around here?"

But George was too furious to answer. He was gnawing at his knuckles and staring across the room at Sir Peregrine with an expression of utter fury.

At that moment, Catriona made her entrance, escorted by Mr. Charles Schwab, of Bethlehem Steel, and closely followed by Lady Cressworthy and Mr. Paul Hartley, the fifth son of the banking Hartleys, who had once bought the Ingestre Hotel in Vancouver for the sole purpose of sacking the elevator operator, who had irritated him with his glumness.

Catriona was wearing an emerald green crepe dress by Martial et Armand, very simply cut, with long lapels, and a front trimmed with embroidered black crepe. She wore a wide-brimmed white hat with green scalloped silk bands on it to match her dress, teardrop earrings, and green crocodile shoes with T-bar straps. Mr. Schwab wore a suit cut from pearl-grey English wool which had been "built" for him, as he liked to say, by Henry Poole & Sons, at 37 Savile Row. The suit didn't fit, for a gentleman's suits never *fit*. They make the best of a gentleman's attributes, and subtly disguise his shortcomings.

George looked at Catriona keenly, and then bowed his head to her. "Miss Keys," he said.

Catriona slowly and disdainfully turned her head towards him. Her slanted eyes, when she finally caught his stare, were like cold chips of some dark and adamant mineral. "Why," she said. "It's Mr. Waterman."

George, at that moment, had no choice. Boorish and crude as he could be, he was still a man of his time, and of the etiquette of his time. He had been openly refused a place at the captain's table, and now Catriona had purposely mispronounced his name. He said, "Excuse me," and walked out of the dining lounge with abrupt mechanical strides.

Charles Schwab said, "What's eating *him?*"

Catriona smiled. "I don't know. I think he just saw a ghost."

Charles Schwab happily drew Catriona's arm closer. "Do you know something?" he said. "There are two things in this world that make me feel happy. The sight of a furnace chimney at night when the red fire's pouring out of it like hell itself, and a pretty girl."

"In that order?" put in Paul Hartley. He was skinny, and his moustache was wispy and blond, but in five years' time he would undoubtedly grow up to be more than passably handsome.

"What are you?" Charles Schwab demanded. "Some kind of philosopher or something? Plato maybe? Who cares what order? A furnace is a furnace, and a girl is a girl. They're both hot stuff. Who cares what order? What order! You're going to tell me whether your father prefers your mother to money? How do you know? How does *he* know?"

Catriona giggled. It was the first time she had really laughed since George had assaulted her. Charles Schwab, smiling at his own outburst, patted her arm and then kissed her on the cheek.

At the far end of Sir Peregrine's table, Edgar Deacon was deep in conversation with Mr. Denis O'Hara, from the Eire Credit Bank, and it was during the course of this conversation that the most crucial decisions of that whole noonday hour were finally reached.

Fifty-five

As the first-class passengers filed into luncheon, Mademoiselle Louise Narron was still in her stateroom staring at her three reflections in the triple looking glass on her dressing table. Each reflection looked more bleary and more devastated than the next. She had been crying for a whole hour, a monotonous and wearisome series of high yelps, as if a Pomeranian bitch had caught her leg in an automobile door.

Her stewardess, Madge, was waiting patiently beside her bed, where the diva's clothes were laid out for luncheon. Madge would have done almost anything for a cup of tea, as long as it was reasonably moral. The chief steward always seemed to give her the hysterical ones to look after. Once, on the *Fatidical*, she had been allocated the wife of a Brazilian politician who had thrown fits of dramatic rage at the slightest provocation, and had once ripped her evening gown down to her waist during a diplomatic cocktail party in the Crystal Lounge. Then there had been Mrs. Wuldorf, the wife of the catering billionaire, who had insisted on changing her dress every three hours every day. During the whole four-and-a-half-day voyage across the Atlantic, she had never worn the same dress twice.

Louise at last said, "Madge, will you bring me a cigarette?"

Madge did as she was told, but as she offered Louise the open silver cigarette box, she said, "You did tell me you weren't supposed to smoke. Bad for your voice, and all that."

Louise stared at herself in the mirror. "Who cares about my voice? I have lost the man I was going to marry. *Je suis désolée.* Do you know what that means?"

"You feel fed up, I suppose."

"Fed up? It means my entire world has collapsed around me." She pronounced it "coll-upsed," as in "scallops."

"Did he really ask you to marry him?" said Madge, striking a match.

Louise lifted her cigarette to the flame and nodded. "We plighted our troth by the light of the moon. I shall never be able to go out in the moonlight again."

She smoked one or two puffs, and then began to sing, " 'And ere now thy glowing eye have I seen: the man whose glance solaced my grief; When he greeted me had that eye—I knew him because of his eye.' "

She crushed out the cigarette and made a face. "Sieglinde, from *Die Walküre.* Poor Sieglinde. Poor me."

There was a knock at her stateroom door. Madge said, "Shall I answer it, mum?"

"Oh . . . if you wish," said Louise. She felt as if madness were stealing up on her. She had done so much to persuade herself to love Rudyard. She had turned herself inside out. And now there was no purpose in it, because he was drowned, and gone forever, taking with him below the surface of the ocean all of her efforts to forget Raymond.

She had seen Rudyard's discarded shoes and jacket on the bridge. She had let out a howl of anguish, one of those incredible operatic shrieks that make wineglasses ring, and milk turn sour, and bodies rise to the surface of ponds. It had made Ralph Peel's hair stand on end, all of it. But it had also brought this magnificent red-haired Amazon to his immediate attention again. And so it was that when Madge went to open the door of Louise Narron's stateroom, Ralph was there, with a small posy of white flowers and a look on his face that could only be described as sly sympathy.

"Mademoiselle . . . so sorry to intrude . . . but this is just a small personal gesture . . . . considering how Mr. Philips and I were such close friends."

"Oh," said Louise, sitting bolt upright in her clashing orange bathrobe. Then, "Oh, you'd better come in. Why, that's most thoughtful of you. Flowers! You Englishmen are all such gentlemen! That is what I told poor Rudyard when—Well, I don't know when it was. My mind has been smashed to tiny pieces, like a broken mirror."

"Yes," said Ralph, unsure of what any of this meant.

"Have a drink," suggested Louise. "Can you help yourself?"

"Well," said Ralph, "I'm not really supposed to. But considering the

416

tragic circumstances . . ."

He set down the posy of flowers on the table and went stiffly across to the cocktail cabinet, where he picked up one decanter after another, sniffing them carefully until he found the single-malt whisky. He poured himself a very large glassful, and swallowed half of it straight down, with his back still turned, so that Louise wouldn't see how much he had.

"Would you like one?" he asked her.

Louise tossed her fiery red hair. "Drink is no consolation."

"Well, no," said Ralph. "But it's better than a poke in the eye with a burnt stick."

Louise turned on her dressing table stool and stared at him. He gave her an uncomfortable smile, which soon died away.

"Do you know what it is to be loved?" she demanded.

Ralph didn't answer.

Louise stood up and swept across the room in her orange robe, until she was towering over him. Ralph looked down and her right breast was almost level with his chin.

"Do you know what it is to lose everything you have?" asked Louise.

Ralph hesitated, and then said, "I lost my wage packet once."

"Oh, you British men! You are all so cold! Ice runs in your veins!"

Ralph, embarrassed, looked down at his drink, and then across at Madge. Madge gave him a slow, exaggerated wink, which plainly meant Never mind the theatricals. Just keep on acting English, and you'll be all right.

Ralph coughed. "Mademoiselle Narron," he said, "perhaps I could escort you in to luncheon?"

"I have nothing black to wear. Nothing suitable, anyway."

"I don't really think that matters, Mademoiselle. Not many people knew that you and Rudyard were—well, you know, friends of any kind. Perhaps it's better not to advertise the fact."

Mademoiselle Narron slowly nodded. Then she reached out and touched the back of Ralph's hand, which was patterned with dark whorls of fur.

"You are so hairy," she whispered. "I have always wondered what it would be like to be . . . touched by a hairy man."

Madge puffed her cheeks out in exasperation. Ralph said, in a voice that for him sounded oddly cultured, "It was a pity about Rudyard, don't you think? It should never have happened, really. There wasn't any point."

"Is there a point to anything?" asked Louise.

Ralph leaned forward and kissed her cheek. "To me there is," he said, ambiguously, and waited for the quiet flicker of understanding which eventually appeared in her eyes.

She said, "Perhaps I could learn to love moonlight again. Do you think so?"

Fifty-six

On his way to the dining lounge with Grace Bunyon, his admirer and second, Mr. Duncan Wilkes was intercepted by Dr. Fields.

"May I have a private word with you?" asked Dr. Fields. "I do apologise, Miss Bunyon, but it's rather important."

Mr. Wilkes beckoned to the chief steward. "Will you escort this lady into luncheon, please?" he asked, then, to Grace, "I won't be more than a minute, my dear. Please excuse me."

Dr. Fields led Mr. Wilkes by the arm to the small sofa in the anteroom and offered him a seat.

"If you're thinking that you're going to persuade me to give up this contest because of my health," he said, "I'm afraid you've got yourself another think coming. I know what's wrong with me. Heart, blood pressure, all that kind of thing. But this is a challenge, and I've never given up on a challenge in the whole of my life, no matter what it's done to my health. I'm going to see this through to the bitter end."

But Dr. Fields was more subtle than to tackle Mr. Wilkes head-on. Instead, he said thoughtfully, "It's not *your* health that I'm concerned about, Mr. Wilkes. I can see that you're suffering from a heart condition. But you're a big, strong fellow. A few extra meals won't hurt you, as long as you take care to lose all the surplus weight when you get back to America. No, it's Mr. Kretchmer's health that concerns me more. I'm afraid that one or two more meals and he's going to become seriously ill. If not fatally ill."

Duncan Wilkes made a suspicious face. "Are you serious? What's the matter with him?"

Dr. Fields said softly, "Beebe's Syndrome."

Duncan Wilkes waited for Dr. Fields to say more, but he didn't. Instead, he looked at the newspaper proprietor over his crescent-shaped half-glasses and pursed his lips as if he had just uttered the terrible and immortal words of the British death sentence: *You shall be taken from there to a place of execution . . .*

"Well," puffed Duncan Wilkes. He tugged out his handkerchief and mopped his face and his neck. "Beebe's Syndrome, hey?"

Dr. Fields nodded.

"And it could be fatal?"

"I would have thought so. And quite soon, if Mr. Kretchmer doesn't give up this excessive eating."

"Have you spoken to Mr. Kretchmer?"

"How can I?" asked Dr. Fields. "I'm not his personal doctor. I'm only a ship's sawbones. It would be quite improper of me to give him my diagnosis without conferring with his own practitioner first; and, of course, that's impossible."

Duncan Wilkes said, "This . . . Beebe's Syndrome. What exactly is it?"

Dr. Fields lowered his gaze. "It's a degeneration of the pancreatic effulgence brought about by the overinducement of fats. There's no cure, apart from a strict vegetarian diet, and plenty of mineral water."

Duncan Wilkes thought about this fiercely for a long time, then took out a cigar from an embossed alligator case and gripped it between his teeth. "And one more meal could kill him, hey?"

Dr. Fields nodded, with even greater solemnity.

"He did go in for this contest of his own free will," argued Duncan Wilkes. "He must have known there were risks to his health, just as I know that there's a risk to mine."

"Unless his doctor has already told him that he's suffering from Beebe's Syndrome, he wouldn't necessarily be aware that there's anything wrong with him," said Dr. Fields, quietly.

"I see," said Duncan Wilkes. "So what you're saying is that if I continue with this contest, knowing that he's sick that way, I may personally be responsible for killing him? A kind of gastronomic homicide?"

"You would certainly be morally liable, if not legally," said Dr. Fields.

Duncan Wilkes took his cigar out of his mouth and shook his head. "I sure do hate to have to give up on a challenge," he said. "If I throw my towel in now, because of this, then I can tell you that it's the first time in my life I've ever given in."

Dr. Fields raised his eyes again. "I'm sure the Lord God won't see it as giving in. The Lord God will see it as a truly Christian act. It's called self-sacrifice."

"Well, I suppose you're right. I'd hate to have to account for Mr. Kretchmer's death at the Pearly Gates."

He hesitated for a moment more, and then he said, "All right. You win. I'll concede the contest. I'm just about sick up to here with all this rich French cooking anyhow. It'll be quite a luxury to eat a dry cracker and drink a glass of water, and nothing else."

Dr. Fields said, "You're a man in a million, Mr. Wilkes. I thank you. You can be sure that what you've done today won't be forgotten."

Mr. Wilkes shook Dr. Fields by the hand and then went into luncheon. The dining lounge was already crowded, and there was a spatter of applause as Mr. Wilkes walked between the tables to the corner where he and Mr. Kretchmer had been sitting for the past two days. Instead of sitting down, however, Mr. Wilkes leaned forward and whispered something in Grace Bunyon's ear. Grace Bunyon frowned at first, but then she smiled and nodded.

"Mr. Kretchmer, Miss Chibnall," she announced, in her clearest, most dramatic voice. "Mr. Wilkes has decided to surrender the eating contest. He offers you his heartiest congratulations, and hopes that you will join him in some Melba toast and Spa water."

There was a great deal of cheering and hand-shaking, and a babble of conversation that almost drowned the orchestra's unsteady version of "When Irish Eyes Are Smiling." Mr. Wilkes and Mr. Kretchmer shook hands. Mr. Wilkes kissed Henrietta Chibnall, who cried. Mr. Kretchmer shook hands with the chief steward and with Oliver Lennox, the quartermaster, and then with Lord Willunshaw. Mary Pickford kissed Mr. Wilkes, and Douglas Fairbanks kissed Grace Bunyon. Grace Bunyon kissed Philip Carter-Helm, and Claude Graham-White kissed Catriona. Catriona shook hands with both Mr. Wilkes and Mr. Kretchmer.

Mark Beeney didn't appear at luncheon; he was still working in his stateroom with John Crombey. George Welterman also stayed in his stateroom, dictating a series of furious letters to Keys' major investors, and also to the New York newspapers, deploring the treatment he had received aboard the *Arcadia* (although he would later tear most of them up).

But it was Maurice Peace who was happiest of all that lunchtime. Not only had he won £1,654 when Mr. Duncan Wilkes had conceded the eating contest, but he had managed to do so without Mr. Duncan Wilkes having to suffer a heart attack. And to top everything, he adored brill.

He was seated next to Mr. Kearney, from the Association of Irish Underwriters, and between mouthfuls of fresh-baked bread roll and brill, he told him about the time he had made a living selling Irish sweepstakes tickets in Paris. "At one time, just before the draw, I had a single solitary two-dollar ticket left, and I took it into the men's bar at the Paris Ritz. But nobody was interested. They were either anti-Irish, or they were anti-gambling. Well, I went on and on trying to sell this one ticket until a gentleman at the other end of the bar who was heartily sick of my sales pitch gave me two dollars for it, just to shut me up. That ticket won him $139,000. And do you know who he was? Mr. William C. Procter, the president of Procter and Gamble, who personally owned ninety-nine and forty-four hundredths per cent of Ivory soap."

Fifty-seven

After luncheon was over, many of the passengers took to their cabins to doze off the effects of the special Irish celebration. The first course had brought before them a selection of asparagus soup, crimped salmon, fillets of gurnet, flamed brill, and *soles aux fines herbes*. This had been followed by lamb cutlets, *tendrons de veau au jardinière*, lobster patties, and larded sweetbreads. Then the stewards had brought on boiled capons, saddle of lamb, boiled calf's head, ham, and roasted chickens. And for any passenger with any appetite left, there had been roasted leverets, broiled goslings, prawns, cheesecakes, custards, fondues, and plovers' eggs. Coffee, chocolates, ices, and fruit had been served to those still upright.

"The terrible beauty of it is," wrote Julius Briggs, "that one retires to one's bed, with the shades tightly drawn so that passing promenaders may not peek in and marvel at the size of one's distended corporation; and even as one lies there in the twilight, breathless and exhausted, one is conscious that within one and a half hours, tea will be served in the Palm Court, with whipped-cream fancies and anchovies on toast and cucumber sandwiches, and that only three hours after that it will be time for a fancy-dress dinner, which tonight will feature lobster rissoles, mutton cutlets *à la maintenon,* ragoût of duck and green peas, and trout *à la Génévése.* One cries to whatever gods there may be to curb the salaciousness of one's appetite, and to ease the strenuousness of one's digestion!"

That may have been the terrible beauty of it, but the strange *truth* of it was that none of the first-class passengers would manage to eat their way through more than fifty pounds' worth of food in four and a half days. Keys could have cut the first-class fare by more than three hundred pounds and still made a moderate profit. Stanley Keys' philosophy about serving food in first class had always been: Give them more than they can possibly eat, because then they'll feel that they've had their money's worth. "The cost of throwing away a few ducks and a few joints of beef, at wholesale prices," he had written, "is nothing compared with the profit we will make if our first-class passengers feel they have been outrageously spoilt and will book with us again."

Edgar Deacon went back to his stateroom to work on a lengthy draft agreement. Percy Fearson had been waiting for him, but had fallen asleep in one of his armchairs, and was snoring with a ducklike quacking of his lips, followed by a loud whistling whoop. Edgar stood beside him and listened to him for a while, and then smiled. He felt quite tired himself, although he had been careful only to eat a little sole, and a couple of slices of chicken breast. He mixed himself a gin and French and crossed his living room to his desk.

There was a knock at his door. He called, "Come in!" but when nobody did, he went over to answer it. Outside in the corridor was a tall man with thinning white hair, and the look about him of a rather destitute aristocrat. He said, "Mr. Keys, is it?" in the booming voice of someone who has never had to speak quietly.

"Mr. Keys passed away last week," said Edgar.

"Ah!" said the man. "So who are you?"

"My name is Edgar Deacon. I'm the managing director of Keys Shipping, for the time being."

The tall man stepped uninvited into Edgar's living room, propped his hands on his hips, and looked around. When he saw Percy Fearson fast asleep in an armchair, he raised a questioning eyebrow.

"Mr. Fearson," explained Edgar. "He's been working all night. I thought he deserved a nap."

"Well, I'm glad *somebody* thinks they can afford to nap on this ship," said the tall man, in his loud, unmodulated voice. "Because it seems to me that the rest of us can't, on account of what might happen to our lady-folk if we do."

Edgar closed the stateroom door. "I beg your pardon?" he said.

"Well, you might do," said the man, stalking around the room with his hands still perched on his hips, and his lower lip stuck out. "You might *indeed* beg my pardon. But an apology won't really help."

"Do I know you?" asked Edgar.

"You should do," the man retorted. "I've been travelling on this Godforsaken ship of yours since it left Liverpool."

"I'm sorry you feel that way," said Edgar carefully.

"Sorry! It's not for *you* to be sorry! *I'm* the one who's sorry! Sorry I ever let my wife travel by Keys Shipping. That's what I'm sorry about!"

Edgar said patiently, "Do you think you could explain yourself? You appear to have some complaint about the ship, but I'm not sure what it is."

"It's my wife!" the man exclaimed.

"Yes, sir," said Edgar, "but who is your wife?"

"You don't know my wife? You call yourselves a luxury shipping line, and you don't know my wife?"

"If I knew who *you* were, sir, I might—"

"Well, that's it, isn't it!" the man declaimed. "You don't even know who *I* am! And that's the trouble! It seems to me that you don't know a damn thing! Stupidity one can forgive, but not ignorance!"

Edgar said, "Would you care for a drink, Mr.—?"

"Mister!" exclaimed the man. "That's just it! Mister!"

Percy Fearson woke up now and stared around him in bewilderment. Edgar said, "Percy! This gentleman is insisting that we should know him. Are you familiar with him?"

Percy rubbed at his eyes and tried to focus. But before he could make a guess at the identity of their irate visitor, the man himself said, "I am Lord Thomas FitzPerry. I have been travelling on the *Arcadia* in a certain disguise, in order to avoid publicity."

Edgar clicked the heels of his deck shoes together and gave Lord FitzPerry a nod of understanding and welcome. "In that case, sir, we're delighted to have you aboard. Now I come to think of it, you must have been the gentleman in the wig and the sunglasses and the silk scarf."

"Indeed I was, and nobody recognised me. But what a penalty I have paid!"

"What's up?" asked Percy Fearson, easing himself out of the arm-chair and brushing his crumpled tweed trousers. "You don't have anything to complain about, surely?"

"I suppose it depends on your moral outlook," said Lord FitzPerry. "But I have evidence that one of your officers set his hat at my wife, whom he believed to be travelling alone, and therefore unprotected, and then went about seducing her in the most calculating and inhuman fashion, a seduction which included practices so degrading that one could not even mention them out loud in a court of law. And more's the pity, because a court of law is where your officer's infamous behaviour is going to be judged."

Edgar was no longer smiling. "This is a very serious allegation, Lord FitzPerry."

"You may be sure that it is," Lord FitzPerry told him. "If it comes out in the yellow press that no woman is safe aboard the *Arcadia* because of the unbounded lechery of her officers, then your trade across the Atlantic is going to decline as rapidly as it deserves to! You have a crew of blackguards, Mr. Deacon! Blackguards and bounders! Not to mention cads!"

Percy Fearson said, "Who, exactly, is the officer concerned?"

Lord FitzPerry flared his nostrils, like an irate Arabian horse. "He calls himself Dicky. Or so I've been led to believe."

"Dick Charles," said Percy, in some surprise, looking across at Edgar. "I wouldn't have thought it of him. Too much of a dark horse, that lad."

"Even dark horses seem to harbour the desire to be stallions," said Lord FitzPerry caustically. "At least this one certainly does. He set upon my wife from the moment she came on board. Fortunately, she told me about the outrage, and I took the trouble to borrow the Edison recording machine from the ship's library and conceal it beneath her bed the following night."

He held up a phonograph cylinder. "Here, Mr. Deacon, is your evidence. The voice of your officer as he avails himself of my wife! He speaks words to her that would make any respectable person faint."

"Did he make your wife faint?" asked Edgar gently.

Lord FitzPerry didn't answer that, but shook the wax cylinder in the air. "The evidence is here, Mr. Deacon. There's no getting away from it."

Edgar stayed silent for more than two minutes. When Percy Fearson tried to say something, he raised his hand and quickly shook his head, making it clear that Percy ought to keep his opinions to himself. Then at last he said, "How much do you want for that cylinder, Lord FitzPerry?"

Lord FitzPerry twisted around in a parody of that classic sculptural position known as *contrapposto*. "How *much?* Do you honestly believe that I'm trying to blackmail you?"

"Yes," said Edgar. "I believe that you are."

"I wouldn't accept a thousand pounds for this cylinder. I want to see you dragged into court, and punished as you ought to be punished."

"Would you accept fifteen hundred?"

"Absolutely not."

Edgar said in a measured voice, "I *am* trying to be accommodating, Lord FitzPerry."

"Accommodating? When your officers behave like creatures from some Darwinian pre-history?"

"It just strikes me," put in Percy Fearson, in his stolid Northern accent, "it just strikes me that if you were as upset about what Mr. Charles was doing with your wife as you pretend to be, then you'd have waited behind the cabin door for him and punched him on the nose, rather than left an Edison recording machine under the bed."

There was a silence. Then Lord FitzPerry said, "I won't accept anything less than six thousand pounds and a written apology."

"Fifteen hundred's my limit," said Edgar.

"Well, then," said Lord FitzPerry, "it's obviously going to have to be court."

Edgar said very gently, "I'm giving you one last chance, Lord FitzPerry."

"You're giving *me* one last chance!" declared Lord FitzPerry, puffing up his starched shirtfront like a belligerent pigeon.

"Lord FitzPerry," said Edgar, "it hasn't escaped my notice that you are a regular and notorious gambler. Neither has it escaped my notice that you recently sold most of the furniture from Wrekin Hall to pay off some of your creditors. I do read an occasional newspaper, you know. I don't know what you and Lady FitzPerry are actually playing at, but it strikes me that you are both engaged in what I can only call a game of extortion. You had to leave England for a while, to escape bankruptcy proceedings, and in the process you thought you'd make yourself a little extra money."

"I shall sue you for slander, as well as indecency," bellowed Lord FitzPerry.

"You may certainly try," said Edgar. "But you'll have a difficult time proving either."

"I have this cylinder."

"The cylinder, Lord FitzPerry, belongs to the Keys Shipping Line. If you examine it closely, you will see the words Property of Keys Shipping Company Limited stamped around the end. If you attempt to remove that cylinder from this vessel, I will have you arrested for petty theft."

Lord FitzPerry began to look uncertain. "Nonetheless," he puffed, "what your officer did to my wife was inexcusable."

"Any more inexcusable than anything else your wife has done during the past ten years?"

Lord FitzPerry at last sat down. He said under his breath, "It's quite barbaric, of course."

"You know what they say," replied Edgar. "We live in barbaric times."

Lord FitzPerry didn't know what to say. Edgar glanced across at Percy Fearson, and Percy Fearson shrugged. It was quite obvious to both of them who had devised this little scheme: Lady Diana FitzPerry herself. To seduce a ship's officer and then try to claim compensation from the shipping line was just her style. Most of her jewellery and her furs had probably been gifts from eminent suitors who had been alarmed at the prospect of their wives and colleagues finding out about their liaison with her. It was well known in Fleet Street that her diamond necklace had been given to her by the Standard Assurance Company, after she had amused herself with their chairman. Silence, in Lady Diana FitzPerry's book, was golden.

Edgar said, "I'll give you a cheque for fifteen hundred now, and in return you'll give me that cylinder. What's more, you'll agree to press no charges of assault."

Lord FitzPerry sighed.

"This is your last opportunity," said Edgar. "If you don't say yes now, then I'll have you thrown out of my stateroom, and you won't get a penny. If you want anything, you'll have to fight for it in the courts."

"Very well," said Lord FitzPerry at last. "Although I don't know what her ladyship will say."

Edgar went to his desk, sat down, and opened a drawer to take out a Keys chequebook. He wrote a cheque in green ink for £1,500; blotted it dry, and held it up to Lord FitzPerry. Lord FitzPerry accepted it glumly, and then handed over the Edison cylinder.

"There's one more thing," said Edgar. "I don't expect either you or Lady FitzPerry to travel on a Keys steamer again. If you apply for a cabin, I regret that all the accommodation will be filled."

Lord FitzPerry folded the cheque, tucked it into his breast pocket, and went to the door.

"I'm sorry your wife went to so much trouble for so little," said Edgar. "I just hope that our officer gave her some amusement, along with the work. Good afternoon."

Lord FitzPerry hesitated, as if he wanted to say something. But then he went out and closed the door very precisely behind him.

Fifty-eight

Catriona was dressing to go out on deck that afternoon when Trimmer knocked on her door, and said, "Decent, Miss Keys? Might I come in?"

"Of course. I'm only doing my hair."

Alice said irritably, "Couldn't it wait?"

"I'm sorry, miss," said Trimmer. "I'ave to get down to the laundry before the shift changes, just to make sure we get the right linen. Chaos it was yesterday."

"That Monty Willowby's been very *lax* this trip, I've noticed," said Alice. "Not like his usual self, not at all."

"Be fair, Alice," put in Trimmer. "The *Arcadia*'s more than most pursers could 'andle."

"Is that for me?" Catriona asked him, nodding towards the brown envelope he was carrying.

"Ah, yes, Miss Keys. Found it in me scrapbook. Didn't know I kept a scrapbook, did you? Hevery trip I've been hon, I've halways kept a souvenir, something what reminds me hof heverything that 'appened."

"What will you keep from this trip?" asked Catriona, smiling.

"I 'opes to take a Blue Riband, Miss Keys, if we wins it. That'll be something, to beat the *Mauretania*, now won't it?"

He opened the envelope and produced a ship's cruising menu, printed in blue, with a colour painting of the ship pasted onto the front of it. Printed in silver script was the title SS *Orange*, and underneath "Mediterranean Cruise, 1911." Inside, there was a menu for Solferino Soup, Fried Fish with Orly Sauce, Prawn Curry, Sheep's Trotters, and

Tapioca Pudding.

"That was the *Orange*. Thought you'd like to see 'ow she looked. Just has a matter hof hinterest."

"Well, thank you," said Catriona. "Do you mind if I keep this, and show it to Mr. Beeney?"

"By hall means, miss."

Mark Beeney came to call for Catriona at three; and together they promenaded gracefully around the first-class decks, Catriona wearing a blue rep dress suit, checked socks, and white golf shoes, and Mark in a blue and white striped yachting blazer and white ducks. It was a warm and exhilarating day. The Atlantic sparkled as brightly as if every lady in cabin class had tossed her diamonds into the ocean, and the orchestra played swooning tunes of love and silliness and youth.

> *I'm no chicken,*
> *But I'll talk turkey,*
> *If you'll talk turkey too-oo-ooh!*

Mark led her at last to the rail, and they looked back at the wide white wake that foamed ceaselessly from the *Arcadia*'s stern. "This is when I love the sea," he said. "Look at it . . . it's marvellous."

Catriona said, "It always looks so lonely and empty to me."

"You don't feel lonely, do you?"

"A little."

He smiled. "That's not much of a compliment to me."

"Oh, I didn't mean that. I'm sorry. I was just thinking about my father. He put his heart and soul into this ship, and he never saw it cross the Atlantic. He would have been so proud."

Mark took out his cigarette case and offered Catriona a Sobranie.

"How's Marcia?" asked Catriona, trying to change the subject so that they wouldn't become too entangled in emotional arguments.

"Jumping off an ocean liner into mid-Atlantic is pretty serious."

"Well, maybe. But she was rescued, wasn't she?"

Catriona touched his hand. "You don't have to feel *quite* so guilty about it, you know. I don't think anybody really blames you. In fact, some of the women seem to think it makes you even more glamorous. They love a hint of danger."

"Danger, huh?" said Mark. He drew hard on his cigarette.

"By the way," said Catriona, opening her bag, "do you remember this ship?"

"Sure," said Mark, examining the menu with narrowed eyes. "The *Orange*. Sank off the Indian coast, didn't she, four or five years ago? Just after the Armistice, anyway. Why?"

"Well, you know Philip Carter-Helm, don't you?"

"Sure. Not intimately, of course, but we seem to be getting on pretty reasonably together."

Catriona held her hat against a sudden gust of wind. "Do you have any idea why Philip Carter-Helm should have been arguing with my father about the *Orange* only a week or two before she sank?"

Mark studied the picture again, then looked back at Catriona. "No," he said slowly.

"He's in marine insurance, isn't he, Philip?"

"That's right. Well, that's what he tells me."

"Well, you don't think—"

Mark gave a quick glance over his shoulder, the instinctive reaction of a businessman who wants to make sure that nobody can overhear him. "You're not trying to suggest that your father and Philip Carter-Helm arranged to sink the *Orange* deliberately?"

"I don't know. But I've been thinking about it and thinking about it. I may be completely screwy. But the *Orange* sank without any loss of life at all, in calm water; and when the insurance money was paid by Lloyd's, that did give father sufficient capital to lay down the keel of the *Arcadia*."

"It could have been coincidence."

"Well, yes, of course it could. And I don't have any means of proving it. But somehow the idea just won't seem to go away."

Mark took another deep suck at his cigarette. Then he flicked it, so that the butt spun out to sea. "Never did like smoking in the open air. You might just as well light a bonfire and breathe *that* in."

"But don't you think it's possible?" Catriona insisted. "Don't you think that the *Orange* could have been sunk for the money, and nothing else?"

Mark shrugged. "I don't really know what to say. Stanley Keys was *your* old man, not mine."

"And your old man would never have done anything so underhand, is that it?"

"Do you think *yours* would?" asked Mark. "Come on, you know what a reputation he had for honesty. 'Stanley the Straight.'"

"I know. But somehow—I can't really explain it—I seem to think that he *could* have done it. He was a very passionate man, you know; and when he wanted something, he did everything he possibly could to get it. He treated his workers exceptionally well, of course. They all respected him and admired him. But I wonder whether he did that only because he knew that was the best way to get them to work extra hard, and put in hours of overtime without being paid. I keep thinking about the woman that Edgar Deacon took me to see before we boarded. Father had done so much for her. In fact, in some ways, he seemed to have lavished more care on her than he ever did on my mother. Although he loved his own family, every one of us, I can't say he didn't—I think he considered that we were a nuisance, too, because we expected to be supported without making any real contribution to the company. There was something else that poor woman said, too, that her husband would have adored to have sailed on the *Arcadia*'s maiden voyage. He'd put so much skill into building her, it seemed almost criminal that he wasn't allowed to sail on her. And you know, there isn't a single Keys workman on this ship, apart from her maintenance crew. My father never gave anything away. Nothing. Not even his friendship."

Mark leaned back against the rail. "Don't you think you're being a little bit too harsh on him?"

"I don't know. Perhaps I am."

"Maybe we should go and find ourselves some tea," Mark suggested. "Would you care for some tea?" he asked her, in a carefully studied English accent.

Catriona reached out and took his hand. "Yes, I would."

They walked along the deck to the staircase; but just as they were about to go down to the Orchid Lounge, they were hailed by John Crombey. "Mark, I really *have* to speak to you about those refit charges at Newport News."

"Does it have to be now?" asked Mark impatiently. "Miss Keys and I were just going down for tea."

"I won't take more than a minute," John Crombey insisted.

They went downstairs together, John Crombey rattling through statistic after statistic: how the shipfitters were overcharging on hinges, pipework, underlay, and veneer work; how the suppliers were giving them short loads. "You have to understand, Mark, that for the cost of materials which we never get to see, we could build outselves another small ship."

John Crombey was still going through figures when they sat down. "We could halve the cost of turbine seals if we went to Oppenheimer's; and we could cut the cost of linoleum by over a third if we went to Indiana Flooring. We could save ourselves nearly $100,000 if we had the sheet-metal work done by US Weld instead of Appalachian; and—what's that?"

There was an awkward pause. Then Mark said, blinking, nonplussed, "What's what?"

John Crombey reached across the table and picked up the menu of the SS *Orange*. "That's remarkable," he said.

"What's remarkable about it?" asked Mark.

"Well, it says SS *Orange*. And, yes, I guess it is the SS *Orange*. But it's not the *Orange* at all."

"I beg your pardon?" asked Catriona.

"What I mean is that this ship is sailing around the South China Sea, this identical ship, and yet she isn't called SS *Orange* at all. As far as I recall, she's called the *Funabashi*, and she belongs to the Kyoto Shipping and Trading Company."

"John," said Mark patiently, "the *Orange* was sunk nearly five years ago."

"I know that," said John Crombey, twitching his neat little moustache. "But the fact remains that this *is* the *Funabashi*. Look, you can tell by the notched effect on the stern counter. There is no other ship in the world that has that notch. It was designed specifically for the loading and offloading of cargoes of teak at Moulmein."

Mark looked across at Catriona, and she could see by the expression on his face that he was wondering how to prepare her for the thought that her father might have been very much less than the maritime hero he had always appeared to be.

Catriona saved his feelings by saying it out loud for both of them. "If the *Funabashi* is the *Orange*, then the *Orange* didn't sink at all; and yet Keys claimed the full insurance on her."

John Crombey stared at Mark worriedly, unused to a business competitor being so frank. Then, quite abruptly, he said, "It happens all the time, you know. It's not unusual, particularly with a ship that needs a refit. Well, available cash being what it is these days. All you have to do is take your ship out somewhere, open the seacocks, half flood the holds, and then allow yourself to be conveniently 'discovered' by the ship of a friendly accomplice, so that all of your crew can be taken off to safety. You take photographs of the ship foundering, of course, to prove what happened; but immediately the 'rescue vessel' is out of sight, you pump out the seawater, refloat your ship, paint over her name, and sail her at top speed to a prearranged dry dock to have her repainted and refitted. You leave as much debris floating on the ocean as you can; deck chairs with the ship's name stencilled on them, things like that; and with any luck you can claim your full insurance within two or three months, as well as the money you made from selling her off. You remember that Greek chap, what was his name, Kostas, he sank the *Iolanthe* six times before they caught up with him; and he had the gall to keep selling her back to his own company."

There was a lengthy and difficult silence. John Crombey cleared his throat several times, a worrying little noise, as if he were trying to start up the engine of a model boat.

Mark said, "You realise that if your father was involved in sinking the *Orange* for the insurance money, then Edgar Deacon was probably involved, too."

"And Philip Carter-Helm?" said Catriona. "Perhaps Philip Carter-Helm was the one who put them up to it."

"I don't know. John, what do you know about the Kyoto Shipping and Trading Company? Is there anybody there we could contact by telegraph? How about Takemitsu? Didn't he use to work for them once?"

"Well, he used to," said John. "But Kyoto Shipping was taken over about four years ago by International Mercantile Marine, or at least by their Far East people."

Catriona frowned. "But that means that IMM probably know about the *Orange* too."

"They very well might," agreed John Crombey. "But a ship that's sold off after an insurance fraud usually comes pretty cheap; and it's not like IMM to look a gift horse in the mouth. Ask no questions, hear no lies."

The waitress brought them China tea and a silver plate arranged with crystallised plums and apricots, Bakewell tarts, and Maids of Honour. Mark took a Bakewell tart and bit into it unselfconsciously, with crumbs on his chin. "Who was Far Eastern director of IMM in those days? Don't tell me it was George Welterman."

John Crombey smiled tightly and nodded. "Who else? George Welterman."

"So, let's work this out. Why is Edgar Deacon so anxious to let Keys go for eighteen million to George Welterman? And why is George Welterman so wonderfully anxious to buy? IMM could certainly do with some of your ships, but do they really need the whole fleet, including the *Arcadia*, when they've already got the *Mauretania*? And why does it all have to be done in such indecent haste, so that the fleet's sold off before anyone has a chance to do any real deep digging in the company's books and records?

"This may be hogwash. Edgar Deacon may be the honest man that Diogenes was always looking for. But it wouldn't surprise me if Edgar Deacon is so enthusiastic to sell and George Welterman so enthusiastic to buy because both of them were parties to the *Orange* fraud, if there *was* a fraud, and because the only way in which they can keep it quiet is to keep the books to themselves. What do you think about that, John?"

John Crombey peered at the illustration of the SS *Orange* and shrugged. "It's impossible to say. But the facts do appear to speak for themselves, don't they? There's no question in my mind that the *Orange* and the *Funabashi* are one and the same ship."

"Catriona?" asked Mark.

Catriona reached over and plucked the *Orange*'s menu out of John Crombey's hands. "I don't know," she said. "But I'm going to find out. I think I've allowed myself to be Edgar Deacon's ornament for a little too long."

Mark encouragingly held her hand. "You may have to face up to the fact that the *Orange* was just the tip of the iceberg."

"The *Titanic* was sunk by an iceberg," said Catriona, in a level voice.

"Well, let's make sure that the *Arcadia* doesn't go the same way."

"What will you do now?" John Crombey asked, picking an S-shaped thread from the knee of his immaculately pressed trousers. "I mean, I'm not trying to be presumptuous. We are rival companies. But since you've been so open with us . . ."

"I'm not sure," said Catriona. "But I expect that you'll be the first to know."

They finished their tea, and then Catriona said, "Let's continue that walk on the deck, Mark. I feel like some fresh air."

They walked along the starboard promenade deck, sheltered from the wind, with their hands in their pockets, a little way apart.

"You realise that all of this *Orange* business may be nothing more than an uninformed guess," said Mark. "We may all end up eating Embarrassment Pie."

"I don't think so," said Catriona, staring at the sea.

Mark took her arm. "If it's true, well, there are hundreds of guys who have done the same kind of thing, to keep their business going, to protect their families. Life is a jungle, you know that already; and businessmen are the lions and tigers."

"And the jackals," said Catriona.

They walked on a little further, until they were sheltered from the wind by the gymnasium. The clatter of mechanical horses and rowing machines could be heard through the open ventilators, and the intermittent squeaking of plimsolls on the polished oak floor.

Mark said, trying to be encouraging, "You'll love Boston. I have a house on Commonwealth Avenue. We can take the old horse-drawn carriage out and have codfish and brown bread and beans at the Bell in Hand."

Catriona said, "Can I trust you?"

"Trust me? Of course you can trust me. I'm the soul of discretion, incarnate."

"I didn't really mean that. Can I trust you not to take advantage of the way I feel about you? I know it sounds awful, but I don't want to wake up from some romantic dream, only to find that you've taken everything away from me without my knowing."

"Catriona, I can't make any secret of the fact that I want the *Arcadia.*"

"I know. But don't do it sneakily."

Mark held her hand. Then he bent forward and kissed her, quite lightly, on the lips. He looked very closely into her eyes and said, "Do you really think I could do anything to harm you?"

"No," said Catriona. Then, "I don't know. You've got so many other things to consider."

"I've fallen in love with you, Catriona."

She turned away and looked out across the ocean. She felt alarmed by Mark's affection for her, but proud and happy at the same time. When she turned back to him and saw him standing there with such a warm and caring expression on his face, and the breeze blowing his curly hair, she knew that if she didn't love him already, she easily could.

"You know what my father used to say?" she said.

Mark shook his head.

"He used to say, 'Never fall in love with anybody you don't feel a little bit frightened of.'"

"Are you frightened of me?"

"A little. Not *too* much. But a little."

It wouldn't have been proper for them to kiss on deck, in front of everybody, but Mark took her hand and squeezed it, and the look on his face was as good as a kiss. They walked hand in hand to the forward part of the promenade deck, which was enclosed, and there they sat for another half-hour talking softly and laughing, and never taking their eyes off each other. Sir Peregrine, who was limping around the deck with Nurse Queensland to show everybody that he was still in command, saw them from the companionway amidships and let out a grunt of disapproval.

"Damn canoodling with the enemy," he remarked.

"Well, I think it's wonderful," said Nurse Queensland. "I think everybody should fall in love when they cross the Atlantic. I wish I could fall in love myself."

"Not with *me*, I sincerely trust," said Sir Peregrine.

Nurse Queensland said nothing, but thought of what Sir Peregrine had murmured in his coma, about Maude; and she forgave him his crustiness, because she knew how deeply his devotion really could run.

Fifty-nine

George Welterman was taken down to the automobile hold by Monty Willowby so that he could inspect Mark Beeney's car. Maurice Peace came along, too, eating a peach, and walked around the gleaming length of it with undisguised admiration, and not a little jealousy.

"You're a swine, winning this," he said. "You're even more of a swine if you're thinking of destroying it. Why don't you give it to a good cause, like the Cincinnati Hospital for the Deaf, or better still, to me?"

George drummed his fingers on the hood. "No, Mr. Peace. This is my revenge. I want to take this back to my office in New York, triumphant."

"Well, that's very Roman of you," said Maurice, wiping his juicy mouth with his handkerchief. "Are you sure you don't want me to dance in front of you up Fifth Avenue, throwing garlands of flowers under your wheels?"

Monty Willowby said, "Do you want to see inside, sir? I've got the keys."

George glanced down at his watch. "Just for a moment, then. I have some pressing business to attend to."

Monty Willowby opened up the driver's door and George Welterman peered inside. There was a strong aroma of thick hide, brandy, and some peppery man's cologne. The steering wheel was made of shaped and laminated avodire wood, in light grey, on a sterling silver base. The dashboard was made from highly polished satinwood, which was usually considered so expensive that it was used only for making small boxes and picture frames. Each dial—speedometer, oil pressure gauge, revolution counter, and mileage recorder—was made of raised gold figures on a background of lapis lazuli. The gold and silver gearshift knob alone could have been traded for a large semi-detached house in a good suburb of London.

"Now that's what I call a motorcar," said Maurice. "Are you sure you don't want to give it to the Cincinnati Home for the Deaf?"

But George Welterman was in no mood for jokes. He took out his wallet, gave Monty Willowby a one-pound tip, and then said, "Let's get back upstairs. Maybe I'll come and have another gloat tomorrow."

"Ah, well," said Maurice, touching the silver-plated headlamps with affectionate resignation.

Monty Willowby locked the Marmon up again and followed along behind, whistling "In a Monastery Garden," but on the way back across the hold, he caught hold of George Welterman's sleeve. "I hope you don't think I'm being presumptuous, Mr. Welterman," he said, "but it you're taking that automobile with you when you leave the ship, I wonder if you could do me a small favour."

George Welterman, without breaking his stride, looked down at Monty and raised one eyebrow.

"I've got a few items which need to be unloaded in New York, you see," said Monty, "and the problem is that they're quite fragile. I wouldn't like them to be manhandled by the longshoremen in New York and broken. Pieces of antique furniture, if you get my meaning."

"Illicitly exported?" asked George.

"Oh, no, sir. Nothing like that. Just fragile."

George paused and thought. Then he said, "All right. Whatever they are, just wrap them up and leave them in the trunk, or on the back seat. I'll make sure they clear customs without any trouble."

"Well, sir, that's very big of you, sir," said Monty. "If there's any thing I can do in return . . ."

"Oh, just a small matter," said George. "Make sure I'm sitting at the captain's table tonight at dinner, and at every other meal."

"Well, sir, I'm not sure I can—"

George smiled. Monty heard the vipers hissing in his head. "Very well, sir," he said. "The captain's table it is."

When George had gone, Monty locked up the automobile hold and breathed a deep sigh of relief. He had seventeen lavatory seats now, each one labelled according to the celebrity who had sat on it, and he was sure that Mr. Fribourg would be satisfied with that. Not only did he have the seats, but he had a means of getting them undetected off the ship, so that there would be no risk of being arrested for petty theft.

Life was beginning to look up. Apart from Mr. Fribourg's seats, the voyage had already yielded a dozen cases of Perrier-Jouët champagne for sale in New York restaurants, eighteen sides of best Scotch beef, fifteen sides of smoked salmon, more pounds of Malossol caviar than he could weigh, plus a whole variety of other sundries, and nearly £850 in gratuities, cash.

He was beginning to feel like an emperor again. All he had to do now was to lean on Sir Peregrine and make sure that George Welterman was invited to the top table tonight.

Sixty

When George Welterman opened the door of his stateroom and found Catriona standing there, with Alice beside her, his eyes widened in displeased surprise; but that was all. He was too experienced to show how unexpected her visit was, too experienced and too vain.

"Miss Keys," he said, a little hoarsely. He was holding a glass of seven-year-old Golden Wedding whisky in his hand. "This *is* a pleasure. Well, I hope it is."

Catriona found herself unable to speak for one throat-tightening moment, but then she managed to say, "I think we still have unfinished business, Mr. Welterman."

"Come in," said George, opening the door wider. Catriona hesitated, and then walked in, with Alice keeping unnaturally close behind her, and glaring at George with unabashed distaste. George tried to smile at her, but gradually his smile collapsed into a melting snarl.

"You'll have a drink?" he asked. "I'm afraid my man is out running an errand for me at the moment."

"A gin and bitters, please," said Catriona.

"And your—?" indicating Alice.

"Nothing for me, thanks very much, sir," snapped Alice, clutching her bag tightly and tilting up her nose.

"Sit down," George invited them. "You know something, I've been hoping that we could get back together on speaking terms before the voyage ended. There really isn't any way I can express how sorry I feel. It was all a terrible misunderstanding, I hope you realise that."

"Well, perhaps it was," Catriona replied, sitting down and crossing her legs tidily. "But in any case, you and I are going to have to work together, aren't we, if we decide to sell Keys to IMM?"

"That's right," George agreed. He brought over her drink and held it out for her. "I'm glad you see it that way. A lot of girls would have been hysterical."

Catriona sipped her drink. George had mixed it too strong, with too much Gordon's. "I'm all kinds of things, Mr. Welterman, but I'm never hysterical"

"Can't you find it in your heart to call me George?"

"Perhaps."

George sat down, uncomfortably close. "You're feeling . . . well, you're feeling okay? No harm done?"

"Not so far," said Catriona.

"But you haven't just called by for the sake of your health."

"No, I've called by to talk about the *Orange*."

George slowly sat back in his chair, cupping his whisky glass in both hands. Catriona watched him tensely; this was the only card that she had to play against him, apart from the sheer surprise of her visit, and if he were to deny all knowledge of the *Orange* then she wasn't at all sure what she was going to do next.

"Have you discussed it with Edgar?" asked George, pronouncing his words with care.

"Not yet."

"But I assume that you know all about it?"

Catriona nodded.

There was a long silence. George stared at her intently for a while, and then stood up and paced across the room. "How much do you know?" he asked her.

"I know about a remarkably similar ship called the *Funabashi*."

"Well . . . do you now?" George replied. "You're better informed than I thought."

"I own a quarter of Keys Shipping, Mr. Welterman. Don't you think it's my business to know?"

George shrugged. Then he said, "You understand now why you *have* to sell Keys Shipping to me."

"Of course."

"Your father's reputation . . . poor old Edgar's reputation . . . and, of course my *own* reputation, although I would always have been able to protest that we bought the *Orange* in good faith, not realising that she was supposed to have been sunk. They refitted her at Calcutta, you know, in Edgar Deacon's own yards. And did a fine job on her, too."

"Obviously I'm going to have to agree to give you my support," said Catriona, more coldly than she had meant to.

George looked at her narrowly. "I don't want you to feel that I'm exerting any undue pressure on you, Catriona. I don't want you to go away saying that you've been blackmailed, or anything unpleasant like that. Because, you know, it simply wouldn't be true."

"No," said Catriona. "I know."

He came and sat down again, just as close as before. "I'm offering eighteen million for the entire fleet; and that's an excellent price, considering how old most of your ships actually are. My accountants will go through the books and reconcile any little problems that might have cropped up in the past, and that will be that."

"And you'll keep the fleet together?"

"As far as commercially possible."

Catriona lowered her eyes. George raised a hand for a moment, a little way above her knee, but then Alice sniffed loudly, and fixed him with a stare like an outraged peregrine falcon, and he withdrew it.

"I don't want you to tell Edgar what we've discussed," said Catriona. "He likes to think of himself as my guardian, you know, now that my father's gone. If he knew that I'd found out about the *Orange* . . . well, I think it would embarrass him terribly. So, please don't say anything. I'll go and talk to him later and tell him that I've decided to support the sale to IMM."

George couldn't help smiling. "You're a brave, intelligent girl. I misjudged you. I admit it. You have style, Do you mind if I kiss you?"

"You can kiss me."

George leaned forward and, with difficulty, pecked Catriona's cheek. The feeling of his lips against her face made her skin tighten with coldness; but she was determined this time that he was going to dance to her tune; yes, and Edgar, too.

"I'll have to go now," she said. "But it's the fancy-dress ball tonight, and I'm sure I'll see you there. Have you decided on a costume?"

"I thought it was supposed to be a surprise."

"It is. But I rather saw you as Cyrano de Bergerac."

George let out a short, uncomfortable laugh. "Did you?" he said loudly. Then, more reflectively, "Did you?"

Sixty-one

Catriona was very quiet while Alice dressed her for the fancy-dress ball. She was going as Cinderella, in a white satin fairy-tale gown with a flounced crinoline skirt tied with ribbons, and a tight low-cut bodice that pushed her breasts into a deep dramatic cleavage, and which was panelled in the front with ruffles of Brussels lace and sewn with seed pearls. She wore a high white wig, bedecked with bows and mother-of-pearl combs, and festooned with pearls, and her cheeks were rouged and accentuated with beauty spots. She felt ridiculously overdressed and extravagant, and ravishingly, archaically beautiful.

She was still thinking about George Welterman, though, and Edgar, and the strange history of the SS *Orange*. She knew now that it was true; George had confirmed that. And although it hurt her to have discovered that her father had been involved in illegal conspiracy in order to raise enough money to start building the *Arcadia*, it was a peculiar relief, too, to have had her doubts confirmed. She smoked a cigarette and watched herself in the mirror as Alice teased her wig, and thought about what she could do next.

The past three days on the *Arcadia* had aroused in her a feeling which she could not yet fully understand; but a feeling which was strong and deeply emotional nonetheless. It was partly pride, partly arrogance, partly ambition; and it was certainly a feeling which she had inherited from her father. But it was something else, as well, something more valuable, and she was unable fully to understand it because she had never experienced it before. It was, in the very broadest sense, a feeling of responsibility.

It alarmed her. It gave her a sense of vertigo, because all the security to which she had been accustomed all her life had suddenly dropped away from under her silk-slippered feet.

It could have been brought on by George Welterman's brutal rape. Or perhaps it was the genuine love which she was beginning to feel for Mark Beeney. The abrupt discovery that her straight and saintly father had been less than honest may also have had something to do with it; as

438

well as the realisation that shipping, for all its glamour was one of the fiercest and most unscrupulous businesses in the world.

But Catriona was growing up, flowering, maturing. And instead of playing, she was beginning to assert herself as a woman, and to feel the need to do it, too.

Without knowing how, she had begun to think that Keys Shipping *could* survive; and that they could keep the *Arcadia,* too. Her father must have believed it, or he wouldn't have built her. Her father must have seen her as his single greatest hope for the company's future. And if her father had considered that it was possible to keep the company going, why shouldn't she?

It might be absurd; the debts might be far too great; but why had her father believed so passionately in the *Arcadia* and Keys Shipping if there hadn't been a chance of winning through?

She had only a vaguest idea of what she was going to do, and how she was going to do it. But she wanted Edgar and George Welterman to continue to believe that all was well, and at the same time see if she could find some irrefutable evidence to show that all of them had been involved in the "sinking" of the *Orange.* She would have only to convince her mother that Keys could keep going as an independent company, and together they would have a majority vote.

Whether that majority would be worth anything in the face of bankruptcy, she didn't know. But she didn't want Keys sold off in an underhand rush; not yet, not to conceal the commercial sins of Edgar Deacon and George Welterman, and the moral sins of her father.

She didn't really want to sell the *Arcadia* to Mark Beeney, either, if she could possibly help it, however fondly she felt about him.

She was almost ready for the ball when there was a knock at her stateroom door. She heard Trimmer talking to somebody outside, and she called, "Who is it?"

"Mr. Philip Carter-'Elm, miss," Trimmer called back.

"Oh, good. Tell him to come in."

Philip Carter-Helm was dressed as D'Artagnan, with a plumed hat and britches. He raised his hat and gave Catriona a sweeping bow. "You summoned me," he said with mock pomposity.

"Yes." Catriona smiled, bobbing him a curtsey.

"Well?" asked Philip. "Was it anything in particular? Or did you want me to escort you to the ball?"

Catriona walked across the room with a sibilant rustle of silk skirts. "That's very kind of you, but Mr. Beeney will be taking me into the ball tonight."

"I'm disappointed, Miss Keys. I can't say that I'm not. But, well, I'm not an unsporting loser. I must say, though, that you look absolutely stunning. Marie Antoinette?"

439

"Cinderella."

"Well, that's appropriate enough, under the circumstances."

Catriona gave him a sharp, questioning look, and he tried to cover his discomfiture at what he had said by sweeping his cloak around him and saying, "All for one and one for all, don't you think?"

Catriona said, "Why did you and my father argue about the *Orange?*"

Philip remained where he was, his cloak wrapped around him like a protective shroud. He said nothing—nothing at all—and the silence was so uncomfortable and so obvious that even Trimmer looked up from the cocktail cabinet, where he was pouring them both a drink.

Catriona circled around Philip with long, stately steps.

"I want to know why you and my father argued about the *Orange.* Do you think that's too much to ask?"

"Whoever said that we argued about the *Orange!*"

"Mr. Trimmer here was chauffeuring you at the time. He heard everything."

"Did he now?" asked Philip cuttingly, without raising his eyes or looking anywhere near Trimmer. "Well, even limousines have ears."

Catriona said, more gently, "I know about the *Orange*, Mr. Carter-Helm. I know everything that happened. I know that she's still sailing as the *Funabashi.*"

"I see."

"Well, don't you think you'd better tell me about it?"

"Why should I?" retorted Philip, with surprising sharpness.

"Because you're a guest on this ship, that's why. And because I happen to be my father's daughter; and everything that my father did is my concern."

Philip held up the note which Trimmer had slipped under his door, asking him to come to Catriona's cabin. "This particular matter is none of your business whatsoever, I regret to say. And forgive me for being so forthright, when I'm nothing but a guest."

"Mr. Carter-Helm—"

"Miss Keys, I have nothing to say to you on the subject. Your father and I did have some discussions, yes, but I am not obliged to disclose what they were, and I have absolutely no intention of doing so."

Catriona stared at him, feeling cold and angry as a princess, especially in the costume she was wearing.

"Mr. Carter-Helm, the future of the whole of Keys Shipping is at risk."

"I've already given you my advice. Sell the *Arcadia* to Mark Beeney."

"But the *Orange* is crucial to the whole thing, the whole sale."

"Be that as it may, there's nothing more that I'm prepared to say. I really think I ought to be going."

440

"Mr. Carter-Helm—"

"Miss Keys," said Philip, "remember the old nursery rhyme?

> "Where the fish swim free, child
> And never bite the line;
> Keep your nose in your own soup
> And keep it out of mine."

"What did you say?" asked Catriona, shocked.

Philip replaced his hat and stalked to the door. "I'm telling you in the politest way that I know how to, Miss Keys, that you should try to mind your own business."

With that, he left the stateroom and closed the door firmly behind him.

" 'E was rather hoffand," remarked Trimmer.

"Yes," said Catriona.

"Are you all right, miss?" asked Alice. "You're looking a little queer."

"Yes, I'm all right," said Catriona. "In fact I think I'm better than ever."

Sixty-two

As the first-class passengers assembled in the Grand Lounge for the beginning of the fancy-dress ball, two significant conversations took place. One was between the Knave of Hearts, who looked distinctly like Maurice Peace, and Julius Caesar, who bore an uncanny resemblance to Derek Holdsworth. Maurice was eating an anchovy-and-cheese sandwich, and holding a pint tankard of Mumm's champagne. Derek Holdsworth was eating nothing at all, and looking anxiously around for Harry Pakenow. He was very unhappy that he had let Harry go, especially since Mrs. Chalk-Herbert had reported earlier this evening that one of her diamond bracelets was missing. Derek's father had divided the human race into three, like a cheese. There were decent sorts, he had averred, and bad lots, and women. That was all. Before you made up your mind about anybody, you had to work out into which category they fell, and after that it was easy. Harry Pakenow, quite obviously, was a bad lot. He certainly wasn't a woman. The only exception to Derek's father's rule had been Derek's mother, who had somehow contrived to be a woman and a decent sort both at once. As a boy, Derek had found that mystifying. It still mystified him slightly.

Maurice said, "Odd that, about yesterday's run."

"What was odd about it?" asked Derek Holdsworth, abstractedly.

"Odd that we managed to sail so far, even though we stopped to rescue Miss Conroy."

Derek frowned. "The *Arcadia* is a very fast vessel, Mr. Peace."

"Well, I'm aware of that. But six hundred and thirty-five miles? It doesn't really seem possible."

"You don't think so?"

Maurice finished his sandwich and licked his fingers. "I just thought it was a little fishy, that's all."

"Well try one without anchovies in."

"I meant the mileage, Mr. Holdsworth, not the cheese sandwiches."

Derek Holdsworth blinked. Then he said, "Oh, the mileage. Oh, *well.* You know what happened about that."

"No," said Maurice, suspiciously. "What happened about that?"

"It was all something to do with daily averages, Mr. Deacon said. We had to turn in fairly similar figures for each day's sailing, in order to satisfy the investors that we were running smoothly. That's why we entered six hundred and thirty-five for the last twenty-four hours; and that's why we're steaming ahead so fast now to make up the actual distance."

Maurice looked at him with his head inquisitively cocked to one side.

"You mean we didn't actually sail six hundred and thirty-five miles?"

Derek Holdsworth nodded. "But don't tell anyone I told you. Strictly hush-hush."

Maurice made a thoughtful face. "I wouldn't dream of telling any-body you told me. Not a soul."

Just then, Lord Willunshaw came across the crowded lounge in a long white toga, dressed as Diogenes. He was carrying a brass lamp in one hand and a glass of champagne in the other.

"Are you looking for an honest man or an alcoholic?" asked Maurice.

"I'm looking for neither, as a matter of fact. I'm looking for you. Do you fancy a return game of poker tonight? Give a chap a chance to win some of his money back?"

"Lord Willunshaw, I'm going to try to put this nicely," said Maurice. "I've been gambling all my life and you're not really in my league. I don't want to see you lose any more. I've already won two of your loose-boxes, a sofa, and one of your servants' cottages. Next you'll be staking your horses, or your daughters, or something."

Lord Willunshaw cleared his throat loudly. "Damn it," he said, "you can have me daughters any time. But not me damn horses."

Across the lounge, under the sparkling lights, through the laughing

442

crowds of cavaliers and pierrots and punchinellos, through the bright and hilarious group who were blacked up as ebony steppers from a Harlem nightclub, through the mermaids and kings and harlequins, Harry Pakenow made his uncertain way. He had no fancy-dress costume of his own, but his steward, a miniature ginger-haired man of intense dapperness, had managed to borrow on his behalf a clown's costume, in silvery satin, with black diamond patches on it, and black ruffles at the neck and cuffs, and a black skullcap. Unhappy, lonely, and uncertain, Harry skirted around the edge of the lounge, smiling back at anyone who waved to him, but feeling completely isolated from all this wealth and gaiety and swinging music.

At length, he stood by one of the lounge's reflecting pillars, drinking his third glass of champagne more quickly than he ought to, and eating a kidney wrapped in bacon. He saw Catriona arrive down the staircase, in her dazzling white fairy-tale crinoline and her tall white elaborate wig; and Mark Beeney, as Prince Charming, in a midnight-blue Regency frock coat, and tight white breeches which Harry (with his glum but uncompromising eye for life's realities) thought far too revealing to the assembled company of the side which Mark Beeney dressed. He finished his champagne, and a steward immediately took away his glass and gave him another one. Tonight, he thought, I'm going to get extremely pissed. Or spifflicated, as most of the young people in cabin class called it.

"Hallo," said a voice by Harry's elbow. He looked around, and it was Lucille Foster, dressed in pink, as the Sugar Plum Fairy.

"Hallo," said Harry. "I didn't know you were allowed up so late. You look marvellous."

"Mrs. Hall said I could stay until half past ten, as a treat. Mind you, mother always used to let me stay up until midnight. She said what did it matter what time children went to bed? If they're tired, she said, they'll sleep."

"Well, I suppose there's some sense in that," said Harry, whose own mother, a small plain woman who had always seemed to smell of lavender, had insisted that he was in bed by seven; so that he had often lain there under his cheap maroon blanket with the sun shining through the curtains, his younger brother fast asleep beside him, but his friends playing noisily in the street outside.

Lucille unselfconsciously linked arms with Harry and said, "You don't think I'm a terrible person, do you?"

"No," said Harry. He didn't laugh at her for asking. There were times in everybody's life when they needed to know the answer to a question like that. "I think you're very thoughtful, and very nice; and besides all of that, I think you're very pretty, too."

"I suppose I'm too young for you to think of marrying me."

Harry looked down at her through his round spectacles, and there she was so rich and so young, with a way of life that Harry couldn't even start to imagine in pieces all around her. She had drunk highballs in Paris, dressed in silk, eaten ortolan, and walked along the pathways of the Palace of Versailles in white organdie summer dresses. For a mother, she had once been blessed or cursed with one of the most fashionable and outrageous women of the 1920s. And here she was, at this noisy fancy-dress ball on the *Arcadia,* talking of marriage. To *him,* to Harry Pakenow.

He said, in a voice which was slightly hoarse, "I couldn't marry you, Lucille. I wish I could. I think you're the most beautiful girl on earth. You made a friend of me when nobody else would. You trusted me. You believed in me, too; and that's a lot more than most married people do."

Lucille stared up at him. "Mother always used to say that you can tell a good friend in the first minute you meet them."

"Mother was right. But I can only be your friend, nothing more. We don't belong in the same world, you and me. I've got other things to do with my life, apart from drinking champagne and dancing the fox trot."

Lucille said, "I have, too. But sometimes I don't know what they are."

"You'll find out," Harry told her gently. "That's if there *are* any other things of course. There may not be. Some people are born to fox-trot, and nothing else. In which case, you'll have to kick up your heels, enjoy yourself, and make the best of it."

"You could come *with* us," said Lucille seriously.

"What do you mean?"

"Well . . . you could come with us to the Halls'. They have a huge house. They're bound to need some extra help there. Then we could be together."

"I couldn't do that."

"Why not? They'd pay you well. I know Mrs. Hall is a bit funny sometimes, but she's quite nice really. Do say you'll come."

Harry thought of his thirty unexploded sticks of dynamite in the trunk of Mark Beeney's Marmon. He thought of his Socialist friends in New York, the Communists and the Wobblies. He thought of Janice, and the flat in Bootle, with the washing flickering through the hammered-glass window like a motion picture, except that it had sound. The sound of children playing in weedy Victorian gardens. The sound of electric trams, grizzling along the metal tracks to Liverpool. The sound of Janice singing.

He understood then that the rich had won. They would always win. They had won because they ruled the world in ways he had only been able to guess at. If you were too poor to be admitted to the right social and political clubs; if you were too poor to play checkers with the Mellons or dine with the Rockefellers; if you didn't have a mansion on Long Island and a string of thoroughbred racehorses in Kentucky; if you didn't own a Dodge motorboat or a Buhl Air-Sedan, then you were licked. A whisper in the right ear at the right club would always have a far more devastating

444

effect on world affairs than the largest bomb. It didn't matter what you blew up. You could demolish the Woolworth Building, and Woolworth's would still go on making profits at their 1,200 five-and-dimes throughout the country. You could blow up the *Arcadia,* and luxury liners would still continue to cross the Atlantic. You could affect the way that rich people thought about life by letting off bombs, certainly. You could frighten them. But their vast resources of money made them adaptable beyond anything that the poor could dream of. If London was unsafe, they could always go and live in Paris. If Paris burned, then Biarritz.

Harry said to Lucille, "I don't know what I'm going to do."

"I wish you'd come," said Lucille. "You could always leave if you didn't like it. But I know you would."

"Do you think Mrs. Hall—"

"Leave Mrs. Hall to me."

"Lucille—" said Harry, but she was already skipping off through the crowds with a wave of her fairy wand. Harry watched her disappear, and then snapped his fingers at a steward to bring him another glass of champagne. He felt ashamed as he took the glass; and the way the steward said obsequiously, "Thank you, sir," made him feel even worse. He felt like tugging the man's sleeve and saying, Don't call me sir. I'm just Harry. I'm the same as you. All right? But he knew that he would only make the steward feel worse, and make a fool of himself. He went over to one of the tables and took a blue cocktail cigarette out of a crystal holder. A steward instantly came across and lit it for him.

As he blew out smoke, he thought, I'm *lost.* And it was only when Sabran stared at him over his shoulder that he realised that he had spoken out loud.

The fancy-dress ball was an extravagant success. Before dinner, there was a parade in which everybody linked arms and strutted around the floor of the Grand Lounge to show off their costumes while the orchestra played Strauss marches, and the young girls who had danced at breakfast appeared in flower costumes and tossed over four hundred pounds' worth of purple orchids over them. Then the passengers went through to dinner, a fifteen-course, four-hour banquet that included consommé Fleury, deviled crabs *à la créole,* boiled cod in oyster sauce, samis of wild duck, boned capon *truffée,* ham with champagne sauce, broiled quails on toast, and strawberry *Bavaroise.*

Somehow, dressing up in fancy costumes made the first-class passengers all the more flirtatious, and even Sabran (who was dressed in scarlet tights, as a demon, with papier-maché horns and a silver-painted pitchfork) found enough courage to desert the baroness for twenty minutes and dance the apache with the prettiest of the blacked-up steppers. Ralph Peel, wearing furry donkey's ears, as Bottom, was escorting Louise Narron, in eight layers of white muslin, as Titania, in a manner which sob sister

Marjorie Driscoll described in the *Los Angeles Examiner* as "coochy."

Edgar Deacon was dressed as a buccaneer, with a shabby black tricorn hat and a patch over his eye; Percy Fearson, in a yellow silk turban, was Ali-Baba; and Claude Graham-White appeared in white cardboard armour as Parsifal. Lady Diana FitzPerry, apparently undaunted by her unsuccessful attempt to blackmail the Keys Shipping Line out of £6,000, made a stunning entrance in an extremely diaphanous pink organdie dress, with a coronet of golden leaves around her head, and a rather flaccid asp around her neck. Behind her, looking mournful and chastened, Lord Thomas FitzPerry wore only his formal supper dress.

Baroness Zawisza stunned the assembly by wearing almost nothing except two gold-painted leaves over her breasts, and a slightly larger gold-painted leaf between her legs, held with nothing but the thinnest gold ballet-shoe laces, and leaving her bottom quite bare. On her head she wore a pyramid of gold-painted apples; and on her feet the highest of golden slippers. To anyone who had the courage to inquire, she was attending the fancy-dress ball as the golden apples of the sun. Julius Briggs remarked that "only a lady so utterly confident of her beauty and her wealth could have appeared in company as naked as this; and the remarkable part about it was that in spite of the fact that she had quite a few of the gentlemen in a tizzy, and scandalised one or two of the older women; most of the other ladies appeared to be covetously envious; as if they too had a secret dream of dining and dancing with practically nothing on at all."

As a couple, however, it was Catriona and Mark Beeney who entranced the company the most. Catriona had never felt so gracious or so pretty. Her crinoline gown was like a sparkling cloud of frost from which her narrow waist curved up in silk and lace, and her full breasts were cupped so high in the bones of her bodice that her ruby and diamond necklace, the necklace which Mark had given her, was spread out almost horizontally. The natural slant of her eyes had been accentuated by dark eye cosmetics, and by the height of her fancy wig.

Mark, at her side, looked taller and more dandified than ever, and he responded to the formality of his dress by behaving towards Catriona with even more courtesy and consideration than he usually did.

When they danced together around the Grand Lounge after dinner, Catriona held up her skirts and petticoats in one hand, while the other hand lightly rested on Mark's shoulder. The orchestra played "Tales from the Vienna Woods," beautifully and delicately, as it should be played; and with a zither, which most interpretations leave out. And only two or three other couples took to the floor, because the sight of Mark and Catriona together was a glittering picture which most of the passengers wanted to savour and remember.

Afterwards, Mark and Catriona went out on deck, to that small private corner behind the Palm Court where they could watch the *Arcadia*'s phosphorescent wash on the indigo reaches of the sea. A steward brought them a bottle of Veuve Clicquot on a silver tray, and a selection of mints.

Catriona said, "This has been the most wonderful evening I can ever remember."

"Me too," said Mark. His face was in shadow, but she could tell by the warmth of his voice how much he meant it.

"Do you know something?" said Catriona. "I don't even care how long this lasts. Even if it lasts for tonight and no longer, that's all I want."

Mark took her in his arms and held her close. Then he lowered his head and kissed her, his firm tongue pushing deep into her mouth. She sucked at it, even nipped at it with her teeth, until they could both taste blood.

It was one of those kisses from which she wished she never had to emerge; and she wouldn't let him go. She gripped the hair at the back of his neck, and tugged and twisted at the braid on his jacket. Her eyes were closed, because she wanted to concentrate all of the feelings he gave her inside of her head, in that private blackness where her passion lived. He tasted irresistible, and she fed from his lips as if she were eating a sweet and narcotic fruit. She wanted him so much she could have devoured him. His fingers touched her cheek, and then they ran chillingly and thrillingly down the side of her neck; and when at last he slid his hand into the frilly bodice of her dress and held her bare nipple against the sensitive palm, she shivered and murmured and said, "Mark . . ." in that strange clotted voice that sleep talkers use.

For one second, her hand brushed against the swelling in his white breeches, but then she knew she had to turn away and take a deep breath to control herself, because she could feel the breeze-cooled moisture in the silk between her warm thighs, and this time she knew how important it was to resist. There were too many other considerations. Too much business. Too many complications. To become Mark's mistress tonight would be to jeopardise everything that her father's death had given her.

Mark said, "What's wrong?"

"Nothing," she told him. "Everything's exactly right."

He leaned his elbows on the rail. "You said you were a little bit frightened of me. I hope you're not a little bit frightened of yourself as well."

"Isn't everybody?"

"I don't know. Maybe so. The only thing that frightens me is the prospect of growing old."

Catriona picked up her glass of champagne. It was very dry, and very cold. The best champagne, one of Nigel's lounge-lizard friends had told her, should taste like the dust from an Egyptian mummy's bandages.

"Growing old doesn't matter so much when you're rich," she said.

"On the contrary," said Mark. "I think it's far better to grow old when you're poor. Can you imagine the frustration of having millions and millions of dollars, and knowing that all of those millions can do nothing at all to hold back time and make you young again."

"You're being very morbid."

"Not really. I guess I'm just upset."

"Because of me?" asked Catriona.

"A little. I love you, but you seem to be keeping yourself aloof."

Catriona smiled at him. "I love you, too. I think you're the berries, if you must know. But there's all this business going on. You're trying to buy the *Arcadia,* and George Welterman's trying to buy us up completely, and I just need a little time to think."

Sixty-three

Early the following day, Catriona sent three wireless messages; and by teatime, when she was sitting out on deck with Mary Pickford and Mark, Willis the Wireless brought her two replies.

Mark popped an olive into his mouth, and said, "You've been very mysterious today, my love."

"A woman's entitled to be mysterious," retorted Mary Pickford. "In fact, she's *obliged* to be mysterious."

"There's mysterious and there's mysterious," put in Baroness Zawisza, who had eavesdropped on them as she was gliding past in a daring dress by Beer. "There's mysterious ignorant and mysterious knowledgeable." Her tongue lightly rapped the "k" of "knowledgeable" so that it sounded like a Polish translation.

Sabran, just behind her, sniffed the sea air insolently, as if it were vulgar even to breathe it.

Catriona read her messages and then folded them up again and tucked them into her purse.

"You'll have to forgive my outrageous curiosity," said Mark.

"I forgive it." Catriona smiled. "I'd be curious too, if I were you; particularly if the messages said what *these* messages say."

"You're teasing me."

"No," said Catriona in a voice which told him that she meant it, that he wasn't to ask any more. He shrugged and popped in another olive and looked out towards the sparkling ocean. America was only a day and a half away now; and there was a restlessness on board the *Arcadia*, an impatience to arrive. With Sir Peregrine at the helm, the ship had been making tremendous time, and there was a rumour already rife in the smoking lounge that if they kept going at their present speed, they would finally take the Blue Riband away from the *Mauretania*, after thirteen years.

Mark said, "You're pleased? You're upset?"

"I don't know," said Catriona. "Will you excuse me for a while? I think the sunlight's bringing on my headache."

"You didn't tell me you had headaches."

"*Mark*," insisted Catriona firmly; and Mark raised his hands in surrender and stood up to help her out between the deck chairs.

She went first to Philip Carter-Helm's stateroom; but it was locked, and there was no reply when she knocked. She went through to the smoking lounge and down to the library; but she found him at last sitting by himself by the swimming pool reading a copy of *Babbitt*. He was wearing half-glasses, and looked unusually boyish and vulnerable, especially after the testy way in which he had behaved when he had last spoken to her.

"Mr. Carter-Helm," she said quite softly.

He turned around. "Miss Keys," he replied. He folded over the edge of the page which he had been reading, and closed the book.

"Don't get up," she told him, although it was obvious that he hadn't been going to. He half lifted his bottom, in a belated attempt to correct his breach of etiquette, and then sat back again. Catriona drew across the next deck chair and sat quite close to him. The knees of her silk stockings shone in the sunlight.

"I've been wondering and wondering about you," she said.

"Yes? Why were you doing that?"

"Oh, you don't have to be so *gruff*," she told him. "I'm not being critical. I've been wondering about you because of what you said to me yesterday evening."

"I apologize if I was offhand. I wasn't feeling particularly well."

"Don't even think about it. I wasn't offended. I was more curious than offended."

"Curious?" he asked her. He took off his half-glasses and folded them.

"Well, you seemed to be showing such an interest in whether I should sell Keys Shipping or not, and to whom, and for how much. You seemed to have such a personal interest in the *Arcadia*. That's what made me wonder."

"I'm in shipping," said Philip, staring at her with that foxy-eyed look common to people who have just removed their spectacles. "Of course

I'm interested. Everybody in shipping from London to Tokyo is interested in what happens to Keys."

"Not as personally as you."

"I'm not sure that I follow you."

Catriona reached across and touched Philip's arm. He looked slowly down at her hand and then back up at her face again, and she could see then that he realized the masquerading was over.

"The very best thing happened," she said. "Nobody gave you away but yourself."

"What do you mean?"

"Philip, I know who you are." She lifted up the radio messages which she had just received. "I've had confirmation from England. You can't deny it. And I'm pleased. Do you understand me? I'm delighted."

"Why should you be?" he asked her aggressively. "There's nothing for you to be delighted about."

Catriona tugged insistently at his sleeve. "It was the nursery rhyme that gave you away. I thought that I'd seen you somewhere before; there was something about you which struck a chord; and of *course* I'd seen you before. You look just like him; you look more like him than I do."

Philip let out a long, controlled breath. "I didn't really want you to know."

"I know you didn't. But the nursery rhyme. 'Where the fish swim free, child.' I don't know if ever he told you, but he made that up himself. Nobody else knows it but you and me. Until you recited it to me yesterday, I thought I was the only one."

Philip said, "It's a mess, isn't it?"

"Why is it a mess? How can you say that it's a mess?"

He covered his mouth with his hand for almost a minute, as if he didn't trust himself to speak. Then he said, "The *Orange* was the last straw."

"I don't understand."

"We'd argued and argued for more than a year about building the *Arcadia*. He was determined to do it. Determined! He had to challenge White Star and Cunard. Keys was going to be greater than both of them. He didn't seem to realise that he didn't have the assets, and he didn't have the backing. He didn't seem to understand that he lacked some essential talent when it came to running a shipping line. I don't know what it was, quite. He had genius, of a kind. Everybody said he was a genius. He knew how to get the best out of people, and pay them hardly anything in return. That was a talent in itself. He knew how to build ships, too. You only have to look at the *Aurora;* that's a beautiful ship. But he didn't have that gift of being able to attend to every detail at once, and so many sides of the company began to suffer from neglect, and overmanning, and sheer bad management. In 1919, when so many shipping companies were making a roaring profit, we were scarcely breaking even, and all because of top-heavy management and *this* lady, this bitch, the *Arcadia.* They say that she cost four million pounds, but believe me, she cost nearly twice as much as that, when you write in all the waste, and all the bad planning, and all the extravagance. Six first-class staterooms were fitted out, and then stripped again, right back to the bulkheads, because he didn't like the decoration. Can you imagine what that cost? And they had the engines in and out of the hull about fourteen times before he would pass them. He was a perfectionist, like most geniuses are. But he squandered so much time and so much money on achieving perfection; and when it came down to it, it wasn't even worth it. Have you noticed that the inlays in your cupboard doors are abura, and not mahogany?"

"But the *Orange,*" said Catriona.

"Yes," said Philip, "the *Orange.* And not just the *Orange,* but the *Hecate,* and the *Phyllis,* and the *Daphne,* and the *Equitable.*"

Catriona frowned. "You don't mean—?"

"All of them,"—Philip nodded—"all sunk. And all of them, except the *Phyllis,* which caught fire off Honduras about three years ago, all of them still afloat, in various guises."

"Oh, no," whispered Catriona.

"Oh, yes. Can you wonder that I argued with him, when he suggested the *Orange?* But we were running out of money, and he wanted the *Arcadia*'s keel laid down; and he wouldn't take no for an answer. That's when I told him that I resigned; and that's when he cut me off without the proverbial penny."

"I can't believe it."

"Well, it's true; and in a way I'm glad you've found out. Perhaps someone can now put the record straight on the great and honest Stanley Keys. He was sinking his own ships and robbing his own warehouses and setting fire to his own wharfs, anything for extra money, anything to build this ridiculous floating fun palace."

Philip said this with such bitterness that Catriona scarcely knew what to say. He stared at her fiercely for a moment, and then he stood up and swung back his arm and threw his book as far out to sea as he possibly could, the pages fluttering in the afternoon breeze like a falling bird.

"Father was like Babbit in reverse," he said vehemently. "A man who knew the value of everything and the price of nothing. But life isn't like that anymore; the grand Edwardian days are gone. He never understood that. He thought he was Brunel reborn. I don't know. I don't know what he thought he was. But he made sure that he ruined my career. He went ahead and sank the *Orange,* and as far as I was concerned, that was the end. He was stealing; and the *Arcadia* was built out of nothing but stolen and borrowed money. She doesn't belong to Keys Shipping, not one single bolt of her, not one plate, not one plank. And not much else of Keys

Shipping belongs to us, either."

Catriona said, "That's why you wanted to sell her to American Trans-Atlantic?"

Philip nodded. "We have to pay some of this money back, Miss Keys. Or perhaps I should call you Catriona."

"You can call me Catriona."

He looked out to sea. His hands were thrust deep into his pockets, his shoulders hunched. "Honour is a difficult animal, you know. Perhaps it's the privilege of the young to be able to handle it, or at least to believe that we can. But if you want to know the truth, I intended to persuade you as far as I could to support the selling of the *Arcadia* to Mark Beeney, so that at least she would have a good home. No matter how unethical her origins, she's a very fine ship, the finest in the world, and I think Father deserves at least that much of a memorial, for all his sins. But you may have realised that the proceeds from selling her would only delay the death of the rest of the Keys fleet. It would pay off a few creditors who honestly deserve to be paid, and then the fleet would have to be dismantled, and everybody else would have to scramble for what they could get."

"And where would that leave me, and my mother?" asked Catriona, keeping her voice controlled.

Philip twisted around and smiled at her. "I can't say that I care. I'm sorry. Sibling jealousy, I suppose. *You* never worked for him. *You* didn't spend five years of your life greasing propeller shafts and sorting out bills of lading, only to be disinherited and thrown out on your ear. You were always his darling favourite, weren't you? He talked about you all the time —how self-willed you were, how pretty you were. Well, he was right. But that didn't make it any easier for me to accept it. You were spoiled, in spite of your behaviour. The Flapper of the Seas, my God. And if you lose whatever he left you, it won't do you any harm at all. It didn't do *me* any harm; being disinherited; or if it did, it's too darned bad."

Catriona said, "What if I vote for selling out to IMM?"

Philip rocked with silent, overexaggerated laughter. "Same thing, only worse! IMM will probably delay payment, almost indefinitely. George Welterman will think up some excuse; some contractual snag or other; or else he'll say that the Keys fleet was not up to the standard represented by you when you sold it to them. They'll prevent you from moving one single ship, because they'll claim the transaction is under legal dispute, and then they'll sit back and gradually watch your ruination. They've done it before, and they'll do it again. In the end, you'll happily settle for a few million pounds, and that'll be the finish of it. All I can say is that at least if you do things my way the *Arcadia* will continue to cross the Atlantic, and most of our creditors will get a few pennies to remember Stanley Keys by; even if it's only two and six in the pound. That's something; and that's honour, if you can understand the meaning of the word."

"Mark Beeney doesn't know anything about this, does he?" asked Catriona. "I mean, he doesn't know why you're so keen to help him buy the *Arcadia?*"

Philip said nothing.

"I don't know why you bothered to intervene at all," said Catriona. "If George Welterman intends to ruin Keys anyway, why should it matter to you? You had your revenge when Father died. What more do you need?"

"I happen to own a few shares in Keys myself; and so do my friends. Nineteen per cent, altogether. I tried three years ago to take the company over, or at least have a powerful say in how it was managed. Well, that didn't really work out; but I don't intend to be utterly ruined when Keys collapses, and I don't want my friends ruined, either."

Catriona looked at him sceptically.

"Well, that's not the only reason," he said, less assertively. "I suppose the most important reason is that I don't want George Welterman to have the *Arcadia.*"

"A ship built with stolen and borrowed money? Why should you care *who* has her?"

"You know as well as I do."

"Tell me." Catriona insisted.

Philip rubbed his hand along the varnished rail. Standing as he was in the falling afternoon light, with his hair blowing in the breeze, he looked so much like his father that Catriona found herself attracted, and fascinated, as if this were all a peculiar dream. Even his voice, now that he was speaking so unselfconsciously, had the same cadence and bluntness.

"It's *his* ship, that's why; no matter how much I argued against him building it; no matter how much I disapproved of what he was doing with the *Orange,* and all those other ships. It's his ship, and she must run across the Atlantic, because if she doesn't, she'll die, and his whole life, the whole purpose of his whole life, will die right along beside her, inside her, with her. I don't believe in ghosts, Catriona; but the *Arcadia* is the ghost of Stanley Keys, if ever there was one. And his spirit, too."

He paused for a while, and then said, "It all sounds like rot, doesn't it? You probably think that I'm completely cuckoo."

"I don't think that," said Catriona passionately, "I just don't understand what you want."

Philip said, "Your name's Keys, isn't it? For as long as you remain unmarried, anyway. Well, mine was never Keys, and it never can be. Father used to introduce me as the son of an old friend of his. Even Edgar Deacon never found out who I was. Father didn't want Doris to know, of course. I've never met her, but Father always used to tell me that she was very sensitive; and if she'd ever found out that Father had had an affair with Isabelle before they got married, not to mention an illegitimate son . . . Well, 'rocking the boat,' that's what he used to call it. 'We'd better not rock the boat, old man.' "

"Are you really *so* jealous of me?" Catriona asked him.

"I don't know. I don't think it's jealousy. It's just that I think that it's time for the name of Keys to be put to rest; at least as far as shipping's concerned. My name's Carter-Helm, Catriona. Carter, after the doctor who delivered me, and Helm after the helm of a ship. A proud name, don't you think?"

"Philip—" said Catriona.

"No," he said. "It's no damned use, is it? No damned use at all."

"Philip, listen. Supposing we *don't* sell out to IMM, supposing we *don't* sell the *Arcadia* to Mark Beeney, either, supposing we keep the company independent, and worked together to make it profitable, *you and I* Philip. If she takes the Blue Riband, she'll be the most popular liner on the Atlantic. She's beautiful, anyway. You know that. Father must have believed there was a way to keep the company running. He *must* have, or else he wouldn't have invested so much money and so much time into the *Arcadia.*"

Philip ran his hand through his hair. "You didn't even know him, did you? They should have called this ship the *Megalomania,* not the *Arcadia.* He didn't build it because he believed that the company could be saved by launching a huge new liner. It was nothing to do with economics. It was all to do with pride. And I think, in our different ways, we're both as proud as he was. Arrogant, too. My God, just listen to us."

Catriona said, "Philip, ever since I realised who you were, I've been thinking this over and over. I want you to work with me, to make this company successful again. At least let's try it."

"In spite of what I was going to do to you?"

"You didn't know me then. Not face-to-face. You only knew me through Father. I can understand how you must have felt."

"Oh, can you?" said Philip, biting his lip. "Well, I don't really believe that you can. I'm sorry. Many regrets."

"Philip, if you don't help me, I'll have to sell Keys to IMM. I'll *have* to, whatever you say about them."

Philip said, "In that case, I'm very sorry."

"I have to think of the people who work for Keys, and Edgar said that at least they'll keep their jobs."

"If that's what you believe."

"Philip, don't be so bitter, please."

Philip turned towards her, and to Catriona's distress there were tears in his eyes. "You never got on with him, did you? Not that much. You scarcely knew him. Well, I did, or at least I thought I did. I worshipped the bloody man, if you'll excuse my French. I would have done anything for him. And then he wanted to build this bloody ship. It obsessed him; day and night he wouldn't talk about anything else. I think he would have murdered people to build this ship, and in the end I suppose he did in a way. He certainly murdered me. I hate this bloody ship; and yet I love her, too. I hate you, and I hate everything with the name Keys; and yet I feel pride when I see that flag flying with the cross keys on it. I wanted to persuade you to sell the *Arcadia* to Mark Beeney, just to save her; but, well, if you won't, then I think that's all there is to say."

Philip turned away, and began to walk quickly along the promenade deck towards the staircase.

Catriona nearly called after him; but then she didn't. He had probably had enough agony for one afternoon. She sat back in her deck chair and wondered what on earth she was going to say to Edgar Deacon.

She was frightened by what she had done, and yet excited, too. Perhaps the company would still collapse; perhaps George Welterman would still take it over. But at least it would have been done openly and bravely; and at least her father's misdeeds would have been confessed, so that they might be understood and forgiven.

She unfolded the two messages she had received from London. One was from Nigel, and it read: "Philip Carter-Helm is partner in Drago, Cox, & Carter-Helm, Shipping Insurers. Age twenty-nine or thirty as far as his secretary recalls. She thinks he was born Cheshire. Miss you madly. Love, N." The second message was from Millicent Furr, a girl she had known at school. It said, "Philip Stanley George Walmsley was born on February 2, 1895, at Winsford Nursing Home, Cheshire, and registered at Winsford by Isabelle Mary Walmsley, spinster, and Stanley Everett Keys, marine engineer. Sounds intriguing! And when am I going to see you again and catch up on all the gossip? Hope the info's enough. Best, Millie."

She remembered her father saying, "Always such a tease, your Aunt Isabelle," and wondering what he meant. Now she knew. She folded up the messages again, and then tore them into tiny pieces and opened her hand so that the wind could blow them out over the Atlantic.

Sixty-four

Marcia Conroy had been watching Catriona and Philip from further along the deck. When Philip left, she was almost tempted to go and talk to Catriona. She wasn't sure why. Perhaps she wanted to reassure her that she didn't really blame her for what had happened. But then Catriona turned away, too, and disappeared inside, and Marcia decided that perhaps it wasn't quite the right moment anyway.

Marcia was allowed out now for a quarter of an hour twice a day, but although she didn't know it, Dr. Fields had asked Sir Peregrine to detail a crew member to keep a watchful eye on her, particularly when she went close to the rail. Dr. Fields believed that her suicidal mood was past; but he knew from experience that real suicides can be cunning, and that they frequently mislead their friends and relatives into thinking that all their difficulties are over, simply for the chance of being left alone again.

She felt melancholy, as a matter of fact, but not despairing. In her white cloche hat and her fur-trimmed afternoon coat, she looked like a mannequin, elegant, aloof, slightly world-weary. She had taken breakfast that morning, two lightly scrambled eggs and a cup of China tea and a fig, and she surprised herself by thinking that she would enjoy doing something erotic.

She had already decided that she had inhaled enough fresh air when Sabran came back on deck and leaned against the rail quite near her, aggressively posing in a tight black military-style jacket and flappy white silk trousers. He wore rope sandals, and his toenails were painted.

"You are looking sad," he said.

Marcia gave him a brief British smile.

"I too am down in the clumps."

"Dumps," she corrected him.

"Dumps?" He frowned. He lit a cigarette and breathed smoke out of his nostrils. Marcia had the feeling that he would have blown it out of his ears as well if it had been possible. "That Baroness, she expects a slave, not a lover. Do I look like a slave? I am too spee-fee to be a slave."

"Yes," agreed Marcia, "I think you are."

"I will be a picture star, like Valentino, only many more women will swill at my feet."

456

"I think you mean swoon."

"Yes, very swoon. As swoon as I get to Hollywood, USA. Besides, I think you are hotsy-totsy."

"You do?" Marcia smiled.

"Please, do not misunderstand. I am not saying you are a pullover."

"I'm not," said Marcia, and found herself laughing for the first time in two days. "I'm not a pushover, either."

Quite unexpectedly, Sabran dropped to his knees and held her hand. "Please, I wish you would have a gin feez with me."

Marcia touched his cheek with her fingertips. His skin was smooth, quite soft. "All right," she agreed. "Let's go and have a gin feez."

"And then . . .?" asked Sabran.

"Oh, I don't know," said Marcia. "Let's just have the feez, and think about the after after."

Sixty-five

Edgar was having tea with George Welterman when Catriona appeared at his stateroom door. George rose from his seat and bowed and said, "Well, well. The Queen of the Atlantic, in person."

Catriona allowed him to kiss her hand. Then she sat down and took off her hat and said lightly, "Don't let me interrupt you, please."

"We were simply going over the inventory," said Edgar. "George wants to know exactly what he's going to be getting for his eighteen million. It runs into three hundred seventy pages—from the *Arcadia* herself, to three hundred stokers' shovels."

"I see," said Catriona. "No, no tea for me, thank you. I'd rather have a drink."

"Always hard for me to consider drinking before the sun goes down past the yardarm," said Edgar. "Old Anglo-Indian custom, of course. Only way we could keep a check on chaps who would have drunk all day, morning till night." He sucked in his cheeks and then said, "Lot of them still did, of course."

George said, "Edgar's very pleased that you decided to see things his way, Catriona."

"Hm," said Catriona, trying to sound disinterested and vague; but she listened closely as Edgar and George worked out between them how their lawyers could meet as soon as the *Arcadia* docked in New York; and how IMM's accountants could go through the books in a matter of days; so that Keys could be transferred to IMM's British holding company as quickly as possible.

"How many of our executive staff will you be retaining, do you think?" asked Catriona. "Mr. Deacon here, I hope?"

George stood up and smiled and put his arm round Edgar's shoulders. "Mr. Deacon will get the reward he was promised, the deputy managing directorship of all of IMM's British operations. And he deserves it, too. As soon as your poor father died, he acted promptly and properly; and believe me he's going to save us all a great deal of money and legal difficulty." He winked at Catriona to make it clear he was talking about the *Orange.*

"What about Mr. Fearson?"

"Well . . . you have to admit that Percy's getting a little long in the tooth. It isn't going to be easy to find a place for him. But I'm sure we can come to some arrangement."

"And me?"

"You, Miss Keys?" Edgar laughed crisply. "You will be able to go back to London and play with your theatre folk."

Sixty-six

After dinner that evening, she sat with Mark in the cocktail lounge while a somnambulant pianist played slowed-down selections from the show *Big Boy,* including "If You Knew Susie." Catriona wore a shimmering Poiret dress like a silver waterfall, and a glittering headband with a silver-sparkling plume in it. They drank the special cocktail of the evening, Atlantic Punch.

"You haven't seen Philip Carter-Helm, have you?" asked Catriona.

"He wasn't at dinner," said Mark. "But I did see Marcia playing footsy with that fellow Sabran. And believe me, that Polish baroness lady didn't care for it one bit. I think she could have bitten his head off."

Catriona reached across the table and took Mark's hand. "Anyway," she said, "I have something to say to you; something really remarkable, and a proposition to make, too."

"Do you know something," Mark smiled. "I just love that clipped

British way you say *remarkable.*"

"Listen," Catriona insisted; but Mark shushed her.

"You listen first," he told her. "I have something really re-*mark*-able to say, too; and I have a proposition to make. And since I'm the guest around here, and you're the hostess, I think I have first bite at it, don't you?"

Catriona looked into his eyes; and his eyes were sparkling with affection and good humour; and so she said, "Very well. But don't take all night over it."

"Okay," said Mark, adjusting his necktie. "You see, the truth is, I've been giving this business some careful consideration. Normally, I'm impetuous. I take a fancy to something and I have to have it straight away, no arguments, no poodle-dogging around. But this is one of those decisions that are going to affect my whole life, and maybe yours, too, and so I've really think this one out."

"Go on," said Catriona. She couldn't think why her heart was rising so high. She couldn't think why she felt so tense, and thrilled.

Mark reached into his pocket and produced a black ring box. He opened it; and there, nestling in black silk, was a gold ring set with a trio of diamonds, the largest of which must have weighed three or four carats.

"Catriona, I want you to marry me, that's my proposition. I don't believe that I'm a particularly bad catch. I'm extremely rich, and not too ugly, and apart from that I've fallen in love with you like I've never fallen in love with anybody before. Let me tell you something, Catriona, when you come out in the evening, the stars have to hide themselves in shame, and that's a scientific fact."

Catriona suddenly found that there were tears in her eyes.

"You're not upset, are you?" asked Mark worriedly.

Catriona shook her head. "I'm delighted," she choked.

"You mean—"

She nodded. "Yes, you idiot. Of course I do."

Mark picked the ring carefully out of the box, held Catriona's hand, and slid the ring onto her finger. Then he sat back, took out his handkerchief, and mopped at his forehead. "Phew," he said. "I thought for one moment there . . ."

She reached across the table and squeezed his hand tight.

"Shall we make an announcement?" asked Mark. "We could at least persuade the pianist to play something less dreary."

"Not yet," Catriona asked him. "Let me tell you my proposition first."

"You mean you weren't going to ask *me* to marry *you?*"

"I don't know. Sort of. Listen."

She talked to him for almost a quarter of an hour, while he listened intently, his head slightly lowered. Then later they walked hand in hand to the first-class staircase, where they stood for a moment under the towering illuminated funnels, and under the stars, which like the stars in Yeats' poem, had been blown across the sky like sparks from a smithy. There was a scent in the air which was peculiar to luxury Atlantic liners —of expensive fragrances, of fuel oil, and Turkish tobacco, all mingled with ozone and salt.

"If only my father could have been here tonight," said Catriona, although not regretfully; for in a strange way she felt that he was.

Sixty-seven

It was well past one o'clock on Friday morning, and the *Arcadia* was now steaming ahead at full speed, with only a light southwesterly on her port quarter to resist her, and the vibration of her turbines thrilling through everything on board, from the vases of fresh roses on the tables, to the ice cubes in the cocktails, which had been freshly mixed by Henry's steward to sustain them through their discussions.

Tonight the *Arcadia* was alive, and thrusting her way through the ocean at nearly twenty-nine knots. Sir Peregrine had left the fancy-dress ball and was now commanding the bridge personally. Although he would never have admitted it, not even to Nurse Queensland, he was determined that the *Arcadia* should win the Blue Riband on her maiden voyage. He wasn't only fighting for the *Arcadia*, nor for the future of Keys Shipping. He was fighting for himself. Docking in New York in record time was his only hope of retaining his position as commodore of the Keys fleet—if there could be any hope. And, by God, he needed to be commodore. He needed the sea. What would he do without it? Sit in his gloomy Victorian house in Lytham St. Anne's, listening to his housekeeper warbling while she boiled him up a mutton and lentil soup? Pace the corridors afternoon after afternoon, listening to the steady tick of the Viennese clock, and staring back at the sullen dogs which peered at him from all those cracked oil paintings in the hall?

Dream of Maude? No, never. Not dream of Maude. The sea was all that had mercifully kept him from dreaming of Maude every night and every day for all these years. He had been too busy commanding his ships, and too busy entertaining his passengers, to dream of Maude. Maude was a lost love, a letter left unopened on a mantelpiece in some Victorian room, a girl seen from afar in a soft dress and a picture hat, while children played around her with hoops and sticks. Maude was a memory from a time that had disappeared forever behind a slowly closing diaphragm, a time before flappers and automobiles and airplanes and jazz and electric light. A time before anybody knew what "heebie-jeebies" meant and girls dared to show their ankles.

Maude, Maude. The *Arcadia* surged forward to the rhythm of Maude. And all the while she did so, with Sir Peregrine standing so proudly and so lopsidedly on the bridge, and with Harry Pakenow gnawing his fingernails in his first-class bedroom, the timing device in the trunk of Mark Beeney's Marmon turned around to twelve o'clock again, and this time the sear was nudged so closely by the moving hands that there was an audible click. The clock was running down, but there was a chance that it would continue to run until twelve o'clock noon on Friday, and even twelve o'clock midnight, and possibly beyond. So there were at least two chances for the hands to tip the boomerang-shaped sear so that it connected with the trigger and exploded the dynamite. Harry Pakenow could only wait and worry, while everybody else on the *Arcadia* drank and danced and cooed and copulated, or stared hopelessly out into the night.

Sixty-eight

Coney Island appeared through the warm summer mist at 7:56 on Sunday morning, after a Saturday afternoon that had been almost unnaturally calm, and a Saturday night when the ocean had been warm and dark as treacle, with the *Arcadia* sliding over her at high speed. To Catriona, as she stood with Mark by the forward rail to catch her first glimpse of the Statue of Liberty, the *Arcadia*'s maiden voyage now seemed to have been curiously short; a strange abrupt interval of fantasy, what the German passengers would have called an *Augenblick,* a blink of the eye.

After hearing last night who Philip Carter-Helm really was, and what Catriona proposed to do, Mark had agreed, a little reluctantly, to postpone the announcement of their engagement. But this morning when she had woken up, the ship's florist had brought her heaps of trembling gardenias, over a hundred of them, with the message "I Adore You. So There."

Catriona had left a note under Philip's door begging him to call her; and she had asked Monty Willowby to catch his arm if he should see him.

But there had been no reply to the note, and Philip had not appeared at breakfast. As the *Arcadia* neared New York, Catriona was beginning to grow anxious that she would not be able to find him; let alone persuade him to help her with her proposition. Once the ship had docked and he had gone ashore, it could very well be too late; and she was terrified that Keys might have to go to George Welterman by default.

"Maybe I'd better go hunt for him," suggested Mark.

"If he doesn't want to be found, he won't be," said Catriona. "You might just as well try and look for someone in the middle of Fulham on market day."

"But we have to try."

"I don't know. I have a feeling that he'll turn up," said Catriona. "If he doesn't, we'll just have to wait by the gangplanks when the passengers disembark."

"He has to be somewhere."

"Well, he's probably in his stateroom thinking things over. He's just not answering, that's all."

"Maybe Willowby could use his passkey."

"I suppose he could. But I don't want to upset him. He was upset enough as it was."

They smoked cigarettes and waited for twenty minutes longer. "That's Ambrose Light," said Mark. "It won't be long now, and you'll see the Statue of Liberty."

"Do you think we've won the Blue Riband?" Catriona asked.

Dick Charles, who was standing quite close behind her, said, "D-don't t-tempt fate, Miss K-Keys; but I th-think that Sir Peregrine has been k-keeping us up to twenty-eight knots for the past twenty-four hours. So we m-may . . ."

At that moment, however, a swirl of sharp-smelling smoke blew around the deck, and almost simultaneously a woman screeched out, "Fire! My God, there's a fire in the first-class cabins!"

Mark gripped Catriona's arm and ordered, "Stay here!" but Catriona followed closely behind him as he hurried through the crowds of cabin-class passengers who were lining the rail. Ralph Peel came out on deck as they reached the first-class staircase, and he was holding a megaphone.

"Nothing to worry about!" he called. "Just a bit of carpet! No need to disturb yourselves, ladies and gentlemen!"

Catriona panted, "What's happening?"

"Don't quite know, Miss Keys, to tell you the truth. But Monty Willowby said there was someone locked in a first-class stateroom, and smoke pouring out from under the door. They've got four or five chaps down there now, trying to break the door down."

"Oh, my God," said Catriona. "It's Philip."

"What?" Mark frowned.

462

"It's Philip!" said Catriona. "It must be!"

Without waiting, she hurried down the staircase, kicked off her shoes, and ran on stockinged feet along the first-class corridor. As she ran, the fire siren began hooting, loudly and plaintively, like a tortured sea lion, and there was the sound of running feet on the deck above them.

The corridor was already half filled with smoke, and as Catriona turned the corner, with Mark running close up behind her, there was a sudden billow of dense, thick-smelling fumes, so that she could hardly make out what was happening.

Her intuition had been right. The smoke was pouring from under the door of Philip Carter-Helm's cabin; and Monty Willowby and four seamen were hacking at the woodwork with fire axes. So far, they had made little impression on it. It was built of solid mahogany, with bronze panelling, and it had been firmly locked and bolted from the inside.

"No place for you here, miss," said Monty Willowby, raising his arm to keep Catriona away. "He must have a right old blaze going on in there, judging by the smoke. Regular bonfire."

"Have you heard anything from him?" asked Catriona. "Has anybody spoken to him?"

"Timmins heard him say to go away, but that was all, miss."

"Well, please, let me get near. I must try and talk to him."

Monty looked over Catriona's shoulder at Mark. "Got to watch this smoke, miss. Smoke can choke you quicker'n fire can burn you."

"Just for one minute," Catriona insisted.

Mark nodded, and Monty called out to the seamen, "Belay it with the axes there, you chaps!"

The chopping and banging stopped, and Catriona went right up to the cabin door.

"Philip!" she called. "Philip! It's Catriona!"

There was no answer; but from inside the cabin they could hear a popping, crackling sound, as if the furniture and curtains were well alight.

"Philip! You must open the door! We've thought of a way to work everything out!"

Still there was no answer. Monty Willowby took Catriona's arm and said, "Better let us try to get in there, Miss Keys. Poor fellow must be suffocated by now, and we have to think of the ship."

Catriona called out once more, "Philip, please! For Father's sake! Please!"

Without warning, the cabin door was unlocked; it opened a little way, but held on its security chain. Philip appeared, red-eyed, naked to the waist, and sweating. Behind him, smoke was gushing out from the bedroom, and Catriona could see the bright flicker of flames licking up the curtains.

"Philip, for God's sake open the door!"

Philip coughed, and shook his head. "Leave me alone. I know what I'm doing. Go away."

"But Philip, the ship! You're going to burn the ship!"

"That's exactly what I intend to do. Now go away. I'm going to close the door."

Catriona reached quickly into the gap, and clung on to the edge of the door. "You'll have to close it on my fingers if you do. You're my brother, Philip, and I'm not going to let you die."

"Half-brother," said Philip slurrily. "Now get your hand out of there."

"Philip, listen," said Catriona. Her eyes were streaming from the smoke, and she could feel the heat of the air which was pouring out of the gap in the doorway.

"No, Miss Keys, *you* listen," he told her. He sounded drugged and asthmatic from the smoke. "You listen to someone who really knew what kind of a man your father was. Cut me off, after all those years; cut me off and told me never to come near him again. A son should support his father without question, that's what he said. But you . . . you got every-thing—and you didn't even have to love him."

He went into a short hacking coughing fit. Monty Willowby said, "Please, Miss Keys," but Catriona raised her hand to keep him back.

Philip leaned against the side of the door. "Cut me off," he said, and coughed again. "And if you sold Keys to IMM . . . well, you and your mother would still be rich, out of money that I worked for . . . an inheritance that should have been mine. . . . Couldn't have that. . . . But if you *won't* sell to Mark Beeney, then you won't . . . won't give me the pleasure of watching Keys Shipping being ruined . . . so—"

There was a flare-up of flames inside the cabin. Philip turned to try and close the door, but he collapsed, first onto his knees, then onto his back.

Monty Willowby said, "Bill, there you are," and with one blow the burliest of the four seamen had chopped through the security chain on the door and opened it.

Mark came forward abruptly and said, "Here, I'll take him," and hefted Philip onto his shoulders. Catriona stayed close beside him as he carried Philip along the corridor and up the staircase into the fresh air.

"Get me a blanket!" he called; and Baroness Zawisza swept across with a plaid deck-chair rug, which Mark spread out on the deck. He laid Philip carefully down on it and quickly checked his respiration and his pulse. Philip coughed and snuffled and groaned.

"He's all right," said Mark. "Breathed in some smoke, that's all. But he should get over it."

The first-class passengers crowded round in curiosity and consterna-tion. Sir Terence Harding-Crump said, "Do wish they'd tone the whole thing down a bit. Storms, fires. Might as well sail on an Italian ship."

Dr. Fields came up with his bag and examined Philip as he lay on the deck. He lifted his eyelids with his thumb and said, "Have you been taking any pills, old man?"

Philip nodded.

"Well, then, we'd better get you straight down to the ship's hospital. I'm afraid I'm going to have to empty your stomach for you. Can't have chaps dying, you know. It's against regulations."

Philip turned to Catriona, who was kneeling close beside him. "I suppose I ought to say that I'm sorry," he said through thick lips.

"Yes," said Catriona, taking his hand. "I think you ought to."

At that moment, George Welterman appeared to see what was going on; and he timed his arrival perfectly. Standing as he was quite close to Catriona, in anticipation of being able to help her up, and perhaps to take her hand, he was able to hear her quite clearly as she told Philip what she and Mark had decided.

"We're not going to sell Keys Shipping to IMM. Never. And we're not going to hide what happened to the *Orange,* and all of those other ships, either. Perhaps it'll ruin Father's reputation; but then he didn't really deserve that reputation, did he? The *Arcadia* will still be sailing across the Atlantic long after all of this is forgotten, and *she* can be his reputation."

"What will you do?" asked Philip. Two seamen had brought over a stretcher now and were unfolding it beside him.

"I'll tell you all the details later." Catriona smiled. "But Mark will buy the *Arcadia;* and he'll guarantee Keys' debts for five years, in exchange for a twenty-five per cent share of common stock. *My* stock, which I'm quite happy to give him. Particularly since we're going to be married.

"And there's one thing more. Mark would like to see someone really competent put in charge of Keys Shipping, someone who could oversee all the refitting of old ships, and plan to build new ships, and make the company profitable again. Someone who really cares about the company."

George Welterman was staring at Catriona with a face like a white theatrical mask; and when Edgar Deacon appeared next to him, he clutched Edgar's wrist so tightly that Edgar yelped, "What? What is it?" and tried to tug himself away.

The two seamen were carrying Philip down to the hospital now. Catriona touched his grimy forehead and said very softly, "I need you, Philip. I want you to succeed where Father failed. *Our* Father."

Mark and Catriona watched Philip taken away. But then Edgar came up to them and he was stiff and pale and his fists were clenched.

"George just told me what you've been saying," he announced.

Mark put his arm around Catriona and grinned. "George was always excellent at eavesdropping. But, yes, it's true."

"For your information, Miss Keys, you have neither the authority nor the voting power to do it."

Mark turned to Catriona and beamed even more broadly. "I think you'll find, Mr. Deacon, that Miss Keys has all the supporting votes she needs. Her own twenty-five per cent, plus Thistle Maritime, with five per cent, plus a little collection of trusts and insurance companies who all happen to be colleagues and associates of Mr. Philip Carter-Helm, with nineteen per cent."

Edgar said stiffly, "I think you'll find that you're still a fraction short of a majority, Miss Keys. I already have your mother's assurance that she will support whatever course of action I recommend. And I scarcely think that she will be in favour of passing the management of the company into the hands of Mr. Keys' illegitimate son by her own sister, do you?"

Catriona said, "Whatever *my* mother thinks, Philip Carter-Helm's mother thinks differently. I'm sorry, Mr. Deacon, but this plan is a *fait-accompli.* I've already had a wireless message this morning from Aunt Isabelle saying that she will vote in favour of selling the *Arcadia* to American TransAtlantic. Her two per cent gives us at least fifty-one per cent; and that's even supposing that Mr. Fearson and Mr. Thurrock don't vote with us, which I believe they will."

Mark said to Edgar, "Miss Keys, you see, will remain mistress of the *Arcadia;* and after winning the ship herself, that's what I wanted more than anything."

Edgar stood where he was, saying nothing at all. His eyes were like two black stones.

At last he said, "Don't think for one moment that you've heard the end of this," and he turned on his heel and stalked off.

"British India to the finish," said Mark, and he hugged Catriona close.

Sixty-nine

They were in sight of the Statue of Liberty now, but the fire in the first-class cabins was still burning out of control. Dick Charles had taken charge of the firefighting, and he had twenty crewmen forming a bucket chain from the outside swimming pool, while ten more were inside the first-class section frantically spraying the walls and ceiling with fire extinguishers.

As the *Arcadia* steamed majestically through the Verrazano Narrows into Upper Bay, accompanied by dozens of pleasure boats and yachts, and flanked on the starboard side by plumes of water from New York fireboats, black smoke was belching out of her port superstructure, and fragments of blazing curtains were whirling through the air.

"She's taken the Blue Riband," announced the reporter for WEAF News, "but there's something wrong there. She has smoke pouring out of her upper decks, and she's coming in to dock at what I would judge to be a very high speed—maybe ten or fifteen knots. . . . She's approaching the Battery like an express train."

Up on the bridge, Sir Peregrine stood beside the helmsman with a grim, magnificent expression on his face. Ralph Peel stood close beside him, trying to keep as calm as possible.

"Sir Peregrine, our speed," he suggested.

From the forward windows of the bridge, it looked as if the *Arcadia* was already towering over Battery Park and about to sail right up Broadway, but she was still short of Governors Island on her starboard side, and hadn't yet passed Liberty Island to port.

"Forward speed, Mr. Peel?" asked Sir Peregrine.

"Seven knots, sir."

"How's the fire?"

Ralph Peel looked back along the *Arcadia*'s superstructure. "Still burning, sir. Looks serious. Shall we call the New York fire people, sir?"

"No need, Mr. Peel," said Sir Peregrine, nodding towards the fireboats. "They're already with us."

"I'll signal them round to our port side, sir."

"No need, Mr. Peel," said Sir Peregrine. "Hard to port."

"I beg your pardon, sir?"

"Hard to port, Mr. Peel. On the double."

"Yes, sir. At once, sir. Helmsman, hard to port."

"Hard to port it is, sir."

Ralph Peel knew exactly what Sir Peregrine was doing. It was a last spectacular act of seamanship to end a voyage in which he had vindicated himself as one of the greatest ship's masters in modern maritime history. It would have been far more practical to call up the New York fireboats to their port side than to have turned the *Arcadia* through 180 degrees in Upper Bay, especially when she was so closely surrounded by cheering spectators in hundreds of small pleasure craft; but Sir Peregrine was not interested in practicalities; and he believed that anyone who was foolish enough to sail close to a giant ocean liner in a fifteen-foot dinghy deserved whatever swamping they happened to get.

Blasting her whistle so that it echoed all the way to Harlem and out to Brooklyn and Elizabeth, New Jersey, the *Arcadia* swung around with her starboard propellers churning up tumultuous geysers of spray, the entire 960-foot ship like a floating cliff moving around on her axis until she was broadside across the bay, and was at last facing back out towards the Verrazano Narrows, with her high stern counter only hundreds of feet away from the shore of Governors Island.

"Mr. Peel," said Sir Peregrine. "You may now summon those fire-boats. Warn the men that we are seeking assistance from outside; I don't want anyone hosed overboard. And you may break out those half-bottles of champagne for the passengers."

"Sir?"

"Mr. Willowby knows where they are, Mr. Peel. Each one of them has a Blue Riband tied around the neck."

"Very fortuitous, sir," said Ralph Peel.

"And Mr. Peel?"

"Yes, sir."

"Please instruct the stewards that the third toast, after the King and the *Arcadia*—the third toast is to be drunk to the memory of Mr. Rudyard Philips."

There was a pause. Then Ralph Peel said, "Yes, sir."

Seventy

It took two hours to extinguish the fire. Then, smoke-stained but still magnificent, the *Arcadia* was manoeuvred towards the Keys Shipping pier. The ship's orchestra was out on deck playing "Land of Hope and Glory," and the passengers crowded the decks singing and cheering. A BBC microphone was lowered over the stern to make a recording of her propellers for listeners in England.

Mark and Catriona stood on the promenade deck, arm in arm, gazing at New York's towers—the Flatiron Building, the Times Building, the City Investing Company Building, the Singer Building, and the breath-taking Woolworth Building. Grey spires of wealth and romance, rising like castles in the summer mist. Catriona saw them through a blur of happy tears.

George Welterman was one of the first to disembark. Furious, speechless with disappointment and humiliation, he stood on the dock with a grey summer coat thrown over his shoulders, impatiently tapping

468

his cane while they unloaded Mark Beeney's Marmon for him. He was still vengefully determined to drive it up Third Avenue.

Two people had come to George Welterman's cabin while he was packing the last of his possessions. One had been Maurice Peace, to collect a banker's draft for $25,000, as his "consultation fee" for keeping the real mileage of the *Arcadia* on the second day of her sailing a secret. The other was Monty Willowby, to thank George for stowing his priceless relics on the automobile's rear seat (the trunk had been inexplicably jammed) and to promise him that he would be rewarded in Heaven, if not in Weehawken.

"Well," said Mark as George Welterman drove away from the dock with a squeal of tyres. "There goes my dream motor."

"Do you really mind?" asked Catriona.

Mark thought about it, and then said, "Yes. I think I do."

They both laughed.

An ambulance had already parked on the dock to take Philip off to the East Side Clinic; and a long black Austro-Daimler arrived a few minutes afterwards. "That's ours," said Mark. "I bought it by wireless as soon as I lost the Marmon."

"It's very *staid*," said Catriona sniffily.

"That's okay, Mrs. Beeney-to-be. We can always trade it in for a Pierce-Arrow Runabout."

After the Austro-Daimler came a procession of Cadillacs and Rolls-Royces and Hispano-Suizas, in every conceivable hue, from sable to iris. The rich had arrived in New York, and were being swept away in the manner to which they were accustomed.

Just then, a pageboy came up, and said, "Miss Keys?"

"Yes?"

"Flowers, Miss Keys. From Mr. Welterman."

They were orchids in cellophane. A huge spray of twenty or thirty of them, purple and white. The note which was tied to them read, "These are a particularly rare flower known as Enid Cattleya, a cross of Mossiae and Warscewiczii. As rare, and as perverse, as you. With all my adoration, George."

"Well, what do you think about that?" asked Mark, reading the card.

Catriona lowered her eyes. "I don't know," she said. "I think I would rather have had a wreath."

George Welterman drove away from the pier clumsily and impatiently, scraping the Marmon's side against a metal railing. He wasn't used to the car's gearshift, and he drove it erratically and badly until he reached 25th Street, when he began to get the hang of the clutch and drove more smoothly. He reached the intersection of Third Avenue and 28th Street at twelve noon precisely, and sat waiting for a red light, drumming his fingers on the car's steering wheel and wishing he was already changed and bathed and back in the office. He glanced towards the back seat, where Monty Willowby had left an untidy collection of brown-paper parcels.

That was the last voluntary movement of his life. For the sear in the timing device in Harry Pakenow's bomb, jolted back into position by the offloading of the Marmon from the *Arcadia*'s automobile hold, triggered the mechanism which exploded the dynamite. Right in the middle of Third Avenue, the Marmon blew up in a huge cloud of brown smoke, and a shower of metal, mudguards, silver, glass, and splinters of lavatory seat. It stood blazing for over ten minutes before the fire department arrived, with the charred body of George Welterman still gripping the steering wheel, his face fixed in a cindered grin. The noise was heard for twenty blocks, and windows were broken in the Haslett Building, two blocks away.

Two poignant moments finish the story of the *Arcadia*'s maiden voyage. The first was when Harry Pakenow, waving goodbye to Philly, ran across the pier with his suitcase, his cap pulled down over his eyes, looking for the Halls' Rolls-Royce. He caught sight of it just as it was pulling away from the customs shed. Lucille Foster was sitting in the back with Mrs. Hall and another woman in furs. She was wearing a cream-coloured cloche hat, and she looked suddenly very poised and mature. Harry cantered up to the car as it drove sedately along by the waterfront, and waved, and whistled. When nobody took any notice of him, he banged on the window.

"Lucille! It's me! Harry!"

The Rolls-Royce drew to a halt, with Harry running along beside it. The window was wound down, and Mrs. Hall looked out. Her face was white with powder.

"The job," said Harry, smiling expectantly. "You didn't forget, did you?"

"The job?"

"Lucille said—" began Harry; but then he paused, because he could see from the expression on Lucille's face that it had all been a fantasy, a way of being nice to him, a childish favour without any substance.

"It's okay," he said, stepping away from the car. "Wrong car, I guess. Sorry."

Mrs. Hall gave him an uncomprehending twitch that was the nearest she could manage to a smile, and she tapped on the partition with her diamond rings for the driver to pull away. But Lucille suddenly sat up in her seat and cried, "Harry!"

Harry hesitated, and then stepped back up to the side of the car again. "Lucille," he said gently.

There were tears in her eyes. "I'm sorry, Harry."

"You don't have to be. What was it? Nothing. Just one of those shipboard romances."

"Please forgive me," she said. "I didn't mean to hurt you."

He shook his head. "Don't think anything of it. I'm thinking of catching the next boat home, in any case. I've got somebody waiting for me, too."

Then there was the moment when Catriona, still carrying the orchids which she had been given, by George Welterman, met Edgar Deacon on the promenade deck, overlooking the Hudson.

"Mr. Deacon?"

He turned. Then he looked away again and said, "Miss Keys?"

She stood beside him; and for four or five minutes they said nothing, listening to the tooting of tugs, the distant warbling of jazz music, and the sound of New York's traffic.

She said, "I didn't mean to hurt you, you know."

He gave a quick grimace. "You didn't. Not really."

"What will you do now?"

"Oh, well, I don't know. With your permission, perhaps I'll stay here in America for a while. Out of jurisdiction's way, if you know what I mean. Then, I don't know. Perhaps I'll go back to India. Friend of mine plants tea; always said that he'd like me to give him a hand."

There was another pause, and then he said, "Always knew that I'd die in India, you know. Always knew it."

Catriona said, "I'm sorry."

"Don't have to be. Luck of the game. And you *are* Stanley's daughter, after all. Good old Stanley. Straight as a die, old Stanley."

Catriona touched his shoulder. "I'm going now," she said. "Mark's waiting for me downstairs."

"Yes, well, good luck," said Edgar. "And, by the way, there's a little place on 26th Street, between Madison and Third, if I remember. They sell lead soldiers, there; specialise in them. Don't forget to take one back for the Colehill boy."

"No," said Catriona. "No, I won't."

He hesitated, and then, one by one, she threw the orchids that George Welterman had given her into the river, until they were all scattered over the oily surface.

The flowers turned, and whirled, and crowded together when the wash from a passing boat flowed between the *Arcadia* and the next pier. Catriona watched them for a while, and then went to find Mark.